P. G. Wodehouse
The World of Psmith

P.G. Wodehouse

The World of Psmith

The Psmith Omnibus

An omnibus volume containing
Psmith in the City
Psmith Journalist
Leave it to Psmith

PENGUIN BOOKS

PENGUIN BOOKS

Published by the Penguin Group
Penguin Books Ltd, 27 Wrights Lane, London w8 5tz, England
Penguin Putnam Inc., 375 Hudson Street, New York, New York 10014, USA
Penguin Books Australia Ltd, Ringwood, Victoria, Australia
Penguin Books Canada Ltd, 10 Alcorn Avenue, Toronto, Ontario, Canada 4v 3b2
Penguin Books (NZ) Ltd, Private Bag 102902, NSMC, Auckland, New Zealand

Penguin Books Ltd, Registered Offices: Harmondsworth, Middlesex, England .

All rights reserved
Set in 9/11pt Monotype Trump
Phototypeset by Intype London Ltd
Printed in England by Clays Ltd, St Ives plc

Contents

Psmith in the City

TO LESLIE HAVERGAL BRADSHAW

Contents

1 — Mr Bickersdyke Walks behind the Bowler's Arm

Considering what a prominent figure Mr John Bickersdyke was to be in Mike Jackson's life, it was only appropriate that he should make a dramatic entry into it. This he did by walking behind the bowler's arm when Mike had scored ninety-eight, causing him thereby to be clean bowled by a long-hop.

It was the last day of the Ilsworth cricket week, and the house team were struggling hard on a damaged wicket. During the first two matches of the week all had been well. Warm sunshine, true wickets, tea in the shade of the trees. But on the Thursday night, as the team champed their dinner contentedly after defeating the Incogniti by two wickets, a pattering of rain made itself heard upon the windows. By bedtime it had settled to a steady downpour. On Friday morning, when the team of the local regiment arrived in their brake, the sun was shining once more in a watery, melancholy way, but play was not possible before lunch. After lunch the bowlers were in their element. The regiment, winning the toss, put together a hundred and thirty, due principally to a last wicket stand between two enormous corporals, who swiped at everything and had luck enough for two whole teams. The house team followed with seventy-eight, of which Psmith, by his usual golf methods, claimed thirty. Mike, who had gone in first as the star bat of the side, had been run out with great promptitude off the first ball of the innings, which his partner had hit in the immediate neighbourhood of point. At close of play the regiment had made five without loss. This, on the Saturday morning, helped by another shower of rain which made

the wicket easier for the moment, they had increased to
a hundred and forty-eight, leaving the house just two
hundred to make on a pitch which looked as if it were
made of linseed.

It was during this week that Mike had first made the
acquaintance of Psmith's family. Mr Smith had moved
from Shropshire, and taken Ilsworth Hall in a
neighbouring county. This he had done, as far as could
be ascertained, simply because he had a poor opinion of
Shropshire cricket. And just at the moment cricket
happened to be the pivot of his life.

'My father,' Psmith had confided to Mike, meeting
him at the station in the family motor on the Monday,
'is a man of vast but volatile brain. He has not that calm,
dispassionate outlook on life which marks your true
philosopher, such as myself. I – '

'I say,' interrupted Mike, eyeing Psmith's movements
with apprehension, 'you aren't going to drive, are
you?'

'Who else? As I was saying, I am like some contented
spectator of a Pageant. My pater wants to jump in and
stage-manage. He is a man of hobbies. He never has more
than one at a time, and he never has that long. But while
he has it, it's all there. When I left the house this
morning he was all for cricket. But by the time we get to
the ground he may have chucked cricket and taken up
the Territorial Army. Don't be surprised if you find the
wicket being dug up into trenches, when we arrive, and
the pro. moving in echelon towards the pavilion. No,'
he added, as the car turned into the drive, and they caught
a glimpse of white flannels and blazers in the distance, and
heard the sound of bat meeting ball, 'cricket seems still
to be topping the bill. Come along, and I'll show you
your room. It's next to mine, so that, if brooding on Life
in the still hours of the night, I hit on any great truth, I
shall pop in and discuss it with you.'

While Mike was changing, Psmith sat on his bed, and continued to discourse.

'I suppose you're going to the 'Varsity?' he said.

'Rather,' said Mike, lacing his boots. 'You are, of course? Cambridge, I hope. I'm going to King's.'

'Between ourselves,' confided Psmith, 'I'm dashed if I know what's going to happen to me. I am the thingummy of what's-its-name.'

'You look it,' said Mike, brushing his hair.

'Don't stand there cracking the glass,' said Psmith. 'I tell you I am practically a human three-shies-a-penny ball. My father is poising me lightly in his hand, preparatory to flinging me at one of the milky cocos of Life. Which one he'll aim at I don't know. The least thing fills him with a whirl of new views as to my future. Last week we were out shooting together, and he said that the life of the gentleman-farmer was the most manly and independent on earth, and that he had a good mind to start me on that. I pointed out that lack of early training had rendered me unable to distinguish between a threshing-machine and a mangel-wurzel, so he chucked that. He has now worked round to Commerce. It seems that a blighter of the name of Bickersdyke is coming here for the week-end next Saturday. As far as I can say without searching the Newgate Calendar, the man Bickersdyke's career seems to have been as follows. He was at school with my pater, went into the City, raked in a certain amount of doubloons – probably dishonestly – and is now a sort of Captain of Industry, manager of some bank or other, and about to stand for Parliament. The result of these excesses is that my pater's imagination has been fired, and at time of going to press he wants me to imitate Comrade Bickersdyke. However, there's plenty of time. That's one comfort. He's certain to change his mind again. Ready? Then suppose we filter forth into the arena?'

Out on the field Mike was introduced to the man of hobbies. Mr Smith, senior, was a long, earnest-looking

7

man who might have been Psmith in a grey wig but for his obvious energy. He was as wholly on the move as Psmith was wholly statuesque. Where Psmith stood like some dignified piece of sculpture, musing on deep questions with a glassy eye, his father would be trying to be in four places at once. When Psmith presented Mike to him, he shook hands warmly with him and started a sentence, but broke off in the middle of both performances to dash wildly in the direction of the pavilion in an endeavour to catch an impossible catch some thirty yards away. The impetus so gained carried him on towards Bagley, the Ilsworth Hall ground-man, with whom a moment later he was carrying on an animated discussion as to whether he had or had not seen a dandelion on the field that morning. Two minutes afterwards he had skimmed away again. Mike, as he watched him, began to appreciate Psmith's reasons for feeling some doubt as to what would be his future walk in life.

At lunch that day Mike sat next to Mr Smith, and improved his acquaintance with him; and by the end of the week they were on excellent terms. Psmith's father had Psmith's gift of getting on well with people.

On this Saturday, as Mike buckled on his pads, Mr Smith bounded up, full of advice and encouragement.

'My boy,' he said, 'we rely on you. These others' – he indicated with a disparaging wave of the hand the rest of the team, who were visible through the window of the changing-room – 'are all very well. Decent club bats. Good for a few on a billiard-table. But you're our hope on a wicket like this. I have studied cricket all my life' – till that summer it is improbable that Mr Smith had ever handled a bat – 'and I know a first-class batsman when I see one. I've seen your brothers play. Pooh, you're better than any of them. That century of yours against the Green Jackets was a wonderful innings, wonderful. Now look here, my boy. I want you to be careful. We've a lot

of runs to make, so we mustn't take any risks. Hit
plenty of boundaries, of course, but be careful. Careful.
Dash it, there's a youngster trying to climb up the elm.
He'll break his neck. It's young Giles, my keeper's boy.
Hi! Hi, there!'

He scudded out to avert the tragedy, leaving Mike to
digest his expert advice on the art of batting on bad
wickets.

Possibly it was the excellence of this advice which
induced Mike to play what was, to date, the best innings
of his life. There are moments when the batsman feels an
almost super-human fitness. This came to Mike now.
The sun had begun to shine strongly. It made the wicket
more difficult, but it added a cheerful touch to the scene.
Mike felt calm and masterful. The bowling had no terrors
for him. He scored nine off his first over and seven off
his second, half-way through which he lost his partner.
He was to undergo a similar bereavement several times
that afternoon, and at frequent intervals. However simple
the bowling might seem to him, it had enough sting in
it to worry the rest of the team considerably. Batsmen
came and went at the other end with such rapidity that
it seemed hardly worth while their troubling to come in
at all. Every now and then one would give promise of
better things by lifting the slow bowler into the pavilion
or over the boundary, but it always happened that a
similar stroke, a few balls later, ended in an easy catch.
At five o'clock the Ilsworth score was eighty-one for
seven wickets, last man nought, Mike not out fifty-nine.
As most of the house team, including Mike, were
dispersing to their homes or were due for visits at other
houses that night, stumps were to be drawn at six. It
was obvious that they could not hope to win. Number
nine on the list, who was Bagley, the ground-man, went
in with instructions to play for a draw, and minute advice
from Mr Smith as to how he was to do it. Mike had now
begun to score rapidly, and it was not to be expected that

he could change his game; but Bagley, a dried-up little man of the type which bowls for five hours on a hot August day without exhibiting any symptoms of fatigue, put a much-bound bat stolidly in front of every ball he received; and the Hall's prospects of saving the game grew brighter.

At a quarter to six the professional left, caught at very silly point for eight. The score was a hundred and fifteen, of which Mike had made eighty-five.

A lengthy young man with yellow hair, who had done some good fast bowling for the Hall during the week, was the next man in. In previous matches he had hit furiously at everything, and against the Green Jackets had knocked up forty in twenty minutes while Mike was putting the finishing touches to his century. Now, however, with his host's warning ringing in his ears, he adopted the unspectacular, or Bagley, style of play. His manner of dealing with the ball was that of one playing croquet. He patted it gingerly back to the bowler when it was straight, and left it icily alone when it was off the wicket. Mike, still in the brilliant vein, clumped a half-volley past point to the boundary, and with highly scientific late cuts and glides brought his score to ninety-eight. With Mike's score at this, the total at a hundred and thirty, and the hands of the clock at five minutes to six, the yellow-haired croquet exponent fell, as Bagley had fallen, a victim to silly point, the ball being the last of the over.

Mr Smith, who always went in last for his side, and who so far had not received a single ball during the week, was down the pavilion steps and half-way to the wicket before the retiring batsman had taken half a dozen steps.

'Last over,' said the wicket-keeper to Mike. 'Any idea how many you've got? You must be near your century, I should think.'

'Ninety-eight,' said Mike. He always counted his runs.

'By Jove, as near as that? This is something like a finish.'

Mike left the first ball alone, and the second. They were too wide of the off-stump to be hit at safely. Then he felt a thrill as the third ball left the bowler's hand. It was a long-hop. He faced square to pull it.

And at that moment Mr John Bickersdyke walked into his life across the bowling-screen.

He crossed the bowler's arm just before the ball pitched. Mike lost sight of it for a fraction of a second, and hit wildly. The next moment his leg stump was askew; and the Hall had lost the match.

'I'm sorry,' he said to Mr Smith. 'Some silly idiot walked across the screen just as the ball was bowled.'

'What!' shouted Mr Smith. 'Who was the fool who walked behind the bowler's arm?' he yelled appealingly to Space.

'Here he comes, whoever he is,' said Mike.

A short, stout man in a straw hat and a flannel suit was walking towards them. As he came nearer Mike saw that he had a hard, thin-lipped mouth, half-hidden by a rather ragged moustache, and that behind a pair of gold spectacles were two pale and slightly protruding eyes, which, like his mouth, looked hard.

'How are you, Smith,' he said.

'Hullo, Bickersdyke.' There was a slight internal struggle, and then Mr Smith ceased to be the cricketer and became the host. He chatted amiably to the new-comer.

'You lost the game, I suppose,' said Mr Bickersdyke.

The cricketer in Mr Smith came to the top again, blended now, however, with the host. He was annoyed, but restrained in his annoyance.

'I say, Bickersdyke, you know, my dear fellow,' he said complainingly, 'you shouldn't have walked across the screen. You put Jackson off, and made him get bowled.'

'The screen?'

'That curious white object,' said Mike. 'It is not put up merely as an ornament. There's a sort of rough idea of giving the batsman a chance of seeing the ball, as well. It's a great help to him when people come charging across it just as the bowler bowls.'

Mr Bickersdyke turned a slightly deeper shade of purple, and was about to reply, when what sporting reporters call 'the veritable ovation' began.

Quite a large crowd had been watching the game, and they expressed their approval of Mike's performance.

There is only one thing for a batsman to do on these occasions. Mike ran into the pavilion, leaving Mr Bickersdyke standing.

2 — Mike Hears Bad News

It seemed to Mike, when he got home, that there was a touch of gloom in the air. His sisters were as glad to see him as ever. There was a good deal of rejoicing going on among the female Jacksons because Joe had scored his first double century in first-class cricket. Double centuries are too common, nowadays, for the papers to take much notice of them; but, still, it is not everybody who can make them, and the occasion was one to be marked. Mike had read the news in the evening paper in the train, and had sent his brother a wire from the station, congratulating him. He had wondered whether he himself would ever achieve the feat in first-class cricket. He did not see why he should not. He looked forward through a long vista of years of county cricket. He had a birth qualification for the county in which Mr Smith had settled, and he had played for it once already at the beginning of the holidays. His *début* had not been sensational, but it had been promising. The fact that two members of the team had made centuries, and a third seventy odd, had rather eclipsed his own twenty-nine not out; but it had been a faultless innings, and nearly all the papers had said that here was yet another Jackson, evidently well up to the family standard, who was bound to do big things in the future.

The touch of gloom was contributed by his brother Bob to a certain extent, and by his father more noticeably. Bob looked slightly thoughtful. Mr Jackson seemed thoroughly worried.

Mike approached Bob on the subject in the billiard-room after dinner. Bob was practising cannons in rather a listless way.

'What's up, Bob?' asked Mike.

Bob laid down his cue.

'I'm hanged if I know,' said Bob. 'Something seems to be. Father's worried about something.'

'He looked as if he'd got the hump rather at dinner.'

'I only got here this afternoon, about three hours before you did. I had a bit of a talk with him before dinner. I can't make out what's up. He seemed awfully keen on my finding something to do now I've come down from Oxford. Wanted to know whether I couldn't get a tutoring job or a mastership at some school next term. I said I'd have a shot. I don't see what all the hurry's about, though. I was hoping he'd give me a bit of travelling on the Continent somewhere before I started in.'

'Rough luck,' said Mike. 'I wonder why it is. Jolly good about Joe, wasn't it? Let's have fifty up, shall we?'

Bob's remarks had given Mike no hint of impending disaster. It seemed strange, of course, that his father, who had always been so easy-going, should have developed a hustling Get On or Get Out spirit, and be urging Bob to Do It Now; but it never occurred to him that there could be any serious reason for it. After all, fellows had to start working some time or other. Probably his father had merely pointed this out to Bob, and Bob had made too much of it.

Half-way through the game Mr Jackson entered the room, and stood watching in silence.

'Want a game, father?' asked Mike.

'No, thanks, Mike. What is it? A hundred up?'

'Fifty.'

'Oh, then you'll be finished in a moment. When you are, I wish you'd just look into the study for a moment, Mike. I want to have a talk with you.'

'Rum,' said Mike, as the door closed. 'I wonder what's up?'

For a wonder his conscience was free. It was not as if a bad school-report might have arrived in his absence. His Sedleigh report had come at the beginning of the holidays, and had been, on the whole, fairly decent – nothing startling either way. Mr Downing, perhaps through remorse at having harried Mike to such an extent during the Sammy episode, had exercised a studied moderation in his remarks. He had let Mike down far more easily than he really deserved. So it could not be a report that was worrying Mr Jackson. And there was nothing else on his conscience.

Bob made a break of sixteen, and ran out. Mike replaced his cue, and walked to the study.

His father was sitting at the table. Except for the very important fact that this time he felt that he could plead Not Guilty on every possible charge, Mike was struck by the resemblance in the general arrangement of the scene to that painful ten minutes at the end of the previous holidays, when his father had announced his intention of taking him away from Wrykyn and sending him to Sedleigh. The resemblance was increased by the fact that, as Mike entered, Mr Jackson was kicking at the waste-paper basket – a thing which with him was an infallible sign of mental unrest.

'Sit down, Mike,' said Mr Jackson. 'How did you get on during the week?'

'Topping. Only once out under double figures. And then I was run out. Got a century against the Green Jackets, seventy-one against the Incogs, and today I made ninety-eight on a beast of a wicket, and only got out because some silly goat of a chap – '

He broke off. Mr Jackson did not seem to be attending. There was a silence. Then Mr Jackson spoke with an obvious effort.

'Look here, Mike, we've always understood one another, haven't we?'

'Of course we have.'

'You know I wouldn't do anything to prevent you having a good time, if I could help it. I took you away from Wrykyn, I know, but that was a special case. It was necessary. But I understand perfectly how keen you are to go to Cambridge, and I wouldn't stand in the way for a minute, if I could help it.'

Mike looked at him blankly. This could only mean one thing. He was not to go to the Varsity. But why? What had happened? When he had left for the Smith's cricket week, his name had been down for King's, and the whole thing settled. What could have happened since then?

'But I can't help it,' continued Mr Jackson.

'Aren't I going up to Cambridge, father?' stammered Mike.

'I'm afraid not, Mike. I'd manage it if I possibly could. I'm just as anxious to see you get your Blue as you are to get it. But it's kinder to be quite frank. I can't afford to send you to Cambridge. I won't go into details which you would not understand; but I've lost a very large sum of money since I saw you last. So large that we shall have to economize in every way. I shall let this house and take a much smaller one. And you and Bob, I'm afraid, will have to start earning your living. I know it's a terrible disappointment to you, old chap.'

'Oh, that's all right,' said Mike thickly. There seemed to be something sticking in his throat, preventing him from speaking.

'If there was any possible way – '

'No, it's all right, father, really. I don't mind a bit. It's awfully rough luck on you losing all that.'

There was another silence. The clock ticked away energetically on the mantelpiece, as if glad to make itself heard at last. Outside, a plaintive snuffle made itself heard. John, the bull-dog, Mike's inseparable companion, who had followed him to the study, was getting tired of waiting on the mat. Mike got up and opened the door. John lumbered in.

The movement broke the tension.

'Thanks, Mike,' said Mr Jackson, as Mike started to leave the room, 'you're a sportsman.'

3 — The New Era Begins

Details of what were in store for him were given to Mike
next morning. During his absence at Ilsworth a vacancy
had been got for him in that flourishing institution, the
New Asiatic Bank; and he was to enter upon his duties,
whatever they might be, on the Tuesday of the following
week. It was short notice, but banks have a habit of
swallowing their victims rather abruptly. Mike
remembered the case of Wyatt, who had had just about
the same amount of time in which to get used to the
prospect of Commerce.

On the Monday morning a letter arrived from Psmith.
Psmith was still perturbed. 'Commerce,' he wrote,
'continues to boom. My pater referred to Comrade
Bickersdyke last night as a Merchant Prince. Comrade B.
and I do not get on well together. Purely for his own good,
I drew him aside yesterday and explained to him at great
length the frightfulness of walking across the bowling-
screen. He seemed restive, but I was firm. We parted
rather with the Distant Stare than the Friendly Smile.
But I shall persevere. In many ways the casual observer
would say that he was hopeless. He is a poor performer
at Bridge, as I was compelled to hint to him on Saturday
night. His eyes have no animated sparkle of intelligence.
And the cut of his clothes jars my sensitive soul to its
foundations. I don't wish to speak ill of a man behind his
back, but I must confide in you, as my Boyhood's Friend,
that he wore a made-up tie at dinner. But no more of a
painful subject. I am working away at him with a brave
smile. Sometimes I think that I am succeeding. Then he
seems to slip back again. However,' concluded the letter,

ending on an optimistic note, 'I think that I shall make a man of him yet – some day.'

Mike re-read this letter in the train that took him to London. By this time Psmith would know that his was not the only case in which Commerce was booming. Mike had written to him by return, telling him of the disaster which had befallen the house of Jackson. Mike wished he could have told him in person, for Psmith had a way of treating unpleasant situations as if he were merely playing at them for his own amusement. Psmith's attitude towards the slings and arrows of outrageous Fortune was to regard them with a bland smile, as if they were part of an entertainment got up for his express benefit.

Arriving at Paddington, Mike stood on the platform, waiting for his box to emerge from the luggage-van, with mixed feelings of gloom and excitement. The gloom was in the larger quantities, perhaps, but the excitement was there, too. It was the first time in his life that he had been entirely dependent on himself. He had crossed the Rubicon. The occasion was too serious for him to feel the same helplessly furious feeling with which he had embarked on life at Sedleigh. It was possible to look on Sedleigh with quite a personal enmity. London was too big to be angry with. It took no notice of him. It did not care whether he was glad to be there or sorry, and there was no means of making it care. That is the peculiarity of London. There is a sort of cold unfriendliness about it. A city like New York makes the new arrival feel at home in half an hour; but London is a specialist in what Psmith in his letter had called the Distant Stare. You have to buy London's goodwill.

Mike drove across the Park to Victoria, feeling very empty and small. He had settled on Dulwich as the spot to get lodgings, partly because, knowing nothing about London, he was under the impression that rooms anywhere inside the four-mile radius were very expensive, but principally because there was a school at Dulwich, and it would be a comfort being near a school. He might get a game of fives there sometimes, he thought, on a Saturday afternoon, and, in the summer, occasional cricket.

Wandering at a venture up the asphalt passage which leads from Dulwich station in the direction of the College, he came out into Acacia Road. There is something about Acacia Road which inevitably suggests furnished apartments. A child could tell at a glance that it was bristling with bed-sitting rooms.

Mike knocked at the first door over which a card hung.

There is probably no more depressing experience in the world than the process of engaging furnished apartments. Those who let furnished apartments seem to take no joy in the act. Like Pooh-Bah, they do it, but it revolts them.

In answer to Mike's knock, a female person opened the door. In appearance she resembled a pantomime 'dame', inclining towards the restrained melancholy of Mr Wilkie Bard rather than the joyous abandon of Mr George Robey. Her voice she had modelled on the gramophone. Her most recent occupation seemed to have been something with a good deal of yellow soap in it. As a matter of fact – there are no secrets between our readers and ourselves – she had been washing a shirt. A useful occupation, and an honourable, but one that tends to produce a certain homeliness in the appearance.

She wiped a pair of steaming hands on her apron, and regarded Mike with an eye which would have been markedly expressionless in a boiled fish.

'Was there anything?' she asked.

Mike felt that he was in for it now. He had not sufficient ease of manner to back gracefully away and disappear, so he said that there was something. In point of fact, he wanted a bed-sitting room.

'Orkup stays,' said the pantomime dame. Which Mike interpreted to mean, would he walk upstairs?

The procession moved up a dark flight of stairs until it came to a door. The pantomime dame opened this, and shuffled through. Mike stood in the doorway, and looked in.

It was a repulsive room. One of those characterless rooms which are only found in furnished apartments. To Mike, used to the comforts of his bedroom at home and the cheerful simplicity of a school dormitory, it seemed about the most dismal spot he had ever struck. A sort of Sargasso Sea among bedrooms.

He looked round in silence. Then he said: 'Yes.' There did not seem much else to say.

'It's a nice room,' said the pantomime dame. Which was a black lie. It was not a nice room. It never had been a nice room. And it did not seem at all probable that it ever would be a nice room. But it looked cheap. That was the great thing. Nobody could have the assurance to charge much for a room like that. A landlady with a conscience might even have gone to the length of paying people some small sum by way of compensation to them for sleeping in it.

'About what?' queried Mike. Cheapness was the great consideration. He understood that his salary at the bank would be about four pounds ten a month, to begin with, and his father was allowing him five pounds a month. One does not do things *en prince* on a hundred and fourteen pounds a year.

The pantomime dame became slightly more animated. Prefacing her remarks by a repetition of her statement that it was a nice room, she went on to say that she could 'do' it at seven and sixpence per week 'for him' – giving him to understand, presumably, that, if the Shah of Persia or Mr Carnegie ever applied for a night's rest, they would sigh in vain for such easy terms. And that included lights.

Coals were to be looked on as an extra. 'Sixpence a scuttle.' Attendance was thrown in.

Having stated these terms, she dribbled a piece of fluff under the bed, after the manner of a professional Association footballer, and relapsed into her former moody silence.

Mike said he thought that would be all right. The pantomime dame exhibited no pleasure.

''Bout meals?' she said. 'You'll be wanting breakfast. Bacon, aigs, an' that, I suppose?'

Mike said he supposed so.

'That'll be extra,' she said. 'And dinner? A chop, or a nice steak?'

Mike bowed before this original flight of fancy. A chop or a nice steak seemed to be about what he might want.

'That'll be extra,' said the pantomime dame in her best Wilkie Bard manner.

Mike said yes, he supposed so. After which, having put down seven and sixpence, one week's rent in advance, he was presented with a grubby receipt and an enormous latchkey, and the *séance* was at an end.

Mike wandered out of the house. A few steps took him to the railings that bounded the College grounds. It was late August, and the evenings had begun to close in. The cricket-field looked very cool and spacious in the dim light, with the school buildings looming vague and shadowy through the slight mist. The little gate by the railway bridge was not locked. He went in, and walked slowly across the turf towards the big clump of trees which marked the division between the cricket and football fields. It was all very pleasant and soothing after the pantomime dame and her stuffy bed-sitting room. He sat down on a bench beside the second eleven telegraph-board, and looked across the ground at the pavilion. For the first time that day he began to feel really home-sick. Up till now the excitement of a strange venture had borne him up; but the cricket-field and the pavilion reminded him so sharply of Wrykyn. They brought home to him with a cutting distinctness, the absolute finality of his break with the old order of things. Summers would come and go, matches would be played on this ground with all the glory of big scores and keen finishes; but he was done. 'He was a jolly good bat at school. Top of the Wrykyn averages two years. But didn't do anything after he left. Went into the city or something.' That was what they would say of him, if they didn't quite forget him.

The clock on the tower over the senior block chimed quarter after quarter, but Mike sat on, thinking. It was quite late when he got up, and began to walk back to Acacia Road. He felt cold and stiff and very miserable.

4 — First Steps in a Business Career

The City received Mike with the same aloofness with which the more western portion of London had welcomed him on the previous day. Nobody seemed to look at him. He was permitted to alight at St Paul's and make his way up Queen Victoria Street without any demonstration. He followed the human stream till he reached the Mansion House, and eventually found himself at the massive building of the New Asiatic Bank, Limited.

The difficulty now was to know how to make an effective entrance. There was the bank, and here was he. How had he better set about breaking it to the authorities that he had positively arrived and was ready to start earning his four pound ten *per mensem*? Inside, the bank seemed to be in a state of some confusion. Men were moving about in an apparently irresolute manner. Nobody seemed actually to be working. As a matter of fact, the business of a bank does not start very early in the morning. Mike had arrived before things had really begun to move. As he stood near the doorway, one or two panting figures rushed up the steps, and flung themselves at a large book which stood on the counter near the door. Mike was to come to know this book well. In it, if you were an employé of the New Asiatic Bank, you had to inscribe your name every morning. It was removed at ten sharp to the accountant's room, and if you reached the bank a certain number of times in the year too late to sign, bang went your bonus.

After a while things began to settle down. The stir and confusion gradually ceased. All down the length of the bank, figures could be seen, seated on stools and writing hieroglyphics in large letters. A benevolent-looking man, with spectacles and a straggling grey beard, crossed the gangway close to where Mike was standing. Mike put the thing to him, as man to man.

'Could you tell me,' he said, 'what I'm supposed to do? I've just joined the bank.' The benevolent man stopped, and looked at him with a pair of mild blue eyes. 'I think, perhaps, that your best plan would be to see the manager,' he said. 'Yes, I should certainly do that. He will tell you what work you have to do. If you will permit me, I will show you the way.'

'It's awfully good of you,' said Mike. He felt very grateful. After his experience of London, it was a pleasant change to find someone who really seemed to care what happened to him. His heart warmed to the benevolent man.

'It feels strange to you, perhaps, at first, Mr – '

'Jackson.'

'Mr Jackson. My name is Waller. I have been in the City some time, but I can still recall my first day. But one shakes down. One shakes down quite quickly. Here is the manager's room. If you go in, he will tell you what to do.'

'Thanks awfully,' said Mike.

'Not at all.' He ambled off on the quest which Mike had interrupted, turning, as he went, to bestow a mild smile of encouragement on the new arrival. There was something about Mr Waller which reminded Mike pleasantly of the White Knight in 'Alice through the Looking-glass'.

Mike knocked at the managerial door, and went in.

Two men were sitting at the table. The one facing the door was writing when Mike went in. He continued to write all the time he was in the room. Conversation between other people in his presence had apparently no interest for him, nor was it able to disturb him in any way.

The other man was talking into a telephone. Mike waited till he had finished. Then he coughed. The man turned round. Mike had thought, as he looked at his back and heard his voice, that something about his appearance or his way of speaking was familiar. He was right. The man in the chair was Mr Bickersdyke, the cross-screen pedestrian.

These reunions are very awkward. Mike was frankly unequal to the situation. Psmith, in his place, would have opened the conversation, and relaxed the tension with some remark on the weather or the state of the crops. Mike merely stood wrapped in silence, as in a garment.

That the recognition was mutual was evident from Mr Bickersdyke's look. But apart from this, he gave no sign of having already had the pleasure of making Mike's acquaintance. He merely stared at him as if he were a blot on the arrangement of the furniture, and said, 'Well?'

The most difficult parts to play in real life as well as on the stage are those in which no 'business' is arranged for the performer. It was all very well for Mr Bickersdyke. He had been 'discovered sitting'. But Mike had had to enter, and he wished now that there was something he could do instead of merely standing and speaking.

'I've come,' was the best speech he could think of. It was not a good speech. It was too sinister. He felt that even as he said it. It was the sort of thing Mephistopheles would have said to Faust by way of opening conversation. And he was not sure, either, whether he ought not to have added, 'Sir'.

Apparently such subtleties of address were not necessary, for Mr Bickersdyke did not start up and shout, 'This language to me!' or anything of that kind. He merely said, 'Oh! And who are you?'

'Jackson,' said Mike. It was irritating, this assumption

26

on Mr Bickersdyke's part that they had never met before.

'Jackson? Ah, yes. You have joined the staff?'

Mike rather liked this way of putting it. It lent a certain dignity to the proceedings, making him feel like some important person for whose services there had been strenuous competition. He seemed to see the bank's directors being reassured by the chairman. ('I am happy to say, gentlemen, that our profits for the past year are £3,000,006–2–2$\frac{1}{2}$ – (cheers) – and' impressively – 'that we have finally succeeded in inducing Mr Mike Jackson – (sensation) – to – er – in fact, to join the staff!' (Frantic cheers, in which the chairman joined.))

'Yes,' he said.

Mr Bickersdyke pressed a bell on the table beside him, and picking up a pen, began to write. Of Mike he took no further notice, leaving that toy of Fate standing stranded in the middle of the room.

After a few moments one of the men in fancy dress, whom Mike had seen hanging about the gangway, and whom he afterwards found to be messengers, appeared. Mr Bickersdyke looked up.

'Ask Mr Bannister to step this way,' he said.

The messenger disappeared, and presently the door opened again to admit a shock-headed youth with paper cuff-protectors round his wrists.

'This is Mr Jackson, a new member of the staff. He will take your place in the postage department. You will go into the cash department, under Mr Waller. Kindly show him what he has to do.'

Mike followed Mr Bannister out. On the other side of the door the shock-headed one became communicative.

'Whew!' he said, mopping his brow. 'That's the sort of thing which gives me the pip. When William came and said old Bick wanted to see me, I said to him, "William, my boy, my number is up. This is the sack." I made certain that Rossiter had run me in for something. He's been waiting for a chance to do it for weeks, only I've

been as good as gold and haven't given it him. I pity you
going into the postage. There's one thing, though. If
you can stick it for about a month, you'll get through all
right. Men are always leaving for the East, and then you
get shunted on into another department, and the next
new man goes into the postage. That's the best of this
place. It's not like one of those banks where you stay in
London all your life. You only have three years here, and
then you get your orders, and go to one of the branches
in the East, where you're the dickens of a big pot straight
away, with a big screw and a dozen native Johnnies under
you. Bit of all right, that. I shan't get my orders for
another two and a half years and more, worse luck. Still,
it's something to look forward to.'

'Who's Rossiter?' asked Mike.

'The head of the postage department. Fussy little brute.
Won't leave you alone. Always trying to catch you on
the hop. There's one thing, though. The work in the
postage is pretty simple. You can't make many mistakes,
if you're careful. It's mostly entering letters and stamping
them.'

They turned in at the door in the counter, and arrived
at a desk which ran parallel to the gangway. There was
a high rack running along it, on which were several
ledgers. Tall, green-shaded electric lamps gave it rather a
cosy look.

As they reached the desk, a little man with short, black
whiskers buzzed out from behind a glass screen, where
there was another desk.

'Where have you been, Bannister, where have you
been? You must not leave your work in this way. There
are several letters waiting to be entered. Where have you
been?'

'Mr Bickersdyke sent for me,' said Bannister, with the
calm triumph of one who trumps an ace.

'Oh! Ah! Oh! Yes, very well. I see. But get to work, get
to work. Who is this?'

'This is a new man. He's taking my place. I've been moved on to the cash.'

'Oh! Ah! Is your name Smith?' asked Mr Rossiter, turning to Mike.

Mike corrected the rash guess, and gave his name. It struck him as a curious coincidence that he should be asked if his name were Smith, of all others. Not that it is an uncommon name.

'Mr Bickersdyke told me to expect a Mr Smith. Well, well, perhaps there are two new men. Mr Bickersdyke knows we are short-handed in this department. But, come along, Bannister, come along. Show Jackson what he has to do. We must get on. There is no time to waste.'

He buzzed back to his lair. Bannister grinned at Mike. He was a cheerful youth. His normal expression was a grin.

'That's a sample of Rossiter,' he said. 'You'd think from the fuss he's made that the business of the place was at a standstill till we got to work. Perfect rot! There's never anything to do here till after lunch, except checking the stamps and petty cash, and I've done that ages ago. There are three letters. You may as well enter them. It all looks like work. But you'll find the best way is to wait till you get a couple of dozen or so, and then work them off in a batch. But if you see Rossiter about, then start stamping something or writing something, or he'll run you in for neglecting your job. He's a nut. I'm jolly glad I'm under old Waller now. He's the pick of the bunch. The other heads of departments are all nuts, and Bickersdyke's the nuttiest of the lot. Now, look here. This is all you've got to do. I'll just show you, and then you can manage for yourself. I shall have to be shunting off to my own work in a minute.'

5 — The Other Man

As Bannister had said, the work in the postage department
was not intricate. There was nothing much to do except
enter and stamp letters, and, at intervals, take them down
to the post office at the end of the street. The nature of
the work gave Mike plenty of time for reflection.

His thoughts became gloomy again. All this was very
far removed from the life to which he had looked
forward. There are some people who take naturally to a
life of commerce. Mike was not of these. To him the
restraint of the business was irksome. He had been used
to an open-air life, and a life, in its way, of excitement.
He gathered that he would not be free till five o'clock,
and that on the following day he would come at ten and
go at five, and the same every day, except Saturdays
and Sundays, all the year round, with a ten days' holiday.
The monotony of the prospect appalled him. He was not
old enough to know what a narcotic is Habit, and that
one can become attached to and interested in the most
unpromising jobs. He worked away dismally at his
letters till he had finished them. Then there was nothing
to do except sit and wait for more.

He looked through the letters he had stamped, and re-
read the addresses. Some of them were directed to people
living in the country, one to a house which he knew quite
well, near to his own home in Shropshire. It made him
home-sick, conjuring up visions of shady gardens and
country sounds and smells, and the silver Severn
gleaming in the distance through the trees. About now,
if he were not in this dismal place, he would be lying in
the shade in the garden with a book, or wandering down

to the river to boat or bathe. That envelope addressed to the man in Shropshire gave him the worst moment he had experienced that day.

The time crept slowly on to one o'clock. At two minutes past Mike awoke from a day-dream to find Mr Waller standing by his side. The cashier had his hat on.

'I wonder,' said Mr Waller, 'if you would care to come out to lunch. I generally go about this time, and Mr Rossiter, I know, does not go out till two. I thought perhaps that, being unused to the City, you might have some difficulty in finding your way about.'

'It's awfully good of you,' said Mike. 'I should like to.'

The other led the way through the streets and down obscure alleys till they came to a chop-house. Here one could have the doubtful pleasure of seeing one's chop in its various stages of evolution. Mr Waller ordered lunch with the care of one to whom lunch is no slight matter. Few workers in the City do regard lunch as a trivial affair. It is the keynote of their day. It is an oasis in a desert of ink and ledgers. Conversation in city office deals, in the morning, with what one is going to have for lunch, and in the afternoon with what one has had for lunch.

At intervals during the meal Mr Waller talked. Mike was content to listen. There was something soothing about the grey-bearded one.

'What sort of a man is Bickersdyke?' asked Mike.

'A very able man. A very able man indeed. I'm afraid he's not popular in the office. A little inclined, perhaps, to be hard on mistakes. I can remember the time when he was quite different. He and I were fellow clerks in Morton and Blatherwick's. He got on better than I did. A great fellow for getting on. They say he is to be the Unionist candidate for Kenningford when the time comes. A great worker, but perhaps not quite the sort of man to be generally popular in an office.'

'He's a blighter,' was Mike's verdict. Mr Waller made no comment. Mike was to learn later that the manager and the cashier, despite the fact that they had been together in less prosperous days – or possibly because of it – were not on very good terms. Mr Bickersdyke was a man of strong prejudices, and he disliked the cashier, whom he looked down upon as one who had climbed to a lower rung of the ladder than he himself had reached.

As the hands of the chop-house clock reached a quarter to two, Mr Waller rose, and led the way back to the office, where they parted for their respective desks. Gratitude for any good turn done to him was a leading characteristic of Mike's nature, and he felt genuinely grateful to the cashier for troubling to seek him out and be friendly to him.

His three-quarters-of-an-hour absence had led to the accumulation of a small pile of letters on his desk. He sat down and began to work them off. The addresses continued to exercise a fascination for him. He was miles away from the office, speculating on what sort of a man J. B. Garside, Esq, was, and whether he had a good time at his house in Worcestershire, when somebody tapped him on the shoulder.

He looked up.

Standing by his side, immaculately dressed as ever, with his eye-glass fixed and a gentle smile on his face, was Psmith.

Mike stared.

'Commerce,' said Psmith, as he drew off his lavender gloves, 'has claimed me for her own. Comrade of old, I, too, have joined this blighted institution.'

As he spoke, there was a whirring noise in the immediate neighbourhood, and Mr Rossiter buzzed out from his den with the *esprit* and animation of a clock-work toy.

'Who's here?' said Psmith with interest, removing his eye-glass, polishing it, and replacing it in his eye.

'Mr Jackson,' exclaimed Mr Rossiter. 'I really must ask you to be good enough to come in from your lunch at the proper time. It was fully seven minutes to two when you returned, and – '

'That little more,' sighed Psmith, 'and how much is it!'

'Who are you?' snapped Mr Rossiter, turning on him.

'I shall be delighted, Comrade – '

'Rossiter,' said Mike, aside.

'Comrade Rossiter. I shall be delighted to furnish you with particulars of my family history. As follows. Soon after the Norman Conquest, a certain Sieur de Psmith grew tired of work – a family failing, alas – and settled down in this country to live peacefully for the remainder of his life on what he could extract from the local peasantry. He may be described as the founder of the family which ultimately culminated in Me. Passing on – '

Mr Rossiter refused to pass on.

'What are you doing here? What have you come for?'

'Work,' said Psmith, with simple dignity. 'I am now a member of the staff of this bank. Its interests are my interests. Psmith, the individual, ceases to exist, and there springs into being Psmith, the cog in the wheel of the New Asiatic Bank; Psmith, the link in the bank's chain; Psmith, the Worker. I shall not spare myself,' he proceeded earnestly. 'I shall toil with all the accumulated energy of one who, up till now, has only known what work is like from hearsay. Whose is that form sitting on the steps of the bank in the morning, waiting eagerly for the place to open? It is the form of Psmith, the Worker. Whose is that haggard, drawn face which bends over a ledger long after the other toilers have sped blithely westwards to dine at Lyons' Popular Café? It is the face of Psmith, the Worker.'

'I – ' began Mr Rossiter.

'I tell you,' continued Psmith, waving aside the interruption and tapping the head of the department rhythmically in the region of the second waistcoat-button with a long finger, 'I tell *you*, Comrade Rossiter, that you

33

have got hold of a good man. You and I together, not forgetting Comrade Jackson, the pet of the Smart Set, will toil early and late till we boost up this Postage Department into a shining model of what a Postage Department should be. What that is, at present, I do not exactly know. However. Excursion trains will be run from distant shires to see this Postage Department. American visitors to London will do it before going on to the Tower. And now,' he broke off, with a crisp, businesslike intonation, 'I must ask you to excuse me. Much as I have enjoyed this little chat, I fear it must now cease. The time has come to work. Our trade rivals are getting ahead of us. The whisper goes round, "Rossiter and Psmith are talking, not working," and other firms prepare to pinch our business. Let me Work.'

Two minutes later, Mr Rossiter was sitting at his desk with a dazed expression, while Psmith, perched gracefully on a stool, entered figures in a ledger.

6 — Psmith Explains

For the space of about twenty-five minutes Psmith sat in silence, concentrated on his ledger, the picture of the model bank-clerk. Then he flung down his pen, slid from his stool with a satisfied sigh, and dusted his waistcoat. 'A commercial crisis,' he said, 'has passed. The job of work which Comrade Rossiter indicated for me has been completed with masterly skill. The period of anxiety is over. The bank ceases to totter. Are you busy, Comrade Jackson, or shall we chat awhile?'

Mike was not busy. He had worked off the last batch of letters, and there was nothing to do but to wait for the next, or – happy thought – to take the present batch down to the post, and so get out into the sunshine and fresh air for a short time. 'I rather think I'll nip down to the post-office,' said he, 'You couldn't come too, I suppose?'

'On the contrary,' said Psmith, 'I could, and will. A stroll will just restore those tissues which the gruelling work of the last half-hour has wasted away. It is a fearful strain, this commercial toil. Let us trickle towards the post office. I will leave my hat and gloves as a guarantee of good faith. The cry will go round, "Psmith has gone! Some rival institution has kidnapped him!" Then they will see my hat,' – he built up a foundation of ledgers, planted a long ruler in the middle, and hung his hat on it – 'my gloves,' – he stuck two pens into the desk and hung a lavender glove on each – 'and they will sink back swooning with relief. The awful suspense will be over. They will say, "No, he has not gone permanently. Psmith will return. When the fields are white with daisies he'll return.'' And now, Comrade Jackson, lead me to this picturesque little post-office of yours of which I have heard so much.'

Mike picked up the long basket into which he had thrown the letters after entering the addresses in his ledger, and they moved off down the aisle. No movement came from Mr Rossiter's lair. Its energetic occupant was hard at work. They could just see part of his hunched-up back.

'I wish Comrade Downing could see us now,' said Psmith. 'He always set us down as mere idlers. Triflers. Butterflies. It would be a wholesome corrective for him to watch us perspiring like this in the cause of Commerce.'

'You haven't told me yet what on earth you're doing here,' said Mike. 'I thought you were going to the 'Varsity. Why the dickens are you in a bank? Your pater hasn't lost his money, has he?'

'No. There is still a tolerable supply of doubloons in the old oak chest. Mine is a painful story.'

'It always is,' said Mike.

'You are very right, Comrade Jackson. I am the victim of Fate. Ah, so you put the little chaps in there, do you?' he said, as Mike, reaching the post-office, began to bundle the letters into the box. 'You seem to have grasped your duties with admirable promptitude. It is the same with me. I fancy we are both born men of Commerce. In a few years we shall be pinching Comrade Bickersdyke's job. And talking of Comrade B. brings me back to my painful story. But I shall never have time to tell it to you during our walk back. Let us drift aside into this tea-shop. We can order a buckwheat cake or a butter-nut, or something equally succulent, and carefully refraining from consuming these dainties, I will tell you all.'

'Right O!' said Mike.

'When last I saw you,' resumed Psmith, hanging Mike's basket on the hat-stand and ordering two portions of

36

porridge, 'you may remember that a serious crisis in my
affairs had arrived. My father inflamed with the idea of
Commerce had invited Comrade Bickersdyke – '

'When did you know he was a manager here?' asked
Mike.

'At an early date. I have my spies everywhere.
However, my pater invited Comrade Bickersdyke to our
house for the week-end. Things turned out rather
unfortunately. Comrade B. resented my purely altruistic
efforts to improve him mentally and morally. Indeed, on
one occasion he went so far as to call me an impudent
young cub, and to add that he wished he had me under
him in his bank, where, he asserted, he would knock
some of the nonsense out of me. All very painful. I tell
you, Comrade Jackson, for the moment it reduced my
delicately vibrating ganglions to a mere frazzle.
Recovering myself, I made a few blithe remarks, and we
then parted. I cannot say that we parted friends, but at
any rate I bore him no ill-will. I was still determined to
make him a credit to me. My feelings towards him were
those of some kindly father to his prodigal son. But he,
if I may say so, was fairly on the hop. And when my pater,
after dinner the same night, played into his hands by
mentioning that he thought I ought to plunge into a career
of commerce, Comrade B. was, I gather, all over him.
Offered to make a vacancy for me in the bank, and to take
me on at once. My pater, feeling that this was the real
hustle which he admired so much, had me in, stated his
case, and said, in effect, "How do we go?" I intimated
that Comrade Bickersdyke was my greatest chum on
earth. So the thing was fixed up and here I am. But you
are not getting on with your porridge, Comrade Jackson.
Perhaps you don't care for porridge? Would you like a
finnan haddock, instead? Or a piece of shortbread? You
have only to say the word.'

'It seems to me,' said Mike gloomily, 'that we are in
for a pretty rotten time of it in this bally bank. If

Bickersdyke's got his knife into us, he can make it jolly
warm for us. He's got his knife into me all right about
that walking-across-the-screen business.'

'True,' said Psmith, 'to a certain extent. It is an
undoubted fact that Comrade Bickersdyke will have a jolly
good try at making life a nuisance to us; but, on the other
hand, I propose, so far as in me lies, to make things
moderately unrestful for him, here and there.'

'But you can't,' objected Mike. 'What I mean to say is,
it isn't like a school. If you wanted to score off a master
at school, you could always rag and so on. But here you
can't. How can you rag a man who's sitting all day in a
room of his own while you're sweating away at a desk at
the other end of the building?'

'You put the case with admirable clearness, Comrade
Jackson,' said Psmith approvingly. 'At the hard-headed,
common-sense business you sneak the biscuit every time
with ridiculous ease. But you do not know all. I do not
propose to do a thing in the bank except work. I shall be
a model as far as work goes. I shall be flawless. I shall
bound to do Comrade Rossiter's bidding like a highly
trained performing dog. It is outside the bank, when I
have staggered away dazed with toil, that I shall resume
my attention to the education of Comrade Bickersdyke.'

'But, dash it all, how can you? You won't see him.
He'll go off home, or to his club, or – '

Psmith tapped him earnestly on the chest.

'There, Comrade Jackson,' he said, 'you have hit the
bull's-eye, rung the bell, and gathered in the cigar or
cocoanut according to choice. He *will* go off to his club.
And I shall do precisely the same.'

'How do you mean?'

'It is this way. My father, as you may have noticed
during your stay at our stately home of England, is a
man of a warm, impulsive character. He does not always
do things as other people would do them. He has his
own methods. Thus, he has sent me into the City to do

the hard-working, bank-clerk act, but at the same time
he is allowing me just as large an allowance as he would
have given me if I had gone to the 'Varsity. Morever,
while I was still at Eton he put my name up for his clubs,
the Senior Conservative among others. My pater belongs
to four clubs altogether, and in course of time, when my
name comes up for election, I shall do the same.
Meanwhile, I belong to one, the Senior Conservative. It
is a bigger club than the others, and your name comes
up for election sooner. About the middle of last month a
great yell of joy made the West End of London shake like
a jelly. The three thousand members of the Senior
Conservative had just learned that I had been elected.'

Psmith paused, and ate some porridge.

'I wonder why they call this porridge,' he observed
with mild interest. 'It would be far more manly and
straightforward of them to give it its real name. To
resume. I have gleaned, from casual chit-chat with my
father, that Comrade Bickersdyke also infests the Senior
Conservative. You might think that that would make
me, seeing how particular I am about whom I mix with,
avoid the club. Error. I shall go there every day. If
Comrade Bickersdyke wishes to emend any little traits
in my character of which he may disapprove, he shall
never say that I did not give him the opportunity. I
shall mix freely with Comrade Bickersdyke at the Senior
Conservative Club. I shall be his constant companion. I
shall, in short, haunt the man. By these strenuous means
I shall, as it were, get a bit of my own back. And now,'
said Psmith, rising, 'it might be as well, perhaps, to
return to the bank and resume our commercial duties. I
don't know how long you are supposed to be allowed for
your little trips to and from the post-office, but, seeing
that the distance is about thirty yards, I should say at a
venture not more than half an hour. Which is exactly the
space of time which has flitted by since we started out
on this important expedition. Your devotion to porridge,

Comrade Jackson, has led to our spending about twenty-five minutes in this hostelry.'

'Great Scott,' said Mike, 'there'll be a row.'

'Some slight temporary breeze, perhaps,' said Psmith. 'Annoying to men of culture and refinement, but not lasting. My only fear is lest we may have worried Comrade Rossiter at all. I regard Comrade Rossiter as an elder brother, and would not cause him a moment's heart-burning for worlds. However, we shall soon know,' he added, as they passed into the bank and walked up the aisle, 'for there is Comrade Rossiter waiting to receive us in person.'

The little head of the Postage Department was moving restlessly about in the neighbourhood of Psmith's and Mike's desk.

'Am I mistaken,' said Psmith to Mike, 'or is there the merest suspicion of a worried look on our chief's face? It seems to me that there is the slightest soupçon of shadow about that broad, calm brow.'

7 — Going into Winter Quarters

There was.

Mr Rossiter had discovered Psmith's and Mike's absence about five minutes after they had left the building. Ever since then, he had been popping out of his lair at intervals of three minutes, to see whether they had returned. Constant disappointment in this respect had rendered him decidedly jumpy. When Psmith and Mike reached the desk, he was a kind of human soda-water bottle. He fizzed over with questions, reproofs, and warnings.

'What does it mean? What does it mean?' he cried. 'Where have you been? Where have you been?'

'Poetry,' said Psmith approvingly.

'You have been absent from your places for over half an hour. Why? Why? Why? Where have you been? Where have you been? I cannot have this. It is preposterous. Where have you been? Suppose Mr Bickersdyke had happened to come round here. I should not have known what to say to him.'

'Never an easy man to chat with, Comrade Bickersdyke,' agreed Psmith.

'You must thoroughly understand that you are expected to remain in your places during business hours.'

'Of course,' said Psmith, 'that makes it a little hard for Comrade Jackson to post letters, does it not?'

'Have you been posting letters?'

'We have,' said Psmith. 'You have wronged us. Seeing our absent places you jumped rashly to the conclusion that we were merely gadding about in pursuit of pleasure.

Error. All the while we were furthering the bank's best interests by posting letters.'

'You had no business to leave your place. Jackson is on the posting desk.'

'You are very right,' said Psmith, 'and it shall not occur again. It was only because it was the first day. Comrade Jackson is not used to the stir and bustle of the City. His nerve failed him. He shrank from going to the post-office alone. So I volunteered to accompany him. And,' concluded Psmith, impressively, 'we won safely through. Every letter has been posted.'

'That need not have taken you half an hour.'

'True. And the actual work did not. It was carried through swiftly and surely. But the nerve-strain had left us shaken. Before resuming our more ordinary duties we had to refresh. A brief breathing-space, a little coffee and porridge, and here we are, fit for work once more.'

'If it occurs again, I shall report the matter to Mr Bickersdyke.'

'And rightly so,' said Psmith, earnestly. 'Quite rightly so. Discipline, discipline. That is the cry. There must be no shirking of painful duties. Sentiment must play no part in business. Rossiter, the man, may sympathise, but Rossiter, the Departmental head, must be adamant.'

Mr Rossiter pondered over this for a moment, then went off on a side-issue.

'What is the meaning of this foolery?' he asked, pointing to Psmith's gloves and hat. 'Suppose Mr Bickersdyke had come round and seen them, what should I have said?'

'You would have given him a message of cheer. You would have said, " All is well. Psmith has not left us. He will come back. And Comrade Bickersdyke, relieved, would have – '

'You do not seem very busy, Mr Smith.'

Both Psmith and Mr Rossiter were startled.

Mr Rossiter jumped as if somebody had run a gimlet

42

into him, and even Psmith started slightly. They had not heard Mr Bickersdyke approaching. Mike, who had been stolidly entering addresses in his ledger during the latter part of the conversation, was also taken by surprise.

Psmith was the first to recover. Mr Rossiter was still too confused for speech, but Psmith took the situation in hand.

'Apparently no,' he said, swiftly removing his hat from the ruler. 'In reality, yes. Mr Rossiter and I were just scheming out a line of work for me as you came up. If you had arrived a moment later, you would have found me toiling.'

'H'm. I hope I should. We do not encourage idling in this bank.'

'Assuredly not,' said Psmith warmly. 'Most assuredly not. I would not have it otherwise. I am a worker. A bee, not a drone. A *Lusitania*, not a limpet. Perhaps I have not yet that grip on my duties which I shall soon acquire; but it is coming. It is coming. I see daylight.'

'H'm. I have only your word for it.' He turned to Mr Rossiter, who had now recovered himself, and was as nearly calm as it was in his nature to be. 'Do you find Mr Smith's work satisfactory, Mr Rossiter?'

Psmith waited resignedly for an outburst of complaint respecting the small matter that had been under discussion between the head of the department and himself; but to his surprise it did not come.

'Oh – ah – quite, quite, Mr Bickersdyke. I think he will very soon pick things up.'

Mr Bickersdyke turned away. He was a conscientious bank manager, and one can only suppose that Mr Rossiter's tribute to the earnestness of one of his employés was gratifying to him. But for that, one would have said that he was disappointed.

'Oh, Mr Bickersdyke,' said Psmith.

The manager stopped.

'Father sent his kind regards to you,' said Psmith
benevolently.

Mr Bickersdyke walked off without comment.

'An uncommonly cheery, companionable feller,'
murmured Psmith, as he turned to his work.

The first day anywhere, if one spends it in a sedentary
fashion, always seemed unending; and Mike felt as if he
had been sitting at his desk for weeks when the hour for
departure came. A bank's day ends gradually,
reluctantly, as it were. At about five there is a sort of stir,
not unlike the stir in a theatre when the curtain is on
the point of falling. Ledgers are closed with a bang. Men
stand about and talk for a moment or two before going
to the basement for their hats and coats. Then, at irregular
intervals, forms pass down the central aisle and out
through the swing doors. There is an air of relaxation over
the place, though some departments are still working as
hard as ever under a blaze of electric light. Somebody
begins to sing, and an instant chorus of protests and
maledictions rises from all sides. Gradually, however, the
electric lights go out. The procession down the centre
aisle becomes more regular; and eventually the place is
left to darkness and the night watchman.

The postage department was one of the last to be freed
from duty. This was due to the inconsiderateness of the
other departments, which omitted to disgorge their
letters till the last moment. Mike, as he grew familiar
with the work, and began to understand it, used to prowl
round the other departments during the afternoon and
wrest letters from them, usually receiving with them
much abuse for being a nuisance and not leaving honest
workers alone. Today, however, he had to sit on till
nearly six, waiting for the final batch of correspondence.

Psmith, who had waited patiently with him, though
his own work was finished, accompanied him down to

the post office and back again to the bank to return the letter basket; and they left the office together.

'By the way,' said Psmith, 'what with the strenuous labours of the bank and the disturbing interviews with the powers that be, I have omitted to ask you where you are digging. Wherever it is, of course you must clear out. It is imperative, in this crisis, that we should be together. I have acquired a quite snug little flat in Clement's Inn. There is a spare bedroom. It shall be yours.'

'My dear chap,' said Mike, 'it's all rot. I can't sponge on you.'

'You pain me, Comrade Jackson. I was not suggesting such a thing. We are business men, hard-headed young bankers. I make you a business proposition. I offer you the post of confidential secretary and adviser to me in exchange for a comfortable home. The duties will be light. You will be required to refuse invitations to dinner from crowned heads, and to listen attentively to my views on Life. Apart from this, there is little to do. So that's settled.'

'It isn't,' said Mike. 'I – '

'You will enter upon your duties tonight. Where are you suspended at present?'

'Dulwich. But, look here – '

'A little more, and you'll get the sack. I tell you the thing is settled. Now, let us hail yon taximeter cab, and desire the stern-faced aristocrat on the box to drive us to Dulwich. We will then collect a few of your things in a bag, have the rest off by train, come back in the taxi, and go and bite a chop at the Carlton. This is a momentous day in our careers, Comrade Jackson. We must buoy ourselves up.'

Mike made no further objections. The thought of that bed-sitting room in Acacia Road and the pantomime dame rose up and killed them. After all, Psmith was not like any ordinary person. There would be no question of charity. Psmith had invited him to the flat in exactly the

same spirit as he had invited him to his house for
the cricket week.

'You know,' said Psmith, after a silence, as they flitted
through the streets in the taximeter, 'one lives and
learns. Were you so wrapped up in your work this
afternoon that you did not hear my very entertaining
little chat with Comrade Bickersdyke, or did it happen to
come under your notice? It did? Then I wonder if you
were struck by the singular conduct of Comrade
Rossiter?'

'I thought it rather decent of him not to give you away
to that blighter Bickersdyke.'

'Admirably put. It was precisely that that struck me.
He had his opening, all ready made for him, but he
refrained from depositing me in the soup. I tell you,
Comrade Jackson, my rugged old heart was touched. I said
to myself, "There must be good in Comrade Rossiter,
after all. I must cultivate him." I shall make it my
business to be kind to our Departmental head. He
deserves the utmost consideration. His action shone
like a good deed in a wicked world. Which it was, of
course. From today onwards I take Comrade Rossiter
under my wing. We seem to be getting into a tolerably
benighted quarter. Are we anywhere near? "Through
Darkest Dulwich in a Taximeter."'

The cab arrived at Dulwich station, and Mike stood
up to direct the driver. They whirred down Acacia Road.
Mike stopped the cab and got out. A brief and somewhat
embarrassing interview with the pantomime dame,
during which Mike was separated from a week's rent in
lieu of notice, and he was in the cab again, bound for
Clement's Inn.

His feelings that night differed considerably from the
frame of mind in which he had gone to bed the night
before. It was partly a very excellent dinner and partly
the fact that Psmith's flat, though at present in some
disorder, was obviously going to be extremely

comfortable, that worked the change. But principally it was due to his having found an ally. The gnawing loneliness had gone. He did not look forward to a career of Commerce with any greater pleasure than before; but there was no doubt that with Psmith, it would be easier to get through the time after office hours. If all went well in the bank he might find that he had not drawn such a bad ticket after all.

8 — The Friendly Native

'The first principle of warfare,' said Psmith at breakfast next morning, doling out bacon and eggs with the air of a medieval monarch distributing largesse, 'is to collect a gang, to rope in allies, to secure the cooperation of some friendly native. You may remember that at Sedleigh it was partly the sympathetic cooperation of that record blitherer, Comrade Jellicoe, which enabled us to nip the pro-Spiller movement in the bud. It is the same in the present crisis. What Comrade Jellicoe was to us at Sedleigh, Comrade Rossiter must be in the City. We must make an ally of that man. Once I know that he and I are as brothers, and that he will look with a lenient and benevolent eye on any little shortcomings in my work, I shall be able to devote my attention whole-heartedly to the moral reformation of Comrade Bickersdyke, that man of blood. I look on Comrade Bickersdyke as a bargee of the most pronounced type; and anything I can do towards making him a decent member of Society shall be done freely and ungrudgingly. A trifle more tea, Comrade Jackson?'

'No, thanks,' said Mike. 'I've done. By Jove, Smith, this flat of yours is all right.'

'Not bad,' assented Psmith, 'not bad. Free from squalor to a great extent. I have a number of little objects of *vertu* coming down shortly from the old homestead. Pictures, and so on. It will be by no means un-snug when they are up. Meanwhile, I can rough it. We are old campaigners, we Psmiths. Give us a roof, a few comfortable chairs, a sofa or two, half a dozen cushions, and decent meals, and we do not repine. Reverting once more to Comrade Rossiter – '

'Yes, what about him?' said Mike. 'You'll have a pretty tough job turning him into a friendly native, I should think. How do you mean to start?'

Psmith regarded him with a benevolent eye.

'There is but one way,' he said. 'Do you remember the case of Comrade Outwood, at Sedleigh? How did we corral him, and become to him practically as long-lost sons?'

'We got round him by joining the Archaeological Society.'

'Precisely,' said Psmith. 'Every man has his hobby. The thing is to find it out. In the case of comrade Rossiter, I should say that it would be either postage stamps, dried seaweed, or Hall Caine. I shall endeavour to find out today. A few casual questions, and the thing is done. Shall we be putting in an appearance at the busy hive now? If we are to continue in the running for the bonus stakes, it would be well to start soon.'

Mike's first duty at the bank that morning was to check the stamps and petty cash. While he was engaged on this task, he heard Psmith conversing affably with Mr Rossiter.

'Good morning,' said Psmith.

'Morning,' replied his chief, doing sleight-of-hand tricks with a bundle of letters which lay on his desk 'Get on with your work, Psmith. We have a lot before us.'

'Undoubtedly. I am all impatience. I should say that in an institution like this, dealing as it does with distant portions of the globe, a philatelist would have excellent opportunities of increasing his collection. With me, stamp-collecting has always been a positive craze. I – '

'I have no time for nonsense of that sort myself,' said Mr Rossiter. 'I should advise you, if you mean to get on, to devote more time to your work and less to stamps.'

'I will start at once. Dried seaweed, again – '

'Get on with your work, Smith.'

Psmith retired to his desk.

'This,' he said to Mike, 'is undoubtedly something in the nature of a set-back. I have drawn blank. The papers bring out posters, "Psmith Baffled." I must try again. Meanwhile, to work. Work, the hobby of the philosopher and the poor man's friend.'

The morning dragged slowly on without incident. At twelve o'clock Mike had to go out and buy stamps, which he subsequently punched in the punching-machine in the basement, a not very exhilarating job in which he was assisted by one of the bank messengers, who discoursed learnedly on roses during the *séance*. Roses were his hobby. Mike began to see that Psmith had reason in his assumption that the way to every man's heart was through his hobby. Mike made a firm friend of William, the messenger, by displaying an interest and a certain knowledge of roses. At the same time the conversation had the bad effect of leading to an acute relapse in the matter of home-sickness. The rose-garden at home had been one of Mike's favourite haunts on a summer afternoon. The contrast between it and the basement of the new Asiatic Bank, the atmosphere of which was far from being roselike, was too much for his feelings. He emerged from the depths, with his punched stamps, filled with bitterness against Fate.

He found Psmith still baffled.

'Hall Caine,' said Psmith regretfully, 'has also proved a frost. I wandered round to Comrade Rossiter's desk just now with a rather brainy excursus on "The Eternal City", and was received with the Impatient Frown rather than the Glad Eye. He was in the middle of adding up a rather tricky column of figures, and my remarks caused him to drop a stitch. So far from winning the man over, I have gone back. There now exists between Comrade Rossiter and myself a certain coldness. Further investigations will be postponed till after lunch.'

The postage department received visitors during the

morning. Members of other departments came with letters, among them Bannister. Mr Rossiter was away in the manager's room at the time.

'How are you getting on?' said Bannister to Mike.

'Oh, all right,' said Mike.

'Had any trouble with Rossiter yet?'

'No, not much.'

'He hasn't run you in to Bickersdyke?'

'No.'

'Pardon my interrupting a conversation between old college chums,' said Psmith courteously, 'but I happened to overhear, as I toiled at my desk, the name of Comrade Rossiter.'

Bannister looked somewhat startled. Mike introduced them.

'This is Smith,' he said. 'Chap I was at school with. This is Bannister, Smith, who used to be on here till I came.'

'In this department?' asked Psmith.

'Yes.'

'Then, Comrade Bannister, you are the very man I have been looking for. Your knowledge will be invaluable to us. I have no doubt that, during your stay in this excellently managed department, you had many opportunities of observing Comrade Rossiter?'

'I should jolly well think I had,' said Bannister with a laugh. 'He saw to that. He was always popping out and cursing me about something.'

'Comrade Rossiter's manners are a little restive,' agreed Psmith. 'What used you to talk to him about?'

'What used I to talk to him about?'

'Exactly. In those interviews to which you have alluded, how did you amuse, entertain Comrade Rossiter?'

'I didn't. He used to do all the talking there was.'

Psmith straightened his tie, and clicked his tongue, disappointed.

'This is unfortunate,' he said, smoothing his hair. 'You see, Comrade Bannister, it is this way. In the course of my professional duties, I find myself continually coming into contact with Comrade Rossiter.'

'I bet you do,' said Bannister.

'On these occasions I am frequently at a loss for entertaining conversation. He has no difficulty, as apparently happened in your case, in keeping up his end of the dialogue. The subject of my shortcomings provides him with ample material for speech. I, on the other hand, am dumb. I have nothing to say.'

'I should think that was a bit of a change for you, wasn't it?'

'Perhaps, so,' said Psmith, 'perhaps so. On the other hand, however restful it may be to myself, it does not enable me to secure Comrade Rossiter's interest and win his esteem.'

'What Smith wants to know,' said Mike, 'is whether Rossiter has any hobby of any kind. He thinks, if he has, he might work it to keep in with him.'

Psmith, who had been listening with an air of pleased interest, much as a father would listen to his child prattling for the benefit of a visitor, confirmed this statement.

'Comrade Jackson,' he said, 'has put the matter with his usual admirable clearness. That is the thing in a nutshell. Has Comrade Rossiter any hobby that you know of? Spillikins, brass-rubbing, the Near Eastern Question, or anything like that? I have tried him with postage-stamps (which you'd think, as head of a postage department, he ought to be interested in), and dried seaweed, Hall Caine, but I have the honour to report total failure. The man seems to have no pleasures. What does he do with himself when the day's toil is ended? That giant brain must occupy itself somehow.'

'I don't know,' said Bannister, 'unless it's football. I saw him once watching Chelsea. I was rather surprised.'

'Football,' said Psmith thoughtfully, 'football. By no means a scaly idea. I rather fancy, Comrade Bannister, that you have whanged the nail on the head. Is he strong on any particular team? I mean, have you ever heard him, in the intervals of business worries, stamping on his desk and yelling, "Buck up Cottagers!" or "Lay 'em out, Pensioners!" or anything like that? One moment.' Psmith held up his hand. 'I will get my Sherlock Holmes system to work. What was the other team in the modern gladiatorial contest at which you saw Comrade Rossiter?'

'Manchester United.'

'And Comrade Rossiter, I should say, was a Manchester man.'

'I believe he is.'

'Then I am prepared to bet a small sum that he is nuts on Manchester United. My dear Holmes, how – ! Elementary, my dear fellow, quite elementary. But here comes the lad in person.'

Mr Rossiter turned in from the central aisle through the counter-door, and, observing the conversational group at the postage-desk, came bounding up. Bannister moved off.

'Really, Smith,' said Mr Rossiter, 'you always seem to be talking. I have overlooked the matter once, as I did not wish to get you into trouble so soon after joining, but, really, it cannot go on. I must take notice of it.'

Psmith held up his hand.

'The fault was mine,' he said, with manly frankness. 'Entirely mine. Bannister came in a purely professional spirit to deposit a letter with Comrade Jackson. I engaged him in conversation on the subject of the Football League, and I was just trying to correct his view that Newcastle United were the best team playing, when you arrived.'

'It is perfectly absurd,' said Mr Rossiter, 'that you

should waste the bank's time in this way. The bank pays you to work, not to talk about professional football.'

'Just so, just so,' murmured Psmith.

'There is too much talking in this department.'

'I fear you are right.'

'It is nonsense.'

'My own view,' said Psmith, 'was that Manchester United were by far the finest team before the public.'

'Get on with your work, Smith.'

Mr Rossiter stumped off to his desk, where he sat as one in thought.

'Smith,' he said at the end of five minutes.

Psmith slid from his stool, and made his way deferentially towards him.

'Bannister's a fool,' snapped Mr Rossiter.

'So I thought,' said Psmith.

'A perfect fool. He always was.'

Psmith shook his head sorrowfully, as who should say, 'Exit Bannister.'

'There is no team playing today to touch Manchester United.'

'Precisely what I said to Comrade Bannister.'

'Of course. You know something about it.'

'The study of League football,' said Psmith, 'has been my relaxation for years.'

'But we have no time to discuss it now.'

'Assuredly not, sir. Work before everything.'

'Some other time, when – '

' – We are less busy. Precisely.'

Psmith moved back to his seat.

'I fear,' he said to Mike, as he resumed work, 'that as far as Comrade Rossiter's friendship and esteem are concerned, I have to a certain extent landed Comrade Bannister in the bouillon, but it was in a good cause. I fancy we have won through. Half an hour's thoughtful perusal of the "Footballers' Who's Who", just to find out some elementary facts about Manchester United, and

I rather think the friendly Native is corralled. And now once more to work. Work, the hobby of the hustler and the deadbeat's dread.'

9 — The Haunting of Mr Bickersdyke

Anything in the nature of a rash and hasty move was
wholly foreign to Psmith's tactics. He had the patience
which is the chief quality of the successful general. He
was content to secure his base before making any
offensive movement. It was a fortnight before he turned
his attention to the education of Mr Bickersdyke. During
that fortnight he conversed attractively, in the intervals
of work, on the subject of League football in general and
Manchester United in particular. The subject is not hard
to master if one sets oneself earnestly to it; and Psmith
spared no pains. The football editions of the evening
papers are not reticent about those who play the game:
and Psmith drank in every detail with the thoroughness
of the conscientious student. By the end of the fortnight
he knew what was the favourite breakfast-food of J.
Turnbull; what Sandy Turnbull wore next his skin; and
who, in the opinion of Meredith, was England's leading
politician. These facts, imparted to and discussed with
Mr Rossiter, made the progress of the *entente cordiale*
rapid. It was on the eighth day that Mr Rossiter consented
to lunch with the Old Etonian. On the tenth he played
the host. By the end of the fortnight the flapping of the
white wings of Peace over the Postage Department was
setting up a positive draught. Mike, who had been
introduced by Psmith as a distant relative of Moger, the
goalkeeper, was included in the great peace.

'So that now,' said Psmith, reflectively polishing his
eye-glass, 'I think that we may consider ourselves free
to attend to Comrade Bickersdyke. Our bright little
Mancunian friend would no more run us in now than if

we were the brothers Turnbull. We are as inside forwards to him.'

The club to which Psmith and Mr Bickersdyke belonged was celebrated for the steadfastness of its political views, the excellence of its cuisine, and the curiously Gorgonzolaesque marble of its main staircase. It takes all sorts to make a world. It took about four thousand of all sorts to make the Senior Conservative Club. To be absolutely accurate, there were three thousand seven hundred and eighteen members.

To Mr Bickersdyke for the next week it seemed as if there was only one.

There was nothing crude or overdone about Psmith's methods. The ordinary man, having conceived the idea of haunting a fellow clubman, might have seized the first opportunity of engaging him in conversation. Not so Psmith. The first time he met Mr Bickersdyke in the club was on the stairs after dinner one night. The great man, having received practical proof of the excellence of cuisine referred to above, was coming down the main staircase at peace with all men, when he was aware of a tall young man in the 'faultless evening dress' of which the female novelist is so fond, who was regarding him with a fixed stare through an eye-glass. The tall young man, having caught his eye, smiled faintly, nodded in a friendly but patronizing manner, and passed on up the staircase to the library. Mr Bickersdyke sped on in search of a waiter.

As Psmith sat in the library with a novel, the waiter entered, and approached him.

'Beg pardon, sir,' he said. 'Are you a member of this club?'

Psmith fumbled in his pocket and produced his eye-glass, through which he examined the waiter, button by button.

'I am Psmith,' he said simply.

'A member, sir?'

'*The* member,' said Psmith. 'Surely you participated
in the general rejoicings which ensued when it was
announced that I had been elected? But perhaps you were
too busy working to pay any attention. If so, I respect
you. I also am a worker. A toiler, not a flatfish. A sizzler,
not a squab. Yes, I am a member. Will you tell Mr
Bickersdyke that I am sorry, but I have been elected, and
have paid my entrance fee and subscription.'

'Thank you, sir.'

The waiter went downstairs and found Mr Bickersdyke
in the lower smoking-room.

'The gentleman says he is, sir.'

'H'm,' said the bank-manager. 'Coffee and Bene-
dictine, and a cigar.'

'Yes, sir.'

On the following day Mr Bickersdyke met Psmith in
the club three times, and on the day after that seven.
Each time the latter's smile was friendly, but patronizing.
Mr Bickersdyke began to grow restless.

On the fourth day Psmith made his first remark. The
manager was reading the evening paper in a corner, when
Psmith sinking gracefully into a chair beside him, caused
him to look up.

'The rain keeps off,' said Psmith.

Mr Bickersdyke looked as if he wished his employee
would imitate the rain, but he made no reply.

Psmith called a waiter.

'Would you mind bringing me a small cup of coffee?'
he said. 'And for you,' he added to Mr Bickersdyke.

'Nothing,' growled the manager.

'And nothing for Mr Bickersdyke.'

The waiter retired. Mr Bickersdyke became absorbed
in his paper.

'I see from my morning paper,' said Psmith, affably,
'that you are to address a meeting at the Kenningford Town
Hall next week. I shall come and hear you. Our politics
differ in some respects, I fear – I incline to the Socialist

view – but nevertheless I shall listen to your remarks with great interest, great interest.'

The paper rustled, but no reply came from behind it.

'I heard from father this morning,' resumed Psmith.

Mr Bickersdyke lowered his paper and glared at him.

'I don't wish to hear about your father,' he snapped.

An expression of surprise and pain came over Psmith's face.

'What!' he cried. 'You don't mean to say that there is any coolness between my father and you? I am more grieved than I can say. Knowing, as I do, what a genuine respect my father has for your great talents, I can only think that there must have been some misunderstanding. Perhaps if you would allow me to act as a mediator – '

Mr Bickersdyke put down his paper and walked out of the room.

Psmith found him a quarter of an hour later in the card-room. He sat down beside his table, and began to observe the play with silent interest. Mr Bickersdyke, never a great performer at the best of times, was so unsettled by the scrutiny that in the deciding game of the rubber he revoked, thereby presenting his opponents with the rubber by a very handsome majority of points. Psmith clicked his tongue sympathetically.

Dignified reticence is not a leading characteristic of the bridge-player's manner at the Senior Conservative Club on occasions like this. Mr Bickersdyke's partner did not bear his calamity with manly resignation. He gave tongue on the instant. 'What on earth's,' and 'Why on earth's' flowed from his mouth like molten lava. Mr Bickersdyke sat and fermented in silence. Psmith clicked his tongue sympathetically throughout.

Mr Bickersdyke lost that control over himself which every member of a club should possess. He turned on Psmith with a snort of frenzy.

'How can I keep my attention fixed on the game when you sit staring at me like a – like a – '

'I am sorry,' said Psmith gravely, 'if my stare falls short in any way of your ideal of what a stare should be; but I appeal to these gentlemen. Could I have watched the game more quietly?'

'Of course not,' said the bereaved partner warmly. 'Nobody could have any earthly objection to your behaviour. It was absolute carelessness. I should have thought that one might have expected one's partner at a club like this to exercise elementary – '

But Mr Bickersdyke had gone. He had melted silently away like the driven snow.

Psmith took his place at the table.

'A somewhat nervous excitable man, Mr Bickersdyke, I should say,' he observed.

'A somewhat dashed, blanked idiot,' emended the bank-manager's late partner. 'Thank goodness he lost as much as I did. That's some light consolation.'

Psmith arrived at the flat to find Mike still out. Mike had repaired to the Gaiety earlier in the evening to refresh his mind after the labours of the day. When he returned, Psmith was sitting in an armchair with his feet on the mantelpiece, musing placidly on Life.

'Well?' said Mike.

'Well? And how was the Gaiety? Good show?'

'Jolly good. What about Bickersdyke?'

Psmith looked sad.

'I cannot make Comrade Bickersdyke out,' he said. 'You would think that a man would be glad to see the son of a personal friend. On the contrary, I may be wronging Comrade B., but I should almost be inclined to say that my presence in the Senior Conservative Club tonight irritated him. There was no *bonhomie* in his manner. He seemed to me to be giving a spirited imitation of a man about to foam at the mouth. I did my best to entertain him. I chatted. His only reply was to leave the room. I followed him to the card-room, and watched his very remarkable and brainy tactics at bridge, and he accused me of causing him to revoke. A very curious personality, that of Comrade Bickersdyke. But let us dismiss him from our minds. Rumours have reached me,' said Psmith, 'that a very decent little supper may be obtained at a quaint, old-world eating-house called the Savoy. Will you accompany me thither on a tissue-restoring expedition? It would be rash not to probe these rumours to their foundation, and ascertain their exact truth.'

10 — Mr Bickersdyke Addresses His Constituents

It was noted by the observant at the bank next morning that Mr Bickersdyke had something on his mind. William, the messenger, knew it, when he found his respectful salute ignored. Little Briggs, the accountant, knew it when his obsequious but cheerful 'Good morning' was acknowledged only by a 'Morn'' which was almost an oath. Mr Bickersdyke passed up the aisle and into his room like an east wind. He sat down at his table and pressed the bell. Harold, William's brother and co-messenger, entered with the air of one ready to duck if any missile should be thrown at him. The reports of the manager's frame of mind had been circulated in the office, and Harold felt somewhat apprehensive. It was on an occasion very similar to this that George Barstead, formerly in the employ of the New Asiatic Bank in the capacity of messenger, had been rash enough to laugh at what he had taken for a joke of Mr Bickersdyke's, and had been instantly presented with the sack for gross impertinence.

'Ask Mr Smith – ' began the manager. Then he paused. 'No, never mind,' he added.

Harold remained in the doorway, puzzled.

'Don't stand there gaping at me, man,' cried Mr Bickersdyke, 'Go away.'

Harold retired and informed his brother, William, that in his, Harold's, opinion, Mr Bickersdyke was off his chump.

'Off his onion,' said William, soaring a trifle higher in poetic imagery.

'Barmy,' was the terse verdict of Samuel Jakes, the

third messenger. 'Always said so.' And with that the
New Asiatic Bank staff of messengers dismissed Mr
Bickersdyke and proceeded to concentrate themselves
on their duties, which consisted principally of hanging
about and discussing the prophecies of that modern seer,
Captain Coe.

What had made Mr Bickersdyke change his mind so
abruptly was the sudden realization of the fact that he
had no case against Psmith. In his capacity of manager of
the bank he could not take official notice of Psmith's
behaviour outside office hours, especially as Psmith had
done nothing but stare at him. It would be impossible
to make anybody understand the true inwardness of
Psmith's stare. Theoretically, Mr Bickersdyke had the
power to dismiss any subordinate of his whom he did not
consider satisfactory, but it was a power that had to be
exercised with discretion. The manager was accountable
for his actions to the Board of Directors. If he dismissed
Psmith, Psmith would certainly bring an action against
the bank for wrongful dismissal, and on the evidence he
would infallibly win it. Mr Bickersdyke did not welcome
the prospect of having to explain to the Directors that
he had let the shareholders of the bank in for a fine of
whatever a discriminating jury cared to decide upon,
simply because he had been stared at while playing bridge.
His only hope was to catch Psmith doing his work
badly.

He touched the bell again, and sent for Mr Rossiter.

The messenger found the head of the Postage
Department in conversation with Psmith. Manchester
United had been beaten by one goal to nil on the previous
afternoon, and Psmith was informing Mr Rossiter that
the referee was a robber, who had evidently been
financially interested in the result of the game. The way
he himself looked at it, said Psmith, was that the thing
had been a moral victory for the United. Mr Rossiter
said yes, he thought so too. And it was at this moment

that Mr Bickersdyke sent for him to ask whether Psmith's work was satisfactory.

The head of the Postage Department gave his opinion without hesitation. Psmith's work was about the hottest proposition he had ever struck. Psmith's work – well, it stood alone. You couldn't compare it with anything. There are no degrees in perfection. Psmith's work was perfect, and there was an end to it.

He put it differently, but that was the gist of what he said.

Mr Bickersdyke observed he was glad to hear it, and smashed a nib by stabbing the desk with it.

It was on the evening following this that the bank-manager was due to address a meeting at the Kenningford Town Hall. He was looking forward to the event with mixed feelings. He had stood for Parliament once before, several years back, in the North. He had been defeated by a couple of thousand votes, and he hoped that the episode had been forgotten. Not merely because his defeat had been heavy. There was another reason. On that occasion he had stood as a Liberal. He was standing for Kenningford as a Unionist. Of course, a man is at perfect liberty to change his views, if he wishes to do so, but the process is apt to give his opponents a chance of catching him (to use the inspired language of the music-halls) on the bend. Mr Bickersdyke was rather afraid that the light-hearted electors of Kenningford might avail themselves of this chance.

Kenningford, S. E., is undoubtedly by way of being a tough sort of place. Its inhabitants incline to a robust type of humour, which finds a verbal vent in catch phrases and expends itself physically in smashing shop-windows and kicking policemen. He feared that the meeting at the Town Hall might possibly be a trifle rowdy.

All political meetings are very much alike. Somebody

gets up and introduces the speaker of the evening, and then the speaker of the evening says at great length what he thinks of the scandalous manner in which the Government is behaving or the iniquitous goings-on of the Opposition. From time to time confederates in the audience rise and ask carefully rehearsed questions, and are answered fully and satisfactorily by the orator. When a genuine heckler interrupts, the orator either ignores him, or says haughtily that he can find him arguments but cannot find him brains. Or, occasionally, when the question is an easy one, he answers it. A quietly conducted political meeting is one of England's most delightful indoor games. When the meeting is rowdy, the audience has more fun, but the speaker a good deal less.

Mr Bickersdyke's introducer was an elderly Scotch peer, an excellent man for the purpose in every respect, except that he possessed a very strong accent.

The audience welcomed that accent uproariously. The electors of Kenningford who rarely had any definite opinions on politics were fairly equally divided. There were about as many earnest Liberals as there were earnest Unionists. But besides these there was a strong contingent who did not care which side won. These looked on elections as Heaven-sent opportunities for making a great deal of noise. They attended meetings in order to extract amusement from them; and they voted, if they voted at all, quite irresponsibly. A funny story at the expense of one candidate told on the morning of the polling, was quite likely to send these brave fellows off in dozens filling in their papers for the victim's opponent.

There was a solid block of these gay spirits at the back of the hall. They received the Scotch peer with huge delight. He reminded them of Harry Lauder and they said so. They addressed him affectionately as 'Arry', throughout his speech, which was rather long. They implored him to be a pal and sing 'The Saftest of the

Family'. Or, failing that, 'I love a lassie'. Finding they
could not induce him to do this, they did it themselves.
They sang it several times. When the peer, having finished
his remarks on the subject of Mr Bickersdyke, at length
sat down, they cheered for seven minutes, and demanded
an encore.

The meeting was in excellent spirits when Mr
Bickersdyke rose to address it.

The effort of doing justice to the last speaker had left
the free and independent electors at the back of the hall
slightly limp. The bank-manager's opening remarks were
received without any demonstration.

Mr Bickersdyke spoke well. He had a penetrating, if
harsh, voice, and he said what he had to say forcibly.
Little by little the audience came under his spell. When,
at the end of a well-turned sentence, he paused and took
a sip of water, there was a round of applause, in which
many of the admirers of Mr Harry Lauder joined.

He resumed his speech. The audience listened
intently. Mr Bickersdyke, having said some nasty things
about Free Trade and the Alien Immigrant, turned to the
Needs of the Navy and the necessity of increasing
the fleet at all costs.

'This is no time for half-measures,' he said. 'We must
do our utmost. We must burn our boats – '

'Excuse me,' said a gentle voice.

Mr Bickersdyke broke off. In the centre of the hall a
tall figure had risen. Mr Bickersdyke found himself
looking at a gleaming eye-glass which the speaker had
just polished and inserted in his eye.

The ordinary heckler Mr Bickersdyke would have
taken in his stride. He had got his audience, and simply by
continuing and ignoring the interruption, he could have
won through in safety. But the sudden appearance of
Psmith unnerved him. He remained silent.

'How,' asked Psmith, 'do you propose to strengthen
the Navy by burning boats?'

The inanity of the question enraged even the pleasure-seekers at the back.

'Order! Order!' cried the earnest contingent.

'Sit down, fice!' roared the pleasure-seekers.

Psmith sat down with a patient smile.

Mr Bickersdyke resumed his speech. But the fire had gone out of it. He had lost his audience. A moment before, he had grasped them and played on their minds (or what passed for minds down Kenningford way) as on a stringed instrument. Now he had lost his hold.

He spoke on rapidly, but he could not get into his stride. The trivial interruption had broken the spell. His words lacked grip. The dead silence in which the first part of his speech had been received, that silence which is a greater tribute to the speaker than any applause, had given place to a restless medley of little noises; here a cough; there a scraping of a boot along the floor, as its wearer moved uneasily in his seat; in another place a whispered conversation. The audience was bored.

Mr Bickersdyke left the Navy, and went on to more general topics. But he was not interesting. He quoted figures, saw a moment later that he had not quoted them accurately, and instead of carrying on boldly, went back and corrected himself.

'Gow up top!' said a voice at the back of the hall, and there was a general laugh.

Mr Bickersdyke galloped unsteadily on. He condemned the Government. He said they had betrayed their trust.

And then he told an anecdote.

'The Government, gentlemen,' he said, 'achieves nothing worth achieving, and every individual member of the Government takes all the credit for what is done to himself. Their methods remind me, gentlemen, of an amusing experience I had while fishing one summer in the Lake District.'

In a volume entitled 'Three Men in a Boat' there is a

story of how the author and a friend go into a riverside inn and see a very large trout in a glass case. They make inquiries about it. Five men assure them, one by one, that the trout was caught by themselves. In the end the trout turns out to be made of plaster of Paris.

Mr Bickersdyke told that story as an experience of his own while fishing one summer in the Lake District.

It went well. The meeting was amused. Mr Bickersdyke went on to draw a trenchant comparison between the lack of genuine merit in the trout and the lack of genuine merit in the achievements of His Majesty's Government.

There was applause.

When it had ceased, Psmith rose to his feet again.

'Excuse me,' he said.

11 — Misunderstood

Mike had refused to accompany Psmith to the meeting that evening, saying that he got too many chances in the ordinary way of business of hearing Mr Bickersdyke speak, without going out of his way to make more. So Psmith had gone off to Kenningford alone, and Mike, feeling too lazy to sally out to any place of entertainment, had remained at the flat with a novel.

He was deep in this, when there was the sound of a key in the latch, and shortly afterwards Psmith entered the room. On Psmith's brow there was a look of pensive care, and also a slight discoloration. When he removed his overcoat, Mike saw that his collar was burst and hanging loose and that he had no tie. On his erstwhile speckless and gleaming shirt front were a number of finger-impressions, of a boldness and clearness of outline which would have made a Bertillon expert leap with joy.

'Hullo!' said Mike dropping his book.

Psmith nodded in silence, went to his bedroom, and returned with a looking-glass. Propping this up on a table, he proceeded to examine himself with the utmost care. He shuddered slightly as his eye fell on the finger-marks; and without a word he went into his bathroom again. He emerged after an interval of ten minutes in sky-blue pyjamas, slippers, and an Old Etonian blazer. He lit a cigarette; and, sitting down, stared pensively into the fire.

'What the dickens have you been playing at?' demanded Mike.

Psmith heaved a sigh.

'That,' he replied, 'I could not say precisely. At one

69

Psmith in the City

moment it seemed to be Rugby football, at another a jiu-
jitsu *séance*. Later, it bore a resemblance to a pantomime
rally. However, whatever it was, it was all very bright
and interesting. A distinct experience.'

'Have you been scrapping?' asked Mike. 'What
happened? Was there a row?'

'There was,' said Psmith, 'in a measure what might be
described as a row. At least, when you find a perfect
stranger attaching himself to your collar and pulling, you
begin to suspect that something of that kind is on the
bill.'

'Did they do that?'

Psmith nodded.

'A merchant in a moth-eaten bowler started warbling
to a certain extent with me. It was all very trying for a
man of culture. He was a man who had, I should say,
discovered that alcohol was a food long before the doctors
found it out. A good chap, possibly, but a little boisterous
in his manner. Well, well.'

Psmith shook his head sadly.

'He got you one on the forehead,' said Mike, 'or
somebody did. Tell us what happened. I wish the dickens
I'd come with you. I'd no notion there would be a rag of
any sort. What did happen?'

'Comrade Jackson,' said Psmith sorrowfully, 'how sad
it is in this life of ours to be consistently misunderstood.
You know, of course, how wrapped up I am in Comrade
Bickersdyke's welfare. You know that all my efforts are
directed towards making a decent man of him; that, in
short, I am his truest friend. Does he show by so much
as a word that he appreciates my labours? Not he. I believe
that man is beginning to dislike me, Comrade Jackson.'

'What happened, anyhow? Never mind about
Bickersdyke.'

'Perhaps it was mistaken zeal on my part . . . Well, I
will tell you all. Make a long arm for the shovel, Comrade
Jackson, and pile on a few more coals. I thank you. Well,

all went quite smoothly for a while. Comrade B. in quite good form. Got his second wind, and was going strong for the tape, when a regrettable incident occurred. He informed the meeting, that while up in the Lake country, fishing, he went to an inn and saw a remarkably large stuffed trout in a glass case. He made inquiries, and found that five separate and distinct people had caught – '

'Why, dash it all,' said Mike, 'that's a frightful chestnut.'

Psmith nodded.

'It certainly has appeared in print,' he said. 'In fact I should have said it was rather a well-known story. I was so interested in Comrade Bickersdyke's statement that the thing had happened to himself that purely out of good-will towards him, I got up and told him that I thought it was my duty, as a friend, to let him know that a man named Jerome had pinched his story, put it in a book, and got money by it. Money, mark you, that should by rights have been Comrade Bickersdyke's. He didn't appear to care much about sifting the matter thoroughly. In fact, he seemed anxious to get on with his speech, and slur the matter over, But, tactlessly perhaps, I continued rather to harp on the thing. I said that the book in which the story had appeared was published in 1889. I asked him how long ago it was that he had been on his fishing tour, because it was important to know in order to bring the charge home against Jerome. Well, after a bit, I was amazed, and pained, too, to hear Comrade Bickersdyke urging certain bravoes in the audience to turn me out. If ever there was a case of biting the hand that fed him . . . Well, well . . . By this time the meeting had begun to take sides to some extent. What I might call my party, the Earnest Investigators, were whistling between their fingers, stamping on the floor, and shouting, "Chestnuts!" while the opposing party, the bravoes, seemed to be trying, as I say, to do jui-jitsu tricks with me. It was a painful situation. I know the cultivated man of affairs should

have passed the thing off with a short, careless laugh;
but, owing to the above-mentioned alcohol-expert having
got both hands under my collar, short, careless laughs
were off. I was compelled, very reluctantly, to conclude
the interview by tapping the bright boy on the jaw. He
took the hint, and sat down on the floor. I thought
no more of the matter, and was making my way
thoughtfully to the exit, when a second man of wrath put
the above on my forehead. You can't ignore a thing like
that. I collected some of his waistcoat and one of his legs,
and hove him with some vim into the middle distance.
By this time a good many of the Earnest Investigators
were beginning to join in; and it was just there that the
affair began to have certain points of resemblance to a
pantomime rally. Everybody seemed to be shouting a good
deal and hitting everybody else. It was no place for a man
of delicate culture, so I edged towards the door, and
drifted out. There was a cab in the offing. I boarded it.
And, having kicked a vigorous politician in the stomach,
as he was endeavouring to climb in too, I drove off home.'

Psmith got up, looked at his forehead once more in the
glass, sighed, and sat down again.

'All very disturbing,' he said.

'Great Scott,' said Mike, 'I wish I'd come. Why on
earth didn't you tell me you were going to rag? I think
you might as well have done. I wouldn't have missed it
for worlds.'

Psmith regarded him with raised eyebrows.

'Rag!' he said. 'Comrade Jackson, I do not understand
you. You surely do not think that I had any other object in
doing what I did than to serve Comrade Bickersdyke? It's
terrible how one's motives get distorted in this world of
ours.'

'Well,' said Mike, with a grin, 'I know one person
who'll jolly well distort your motives, as you call it, and
that's Bickersdyke.'

Psmith looked thoughtful.

'True,' he said, 'true. There is that possibility. I tell you, Comrade Jackson, once more that my bright young life is being slowly blighted by the frightful way in which that man misunderstands me. It seems almost impossible to try to do him a good turn without having the action misconstrued.'

'What'll you say to him tomorrow?'

'I shall make no allusion to the painful affair. If I happen to meet him in the ordinary course of business routine, I shall pass some light, pleasant remark – on the weather, let us say, or the Bank Rate – and continue my duties.'

'How about if he sends for you, and wants to do the light, pleasant remark business on his own?'

'In that case I shall not thwart him. If he invites me into his private room, I shall be his guest, and shall discuss, to the best of my ability, any topic which he may care to introduce. There shall be no constraint between Comrade Bickersdyke and myself.'

'No, I shouldn't think there would be. I wish I could come and hear you.'

'I wish you could,' said Psmith courteously.

'Still, it doesn't matter much to you. You don't care if you do get sacked.'

Psmith rose.

'In that way possibly, as you say, I am agreeably situated. If the New Asiatic Bank does not require Psmith's services, there are other spheres where a young man of spirit may carve a place for himself. No, what is worrying me, Comrade Jackson, is not the thought of the push. It is the growing fear that Comrade Bickersdyke and I will never thoroughly understand and appreciate one another. A deep gulf lies between us. I do what I can do to bridge it over, but he makes no response. On his side of the gulf building operations appear to be at an entire standstill. That is what is carving these lines of care on my forehead, Comrade Jackson. That is what is painting

73

these purple circles beneath my eyes. Quite inadvertently to be disturbing Comrade Bickersdyke, annoying him, preventing him from enjoying life. How sad this is. Life bulges with these tragedies.'

Mike picked up the evening paper.

'Don't let it keep you awake at night,' he said. 'By the way did you see that Manchester United were playing this afternoon? They won. You'd better sit down and sweat up some of the details. You'll want them tomorrow.'

'You are very right, Comrade Jackson,' said Psmith, re-seating himself. 'So the Mancunians pushed the bulb into the meshes beyond the uprights no fewer than four times, did they? Bless the dear boys, what spirits they do enjoy, to be sure. Comrade Jackson, do not disturb me. I must concentrate myself. These are deep waters.'

12 — In a Nutshell

Mr Bickersdyke sat in his private room at the New
Asiatic Bank with a pile of newspapers before him. At
least, the casual observer would have said that it
was Mr Bickersdyke. In reality, however, it was an active
volcano in the shape and clothes of the bank-manager.
It was freely admitted in the office that morning that the
manager had lowered all records with ease. The staff had
known him to be in a bad temper before – frequently; but
his frame of mind on all previous occasions had been,
compared with his present frame of mind, that of a rather
exceptionally good-natured lamb. Within ten minutes of
his arrival the entire office was on the jump. The
messengers were collected in a pallid group in the
basement, discussing the affair in whispers and
endeavouring to restore their nerve with about
sixpenn'orth of the beverage known as 'unsweetened'.
The heads of departments, to a man, had bowed before
the storm. Within the space of seven minutes and a
quarter Mr Bickersdyke had contrived to find some fault
with each of them. Inward Bills was out at an A. B. C.
shop snatching a hasty cup of coffee, to pull him together
again. Outward Bills was sitting at his desk with the
glazed stare of one who has been struck in the thorax by
a thunderbolt. Mr Rossiter had been torn from Psmith in
the middle of a highly technical discussion of the
Manchester United match, just as he was showing – with
the aid of a ball of paper – how he had once seen Meredith
centre to Sandy Turnbull in a Cup match, and was now
leaping about like a distracted grasshopper. Mr Waller,
head of the Cash Department, had been summoned to

75

the Presence, and after listening meekly to a rush of criticism, had retired to his desk with the air of a beaten spaniel.

Only one man of the many in the building seemed calm and happy – Psmith.

Psmith had resumed the chat about Manchester United, on Mr Rossiter's return from the lion's den, at the spot where it had been broken off; but, finding that the head of the Postage Department was in no mood for discussing football (or anything else), he had postponed his remarks and placidly resumed his work.

Mr Bickersdyke picked up a paper, opened it, and began searching the columns. He had not far to look. It was a slack season for the newspapers, and his little trouble, which might have received a paragraph in a busy week, was set forth fully in three-quarters of a column.

The column was headed, 'Amusing Heckling'.

Mr Bickersdyke read a few lines, and crumpled the paper up with a snort.

The next he examined was an organ of his own shade of political opinion. It too, gave him nearly a column, headed 'Disgraceful Scene at Kenningford'. There was also a leaderette on the subject.

The leaderette said so exactly what Mr Bickersdyke thought himself that for a moment he was soothed. Then the thought of his grievance returned, and he pressed the bell.

'Send Mr Smith to me,' he said.

William, the messenger, proceeded to inform Psmith of the summons.

Psmith's face lit up.

'I am *always* glad to sweeten the monotony of toil with a chat with Little Clarence,' he said. 'I shall be with him in a moment.'

He cleaned his pen very carefully, placed it beside his ledger, flicked a little dust off his coatsleeve, and made his way to the manager's room.

Mr Bickersdyke received him with the ominous restraint of a tiger crouching for its spring. Psmith stood beside the table with languid grace, suggestive of some favoured confidential secretary waiting for instructions.

A ponderous silence brooded over the room for some moments. Psmith broke it by remarking that the Bank Rate was unchanged. He mentioned this fact as if it afforded him a personal gratification.

Mr Bickersdyke spoke.

'Well, Mr Smith?' he said.

'You wished to see me about something, sir?' inquired Psmith, ingratiatingly.

'You know perfectly well what I wished to see you about. I want to hear your explanation of what occurred last night.'

'May I sit, sir?'

He dropped gracefully into a chair, without waiting for permission, and, having hitched up the knees of his trousers, beamed winningly at the manager.

'A deplorable affair,' he said, with a shake of his head. 'Extremely deplorable. We must not judge these rough, uneducated men too harshly, however. In a time of excitement the emotions of the lower classes are easily stirred. Where you or I would – '

Mr Bickersdyke interrupted.

'I do not wish for any more buffoonery, Mr Smith – '

Psmith raised a pained pair of eyebrows.

'Buffoonery, sir!'

'I cannot understand what made you act as you did last night, unless you are perfectly mad, as I am beginning to think.'

'But, surely, sir, there was nothing remarkable in my behaviour? When a merchant has attached himself to your collar, can you do less than smite him on the other cheek? I merely acted in self-defence. You saw for yourself – '

77

'You know what I am alluding to. Your behaviour
during my speech.'

'An excellent speech,' murmured Psmith courteously.

'Well?' said Mr Bickersdyke.

'It was, perhaps, mistaken zeal on my part, sir, but
you must remember that I acted purely from the best
motives. It seemed to me – '

'That is enough, Mr Smith. I confess that I am
absolutely at a loss to understand you – '

'It is too true, sir,' sighed Psmith.

'You seem,' continued Mr Bickersdyke, warming to
his subject, and turning gradually a richer shade of
purple, 'you seem to be determined to endeavour to annoy
me.' ('No no,' from Psmith.) 'I can only assume that you
are not in your right senses. You follow me about in my
club – '

'Our club, sir,' murmured Psmith.

'Be good enough not to interrupt me, Mr Smith. You
dog my footsteps in my club – '

'Purely accidental, sir. We happen to meet – that is
all.'

'You attend meetings at which I am speaking, and
behave in a perfectly imbecile manner.'

Psmith moaned slightly.

'It may seem humorous to you, but I can assure you it
is extremely bad policy on your part. The New Asiatic
Bank is no place for humour, and I think – '

'Excuse me, sir,' said Psmith.

The manager started at the familiar phrase. The plum-
colour of his complexion deepened.

'I entirely agree with you, sir,' said Psmith, 'that this
bank is no place for humour.'

'Very well, then. You – '

'And I am never humorous in it. I arrive punctually in
the morning, and I work steadily and earnestly till my
labours are completed. I think you will find, on inquiry,
that Mr Rossiter is satisfied with my work.'

'That is neither here nor – '

'Surely, sir,' said Psmith, 'you are wrong? Surely your jurisdiction ceases after office hours? Any little misunderstanding we may have at the close of the day's work cannot affect you officially. You could not, for instance, dismiss me from the service of the bank if we were partners at bridge at the club and I happened to revoke.'

'I can dismiss you, let me tell you, Mr Smith, for studied insolence, whether in the office or not.'

'I bow to superior knowledge,' said Psmith politely, 'but I confess I doubt it. And,' he added, 'there is another point. May I continue to some extent?'

'If you have anything to say, say it.'

Psmith flung one leg over the other, and settled his collar.

'It is perhaps a delicate matter,' he said, 'but it is best to be frank. We should have no secrets. To put my point quite clearly, I must go back a little, to the time when you paid us that very welcome week-end visit at our house in August.'

'If you hope to make capital out of the fact that I have been a guest of your father – '

'Not at all,' said Psmith deprecatingly. 'Not at all. You do not take me. My point is this. I do not wish to revive painful memories, but it cannot be denied that there was, here and there, some slight bickering between us on that occasion. The fault,' said Psmith magnanimously, 'was possibly mine. I may have been too exacting, too capricious. Perhaps so. However, the fact remains that you conceived the happy notion of getting me into this bank, under the impression that, once I was in, you would be able to – if I may use the expression – give me beans. You said as much to me, if I remember. I hate to say it, but don't you think that if you give me the sack, although my work is satisfactory to the head of my department, you will be by way of admitting that you bit off rather more than you could chew? I merely make the suggestion.'

Mr Bickersdyke half rose from his chair.

'You – '

'Just so, just so, but – to return to the main point – don't you? The whole painful affair reminds me of the story of Agesilaus and the Petulant Pterodactyl, which as you have never heard, I will now proceed to relate. Agesilaus – '

Mr Bickersdyke made a curious clucking noise in his throat.

'I am boring you,' said Psmith, with ready tact. 'Suffice it to say that Comrade Agesilaus interfered with the pterodactyl, which was doing him no harm; and the intelligent creature, whose motto was "Nemo me impune lacessit", turned and bit him. Bit him good and hard, so that Agesilaus ever afterwards had a distaste for pterodactyls. His reluctance to disturb them became quite a by-word. The Society papers of the period frequently commented upon it. Let us draw the parallel.'

Here Mr Bickersdyke, who had been clucking throughout this speech, essayed to speak; but Psmith hurried on.

'You are Agesilaus,' he said. 'I am the Petulant Pterodactyl. You, if I may say so, butted in of your own free will, and took me from a happy home, simply in order that you might get me into this place under you, and give me beans. But, curiously enough, the major portion of that vegetable seems to be coming to you. Of course, you can administer the push if you like; but, as I say, it will be by way of a confession that your scheme has sprung a leak. Personally,' said Psmith, as one friend to another, 'I should advise you to stick it out. You never know what may happen. At any moment I may fall from my present high standard of industry and excellence; and then you have me, so to speak, where the hair is crisp.'

He paused. Mr Bickersdyke's eyes, which even in their normal state protruded slightly, now looked as if they might fall out at any moment. His face had passed from the plum-coloured stage to something beyond. Every now and then he made the clucking noise, but except for that he was silent. Psmith, having waited for some time for something in the shape of comment or criticism on his remarks, now rose.

'It has been a great treat to me, this little chat,' he said affably, 'but I fear that I must no longer allow purely social enjoyments to interfere with my commercial pursuits. With your permission, I will rejoin my department, where my absence is doubtless already causing comment and possibly dismay. But we shall be meeting at the club shortly, I hope. Good-bye, sir, good-bye.'

He left the room, and walked dreamily back to the Postage Department, leaving the manager still staring glassily at nothing.

13 — Mike is Moved On

This episode may be said to have concluded the first act of the commercial drama in which Mike and Psmith had been cast for leading parts. And, as usually happens after the end of an act, there was a lull for a while until things began to work up towards another climax. Mike, as day succeeded day, began to grow accustomed to the life of the bank, and to find that it had its pleasant side after all. Whenever a number of people are working at the same thing, even though that thing is not perhaps what they would have chosen as an object in life, if left to themselves, there is bound to exist an atmosphere of good-fellowship; something akin to, though a hundred times weaker than, the public school spirit. Such a community lacks the main motive of the public school spirit, which is pride in the school and its achievements. Nobody can be proud of the achievements of a bank. When the business of arranging a new Japanese loan was given to the New Asiatic Bank, its employees did not stand on stools, and cheer. On the contrary, they thought of the extra work it would involve; and they cursed a good deal, though there was no denying that it was a big thing for the bank – not unlike winning the Ashburton would be to a school. There is a cold impersonality about a bank. A school is a living thing.

Setting aside this important difference, there was a good deal of the public school about the New Asiatic Bank. The heads of departments were not quite so autocratic as masters, and one was treated more on a grown-up scale, as man to man; but, nevertheless, there remained a distinct flavour of a school republic. Most of the men in the bank, with the exception of certain hard-headed Scotch youths drafted in from other establishments in the City, were old public school men. Mike found two Old Wrykinians in the first week. Neither was well known to him. They had left in his second year in the team. But it was pleasant to have them about, and to feel that they had been educated at the right place.

As far as Mike's personal comfort went, the presence of these two Wrykinians was very much for the good. Both of them knew all about his cricket, and they spread the news. The New Asiatic Bank, like most London banks, was keen on sport, and happened to possess a cricket team which could make a good game with most of the second-rank clubs. The disappearance to the East of two of the best bats of the previous season caused Mike's advent to be hailed with a good deal of enthusiasm. Mike was a county man. He had only played once for his county, it was true, but that did not matter. He had passed the barrier which separates the second-class bat from the first-class, and the bank welcomed him with awe. County men did not come their way every day.

Mike did not like being in the bank, considered in the light of a career. But he bore no grudge against the inmates of the bank, such as he had borne against the inmates of Sedleigh. He had looked on the latter as bound up with the school, and, consequently, enemies. His fellow workers in the bank he regarded as companions in misfortune. They were all in the same boat together. There were men from Tonbridge, Dulwich, Bedford, St Paul's, and a dozen other schools. One or two of them he knew by repute from the pages of Wisden. Bannister, his cheerful predecessor in the Postage Department, was the Bannister, he recollected now, who had played for Geddington against Wrykyn in his second year in the Wrykyn team. Munroe, the big man in the Fixed Deposits, he remembered as leader of the Ripton pack. Every day brought fresh discoveries of this sort, and each made

Mike more reconciled to his lot. They were a pleasant set of fellows in the New Asiatic Bank, and but for the dreary outlook which the future held – for Mike, unlike most of his fellow workers, was not attracted by the idea of a life in the East – he would have been very fairly content.

The hostility of Mr Bickersdyke was a slight drawback. Psmith had developed a habit of taking Mike with him to the club of an evening; and this did not do anything towards wiping out of the manager's mind the recollection of his former passage of arms with the Old Wrykinian. The glass remaining Set Fair as far as Mr Rossiter's approval was concerned, Mike was enabled to keep off the managerial carpet to a great extent; but twice, when he posted letters without going through the preliminary formality of stamping them, Mr Bickersdyke had opportunities of which he availed himself. But for these incidents life was fairly enjoyable. Owing to Psmith's benevolent efforts, the Postage Department became quite a happy family, and ex-occupants of the postage desk, Bannister especially, were amazed at the change that had come over Mr Rossiter. He no longer darted from his lair like a pouncing panther. To report his subordinates to the manager seemed now to be a lost art with him. The sight of Psmith and Mr Rossiter proceeding high and disposedly to a mutual lunch became quite common, and ceased to excite remark.

'By kindness,' said Psmith to Mike, after one of these expeditions. 'By tact and kindness. That is how it is done. I do not despair of training Comrade Rossiter one of these days to jump through paper hoops.'

So that, altogether, Mike's life in the bank had become very fairly pleasant.

Out of office-hours he enjoyed himself hugely. London was strange to him, and with Psmith as a companion, he extracted a vast deal of entertainment from it. Psmith was not unacquainted with the West End, and he proved an excellent guide. At first Mike expostulated with unfailing regularity at the other's habit of paying for everything, but Psmith waved aside all objections with languid firmness.

'I need you, Comrade Jackson,' he said, when Mike lodged a protest on finding himself bound for the stalls for the second night in succession. 'We must stick together. As my confidential secretary and adviser, your place is by my side. Who knows but that between the acts tonight I may not be seized with some luminous thought? Could I utter this to my next-door neighbour or the programme-girl? Stand by me, Comrade Jackson, or we are undone.'

So Mike stood by him.

By this time Mike had grown so used to his work that he could tell to within five minutes when a rush would come; and he was able to spend a good deal of his time reading a surreptitious novel behind a pile of ledgers, or down in the tea-room. The New Asiatic Bank supplied tea to its employees. In quality it was bad, and the bread-and-butter associated with it was worse. But it had the merit of giving one an excuse for being away from one's desk. There were large printed notices all over the tea-room, which was in the basement, informing gentlemen that they were only allowed ten minutes for tea, but one took just as long as one thought the head of one's department would stand, from twenty-five minutes to an hour and a quarter.

This state of things was too good to last. Towards the beginning of the New Year a new man arrived, and Mike was moved on to another department.

14 — Mr Waller Appears in a New Light

The department into which Mike was sent was the Cash, or, to be more exact, that section of it which was known as Paying Cashier. The important task of shooting doubloons across the counter did not belong to Mike himself, but to Mr Waller. Mike's work was less ostentatious, and was performed with pen, ink, and ledgers in the background. Occasionally, when Mr Waller was out at lunch, Mike had to act as substitute for him, and cash cheques; but Mr Waller always went out at a slack time, when few customers came in, and Mike seldom had any very startling sum to hand over.

He enjoyed being in the Cash Department. He liked Mr Waller. The work was easy; and when he did happen to make mistakes, they were corrected patiently by the grey-bearded one, and not used as levers for boosting him into the presence of Mr Bickersdyke, as they might have been in some departments. The cashier seemed to have taken a fancy to Mike; and Mike, as was usually the way with him when people went out of their way to be friendly, was at his best. Mike at his ease and unsuspicious of hostile intentions was a different person from Mike with his prickles out.

Psmith, meanwhile, was not enjoying himself. It was an unheard-of thing, he said, depriving a man of his confidential secretary without so much as asking his leave.

'It has caused me the greatest inconvenience,' he told Mike, drifting round in a melancholy way to the Cash Department during a slack spell one afternoon. 'I miss you at every turn. Your keen intelligence and ready sympathy were invaluable to me. Now where am I? In the cart. I evolved a slightly bright thought on life just now. There was nobody to tell it to except the new man. I told it him, and the fool gaped. I tell you, Comrade Jackson, I feel like some lion that has been robbed of its cub. I feel as Marshall would feel if they took Snelgrove away from him, or as Peace might if he awoke one morning to find Plenty gone. Comrade Rossiter does his best. We still talk brokenly about Manchester United – they got routed in the first round of the Cup yesterday and Comrade Rossiter is wearing black – but it is not the same. I try work, but that is no good either. From ledger to ledger they hurry me, to stifle my regret. And when they win a smile from me, they think that I forget. But I don't. I am a broken man. That new exhibit they've got in your place is about as near to the Extreme Edge as anything I've ever seen. One of Nature's blighters. Well, well, I must away. Comrade Rossiter awaits me.'

Mike's successor, a youth of the name of Bristow, was causing Psmith a great deal of pensive melancholy. His worst defect – which he could not help – was that he was not Mike. His others – which he could – were numerous. His clothes were cut in a way that harrowed Psmith's sensitive soul every time he looked at them. The fact that he wore detachable cuffs, which he took off on beginning work and stacked in a glistening pile on the desk in front of him, was no proof of innate viciousness of disposition, but it prejudiced the Old Etonian against him. It was part of Psmith's philosophy that a man who wore detachable cuffs had passed beyond the limit of human toleration. In addition, Bristow wore a small black moustache and a ring and that, as Psmith informed Mike, put the lid on it.

Mike would sometimes stroll round to the Postage Department to listen to the conversations between the two. Bristow was always friendliness itself. He habitually addressed Psmith as Smithy, a fact which entertained

Mike greatly but did not seem to amuse Psmith to any
overwhelming extent. On the other hand, when, as he
generally did, he called Mike 'Mister Cricketer', the
humour of the thing appeared to elude Mike, though
the mode of address always drew from Psmith a pale, wan
smile, as of a broken heart made cheerful against its own
inclination.

The net result of the coming of Bristow was that
Psmith spent most of his time, when not actually
oppressed by a rush of work, in the precincts of the Cash
Department, talking to Mike and Mr Waller. The latter
did not seem to share the dislike common among the
other heads of departments of seeing his subordinates
receiving visitors. Unless the work was really heavy, in
which case a mild remonstrance escaped him, he offered
no objection to Mike being at home to Psmith. It was this
tolerance which sometimes got him into trouble with
Mr Bickersdyke. The manager did not often perambulate
the office, but he did occasionally, and the interview
which ensued upon his finding Hutchinson, the underling
in the Cash Department at that time, with his stool
tilted comfortably against the wall, reading the sporting
news from a pink paper to a friend from the Outward
Bills Department who lay luxuriously on the floor beside
him, did not rank among Mr Waller's pleasantest
memories. But Mr Waller was too soft-hearted to interfere
with his assistants unless it was absolutely necessary.
The truth of the matter was that the New Asiatic Bank
was over-staffed. There were too many men for the work.
The London branch of the bank was really only a nursery.
New men were constantly wanted in the Eastern
branches, so they had to be put into the London branch
to learn the business, whether there was any work for
them to do or not.

It was after one of these visits of Psmith's that Mr
Waller displayed a new and unsuspected side to his
character. Psmith had come round in a state of some

depression to discuss Bristow, as usual. Bristow, it seemed, had come to the bank that morning in a fancy waistcoat of so emphatic a colour-scheme that Psmith stoutly refused to sit in the same department with it.

'What with Comrades Bristow and Bickersdyke combined,' said Psmith plaintively, 'the work is becoming too hard for me. The whisper is beginning to circulate, "Psmith's number is up. As a reformer he is merely among those present. He is losing his dash." But what can I do? I cannot keep an eye on both of them at the same time. The moment I concentrate myself on Comrade Bickersdyke for a brief spell, and seem to be doing him a bit of good, what happens? Why, Comrade Bristow sneaks off and buys a sort of woollen sunset. I saw the thing unexpectedly. I tell you I was shaken. It is the suddenness of that waistcoat which hits you. It's discouraging, this sort of thing. I try always to think well of my fellow man. As an energetic Socialist, I do my best to see the good that is in him, but it's hard. Comrade Bristow's the most striking argument against the equality of man I've ever come across.'

Mr Waller intervened at this point.

'I think you must really let Jackson go on with his work, Smith,' he said. 'There seems to be too much talking.'

'My besetting sin,' said Psmith sadly. 'Well, well, I will go back and do my best to face it, but it's a tough job.'

He tottered wearily away in the direction of the Postage Department.

'Oh, Jackson,' said Mr Waller, 'will you kindly take my place for a few minutes? I must go round and see the Inward Bills about something. I shall be back very soon.'

Mike was becoming accustomed to deputizing for the cashier for short spaces of time. It generally happened that he had to do so once or twice a day. Strictly speaking, perhaps, Mr Waller was wrong to leave such an

important task as the actual cashing of cheques to
an inexperienced person of Mike's standing; but the
New Asiatic Bank differed from most banks in that there
was not a great deal of cross-counter work. People came
in fairly frequently to cash cheques of two or three pounds,
but it was rare that any very large dealings took
place.

Having completed his business with the Inward Bills,
Mr Waller made his way back by a circuitous route, taking
in the Postage desk.

He found Psmith with a pale, set face, inscribing
figures in a ledger. The Old Etonian greeted him with
the faint smile of a persecuted saint who is determined
to be cheerful even at the stake.

'Comrade Bristow,' he said.

'Hullo, Smithy?' said the other, turning.

Psmith sadly directed Mr Waller's attention to the
waistcoat, which was certainly definite in its colouring.

'Nothing,' said Psmith. 'I only wanted to look at you.'

'Funny ass,' said Bristow, resuming his work. Psmith
glanced at Mr Waller, as who should say, 'See what I
have to put up with. And yet I do not give way.'

'Oh – er – Smith,' said Mr Waller, 'when you were
talking to Jackson just now – '

'Say no more,' said Psmith. 'It shall not occur again.
Why should I dislocate the work of your department in
my efforts to win a sympathetic word? I will bear
Comrade Bristow like a man here. After all, there are
worse things at the Zoo.'

'No, no,' said Mr Waller hastily, 'I did not mean that.
By all means pay us a visit now and then, if it does not
interfere with your own work. But I noticed just now that
you spoke to Bristow as Comrade Bristow.'

'It is too true,' said Psmith. 'I must correct myself of
the habit. He will be getting above himself.'

'And when you were speaking to Jackson, you spoke
of yourself as a Socialist.'

'Socialism is the passion of my life,' said Psmith.

Mr Waller's face grew animated. He stammered in his eagerness.

'I am delighted,' he said. 'Really, I am delighted. I also – '

'A fellow worker in the Cause?' said Psmith.

'Er – exactly.'

Psmith extended his hand gravely. Mr Waller shook it with enthusiasm.

'I have never liked to speak of it to anybody in the office,' said Mr Waller, 'but I, too, am heart and soul in the movement.'

'Yours for the Revolution?' said Psmith.

'Just so. Just so. Exactly. I was wondering – the fact is, I am in the habit of speaking on Sundays in the open air, and – '

'Hyde Park?'

'No. No. Clapham Common. It is – er – handier for me where I live. Now, as you are interested in the movement, I was thinking that perhaps you might care to come and hear me speak next Sunday. Of course, if you have nothing better to do.'

'I should like to excessively,' said Psmith.

'Excellent. Bring Jackson with you, and both of you come to supper afterwards, if you will.'

'Thanks very much.'

'Perhaps you would speak yourself?'

'No,' said Psmith. 'No. I think not. My Socialism is rather of the practical sort. I seldom speak. But it would be a treat to listen to you. What – er – what type of oratory is yours?'

'Oh, well,' said Mr Waller, pulling nervously at his beard, 'of course I – . Well, I am perhaps a little bitter – '

'Yes, yes.'

'A little mordant and ironical.'

'You would be,' agreed Psmith. 'I shall look forward

to Sunday with every fibre quivering. And Comrade Jackson shall be at my side.'

'Excellent,' said Mr Waller. 'I will go and tell him now.'

15 — Stirring Times on the Common

'The first thing to do,' said Psmith, 'is to ascertain that such a place as Clapham Common really exists. One has heard of it, of course, but has its existence ever been proved? I think not. Having accomplished that, we must then try to find out how to get to it. I should say at a venture that it would necessitate a sea-voyage. On the other hand, Comrade Waller, who is a native of the spot, seems to find no difficulty in rolling to the office every morning. Therefore – you follow me, Jackson? – it must be in England. In that case, we will take a taximeter cab, and go out into the unknown, hand in hand, trusting to luck.'

'I expect you could get there by tram,' said Mike.

Psmith suppressed a slight shudder.

'I fear, Comrade Jackson,' he said, 'that the old *noblesse oblige* traditions of the Psmiths would not allow me to do that. No. We will stroll gently, after a light lunch, to Trafalgar Square, and hail a taxi.'

'Beastly expensive.'

'But with what an object! Can any expenditure be called excessive which enables us to hear Comrade Waller being mordant and ironical at the other end?'

'It's a rum business,' said Mike. 'I hope the dickens he won't mix us up in it. We should look frightful fools.'

'I may possibly say a few words,' said Psmith carelessly, 'if the spirit moves me. Who am I that I should deny people a simple pleasure?'

Mike looked alarmed.

'Look here,' he said, 'I say, if you *are* going to play the

93

goat, for goodness' sake don't go lugging me into it. I've got heaps of troubles without that.'

Psmith waved the objection aside.

'You,' he said, 'will be one of the large, and, I hope, interested audience. Nothing more. But it is quite possible that the spirit may not move me. I may not feel inspired to speak. I am not one of those who love speaking for speaking's sake. If I have no message for the many-headed, I shall remain silent.'

'Then I hope the dickens you won't have,' said Mike. Of all things he hated most being conspicuous before a crowd – except at cricket, which was a different thing – and he had an uneasy feeling that Psmith would rather like it than otherwise.

'We shall see,' said Psmith absently. 'Of course, if in the vein, I might do something big in the way of oratory. I am a plain, blunt man, but I feel convinced that, given the opportunity, I should haul up my slacks to some effect. But – well, we shall see. We shall see.'

And with this ghastly state of doubt Mike had to be content.

It was with feelings of apprehension that he accompanied Psmith from the flat to Trafalgar Square in search of a cab which should convey them to Clapham Common.

They were to meet Mr Waller at the edge of the Common nearest the old town of Clapham. On the journey down Psmith was inclined to be *débonnaire*. Mike, on the other hand, was silent and apprehensive. He knew enough of Psmith to know that, if half an opportunity were offered him, he would extract entertainment from this affair after his own fashion; and then the odds were that he himself would be dragged into it. Perhaps – his scalp bristled at the mere idea – he would even be let in for a speech.

This grisly thought had hardly come into his head, when Psmith spoke.

'I'm not half sure,' he said thoughtfully, 'I shan't call on you for a speech, Comrade Jackson.'

'Look here, Psmith – ' began Mike agitatedly.

'I don't know. I think your solid, incisive style would rather go down with the masses. However, we shall see, we shall see.'

Mike reached the Common in a state of nervous collapse.

Mr Waller was waiting for them by the railings near the pond. The apostle of the Revolution was clad soberly in black, except for a tie of vivid crimson. His eyes shone with the light of enthusiasm, vastly different from the mild glow of amiability which they exhibited for six days in every week. The man was transformed.

'Here you are,' he said. 'Here you are. Excellent. You are in good time. Comrades Wotherspoon and Prebble have already begun to speak. I shall commence now that you have come. This is the way. Over by these trees.'

They made their way towards a small clump of trees, near which a fair-sized crowd had already begun to collect. Evidently listening to the speakers was one of Clapham's fashionable Sunday amusements. Mr Walker talked and gesticulated incessantly as he walked. Psmith's demeanour was perhaps a shade patronizing, but he displayed interest. Mike proceeded to the meeting with the air of an about-to-be-washed dog. He was loathing the whole business with a heartiness worthy of a better cause. Somehow, he felt he was going to be made to look a fool before the afternoon was over. But he registered a vow that nothing should drag him on to the small platform which had been erected for the benefit of the speaker.

As they drew nearer, the voices of Comrades Wotherspoon and Prebble became more audible. They had been audible all the time, very much so, but now they grew in volume. Comrade Wotherspoon was a tall, thin man with side-whiskers and a high voice. He

scattered his aitches as a fountain its sprays in a strong
wind. He was very earnest. Comrade Prebble was earnest,
too. Perhaps even more so than Comrade Wotherspoon.
He was handicapped to some extent, however, by not
having a palate. This gave to his profoundest thoughts a
certain weirdness, as if they had been uttered in an
unknown tongue. The crowd was thickest round his
platform. The grown-up section plainly regarded him as
a comedian, pure and simple, and roared with happy
laughter when he urged them to march upon Park Lane
and loot the same without mercy or scruple. The children
were more doubtful. Several had broken down, and been
led away in tears.

When Mr Waller got up to speak on platform number
three, his audience consisted at first only of Psmith,
Mike, and a fox-terrier. Gradually however, he attracted
others. After wavering for a while, the crowd finally
decided that he was worth hearing. He had a method of
his own. Lacking the natural gifts which marked
Comrade Prebble out as an entertainer, he made up for
this by his activity. Where his colleagues stood
comparatively still, Mr Waller behaved with the vivacity
generally supposed to belong only to peas on shovels
and cats on hot bricks. He crouched to denounce the
House of Lords. He bounded from side to side while
dissecting the methods of the plutocrats. During an
impassioned onslaught on the monarchical system he
stood on one leg and hopped. This was more the sort of
thing the crowd had come to see. Comrade Wotherspoon
found himself deserted, and even Comrade Prebble's
shortcomings in the way of palate were insufficient to
keep his flock together. The entire strength of the
audience gathered in front of the third platform.

Mike, separated from Psmith by the movement of the
crowd, listened with a growing depression. That feeling
which attacks a sensitive person sometimes at the theatre
when somebody is making himself ridiculous on the

stage – the illogical feeling that it is he and not the actor who is floundering – had come over him in a wave. He liked Mr Waller, and it made his gorge rise to see him exposing himself to the jeers of a crowd. The fact that Mr Waller himself did not know that they were jeers, but mistook them for applause, made it no better. Mike felt vaguely furious.

His indignation began to take a more personal shape when the speaker, branching off from the main subject of Socialism, began to touch on temperance. There was no particular reason why Mr Waller should have introduced the subject of temperance, except that he happened to be an enthusiast. He linked it on to his remarks on Socialism by attributing the lethargy of the masses to their fondness for alcohol; and the crowd, which had been inclined rather to pat itself on the back during the assaults on Rank and Property, finding itself assailed in its turn, resented it. They were there to listen to speakers telling them that they were the finest fellows on earth, not pointing out their little failings to them. The feeling of the meeting became hostile. The jeers grew more frequent and less good-tempered.

'Comrade Waller means well,' said a voice in Mike's ear, 'but if he shoots it at them like this much more there'll be a bit of an imbroglio.'

'Look here, Smith,' said Mike quickly, 'can't we stop him? These chaps are getting fed up, and they look bargees enough to do anything. They'll be going for him or something soon.'

'How can we switch off the flow? I don't see. The man is wound up. He means to get it off his chest if it snows. I feel we are by way of being in the soup once more, Comrade Jackson. We can only sit tight and look on.'

The crowd was becoming more threatening every minute. A group of young men of the loafer class who stood near Mike were especially fertile in comment. Psmith's eyes were on the speaker; but Mike was watching

97

this group closely. Suddenly he saw one of them, a thick-set youth wearing a cloth cap and no collar, stoop.

When he rose again there was a stone in his hand.

The sight acted on Mike like a spur. Vague rage against nobody in particular had been simmering in him for half an hour. Now it concentrated itself on the cloth-capped one.

Mr Waller paused momentarily before renewing his harangue. The man in the cloth cap raised his hand. There was a swirl in the crowd, and the first thing that Psmith saw as he turned was Mike seizing the would-be marksman round the neck and hurling him to the ground, after the manner of a forward at football tackling an opponent during a line-out from touch.

There is one thing which will always distract the attention of a crowd from any speaker, and that is a dispute between two of its units. Mr Waller's views on temperance were forgotten in an instant. The audience surged round Mike and his opponent.

The latter had scrambled to his feet now, and was looking round for his assailant.

'That's 'im, Bill!' cried eager voices, indicating Mike.

''E's the bloke wot 'it yer, Bill,' said others, more precise in detail.

Bill advanced on Mike in a sidelong, crab-like manner.

''Oo're you, I should like to know?' said Bill.

Mike, rightly holding that this was merely a rhetorical question and that Bill had no real thirst for information as to his family history, made no reply. Or, rather, the reply he made was not verbal. He waited till his questioner was within range, and then hit him in the eye. A reply far more satisfactory, if not to Bill himself, at any rate to the interested onlookers, than any flow of words.

A contented sigh went up from the crowd. Their Sunday afternoon was going to be spent just as they considered Sunday afternoons should be spent.

'Give us your coat,' said Psmith briskly, 'and try and get it over quick. Don't go in for any fancy sparring. Switch it on, all you know, from the start. I'll keep a thoughtful eye open to see that none of his friends and relations join in.'

Outwardly Psmith was unruffled, but inwardly he was not feeling so composed. An ordinary turn-up before an impartial crowd which could be relied upon to preserve the etiquette of these matters was one thing. As regards the actual little dispute with the cloth-capped Bill, he felt that he could rely on Mike to handle it satisfactorily. But there was no knowing how long the crowd would be content to remain mere spectators. There was no doubt which way its sympathies lay. Bill, now stripped of his coat and sketching out in a hoarse voice a scenario of what he intended to do – knocking Mike down and stamping him into the mud was one of the milder feats he promised to perform for the entertainment of an indulgent audience – was plainly the popular favourite.

Psmith, though he did not show it, was more than a little apprehensive.

Mike, having more to occupy his mind in the immediate present, was not anxious concerning the future. He had the great advantage over Psmith of having lost his temper. Psmith could look on the situation as a whole, and count the risks and possibilities. Mike could only see Bill shuffling towards him with his head down and shoulders bunched.

'Gow it, Bill!' said someone.

'Pliy up, the Arsenal!' urged a voice on the outskirts of the crowd.

A chorus of encouragement from kind friends in front: 'Step up, Bill!'

And Bill stepped.

16 — Further Developments

Bill (surname unknown) was not one of your ultra-scientific fighters. He did not favour the American crouch and the artistic feint. He had a style wholly his own. It seemed to have been modelled partly on a tortoise and partly on a windmill. His head he appeared to be trying to conceal between his shoulders, and he whirled his arms alternately in circular sweeps.

Mike, on the other hand, stood upright and hit straight, with the result that he hurt his knuckles very much on his opponent's skull, without seeming to disturb the latter to any great extent. In the process he received one of the windmill swings on the left ear. The crowd, strong pro-Billites, raised a cheer.

This maddened Mike. He assumed the offensive. Bill, satisfied for the moment with his success, had stepped back, and was indulging in some fancy sparring, when Mike sprang upon him like a panther. They clinched, and Mike, who had got the under grip, hurled Bill forcibly against a stout man who looked like a publican. The two fell in a heap, Bill underneath.

At the same time Bill's friends joined in.

The first intimation Mike had of this was a violent blow across the shoulders with a walking-stick. Even if he had been wearing his overcoat, the blow would have hurt. As he was in his jacket it hurt more than anything he had ever experienced in his life. He leapt up with a yell, but Psmith was there before him. Mike saw his assailant lift the stick again, and then collapse as the old Etonian's right took him under the chin.

He darted to Psmith's side.

'This is no place for us,' observed the latter sadly. 'Shift ho, I think. Come on.'

They dashed simultaneously for the spot where the crowd was thinnest. The ring which had formed round Mike and Bill had broken up as the result of the intervention of Bill's allies, and at the spot for which they ran only two men were standing. And these had apparently made up their minds that neutrality was the best policy, for they made no movement to stop them. Psmith and Mike charged through the gap, and raced for the road.

The suddenness of the move gave them just the start they needed. Mike looked over his shoulder. The crowd, to a man, seemed to be following. Bill, excavated from beneath the publican, led the field. Lying a good second came a band of three, and after them the rest in a bunch.

They reached the road in this order.

Some fifty yards down the road was a stationary tram. In the ordinary course of things it would probably have moved on long before Psmith and Mike could have got to it; but the conductor, a man with sporting blood in him, seeing what appeared to be the finish of some Marathon Race, refrained from giving the signal, and moved out into the road to observe events more clearly, at the same time calling to the driver, who joined him. Passengers on the roof stood up to get a good view. There was some cheering.

Psmith and Mike reached the tram ten yards to the good; and, if it had been ready to start then, all would have been well. But Bill and his friends had arrived while the driver and conductor were both out in the road.

The affair now began to resemble the doings of Horatius on the bridge. Psmith and Mike turned to bay on the platform at the foot of the tram steps. Bill, leading by three yards, sprang on to it, grabbed Mike, and fell with him on to the road. Psmith, descending with a dignity somewhat lessened by the fact that his hat was on the side of his head, was in time to engage the runners-up.

Psmith, as pugilist, lacked something of the calm majesty which characterized him in the more peaceful moments of life, but he was undoubtedly effective. Nature had given him an enormous reach and a lightness on his feet remarkable in one of his size; and at some time in his career he appeared to have learned how to use his hands. The first of the three runners, the walking-stick manipulator, had the misfortune to charge straight into the old Etonian's left. It was a well-timed blow, and the force of it, added to the speed at which the victim was running, sent him on to the pavement, where he spun round and sat down. In the subsequent proceedings he took no part.

The other two attacked Psmith simultaneously, one on each side. In doing so, the one on the left tripped over Mike and Bill, who were still in the process of sorting themselves out, and fell, leaving Psmith free to attend to the other. He was a tall, weedy youth. His conspicuous features were a long nose and a light yellow waistcoat. Psmith hit him on the former with his left and on the latter with his right. The long youth emitted a gurgle, and collided with Bill, who had wrenched himself free from Mike and staggered to his feet. Bill, having received a second blow in the eye during the course of his interview on the road with Mike, was not feeling himself. Mistaking the other for an enemy, he proceeded to smite him in the parts about the jaw. He had just upset him, when a stern official voice observed, ''Ere, now, what's all this?'

There is no more unfailing corrective to a scene of strife than the 'What's all this?' of the London policeman. Bill abandoned his intention of stamping on the prostrate one, and the latter, sitting up, blinked and was silent.

'What's all this?' asked the policeman again. Psmith,

adjusting his hat at the correct angle again, undertook the explanations.

'A distressing scene, officer,' he said. 'A case of that unbridled brawling which is, alas, but too common in our London streets. These two, possibly till now the closest friends, fall out over some point, probably of the most trivial nature, and what happens? They brawl. They – '

'He 'it me,' said the long youth, dabbing at his face with a handkerchief and pointing an accusing finger at Psmith, who regarded him through his eyeglass with a look in which pity and censure were nicely blended.

Bill, meanwhile, circling round restlessly, in the apparent hope of getting past the Law and having another encounter with Mike, expressed himself in a stream of language which drew stern reproof from the shocked constable.

'You 'op it,' concluded the man in blue. 'That's what you do. You 'op it.'

'I should,' said Psmith kindly. 'The officer is speaking in your best interests. A man of taste and discernment, he knows what is best. His advice is good, and should be followed.'

The constable seemed to notice Psmith for the first time. He turned and stared at him. Psmith's praise had not had the effect of softening him. His look was one of suspicion.

'And what might *you* have been up to?' he inquired coldly. 'This man says you hit him.'

Psmith waved the matter aside.

'Purely in self-defence,' he said, 'purely in self-defence. What else could the man of spirit do? A mere tap to discourage an aggressive movement.'

The policeman stood silent, weighing matters in the balance. He produced a notebook and sucked his pencil. Then he called the conductor of the tram as a witness.

'A brainy and admirable step,' said Psmith,

approvingly. 'This rugged, honest man, all unused to verbal subtleties, shall give us his plain account of what happened. After which, as I presume this tram – little as I know of the habits of trams – has got to go somewhere today, I would suggest that we all separated and moved on.'

He took two half-crowns from his pocket, and began to clink them meditatively together. A slight softening of the frigidity of the constable's manner became noticeable. There was a milder beam in the eyes which gazed into Psmith's.

Nor did the conductor seem altogether uninfluenced by the sight,

The conductor deposed that he had bin on the point of pushing on, seeing as how he'd hung abart long enough, when he see'd them two gents, the long 'un with the heye-glass (Psmith bowed) and t'other 'un, a-legging of it dahn the road towards him, with the other blokes pelting after 'em. He added that, when they reached the trem, the two gents had got aboard, and was then set upon by the blokes. And after that, he concluded, well, there was a bit of a scrap, and that's how it was.

'Lucidly and excellently put,' said Psmith. 'That is just how it was. Comrade Jackson, I fancy we leave the court without a stain on our characters. We win through. Er – constable, we have given you a great deal of trouble. Possibly – ?'

'Thank you, sir.' There was a musical clinking. 'Now then, all of you, you 'op it. You've all bin poking your noses in 'ere long enough. Pop off. Get on with that tram, conductor.'

Psmith and Mike settled themselves in a seat on the roof. When the conductor came along, Psmith gave him half a crown, and asked after his wife and the little ones at home. The conductor thanked goodness that he was a bachelor, punched the tickets, and retired.

'Subject for a historical picture,' said Psmith.

'Wounded leaving the field after the Battle of Clapham Common. How are your injuries, Comrade Jackson?'

'My back's hurting like blazes,' said Mike. 'And my ear's all sore where that chap got me. Anything the matter with you?'

'Physically,' said Psmith, 'no. Spiritually much. Do you realize, Comrade Jackson, the thing that has happened? I am riding in a tram. I, Psmith, have paid a penny for a ticket on a tram. If this should get about the clubs! I tell you, Comrade Jackson, no such crisis has ever occurred before in the course of my career.'

'You can always get off, you know,' said Mike.

'He thinks of everything,' said Psmith, admiringly. 'You have touched the spot with an unerring finger. Let us descend. I observe in the distance a cab. That looks to me more the sort of thing we want. Let us go and parley with the driver.'

17 — Sunday Supper

The cab took them back to the flat, at considerable expense, and Psmith requested Mike to make tea, a performance in which he himself was interested purely as a spectator. He had views on the subject of tea-making which he liked to expound from an armchair or sofa, but he never got further than this. Mike, his back throbbing dully from the blow he had received, and feeling more than a little sore all over, prepared the Etna, fetched the milk, and finally produced the finished article.

Psmith sipped meditatively.

'How pleasant,' he said, 'after strife is rest. We shouldn't have appreciated this simple cup of tea had our sensibilities remained unstirred this afternoon. We can now sit at our ease, like warriors after the fray, till the time comes for setting cut to Comrade Waller's once more.'

Mike looked up.

'What! You don't mean to say you're going to sweat out to Clapham again?'

'Undoubtedly. Comrade Waller is expecting us to supper.'

'What absolute rot! We can't fag back there.'

'Noblesse oblige. The cry has gone round the Waller household, " Jackson and Psmith are coming to supper," and we cannot disappoint them now. Already the fatted blanc-mange has been killed, and the table creaks beneath what's left of the midday beef. We must be there; besides, don't you want to see how the poor man is? Probably we shall find him in the act of emitting his last breath. I expect he was lynched by the enthusiastic mob.'

'Not much,' grinned Mike. 'They were too busy with us. All right, I'll come if you really want me to, but it's awful rot.'

One of the many things Mike could never understand in Psmith was his fondness for getting into atmospheres that were not his own. He would go out of his way to do this. Mike, like most boys of his age, was never really happy and at his ease except in the presence of those of his own years and class. Psmith, on the contrary, seemed to be bored by them, and infinitely preferred talking to somebody who lived in quite another world. Mike was not a snob. He simply had not the ability to be at his ease with people in another class from his own. He did not know what to talk to them about, unless they were cricket professionals. With them he was never at a loss.

But Psmith was different. He could get on with anyone. He seemed to have the gift of entering into their minds and seeing things from their point of view.

As regarded Mr Waller, Mike liked him personally, and was prepared, as we have seen, to undertake considerable risks in his defence; but he loathed with all his heart and soul the idea of supper at his house. He knew that he would have nothing to say. Whereas Psmith gave him the impression of looking forward to the thing as a treat.

The house where Mr Waller lived was one of a row of semi-detached villas on the north side of the Common. The door was opened to them by their host himself. So far from looking battered and emitting last breaths, he appeared particularly spruce. He had just returned from Church, and was still wearing his gloves and tall hat. He squeaked with surprise when he saw who were standing on the mat.

'Why, dear me, dear me,' he said. 'Here you are! I have been wondering what had happened to you. I was afraid that you might have been seriously hurt. I was afraid those ruffians might have injured you. When last I saw you, you were being – '

'Chivvied,' interposed Psmith, with dignified melancholy. 'Do not let us try to wrap the fact up in pleasant words. We were being chivvied. We were legging it with the infuriated mob at our heels. An ignominious position for a Shropshire Psmith, but, after all, Napoleon did the same.'

'But what happened? I could not see. I only know that quite suddenly the people seemed to stop listening to me, and all gathered round you and Jackson. And then I saw that Jackson was engaged in a fight with a young man.'

'Comrade Jackson, I imagine, having heard a great deal about all men being equal, was anxious to test the theory, and see whether Comrade Bill was as good a man as he was. The experiment was broken off prematurely, but I personally should be inclined to say that Comrade Jackson had a shade the better of the exchanges.'

Mr Waller looked with interest at Mike, who shuffled and felt awkward. He was hoping that Psmith would say nothing about the reason of his engaging Bill in combat. He had an uneasy feeling that Mr Waller's gratitude would be effusive and overpowering, and he did not wish to pose as the brave young hero. There are moments when one does not feel equal to the *rôle*.

Fortunately, before Mr Waller had time to ask any further questions, the supper-bell sounded, and they went into the dining-room.

Sunday supper, unless done on a large and informal scale, is probably the most depressing meal in existence. There is a chill discomfort in the round of beef, an icy severity about the open jam tart. The blancmange shivers miserably.

Spirituous liquor helps to counteract the influence of these things, and so does exhilarating conversation. Unfortunately, at Mr Waller's table there was neither.

The cashier's views on temperance were not merely for the platform; they extended to the home. And the company was not of the exhilarating sort. Besides Psmith and Mike and their host, there were four people present – Comrade Prebble, the orator; a young man of the name of Richards; Mr Waller's niece, answering to the name of Ada, who was engaged to Mr Richards; and Edward.

Edward was Mr Waller's son. He was ten years old, wore a very tight Eton suit, and had the peculiarly loathsome expression which a snub nose sometimes gives to the young.

It would have been plain to the most casual observer that Mr Waller was fond and proud of his son. The cashier was a widower, and after five minutes' acquaintance with Edward, Mike felt strongly that Mrs Waller was the lucky one. Edward sat next to Mike, and showed a tendency to concentrate his conversation on him. Psmith, at the opposite end of the table, beamed in a fatherly manner upon the pair through his eye-glass.

Mike got on with small girls reasonably well. He preferred them at a distance, but, if cornered by them, could put up a fairly good show. Small boys, however, filled him with a sort of frozen horror. It was his view that a boy should not be exhibited publicly until he reached an age when he might be in the running for some sort of colours at a public school.

Edward was one of those well-informed small boys. He opened on Mike with the first mouthful.

'Do you know the principal exports of Marseilles?' he inquired.

'What?' said Mike coldly.

'Do you know the principal exports of Marseilles? I do.'

'Oh?' said Mike.

'Yes. Do you know the capital of Madagascar?'

Mike, as crimson as the beef he was attacking, said he did not.

'I do.'

'Oh?' said Mike.

'Who was the first king – '

'You mustn't worry Mr Jackson, Teddy,' said Mr
Waller, with a touch of pride in his voice, as who should
say 'There are not many boys of his age, I can tell you,
who *could* worry you with questions like that.'

'No, no, he likes it,' said Psmith, unnecessarily. 'He
likes it. I always hold that much may be learned by
casual chit-chat across the dinner-table. I owe much of
my own grasp of – '

'I bet *you* don't know what's the capital of Madagascar,'
interrupted Mike rudely.

'I do,' said Edward. 'I can tell you the kings of Israel?'
he added, turning to Mike. He seemed to have no
curiosity as to the extent of Psmith's knowledge. Mike's
appeared to fascinate him.

Mike helped himself to beetroot in moody silence.

His mouth was full when Comrade Prebble asked him
a question. Comrade Prebble, as has been pointed out in
an earlier part of the narrative, was a good chap, but had
no roof to his mouth.

'I beg your pardon?' said Mike.

Comrade Prebble repeated his observation. Mike
looked helplessly at Psmith, but Psmith's eyes were on
his plate.

Mike felt he must venture on some answer.

'No,' he said decidedly.

Comrade Prebble seemed slightly taken aback. There
was an awkward pause. Then Mr Waller, for whom his
fellow Socialist's methods of conversation held no
mysteries, interpreted.

'The mustard, Prebble? Yes, yes. Would you mind
passing Prebble the mustard, Mr Jackson?'

'Oh, sorry,' gasped Mike, and, reaching out, upset the
water-jug into the open jam-tart.

Through the black mist which rose before his eyes as

he leaped to his feet and stammered apologies came the
dispassionate voice of Master Edward Waller reminding
him that mustard was first introduced into Peru by
Cortez.

His host was all courtesy and consideration. He passed
the matter off genially. But life can never be quite the same
after you have upset a water-jug into an open jam-tart at
the table of a comparative stranger. Mike's nerve had gone.
He ate on, but he was a broken man.

At the other end of the table it became gradually
apparent that things were not going on altogether as
they should have done. There was a sort of bleakness in
the atmosphere. Young Mr Richards was looking like a
stuffed fish, and the face of Mr Waller's niece was cold
and set.

'Why, come, come, Ada,' said Mr Waller, breezily,
'what's the matter? You're eating nothing. What's
George been saying to you?' he added jocularly.

'Thank you, uncle Robert,' replied Ada precisely,
'there's nothing the matter. Nothing that Mr Richards
can say to me can upset me.'

'Mr Richards!' echoed Mr Waller in astonishment.
How was he to know that, during the walk back from
church, the world had been transformed, George had
become Mr Richards, and all was over?

'I assure you, Ada – ' began that unfortunate young
man. Ada turned a frigid shoulder towards him.

'Come, come,' said Mr Waller disturbed. 'What's all
this? What's all this?'

His niece burst into tears and left the room.

If there is anything more embarrassing to a guest than
a family row, we have yet to hear of it. Mike, scarlet to
the extreme edges of his ears, concentrated himself on
his plate. Comrade Prebble made a great many remarks,
which were probably illuminating, if they could have
been understood. Mr Waller looked, astonished, at Mr
Richards. Mr Richards, pink but dogged, loosened his

collar, but said nothing. Psmith, leaning forward, asked
Master Edward Waller his opinion on the Licensing Bill.

'We happened to have a word or two,' said Mr Richards
at length, 'on the way home from church on the subject
of Women's Suffrage.'

'That fatal topic!' murmured Psmith.

'In Australia – ' began Master Edward Waller.

'I was rayther – well, rayther facetious about it,'
continued Mr Richards.

Psmith clicked his tongue sympathetically.

'In Australia – ' said Edward.

'I went talking on, laughing and joking, when all of a
sudden she flew out at me. How was I to know she was
'eart and soul in the movement? You never told me,' he
added accusingly to his host.

'In Australia – ' said Edward.

'I'll go and try and get her round. How was I to know?'

Mr Richards thrust back his chair and bounded from
the room.

'Now, iawinyaw, iear oller – ' said Comrade Prebble
judicially, but was interrupted.

'How very disturbing!' said Mr Waller. 'I am so sorry
that this should have happened. Ada is such a touchy,
sensitive girl. She – '

'In Australia,' said Edward in even tones, 'they've *got*
Women's Suffrage already. Did *you* know that?' he said
to Mike.

Mike made no answer. His eyes were fixed on his plate.
A bead of perspiration began to roll down his forehead.
If his feelings could have been ascertained at that
moment, they would have been summed up in the
words, 'Death, where is thy sting?'

18 — Psmith Makes a Discovery

'Women,' said Psmith, helping himself to trifle, and
speaking with the air of one launched upon his special
subject, 'are, one must recollect, like – like – er, well, in
fact, just so. Passing on lightly from that conclusion, let
us turn for a moment to the Rights of Property, in
connection with which Comrade Prebble and yourself
had so much that was interesting to say this afternoon.
Perhaps you' – he bowed in Comrade Prebble's direction –
'would resume, for the benefit of Comrade Jackson – a
novice in the Cause, but earnest – your very lucid – '

Comrade Prebble beamed, and took the floor. Mike
began to realize that, till now, he had never known what
boredom meant. There had been moments in his life
which had been less interesting than other moments, but
nothing to touch this for agony. Comrade Prebble's
address streamed on like water rushing over a weir.
Every now and then there was a word or two which was
recognizable, but this happened so rarely that it
amounted to little. Sometimes Mr Waller would interject
a remark, but not often. He seemed to be of the opinion
that Comrade Prebble's was the master mind and that to
add anything to his views would be in the nature of
painting the lily and gilding the refined gold. Mike himself
said nothing. Psmith and Edward were equally silent.
The former sat like one in a trance, thinking his own
thoughts, while Edward, who, prospecting on the
sideboard, had located a rich biscuit-mine, was too
occupied for speech.

After about twenty minutes, during which Mike's
discomfort changed to a dull resignation, Mr Waller

suggested a move to the drawing-room, where Ada, he
said, would play some hymns.

The prospect did not dazzle Mike, but any change, he
thought, must be for the better. He had sat staring at the
ruin of the blancmange so long that it had begun to
hypnotize him. Also, the move had the excellent result
of eliminating the snub-nosed Edward, who was sent to
bed. His last words were in the form of a question,
addressed to Mike, on the subject of the hypotenuse and
the square upon the same.

'A remarkably intelligent boy,' said Psmith. 'You must
let him come to tea at our flat one day. I may not be in
myself – I have many duties which keep me away – but
Comrade Jackson is sure to be there, and will be delighted
to chat with him.'

On the way upstairs Mike tried to get Psmith to
himself for a moment to suggest the advisability of an
early departure; but Psmith was in close conversation
with his host. Mike was left to Comrade Prebble, who,
apparently, had only touched the fringe of his subject in
his lecture in the dining-room.

When Mr Waller had predicted hymns in the drawing-
room, he had been too sanguine (or too pessimistic). Of
Ada, when they arrived, there were no signs. It seemed
that she had gone straight to bed. Young Mr Richards
was sitting on the sofa, moodily turning the leaves of a
photograph album, which contained portraits of Master
Edward Waller in geometrically progressing degrees of
repulsiveness – here, in frocks, looking like a gargoyle;
there, in sailor suit, looking like nothing on earth. The
inspection of these was obviously deepening Mr Richards'
gloom, but he proceeded doggedly with it.

Comrade Prebble backed the reluctant Mike into a
corner, and, like the Ancient Mariner, held him with
a glittering eye. Psmith and Mr Waller, in the opposite
corner, were looking at something with their heads close
together. Mike definitely abandoned all hope of a rescue

from Psmith, and tried to buoy himself up with the reflection that this could not last for ever.

Hours seemed to pass, and then at last he heard Psmith's voice saying good-bye to his host.

He sprang to his feet. Comrade Prebble was in the middle of a sentence, but this was no time for polished courtesy. He felt that he must get away, and at once. 'I fear,' Psmith was saying, 'that we must tear ourselves away. We have greatly enjoyed our evening. You must look us up at our flat one day, and bring Comrade Prebble. If I am not in, Comrade Jackson is certain to be, and he will be more than delighted to hear Comrade Prebble speak further on the subject of which he is such a master.' Comrade Prebble was understood to say that he would certainly come. Mr Waller beamed. Mr Richards, still steeped in gloom, shook hands in silence.

Out in the road, with the front door shut behind them, Mike spoke his mind.

'Look here, Smith,' he said definitely, 'if being your confidential secretary and adviser is going to let me in for any more of that sort of thing, you can jolly well accept my resignation.'

'The orgy was not to your taste?' said Psmith sympathetically.

Mike laughed. One of those short, hollow, bitter laughs.

'I am at a loss, Comrade Jackson,' said Psmith, 'to understand your attitude. You fed sumptuously. You had fun with the crockery – that knockabout act of yours with the water-jug was alone worth the money – and you had the advantage of listening to the views of a master of his subject. What more do you want?'

'What on earth did you land me with that man Prebble for?'

'Land you! Why, you courted his society. I had practically to drag you away from him. When I got up to say good-bye, you were listening to him with bulging eyes. I never saw such a picture of rapt attention. Do you mean to tell me, Comrade Jackson, that your appearance belied you, that you were not interested? Well, well. How we misread our fellow creatures.'

'I think you might have come and lent a hand with Prebble. It was a bit thick.'

'I was too absorbed with Comrade Waller. We were talking of things of vital moment. However, the night is yet young. We will take this cab, wend our way to the West, seek a café, and cheer ourselves with light refreshments.'

Arrived at a café whose window appeared to be a sort of museum of every kind of German sausage, they took possession of a vacant table and ordered coffee. Mike soon found himself soothed by his bright surroundings, and gradually his impressions of blancmange, Edward, and Comrade Prebble faded from his mind. Psmith, meanwhile, was preserving an unusual silence, being deep in a large square book of the sort in which Press cuttings are pasted. As Psmith scanned its contents a curious smile lit up his face. His reflections seemed to be of an agreeable nature.

'Hullo,' said Mike, 'what have you got hold of there? Where did you get that?'

'Comrade Waller very kindly lent it to me. He showed it to me after supper, knowing how enthusiastically I was attached to the Cause. Had you been less tensely wrapped up in Comrade Prebble's conversation, I would have desired you to step across and join us. However, you now have your opportunity.'

'But what is it?' asked Mike.

'It is the record of the meetings of the Tulse Hill Parliament,' said Psmith impressively. 'A faithful record of all they said, all the votes of confidence they passed in the Government, and also all the nasty knocks they gave it from time to time.'

'What on earth's the Tulse Hill Parliament?'

'It is, alas,' said Psmith in a grave, sad voice, 'no more. In life it was beautiful, but now it has done the Tom Bowling act. It has gone aloft. We are dealing, Comrade Jackson, not with the live, vivid present, but with the far-off, rusty past. And yet, in a way, there is a touch of the live, vivid present mixed up in it.'

'I don't know what the dickens you're talking about,' said Mike. 'Let's have a look, anyway.'

Psmith handed him the volume, and, leaning back, sipped his coffee, and watched him. At first Mike's face was bored and blank, but suddenly an interested look came into it.

'Aha!' said Psmith.

'Who's Bickersdyke? Anything to do with our Bickersdyke?'

'No other than our genial friend himself.'

Mike turned the pages, reading a line or two on each.

'Hullo!' he said, chuckling. 'He lets himself go a bit, doesn't he!'

'He does,' acknowledged Psmith. 'A fiery, passionate nature, that of Comrade Bickersdyke.'

'He's simply cursing the Government here. Giving them frightful beans.'

Psmith nodded.

'I noticed the fact myself.'

'But what's it all about?'

'As far as I can glean from Comrade Waller,' said Psmith, 'about twenty years ago, when he and Comrade Bickersdyke worked hand-in-hand as fellow clerks at the New Asiatic, they were both members of the Tulse Hill Parliament, that powerful institution. At that time Comrade Bickersdyke was as fruity a Socialist as Comrade Waller is now. Only, apparently, as he began to get on a bit in the world, he altered his views to some extent as regards the iniquity of freezing on to a decent share of the doubloons. And that, you see, is where the dim and rusty past begins to get mixed up with the live,

vivid present. If any tactless person were to publish those
very able speeches made by Comrade Bickersdyke when
a bulwark of the Tulse Hill Parliament, our revered chief
would be more or less caught bending, if I may employ
the expression, as regards his chances of getting in as
Unionist candidate at Kenningford. You follow me,
Watson? I rather fancy the light-hearted electors of
Kenningford, from what I have seen of their rather acute
sense of humour, would be, as it were, all over it. It
would be very, very trying for Comrade Bickersdyke if
these speeches of his were to get about.'

'You aren't going to – !'

'I shall do nothing rashly. I shall merely place this
handsome volume among my treasured books. I shall
add it to my "Books that have helped me" series. Because
I fancy that, in an emergency, it may not be at all a bad
thing to have about me. And now,' he concluded, 'as the
hour is getting late, perhaps we had better be shoving
off for home.'

19 — The Illness of Edward

Life in a bank is at its pleasantest in the winter. When all
the world outside is dark and damp and cold, the light
and warmth of the place are comforting. There is a
pleasant air of solidity about the interior of a bank. The
green shaded lamps look cosy. And, the outside world
offering so few attractions, the worker, perched on his
stool, feels that he is not so badly off after all. It is when
the days are long and the sun beats hot on the pavement,
and everything shouts to him how splendid it is out in
the country, that he begins to grow restless.

Mike, except for a fortnight at the beginning of his
career in the New Asiatic Bank, had not had to stand the
test of sunshine. At present, the weather being cold and
dismal, he was almost entirely contented. Now that he
had got into the swing of his work, the days passed very
quickly; and with his life after office-hours he had no
fault to find at all.

His life was very regular. He would arrive in the
morning just in time to sign his name in the attendance-
book before it was removed to the accountant's room.
That was at ten o'clock. From ten to eleven he would
potter. There was nothing going on at that time in his
department, and Mr Waller seemed to take it for granted
that he should stroll off to the Postage Department and
talk to Psmith, who had generally some fresh grievance
against the ring-wearing Bristow to air. From eleven to
half past twelve he would put in a little gentle work. Lunch,
unless there was a rush of business or Mr Waller happened
to suffer from a spasm of conscientiousness, could be
spun out from half-past twelve to two. More work from

two till half past three. From half past three till half past four tea in the tea-room, with a novel. And from half past four till five either a little more work or more pottering, according to whether there was any work to do or not. It was by no means an unpleasant mode of spending a late January day.

Then there was no doubt that it was an interesting little community, that of the New Asiatic Bank. The curiously amateurish nature of the institution lent a certain air of light-heartedness to the place. It was not like one of those banks whose London office is their main office, where stern business is everything and a man becomes a mere machine for getting through a certain amount of routine work. The employees of the New Asiatic Bank, having plenty of time on their hands, were able to retain their individuality. They had leisure to think of other things besides their work. Indeed, they had so much leisure that it is a wonder they thought of their work at all.

The place was full of quaint characters. There was West, who had been requested to leave Haileybury owing to his habit of borrowing horses and attending meets in the neighbourhood, the same being always out of bounds and necessitating a complete disregard of the rules respecting evening chapel and lock-up. He was a small, dried-up youth, with black hair plastered down on his head. He went about his duties in a costume which suggested the sportsman of the comic papers.

There was also Hignett, who added to the meagre salary allowed him by the bank by singing comic songs at the minor music halls. He confided to Mike his intention of leaving the bank as soon as he had made a name, and taking seriously to the business. He told him that he had knocked them at the Bedford the week before, and in support of the statement showed him a cutting from the *Era*, in which the writer said that 'Other acceptable turns were the Bounding Zouaves,

Steingruber's Dogs, and Arthur Hignett.' Mike wished him luck.

And there was Raymond who dabbled in journalism and was the author of 'Straight Talks to Housewives' in *Trifles*, under the pseudonym of 'Lady Gussie'; Wragge, who believed that the earth was flat, and addressed meetings on the subject in Hyde Park on Sundays; and many others, all interesting to talk to of a morning when work was slack and time had to be filled in.

Mike found himself, by degrees, growing quite attached to the New Asiatic Bank.

One morning, early in February, he noticed a curious change in Mr Waller. The head of the Cash Department was, as a rule, mildly cheerful on arrival, and apt (excessively, Mike thought, though he always listened with polite interest) to relate the most recent sayings and doings of his snub-nosed son, Edward. No action of this young prodigy was withheld from Mike. He had heard, on different occasions, how he had won a prize at his school for General Information (which Mike could well believe); how he had trapped young Mr Richards, now happily reconciled to Ada, with an ingenious verbal catch; and how he had made a sequence of diverting puns on the name of the new curate, during the course of that cleric's first Sunday afternoon visit.

On this particular day, however, the cashier was silent and absent-minded. He answered Mike's good-morning mechanically, and sitting down at his desk, stared blankly across the building. There was a curiously grey, tired look on his face.

Mike could not make it out. He did not like to ask if there was anything the matter. Mr Waller's face had the unreasonable effect on him of making him feel shy and awkward. Anything in the nature of sorrow always dried Mike up and robbed him of the power of speech. Being naturally sympathetic, he had raged inwardly in many a crisis at this devil of dumb awkwardness which

121

possessed him and prevented him from putting his
sympathy into words. He had always envied the cooing
readiness of the hero on the stage when anyone was in
trouble. He wondered whether he would ever acquire that
knack of pouring out a limpid stream of soothing words
on such occasions. At present he could get no farther than
a scowl and an almost offensive gruffness.

The happy thought struck him of consulting Psmith.
It was his hour for pottering, so he pottered round to the
Postage Department, where he found the old Etonian
eyeing with disfavour a new satin tie which Bristow was
wearing that morning for the first time.

'I say, Smith,' he said, 'I want to speak to you for a
second.'

Psmith rose. Mike led the way to a quiet corner of the
Telegrams Department.

'I tell you, Comrade Jackson,' said Psmith, 'I am hard
pressed. The fight is beginning to be too much for me.
After a grim struggle, after days of unremitting toil, I
succeeded yesterday in inducing the man Bristow to
abandon that rainbow waistcoat of his. Today I enter the
building, blythe and buoyant, worn, of course, from
the long struggle, but seeing with aching eyes the dawn
of another, better era, and there is Comrade Bristow in
a satin tie. It's hard, Comrade Jackson, it's hard, I tell you.'

'Look here, Smith,' said Mike, 'I wish you'd go round
to the Cash and find out what's up with old Waller. He's
got the hump about something. He's sitting there looking
absolutely fed up with things. I hope there's nothing up.
He's not a bad sort. It would be rot if anything rotten's
happened.'

Psmith began to display a gentle interest.

'So other people have troubles as well as myself,' he
murmured musingly. 'I had almost forgotten that.
Comrade Waller's misfortunes cannot but be trivial
compared with mine, but possibly it will be as well to

ascertain their nature. I will reel round and make inquiries.'

'Good man,' said Mike. 'I'll wait here.'

Psmith departed, and returned, ten minutes later, looking more serious than when he had left.

'His kid's ill, poor chap,' he said briefly. 'Pretty badly too, from what I can gather. Pneumonia. Waller was up all night. He oughtn't to be here at all today. He doesn't know what he's doing half the time. He's absolutely fagged out. Look here, you'd better nip back and do as much of the work as you can. I shouldn't talk to him much if I were you. Buck along.'

Mike went. Mr Waller was still sitting staring out across the aisle. There was something more than a little gruesome in the sight of him. He wore a crushed, beaten look, as if all the life and fight had gone out of him. A customer came to the desk to cash a cheque. The cashier shovelled the money to him under the bars with the air of one whose mind is elsewhere. Mike could guess what he was feeling, and what he was thinking about. The fact that the snub-nosed Edward was, without exception, the most repulsive small boy he had ever met in this world, where repulsive small boys crowd and jostle one another, did not interfere with his appreciation of the cashier's state of mind. Mike's was essentially a sympathetic character. He had the gift of intuitive understanding, where people of whom he was fond were concerned. It was this which drew to him those who had intelligence enough to see beyond his sometimes rather forbidding manner, and to realize that his blunt speech was largely due to shyness. In spite of his prejudice against Edward, he could put himself into Mr Waller's place, and see the thing from his point of view.

Psmith's injunction to him not to talk much was unnecessary. Mike, as always, was rendered utterly dumb by the sight of suffering. He sat at his desk, occupying himself as best he could with the driblets of work which came to him.

Mr Waller's silence and absentness continued unchanged. The habit of years had made his work mechanical. Probably few of the customers who came to cash cheques suspected that there was anything the matter with the man who paid them their money. After all, most people look on the cashier of a bank as a sort of human slot-machine. You put in your cheque, and out comes money. It is no affair of yours whether life is treating the machine well or ill that day.

The hours dragged slowly by till five o'clock struck, and the cashier, putting on his coat and hat, passed silently out through the swing-doors. He walked listlessly. He was evidently tired out.

Mike shut his ledger with a vicious bang, and went across to find Psmith. He was glad the day was over.

20 — Concerning a Cheque

Things never happen quite as one expects them to. Mike came to the office next morning prepared for a repetition of the previous day. He was amazed to find the cashier not merely cheerful, but even exuberantly cheerful. Edward, it appeared, had rallied in the afternoon, and, when his father had got home, had been out of danger. He was now going along excellently, and had stumped Ada, who was nursing him, with a question about the Thirty Years' War, only a few minutes before his father had left to catch his train. The cashier was overflowing with happiness and goodwill towards his species. He greeted customers with bright remarks on the weather, and snappy views on the leading events of the day: the former tinged with optimism, the latter full of a gentle spirit of toleration. His attitude towards the latest actions of His Majesty's Government was that of one who felt that, after all, there was probably some good even in the vilest of his fellow creatures, if one could only find it.

Altogether, the cloud had lifted from the Cash Department. All was joy, jollity, and song.

'The attitude of Comrade Waller,' said Psmith, on being informed of the change, 'is reassuring. I may now think of my own troubles. Comrade Bristow has blown into the office today in patent leather boots with white kid uppers, as I believe the technical term is. Add to that the fact that he is still wearing the satin tie, the waistcoat, and the ring, and you will understand why I have definitely decided this morning to abandon all hope of his reform. Henceforth my services, for what they are worth, are at the disposal of Comrade Bickersdyke. My

time from now onward is his. He shall have the full
educative value of my exclusive attention. I give Comrade
Bristow up. Made straight for the corner flag, you
understand,' he added, as Mr Rossiter emerged from his
lair, 'and centred, and Sandy Turnbull headed a beautiful
goal. I was just telling Jackson about the match against
Blackburn Rovers,' he said to Mr Rossiter.

'Just so, just so. But get on with your work, Smith. We
are a little behind-hand. I think perhaps it would be as
well not to leave it just yet.'

'I will leap at it at once,' said Psmith cordially.

Mike went back to his department.

The day passed quickly. Mr Waller, in the intervals of
work, talked a good deal, mostly of Edward, his doings,
his sayings, and his prospects. The only thing that seemed
to worry Mr Waller was the problem of how to employ
his son's almost superhuman talents to the best
advantage. Most of the goals towards which the average
man strives struck him as too unambitious for the
prodigy.

By the end of the day Mike had had enough of Edward.
He never wished to hear the name again.

We do not claim originality for the statement that
things never happen quite as one expects them to.
We repeat it now because of its profound truth.
The Edward's pneumonia episode having ended
satisfactorily (or, rather, being apparently certain to end
satisfactorily, for the invalid, though out of danger, was
still in bed), Mike looked forward to a series of days
unbroken by any but the minor troubles of life. For these
he was prepared. What he did not expect was any big
calamity.

At the beginning of the day there were no signs of it.
The sky was blue and free from all suggestions of
approaching thunderbolts. Mr Waller, still chirpy, had
nothing but good news of Edward. Mike went for his
morning stroll round the office feeling that things had

settled down and had made up their mind to run
smoothly.

When he got back, barely half an hour later, the storm
had burst.

There was no one in the department at the moment of
his arrival; but a few minutes later he saw Mr Waller
come out of the manager's room, and make his way down
the aisle.

It was his walk which first gave any hint that
something was wrong. It was the same limp, crushed walk
which Mike had seen when Edward's safety still hung in
the balance.

As Mr Waller came nearer, Mike saw that the cashier's
face was deadly pale.

Mr Waller caught sight of him and quickened his pace.

'Jackson,' he said.

Mike came forward.

'Do you – remember – ' he spoke slowly, and with an
effort, 'do you remember a cheque coming through the
day before yesterday for a hundred pounds, with Sir John
Morrison's signature?'

'Yes. It came in the morning, rather late.'

Mike remembered the cheque perfectly well, owing to
the amount. It was the only three-figure cheque which
had come across the counter during the day. It had been
presented just before the cashier had gone out to lunch. He
recollected the man who had presented it, a tallish man
with a beard. He had noticed him particularly because of
the contrast between his manner and that of the cashier.
The former had been so very cheery and breezy, the
latter so dazed and silent.

'Why,' he said.

'It was a forgery,' muttered Mr Waller, sitting down
heavily.

Mike could not take it in all at once. He was stunned.
All he could understand was that a far worse thing had
happened than anything he could have imagined.

'A forgery?' he said.

'A forgery. And a clumsy one. Oh it's hard. I should have seen it on any other day but that. I could not have missed it. They showed me the cheque in there just now. I could not believe that I had passed it. I don't remember doing it. My mind was far away. I don't remember the cheque or anything about it. Yet there it is.'

Once more Mike was tongue-tied. For the life of him he could not think of anything to say. Surely, he thought, he could find *something* in the shape of words to show his sympathy. But he could find nothing that would not sound horribly stilted and cold. He sat silent.

'Sir John is in there,' went on the cashier. 'He is furious. Mr Bickersdyke, too. They are both furious. I shall be dismissed. I shall lose my place. I shall be dismissed.' He was talking more to himself than to Mike. It was dreadful to see him sitting there, all limp and broken.

'I shall lose my place. Mr Bickersdyke has wanted to get rid of me for a long time. He never liked me. I shall be dismissed. What can I do? I'm an old man. I can't make another start. I am good for nothing. Nobody will take an old man like me.'

His voice died away. There was a silence. Mike sat staring miserably in front of him.

Then, quite suddenly, an idea came to him. The whole pressure of the atmosphere seemed to lift. He saw a way out. It was a curious crooked way, but at that moment it stretched clear and broad before him. He felt lighthearted and excited, as if he were watching the development of some interesting play at the theatre.

He got up, smiling.

The cashier did not notice the movement. Somebody had come in to cash a cheque, and he was working mechanically.

Mike walked up the aisle to Mr Bickersdyke's room, and went in.

The manager was in his chair at the big table. Opposite

him, facing slightly sideways, was a small, round, very red-faced man. Mr Bickersdyke was speaking as Mike entered.

'I can assure you, Sir John – ' he was saying.

He looked up as the door opened.

'Well, Mr Jackson?'

Mike almost laughed. The situation was tickling him.

'Mr Waller has told me – ' he began.

'I have already seen Mr Waller.'

'I know. He told me about the cheque. I came to explain.'

'Explain?'

'Yes. He didn't cash it at all.'

'I don't understand you, Mr Jackson.'

'I was at the counter when it was brought in,' said Mike. 'I cashed it.'

21 — Psmith Makes Inquiries

Psmith, as was his habit of a morning when the fierce
rush of his commercial duties had abated somewhat,
was leaning gracefully against his desk, musing on many
things, when he was aware that Bristow was standing
before him.

Focusing his attention with some reluctance upon this
blot on the horizon, he discovered that the exploiter of
rainbow waistcoats and satin ties was addressing him.

'I say, Smithy,' said Bristow. He spoke in rather an
awed voice.

'Say on, Comrade Bristow,' said Psmith graciously.
'You have our ear. You would seem to have something
on your chest in addition to that Neapolitan ice garment
which, I regret to see, you still flaunt. If it is one tithe
as painful as that, you have my sympathy. Jerk it out,
Comrade Bristow.'

'Jackson isn't half copping it from old Bick.'

'Isn't – ? What exactly did you say?'

'He's getting it hot on the carpet.'

'You wish to indicate,' said Psmith, 'that there is some
slight disturbance, some passing breeze between
Comrades Jackson and Bickersdyke?'

Bristow chuckled.

'Breeze! Blooming hurricane, more like it. I was in
Bick's room just now with a letter to sign, and I tell you,
the fur was flying all over the bally shop. There was old
Bick cursing for all he was worth, and a little red-faced
buffer puffing out his cheeks in an armchair.'

'We all have our hobbies,' said Psmith.

'Jackson wasn't saying much. He jolly well hadn't a

chance. Old Bick was shooting it out fourteen to the dozen.'

'I have been privileged,' said Psmith, 'to hear Comrade Bickersdyke speak both in his sanctum and in public. He has, as you suggest, a ready flow of speech. What, exactly was the cause of the turmoil?'

'I couldn't wait to hear. I was too jolly glad to get away. Old Bick looked at me as if he could eat me, snatched the letter out of my hand, signed it, and waved his hand at the door as a hint to hop it. Which I jolly well did. He had started jawing Jackson again before I was out of the room.'

'While applauding his hustle,' said Psmith, 'I fear that I must take official notice of this. Comrade Jackson is essentially a Sensitive Plant, highly strung, neurotic. I cannot have his nervous system jolted and disorganized in this manner, and his value as a confidential secretary and adviser impaired, even though it be only temporarily. I must look into this. I will go and see if the orgy is concluded. I will hear what Comrade Jackson has to say on the matter. I shall not act rashly, Comrade Bristow. If the man Bickersdyke is proved to have had good grounds for his outbreak, he shall escape uncensured. I may even look in on him and throw him a word of praise. But if I find, as I suspect, that he has wronged Comrade Jackson, I shall be forced to speak sharply to him.'

Mike had left the scene of battle by the time Psmith reached the Cash Department, and was sitting at his desk in a somewhat dazed condition, trying to clear his mind sufficiently to enable him to see exactly how matters stood as concerned himself. He felt confused and rattled. He had known, when he went to the manager's room to make his statement, that there would be trouble. But, then, trouble is such an elastic word. It embraces a hundred degrees of meaning. Mike had expected sentence of dismissal, and he had got it. So far he had nothing to complain of. But he had not expected it to come to him riding high on the crest of a great, frothing wave of verbal denunciation. Mr Bickersdyke, through constantly speaking in public, had developed the habit of fluent denunciation to a remarkable extent. He had thundered at Mike as if Mike had been his Majesty's Government or the Encroaching Alien, or something of that sort. And that kind of thing is a little overwhelming at short range. Mike's head was still spinning.

It continued to spin; but he never lost sight of the fact round which it revolved, namely, that he had been dismissed from the service of the bank. And for the first time he began to wonder what they would say about this at home.

Up till now the matter had seemed entirely a personal one. He had charged in to rescue the harassed cashier in precisely the same way as that in which he had dashed in to save him from Bill, the Stone-Flinging Scourge of Clapham Common. Mike's was one of those direct, honest minds which are apt to concentrate themselves on the crisis of the moment, and to leave the consequences out of the question entirely.

What would they say at home? That was the point.

Again, what could he do by way of earning a living? He did not know much about the City and its ways, but he knew enough to understand that summary dismissal from a bank is not the best recommendation one can put forward in applying for another job. And if he did not get another job in the City, what could he do? If it were only summer, he might get taken on somewhere as a cricket professional. Cricket was his line. He could earn his pay at that. But it was very far from being summer.

He had turned the problem over in his mind till his head ached, and had eaten in the process one-third of a wooden penholder, when Psmith arrived.

'It has reached me,' said Psmith, 'that you and Comrade Bickersdyke have been seen doing the

Hackenschmidt-Gotch act on the floor. When my
informant left, he tells me, Comrade B. had got a half-
Nelson on you, and was biting pieces out of your ear. Is
this so?'

Mike got up. Psmith was the man, he felt, to advise
him in this crisis. Psmith's was the mind to grapple with
his Hard Case.

'Look here, Smith,' he said, 'I want to speak to you.
I'm in a bit of a hole, and perhaps you can tell me what
to do. Let's go out and have a cup of coffee, shall we? I
can't tell you about it here.'

'An admirable suggestion,' said Psmith. 'Things in the
Postage Department are tolerably quiescent at present.
Naturally I shall be missed, if I go out. But my absence
will not spell irretrievable ruin, as it would at a period
of greater commercial activity. Comrades Rossiter and
Bristow have studied my methods. They know how I
like things to be done. They are fully competent to
conduct the business of the department in my absence.
Let us, as you say, scud forth. We will go to a Mecca. Why
so-called I do not know, nor, indeed, do I ever hope to
know. There we may obtain, at a price, a passable cup of
coffee, and you shall tell me your painful story.'

The Mecca, except for the curious aroma which
pervades all Meccas, was deserted. Psmith, moving a
box of dominoes on to the next table, sat down.

'Dominoes,' he said, 'is one of the few manly sports
which have never had great attractions for me. A cousin
of mine, who secured his chess blue at Oxford, would,
they tell me, have represented his University in the
dominoes match also, had he not unfortunately
dislocated the radius bone of his bazooka while training
for it. Except for him, there has been little dominoes
talent in the Psmith family. Let us merely talk. What of
this slight brass-rag-parting to which I alluded just now?
Tell me all.'

He listened gravely while Mike related the incidents

133

which had led up to his confession and the results of the same. At the conclusion of the narrative he sipped his coffee in silence for a moment.

'This habit of taking on to your shoulders the harvest of other people's bloomers,' he said meditatively, 'is growing upon you, Comrade Jackson. You must check it. It is like dram-drinking. You begin in a small way by breaking school rules to extract Comrade Jellicoe (perhaps the supremest of all the blitherers I have ever met) from a hole. If you had stopped there, all might have been well. But the thing, once started, fascinated you. Now you have landed yourself with a splash in the very centre of the Oxo in order to do a good turn to Comrade Waller. You must drop it, Comrade Jackson. When you were free and without ties, it did not so much matter. But now that you are confidential secretary and adviser to a Shropshire Psmith, the thing must stop. Your secretarial duties must be paramount. Nothing must be allowed to interfere with them. Yes. The thing must stop before it goes too far.'

'It seems to me,' said Mike, 'that it has gone too far. I've got the sack. I don't know how much farther you want it to go.'

Psmith stirred his coffee before replying.

'True,' he said, 'things look perhaps a shade rocky just now, but all is not yet lost. You must recollect that Comrade Bickersdyke spoke in the heat of the moment. That generous temperament was stirred to its depths. He did not pick his words. But calm will succeed storm, and we may be able to do something yet. I have some little influence with Comrade Bickersdyke. Wrongly, perhaps,' added Psmith modestly, 'he thinks somewhat highly of my judgment. If he sees that I am opposed to this step, he may possibly reconsider it. What Psmith thinks today, is his motto, I shall think tomorrow. However, we shall see.'

'I bet we shall!' said Mike ruefully.

'There is, moreover,' continued Psmith, 'another

aspect to the affair. When you were being put through
it, in Comrade Bickersdyke's inimitably breezy manner,
Sir John What's-his-name was, I am given to understand,
present. Naturally, to pacify the aggrieved bart., Comrade
B. had to lay it on regardless of expense. In America, as
possibly you are aware, there is a regular post of mistake-
clerk, whose duty it is to receive in the neck anything
that happens to be coming along when customers make
complaints. He is hauled into the presence of the
foaming customer, cursed, and sacked. The customer goes
away appeased. The mistake-clerk, if the harangue has
been unusually energetic, applies for a rise of salary. Now,
possibly, in your case – '

'In my case,' interrupted Mike, 'there was none of that
rot. Bickersdyke wasn't putting it on. He meant every
word. Why, dash it all, you know yourself he'd be only
too glad to sack me, just to get some of his own back
with me.'

Psmith's eyes opened in pained surprise.

'Get some of his own back!' he repeated.

'Are you insinuating, Comrade Jackson, that my
relations with Comrade Bickersdyke are not of the most
pleasant and agreeable nature possible? How do these
ideas get about? I yield to nobody in my respect for our
manager. I may have had occasion from time to time to
correct him in some trifling matter, but surely he is not
the man to let such a thing rankle? No! I prefer to think
that Comrade Bickersdyke regards me as his friend and
well-wisher, and will lend a courteous ear to any proposal
I see fit to make. I hope shortly to be able to prove this
to you. I will discuss this little affair of the cheque with
him at our ease at the club, and I shall be surprised if we
do not come to some arrangement.'

'Look here, Smith,' said Mike earnestly, 'for goodness'
sake don't go playing the goat. There's no earthly need
for you to get lugged into this business. Don't you worry
about me. I shall be all right.'

135

'I think,' said Psmith, 'that you will – when I have chatted with Comrade Bickersdyke.'

22 — And Takes Steps

On returning to the bank, Mike found Mr Waller in the grip of a peculiarly varied set of mixed feelings. Shortly after Mike's departure for the Mecca, the cashier had been summoned once more into the Presence, and had there been informed that, as apparently he had not been directly responsible for the gross piece of carelessness by which the bank had suffered so considerable a loss (here Sir John puffed out his cheeks like a meditative toad), the matter, as far as he was concerned, was at an end. On the other hand – ! Here Mr Waller was hauled over the coals for Incredible Rashness in allowing a mere junior subordinate to handle important tasks like the paying out of money, and so on, till he felt raw all over. However, it was not dismissal. That was the great thing. And his principal sensation was one of relief.

Mingled with the relief were sympathy for Mike, gratitude to him for having given himself up so promptly, and a curiously dazed sensation, as if somebody had been hitting him on the head with a bolster.

All of which emotions, taken simultaneously, had the effect of rendering him completely dumb when he saw Mike. He felt that he did not know what to say to him. And as Mike, for his part, simply wanted to be let alone, and not compelled to talk, conversation was at something of a standstill in the Cash Department.

After five minutes, it occurred to Mr Waller that perhaps the best plan would be to interview Psmith. Psmith would know exactly how matters stood. He could not ask Mike point-blank whether he had been dismissed. But there was the probability that Psmith had been informed and would pass on the information.

Psmith received the cashier with a dignified kindliness.

'Oh, er, Smith,' said Mr Waller, 'I wanted just to ask you about Jackson.'

Psmith bowed his head gravely.

'Exactly,' he said. 'Comrade Jackson. I think I may say that you have come to the right man. Comrade Jackson has placed himself in my hands, and I am dealing with his case. A somewhat tricky business, but I shall see him through.'

'Has he – ?' Mr Waller hesitated.

'You were saying?' said Psmith.

'Does Mr Bickersdyke intend to dismiss him?'

'At present,' admitted Psmith, 'there is some idea of that description floating – nebulously, as it were – in Comrade Bickersdyke's mind. Indeed, from what I gather from my client, the push was actually administered, in so many words. But tush! And possibly bah! we know what happens on these occasions, do we not? You and I are students of human nature, and we know that a man of Comrade Bickersdyke's warm-hearted type is apt to say in the heat of the moment a great deal more than he really means. Men of his impulsive character cannot help expressing themselves in times of stress with a certain generous strength which those who do not understand them are inclined to take a little too seriously. I shall have a chat with Comrade Bickersdyke at the conclusion of the day's work, and I have no doubt that we shall both laugh heartily over this little episode.'

Mr Waller pulled at his beard, with an expression on his face that seemed to suggest that he was not quite so confident on this point. He was about to put his doubts into words when Mr Rossiter appeared, and Psmith, murmuring something about duty, turned again to his ledger. The cashier drifted back to his own department.

It was one of Psmith's theories of Life, which he was accustomed to propound to Mike in the small hours of the morning with his feet on the mantelpiece, that the secret of success lay in taking advantage of one's occasional slices of luck, in seizing, as it were, the happy moment. When Mike, who had had the passage to write out ten times at Wrykyn on one occasion as an imposition, reminded him that Shakespeare had once said something about there being a tide in the affairs of men, which, taken at the flood, &c., Psmith had acknowledged with an easy grace that possibly Shakespeare *had* got on to it first, and that it was but one more proof of how often great minds thought alike.

Though waiving his claim to the copyright of the maxim, he nevertheless had a high opinion of it, and frequently acted upon it in the conduct of his own life.

Thus, when approaching the Senior Conservative Club at five o'clock with the idea of finding Mr Bickersdyke there, he observed his quarry entering the Turkish Baths which stand some twenty yards from the club's front door, he acted on his maxim, and decided, instead of waiting for the manager to finish his bath before approaching him on the subject of Mike, to corner him in the Baths themselves.

He gave Mr Bickersdyke five minutes' start. Then, reckoning that by that time he would probably have settled down, he pushed open the door and went in himself. And, having paid his money, and left his boots with the boy at the threshold, he was rewarded by the sight of the manager emerging from a box at the far end of the room, clad in the mottled towels which the bather, irrespective of his personal taste in dress, is obliged to wear in a Turkish bath.

Psmith made for the same box. Mr Bickersdyke's clothes lay at the head of one of the sofas, but nobody else had staked out a claim. Psmith took possession of the sofa next to the manager's. Then, humming lightly, he undressed, and made his way downstairs to the Hot Rooms. He rather fancied himself in towels. There was something about them which seemed to suit his figure. They gave him, he thought, rather a *débonnaire* look. He paused for a moment before the looking-glass to examine himself, with approval, then pushed open the door of the Hot Rooms and went in.

23 — Mr Bickersdyke Makes a Concession

Mr Bickersdyke was reclining in an easy-chair in the first room, staring before him in the boiled-fish manner customary in a Turkish Bath. Psmith dropped into the next seat with a cheery 'Good evening.' The manager started as if some firm hand had driven a bradawl into him. He looked at Psmith with what was intended to be a dignified stare. But dignity is hard to achieve in a couple of parti-coloured towels. The stare did not differ to any great extent from the conventional boiled-fish look, alluded to above.

Psmith settled himself comfortably in his chair. 'Fancy finding you here,' he said pleasantly. 'We seem always to be meeting. To me,' he added, with a reassuring smile, 'it is a great pleasure. A very great pleasure indeed. We see too little of each other during office hours. Not that one must grumble at that. Work before everything. You have your duties, I mine. It is merely unfortunate that those duties are not such as to enable us to toil side by side, encouraging each other with word and gesture. However, it is idle to repine. We must make the most of these chance meetings when the work of the day is over.'

Mr Bickersdyke heaved himself up from his chair and took another at the opposite end of the room. Psmith joined him.

'There's something pleasantly mysterious, to my mind,' said he chattily, 'in a Turkish Bath. It seems to take one out of the hurry and bustle of the everyday world. It is a quiet backwater in the rushing river of Life. I like to sit and think in a Turkish Bath. Except, of course, when I have a congenial companion to talk to. As now. To me – '

Mr Bickersdyke rose, and went into the next room.

'To me,' continued Psmith, again following, and
seating himself beside the manager, 'there is, too,
something eerie in these places. There is a certain sinister
air about the attendants. They glide rather than walk.
They say little. Who knows what they may be planning
and plotting? That drip-drip again. It may be merely
water, but how are we to know that it is not blood? It
would be so easy to do away with a man in a Turkish
Bath. Nobody has seen him come in. Nobody can trace
him if he disappears. These are uncomfortable thoughts,
Mr Bickersdyke.'

Mr Bickersdyke seemed to think them so. He rose
again, and returned to the first room.

'I have made you restless,' said Psmith, in a voice of
self-reproach, when he had settled himself once more
by the manager's side. 'I am sorry. I will not pursue the
subject. Indeed, I believe that my fears are unnecessary.
Statistics show, I understand, that large numbers of men
emerge in safety every year from Turkish Baths. There
was another matter of which I wished to speak to you. It
is a somewhat delicate matter, and I am only encouraged
to mention it to you by the fact that you are so close a
friend of my father's.'

Mr Bickersdyke had picked up an early edition of an
evening paper, left on the table at his side by a previous
bather, and was to all appearances engrossed in it. Psmith,
however, not discouraged, proceeded to touch upon the
matter of Mike.

'There was,' he said, 'some little friction, I hear, in the
office today in connection with a cheque.' The evening
paper hid the manager's expressive face, but from the fact
that the hands holding it tightened their grip Psmith
deduced that Mr Bickersdyke's attention was not wholly
concentrated on the City news. Moreover, his toes
wriggled. And when a man's toes wriggle, he is interested
in what you are saying.

'All these petty breezes,' continued Psmith sympathetically, 'must be very trying to a man in your position, a man who wishes to be left alone in order to devote his entire thought to the niceties of the higher Finance. It is as if Napoleon, while planning out some intricate scheme of campaign, were to be called upon in the midst of his meditations to bully a private for not cleaning his buttons. Naturally, you were annoyed. Your giant brain, wrenched temporarily from its proper groove, expended its force in one tremendous reprimand of Comrade Jackson. It was as if one had diverted some terrific electric current which should have been controlling a vast system of machinery, and turned it on to annihilate a black-beetle. In the present case, of course, the result is as might have been expected. Comrade Jackson, not realizing the position of affairs, went away with the absurd idea that all was over, that you meant all you said – briefly, that his number was up. I assured him that he was mistaken, but no! He persisted in declaring that all was over, that you had dismissed him from the bank.'

Mr Bickersdyke lowered the paper and glared bulbously at the old Etonian.

'Mr Jackson is perfectly right,' he snapped. 'Of course I dismissed him.'

'Yes, yes,' said Psmith, 'I have no doubt that at the moment you did work the rapid push. What I am endeavouring to point out is that Comrade Jackson is under the impression that the edict is permanent, that he can hope for no reprieve.'

'Nor can he.'

'You don't mean – '

'I mean what I say.'

'Ah, I quite understand,' said Psmith, as one who sees that he must make allowances. 'The incident is too recent. The storm has not yet had time to expend itself. You have not had leisure to think the matter over coolly. It is hard, of course, to be cool in a Turkish Bath. Your ganglions are still vibrating. Later, perhaps – '

'Once and for all,' growled Mr Bickersdyke, 'the thing is ended. Mr Jackson will leave the bank at the end of the month. We have no room for fools in the office.'

'You surprise me,' said Psmith. 'I should not have thought that the standard of intelligence in the bank was extremely high. With the exception of our two selves, I think that there are hardly any men of real intelligence on the staff. And Comrade Jackson is improving every day. Being, as he is, under my constant supervision he is rapidly developing a stranglehold on his duties, which – '

'I have no wish to discuss the matter any further.'

'No, no. Quite so, quite so. Not another word. I am dumb.'

'There are limits you see, to the uses of impertinence, Mr Smith.'

Psmith started.

'You are not suggesting – ! You do not mean that I – !'

'I have no more to say. I shall be glad if you will allow me to read my paper.'

Psmith waved a damp hand.

'I should be the last man,' he said stiffly, 'to force my conversation on another. I was under the impression that you enjoyed these little chats as keenly as I did. If I was wrong – '

He relapsed into a wounded silence. Mr Bickersdyke resumed his perusal of the evening paper, and presently, laying it down, rose and made his way to the room where muscular attendants were in waiting to perform that blend of Jiu-Jitsu and Catch-as-catch-can which is the most valuable and at the same time most painful part of a Turkish Bath.

It was not till he was resting on his sofa, swathed from head to foot in a sheet and smoking a cigarette, that he realized that Psmith was sharing his compartment.

He made the unpleasant discovery just as he had

finished his first cigarette and lighted his second. He
was blowing out the match when Psmith, accompanied
by an attendant, appeared in the doorway, and proceeded
to occupy the next sofa to himself. All that feeling of
dreamy peace, which is the reward one receives for
allowing oneself to be melted like wax and kneaded like
bread, left him instantly. He felt hot and annoyed. To
escape was out of the question. Once one has been
scientifically wrapped up by the attendant and placed
on one's sofa, one is a fixture. He lay scowling at the
ceiling, resolved to combat all attempt at conversation
with a stony silence.

Psmith, however, did not seem to desire conversation.
He lay on his sofa motionless for a quarter of an hour,
then reached out for a large book which lay on the table,
and began to read.

When he did speak, he seemed to be speaking to
himself. Every now and then he would murmur a few
words, sometimes a single name. In spite of himself, Mr
Bickersdyke found himself listening.

At first the murmurs conveyed nothing to him. Then
suddenly a name caught his ear. Strowther was the name,
and somehow it suggested something to him. He could
not say precisely what. It seemed to touch some chord
of memory. He knew no one of the name of Strowther.
He was sure of that. And yet it was curiously familiar.
An unusual name, too. He could not help feeling that at
one time he must have known it quite well.

'Mr Strowther,' murmured Psmith, 'said that the hon.
gentleman's remarks would have been nothing short of
treason, if they had not been so obviously the mere
babblings of an irresponsible lunatic. Cries of "Order,
order," and a voice, "Sit down, fat-head!"'

For just one moment Mr Bickersdyke's memory poised
motionless, like a hawk about to swoop. Then it darted
at the mark. Everything came to him in a flash. The hands
of the clock whizzed back. He was no longer Mr John

Bickersdyke, manager of the London branch of the New
Asiatic Bank, lying on a sofa in the Cumberland Street
Turkish Baths. He was Jack Bickersdyke, clerk in the
employ of Messrs Norton and Biggleswade, standing on
a chair and shouting 'Order! order!' in the Masonic Room
of the 'Red Lion' at Tulse Hill, while the members of
the Tulse Hill Parliament, divided into two camps, yelled
at one another, and young Tom Barlow, in his official
capacity as Mister Speaker, waved his arms dumbly, and
banged the table with his mallet in his efforts to restore
calm.

He remembered the whole affair as if it had happened
yesterday. It had been a speech of his own which had
called forth the above expression of opinion from
Strowther. He remembered Strowther now, a pale,
spectacled clerk in Baxter and Abrahams, an inveterate
upholder of the throne, the House of Lords and all
constituted authority. Strowther had objected to the
socialistic sentiments of his speech in connection with
the Budget, and there had been a disturbance unparalleled
even in the Tulse Hill Parliament, where disturbances
were frequent and loud . . .

Psmith looked across at him with a bright smile. 'They
report you verbatim,' he said. 'And rightly. A more able
speech I have seldom read. I like the bit where you
call the Royal Family "blood-suckers". Even then, it
seems you knew how to express yourself fluently and
well.'

Mr Bickersdyke sat up. The hands of the clock had
moved again, and he was back in what Psmith had called
the live, vivid present.

'What have you got there?' he demanded.

'It is a record,' said Psmith, 'of the meeting of an
institution called the Tulse Hill Parliament. A bright,
chatty little institution, too, if one may judge by these
reports. You in particular, if I may say so, appear to have
let yourself go with refreshing vim. Your political views

have changed a great deal since those days, have they
not? It is extremely interesting. A most fascinating study
for political students. When I send these speeches of
yours to the *Clarion* – '

Mr Bickersdyke bounded on his sofa.

'What!' he cried.

'I was saying,' said Psmith, 'that the *Clarion* will
probably make a most interesting comparison between
these speeches and those you have been making at
Kenningford.'

'I – I – I forbid you to make any mention of these
speeches.'

Psmith hesitated.

'It would be great fun seeing what the papers said,' he
protested.

'Great fun!'

'It is true,' mused Psmith, 'that in a measure, it would
dish you at the election. From what I saw of those light-
hearted lads at Kenningford the other night, I should say
they would be so amused that they would only just have
enough strength left to stagger to the poll and vote for
your opponent.'

Mr Bickersdyke broke out into a cold perspiration.

'I forbid you to send those speeches to the papers,' he
cried.

Psmith reflected.

'You see,' he said at last, 'it is like this. The departure
of Comrade Jackson, my confidential secretary and
adviser, is certain to plunge me into a state of the deepest
gloom. The only way I can see at present by which I can
ensure even a momentary lightening of the inky cloud is
the sending of these speeches to some bright paper like the
Clarion. I feel certain that their comments would wring,
at any rate, a sad, sweet smile from me. Possibly even a
hearty laugh. I must, therefore, look on these very able
speeches of yours in something of the light of an antidote.
They will stand between me and black depression.

Without them I am in the cart. With them I may possibly buoy myself up.'

Mr Bickersdyke shifted uneasily on his sofa. He glared at the floor. Then he eyed the ceiling as if it were a personal enemy of his. Finally he looked at Psmith. Psmith's eyes were closed in peaceful meditation.

'Very well,' said he at last. 'Jackson shall stop.'

Psmith came out of his thoughts with a start. 'You were observing – ?' he said.

'I shall not dismiss Jackson,' said Mr Bickersdyke.

Psmith smiled winningly.

'Just as I had hoped,' he said. 'Your very justifiable anger melts before reflection. The storm subsides, and you are at leisure to examine the matter dispassionately. Doubts begin to creep in. Possibly, you say to yourself, I have been too hasty, too harsh. Justice must be tempered with mercy. I have caught Comrade Jackson bending, you add (still to yourself), but shall I press home my advantage too ruthlessly? No, you cry, I will abstain. And I applaud your action. I like to see this spirit of gentle toleration. It is bracing and comforting. As for these excellent speeches,' he added, 'I shall, of course, no longer have any need of their consolation. I can lay them aside. The sunlight can now enter and illumine my life through more ordinary channels. The cry goes round, "Psmith is himself again."'

Mr Bickersdyke said nothing. Unless a snort of fury may be counted as anything.

24 — The Spirit of Unrest

During the following fortnight, two things happened
which materially altered Mike's position in the bank.

The first was that Mr Bickersdyke was elected a
member of Parliament. He got in by a small majority
amidst scenes of disorder of a nature unusual even in
Kenningford. Psmith, who went down on the polling-day
to inspect the revels and came back with his hat smashed
in, reported that, as far as he could see, the electors of
Kenningford seemed to be in just that state of happy
intoxication which might make them vote for Mr
Bickersdyke by mistake. Also it had been discovered, on
the eve of the poll, that the bank manager's opponent,
in his youth, had been educated at a school in Germany,
and had subsequently spent two years at Heidelberg
University. These damaging revelations were having a
marked effect on the warm-hearted patriots of
Kenningford, who were now referring to the candidate in
thick but earnest tones as 'the German Spy'.

'So that taking everything into consideration,' said
Psmith, summing up, 'I fancy that Comrade Bickersdyke
is home.'

And the papers next day proved that he was right.

'A hundred and fifty-seven,' said Psmith, as he read
his paper at breakfast. 'Not what one would call a
slashing victory. It is fortunate for Comrade Bickersdyke,
I think, that I did not send those very able speeches of
his to the *Clarion*.'

Till now Mike had been completely at a loss to
understand why the manager had sent for him on the
morning following the scene about the cheque, and

informed him that he had reconsidered his decision to
dismiss him. Mike could not help feeling that there was
more in the matter than met the eye. Mr Bickersdyke
had not spoken as if it gave him any pleasure to reprieve
him. On the contrary, his manner was distinctly brusque.
Mike was thoroughly puzzled. To Psmith's statement,
that he had talked the matter over quietly with the manager
and brought things to a satisfactory conclusion, he had
paid little attention. But now he began to see light.

'Great Scott, Smith,' he said, 'did you tell him you'd
send those speeches to the papers if he sacked me?'

Psmith looked at him through his eye-glass, and helped
himself to another piece of toast.

'I am unable,' he said, 'to recall at this moment the
exact terms of the very pleasant conversation I had with
Comrade Bickersdyke on the occasion of our chance
meeting in the Turkish Bath that afternoon; but,
thinking things over quietly now that I have more leisure,
I cannot help feeling that he may possibly have read
some such intention into my words. You know how it is
in these little chats, Comrade Jackson. One leaps to
conclusions. Some casual word I happened to drop may
have given him the idea you mention. At this distance
of time it is impossible to say with any certainty. Suffice
it that all has ended well. He *did* reconsider his resolve.
I shall be only too happy if it turns out that the seed of
the alteration in his views was sown by some careless
word of mine. Perhaps we shall never know.'

Mike was beginning to mumble some awkward words
of thanks, when Psmith resumed his discourse.

'Be that as it may, however,' he said, 'we cannot but
perceive that Comrade Bickersdyke's election has
altered our position to some extent. As you have pointed
out, he may have been influenced in this recent affair
by some chance remark of mine about those speeches.
Now, however, they will cease to be of any value. Now
that he is elected he has nothing to lose by their

publication. I mention this by way of indicating that it
is possible that, if another painful episode occurs, he may
be more ruthless.'

'I see what you mean,' said Mike. 'If he catches me on
the hop again, he'll simply go ahead and sack me.'

'That,' said Psmith, '*is* more or less the position of
affairs.'

The other event which altered Mike's life in the bank
was his removal from Mr Waller's department to the
Fixed Deposits. The work in the Fixed Deposits was less
pleasant, and Mr Gregory, the head of the department
was not of Mr Waller's type. Mr Gregory, before joining
the home-staff of the New Asiatic Bank, had spent a
number of years with a firm in the Far East, where he had
acquired a liver and a habit of addressing those under
him in a way that suggested the mate of a tramp steamer.
Even on the days when his liver was not troubling him,
he was truculent. And when, as usually happened, it did
trouble him, he was a perfect fountain of abuse. Mike
and he hated each other from the first. The work in the
Fixed Deposits was not really difficult, when you got
the hang of it, but there was a certain amount of confusion
in it to a beginner; and Mike, in commercial matters, was
as raw a beginner as ever began. In the two other
departments through which he had passed, he had done
tolerably well. As regarded his work in the Postage
Department, stamping letters and taking them down to
the post office was just about his form. It was the sort of
work on which he could really get a grip. And in the
Cash Department, Mr Waller's mild patience had helped
him through. But with Mr Gregory it was different. Mike
hated being shouted at. It confused him. And Mr Gregory
invariably shouted. He always spoke as if he were
competing against a high wind. With Mike he shouted
more than usual. On his side, it must be admitted that
Mike was something out of the common run of bank
clerks. The whole system of banking was a horrid

mystery to him. He did not understand why things were done, or how the various departments depended on and dove-tailed into one another. Each department seemed to him something separate and distinct. Why they were all in the same building at all he never really gathered. He knew that it could not be purely from motives of sociability, in order that the clerks might have each other's company during slack spells. That much he suspected, but beyond that he was vague.

It naturally followed that, after having grown, little by little, under Mr Waller's easy-going rule, to enjoy life in the bank, he now suffered a reaction. Within a day of his arrival in the Fixed Deposits he was loathing the place as earnestly as he had loathed it on the first morning.

Psmith, who had taken his place in the Cash Department, reported that Mr Waller was inconsolable at his loss.

'I do my best to cheer him up,' he said, 'and he smiles bravely every now and then. But when he thinks I am not looking, his head droops and that wistful expression comes into his face. The sunshine has gone out of his life.'

It had just come into Mike's, and, more than anything else, was making him restless and discontented. That is to say, it was now late spring: the sun shone cheerfully on the City; and cricket was in the air. And that was the trouble.

In the dark days, when everything was fog and slush, Mike had been contented enough to spend his mornings and afternoons in the bank, and go about with Psmith at night. Under such conditions, London is the best place in which to be, and the warmth and light of the bank were pleasant.

But now things had changed. The place had become a prison. With all the energy of one who had been born and bred in the country, Mike hated having to stay indoors on days when all the air was full of approaching summer.

There were mornings when it was almost more than he could do to push open the swing doors, and go out of the fresh air into the stuffy atmosphere of the bank.

The days passed slowly, and the cricket season began. Instead of being a relief, this made matters worse. The little cricket he could get only made him want more. It was as if a starving man had been given a handful of wafer biscuits.

If the summer had been wet, he might have been less restless. But, as it happened, it was unusually fine. After a week of cold weather at the beginning of May, a hot spell set in. May passed in a blaze of sunshine. Large scores were made all over the country.

Mike's name had been down for the M. C. C. for some years, and he had become a member during his last season at Wrykyn. Once or twice a week he managed to get up to Lord's for half an hour's practice at the nets; and on Saturdays the bank had matches, in which he generally managed to knock the cover off rather ordinary club bowling. But it was not enough for him.

June came, and with it more sunshine. The atmosphere of the bank seemed more oppressive than ever.

25 — At the Telephone

If one looks closely into those actions which are
apparently due to sudden impulse, one generally finds that
the sudden impulse was merely the last of a long series
of events which led up to the action. Alone, it would
not have been powerful enough to effect anything. But,
coming after the way has been paved for it, it is
irresistible. The hooligan who bonnets a policeman
is apparently the victim of a sudden impulse. In reality,
however, the bonneting is due to weeks of daily
encounters with the constable, at each of which
meetings the dislike for his helmet and the idea of
smashing it in grow a little larger, till finally they
blossom into the deed itself.

This was what happened in Mike's case. Day by day,
through the summer, as the City grew hotter and stuffier,
his hatred of the bank became more and more the thought
that occupied his mind. It only needed a moderately
strong temptation to make him break out and take the
consequences.

Psmith noticed his restlessness and endeavoured to
soothe it.

'All is not well,' he said, 'with Comrade Jackson, the
Sunshine of the Home. I note a certain wanness of
the cheek. The peach-bloom of your complexion is no
longer up to sample. Your eye is wild; your merry laugh
no longer rings through the bank, causing nervous
customers to leap into the air with startled exclamations.
You have the manner of one whose only friend on earth
is a yellow dog, and who has lost the dog. Why is this,
Comrade Jackson?'

They were talking in the flat at Clement's Inn. The night was hot. Through the open windows the roar of the Strand sounded faintly. Mike walked to the window and looked out.

'I'm sick of all this rot,' he said shortly.

Psmith shot an inquiring glance at him, but said nothing. This restlessness of Mike's was causing him a good deal of inconvenience, which he bore in patient silence, hoping for better times. With Mike obviously discontented and out of tune with all the world, there was but little amusement to be extracted from the evenings now. Mike did his best to be cheerful, but he could not shake off the caged feeling which made him restless.

'What rot it all is!' went on Mike, sitting down again. 'What's the good of it all? You go and sweat all day at a desk, day after day, for about twopence a year. And when you're about eighty-five, you retire. It isn't living at all. It's simply being a bally vegetable.'

'You aren't hankering, by any chance, to be a pirate of the Spanish main, or anything like that, are you?' inquired Psmith.

'And all this rot about going out East,' continued Mike. 'What's the good of going out East?'

'I gather from casual chit-chat in the office that one becomes something of a blood when one goes out East,' said Psmith. 'Have a dozen native clerks under you, all looking up to you as the Last Word in magnificence, and end by marrying the Governor's daughter.'

'End by getting some foul sort of fever, more likely, and being booted out as no further use to the bank.'

'You look on the gloomy side, Comrade Jackson. I seem to see you sitting in an armchair, fanned by devoted coolies, telling some Eastern potentate that you can give him five minutes. I understand that being in a bank in the Far East is one of the world's softest jobs. Millions of natives hang on your lightest word. Enthusiastic rajahs draw you aside and press jewels into your hand as a token of respect and esteem. When on an elephant's back you pass, somebody beats on a booming brass gong! The Banker of Bhong! Isn't your generous young heart stirred to any extent by the prospect? I am given to understand – '

'I've a jolly good mind to chuck up the whole thing and become a pro. I've got a birth qualification for Surrey. It's about the only thing I could do any good at.'

Psmith's manner became fatherly.

'*You're* all right,' he said. 'The hot weather has given you that tired feeling. What you want is a change of air. We will pop down together hand in hand this week-end to some seaside resort. You shall build sand castles, while I lie on the beach and read the paper. In the evening we will listen to the band, or stroll on the esplanade, not so much because we want to, as to give the natives a treat. Possibly, if the weather continues warm, we may even paddle. A vastly exhilarating pastime, I am led to believe, and *so* strengthening for the ankles. And on Monday morning we will return, bronzed and bursting with health, to our toil once more.'

'I'm going to bed,' said Mike, rising.

Psmith watched him lounge from the room, and shook his head sadly. All was not well with his confidential secretary and adviser.

The next day, which was a Thursday, found Mike no more reconciled to the prospect of spending from ten till five in the company of Mr Gregory and the ledgers. He was silent at breakfast, and Psmith, seeing that things were still wrong, abstained from conversation. Mike propped the *Sportsman* up against the hot-water jug, and read the cricket news. His county, captained by brother Joe, had, as he had learned already from yesterday's evening paper, beaten Sussex by five wickets at Brighton. Today they were due to play Middlesex at Lord's. Mike thought that he would try to get off early, and go and see some of the first day's play.

As events turned out, he got off a good deal earlier, and saw a good deal more of the first day's play than he had anticipated.

He had just finished the preliminary stages of the morning's work, which consisted mostly of washing his hands, changing his coat, and eating a section of a pen-holder, when William, the messenger, approached.

'You're wanted on the 'phone, Mr Jackson.'

The New Asiatic Bank, unlike the majority of London banks, was on the telephone, a fact which Psmith found a great convenience when securing seats at the theatre. Mike went to the box and took up the receiver.

'Hullo!' he said.

'Who's that?' said an agitated voice. 'Is that you, Mike? I'm Joe.'

'Hullo, Joe,' said Mike. 'What's up? I'm coming to see you this evening. I'm going to try and get off early.'

'Look here, Mike, are you busy at the bank just now?'

'Not at the moment. There's never anything much going on before eleven.'

'I mean, are you busy today? Could you possibly manage to get off and play for us against Middlesex?'

Mike nearly dropped the receiver.

'What?' he cried.

'There's been the dickens of a mix-up. We're one short, and you're our only hope. We can't possibly get another man in the time. We start in half an hour. Can you play?'

For the space of, perhaps, one minute, Mike thought.

'Well?' said Joe's voice.

The sudden vision of Lord's ground, all green and cool in the morning sunlight, was too much for Mike's resolution, sapped as it was by days of restlessness. The feeling surged over him that whatever happened afterwards, the joy of the match in perfect weather on a perfect wicket would make it worth while. What did it matter what happened afterwards?

'All right, Joe,' he said. 'I'll hop into a cab now, and go and get my things.'

'Good man,' said Joe, hugely relieved.

26 — Breaking the News

Dashing away from the call-box, Mike nearly cannoned into Psmith, who was making his way pensively to the telephone with the object of ringing up the box office of the Haymarket Theatre.

'Sorry,' said Mike. 'Hullo, Smith.'

'Hullo indeed,' said Psmith, courteously. 'I rejoice, Comrade Jackson, to find you going about your commercial duties like a young bomb. How is it, people repeatedly ask me, that Comrade Jackson contrives to catch his employer's eye and win the friendly smile from the head of his department? My reply is that where others walk, Comrade Jackson runs. Where others stroll, Comrade Jackson legs it like a highly-trained mustang of the prairie. He does not loiter. He gets back to his department bathed in perspiration, in level time. He – '

'I say, Smith,' said Mike, 'you might do me a favour.'

'A thousand. Say on.'

'Just look in at the Fixed Deposits and tell old Gregory that I shan't be with him today, will you? I haven't time myself. I must rush!'

Psmith screwed his eyeglass into his eye, and examined Mike carefully.

'What exactly – ?' he began.

'Tell the old ass I've popped off.'

'Just so, just so,' murmured Psmith, as one who assents to a thoroughly reasonable proposition. 'Tell him you have popped off. It shall be done. But it is within the bounds of possibility that Comrade Gregory may inquire further. Could you give me some inkling as to why you are popping?'

'My brother Joe has just rung me up from Lords. The county are playing Middlesex and they're one short. He wants me to roll up.'

Psmith shook his head sadly.

'I don't wish to interfere in any way,' he said, 'but I suppose you realize that, by acting thus, you are to some extent knocking the stuffing out of your chances of becoming manager of this bank? If you dash off now, I shouldn't count too much on that marrying the Governor's daughter scheme I sketched out for you last night. I doubt whether this is going to help you to hold the gorgeous East in fee, and all that sort of thing.'

'Oh, dash the gorgeous East.'

'By all means,' said Psmith obligingly. 'I just thought I'd mention it. I'll look in at Lord's this afternoon. I shall send my card up to you, and trust to your sympathetic cooperation to enable me to effect an entry into the pavilion on my face. My father is coming up to London today. I'll bring him along, too.'

'Right ho. Dash it, it's twenty to. So long. See you at Lord's.'

Psmith looked after his retreating form till it had vanished through the swing-door, and shrugged his shoulders resignedly, as if disclaiming all responsibility.

'He has gone without his hat,' he murmured. 'It seems to me that this is practically a case of running amok. And now to break the news to bereaved Comrade Gregory.'

He abandoned his intention of ringing up the Haymarket Theatre, and turning away from the callbox, walked meditatively down the aisle till he came to the Fixed Deposits Department, where the top of Mr Gregory's head was to be seen over the glass barrier, as he applied himself to his work.

Psmith, resting his elbows on the top of the barrier and holding his head between his hands, eyed the

absorbed toiler for a moment in silence, then emitted a
hollow groan.

Mr Gregory, who was ruling a line in a ledger – most
of the work in the Fixed Deposits Department
consisted of ruling lines in ledgers, sometimes in black
ink, sometimes in red – started as if he had been stung,
and made a complete mess of the ruled line. He lifted a
fiery, bearded face, and met Psmith's eye, which shone
with kindly sympathy,

He found words.

'What the dickens are you standing there for, mooing
like a blanked cow?' he inquired.

'I was groaning,' explained Psmith with quiet dignity.
'And why was I groaning?' he continued. 'Because a
shadow has fallen on the Fixed Deposits Department.
Comrade Jackson, the Pride of the Office, has gone.'

Mr Gregory rose from his seat.

'I don't know who the dickens you are – ' he began.

'I am Psmith,' said the old Etonian.

'Oh, you're Smith, are you?'

'With a preliminary P. Which, however, is not
sounded.'

'And what's all this dashed nonsense about Jackson?'

'He is gone. Gone like the dew from the petal of a
rose.'

'Gone! Where's he gone to?'

'Lord's.'

'What lord's?'

Psmith waved his hand gently.

'You misunderstand me. Comrade Jackson has not
gone to mix with any member of our gay and thoughtless
aristocracy. He has gone to Lord's cricket ground.'

Mr Gregory's beard bristled even more than was its
wont.

'What!' he roared. 'Gone to watch a cricket match!
Gone – !'

'Not to watch. To play. An urgent summons I need not

say. Nothing but an urgent summons could have wrenched him from your very delightful society, I am sure.'

Mr Gregory glared.

'I don't want any of your impudence,' he said.

Psmith nodded gravely.

'We all have these curious likes and dislikes,' he said tolerantly. 'You do not like my impudence. Well, well, some people don't. And now, having broken the sad news, I will return to my own department.'

'Half a minute. You come with me and tell this yarn of yours to Mr Bickersdyke.'

'You think it would interest, amuse him? Perhaps you are right. Let us buttonhole Comrade Bickersdyke.'

Mr Bickersdyke was disengaged. The head of the Fixed Deposits Department stumped into the room. Psmith followed at a more leisurely pace.

'Allow me,' he said with a winning smile, as Mr Gregory opened his mouth to speak, 'to take this opportunity of congratulating you on your success at the election. A narrow but well-deserved victory.'

There was nothing cordial in the manager's manner.

'What do you want?' he said.

'Myself, nothing,' said Psmith. 'But I understand that Mr Gregory has some communication to make.'

'Tell Mr Bickersdyke that story of yours,' said Mr Gregory.

'Surely,' said Psmith reprovingly, 'this is no time for anecdotes. Mr Bickersdyke is busy. He – '

'Tell him what you told me about Jackson.'

Mr Bickersdyke looked up inquiringly.

'Jackson,' said Psmith, 'has been obliged to absent himself from work today owing to an urgent summons from his brother, who, I understand, has suffered a bereavement.'

'It's a lie,' roared Mr Gregory. 'You told me yourself he'd gone to play in a cricket match.'

'True. As I said, he received an urgent summons from his brother.'

'What about the bereavement, then?'

'The team was one short. His brother was very distressed about it. What could Comrade Jackson do? Could he refuse to help his brother when it was in his power? His generous nature is a byword. He did the only possible thing. He consented to play.'

Mr Bickersdyke spoke.

'Am I to understand,' he asked, with sinister calm, 'that Mr Jackson has left his work and gone off to play in a cricket match?'

'Something of that sort has, I believe, happened,' said Psmith. 'He knew, of course,' he added, bowing gracefully in Mr Gregory's direction, 'that he was leaving his work in thoroughly competent hands.'

'Thank you,' said Mr Bickersdyke. 'That will do. You will help Mr Gregory in his department for the time being, Mr Smith. I will arrange for somebody to take your place in your own department.'

'It will be a pleasure,' murmured Psmith.

'Show Mr Smith what he has to do, Mr Gregory,' said the manager.

They left the room.

'How curious, Comrade Gregory,' mused Psmith, as they went, 'are the workings of Fate! A moment back, and your life was a blank. Comrade Jackson, that prince of Fixed Depositors, had gone. How, you said to yourself despairingly, can his place be filled? Then the cloud broke, and the sun shone out again. *I* came to help you. What you lose on the swings, you make up on the roundabouts. Now show me what I have to do, and then let us make this department sizzle. You have drawn a good ticket, Comrade Gregory.'

27 — At Lord's

Mike got to Lord's just as the umpires moved out into the field. He raced round to the pavilion. Joe met him on the stairs.

'It's all right,' he said. 'No hurry. We've won the toss. I've put you in fourth wicket.'

'Right ho,' said Mike. 'Glad we haven't to field just yet.'

'We oughtn't to have to field today if we don't chuck our wickets away.'

'Good wicket?'

'Like a billiard-table. I'm glad you were able to come. Have any difficulty in getting away?'

Joe Jackson's knowledge of the workings of a bank was of the slightest. He himself had never, since he left Oxford, been in a position where there were obstacles to getting off to play in first-class cricket. By profession he was agent to a sporting baronet whose hobby was the cricket of the county, and so, far from finding any difficulty in playing for the county, he was given to understand by his employer that that was his chief duty. It never occurred to him that Mike might find his bank less amenable in the matter of giving leave. His only fear, when he rang Mike up that morning, had been that this might be a particularly busy day at the New Asiatic Bank. If there was no special rush of work, he took it for granted that Mike would simply go to the manager, ask for leave to play in the match, and be given it with a beaming smile.

Mike did not answer the question, but asked one on his own account.

'How did you happen to be short?' he said.

'It was rotten luck. It was like this. We were altering our team after the Sussex match, to bring in Ballard, Keene, and Willis. They couldn't get down to Brighton, as the 'Varsity had a match, but there was nothing on for them in the last half of the week, so they'd promised to roll up.'

Ballard, Keene, and Willis were members of the Cambridge team, all very capable performers and much in demand by the county, when they could get away to play for it.

'Well?' said Mike.

'Well, we all came up by train from Brighton last night. But these three asses had arranged to motor down from Cambridge early today, and get here in time for the start. What happens? Why, Willis, who fancies himself as a chauffeur, undertakes to do the driving; and naturally, being an absolute rotter, goes and smashes up the whole concern just outside St Albans. The first thing I knew of it was when I got to Lord's at half past ten, and found a wire waiting for me to say that they were all three of them crocked, and couldn't possibly play. I tell you, it was a bit of a jar to get half an hour before the match started. Willis has sprained his ankle, apparently; Keene's damaged his wrist; and Ballard has smashed his collar-bone. I don't suppose they'll be able to play in the 'Varsity match. Rotten luck for Cambridge. Well, fortunately we'd had two reserve pros. with us at Brighton, who had come up to London with the team in case they might be wanted, so, with them, we were only one short. Then I thought of you. That's how it was.'

'I see,' said Mike. 'Who are the pros?'

'Davis and Brockley. Both bowlers. It weakens our batting a lot, Ballard or Willis might have got a stack of runs on this wicket. Still, we've got a certain amount of batting as it is. We oughtn't to do badly, if we're careful. You've been getting some practice, I suppose, this season?'

'In a sort of a way. Nets and so on. No matches of any importance.'

'Dash it, I wish you'd had a game or two in decent class cricket. Still, nets are better than nothing, I hope you'll be in form. We may want a pretty long knock from you, if things go wrong. These men seem to be settling down all right, thank goodness,' he added, looking out of the window at the county's first pair, Warrington and Mills, two professionals, who, as the result of ten minutes' play, had put up twenty.

'I'd better go and change,' said Mike, picking up his bag. 'You're in first wicket, I suppose?'

'Yes. And Reggie, second wicket.'

Reggie was another of Mike's brothers, not nearly so fine a player as Joe, but a sound bat, who generally made runs if allowed to stay in.

Mike changed, and went out into the little balcony at the top of the pavilion. He had it to himself. There were not many spectators in the pavilion at this early stage of the game.

There are few more restful places, if one wishes to think, than the upper balconies of Lord's pavilion. Mike, watching the game making its leisurely progress on the turf below, set himself seriously to review the situation in all its aspects. The exhilaration of bursting the bonds had begun to fade, and he found himself able to look into the matter of his desertion and weigh up the consequences. There was no doubt that he had cut the painter once and for all. Even a friendly-disposed management could hardly overlook what he had done. And the management of the New Asiatic Bank was the very reverse of friendly. Mr Bickersdyke, he knew, would jump at this chance of getting rid of him. He realized that he must look on his career in the bank as a closed book. It

was definitely over, and he must now think about the
future.

It was not a time for half-measures. He could not go
home. He must carry the thing through, now that he had
begun, and find something definite to do, to support
himself.

There seemed only one opening for him. What could
he do, he asked himself. Just one thing. He could play
cricket. It was by his cricket that he must live. He would
have to become a professional. Could he get taken on?
That was the question. It was impossible that he should
play for his own county on his residential qualification.
He could not appear as a professional in the same team
in which his brothers were playing as amateurs. He must
stake all on his birth qualification for Surrey.

On the other hand, had he the credentials which
Surrey would want? He had a school reputation. But was
that enough? He could not help feeling that it might not
be.

Thinking it over more tensely than he had ever thought
over anything in his whole life, he saw clearly that
everything depended on what sort of show he made in
this match which was now in progress. It was his big
chance. If he succeeded, all would be well. He did not
care to think what his position would be if he did
not succeed.

A distant appeal and a sound of clapping from the
crowd broke in on his thoughts. Mills was out, caught
at the wicket. The telegraph-board gave the total as
forty-eight. Not sensational. The success of the team
depended largely on what sort of a start the two
professionals made.

The clapping broke out again as Joe made his way
down the steps. Joe, as an All England player, was a
favourite with the crowd.

Mike watched him play an over in his strong, graceful

style: then it suddenly occurred to him that he would
like to know how matters had gone at the bank in his
absence.

He went down to the telephone, rang up the bank, and
asked for Psmith.

Presently the familiar voice made itself heard.

'Hullo, Smith.'

'Hullo. Is that Comrade Jackson? How are things
progressing?'

'Fairly well. We're in first. We've lost one wicket, and
the fifty's just up. I say, what's happened at the bank?'

'I broke the news to Comrade Gregory. A charming
personality. I feel that we shall be friends.'

'Was he sick?'

'In a measure, yes. Indeed, I may say he practically
foamed at the mouth. I explained the situation, but he
was not to be appeased. He jerked me into the presence
of Comrade Bickersdyke, with whom I had a brief but
entertaining chat. He had not a great deal to say, but he
listened attentively to my narrative, and eventually told
me off to take your place in the Fixed Deposits. That
melancholy task I am now performing to the best of my
ability. I find the work a little trying. There is too much
ledger-lugging to be done for my simple tastes. I have
been hauling ledgers from the safe all the morning.
The cry is beginning to go round, "Psmith is willing, but
can his physique stand the strain?" In the excitement of
the moment just now I dropped a somewhat massive
tome on to Comrade Gregory's foot, unfortunately,
I understand, the foot in which he has of late been
suffering twinges of gout. I passed the thing off with
ready tact, but I cannot deny that there was a certain
temporary coolness, which, indeed, is not yet past. These
things, Comrade Jackson, are the whirlpools in the quiet
stream of commercial life.'

'Have I got the sack.'

'No official pronouncement has been made to me as

yet on the subject, but I think I should advise you, if you
are offered another job in the course of the day, to accept
it. I cannot say that you are precisely the pet of the
management just at present. However, I have ideas for
your future, which I will divulge when we meet. I propose
to slide coyly from the office at about four o'clock. I am
meeting my father at that hour. We shall come straight
on to Lord's.'

'Right ho,' said Mike. 'I'll be looking out for you.'

'Is there any little message I can give Comrade Gregory
from you?'

'You can give him my love, if you like.'

'It shall be done. Good-bye.'

'Good-bye.'

Mike replaced the receiver, and went up to his balcony
again.

As soon as his eye fell on the telegraph-board he saw
with a start that things had been moving rapidly in his
brief absence. The numbers of the batsmen on the board
were three and five.

'Great Scott!' he cried. 'Why, I'm in next. What on
earth's been happening?'

He put on his pads hurriedly, expecting every moment
that a wicket would fall and find him unprepared. But
the batsmen were still together when he rose, ready for
the fray, and went downstairs to get news.

He found his brother Reggie in the dressing-
room.

'What's happened?' he said. 'How were you out?'

'L. b. w.,' said Reggie. 'Goodness knows how it
happened. My eyesight must be going. I mistimed the
thing altogether.'

'How was Warrington out?'

'Caught in the slips.'

'By Jove!' said Mike. 'This is pretty rocky. Three for
sixty-one. We shall get mopped.'

'Unless you and Joe do something. There's no earthly

need to get out. The wicket's as good as you want, and
the bowling's nothing special. Well played, Joe!'

A beautiful glide to leg by the greatest of the Jacksons
had rolled up against the pavilion rails. The fieldsmen
changed across for the next over.

'If only Peters stops a bit – ' began Mike, and broke off.
Peters' off stump was lying at an angle of forty-five
degrees.

'Well, he hasn't,' said Reggie grimly. 'Silly ass, why
did he hit at that one? All he'd got to do was to stay in
with Joe. Now it's up to you. Do try and do something,
or we'll be out under the hundred.'

Mike waited till the outcoming batsman had turned
in at the professionals' gate. Then he walked down the
steps and out into the open, feeling more nervous than
he had felt since that far-off day when he had first gone
in to bat for Wrykyn against the M. C. C. He found his
thoughts flying back to that occasion. Today, as then,
everything seemed very distant and unreal. The
spectators were miles away. He had often been to Lord's
as a spectator, but the place seemed entirely unfamiliar
now. He felt as if he were in a strange land.

He was conscious of Joe leaving the crease to meet
him on his way. He smiled feebly. 'Buck up,' said Joe in
that robust way of his which was so heartening. 'Nothing
in the bowling, and the wicket like a shirt-front. Play
just as if you were at the nets. And for goodness' sake
don't try to score all your runs in the first over. Stick in,
and we've got them.'

Mike smiled again more feebly than before, and made
a weird gurgling noise in his throat.

It had been the Middlesex fast bowler who had
destroyed Peters. Mike was not sorry. He did not object
to fast bowling. He took guard, and looked round him,
taking careful note of the positions of the slips.

As usual, once he was at the wicket the paralysed
feeling left him. He became conscious again of his power.

Dash it all, what was there to be afraid of? He was a jolly good bat, and he would jolly well show them that he was, too.

The fast bowler, with a preliminary bound, began his run. Mike settled himself into position, his whole soul concentrated on the ball. Everything else was wiped from his mind.

28 — Psmith Arranges His Future

It was exactly four o'clock when Psmith, sliding unostentatiously from his stool, flicked divers pieces of dust from the leg of his trousers, and sidled towards the basement, where he was wont to keep his hat during business hours. He was aware that it would be a matter of some delicacy to leave the bank at that hour. There was a certain quantity of work still to be done in the Fixed Deposits Department – work in which, by rights, as Mike's understudy, he should have lent a sympathetic and helping hand. 'But what of that?' he mused, thoughtfully smoothing his hat with his knuckles. 'Comrade Gregory is a man who takes such an enthusiastic pleasure in his duties that he will go singing about the office when he discovers that he has got a double lot of work to do.'

With this comforting thought, he started on his perilous journey to the open air. As he walked delicately, not courting observation, he reminded himself of the hero of 'Pilgrim's Progress'. On all sides of him lay fearsome beasts, lying in wait to pounce upon him. At any moment Mr Gregory's hoarse roar might shatter the comparative stillness, or the sinister note of Mr Bickersdyke make itself heard.

'However,' said Psmith philosophically, 'these are Life's Trials, and must be borne patiently.'

A roundabout route, *via* the Postage and Inwards Bills Departments, took him to the swing-doors. It was here that the danger became acute. The doors were well within view of the Fixed Deposits Department, and Mr Gregory had an eye compared with which that of an eagle was more or less bleared.

Psmith looked up. Mr Gregory was leaning over the barrier manner. As he did so a bellow rang through the office, causing a timid customer, who had come in to arrange about an overdraft, to lose his nerve completely and postpone his business till the following afternoon.

Psmith looked up. Mr Gregory was leaning over the barrier which divided his lair from the outer world, and gesticulating violently.

'Where are you going,' roared the head of the Fixed Deposits.

Psmith did not reply. With a benevolent smile and a gesture intended to signify all would come right in the future, he slid through the swing-doors, and began to move down the street at a somewhat swifter pace than was his habit.

Once round the corner he slackened his speed.

'This can't go on,' he said to himself. 'This life of commerce is too great a strain. One is practically a hunted hare. Either the heads of my department must refrain from View Halloos when they observe me going for a stroll, or I abandon Commerce for some less exacting walk in life.'

He removed his hat, and allowed the cool breeze to play upon his forehead. The episode had been disturbing.

He was to meet his father at the Mansion House. As he reached that land-mark he saw with approval that punctuality was a virtue of which he had not the sole monopoly in the Smith family. His father was waiting for him at the tryst.

'Certainly, my boy,' said Mr Smith senior, all activity in a moment, when Psmith had suggested going to Lord's. 'Excellent. We must be getting on. We must not miss a moment of the match. Bless my soul: I haven't seen a first-class match this season. Where's a cab? Hi,

cabby! No, that one's got some one in it. There's another.
Hi! Here, lunatic! Are you blind? Good, he's seen us.
That's right. Here he comes. Lord's Cricket Ground,
cabby, as quick as you can. Jump in, Rupert, my boy,
jump in.'

Psmith rarely jumped. He entered the cab with
something of the stateliness of an old Roman Emperor
boarding his chariot, and settled himself comfortably in
his seat. Mr Smith dived in like a rabbit.

A vendor of newspapers came to the cab thrusting an
evening paper into the interior. Psmith bought it.'

'Let's see how they're getting on,' he said, opening the
paper. 'Where are we? Lunch scores. Lord's. Aha!
Comrade Jackson is in form.'

'Jackson?' said Mr Smith. 'is that the same youngster
you brought home last summer? The batsman? Is he
playing today?'

'He was not out thirty at lunch-time. He would appear
to be making something of a stand with his brother Joe,
who has made sixty-one up to the moment of going to
press. It's possible he may still be in when we get there.
In which case we shall not be able to slide into the
pavilion.'

'A grand bat, that boy. I said so last summer. Better
than any of his brothers. He's in the bank with you, isn't
he?'

'He was this morning. I doubt, however, whether
he can be said to be still in that position.'

'Eh? what? How's that?'

'There was some slight friction between him and the
management. They wished him to be glued to his stool;
he preferred to play for the county. I think we may say
that Comrade Jackson has secured the Order of the Boot.'

'What? Do you mean to say – ?'

Psmith related briefly the history of Mike's departure.
Mr Smith listened with interest.

'Well,' he said at last, 'hang me if I blame the boy. It's

a sin cooping up a fellow who can bat like that in a bank.
I should have done the same myself in his place.'

Psmith smoothed his waistcoat.

'Do you know, father,' he said, 'this bank business is
far from being much of a catch. Indeed, I should describe
it definitely as a bit off. I have given it a fair trial, and I
now denounce it unhesitatingly as a shade too thick.'

'What? Are you getting tired of it?'

'Not precisely tired. But, after considerable reflection,
I have come to the conclusion that my talents lie
elsewhere. At lugging ledgers I am among the also-rans –
a mere cipher. I have been wanting to speak to you about
this for some time. If you have no objection, I should like
to go to the Bar.'

'The Bar? Well – '

'I fancy I should make a pretty considerable hit as a
barrister.'

Mr Smith reflected. The idea had not occurred to him
before. Now that it was suggested, his always easily-
fired imagination took hold of it readily. There was a good
deal to be said for the Bar as a career. Psmith knew his
father, and he knew that the thing was practically as good
as settled. It was a new idea, and as such was bound to
be favourably received.

'What I should do, if I were you,' he went on, as if he
were advising a friend on some course of action certain
to bring him profit and pleasure, 'is to take me away from
the bank at once. Don't wait. There is no time like the
present. Let me hand in my resignation tomorrow. The
blow to the management, especially to Comrade
Bickersdyke, will be a painful one, but it is the truest
kindness to administer it swiftly. Let me resign
tomorrow, and devote my time to quiet study. Then
I can pop up to Cambridge next term, and all will be
well.'

'I'll think it over – ' began Mr Smith.

'Let us hustle,' urged Psmith. 'Let us Do It Now. It is

the only way. Have I your leave to shoot in my resignation to Comrade Bickersdyke tomorrow morning?'

Mr Smith hesitated for a moment, then made up his mind.

'Very well,' he said. 'I really think it is a good idea. There are great opportunities open to a barrister. I wish we had thought of it before.'

'I am not altogether sorry that we did not,' said Psmith. 'I have enjoyed the chances my commercial life has given me of associating with such a man as Comrade Bickersdyke. In many ways a master-mind. But perhaps it is as well to close the chapter. How it happened it is hard to say, but somehow I fancy I did not precisely hit it off with Comrade Bickersdyke. With Psmith, the worker, he had no fault to find; but it seemed to me sometimes, during our festive evenings together at the club, that all was not well. From little, almost imperceptible signs I have suspected now and then that he would just as soon have been without my company. One cannot explain these things. It must have been some incompatibility of temperament. Perhaps he will manage to bear up at my departure. But here we are,' he added, as the cab drew up. 'I wonder if Comrade Jackson is still going strong.'

They passed through the turnstile, and caught sight of the telegraph-board.

'By Jove!' said Psmith, 'he is. I don't know if he's number three or number six. I expect he's number six. In which case he has got ninety-eight. We're just in time to see his century.'

29 — And Mike's

For nearly two hours Mike had been experiencing the
keenest pleasure that it had ever fallen to his lot to feel.
From the moment he took his first ball till the luncheon
interval he had suffered the acutest discomfort. His
nervousness had left him to a great extent, but he had
never really settled down. Sometimes by luck, and
sometimes by skill, he had kept the ball out of his wicket;
but he was scratching, and he knew it. Not for a single
over had he been comfortable. On several occasions he
had edged balls to leg and through the slips in quite an
inferior manner, and it was seldom that he managed to
hit with the centre of the bat.

Nobody is more alive to the fact that he is not playing
up to his true form than the batsman. Even though his
score mounted little by little into the twenties, Mike was
miserable. If this was the best he could do on a perfect
wicket, he felt there was not much hope for him as a
professional.

The poorness of his play was accentuated by the
brilliance of Joe's. Joe combined science and vigour to a
remarkable degree. He laid on the wood with a graceful
robustness which drew much cheering from the crowd.
Beside him Mike was oppressed by that leaden sense of
moral inferiority which weighs on a man who has turned
up to dinner in ordinary clothes when everybody else has
dressed. He felt awkward and conspicuously out of
place.

Then came lunch – and after lunch a glorious change.

Volumes might be written on the cricket lunch and
the influence it has on the run of the game; how it

undoes one man, and sends another back to the fray like a giant refreshed; how it turns the brilliant fast bowler into the sluggish medium, and the nervous bat into the masterful smiter.

On Mike its effect was magical. He lunched wisely and well, chewing his food with the concentration of a thirty-three-bites a mouthful crank, and drinking dry ginger-ale. As he walked out with Joe after the interval he knew that a change had taken place in him. His nerve had come back, and with it his form.

It sometimes happens at cricket that when one feels particularly fit one gets snapped in the slips in the first over, or clean bowled by a full toss; but neither of these things happened to Mike. He stayed in, and began to score. Now there were no edgings through the slips and snicks to leg. He was meeting the ball in the centre of the bat, and meeting it vigorously. Two boundaries in successive balls off the fast bowler, hard, clean drives past extra-cover, put him at peace with all the world. He was on top. He had found himself.

Joe, at the other end, resumed his brilliant career. His century and Mike's fifty arrived in the same over. The bowling began to grow loose.

Joe, having reached his century, slowed down somewhat, and Mike took up the running. The score rose rapidly.

A leg-theory bowler kept down the pace of the run-getting for a time, but the bowlers at the other end continued to give away runs. Mike's score passed from sixty to seventy, from seventy to eighty, from eighty to ninety. When the Smiths, father and son, came on to the ground the total was ninety-eight. Joe had made a hundred and thirty-three.

Mike reached his century just as Psmith and his father took their seats. A square cut off the slow bowler was just too wide for point to get to. By the time third man had sprinted across and returned the ball the batsmen had run two.

Mr Smith was enthusiastic.

'I tell you,' he said to Psmith, who was clapping in a gently encouraging manner, 'the boy's a wonderful bat. I said so when he was down with us. I remember telling him so myself. "I've seen your brothers play," I said, "and you're better than any of them." I remember it distinctly. He'll be playing for England in another year or two. Fancy putting a cricketer like that into the City! It's a crime.'

'I gather,' said Psmith, 'that the family coffers had got a bit low. It was necessary for Comrade Jackson to do something by way of saving the Old Home.'

'He ought to be at the University. Look, he's got that man away to the boundary again. They'll never get him out.'

At six o'clock the partnership was broken, Joe running himself out in trying to snatch a single where no single was. He had made a hundred and eighty-nine.

Mike flung himself down on the turf with mixed feelings. He was sorry Joe was out, but he was very glad indeed of the chance of a rest. He was utterly fagged. A half-day match once a week is no training for first-class cricket. Joe, who had been playing all the season, was as tough as india-rubber, and trotted into the pavilion as fresh as if he had been having a brief spell at the nets. Mike, on the other hand, felt that he simply wanted to be dropped into a cold bath and left there indefinitely. There was only another half-hour's play, but he doubted if he could get through it.

He dragged himself up wearily as Joe's successor arrived at the wickets. He had crossed Joe before the latter's downfall, and it was his turn to take the bowling.

Something seemed to have gone out of him. He could not time the ball properly. The last ball of the over looked like a half-volley, and he hit out at it. But it was just short of a half-volley, and his stroke arrived too soon. The bowler, running in the direction of mid-on, brought off an easy c.-and-b.

Mike turned away towards the pavilion. He heard the gradually swelling applause in a sort of dream. It seemed to him hours before he reached the dressing-room.

He was sitting on a chair, wishing that somebody would come along and take off his pads, when Psmith's card was brought to him. A few moments later the old Etonian appeared in person.

'Hullo, Smith,' said Mike, 'By Jove! I'm done.'

' "How Little Willie Saved the Match," ' said Psmith. 'What you want is one of those gin and ginger-beers we hear so much about. Remove those pads, and let us flit downstairs in search of a couple. Well, Comrade Jackson, you have fought the good fight this day. My father sends his compliments. He is dining out, or he would have come up. He is going to look in at the flat latish.'

'How many did I get?' asked Mike. 'I was so jolly done I didn't think of looking.'

'A hundred and forty-eight of the best,' said Psmith. 'What will they say at the old homestead about this? Are you ready? Then let us test this fruity old ginger-beer of theirs.'

The two batsmen who had followed the big stand were apparently having a little stand all of their own. No more wickets fell before the drawing of stumps. Psmith waited for Mike while he changed, and carried him off in a cab to Simpson's, a restaurant which, as he justly observed, offered two great advantages, namely, that you need not dress, and, secondly, that you paid your half-crown, and were then at liberty to eat till you were helpless, if you felt so disposed, without extra charge.

Mike stopped short of this giddy height of mastication, but consumed enough to make him feel a great deal better. Psmith eyed his inroads on the menu with approval.

'There is nothing,' he said, 'like victualling up before an ordeal.'

'What's the ordeal?' said Mike.

'I propose to take you round to the club anon, where I trust we shall find Comrade Bickersdyke. We have much to say to one another.'

'Look here, I'm hanged – ' began Mike.

'Yes, you must be there,' said Psmith. 'Your presence will serve to cheer Comrade B. up. Fate compels me to deal him a nasty blow, and he will want sympathy. I have got to break it to him that I am leaving the bank.'

'What, are you going to chuck it?'

Psmith inclined his head.

'The time,' he said, 'has come to part. It has served its turn. The startled whisper runs round the City. "Psmith has had sufficient." '

'What are you going to do?'

'I propose to enter the University of Cambridge, and there to study the intricacies of the Law, with a view to having a subsequent dash at becoming Lord Chancellor.'

'By Jove!' said Mike, 'you're lucky. I wish I were coming too.'

Psmith knocked the ash off his cigarette.

'Are you absolutely set on becoming a pro?' he asked.

'It depends on what you call set. It seems to me it's about all I can do.'

'I can offer you a not entirely scaly job,' said Smith, 'if you feel like taking it. In the course of conversation with my father during the match this afternoon, I gleaned the fact that he is anxious to secure your services as a species of agent. The vast Psmith estates, it seems, need a bright boy to keep an eye upon them. Are you prepared to accept the post?'

Mike stared.

'Me! Dash it all, how old do you think I am? I'm only nineteen.'

'I had suspected as much from the alabaster clearness

of your unwrinkled brow. But my father does not wish you to enter upon your duties immediately. There would be a preliminary interval of three, possibly four, years at Cambridge, during which, I presume, you would be learning divers facts concerning spuds, turmuts, and the like. At least,' said Psmith airily, 'I suppose so. Far be it from me to dictate the line of your researches.'

'Then I'm afraid it's off,' said Mike gloomily. 'My pater couldn't afford to send me to Cambridge.'

'That obstacle,' said Psmith, 'can be surmounted. You would, of course, accompany me to Cambridge, in the capacity, which you enjoy at the present moment, of my confidential secretary and adviser. Any expenses that might crop up would be defrayed from the Psmith family chest.'

Mike's eyes opened wide again.

'Do you mean,' he asked bluntly, 'that your pater would pay for me at the 'Varsity? No I say – dash it – I mean, I couldn't – '

'Do you suggest,' said Psmith, raising his eyebrows, 'that I should go to the University *without* a confidential secretary and adviser?'

'No, but I mean – ' protested Mike.

'Then that's settled,' said Psmith. 'I knew you would not desert me in my hour of need, Comrade Jackson. "What will you do," asked my father, alarmed for my safety, "among these wild undergraduates? I fear for my Rupert." "Have no fear, father," I replied. "Comrade Jackson will be beside me." His face brightened immediately. "Comrade Jackson," he said, "is a man in whom I have the supremest confidence. If he is with you I shall sleep easy of nights." It was after that that the conversation drifted to the subject of agents.'

Psmith called for the bill and paid it in the affable manner of a monarch signing a charter. Mike sat silent, his mind in a whirl. He saw exactly what had happened. He could almost hear Psmith talking his father into agreeing with his scheme. He could think of nothing to say. As usually happened in any emotional crisis in his life, words absolutely deserted him. The thing was too big. Anything he could say would sound too feeble. When a friend has solved all your difficulties and smoothed out all the rough places which were looming in your path, you cannot thank him as if he had asked you to lunch. The occasion demanded some neat, polished speech; and neat, polished speeches were beyond Mike.

'I say, Psmith – ' he began.

Psmith rose.

'Let us now,' he said, 'collect our hats and meander to the club, where, I have no doubt, we shall find Comrade Bickersdyke, all unconscious of impending misfortune, dreaming pleasantly over coffee and a cigar in the lower smoking-room.'

30 — The Last Sad Farewells

As it happened, that was precisely what Mr Bickersdyke
was doing. He was feeling thoroughly pleased with life.
For nearly nine months Psmith had been to him a sort of
spectre at the feast inspiring him with an ever-present
feeling of discomfort which he had found impossible to
shake off. And tonight he saw his way of getting rid of
him.

At five minutes past four Mr Gregory, crimson and
wrathful, had plunged into his room with a long
statement of how Psmith, deputed to help in the life and
thought of the Fixed Deposits Department, had left the
building at four o'clock, when there was still another
hour and a half's work to be done.

Moreover, Mr Gregory deposed, the errant one, seen
sliding out of the swinging door, and summoned in a
loud, clear voice to come back, had flatly disobeyed and
had gone upon his way. 'Grinning at me,' said the
aggrieved Mr Gregory, 'like a dashed ape.' A most unjust
description of the sad, sweet smile which Psmith had
bestowed upon him from the doorway.

Ever since that moment Mr Bickersdyke had felt that
there was a silver lining to the cloud. Hitherto Psmith
had left nothing to be desired in the manner in which he
performed his work. His righteousness in the office had
clothed him as in a suit of mail. But now he had slipped.
To go off an hour and a half before the proper time, and
to refuse to return when summoned by the head of his
department – these were offences for which he could be
dismissed without fuss. Mr Bickersdyke looked forward
to tomorrow's interview with his employee.

Meanwhile, having enjoyed an excellent dinner, he was now, as Psmith had predicted, engaged with a cigar and a cup of coffee in the lower smoking-room of the Senior Conservative Club.

Psmith and Mike entered the room when he was about half through these luxuries.

Psmith's first action was to summon a waiter, and order a glass of neat brandy.

'Not for myself,' he explained to Mike. 'For Comrade Bickersdyke. He is about to sustain a nasty shock, and may need a restorative at a moment's notice. For all we know, his heart may not be strong. In any case, it is safest to have a pick-me-up handy.'

He paid the waiter, and advanced across the room, followed by Mike. In his hand, extended at arm's length, he bore the glass of brandy.

Mr Bickersdyke caught sight of the procession, and started. Psmith set the brandy down very carefully on the table, beside the manager's coffee cup, and, dropping into a chair, regarded him pityingly through his eyeglass. Mike, who felt embarrassed, took a seat some little way behind his companion. This was Psmith's affair, and he proposed to allow him to do the talking.

Mr Bickersdyke, except for a slight deepening of the colour of his complexion, gave no sign of having seen them. He puffed away at his cigar, his eyes fixed on the ceiling.

'An unpleasant task lies before us,' began Psmith in a low, sorrowful voice, 'and it must not be shirked. Have I your ear, Mr Bickersdyke?'

Addressed thus directly, the manager allowed his gaze to wander from the ceiling. He eyed Psmith for a moment like an elderly basilisk, than looked back at the ceiling again.

'I shall speak to you tomorrow,' he said.

Psmith heaved a heavy sigh.

'You will not see us tomorrow,' he said, pushing the brandy a little nearer.

Mr Bickersdyke's eyes left the ceiling once more.
'What do you mean?' he said.

'Drink this,' urged Psmith sympathetically, holding
out the glass. 'Be brave,' he went on rapidly. 'Time
softens the harshest blows. Shocks stun us for the
moment, but we recover. Little by little we come to
ourselves again. Life, which we had thought could hold
no more pleasure for us, gradually shows itself not
wholly grey.'

Mr Bickersdyke seemed about to make an observation
at this point, but Psmith, with a wave of the hand, hurried
on.

'We find that the sun still shines, the birds still sing.
Things which used to entertain us resume their
attraction. Gradually we emerge from the soup, and
begin – '

'If you have anything to say to me,' said the manager,
'I should be glad if you would say it, and go.'

'You prefer me not to break the bad news gently?' said
Psmith. 'Perhaps you are wise. In a word, then,' – he
picked up the brandy and held it out to him – 'Comrade
Jackson and myself are leaving the bank.'

'I am aware of that,' said Mr Bickersdyke drily.

Psmith put down the glass.

'You have been told already?' he said. 'That accounts
for your calm. The shock has expended its force on you,
and can do no more. You are stunned. I am sorry, but it
had to be. You will say that it is madness for us to offer
our resignations, that our grip on the work of the bank
made a prosperous career in Commerce certain for us.
It may be so. But somehow we feel that our talents lie
elsewhere. To Comrade Jackson the management of the
Psmith estates seems the job on which he can get the rapid
half-Nelson. For my own part, I feel that my long suit is
the Bar. I am a poor, unready speaker, but I intend to
acquire a knowledge of the Law which shall outweigh
this defect. Before leaving you, I should like to say –

I may speak for you as well as myself, Comrade Jackson – ?'

Mike uttered his first contribution to the conversation – a gurgle – and relapsed into silence again.

'I should like to say,' continued Psmith, 'how much Comrade Jackson and I have enjoyed our stay in the bank. The insight it has given us into your masterly handling of the intricate mechanism of the office has been a treat we would not have missed. But our place is elsewhere.'

He rose. Mike followed his example with alacrity. It occurred to Mr Bickersdyke, as they turned to go, that he had not yet been able to get in a word about their dismissal. They were drifting away with all the honours of war.

'Come back,' he cried.

Psmith paused and shook his head sadly.

'This is unmanly, Comrade Bickersdyke,' he said. 'I had not expected this. That you should be dazed by the shock was natural. But that you should beg us to reconsider our resolve and return to the bank is unworthy of you. Be a man. Bite the bullet. The first keen pang will pass. Time will soften the feeling of bereavement. You must be brave. Come, Comrade Jackson.'

Mike responded to the call without hesitation.

'We will now,' said Psmith, leading the way to the door, 'push back to the flat. My father will be round there soon.' He looked over his shoulder. Mr Bickersdyke appeared to be wrapped in thought.

'A painful business,' sighed Psmith. 'The man seems quite broken up. It had to be, however. The bank was no place for us. An excellent career in many respects, but unsuitable for you and me. It is hard on Comrade Bickersdyke, especially as he took such trouble to get me into it, but I think we may say that we are well out of the place.'

Mike's mind roamed into the future. Cambridge first, and then an open-air life of the sort he had always dreamed of. The Problem of Life seemed to him to be solved. He looked on down the years, and he could see no troubles there of any kind whatsoever. Reason suggested that there were probably one or two knocking about somewhere, but this was no time to think of them. He examined the future, and found it good.

'I should jolly well think,' he said simply, 'that we might.'

Psmith Journalist

Contents

Preface

The conditions of life in New York are so different from those of London that a story of this kind calls for a little explanation. There are several million inhabitants of New York. Not all of them eke out a precarious livelihood by murdering one another, but there is a definite section of the population which murders – not casually, on the spur of the moment, but on definitely commercial lines at so many dollars per murder. The 'gangs' of New York exist in fact. I have not invented them. Most of the incidents in this story are based on actual happenings. The Rosenthal case, where four men, headed by a genial individual calling himself 'Gyp the Blood' shot a fellow-citizen in cold blood in a spot as public and fashionable as Piccadilly Circus and escaped in a motor-car, made such a stir a few years ago that the noise of it was heard all over the world and not, as is generally the case with the doings of the gangs, in New York only. Rosenthal cases on a smaller and less sensational scale are frequent occurrences on Manhattan Island. It was the prominence of the victim rather than the unusual nature of the occurrence that excited the New York press. Most gang victims get a quarter of a column in small type.

P. G. WODEHOUSE   *New York, 1915*

1 — 'Cosy Moments'

The man in the street would not have known it, but a great crisis was imminent in New York journalism.

Everything seemed much as usual in the city. The cars ran blithely on Broadway. Newsboys shouted 'Wux-try!' into the ears of nervous pedestrians with their usual Caruso-like vim. Society passed up and down Fifth Avenue in its automobiles, and was there a furrow of anxiety upon Society's brow? – None. At a thousand street corners a thousand policemen preserved their air of massive superiority to the things of this world. Not one of them showed the least sign of perturbation. Nevertheless, the crisis was at hand. Mr J. Fillken Wilberfloss, editor-in-chief of *Cosy Moments*, was about to leave his post and start on a ten weeks' holiday.

In New York one may find every class of paper which the imagination can conceive. Every grade of society is catered for. If an Esquimau came to New York, the first thing he would find on the book-stalls in all probability would be the *Blubber Magazine*, or some similar production written by Esquimaux for Esquimaux. Everybody reads in New York, and reads all the time. The New Yorker peruses his favourite paper while he is being jammed into a crowded compartment on the subway or leaping like an antelope into a moving street car.

There was thus a public for *Cosy Moments. Cosy Moments*, as its name (an inspiration of Mr Wilberfloss's own) is designed to imply, is a journal for the home. It is the sort of paper which the father of the family is expected to take home with him from his office and read aloud to the chicks before bed-time. It was founded by its

195

proprietor, Mr Benjamin White, as an antidote to yellow journalism. One is forced to admit that up to the present yellow journalism seems to be competing against it with a certain measure of success. Headlines are still of as generous a size as heretofore, and there is no tendency on the part of editors to scamp the details of the last murder-case.

Nevertheless, *Cosy Moments* thrives. It has its public.

Its contents are mildly interesting, if you like that sort of thing. There is a 'Moments in the Nursery' page, conducted by Luella Granville Waterman, to which parents are invited to contribute the bright speeches of their offspring, and which bristles with little stories about the nursery canary, by Jane (aged six), and other works of rising young authors. There is a 'Moments of Meditation' page, conducted by the Reverend Edwin T. Philpotts; a 'Moments Among the Masters' page, consisting of assorted chunks looted from the literature of the past, when foreheads were bulgy and thoughts profound, by Mr Wilberfloss himself; one or two other pages; a short story; answers to correspondents on domestic masters; and a 'Moments of Mirth' page, conducted by an alleged humorist of the name of B. Henderson Asher, which is about the most painful production ever served up to a confiding public.

The guiding spirit of *Cosy Moments* was Mr Wilberfloss. Circumstances had left the development of the paper mainly to him. For the past twelve months the proprietor had been away in Europe, taking the waters at Carlsbad, and the sole control of *Cosy Moments* had passed into the hands of Mr Wilberfloss. Nor had he proved unworthy of the trust or unequal to the duties. In that year *Cosy Moments* had reached the highest possible level of domesticity. Anything not calculated to appeal to the home had been rigidly excluded. And as a result the circulation had increased steadily. Two extra pages had been added, 'Moments Among the Shoppers'

and 'Moments with Society'. And the advertisements
had grown in volume. But the work had told upon the
Editor. Work of that sort carries its penalties with it.
Success means absorption, and absorption spells
softening of the brain. Whether it was the strain of digging
into the literature of the past every week, or the effort
of reading B. Henderson Asher's 'Moments of Mirth' is
uncertain. At any rate, his duties, combined with the
heat of a New York summer, had sapped Mr Wilberfloss's
health to such an extent that the doctor had ordered him
ten weeks' complete rest in the mountains. This Mr
Wilberfloss could, perhaps, have endured, if this had been
all. There are worse places than the mountains of America
in which to spend ten weeks of the tail-end of summer,
when the sun has ceased to grill and the mosquitoes have
relaxed their exertions. But it was not all. The doctor, a
far-seeing man who went down to first causes, had
absolutely declined to consent to Mr Wilberfloss's
suggestion that he should keep in touch with the paper
during his vacation. He was adamant. He had seen copies
of *Cosy Moments* once or twice, and he refused to permit
a man in the editor's state of health to come in contact
with Luella Granville Waterman's 'Moments in the
Nursery' and B. Henderson Asher's 'Moments of Mirth'.
The medicine-man put his foot down firmly.

'You must not see so much as the cover of the paper
for ten weeks,' he said. 'And I'm not so sure that it
shouldn't be longer. You must forget that such a paper
exists. You must dismiss the whole thing from your
mind, live in the open, and develop a little flesh and
muscle.'

To Mr Wilberfloss the sentence was almost equivalent
to penal servitude. It was with tears in his voice that he
was giving his final instructions to his sub-editor, in
whose charge the paper would be left during his absence.
He had taken a long time doing this. For two days he had
been fussing in and out of the office, to the discontent

of its inmates, more especially Billy Windsor, the sub-editor, who was now listening moodily to the last harangue of the series, with the air of one whose heart is not in the subject. Billy Windsor was a tall, wiry, loose-jointed young man, with unkempt hair and the general demeanour of a caged eagle. Looking at him, one could picture him astride of a broncho, rounding up cattle, or cooking his dinner at a camp-fire. Somehow he did not seem to fit into the *Cosy Moments* atmosphere.

'Well, I think that that is all, Mr Windsor,' chirruped the editor. He was a little man with a long neck and large *pince-nez*, and he always chirruped. 'You understand the general lines on which I think the paper should be conducted?' The sub-editor nodded. Mr Wilberfloss made him tired. Sometimes he made him more tired than at other times. At the present moment he filled him with an aching weariness. The editor meant well, and was full of zeal, but he had a habit of covering and re-covering the ground. He possessed the art of saying the same obvious thing in a number of different ways to a degree which is found usually only in politicians. If Mr Wilberfloss had been a politician, he would have been one of those dealers in glittering generalities who used to be fashionable in American politics.

'There is just one thing,' he continued. 'Mrs Julia Burdett Parslow is a little inclined – I may have mentioned this before – '

'You did,' said the sub-editor.

Mr Wilberfloss chirruped on, unchecked.

'A little inclined to be late with her "Moments with Budding Girlhood". If this should happen while I am away, just write her a letter, quite a pleasant letter, you understand, pointing out the necessity of being in good time. The machinery of a weekly paper, of course, cannot run smoothly unless contributors are in good time with their copy. She is a very sensible woman, and she will understand, I am sure, if you point it out to her.'

The sub-editor nodded.

'And there is just one other thing. I wish you would correct a slight tendency I have noticed lately in Mr Asher to be just a trifle – well, not precisely *risky*, but perhaps a shade *broad* in his humour.'

'His what?' said Billy Windsor.

'Mr Asher is a very sensible man, and he will be the first to acknowledge that his sense of humour has led him just a little beyond the bounds. You understand? Well, that is all, I think. Now I must really be going, or I shall miss my train. Good-bye, Mr Windsor.'

'Good-bye,' said the sub-editor thankfully.

At the door Mr Wilberfloss paused with the air of an exile bidding farewell to his native land, sighed, and trotted out.

Billy Windsor put his feet upon the table, and with a deep scowl resumed his task of reading the proofs of Luella Granville Waterman's 'Moments in the Nursery'.

2 — Billy Windsor

Billy Windsor had started life twenty-five years before this story opens on his father's ranch in Wyoming. From there he had gone to a local paper of the type whose Society column consists of such items as 'Pawnee Jim Williams was to town yesterday with a bunch of other cheap skates. We take this opportunity of once more informing Jim that he is a liar and a skunk,' and whose editor works with a revolver on his desk and another in his hip-pocket. Graduating from this, he had proceeded to a reporter's post on a daily paper in a Kentucky town, where there were blood feuds and other Southern devices for preventing life from becoming dull. All this time New York, the magnet, had been tugging at him. All reporters dream of reaching New York. At last, after four years on the Kentucky paper, he had come East, minus the lobe of one ear and plus a long scar that ran diagonally across his left shoulder, and had worked without much success as a free-lance. He was tough and ready for anything that might come his way, but these things are a great deal a matter of luck. The cub-reporter cannot make a name for himself unless he is favoured by fortune. Things had not come Billy Windsor's way. His work had been confined to turning in reports of fires and small street-accidents, which the various papers to which he supplied them cut down to a couple of inches.

Billy had been in a bad way when he had happened upon the sub-editorship of *Cosy Moments*. He despised the work with all his heart, and the salary was infinitesimal. But it was regular, and for a while Billy felt that a regular salary was the greatest thing on earth.

But he still dreamed of winning through to a post on one of the big New York dailies, where there was something doing and a man would have a chance of showing what was in him.

The unfortunate thing, however, was that *Cosy Moments* took up his time so completely. He had no chance of attracting the notice of big editors by his present work, and he had no leisure for doing any other.

All of which may go to explain why his normal aspect was that of a caged eagle.

To him, brooding over the outpourings of Luella Granville Waterman, there entered Pugsy Maloney, the office-boy, bearing a struggling cat.

'Say!' said Pugsy.

He was a nonchalant youth, with a freckled, mask-like face, the expression of which never varied. He appeared unconscious of the cat. Its existence did not seem to occur to him.

'Well?' said Billy, looking up. 'Hello, what have you got there?'

Master Maloney eyed the cat, as if he were seeing it for the first time.

'It's a kitty what I got in de street,' he said.

'Don't hurt the poor brute. Put her down.'

Master Maloney obediently dropped the cat, which sprang nimbly on to an upper shelf of the book-case.

'I wasn't hoitin' her,' he said, without emotion. 'Dere was two fellers in de street sickin' a dawg on to her. An' I come up an' says, "G'wan! What do youse t'ink you're doin', fussin' de poor dumb animal?" An' one of de guys, he says, "G'wan! Who do youse t'ink youse is?" An' I says, "I'm de guy what's goin' to swat youse one on de coco if youse don't quit fussin' de poor dumb animal." So wit dat he makes a break at swattin' me one, but I swats him one, an' I swats de odder feller one, an' den I swats dem bote some more, an' I gets de kitty, an' I brings her in here, cos I t'inks maybe youse'll look after her.'

And having finished this Homeric narrative, Master Maloney fixed an expressionless eye on the ceiling, and was silent.

Billy Windsor, like most men of the plains, combined the toughest of muscle with the softest of hearts. He was always ready at any moment to become the champion of the oppressed on the slightest provocation. His alliance with Pugsy Maloney had begun on the occasion when he had rescued that youth from the clutches of a large Negro, who, probably from the soundest of motives, was endeavouring to slay him. Billy had not inquired into the rights and wrongs of the matter: he had merely sailed in and rescued the office-boy. And Pugsy, though he had made no verbal comment on the affair, had shown in many ways that he was not ungrateful.

'Bully for you, Pugsy!' he cried. 'You're a little sport. Here' – he produced a dollar-bill – 'go out and get some milk for the poor brute. She's probably starving. Keep the change.'

'Sure thing,' assented Master Maloney. He strolled slowly out, while Billy Windsor, mounting a chair, proceeded to chirrup and snap his fingers in the effort to establish the foundations of an *entente cordiale* with the rescued cat.

By the time that Pugsy had returned, carrying a five-cent bottle of milk, the animal had vacated the book-shelf, and was sitting on the table, washing her face. The milk having been poured into the lid of a tobacco-tin, in lieu of a saucer, she suspended her operations and adjourned for refreshments. Billy, business being business, turned again to Luella Granville Waterman, but Pugsy, having no immediate duties on hand, concentrated himself on the cat.

'Say!' he said.

'Well?'

'Dat kitty.'

'What about her?'

'Pipe de leather collar she's wearing.'

Billy had noticed earlier in the proceedings that a narrow leather collar encircled the cat's neck. He had not paid any particular attention to it. 'What about it?' he said.

'Guess I know where dat kitty belongs. Dey all have dose collars. I guess she's one of Bat Jarvis's kitties. He's got a lot of dem for fair, and every one wit one of dem collars round deir neck.'

'Who's Bat Jarvis? Do you mean the gang-leader?'

'Sure. He's a cousin of mine,' said Master Maloney with pride.

'Is he?' said Billy. 'Nice sort of fellow to have in the family. So you think that's his cat?'

'Sure. He's got twenty-t'ree of dem, and dey all has dose collars.'

'Are you on speaking terms with the gentleman?'

'Huh?'

'Do you know Bat Jarvis to speak to?'

'Sure. He's me cousin.'

'Well, tell him I've got the cat, and that if he wants it he'd better come round to my place. You know where I live?'

'Sure.'

'Fancy you being a cousin of Bat's, Pugsy. Why did you never tell us? Are you going to join the gang some day?'

'Nope. Nothin' doin'. I'm goin' to be a cowboy.'

'Good for you. Well, you tell him when you see him. And now, my lad, out you get, because if I'm interrupted any more I shan't get through tonight.'

'Sure,' said Master Maloney, retiring.

'Oh, and Pugsy . . .'

'Huh?'

'Go out and get a good big basket. I shall want one to carry this animal home in.'

'Sure,' said Master Maloney.

3 — At 'The Gardenia'

'It would ill beseem me, Comrade Jackson,' said Psmith, thoughtfully sipping his coffee, 'to run down the metropolis of a great and friendly nation, but candour compels me to state that New York is in some respects a singularly blighted town.'

'What's the matter with it?' asked Mike.

'Too decorous, Comrade Jackson. I came over here principally, it is true, to be at your side, should you be in any way persecuted by scoundrels. But at the same time I confess that at the back of my mind there lurked a hope that stirring adventures might come my way. I had heard so much of the place. Report had it that an earnest seeker after amusement might have a tolerably spacious rag in this modern Byzantium. I thought that a few weeks here might restore that keen edge to my nervous system which the languor of the past term had in a measure blunted. I wished my visit to be a tonic rather than a sedative. I anticipated that on my return the cry would go round Cambridge, "Psmith has been to New York. He is full of oats. For he on honey-dew hath fed, and drunk the milk of Paradise. He is hot stuff. Rah!" But what do we find?'

He paused, and lit a cigarette.

'What do we find?' he asked again.

'I don't know,' said Mike. 'What?'

'A very judicious query, Comrade Jackson. What, indeed? We find a town very like London. A quiet, self-respecting town, admirable to the apostle of social reform, but disappointing to one who, like myself, arrives with a brush and a little bucket of red paint, all eager for a

treat. I have been here a week, and I have not seen a single
citizen clubbed by a policeman. No Negroes dance cake-
walks in the street. No cowboy has let off his revolver
at random in Broadway. The cables flash the
message across the ocean, "Psmith is losing his
illusions." '

Mike had come to America with a team of the M.C.C.
which was touring the cricket-playing section of the
United States. Psmith had accompanied him in a private
capacity. It was the end of their first year at Cambridge,
and Mike, with a century against Oxford to his credit,
had been one of the first to be invited to join the tour.
Psmith, who had played cricket in a rather desultory way
at the University, had not risen to these heights. He had
merely taken the opportunity of Mike's visit to the other
side to accompany him. Cambridge had proved pleasant
to Psmith, but a trifle quiet. He had welcomed the chance
of getting a change of scene.

So far the visit had failed to satisfy him. Mike, whose
tastes in pleasure were simple, was delighted with
everything. The cricket so far had been rather of the picnic
order, but it was very pleasant; and there was no limit
to the hospitality with which the visitors were treated. It
was this more than anything which had caused Psmith's
grave disapproval of things American. He was not a
member of the team, so that the advantages of the
hospitality did not reach him. He had all the
disadvantages. He saw far too little of Mike. When he
wished to consult his confidential secretary and adviser
on some aspect of Life, that invaluable official was
generally absent at dinner with the rest of the team.
Tonight was one of the rare occasions when Mike could
get away. Psmith was becoming bored. New York is a
better city than London to be alone in, but it is never
pleasant to be alone in any big city.

As they sat discussing New York's shortcomings over
their coffee, a young man passed them, carrying a basket,

and seated himself at the next table. He was a tall, loose-jointed young man, with unkempt hair.

A waiter made an ingratiating gesture towards the basket, but the young man stopped him. 'Not on your life, sonny,' he said. 'This stays right here.' He placed it carefully on the floor beside his chair, and proceeded to order dinner.

Psmith watched him thoughtfully.

'I have a suspicion, Comrade Jackson,' he said, 'that this will prove to be a somewhat stout fellow. If possible, we will engage him in conversation. I wonder what he's got in the basket. I must get my Sherlock Holmes system to work. What is the most likely thing for a man to have in a basket? You would reply, in your unthinking way, "sandwiches". Error. A man with a basketful of sandwiches does not need to dine at restaurants. We must try again.'

The young man at the next table had ordered a jug of milk to be accompanied by a saucer. These having arrived, he proceeded to lift the basket on to his lap, pour the milk into the saucer, and remove the lid from the basket. Instantly, with a yell which made the young man's table the centre of interest to all the diners, a large grey cat shot up like a rocket, and darted across the room. Psmith watched with silent interest.

It is hard to astonish the waiters at a New York restaurant, but when the cat performed this feat there was a squeal of surprise all round the room. Waiters rushed to and fro, futile but energetic. The cat, having secured a strong strategic position on the top of a large oil-painting which hung on the far wall, was expressing loud disapproval of the efforts of one of the waiters to drive it from its post with a walking-stick. The young man, seeing these manoeuvres, uttered a wrathful shout, and rushed to the rescue.

'Comrade Jackson,' said Psmith, rising, 'we must be in this.'

When they arrived on the scene of hostilities, the young man had just possessed himself of the walking-stick, and was deep in a complex argument with the head-waiter on the ethics of the matter. The head-waiter, a stout impassive German, had taken his stand on a point of etiquette. 'Id is,' he said, 'to bring gats into der grill-room vorbidden. No gendleman would gats into der grill-room bring. Der gendleman – '

The young man meanwhile was making enticing sounds, to which the cat was maintaining an attitude of reserved hostility. He turned furiously on the head-waiter.

'For goodness' sake,' he cried, 'can't you see the poor brute's scared stiff? Why don't you clear your gang of German comedians away, and give her a chance to come down?'

'Der gendleman – ' argued the head-waiter.

Psmith stepped forward and touched him on the arm.

'May I have a word with you in private?'

'Zo?'

Psmith drew him away.

'You don't know who that is?' he whispered, nodding towards the young man.

'No gendleman he is,' asserted the head-waiter. 'Der gendleman would not der gat into – '

Psmith shook his head pityingly.

'These petty matters of etiquette are not for his Grace – but, hush, he wishes to preserve his incognito.'

'Incognito?'

'You understand. You are a man of the world, Comrade – may I call you Freddie? You understand, Comrade Freddie, that in a man in his Grace's position a few little eccentricities may be pardoned. You follow me, Frederick?'

The head-waiter's eye rested upon the young man with a new interest and respect.

'He is noble?' he inquired with awe.

'He is here strictly incognito, you understand,' said Psmith warningly. The head-waiter nodded.

The young man meanwhile had broken down the cat's reserve, and was now standing with her in his arms, apparently anxious to fight all-comers in her defence. The head-waiter approached deferentially.

'Der gendleman,' he said, indicating Psmith, who beamed in a friendly manner though his eye-glass, 'haf everything exblained. All will now quite satisfactory be.'

The young man looked inquiringly at Psmith, who winked encouragingly. The head-waiter bowed.

'Let me present Comrade Jackson,' said Psmith, 'the pet of our English Smart Set. I am Psmith, one of the Shropshire Psmiths. This is a great moment. Shall we be moving back? We were about to order a second instalment of coffee, to correct the effects of a fatiguing day. Perhaps you would care to join us?'

'Sure,' said the alleged duke.

'This,' said Psmith, when they were seated, and the head-waiter had ceased to hover, 'is a great meeting. I was complaining with some acerbity to Comrade Jackson, before you introduced your very interesting performing-animal speciality, that things in New York were too quiet, too decorous. I have an inkling, Comrade – '

'Windsor's my name.'

'I have an inkling, Comrade Windsor, that we see eye to eye on the subject.'

'I guess that's right. I was raised in the plains, and I lived in Kentucky a while. There's more doing there in a day than there is here in a month. Say, how did you fix it with the old man?'

'With Comrade Freddie? I have a certain amount of influence with him. He is content to order his movements in the main by my judgement. I assured him that all would be well, and he yielded.' Psmith gazed with interest at the cat, which was lapping milk from the saucer. 'Are you training that animal for a show of some kind, Comrade Windsor, or is it a domestic pet?'

'I've adopted her. The office-boy on our paper got her away from a dog this morning, and gave her to me.'

'Your paper?'

'*Cosy Moments*,' said Billy Windsor, with a touch of shame.

'*Cosy Moments*?' said Psmith reflectively. 'I regret that the bright little sheet has not come my way up to the present. I must seize an early opportunity of perusing it.'

'Don't you do it.'

'You've no parental pride in the little journal?'

'It's bad enough to hurt,' said Billy Windsor disgustedly. 'If you really want to see it, come along with me to my place, and I'll show you a copy.'

'It will be a pleasure,' said Psmith. 'Comrade Jackson, have you any previous engagement for tonight?'

'I'm not doing anything,' said Mike.

'Then let us stagger forth with Comrade Windsor. While he is loading up that basket, we will be collecting our hats . . . I am not half sure, Comrade Jackson,' he added, as they walked out, 'that Comrade Windsor may not prove to be the genial spirit for whom I have been searching. If you could give me your undivided company, I should ask no more. But with you constantly away, mingling with the gay throng, it is imperative that I have some solid man to accompany me in my ramblings hither and thither. It is possible that Comrade Windsor may possess the qualifications necessary for the post. But here he comes. Let us foregather with him and observe him in private life before arriving at any premature decision.'

4 — Bat Jarvis

Billy Windsor lived in a single room on East Fourteenth Street. Space in New York is valuable, and the average bachelor's apartments consist of one room with a bathroom opening off it. During the daytime this one room loses all traces of being used for sleeping purposes at night. Billy Windsor's room was very much like a public-school study. Along one wall ran a settee. At night this became a bed; but in the daytime it was a settee and nothing but a settee. There was no space for a great deal of furniture. There was one rocking-chair, two ordinary chairs, a table, a book-stand, a typewriter – nobody uses pens in New York – and on the walls a mixed collection of photographs, drawings, knives, and skins, relics of their owner's prairie days. Over the door was the head of a young bear.

Billy's first act on arriving in this sanctum was to release the cat, which, having moved restlessly about for some moments, finally came to the conclusion that there was no means of getting out, and settled itself on a corner of the settee. Psmith, sinking gracefully down beside it, stretched out his legs and lit a cigarette. Mike took one of the ordinary chairs; and Billy Windsor, planting himself in the rocker, began to rock rhythmically to and fro, a performance which he kept up untiringly all the time.

'A peaceful scene,' observed Psmith. 'Three great minds, keen, alert, restless during business hours, relax. All is calm and pleasant chit-chat. You have snug quarters up here, Comrade Windsor. I hold that there is nothing like one's own roof-tree. It is a great treat to one who, like myself, is located in one of these vast caravanserai – to be exact, the Astor – to pass a few moments in the quiet privacy of an apartment such as this.'

'It's beastly expensive at the Astor,' said Mike.

'The place has that drawback also. Anon, Comrade Jackson, I think we will hunt around for some such cubby-hole as this, built for two. Our nervous systems must be conserved.'

'On Fourth Avenue,' said Billy Windsor, 'you can get quite good flats very cheap. Furnished, too. You should move there. It's not much of a neighbourhood. I don't know if you mind that?'

'Far from it, Comrade Windsor. It is my aim to see New York in all its phases. If a certain amount of harmless revelry can be whacked out of Fourth Avenue, we must dash there with the vim of highly-trained smell-dogs. Are you with me, Comrade Jackson?'

'All right,' said Mike.

'And now, Comrade Windsor, it would be a pleasure to me to peruse that little journal of which you spoke. I have had so few opportunities of getting into touch with the literature of this great country.'

Billy Windsor stretched out an arm and pulled a bundle of papers from the book-stand. He tossed them on to the settee by Psmith's side.

'There you are,' he said, 'if you really feel like it. Don't say I didn't warn you. If you've got the nerve, read on.'

Psmith had picked up one of the papers when there came a shuffling of feet in the passage outside, followed by a knock upon the door. The next moment there appeared in the doorway a short, stout young man. There was an indescribable air of toughness about him partly due to the fact that he wore his hair in a well-oiled fringe almost down to his eyebrows, which gave him the appearance of having no forehead at all. His eyes were small and set close together. His mouth was wide, his

jaw prominent. Not, in short, the sort of man you would
have picked out on sight as a model citizen.

His entrance was marked by a curious sibilant sound,
which, on acquaintance, proved to be a whistled tune.
During the interview which followed, except when he
was speaking, the visitor whistled softly and
unceasingly.

'Mr Windsor?' he said to the company at large.

Psmith waved a hand towards the rocking-chair.
'That,' he said, 'is Comrade Windsor. To your right is
Comrade Jackson, England's favourite son. I am Psmith.'

The visitor blinked furtively, and whistled another
tune. As he looked round the room, his eye fell on the
cat. His face lit up.

'Say!' he said, stepping forward, and touching the cat's
collar, 'mine, mister.'

'Are you Bat Jarvis?' asked Windsor with interest.

'Sure,' said the visitor, not without a touch of
complacency, as of a monarch abandoning his incognito.

For Mr Jarvis was a celebrity.

By profession he was a dealer in animals, birds and
snakes. He had a fancier's shop in Groome Street, in the
heart of the Bowery. This was on the ground-floor. His
living abode was in the upper storey of that house, and
it was there that he kept the twenty-three cats whose
necks were adorned with leather collars, and whose
numbers had so recently been reduced to twenty-two.
But it was not the fact that he possessed twenty-three cats
with leather collars that made Mr Jarvis a celebrity. A
man may win a purely local reputation, if only for
eccentricity, by such means. But Mr Jarvis's reputation
was far from being purely local. Broadway knew him,
and the Tenderloin. Tammany Hall knew him. Long
Island City knew him. In the underworld of New York
his name was a byword. For Bat Jarvis was the leader of
the famous Groome Street Gang, the most noted of all
New York's collections of Apaches. More, he was the

founder and originator of it. And, curiously enough, it had
come into being from motives of sheer benevolence. In
Groome Street in those days there had been a dance-
hall, named the Shamrock and presided over by one
Maginnis, an Irishman and a friend of Bat's. At the
Shamrock nightly dances were given and well attended
by the youth of the neighbourhood at ten cents a head.
All might have been well, had it not been for certain other
youths of the neighbourhood who did not dance and so had
to seek other means of getting rid of their surplus energy.
It was the practice of these light-hearted sportsmen to pay
their ten cents for admittance, and once in, to make hay.
And this habit, Mr Maginnis found, was having a marked
effect on his earnings. For genuine lovers of the dance
fought shy of a place where at any moment Philistines
might burst in and break heads and furniture. In this crisis
the proprietor thought of his friend Bat Jarvis. Bat at that
time had a solid reputation as a man of his hands. It is
true that, as his detractors pointed out, he had killed no
one – a defect which he had subsequently corrected; but
his admirers based his claim to respect on his many
meritorious performances with fists and with the black-
jack. And Mr Maginnis for one held him in the very
highest esteem. To Bat accordingly he went, and laid his
painful case before him. He offered him a handsome
salary to be on hand at the nightly dances and check
undue revelry by his own robust methods. Bat had
accepted the offer. He had gone to Shamrock Hall; and
with him, faithful adherents, had gone such stalwarts
as Long Otto, Red Logan, Tommy Jefferson, and Pete
Brodie. Shamrock Hall became a place of joy and order;
and – more important still – the nucleus of the Groome
Street Gang had been formed. The work progressed. Off-
shoots of the main gang sprang up here and there about
the East Side. Small thieves, pickpockets and the like,
flocked to Mr Jarvis as their tribal leader and protector
and he protected them. For he, with his followers, were

of use to the politicians. The New York gangs, and especially the Groome Street Gang, have brought to a fine art the gentle practice of 'repeating'; which, broadly speaking, is the art of voting a number of different times at different polling-stations on election days. A man who can vote, say, ten times in a single day for you, and who controls a great number of followers who are also prepared, if they like you, to vote ten times in a single day for you, is worth cultivating. So the politicians passed the word to the police, and the police left the Groome Street Gang unmolested and they waxed fat and flourished.

Such was Bat Jarvis.

'Pipe de collar,' said Mr Jarvis, touching the cat's neck. 'Mine, mister.'

'Pugsy said it must be,' said Billy Windsor. 'We found two fellows setting a dog on to it, so we took it in for safety.'

Mr Jarvis nodded approval.

'There's a basket here, if you want it,' said Billy.

'Nope. Here, kit.'

Mr Jarvis stooped, and, still whistling softly, lifted the cat. He looked round the company, met Psmith's eye-glass, was transfixed by it for a moment, and finally turned again to Billy Windsor.

'Say!' he said, and paused. 'Obliged,' he added.

He shifted the cat on to his left arm, and extended his right hand to Billy.

'Shake!' he said.

Billy did so.

Mr Jarvis continued to stand and whistle for a few moments more.

'Say!' he said at length, fixing his roving gaze once more upon Billy. 'Obliged. Fond of de kit, I am.'

Psmith nodded approvingly.

'And rightly', he said. 'Rightly, Comrade Jarvis. She is

not unworthy of your affection. A most companionable animal, full of the highest spirits. Her knockabout act in the restaurant would have satisfied the most jaded critic. No diner-out can afford to be without such a cat. Such a cat spells death to boredom.'

Mr Jarvis eyed him fixedly, as if pondering over his remarks. Then he turned to Billy again.

'Say!' he said. 'Any time you're in bad. Glad to be of service. You know the address. Groome Street. Bat Jarvis. Good night. Obliged.'

He paused and whistled a few more bars, then nodded to Psmith and Mike, and left the room. They heard him shuffling downstairs.

'A blithe spirit,' said Psmith. 'Not garrulous, perhaps, but what of that? I am a man of few words myself. Comrade Jarvis's massive silences appeal to me. He seems to have taken a fancy to you, Comrade Windsor.'

Billy Windsor laughed.

'I don't know that he's just the sort of side-partner I'd go out of my way to choose, from what I've heard about him. Still, if one got mixed up with any of that East-Side crowd, he would be a mighty useful friend to have. I guess there's no harm done by getting him grateful.'

'Assuredly not,' said Psmith. 'We should not despise the humblest. And now, Comrade Windsor,' he said, taking up the paper again, 'let me concentrate myself tensely on this very entertaining little journal of yours. Comrade Jackson, here is one for you. For sound, clear-headed criticism,' he added to Billy, 'Comrade Jackson's name is a by-word in our English literary *salons*. His opinion will be both of interest and of profit to you, Comrade Windsor.'

5 – Planning Improvements

'By the way,' said Psmith, 'what is your exact position on this paper? Practically, we know well, you are its back-bone, its life-blood; but what is your technical position? When your proprietor is congratulating himself on having secured the ideal man for your job, what precise job does he congratulate himself on having secured the ideal man for?'

'I'm sub-editor.'

'Merely sub? You deserve a more responsible post than that, Comrade Windsor. Where is your proprietor? I must buttonhole him and point out to him what a wealth of talent he is allowing to waste itself. You must have scope.'

'He's in Europe. At Carlsbad, or somewhere. He never comes near the paper. He just sits tight and draws the profits. He lets the editor look after things. Just at present I'm acting as editor.'

'Ah! then at last you have your big chance. You are free, untrammelled.'

'You bet I'm not,' said Billy Windsor. 'Guess again. There's no room for developing free untrammelled ideas on this paper. When you've looked at it, you'll see that each page is run by some one. I'm simply the fellow who minds the shop.'

Psmith clicked his tongue sympathetically. 'It is like setting a gifted French chef to wash up dishes,' he said. 'A man of your undoubted powers, Comrade Windsor, should have more scope. That is the cry, more scope. I must look into this matter. When I gaze at your broad, bulging forehead, when I see the clear light of intelligence in your eyes, and hear the grey matter splashing restlessly about in your cerebellum, I say to myself without hesitation, "Comrade Windsor must have more scope." ' He looked at Mike, who was turning over the leaves of his copy of *Cosy Moments* in a sort of dull despair. 'Well, Comrade Jackson, and what is your verdict?'

Mike looked at Billy Windsor. He wished to be polite, yet he could find nothing polite to say. Billy interpreted the look.

'Go on,' he said. 'Say it. It can't be worse than what I think.'

'I expect some people would like it awfully,' said Mike.

'They must, or they wouldn't buy it. I've never met any of them yet, though.'

Psmith was deep in Luella Granville Waterman's 'Moments in the Nursery'. He turned to Billy Windsor.

'Luella Granville Waterman,' he said, 'is not by any chance your *nom-de-plume*, Comrade Windsor?'

'Not on your life. Don't think it.'

'I am glad,' said Psmith courteously. 'For, speaking as man to man, I must confess that for sheer, concentrated bilge she gets away with the biscuit with almost insolent ease. Luella Granville Waterman must go.'

'How do you mean?'

'She must go,' repeated Psmith firmly. 'Your first act, now that you have swiped the editorial chair, must be to sack her.'

'But, say, I can't. The editor thinks a heap of her stuff.'

'We cannot help his troubles. We must act for the good of the paper. Moreover, you said, I think, that he was away?'

'So he is. But he'll come back.'

'Sufficient unto the day, Comrade Windsor. I have a suspicion that he will be the first to approve your action. His holiday will have cleared his brain. Make a note of improvement number one – the sacking of Luella Granville Waterman.'

'I guess it'll be followed pretty quick by improvement number two – the sacking of William Windsor. I can't go monkeying about with the paper that way.'

Psmith reflected for a moment.

'Has this job of yours any special attractions for you, Comrade Windsor?'

'I guess not.'

'As I suspected. You yearn for scope. What exactly are your ambitions?'

'I want to get a job on one of the big dailies. I don't see how I'm going to fix it, though, at the present rate.'

Psmith rose, and tapped him earnestly on the chest.

'Comrade Windsor, you have touched the spot. You are wasting the golden hours of your youth. You must move. You must hustle. You must make Windsor of *Cosy Moments* a name to conjure with. You must boost this sheet up till New York rings with your exploits. On the present lines that is impossible. You must strike out a line for yourself. You must show the world that even *Cosy Moments* cannot keep a good man down.'

He resumed his seat.

'How do you mean?' said Billy Windsor.

Psmith turned to Mike.

'Comrade Jackson, if you were editing this paper, is there a single feature you would willingly retain?'

'I don't think there is,' said Mike. 'It's all pretty bad rot.'

'My opinion in a nutshell,' said Psmith, approvingly. 'Comrade Jackson,' he explained, turning to Billy, 'has a secure reputation on the other side for the keenness and lucidity of his views upon literature. You may safely build upon him. In England when Comrade Jackson says "Turn" we all turn. Now, my views on the matter are as follows. *Cosy Moments*, in my opinion (worthless, were it not backed by such a virtuoso as Comrade

Jackson), needs more snap, more go. All these putrid pages must disappear. Letters must be despatched tomorrow morning, informing Luella Granville Waterman and the others (and in particular B. Henderson Asher, who from a cursory glance strikes me as an ideal candidate for a lethal chamber) that, unless they cease their contributions instantly, you will be compelled to place yourself under police protection. After that we can begin to move.'

Billy Windsor sat and rocked himself in his chair without replying. He was trying to assimilate this idea. So far the grandeur of it had dazed him. It was too spacious, too revolutionary. Could it be done? It would undoubtedly mean the sack when Mr J. Fillken Wilberfloss returned and found the apple of his eye torn asunder and, so to speak, deprived of its choicest pips. On the other hand. . . . His brow suddenly cleared. After all, what was the sack? One crowded hour of glorious life is worth an age without a name, and he would have no name as long as he clung to his present position. The editor would be away ten weeks. He would have ten weeks in which to try himself out. Hope leaped within him. In ten weeks he could change *Cosy Moments* into a real live paper. He wondered that the idea had not occurred to him before. The trifling fact that the despised journal was the property of Mr Benjamin White, and that he had no right whatever to tinker with it without that gentleman's approval, may have occurred to him, but, if it did, it occurred so momentarily that he did not notice it. In these crises one cannot think of every-thing.

'I'm on,' he said, briefly.

Psmith smiled approvingly.

'That,' he said, 'is the right spirit. You will, I fancy, have little cause to regret your decision. Fortunately, if I may say so, I happen to have a certain amount of leisure just now. It is at your disposal. I have had little experience of journalistic work, but I foresee that I shall be a quick learner. I will become your sub-editor, without salary.'

'Bully for you,' said Billy Windsor.

'Comrade Jackson,' continued Psmith, 'is unhappily more fettered. The exigencies of his cricket tour will compel him constantly to be gadding about, now to Philadelphia, now to Saskatchewan, anon to Onehorseville, Ga. His services, therefore, cannot be relied upon continuously. From him, accordingly, we shall expect little but moral support. An occasional congratulatory telegram. Now and then a bright smile of approval. The bulk of the work will devolve upon our two selves.'

'Let it devolve,' said Billy Windsor, enthusiastically.

'Assuredly,' said Psmith. 'And now to decide upon our main scheme. You, of course, are the editor, and my suggestions are merely suggestions, subject to your approval. But, briefly, my idea is that *Cosy Moments* should become red-hot stuff. I could wish its tone to be such that the public will wonder why we do not print it on asbestos. We must chronicle all the live events of the day, murders, fires, and the like in a manner which will make our readers' spines thrill. Above all, we must be the guardians of the People's rights. We must be a searchlight, showing up the dark spot in the souls of those who would endeavour in any way to do the PEOPLE in the eye. We must detect the wrong-doer, and deliver him such a series of resentful biffs that he will abandon his little games and become a model citizen. The details of the campaign we must think out after, but I fancy that, if we follow those main lines, we shall produce a bright, readable little sheet which will in a measure make this city sit up and take notice. Are you with me, Comrade Windsor?'

'Surest thing you know,' said Billy with fervour.

6 — The Tenements

To alter the scheme of a weekly from cover to cover is
not a task that is completed without work. The dismissal
of *Cosy Moments'* entire staff of contributors left a gap
in the paper which had to be filled, and owing to the
nearness of press day there was no time to fill it before
the issue of the next number. The editorial staff had to
be satisfied with heading every page with the words 'Look
out! Look out!! Look out!!! See foot of page!!!!' printing
in the space at the bottom the legend 'Next Week! See
Editorial!' and compiling in conjunction a snappy
editorial, setting forth the proposed changes. This was
largely the work of Psmith.

'Comrade Jackson,' he said to Mike, as they set forth
one evening in search of their new flat, 'I fancy I have
found my *métier*. Commerce, many considered, was the
line I should take; and doubtless, had I stuck to that
walk in life, I should soon have become a financial
magnate. But something seemed to whisper to me, even
in the midst of my triumphs in the New Asiatic Bank,
that there were other fields. For the moment it seems to
me that I have found the job for which nature specially
designed me. At last I have Scope. And without Scope,
where are we? Wedged tightly in among the ribstons.
There are some very fine passages in that editorial. The
last paragraph, beginning "*Cosy Moments* cannot be
muzzled", in particular. I like it. It strikes the right note.
It should stir the blood of a free and independent people
till they sit in platoons on the doorstep of our office,
waiting for the next number to appear.'

'How about the next number?' asked Mike. 'Are you and Windsor going to fill the whole paper yourselves?'

'By no means. It seems that Comrade Windsor knows certain stout fellows, reporters on other papers, who will be delighted to weigh in with stuff for a moderate fee.'

'How about Luella What's-her-name and the others? How have they taken it?'

'Up to the present we have no means of ascertaining. The letters giving them the miss-in-baulk in no uncertain voice were only despatched yesterday. But it cannot affect us how they writhe beneath the blow. There is no reprieve.'

Mike roared with laughter.

'It's the rummiest business I ever struck,' he said. 'I'm jolly glad it's not my paper. It's pretty lucky for you two lunatics that the proprietor's in Europe.'

Psmith regarded him with pained surprise.

'I do not understand you, Comrade Jackson. Do you insinuate that we are not acting in the proprietor's best interests? When he sees the receipts after we have handled the paper for a while, he will go singing about his hotel. His beaming smile will be a by-word in Carlsbad. Visitors will be shown it as one of the sights. His only doubt will be whether to send his money to the bank or keep it in tubs and roll in it. We are on to a big thing, Comrade Jackson. Wait till you see our first number.'

'And how about the editor? I should think that first number would bring him back foaming at the mouth.'

'I have ascertained from Comrade Windsor that there is nothing to fear from that quarter. By a singular stroke of good fortune Comrade Wilberfloss – his name is Wilberfloss – has been ordered complete rest during his holiday. The kindly medico, realizing the fearful strain inflicted by reading *Cosy Moments* in its old form, specifically mentioned that the paper was to be withheld from him until he returned.'

'And when he does return, what are you going to do?'

'By that time, doubtless, the paper will be in so
flourishing a state that he will confess how wrong his own
methods were and adopt ours without a murmur. In the
meantime, Comrade Jackson, I would call your attention
to the fact that we seem to have lost our way. In the
exhilaration of this little chat, our footsteps have
wandered. Where we are, goodness only knows. I can only
say that I shouldn't care to have to live here.'

'There's a name up on the other side of that lamp-post.'

'Let us wend in that direction. Ah, Pleasant Street? I
fancy that the master-mind who chose that name must
have had the rudiments of a sense of humour.'

It was indeed a repellent neighbourhood in which they
had arrived. The New York slum stands in a class of its
own. It is unique. The height of the houses and the
narrowness of the streets seem to condense its
unpleasantness. All the smells and noises, which are
many and varied, are penned up in a sort of canyon, and
gain in vehemence from the fact. The masses of dirty
clothes hanging from the fire-escapes increase the
depression. Nowhere in the city does one realize so fully
the disadvantages of a lack of space. New York, being an
island, has had no room to spread. It is a town of human
sardines. In the poorer quarters the congestion is
unbelievable.

Psmith and Mike picked their way through the groups
of ragged children who covered the roadway. There
seemed to be thousands of them.

'Poor kids!' said Mike. 'It must be awful living in a
hole like this.'

Psmith said nothing. He was looking thoughtful. He
glanced up at the grimy buildings on each side. On the
lower floors one could see into dark, bare rooms. These
were the star apartments of the tenement houses, for
they opened on to the street, and so got a little light and
air. The imagination jibbed at the thought of the back
rooms.

223

'I wonder who owns these places,' said Psmith. 'It seems to me that there's what you might call room for improvement. It wouldn't be a scaly idea to turn that *Cosy Moments* searchlight we were talking about on to them.'

They walked on a few steps.

'Look here,' said Psmith, stopping. 'This place makes me sick. I'm going in to have a look round. I expect some muscular householder will resent the intrusion and boot us out, but we'll risk it.'

Followed by Mike, he turned in at one of the doors. A group of men leaning against the opposite wall looked at them without curiosity. Probably they took them for reporters hunting for a story. Reporters were the only tolerably well-dressed visitors Pleasant Street ever entertained.

It was almost pitch dark on the stairs. They had to feel their way up. Most of the doors were shut but one on the second floor was ajar. Through the opening they had a glimpse of a number of women sitting round on boxes. The floor was covered with little heaps of linen. All the women were sewing. Mike, stumbling in the darkness, almost fell against the door. None of the women looked up at the noise. Time was evidently money in Pleasant Street.

On the fourth floor there was an open door. The room was empty. It was a good representative Pleasant Street back room. The architect in this case had given rein to a passion for originality. He had constructed the room without a window of any sort whatsoever. There was a square opening in the door. Through this, it was to be presumed, the entire stock of air used by the occupants was supposed to come.

They stumbled downstairs again and out into the street. By contrast with the conditions indoors the street seemed spacious and breezy.

'This,' said Psmith, as they walked on, 'is where *Cosy Moments* gets busy at a singularly early date.'

'What are you going to do?' asked Mike.

'I propose, Comrade Jackson,' said Psmith, 'if Comrade Windsor is agreeable, to make things as warm for the owner of this place as I jolly well know how. What he wants, of course,' he proceeded in the tone of a family doctor prescribing for a patient, 'is disembowelling. I fancy, however, that a mawkishly sentimental legislature will prevent our performing that national service. We must endeavour to do what we can by means of kindly criticisms in the paper. And now, having settled that important point, let us try and get out of this place of wrath, and find Fourth Avenue.'

7 — Visitors at the Office

On the following morning Mike had to leave with the team for Philadelphia. Psmith came down to the ferry to see him off, and hung about moodily until the time of departure.

'It is saddening to me to a great extent, Comrade Jackson,' he said, 'this perpetual parting of the ways. When I think of the happy moments we have spent hand-in-hand across the seas, it fills me with a certain melancholy to have you flitting off in this manner without me. Yet there is another side to the picture. To me there is something singularly impressive in our unhesitating reply to the calls of Duty. Your Duty summons you to Philadelphia, to knock the cover off the local bowling. Mine retains me here, to play my part in the great work of making New York sit up. By the time you return, with a century or two, I trust, in your bag, the good work should, I fancy, be getting something of a move on. I will complete the arrangements with regard to the flat.'

After leaving Pleasant Street they had found Fourth Avenue by a devious route, and had opened negotiations for a large flat near Thirtieth Street. It was immediately above a saloon, which was something of a drawback, but the landlord had assured them that the voices of the revellers did not penetrate to it.

When the ferry-boat had borne Mike off across the river, Psmith turned to stroll to the office of *Cosy Moments*. The day was fine, and on the whole, despite Mike's desertion, he felt pleased with life. Psmith's was a nature which required a certain amount of stimulus in

the way of gentle excitement; and it seemed to him
that the conduct of the remodelled *Cosy Moments* might
supply this. He liked Billy Windsor, and looked forward
to a not unenjoyable time till Mike should return.

The offices of *Cosy Moments* were in a large building
in the street off Madison Avenue. They consisted of a
sort of outer lair, where Pugsy Maloney spent his time
reading tales of life in the prairies and heading off
undesirable visitors; a small room, which would have
belonged to the stenographer if *Cosy Moments* had
possessed one; and a larger room beyond, which was the
editorial sanctum.

As Psmith passed through the front door, Pugsy
Maloney rose.

'Say!' said Master Maloney.

'Say on, Comrade Maloney,' said Psmith.

'Dey're in dere.'

'Who, precisely?'

'A whole bunch of dem.'

Psmith inspected Master Maloney through his eye-
glass. 'Can you give me any particulars?' he asked
patiently. 'You are well-meaning, but vague, Comrade
Maloney. Who are in there?'

'De whole bunch of dem. Dere's Mr Asher and the Rev.
Philpotts and a gazebo what calls himself Waterman and
about 'steen more of dem.'

A faint smile appeared upon Psmith's face.

'And is Comrade Windsor in there, too, in the middle
of them?'

'Nope. Mr Windsor's out to lunch.'

'Comrade Windsor knows his business. Why did you
let them in?'

'Sure, dey just butted in,' said Master Maloney
complainingly. 'I was sittin' here, readin' me book, when
de foist of de guys blew in. "Boy," says he, "is de editor
in?" "Nope," I says. "I'll go in an' wait," says he.
"Nuttin' doing", says I. "Nix on de goin' in act." I might

227

as well have saved me breat'. In he butts, and he's in der
now. Well, in about t'ree minutes along comes another
gazebo. "Boy," said he, "is de editor in?" "Nope," I says.
"I'll wait," says he lightin' out for de door. Wit dat I sees
de proposition's too fierce for muh. I can't keep dese big
husky guys out if dey's for buttin' in. So when de rest of
de bunch comes along, I don't try to give dem de t'run
down. I says, "Well, gents," I says, "it's up to youse. De
editor ain't in, but if youse wants to join de giddy t'rong,
push t'roo inter de inner room. I can't be boddered." '

'And what more *could* you have said?' agreed Psmith
approvingly. 'Tell me, Comrade Maloney, what was the
general average aspect of these determined spirits?'

'Huh?'

'Did they seem to you to be gay, lighthearted? Did
they carol snatches of song as they went? Or did they
appear to be looking for someone with a hatchet?'

'Dey was hoppin' mad, de-whole bunch of dem.'

'As I suspected. But we must not repine, Comrade
Maloney. These trifling *contretemps* are the penalties we
pay for our high journalistic aims. I will interview these
merchants. I fancy that with the aid of the Diplomatic
Smile and the Honeyed Word I may manage to pull
through. It is as well, perhaps, that Comrade Windsor is
out. The situation calls for the handling of a man of
delicate culture and nice tact. Comrade Windsor would
probably have endeavoured to clear the room with a chair.
If he should arrive during the *séance*, Comrade Maloney,
be so good as to inform him of the state of affairs, and tell
him not to come in. Give him my compliments, and
tell him to go out and watch the snowdrops growing in
Madison Square Garden.'

'Sure,' said Master Maloney.

Then Psmith, having smoothed the nap of his hat and
flicked a speck of dust from his coat-sleeve, walked to
the door of the inner room and went in.

8 — The Honeyed Word

Master Maloney's statement that 'about 'steen visitors'
had arrived in addition to Messrs Asher, Waterman, and
the Rev. Philpotts proved to have been due to a great
extent to a somewhat feverish imagination. There were
only five men in the room.

As Psmith entered, every eye was turned upon him.
To an outside spectator he would have seemed rather
like a very well-dressed Daniel introduced into a den of
singularly irritable lions. Five pairs of eyes were
smouldering with a long-nursed resentment. Five brows
were corrugated with wrathful lines. Such, however, was
the simple majesty of Psmith's demeanour that for a
moment there was a dead silence. Not a word was spoken
as he paced, wrapped in thought, to the editorial chair.
Stillness brooded over the room as he carefully dusted
that piece of furniture, and, having done so to his
satisfaction, hitched up the knees of his trousers and sank
gracefully into a sitting position.

This accomplished, he looked up and started. He gazed
round the room.

'Ha! I am observed!' he murmured.

The words broke the spell. Instantly, the five visitors
burst simultaneously into speech.

'Are you the acting editor of this paper?'

'I wish to have a word with you, sir.'

'Mr Windsor, I presume?'

'Pardon me!'

'I should like a few moments' conversation.'

The start was good and even; but the gentleman who

said 'Pardon me!' necessarily finished first with the rest nowhere.

Psmith turned to him, bowed, and fixed him with a benevolent gaze through his eye-glass.

'Are you Mr Windsor, sir, may I ask?' inquired the favoured one.

The others paused for the reply.

'Alas! no,' said Psmith with manly regret.

'Then who are you?'

'I am Psmith.'

There was a pause.

'Where is Mr Windsor?'

'He is, I fancy, champing about forty cents' worth of lunch at some neighbouring hostelry.'

'When will he return?'

'Anon. But how much anon I fear I cannot say.'

The visitors looked at each other.

'This is exceedingly annoying,' said the man who had said 'Pardon me!' 'I came for the express purpose of seeing Mr Windsor.'

'So did I,' chimed in the rest. 'Same here. So did I.'

Psmith bowed courteously.

'Comrade Windsor's loss is my gain. Is there anything I can do for you?'

'Are you on the editorial staff of this paper?'

'I am acting sub-editor. The work is not light,' added Psmith gratuitously. 'Sometimes the cry goes round, "Can Psmith get through it all? Will his strength support his unquenchable spirit?" But I stagger on. I do not repine. I – '

'Then maybe you can tell me what all this means?' said a small round gentleman who so far had done only chorus work.

'If it is in my power to do so, it shall be done, Comrade – I have not the pleasure of your name?'

'My name is Waterman, sir. I am here on behalf of my wife, whose name you doubtless know.'

'Correct me if I am wrong,' said Psmith, 'but I should say it, also, was Waterman.'

'Luella Granville Waterman, sir,' said the little man proudly. Psmith removed his eye-glass, polished it, and replaced it in his eye. He felt that he must run no risk of not seeing clearly the husband of one who, in his opinion, stood alone in literary circles as a purveyor of sheer bilge.

'My wife,' continued the little man, producing an envelope and handing it to Psmith, 'has received this extraordinary communication from a man signing himself W. Windsor. We are both at a loss to make head or tail of it.'

Psmith was reading the letter.

'It seems reasonably clear to me,' he said.

'It is an outrage. My wife has been a contributor to this journal from its foundation. Her work has given every satisfaction to Mr Wilberfloss. And now, without the slightest warning, comes this peremptory dismissal from W. Windsor. Who is W. Windsor? Where is Mr Wilberfloss?'

The chorus burst forth. It seemed that that was what they all wanted to know: Who was W. Windsor? Where was Mr Wilberfloss?

'I am the Reverend Edwin T. Philpotts, sir,' said a cadaverous-looking man with pale blue eyes and a melancholy face. 'I have contributed "Moments of Meditation" to this journal for a very considerable period of time.'

'I have read your page with the keenest interest,' said Psmith. 'I may be wrong, but yours seems to me work which the world will not willingly let die.'

The Reverend Edwin's frosty face thawed into a bleak smile.

'And yet,' continued Psmith, 'I gather that Comrade Windsor, on the other hand, actually wishes to hurry on its decease. It is these strange contradictions, these

231

clashings of personal taste, which make up what we call life. Here we have, on the one hand – '

A man with a face like a walnut, who had hitherto lurked almost unseen behind a stout person in a serge suit, bobbed into the open, and spoke his piece.

'Where's this fellow Windsor? W. Windsor. That's the man we want to see. I've been working for this paper without a break, except when I had the mumps, for four years, and I've reason to know that my page was as widely read and appreciated as any in New York. And now up comes this Windsor fellow, if you please, and tells me in so many words the paper's got no use for me.'

'These are life's tragedies,' murmured Psmith.

'What's he mean by it? That's what I want to know. And that's what these gentlemen want to know – See here – '

'I am addressing – ?' said Psmith.

'Asher's my name. B. Henderson Asher. I write "Moments of Mirth".'

A look almost of excitement came into Psmith's face, such a look as a visitor to a foreign land might wear when confronted with some great national monument. That he should be privileged to look upon the author of 'Moments of Mirth' in the flesh, face to face, was almost too much.

'Comrade Asher,' he said reverently, 'may I shake your hand?'

The other extended his hand with some suspicion.

'Your "Moments of Mirth",' said Psmith, shaking it, 'have frequently reconciled me to the toothache.'

He reseated himself.

'Gentlemen,' he said, 'this is a painful case. The circumstances, as you will readily admit when you have heard all, are peculiar. You have asked me where Mr Wilberfloss is. I do not know.'

'You don't know!' exclaimed Mr Waterman.

'I don't know. You don't know. They,' said Psmith, indicating the rest with a wave of the hand, 'don't know.

Nobody knows. His locality is as hard to ascertain as that
of a black cat in a coal-cellar on a moonless night. Shortly
before I joined this journal, Mr Wilberfloss, by his doctor's
orders, started out on a holiday, leaving no address. No
letters were to be forwarded. He was to enjoy complete
rest. Where is he now? Who shall say? Possibly legging
it down some rugged slope in the Rockies, with two bears
and a wild cat in earnest pursuit. Possibly in the midst
of some Florida everglade, making a noise like a piece of
meat in order to snare crocodiles. Possibly in Canada,
baiting moose-traps. We have no data.'

Silent consternation prevailed among the audience.
Finally the Rev. Edwin T. Philpotts was struck with an
idea.

'Where is Mr White?' he asked.

The point was well received.

'Yes, where's Mr Benjamin White?' chorused the
rest.

Psmith shook his head.

'In Europe. I cannot say more.'

The audience's consternation deepened.

'Then, do you mean to say,' demanded Mr Asher, 'that
this fellow Windsor's the boss here, that what he says
goes?'

Psmith bowed.

'With your customary clear-headedness, Comrade
Asher, you have got home on the bull's eye first pop.
Comrade Windsor is indeed the boss. A man of intensely
masterful character, he will brook no opposition. I am
powerless to sway him. Suggestions from myself as to the
conduct of the paper would infuriate him. He believes
that radical changes are necessary in the programme of
Cosy Moments, and he means to put them through if it
snows. Doubtless he would gladly consider your work if
it fitted in with his ideas. A snappy account of a glove-
fight, a spine-shaking word picture of a railway smash, or
something on those lines, would be welcomed. But – '

'I have never heard of such a thing,' said Mr Waterman indignantly.

Psmith sighed.

'Some time ago,' he said, ' – how long it seems! – I remember saying to a young friend of mine of the name of Spiller, "Comrade Spiller, never confuse the unusual with the impossible." It is my guiding rule in life. It is unusual for the substitute-editor of a weekly paper to do a Captain Kidd act and take entire command of the journal on his own account; but is it impossible? Alas no. Comrade Windsor has done it. That is where you, Comrade Asher, and you, gentlemen, have landed yourselves squarely in the broth. You have confused the unusual with the impossible.'

'But what is to be done?' cried Mr Asher.

'I fear that there is nothing to be done, except wait. The present *régime* is but an experiment. It may be that when Comrade Wilberfloss, having dodged the bears and eluded the wild cat, returns to his post at the helm of this journal he may decide not to continue on the lines at present mapped out. He should be back in about ten weeks.'

'Ten weeks!'

'I fancy that was to be the duration of his holiday. Till then my advice to you gentlemen is to wait. You may rely on me to keep a watchful eye upon your interests. When your thoughts tend to take a gloomy turn, say to yourselves, "All is well. Psmith is keeping a watchful eye upon our interests." '

'All the same, I should like to see this W. Windsor,' said Mr Asher.

Psmith shook his head.

'I shouldn't,' he said. 'I speak in your best interests. Comrade Windsor is a man of the fiercest passions. He cannot brook interference. Were you to question the wisdom of his plans, there is no knowing what might not happen. He would be the first to regret any violent action, when once he had cooled off, but would that be any consolation to his victim? I think not. Of course, if you wish it, I could arrange a meeting – '

Mr Asher said no, he thought it didn't matter.

'I guess I can wait,' he said.

'That,' said Psmith approvingly, 'is the right spirit. Wait. That is the watch-word. And now,' he added, rising, 'I wonder if a bit of lunch somewhere might not be a good thing? We have had an interesting but fatiguing little chat. Our tissues require restoring. If you gentlemen would care to join me – '

Ten minutes later the company was seated in complete harmony round a table at the Knickerbocker. Psmith, with the dignified bonhomie of a seigneur of the old school was ordering the wine; while B. Henderson Asher, brimming over with good-humour, was relating to an attentive circle an anecdote which should have appeared in his next instalment of 'Moments of Mirth'.

9 — Full Steam Ahead

When Psmith returned to the office, he found Billy
Windsor in the doorway, just parting from a thick-set
young man, who seemed to be expressing his gratitude to
the editor for some good turn. He was shaking him
warmly by the hand.

Psmith stood aside to let him pass.

'An old college chum, Comrade Windsor?' he
asked.

'That was Kid Brady.'

'The name is unfamiliar to me. Another contributor?'

'He's from my part of the country – Wyoming. He
wants to fight anyone in the world at a hundred and
thirty-three pounds.'

'We all have our hobbies. Comrade Brady appears to
have selected a somewhat exciting one. He would find
stamp-collecting less exacting.'

'It hasn't given him much excitement so far, poor
chap,' said Billy Windsor. 'He's in the championship
class, and here he has been pottering about New York for
a month without being able to get a fight. It's always the
way in this rotten East,' continued Billy, warming up as
was his custom when discussing a case of oppression
and injustice. 'It's all graft here. You've got to let half a
dozen brutes dip into every dollar you earn, or you don't
get a chance. If the kid had a manager, he'd get all the
fights he wanted. And the manager would get nearly all
the money. I've told him that we will back him up.'

'You have hit it, Comrade Windsor,' said Psmith with
enthusiasm. '*Cosy Moments* shall be Comrade Brady's
manager. We will give him a much-needed boost up in

our columns. A sporting section is what the paper requires more than anything.'

'If things go on as they've started, what it will require still more will be a fighting-editor. Pugsy tells me you had visitors while I was out.'

'A few,' said Psmith. 'One or two very entertaining fellows. Comrades Asher, Philpotts, and others. I have just been giving them a bite of lunch at the Knickerbocker.'

'Lunch!'

'A most pleasant little lunch. We are now as brothers. I fear I have made you perhaps a shade unpopular with our late contributors; but these things must be. We must clench our teeth and face them manfully. If I were you, I think I should not drop in at the house of Comrade Asher and the rest to take potluck for some little time to come. In order to soothe the squad I was compelled to curse you to some extent.'

'Don't mind me.'

'I think I may say I didn't.'

'Say, look here, you must charge up the price of that lunch to the office. Necessary expenses, you know.'

'I could not dream of doing such a thing, Comrade Windsor. The whole affair was a great treat to me. I have few pleasures. Comrade Asher alone was worth the money. I found his society intensely interesting. I have always believed in the Darwinian theory. Comrade Asher confirmed my views.'

They went into the inner office. Psmith removed his hat and coat.

'And now once more to work,' he said. 'Psmith the *flâneur* of Fifth Avenue ceases to exist. In his place we find Psmith the hard-headed sub-editor. Be so good as to indicate a job of work for me, Comrade Windsor. I am champing at my bit.'

Billy Windsor sat down, and lit his pipe.

'What we want most,' he said thoughtfully, 'is some

237

big topic. That's the only way to get a paper going. Look at *Everybody's Magazine*. They didn't amount to a row of beans till Lawson started his "Frenzied Finance" articles. Directly they began, the whole country was squealing for copies. *Everybody's* put up their price from ten to fifteen cents, and now they lead the field.'

'The country must squeal for *Cosy Moments*,' said Psmith firmly. 'I fancy I have a scheme which may not prove wholly scaly. Wandering yesterday with Comrade Jackson in a search for Fourth Avenue, I happened upon a spot called Pleasant Street. Do you know it?'

Billy Windsor nodded.

'I went down there once or twice when I was a reporter. It's a beastly place.'

'It is a singularly beastly place. We went into one of the houses.'

'They're pretty bad.'

'Who owns them?'

'I don't know. Probably some millionaire. Those tenement houses are about as paying an investment as you can have.'

'Hasn't anybody ever tried to do anything about them?'

'Not so far as I know. It's pretty difficult to get at these fellows, you see. But they're fierce, aren't they, those houses!'

'What,' asked Psmith, 'is the precise difficulty of getting at these merchants?'

'Well, it's this way. There are all sorts of laws about the places, but anyone who wants can get round them as easy as falling off a log. The law says a tenement house is a building occupied by more than two families. Well, when there's a fuss, all the man has to do is to clear out all the families but two. Then, when the inspector fellow comes along, and says, let's say, "Where's your running water on each floor? That's what the law says you've got to have, and here are these people having to go downstairs and out of doors to fetch their water supplies," the landlord simply replies, "Nothing doing. This isn't a tenement house at all. There are only two families here." And when the fuss has blown over, back come the rest of the crowd, and things go on the same as before.'

'I see,' said Psmith. 'A very cheery scheme.'

'Then there's another thing. You can't get hold of the man who's really responsible, unless you're prepared to spend thousands ferreting out evidence. The land belongs in the first place to some corporation or other. They lease it to a lessee. When there's a fuss, they say they aren't responsible, it's up to the lessee. And he lies so low that you can't find out who he is. It's all just like the East. Everything in the East is as crooked as Pearl Street. If you want a square deal, you've got to come out Wyoming way.'

'The main problem, then,' said Psmith, 'appears to be the discovery of the lessee, lad? Surely a powerful organ like *Cosy Moments*, with its vast ramifications, could bring off a thing like that?'

'I doubt it. We'll try, anyway. There's no knowing but what we may have luck.'

'Precisely,' said Psmith. 'Full steam ahead, and trust to luck. The chances are that, if we go on long enough, we shall eventually arrive somewhere. After all, Columbus didn't know that America existed when he set out. All he knew was some highly interesting fact about an egg. What that was, I do not at the moment recall, but it bucked Columbus up like a tonic. It made him fizz ahead like a two-year-old. The facts which will nerve us to effort are two. In the first place, we know that there must be someone at the bottom of the business. Secondly, as there appears to be no law of libel whatsoever in this great and free country, we shall be enabled to haul up our slacks with a considerable absence of restraint.'

'Sure,' said Billy Windsor. 'Which of us is going to write the first article?'

'You may leave it to me, Comrade Windsor. I am no

hardened old journalist, I fear, but I have certain
qualifications for the post. A young man once called at
the office of a certain newspaper, and asked for a job.
"Have you any special line?" asked the editor. "Yes,"
said the bright lad, "I am rather good at invective." "Any
special kind of invective?" queried the man up top. "No,"
replied our hero, "just general invective." Such is my
own case, Comrade Windsor. I am a very fair purveyor of
good, general invective. And as my visit to Pleasant
Street is of such recent date, I am tolerably full of my
subject. Taking full advantage of the benevolent laws of
this country governing libel, I fancy I will produce a screed
which will make this anonymous lessee feel as if he had
inadvertently seated himself upon a tin-tack. Give me
pen and paper, Comrade Windsor, instruct Comrade
Maloney to suspend his whistling till such time as I am
better able to listen to it; and I think we have got a
success.'

10 — Going Some

There was once an editor of a paper in the Far West who was sitting at his desk, musing pleasantly of life, when a bullet crashed through the window and embedded itself in the wall at the back of his head. A happy smile lit up the editor's face. 'Ah,' he said complacently, 'I knew that Personal column of ours was going to be a success!'

What the bullet was to the Far West editor, the visit of Mr Francis Parker to the offices of *Cosy Moments* was to Billy Windsor.

It occurred in the third week of the new *régime* of the paper. *Cosy Moments*, under its new management, had bounded ahead like a motor-car when the throttle is opened. Incessant work had been the order of the day. Billy Windsor's hair had become more dishevelled than ever, and even Psmith had at moments lost a certain amount of his dignified calm. Sandwiched in between the painful case of Kid Brady and the matter of the tenements, which formed the star items of the paper's contents, was a mass of bright reading dealing with the events of the day. Billy Windsor's newspaper friends had turned in some fine, snappy stuff in their best Yellow Journal manner, relating to the more stirring happenings in the city. Psmith, who had constituted himself guardian of the literary and dramatic interests of the paper, had employed his gift of general invective to considerable effect, as was shown by a conversation between Master Maloney and a visitor one morning, heard through the open door.

'I wish to see the editor of this paper,' said the visitor.

'Editor not in,' said Master Maloney, untruthfully.

241

'Ha! Then when he returns I wish you to give him a message.'

'Sure.'

'I am Aubrey Bodkin, of the National Theatre. Give him my compliments, and tell him that Mr Bodkin does not lightly forget.'

An unsolicited testimonial which caused Psmith the keenest satisfaction.

The section of the paper devoted to Kid Brady was attractive to all those with sporting blood in them. Each week there appeared in the same place on the same page a portrait of the Kid, looking moody and important, in an attitude of self-defence, and under the portrait the legend. 'Jimmy Garvin must meet this boy'. Jimmy was the present holder of the light-weight title. He had won it a year before, and since then had confined himself to smoking cigars as long as walking-sticks and appearing nightly as the star in a music-hall sketch entitled 'A Fight for Honour'. His reminiscences were appearing weekly in a Sunday paper. It was this that gave Psmith the idea of publishing Kid Brady's autobiography in *Cosy Moments*, an idea which made the Kid his devoted adherent from then on. Like most pugilists, the Kid had a passion for bursting into print, and his life had been saddened up to the present by the refusal of the press to publish his reminiscences. To appear in print is the fighter's accolade. It signifies that he has arrived. Psmith extended the hospitality of page four of *Cosy Moments* to Kid Brady, and the latter leaped at the chance. He was grateful to Psmith for not editing his contributions. Other pugilists, contributing to other papers, groaned under the supervision of a member of the staff who cut out their best passages and altered the rest into Addisonian English. The readers of *Cosy Moments* got Kid Brady raw.

'Comrade Brady,' said Psmith to Billy, 'has a singularly pure and pleasing style. It is bound to appeal powerfully

to the many-headed. Listen to this bit. Our hero is fighting
Battling Jack Benson in that eminent artist's native town
of Louisville, and the citizens have given their native son
the Approving Hand, while receiving Comrade Brady
with chilly silence. Here is the Kid on the subject: "I
looked around that house, and I seen I hadn't a friend in
it. And then the gong goes, and I says to myself how I has
one friend, my poor old mother way out in Wyoming,
and I goes in and mixes it, and then I seen Benson losing
his goat, so I ups with an awful half-scissor hook to the
plexus, and in the next round I see Benson has a chunk of
yellow, and I gets in with a hay-maker and I picks up
another sleep-producer from the floor and hands it him,
and he takes the count all right." . . . Crisp, lucid, and
to the point. That is what the public wants. If this does
not bring Comrade Garvin up to the scratch, nothing
will.'

But the feature of the paper was the 'Tenement' series.
It was late summer now, and there was nothing much
going on in New York. The public was consequently free
to take notice. The sale of *Cosy Moments* proceeded
briskly. As Psmith had predicted, the change of policy
had the effect of improving the sales to a marked extent.
Letters of complaint from old subscribers poured into the
office daily. But, as Billy Windsor complacently remarked,
they had paid their subscriptions, so that the money was
safe whether they read the paper or not. And, meanwhile,
a large new public had sprung up and was growing every
week. Advertisements came trooping in. *Cosy
Moments*, in short, was passing through an era of
prosperity undreamed of in its history.

'Young blood,' said Psmith nonchalantly, 'young
blood. That is the secret. A paper must keep up to date,
or it falls behind its competitors in the race. Comrade
Wilberfloss's methods were possibly sound, but too
limited and archaic. They lacked ginger. We of the
younger generation have our fingers more firmly on

the public pulse. We read off the public's unspoken wishes as if by intuition. We know the game from A to Z.'

At this moment Master Maloney entered, bearing in his hand a card.

' "Francis Parker"?' said Billy taking it. 'Don't know him.'

'Nor I,' said Psmith. 'We make new friends daily.'

'He's a guy with a tall-shaped hat,' volunteered Master Maloney, 'an' he's wearin' a dude suit an' shiny shoes.'

'Comrade Parker,' said Psmith approvingly, 'has evidently not been blind to the importance of a visit to *Cosy Moments*. He has dressed himself in his best. He has felt, rightly, that this is no occasion for the old straw hat and the baggy flannels. I would not have it otherwise. It is the right spirit. Shall we give him audience, Comrade Windsor?'

'I wonder what he wants.'

'That,' said Psmith, 'we shall ascertain more clearly after a personal interview. Comrade Maloney, show the gentleman in. We can give him three and a quarter minutes.'

Pugsy withdrew.

Mr Francis Parker proved to be a man who might have been any age between twenty-five and thirty-five. He had a smooth, clean-shaven face, and a cat-like way of moving. As Pugsy had stated in effect, he wore a tail-coat, trousers with a crease which brought a smile of kindly approval to Psmith's face, and patent-leather boots of pronounced shininess. Gloves and a tall hat, which he carried, completed an impressive picture.

He moved softly into the room.

'I wished to see the editor.'

Psmith waved a hand towards Billy.

'The treat has not been denied you,' he said. 'Before you is Comrade Windsor, the Wyoming cracker-jack. He is our editor. I myself – I am Psmith – though but a subordinate, may also claim the title in a measure. Technically, I am but a sub-editor; but such is the mutual esteem in which Comrade Windsor and I hold each other that we may practically be said to be inseparable. We have no secrets from each other. You may address us both impartially. Will you sit for a space?'

He pushed a chair towards the visitor, who seated himself with the care inspired by a perfect trouser-crease. There was a momentary silence while he selected a spot on the table on which to place his hat.

'The style of the paper has changed greatly, has it not, during the past few weeks?' he said. 'I have never been, shall I say, a constant reader of *Cosy Moments,* and I may be wrong. But is not its interest in current affairs a recent development?'

'You are very right,' responded Psmith. 'Comrade Windsor, a man of alert and restless temperament, felt that a change was essential if *Cosy Moments* was to lead public thought. Comrade Wilberfloss's methods were good in their way. I have no quarrel with Comrade Wilberfloss. But he did not lead public thought. He catered exclusively for children with water on the brain, and men and women with solid ivory skulls. Comrade Windsor, with a broader view, feels that there are other and larger publics. He refuses to content himself with ladling out a weekly dole of mental predigested breakfast food. He provides meat. He – '

'Then – excuse me – ' said Mr Parker, turning to Billy, 'you, I take it, are responsible for this very vigorous attack on the tenement-house owners?'

'You can take it I am,' said Billy.

Psmith interposed.

'We are both responsible, Comrade Parker. If any husky guy, as I fancy Master Maloney would phrase it, is anxious to aim a swift kick at the man behind those articles, he must distribute it evenly between Comrade Windsor and myself.'

'I see.' Mr Parker paused. 'They are – er – very outspoken articles,' he added.

'Warm stuff,' agreed Psmith. 'Distinctly warm stuff.'

'May I speak frankly?' said Mr Parker.

'Assuredly, Comrade Parker. There must be no secrets, no restraint between us. We would not have you go away and say to yourself, "Did I make my meaning clear? Was I too elusive?" Say on.'

'I am speaking in your best interests.'

'Who would doubt it, Comrade Parker. Nothing has buoyed us up more strongly during the hours of doubt through which we have passed than the knowledge that you wish us well.'

Billy Windsor suddenly became militant. There was a feline smoothness about the visitor which had been jarring upon him ever since he first spoke. Billy was of the plains, the home of blunt speech, where you looked your man in the eye and said it quick. Mr Parker was too bland for human consumption. He offended Billy's honest soul.

'See here,' cried he, leaning forward, 'what's it all about? Let's have it. If you've anything to say about those articles, say it right out. Never mind our best interests. We can look after them. Let's have what's worrying you.'

Psmith waved a deprecating hand.

'Do not let us be abrupt on this happy occasion. To me it is enough simply to sit and chat with Comrade Parker, irrespective of the trend of his conversation. Still, as time is money, and this is our busy day, possibly it might be as well, sir, if you unburdened yourself as soon as convenient. Have you come to point out some flaws in those articles? Do they fall short in any way of your standard for such work?'

Mr Parker's smooth face did not change its expression, but he came to the point.

'I should not go on with them if I were you,' he said.

'Why?' demanded Billy.

'There are reasons why you should not,' said Mr Parker.

'And there are reasons why we should.'

'Less powerful ones.'

There proceeded from Billy a noise not describable in words. It was partly a snort, partly a growl. It resembled more than anything else the preliminary sniffing snarl a bull-dog emits before he joins battle. Billy's cowboy blood was up. He was rapidly approaching the state of mind in which the men of the plains, finding speech unequal to the expression of their thoughts, reach for their guns.

Psmith intervened.

'We do not completely gather your meaning, Comrade Parker. I fear we must ask you to hand it to us with still more breezy frankness. Do you speak from purely friendly motives? Are you advising us to discontinue the articles merely because you fear that they will damage our literary reputation? Or are there other reasons why you feel that they should cease? Do you speak solely as a literary connoisseur? Is it the style or the subject-matter of which you disapprove?'

Mr Parker leaned forward.

'The gentleman whom I represent – '

'Then this is no matter of your own personal taste? You are an emissary?'

'These articles are causing a certain inconvenience to the gentleman whom I represent. Or, rather, he feels that, if continued, they may do so.'

'You mean,' broke in Billy explosively, 'that if we kick up enough fuss to make somebody start a commission to inquire into this rotten business, your friend who owns the private Hades we're trying to get improved, will have to get busy and lose some of his money by making the houses fit to live in? Is that it?'

'It is not so much the money, Mr Windsor, though, of

course, the expense would be considerable. My employer is a wealthy man.'

'I bet he is,' said Billy disgustedly. 'I've no doubt he makes a mighty good pile out of Pleasant Street.'

'It is not so much the money,' repeated Mr Parker, 'as the publicity involved. I speak quite frankly. There are reasons why my employer would prefer not to come before the public just now as the owner of the Pleasant Street property. I need not go into those reasons. It is sufficient to say that they are strong ones.'

'Well, he knows what to do, I guess. The moment he starts to make those houses decent, the articles stop. It's up to him.'

Psmith nodded.

'Comrade Windsor is correct. He has hit the mark and rung the bell. No conscientious judge would withhold from Comrade Windsor a cigar or a coconut, according as his private preference might dictate. That is the matter in a nutshell. Remove the reason for those very scholarly articles, and they cease.'

Mr Parker shook his head.

'I fear that is not feasible. The expense of reconstructing the houses makes that impossible.'

'Then there's no use in talking,' said Billy. 'The articles will go on.'

Mr Parker coughed. A tentative cough, suggesting that the situation was now about to enter upon a more delicate phase. Billy and Psmith waited for him to begin. From their point of view the discussion was over. If it was to be reopened on fresh lines, it was for their visitor to effect that reopening.

'Now, I'm going to be frank, gentlemen,' said he, as who should say, 'We are all friends here. Let us be hearty.' 'I'm going to put my cards on the table, and see if we can't fix something up. Now, see here. We don't want unpleasantness. You aren't in this business for your healths, eh? You've got your living to make, just like everybody else, I guess. Well, see here. This is how it stands. To a certain extent, I don't mind admitting, seeing that we're being frank with one another, you two gentlemen have got us – that's to say, my employer – in a cleft stick. Frankly, those articles are beginning to attract attention, and if they go on there's going to be a lot of inconvenience for my employer. That's clear, I reckon. Well, now, here's a square proposition. How much do you want to stop those articles? That's straight. I've been frank with you, and I want you to be frank with me. What's your figure? Name it, and, if it's not too high, I guess we needn't quarrel.'

He looked expectantly at Billy. Billy's eyes were bulging. He struggled for speech. He had got as far as 'Say!' when Psmith interrupted him. Psmith, gazing sadly at Mr Parker through his monocle, spoke quietly, with the restrained dignity of some old Roman senator dealing with the enemies of the Republic.

'Comrade Parker,' he said, 'I fear that you have allowed constant communication with the conscienceless commercialism of this worldly city to undermine your moral sense. It is useless to dangle rich bribes before our eyes. *Cosy Moments* cannot be muzzled. You doubtless mean well, according to your – if I may say so – somewhat murky lights, but we are not for sale, except at ten cents weekly. From the hills of Maine to the Everglades of Florida, from Sandy Hook to San Francisco, from Portland, Oregon, to Melonsquashville, Tennessee, one sentence is in every man's mouth. And what is that sentence? I give you three guesses. You give it up? It is this: "*Cosy Moments* cannot be muzzled!"'

Mr Parker rose.

'There's nothing more to be done then,' he said.

'Nothing,' agreed Psmith, 'except to make a noise like a hoop and roll away.'

'And do it quick,' yelled Billy, exploding like a fire-cracker.

Psmith bowed.

'Speed,' he admitted, 'would be no bad thing. Frankly
– if I may borrow the expression – your square
proposition has wounded us. I am a man of powerful self-
restraint, one of those strong, silent men, and I can curb
my emotions. But I fear that Comrade Windsor's generous
temperament may at any moment prompt him to start
throwing ink-pots. And in Wyoming his deadly aim with
the ink-pot won him among the admiring cowboys the
sobriquet of Crack-Shot Cuthbert. As man to man,
Comrade Parker, I should advise you to bound swiftly
away.'

'I'm going,' said Mr Parker, picking up his hat. 'And
I'll give you a piece of advice, too. Those articles are
going to be stopped, and if you've any sense between you,
you'll stop them yourselves before you get hurt. That's
all I've got to say, and that goes.'

He went out, closing the door behind him with a bang
that added emphasis to his words.

'To men of nicely poised nervous organization such as
ourselves, Comrade Windsor,' said Psmith, smoothing
his waistcoat thoughtfully, 'these scenes are acutely
painful. We wince before them. Our ganglions quiver
like cinematographs. Gradually recovering command of
ourselves, we review the situation. Did our visitor's final
remarks convey anything definite to you? Were they the
mere casual badinage of a parting guest, or was there
something solid behind them?'

Billy Windsor was looking serious.

'I guess he meant it all right. He's evidently working
for somebody pretty big, and that sort of man would
have a pull with all kinds of Thugs. We shall have to
watch out. Now that they find we can't be bought, they'll
try the other way. They mean business sure enough. But,
by George, let 'em! We're up against a big thing, and I'm
going to see it through if they put every gang in New York
on to us.'

'Precisely, Comrade Windsor. *Cosy Moments*, as I have had occasion to observe before, cannot be muzzled.'

'That's right,' said Billy Windsor. 'And,' he added, with the contented look the Far West editor must have worn as the bullet came through the window, 'we must have got them scared, or they wouldn't have shown their hand that way. I guess we're making a hit. *Cosy Moments* is going some now.'

11 — The Man at the Astor

The duties of Master Pugsy Maloney at the offices of *Cosy Moments* were not heavy; and he was accustomed to occupy his large store of leisure by reading narratives dealing with life in the prairies, which he acquired at a neighbouring shop at cut rates in consideration of their being shop-soiled. It was while he was engrossed in one of these, on the morning following the visit of Mr Parker, that the seedy-looking man made his appearance. He walked in from the street, and stood before Master Maloney.

'Hey, kid,' he said.

Pugsy looked up with some hauteur. He resented being addressed as 'kid' by perfect strangers.

'Editor in, Tommy?' inquired the man.

Pugsy by this time had taken a thorough dislike to him. To be called 'kid' was bad. The subtle insult of 'Tommy' was still worse.

'Nope,' he said curtly, fixing his eyes again on his book. A movement on the part of the visitor attracted his attention. The seedy man was making for the door of the inner room. Pugsy instantly ceased to be the student and became the man of action. He sprang from his seat and wriggled in between the man and the door.

'Youse can't butt in dere,' he said authoritatively. 'Chase yerself.'

The man eyed him with displeasure.

'Fresh kid!' he observed disapprovingly.

'Fade away,' urged Master Maloney.

The visitor's reply was to extend a hand and grasp Pugsy's left ear between a long finger and thumb. Since time began, small boys in every country have had but one answer for this action. Pugsy made it. He emitted a piercing squeal in which pain, fear, and resentment strove for supremacy.

The noise penetrated into the editorial sanctum, losing only a small part of its strength on the way. Psmith, who was at work on a review of a book of poetry, looked up with patient sadness.

'If Comrade Maloney,' he said, 'is going to take to singing as well as whistling, I fear this journal must put up its shutters. Concentrated thought will be out of the question.'

A second squeal rent the air. Billy Windsor jumped up.

'Somebody must be hurting the kid,' he exclaimed.

He hurried to the door and flung it open. Psmith followed at a more leisurely pace. The seedy man, caught in the act, released Master Maloney, who stood rubbing his ear with resentment written on every feature.

On such occasions as this Billy was a man of few words. He made a dive for the seedy man; but the latter, who during the preceding moment had been eyeing the two editors as if he were committing their appearance to memory, sprang back, and was off down the stairs with the agility of a Marathon runner.

'He blows in,' said Master Maloney, aggrieved, 'and asks is de editor dere. I tells him no, 'cos youse said youse wasn't, and he nips me by the ear when I gets busy to stop him gettin' t'roo.'

'Comrade Maloney,' said Psmith, 'you are a martyr. What would Horatius have done if somebody had nipped him by the ear when he was holding the bridge? The story does not consider the possibility. Yet it might have made all the difference. Did the gentleman state his business?'

'Nope. Just tried to butt t'roo.'

'Another of these strong silent men. The world is full of us. These are the perils of the journalistic life. You will be safer and happier when you are rounding up cows on your mustang.'

'I wonder what he wanted,' said Billy, when they were back again in the inner room.

'Who can say, Comrade Windsor? Possibly our autographs. Possibly five minutes' chat on general subjects.'

'I don't like the look of him,' said Billy.

'Whereas what Comrade Maloney objected to was the feel of him. In what respect did his look jar upon you? His clothes were poorly cut, but such things, I know, leave you unmoved.'

'It seems to me,' said Billy thoughtfully, 'as if he came just to get a sight of us.'

'And he got it. Ah, providence is good to the poor.'

'Whoever's behind those tenements isn't going to stick at any odd trifle. We must watch out. That man was probably sent to mark us down for one of the gangs. Now they'll know what we look like, and they can get after us.'

'These are the drawbacks to being public men, Comrade Windsor. We must bear them manfully, without wincing.'

Billy turned again to his work.

'I'm not going to wince,' he said, 'so's you could notice it with a microscope. What I'm going to do is to buy a good big stick. And I'd advise you to do the same.'

It was by Psmith's suggestion that the editorial staff of *Cosy Moments* dined that night in the roof-garden at the top of the Astor Hotel.

'The tired brain,' he said, 'needs to recuperate. To feed on such a night as this in some low-down hostelry on the level of the street, with German waiters breathing heavily down the back of one's neck and two fiddles and a piano whacking out "Beautiful Eyes" about three feet from one's tympanum, would be false economy. Here, fanned by cool breezes and surrounded by fair women and brave men, one may do a bit of tissue-restoring. Moreover, there is little danger up here of being slugged by our moth-eaten acquaintance of this morning. A man with trousers like his would not be allowed in. We shall probably find him waiting for us at the main entrance with a sand-bag, when we leave, but, till then – '

He turned with gentle grace to his soup.

It was a warm night, and the roof-garden was full. From where they sat they could see the million twinkling lights of the city. Towards the end of the meal, Psmith's gaze concentrated itself on the advertisement of a certain brand of ginger-ale in Times Square. It is a mass of electric light arranged in the shape of a great bottle, and at regular intervals there proceed from the bottle's mouth flashes of flame representing ginger-ale. The thing began to exercise a hypnotic effect on Psmith. He came to himself with a start, to find Billy Windsor in conversation with a waiter.

'Yes, my name's Windsor,' Billy was saying.

The waiter bowed and retired to one of the tables where a young man in evening clothes was seated. Psmith recollected having seen this solitary diner looking in their direction once or twice during dinner, but the fact had not impressed him.

'What is happening, Comrade Windsor?' he inquired. 'I was musing with a certain tenseness at the moment, and the rush of events has left me behind.'

'Man at that table wanted to know if my name was Windsor,' said Billy.

'Ah?' said Psmith, interested; 'and was it?'

'Here he comes. I wonder what he wants. I don't know the man from Adam.'

The stranger was threading his way between the tables.

'Can I have a word with you, Mr Windsor?' he said.

Billy looked at him curiously. Recent events had made him wary of strangers.

'Won't you sit down?' he said.

A waiter was bringing a chair. The young man seated himself.

'By the way,' added Billy; 'my friend, Mr Smith.'

'Pleased to meet you,' said the other.

'I don't know your – ' Billy hesitated.

'Never mind about my name,' said the stranger. 'It won't be needed. Is Mr Smith on your paper? Excuse my asking.'

Psmith bowed.

'That's all right, then. I can go ahead.'

He bent forward.

'Neither of you gentlemen are hard of hearing, eh?'

'In the old prairie days,' said Psmith, 'Comrade Windsor was known to the Indians as Boola-Ba-Na-Gosh, which, as you doubtless know, signifies Big-Chief-Who-Can-Hear-A-Fly Clear-Its-Throat. I too can hear as well as the next man. Why?'

'That's all right, then. I don't want to have to shout it. There's some things it's better not to yell.'

He turned to Billy, who had been looking at him all the while with a combination of interest and suspicion. The man might or might not be friendly. In the meantime, there was no harm in being on one's guard. Billy's experience as a cub-reporter had given him the knowledge that is only given in its entirety to police and newspaper men: that there are two New Yorks. One is a modern, well-policed city, through which one may walk from end to end without encountering adventure. The other is a city as full of sinister intrigue, of whisperings and conspiracies, of battle, murder, and sudden death in dark by-ways, as any town of medieval Italy. Given certain conditions, anything may happen to any one in New York. And Billy realized that these conditions now prevailed in his own case. He had come into conflict with New York's underworld. Circumstances had placed him below the surface, where only his wits could help him.

'It's about that tenement business,' said the stranger.

Billy bristled. 'Well, what about it?' he demanded truculently.

The stranger raised a long and curiously delicately shaped hand. 'Don't bite at me,' he said. 'This isn't my funeral. I've no kick coming. I'm a friend.'

'Yet you don't tell us your name.'

'Never mind my name. If you were in my line of business, you wouldn't be so durned stuck on this name thing. Call me Smith, if you like.'

'You could select no nobler pseudonym,' said Psmith cordially.

'Eh? Oh, I see. Well, make it Brown, then. Anything you please. It don't signify. See here, let's get back. About this tenement thing. You understand certain parties have got it against you?'

'A charming conversationalist, one Comrade Parker, hinted at something of the sort,' said Psmith, 'in a recent interview. *Cosy Moments*, however, cannot be muzzled.'

'Well?' said Billy.

'You're up against a big proposition.'

'We can look after ourselves.'

'Gum! you'll need to. The man behind is a big bug.'

Billy leaned forward eagerly.

'Who is he?'

The other shrugged his shoulders.

'I don't know. You wouldn't expect a man like that to give himself away.'

'Then how do you know he's a big bug?'

'Precisely,' said Psmith. 'On what system have you estimated the size of the gentleman's bughood?'

The stranger lit a cigar.

'By the number of dollars he was ready to put up to have you done in.'

Billy's eyes snapped.

'Oh?' he said. 'And which gang has he given the job to?'

'I wish I could tell you. He – his agent, that is – came to Bat Jarvis.'

'The cat-expert?' said Psmith. 'A man of singularly winsome personality.'

'Bat turned the job down.'

'Why was that?' inquired Billy.

'He said he needed the money as much as the next man, but when he found out who he was supposed to lay for, he gave his job the frozen face. Said you were a friend of his and none of his fellows were going to put a finger on you. I don't know what you've been doing to Bat, but he's certainly Willie the Long-Lost Brother with you.'

'A powerful argument in favour of kindness to animals!' said Psmith. 'Comrade Windsor came into possession of one of Comrade Jarvis's celebrated stud of cats. What did he do? Instead of having the animal made into a nourishing soup, he restored it to its bereaved owner. Observe the sequel. He is now as a prize tortoiseshell to Comrade Jarvis.'

'So Bat wouldn't stand for it?' said Billy.

'Not on his life. Turned it down without a blink. And he sent me along to find you and tell you so.'

'We are much obliged to Comrade Jarvis,' said Psmith.

'He told me to tell you to watch out, because another gang is dead sure to take on the job. But he said you were to know he wasn't mixed up in it. He also said that any time you were in bad, he'd do his best for you. You've certainly made the biggest kind of hit with Bat. I haven't seen him so worked up over a thing in years. Well, that's all, I reckon. Guess I'll be pushing along. I've a date to keep. Glad to have met you. Glad to have met you, Mr Smith. Pardon me, you have an insect on your coat.'

He flicked at Psmith's coat with a quick movement. Psmith thanked him gravely.

'Good night,' concluded the stranger, moving off.

For a few moments after he had gone, Psmith and Billy

sat smoking in silence. They had plenty to think about.

'How's the time going?' asked Billy at length.

Psmith felt for his watch, and looked at Billy with some sadness.

'I am sorry to say, Comrade Windsor – '

'Hullo,' said Billy, 'here's that man coming back again.'

The stranger came up to their table, wearing a light overcoat over his dress clothes. From the pocket of this he produced a gold watch.

'Force of habit,' he said apologetically, handing it to Psmith. 'You'll pardon me. Good night, gentlemen, again.'

12 — A Red Taximeter

The Astor Hotel faces on to Times Square. A few paces to the right of the main entrance the Times Building towers to the sky; and at the foot of this the stream of traffic breaks, forming two channels. To the right of the building is Seventh Avenue, quiet, dark, and dull. To the left is Broadway, the Great White Way, the longest, straightest, brightest, wickedest street in the world.

Psmith and Billy, having left the Astor, started to walk down Broadway to Billy's lodgings in Fourteenth Street. The usual crowd was drifting slowly up and down in the glare of the white lights.

They had reached Herald Square, when a voice behind them exclaimed, 'Why, it's Mr Windsor.'

They wheeled round. A flashily dressed man was standing with outstretched hand.

'I saw you come out of the Astor,' he said cheerily. 'I said to myself, "I know that man." Darned if I could put a name to you, though. So I just followed you along, and right here it came to me.'

'It did, did it?' said Billy politely.

'It did, sir. I've never set eyes on you before, but I've seen so many photographs of you that I reckon we're old friends. I know your father very well, Mr Windsor. He showed me the photographs. You may have heard him speak of me – Jack Lake? How is the old man? Seen him lately?'

'Not for some time. He was well when he last wrote.'

'Good for him. He would be. Tough as a plank, old Joe Windsor. We always called him Joe.'

'You'd have known him down in Missouri, of course?'
said Billy.

'That's right. In Missouri. We were side-partners for
years. Now, see here, Mr Windsor, it's early yet. Won't
you and your friend come along with me and have a
smoke and a chat? I live right here in Thirty-Third Street.
I'd be right glad for you to come.'

'I don't doubt it,' said Billy, 'but I'm afraid you'll have
to excuse us.'

'In a hurry, are you?'

'Not in the least.'

'Then come right along.'

'No, thanks.'

'Say, why not? It's only a step.'

'Because we don't want to. Good night.'

He turned, and started to walk away. The other stood
for a moment, staring; then crossed the road.

Psmith broke the silence.

'Correct me if I am wrong, Comrade Windsor,' he said
tentatively, 'but were you not a trifle – shall we say abrupt?
– with the old family friend?'

Billy Windsor laughed.

'If my father's name was Joseph,' he said, 'instead of
being William, the same as mine, and if he'd ever been
in Missouri in his life, which he hasn't, and if I'd
been photographed since I was a kid, which I haven't
been, I might have gone along. As it was. I thought it
better not to.'

'These are deep waters, Comrade Windsor. Do you
mean to intimate – ?'

'If they can't do any better than that, we shan't have
much to worry us. What do they take us for, I wonder?
Farmers? Playing off a comic-supplement bluff like that
on us!'

There was honest indignation in Billy's voice.

'You think, then, that if we had accepted Comrade
Lake's invitation, and gone along for a smoke and a chat,

261

the chat would not have been of the pleasantest nature?'

'We should have been put out of business.'

'I have heard so much,' said Psmith, thoughtfully, 'of the lavish hospitality of the American.'

'Taxi, sir?'

A red taximeter cab was crawling down the road at their side. Billy shook his head.

'Not that a taxi would be an unsound scheme,' said Psmith.

'Not that particular one, if you don't mind.'

'Something about it that offends your aesthetic taste?' queried Psmith sympathetically.

'Something about it makes my aesthetic taste kick like a mule,' said Billy.

'Ah, we highly strung literary men do have these curious prejudices. We cannot help it. We are the slaves of our temperaments. Let us walk, then. After all, the night is fine, and we are young and strong.'

They had reached Twenty-Third Street when Billy stopped. 'I don't know about walking,' he said. 'Suppose we take the Elevated?'

'Anything you wish, Comrade Windsor. I am in your hands.'

They cut across into Sixth Avenue, and walked up the stairs to the station of the Elevated Railway. A train was just coming in.

'Has it escaped your notice, Comrade Windsor,' said Psmith after a pause. 'that, so far from speeding to your lodgings, we are going in precisely the opposite direction? We are in an up-town train.'

'I noticed it,' said Billy briefly.

'Are we going anywhere in particular?'

'This train goes as far as Hundred and Tenth Street. We'll go up to there.'

'And then?'

'And then we'll come back.'

'And after that, I suppose, we'll make a trip to

Philadelphia, or Chicago, or somewhere? Well, well, I am in your hands, Comrade Windsor. The night is yet young. Take me where you will. It is only five cents a go, and we have money in our purses. We are two young men out for reckless dissipation. By all means let us have it.'

At Hundred and Tenth Street they left the train, went down the stairs, and crossed the street. Half-way across Billy stopped.

'What now, Comrade Windsor?' inquired Psmith patiently. 'Have you thought of some new form of entertainment?'

Billy was making for a spot some few yards down the road. Looking in that direction, Psmith saw his objective. In the shadow of the Elevated there was standing a taximeter cab.

'Taxi, sir?' said the driver, as they approached.

'We are giving you a great deal of trouble,' said Billy. 'You must be losing money over this job. All this while you might be getting fares down-town.'

'These meetings, however,' urged Psmith, 'are very pleasant.'

'I can save you worrying,' said Billy. 'My address is 84 East Fourteenth Street. We are going back there now.'

'Search me,' said the driver, 'I don't know what you're talking about.'

'I thought perhaps you did,' replied Billy. 'Good night.'

'These things are very disturbing,' said Psmith, when they were in the train. 'Dignity is impossible when one is compelled to be the Hunted Fawn. When did you begin to suspect that yonder merchant was doing the sleuth-hound act?'

'When I saw him in Broadway having a heart-to-heart talk with our friend from Missouri.'

'He must be something of an expert at the game to have kept on our track.'

'Not on your life. It's as easy as falling off a log. There are only certain places where you can get off an Elevated

263

train. All he'd got to do was to get there before the train, and wait. I didn't expect to dodge him by taking the Elevated. I just wanted to make certain of his game.'

The train pulled up at the Fourteenth Street station. In the roadway at the foot of the opposite staircase was a red taximeter cab.

13 — Reviewing the Situation

Arriving at the bed-sitting-room, Billy proceeded to
occupy the rocking-chair, and, as was his wont, began
to rock himself rhythmically to and fro. Psmith seated
himself gracefully on the couch-bed. There was a
silence.

The events of the evening had been a revelation to
Psmith. He had not realized before the extent of the
ramifications of New York's underworld. That members
of the gangs should crop up in the Astor roof-garden and
in gorgeous raiment in the middle of Broadway was a
surprise. When Billy Windsor had mentioned the gangs, he
had formed a mental picture of low-browed hooligans,
keeping carefully to their own quarter of the town. This
picture had been correct, as far as it went, but it had not
gone far enough. The bulk of the gangs of New York are
of the hooligan class, and are rarely met with outside
their natural boundaries. But each gang has its more
prosperous members; gentlemen, who, like the man of
the Astor roof-garden, support life by more delicate and
genteel methods than the rest. The main body rely for
their incomes, except at election-time, on such primitive
feats as robbing intoxicated pedestrians. The aristocracy
of the gangs soar higher.

It was a considerable time before Billy spoke.

'Say,' he said, 'this thing wants talking over.'

'By all means, Comrade Windsor.'

'It's this way. There's no doubt now that we're up
against a mighty big proposition.'

'Something of the sort would seem to be the case.'

'It's like this. I'm going to see this through. It isn't only that I want to do a bit of good to the poor cusses in those tenements, though I'd do it for that alone. But, as far as I'm concerned, there's something to it besides that. If we win out, I'm going to get a job out of one of the big dailies. It'll give me just the chance I need. See what I mean? Well, it's different with you. I don't see that it's up to you to run the risk of getting yourself put out of business with a blackjack, and maybe shot. Once you get mixed up with the gangs there's no saying what's going to be doing. Well, I don't see why you shouldn't quit. All this has got nothing to do with you. You're over here on a vacation. You haven't got to make a living this side. You want to go about and have a good time, instead of getting mixed up with – '

He broke off.

'Well, that's what I wanted to say, anyway,' he concluded.

Psmith looked at him reproachfully.

'Are you trying to *sack* me, Comrade Windsor?'

'How's that?'

'In various treatises on "How to Succeed in Literature",' said Psmith sadly, 'which I have read from time to time, I have always found it stated that what the novice chiefly needed was an editor who believed in him. In you, Comrade Windsor, I fancied that I had found such an editor.'

'What's all this about?' demanded Billy. 'I'm making no kick about your work.'

'I gathered from your remarks that you were anxious to receive my resignation.'

'Well, I told you why. I didn't want you to be black-jacked.'

'Was that the only reason?'

'Sure.'

'Then all is well,' said Psmith, relieved. 'For the moment I fancied that my literary talents had been weighed in the balance and adjudged below par. If that is all – why, these are the mere everyday risks of the young journalist's life. Without them we should be dull and dissatisfied. Our work would lose its fire. Men such as ourselves, Comrade Windsor, need a certain stimulus, a certain fillip, if they are to keep up their high standards. The knowledge that a low-browed gentleman is waiting round the corner with a sand-bag poised in air will just supply that stimulus. Also that fillip. It will give our output precisely the edge it requires.'

'Then you'll stay in this thing? You'll stick to the work?'

'Like a conscientious leech, Comrade Windsor.'

'Bully for you,' said Billy.

It was not Psmith's habit, when he felt deeply on any subject, to exhibit his feelings; and this matter of the tenements had hit him harder than any one who did not know him intimately would have imagined. Mike would have understood him, but Billy Windsor was too recent an acquaintance. Psmith was one of those people who are content to accept most of the happenings of life in an airy spirit of tolerance. Life had been more or less of a game with him up till now. In his previous encounters with those with whom fate had brought him in contact there had been little at stake. The prize of victory had been merely a comfortable feeling of having had the best of a battle of wits; the penalty of defeat nothing worse than the discomfort of having failed to score. But this tenement business was different. Here he had touched the realities. There was something worth fighting for. His lot had been cast in pleasant places, and the sight of actual raw misery had come home to him with an added force from that circumstance. He was fully aware of the risks that he must run. The words of the man at the Astor, and still more the episodes of the family friend from Missouri and the taximeter cab, had shown him that this thing was on a different plane from anything that had happened to him before. It was a fight without the gloves, and to a finish at that. But he meant to see it through. Somehow or other those tenement houses had got to be cleaned up. If it meant trouble, as it undoubtedly did, that trouble would have to be faced.

'Now that Comrade Jarvis,' he said, 'showing a spirit of forbearance which, I am bound to say, does him credit, has declined the congenial task of fracturing our occiputs, who should you say, Comrade Windsor, would be the chosen substitute?'

Billy shook his head. 'Now that Bat has turned up the job, it might be any one of three gangs. There are four main gangs, you know. Bat's is the biggest. But the smallest of them's large enough to put us away, if we give them the chance.'

'I don't quite grasp the nice points of this matter. Do you mean that we have an entire gang on our trail in one solid mass, or will it be merely a section?'

'Well, a section, I guess, if it comes to that. Parker, or whoever fixed this thing up, would go to the main boss of the gang. If it was the Three Points, he'd go to Spider Reilly. If it was the Table Hill lot, he'd look up Dude Dawson. And so on.'

'And what then?'

'And then the boss would talk it over with his own special partners. Every gang-leader has about a dozen of them. A sort of Inner Circle. They'd fix it up among themselves. The rest of the gang wouldn't know anything about it. The fewer in the game, you see, the fewer to split up the dollars.'

'I see. Then things are not so black. All we have to do is to look out for about a dozen hooligans with a natural dignity in their bearing, the result of intimacy with the main boss. Carefully eluding these aristocrats, we shall win through. I fancy, Comrade Windsor, that all may yet be well. What steps do you propose to take by way of self-defence?'

'Keep out of the middle of the street, and not go off the

Broadway after dark. You're pretty safe on Broadway. There's too much light for them there.'

'Now that our sleuth-hound friend in the taximeter has ascertained your address, shall you change it?'

'It wouldn't do any good. They'd soon find where I'd gone to. How about yours?'

'I fancy I shall be tolerably all right. A particularly massive policeman is on duty at my very doors. So much for our private lives. But what of the day-time? Suppose these sand-bag-specialists drop in at the office during business hours. Will Comrade Maloney's frank and manly statement that we are not in be sufficient to keep them out? I doubt it. All unused to the nice conventions of polite society, these rugged persons will charge through. In such circumstances good work will be hard to achieve. Your literary man must have complete quiet if he is to give the public of his best. But stay. An idea!'

'Well?'

'Comrade Brady. The Peerless Kid. The man *Cosy Moments* is running for the light-weight championship. We are his pugilistic sponsors. You may say that it is entirely owing to our efforts that he has obtained this match with – who exactly is the gentleman Comrade Brady fights at the Highfield Club on Friday night?'

'Cyclone Al. Wolmann, isn't it?'

'You are right. As I was saying, but for us the privilege of smiting Comrade Cyclone Al. Wolmann under the fifth rib on Friday night would almost certainly have been denied to him.'

It almost seemed as if he were right. From the moment the paper had taken up his cause, Kid Brady's star had undoubtedly been in the ascendant. People began to talk about him as a likely man. Edgren, in the *Evening World*, had a paragraph about his chances for the light-weight title. Tad, in the *Journal*, drew a picture of him. Finally, the management of the Highfield Club had signed him for a ten-round bout with Mr Wolmann. There were, therefore, reasons why *Cosy Moments* should feel a claim on the Kid's services.

'He should,' continued Psmith, 'if equipped in any degree with finer feelings, be bubbling over with gratitude towards us. "But for *Cosy Moments*," he should be saying to himself, "where should I be? Among the also-rans." I imagine that he will do any little thing we care to ask of him. I suggest that we approach Comrade Brady, explain the facts of the case, and offer him at a comfortable salary the post of fighting-editor of *Cosy Moments*. His duties will be to sit in the room opening out of ours, girded as to the loins and full of martial spirit, and apply some of those half-scissor hooks of his to the persons of any who overcome the opposition of Comrade Maloney. We, meanwhile, will enjoy the leisure and freedom from interruption which is so essential to the artist.'

'It's not a bad idea,' said Billy.

'It is about the soundest idea,' said Psmith, 'that has ever been struck. One of your newspaper friends shall supply us with tickets, and Friday night shall see us at the Highfield.'

14 — The Highfield

Far up at the other end of the island, on the banks of the
Harlem River, there stands the old warehouse which
modern progress has converted into the Highfield
Athletic and Gymnastic Club. The imagination,
stimulated by the title, conjures up a sort of National
Sporting Club, with pictures on the walls, padding on the
chairs, and a sea of white shirt-fronts from roof to floor.
But the Highfield differs in some respects from this fancy
picture. Indeed, it would be hard to find a respect in which
it does not differ. But these names are so misleading.
The title under which the Highfield used to be known
till a few years back was 'Swifty Bob's'. It was a good,
honest title. You knew what to expect; and if you attended
séances at Swifty Bob's you left your gold watch and
your little savings at home. But a wave of anti-pugilistic
feeling swept over the New York authorities. Promoters
of boxing contests found themselves, to their acute
disgust, raided by the police. The industry began to
languish. People avoided places where at any moment
the festivities might be marred by an inrush of large men
in blue uniforms armed with locust-sticks.

And then some big-brained person suggested the club
idea, which stands alone as an example of American dry
humour. There are now no boxing contests in New York.
Swifty Bob and his fellows would be shocked at the idea
of such a thing. All that happens now is exhibition
sparring bouts between members of the club. It is true
that next day the papers very tactlessly report the friendly
exhibition spar as if it had been quite a serious affair,
but that is not the fault of Swifty Bob.

271

Kid Brady, the chosen of *Cosy Moments*, was billed for a 'ten-round exhibition contest', to be the main event of the evening's entertainment. No decisions are permitted at these clubs. Unless a regrettable accident occurs, and one of the sparrers is knocked out, the verdict is left to the newspapers next day. It is not uncommon to find a man win easily in the *World*, drawn in the *American*, and be badly beaten in the *Evening Mail*. The system leads to a certain amount of confusion, but it has the merit of offering consolation to a much-smitten warrior.

The best method of getting to the Highfield is by the Subway. To see the Subway in its most characteristic mood one must travel on it during the rush-hour, when its patrons are packed into the carriages in one solid jam by muscular guards and policemen, shoving in a manner reminiscent of a Rugby football scrum. When Psmith and Billy entered it on the Friday evening, it was comparatively empty. All the seats were occupied, but only a few of the straps and hardly any of the space reserved by law for the conductor alone.

Conversation on the Subway is impossible. The ingenious gentlemen who constructed it started with the object of making it noisy. Not ordinarily noisy, like a ton of coal falling on to a sheet of tin, but really noisy. So they fashioned the pillars of thin steel, and the sleepers of thin wood, and loosened all the nuts, and now a Subway train in motion suggests a prolonged dynamite explosion blended with the voice of some great cataract.

Psmith, forced into temporary silence by this combination of noises, started to make up for lost time on arriving in the street once more.

'A thoroughly unpleasant neighbourhood,' he said, critically surveying the dark streets. 'I fear me, Comrade Windsor, that we have been somewhat rash in venturing as far into the middle west as this. If ever there was a blighted locality where low-browed desperadoes might be expected to spring with whoops of joy from every corner, this blighted locality is that blighted locality. But we must carry on. In which direction, should you say, does this arena lie?'

It had begun to rain as they left Billy's lodgings. Psmith turned up the collar of his Burberry.

'We suffer much in the cause of Literature,' he said. 'Let us inquire of this genial soul if he knows where the Highfield is.'

The pedestrian referred to proved to be going there himself. They went on together, Psmith courteously offering views on the weather and forecasts of the success of Kid Brady in the approaching contest.

Rattling on, he was alluding to the prominent part *Cosy Moments* had played in the affair, when a rough thrust from Windsor's elbow brought home to him his indiscretion.

He stopped suddenly, wishing he had not said as much. Their connection with that militant journal was not a thing even to be suggested to casual acquaintances, especially in such a particularly ill-lighted neighbourhood as that through which they were now passing.

Their companion, however, who seemed to be a man of small speech, made no comment. Psmith deftly turned the conversation back to the subject of the weather, and was deep in comparison of the respective climates of England and the United States, when they turned a corner and found themselves opposite a gloomy, barn-like building, over the door of which it was just possible to decipher in the darkness the words 'Highfield Athletic and Gymnastic Club'.

The tickets which Billy Windsor had obtained from his newspaper friend were for one of the boxes. These proved to be sort of sheep-pens of unpolished wood, each with four hard chairs in it. The interior of the Highfield Athletic and Gymnastic Club was severely free from anything in the shape of luxury and ornament. Along the four walls were raised benches in tiers. On these were seated as tough-looking a collection of citizens as one might wish to see. On chairs at the ring-side were the reporters, with tickers at their sides, by means of which they tapped details of each round through to their down-town offices, where write-up reporters were waiting to read off and elaborate the messages. In the centre of the room, brilliantly lighted by half a dozen electric chandeliers, was the ring.

There were preliminary bouts before the main event. A burly gentleman in shirt-sleeves entered the ring, followed by two slim youths in fighting costume and a massive person in a red jersey, blue serge trousers, and yellow braces, who chewed gum with an abstracted air throughout the proceedings.

The burly gentleman gave tongue in a voice that cleft the air like a cannon-ball.

'Ex-hib-it-i-on four-round bout between Patsy Milligan and Tommy Goodley, members of this club. Patsy on my right, Tommy on my left. Gentlemen will kindly stop smokin''.'

The audience did nothing of the sort. Possibly they did not apply the description to themselves. Possibly they considered the appeal a mere formula. Somewhere in the background a gong sounded, and Patsy, from the right, stepped briskly forward to meet Tommy, approaching from the left.

The contest was short but energetic. At intervals the combatants would cling affectionately to one another, and on these occasions the red-jerseyed man, still chewing gum and still wearing the same air of being lost in abstract thought, would split up the mass by the simple method of ploughing his way between the pair. Towards the end of the first round Thomas, eluding a left swing, put Patrick neatly to the floor, where the latter remained for the necessary ten seconds.

The remaining preliminaries proved disappointing. So much so that in the last of the series a soured sportsman on one of the benches near the roof began in satirical mood to whistle the 'Merry Widow Waltz'. It was here that the red-jerseyed thinker for the first and last time came out of his meditative trance. He leaned over the ropes, and spoke – without heat, but firmly.

'If that guy whistling back up yonder thinks he can do better than these boys, he can come right down into the ring.'

The whistling ceased.

There was a distinct air of relief when the last preliminary was finished and preparations for the main bout began. It did not commence at once. There were formalities to be gone through, introductions and the like. The burly gentleman re-appeared from nowhere, ushering into the ring a sheepishly-grinning youth in flannel suit.

'In-ter-*doo*-cin' Young Leary,' he bellowed impressively, 'a noo member of this club, who will box some good boy here in September.'

He walked to the other side of the ring and repeated the remark. A raucous welcome was accorded to the new member.

Two other notable performers were introduced in a similar manner, and then the building became suddenly full of noise, for a tall youth in a bath-robe, attended by a little army of assistants, had entered the ring. One of the army carried a bright green bucket, on which were painted in white letters the words 'Cyclone Al. Wolmann'. A moment later there was another, though far lesser, uproar, as Kid Brady, his pleasant face wearing a self-confident smirk, ducked under the ropes and sat down in the opposite corner.

'Ex-hib-it-i-on ten-round bout,' thundered the burly gentleman, 'between Cyclone Al. Wolmann – '

Loud applause. Mr Wolmann was one of the famous, a fighter with a reputation from New York to San Francisco.

275

He was generally considered the most likely man to give the hitherto invincible Jimmy Garvin a hard battle for the light-weight championship.

'Oh, you Al.!' roared the crowd.

Mr Wolmann bowed benevolently.

' – and Kid Brady, members of this – '

There was noticeably less applause for the Kid. He was an unknown. A few of those present had heard of his victories in the West, but these were but a small section of the crowd. When the faint applause had ceased, Psmith rose to his feet.

'Oh, you Kid!' he observed encouragingly. 'I should not like Comrade Brady,' he said, reseating himself, 'to think that he has no friend but his poor old mother, as, you will recollect, occurred on a previous occasion.'

The burly gentleman, followed by the two armies of assistants, dropped down from the ring, and the gong sounded.

Mr Wolmann sprang from his corner as if somebody had touched a spring. He seemed to be of the opinion that if you are a cyclone, it is never too soon to begin behaving like one. He danced round the Kid with an india-rubber agility. The *Cosy Moments* representative exhibited more stolidity. Except for the fact that he was in fighting attitude, with one gloved hand moving slowly in the neighbourhood of his stocky chest, and the other pawing the air on a line with his square jaw, one would have said that he did not realize the position of affairs. He wore the friendly smile of the good-natured guest who is led forward by his hostess to join in some round game.

Suddenly his opponent's long left shot out. The Kid, who had been strolling forward, received it under the chin, and continued to stroll forward as if nothing of note had happened. He gave the impression of being aware that Mr Wolmann had committed a breach of good taste and of being resolved to pass it off with ready tact.

The Cyclone, having executed a backward leap, a
forward leap, and a feint, landed heavily with both hands.
The Kid's genial smile did not even quiver, but he
continued to move forward. His opponent's left flashed
out again, but this time, instead of ignoring the matter,
the Kid replied with a heavy right swing; and Mr
Wolmann, leaping back, found himself against the ropes.
By the time he had got out of that uncongenial position,
two more of the Kid's swings had found their mark. Mr
Wolmann, somewhat perturbed, scuttered out into the
middle of the ring, the Kid following in his self-contained,
solid way.

The Cyclone now became still more cyclonic. He had
a left arm which seemed to open out in joints like a
telescope. Several times when the Kid appeared well out
of distance there was a thud as a brown glove ripped in
over his guard and jerked his head back. But always he
kept boring in, delivering an occasional right to the body
with the pleased smile of an infant destroying a Noah's
Ark with a tack-hammer. Despite these efforts, however,
he was plainly getting all the worst of it. Energetic Mr
Wolmann, relying on his long left, was putting in three
blows to his one. When the gong sounded, ending the first
round, the house was practically solid for the Cyclone.
Whoops and yells rose from everywhere. The building
rang with shouts of, 'Oh, you Al.!'

Psmith turned sadly to Billy.

'It seems to me, Comrade Windsor,' he said, 'that this
merry meeting looks like doing Comrade Brady no good.
I should not be surprised at any moment to see his head
bounce off on to the floor.'

'Wait,' said Billy. 'He'll win yet.'

'You think so?'

'Sure. He comes from Wyoming,' said Billy with
simple confidence.

Rounds two and three were a repetition of round one.
The Cyclone raged almost unchecked about the ring. In

one lightning rally in the third he brought his right across squarely on to the Kid's jaw. It was a blow which should have knocked any boxer out. The Kid merely staggered slightly and returned to business, still smiling.

'See!' roared Billy enthusiastically in Psmith's ear, above the uproar. 'He doesn't mind it! He likes it! He comes from Wyoming!'

With the opening of round four there came a subtle change. The Cyclone's fury was expending itself. That long left shot out less sharply. Instead of being knocked back by it, the *Cosy Moments* champion now took the hits in his stride, and came shuffling in with his damaging body-blows. There were cheers and 'Oh, you Al.'s!' at the sound of the gong, but there was an appealing note in them this time. The gallant sportsmen whose connection with boxing was confined to watching other men fight, and betting on what they considered a certainty, and who would have expired promptly if any one had tapped them sharply on their well-filled waistcoats, were beginning to fear that they might lose their money after all.

In the fifth round the thing became a certainty. Like the month of March, the Cyclone, who had come in like a lion, was going out like a lamb. A slight decrease in the pleasantness of the Kid's smile was noticeable. His expression began to resemble more nearly the gloomy importance of the *Cosy Moments* photographs. Yells of agony from panic-stricken speculators around the ring began to smite the rafters. The Cyclone, now but a gentle breeze, clutched repeatedly, hanging on like a leech till removed by the red-jerseyed referee.

Suddenly a grisly silence fell upon the house. It was broken by a cowboy yell from Billy Windsor. For the Kid, battered, but obviously content, was standing in the middle of the ring, while on the ropes the Cyclone, drooping like a wet sock, was sliding slowly to the floor.

'*Cosy Moments* wins,' said Psmith. 'An omen, I fancy, Comrade Windsor.'

15 — An Addition to the Staff

Penetrating into the Kid's dressing-room some moments later, the editorial staff found the winner of the ten-round exhibition bout between members of the club seated on a chair, having his right leg rubbed by a shock-headed man in a sweater, who had been one of his seconds during the conflict. The Kid beamed as they entered.

'Gents,' he said, 'come right in. Mighty glad to see you.'

'It is a relief to me, Comrade Brady,' said Psmith, 'to find that you *can* see us. I had expected to find that Comrade Wolmann's purposeful biffs had completely closed your star-likes.'

'Sure, I never felt them. He's a good quick boy, is Al., but,' continued the Kid with powerful imagery, 'he couldn't hit a hole in a block of ice-cream, not if he was to use a hammer.'

'And yet at one period in the proceedings, Comrade Brady,' said Psmith, 'I fancied that your head would come unglued at the neck. But the fear was merely transient. When you began to administer those – am I correct in saying? – half-scissor hooks to the body, why, then I felt like some watcher of the skies when a new planet swims into his ken; or like stout Cortez when with eagle eyes he stared at the Pacific.'

The Kid blinked.

'How's that?' he inquired.

'And why did I feel like that, Comrade Brady? I will tell you. Because my faith in you was justified. Because there before me stood the ideal fighting-editor of *Cosy Moments*. It is not a post that any weakling can fill.

There charm of manner cannot qualify a man for the position. No one can hold down the job simply by having a kind heart or being good at farmyard imitations. No. We want a man of thews and sinews, a man who would rather be hit on the head with a half-brick than not. And you, Comrade Brady, are such a man.'

The Kid turned appealingly to Billy.

'Say, this gets past me, Mr Windsor. Put me wise.'

'Can we have a couple of words with you alone, Kid?' said Billy. 'We want to talk over something with you.'

'Sure. Sit down, gents. Jack'll be through in a minute.'

Jack, who during this conversation had been concentrating himself on his subject's left leg, now announced that he guessed that would about do, and having advised the Kid not to stop and pick daisies, but to get into his clothes at once before he caught a chill, bade the company good night and retired.

Billy shut the door.

'Kid,' he said, 'you know those articles about the tenements we've been having in the paper?'

'Sure. I read 'em. They're to the good.'

Psmith bowed.

'You stimulate us, Comrade Brady. This is praise from Sir Hubert Stanley.'

'It was about time some strong josher came and put it across to 'em,' added the Kid.

'So we thought. Comrade Parker, however, totally disagreed with us.'

'Parker?'

'That's what I'm coming to,' said Billy. 'The day before yesterday a man named Parker called at the office and tried to buy us off.'

Billy's voice grew indignant at the recollection.

'You gave him the hook, I guess?' queried the interested Kid.

'To such an extent, Comrade Brady,' said Psmith, 'that he left breathing threatenings and slaughter. And it is for that reason that we have ventured to call upon you.'

'It's this way,' said Billy. 'We're pretty sure by this time that whoever the man is this fellow Parker's working for has put one of the gangs on to us.'

'You don't say!' exclaimed the Kid. 'Gum! Mr Windsor, they're tough propositions, those gangs.'

'We've been followed in the streets, and once they put up a bluff to get us where they could do us in. So we've come along to you. We can look after ourselves out of the office, you see, but what we want is some one to help in case they try to rush us there.'

'In brief, a fighting-editor,' said Psmith. 'At all costs we must have privacy. No writer can prune and polish his sentences to his satisfaction if he is compelled constantly to break off in order to eject boisterous hooligans. We therefore offer you the job of sitting in the outer room and intercepting these bravoes before they can reach us. The salary we leave to you. There are doubloons and to spare in the old oak chest. Take what you need and put the rest – if any – back. How does the offer strike you. Comrade Brady?'

'We don't want to get you in under false pretences, Kid,' said Billy. 'Of course, they may not come anywhere near the office. But still, if they did, there would be something doing. What do you feel about it?'

'Gents,' said the Kid, 'it's this way.'

He stepped into his coat, and resumed.

'Now that I've made good by getting the decision over Al., they'll be giving me a chance of a big fight. Maybe with Jimmy Garvin. Well, if that happens, see what I mean? I'll have to be going away somewhere and getting into training. I shouldn't be able to come and sit with you. But, if you gents feel like it, I'd be mighty glad to come in till I'm wanted to go into training-camp.'

'Great,' said Billy; 'that would suit us all the way up. If you'd do that, Kid, we'd be tickled to death.'

'And touching salary – ' put in Psmith.

'Shucks!' said the Kid with emphasis. 'Nix on the salary thing. I wouldn't take a dime. If it hadn't a been for you gents, I'd have been waiting still for a chance of lining up in the championship class. That's good enough for me. Any old thing you gents want me to do, I'll do it. And glad, too.'

'Comrade Brady,' said Psmith warmly, 'you are, if I may say so, the goods. You are, beyond a doubt, supremely the stuff. We three, then, hand-in-hand, will face the foe; and if the foe has good, sound sense, he will keep right away. You appear to be ready. Shall we meander forth?'

The building was empty and the lights were out when they emerged from the dressing-room. They had to grope their way in darkness. It was still raining when they reached the street, and the only signs of life were a moist policeman and the distant glare of public-house lights down the road.

They turned off to the left, and, after walking some hundred yards, found themselves in a blind alley.

'Hullo!' said Billy. 'Where have we come to?'

Psmith sighed.

'In my trusting way,' he said, 'I had imagined that either you or Comrade Brady was in charge of this expedition and taking me by a known route to the nearest Subway station. I did not think to ask. I placed myself, without hesitation, wholly in your hands.'

'I thought the Kid knew the way,' said Billy.

'I was just taggin' along with you gents,' protested the light-weight, 'I thought you was taking me right. This is the first time I been up here.'

'Next time we three go on a little jaunt anywhere,' said Psmith resignedly, 'it would be as well to take a map and a corps of guides with us. Otherwise we shall start from Broadway and finish up at Minneapolis.'

They emerged from the blind alley and stood in the dark street, looking doubtfully up and down it.

283

'Aha!' said Psmith suddenly, 'I perceive a native. Several natives, in fact. Quite a little covey of them. We will put our case before them, concealing nothing, and rely on their advice to take us to our goal.'

A little knot of men was approaching from the left. In the darkness it was impossible to say how many of them there were. Psmith stepped forward, the Kid at his side.

'Excuse me, sir,' he said to the leader, 'but if you can spare me a moment of your valuable time – '

There was a sudden shuffle of feet on the pavement, a quick movement on the part of the Kid, a chunky sound as of wood striking wood, and the man Psmith had been addressing fell to the ground in a heap.

As he fell, something dropped from his hand on to the pavement with a bump and a rattle. Stooping swiftly, the Kid picked it up, and handed it to Psmith. His fingers closed upon it. It was a short, wicked-looking little bludgeon, the black-jack of the New York tough.

'Get busy,' advised the Kid briefly.

16 — The First Battle

The promptitude and despatch with which the Kid had attended to the gentleman with the black-jack had not been without its effect on the followers of the stricken one. Physical courage is not an outstanding quality of the New York hooligan. His personal preference is for retreat when it is a question of unpleasantness with a stranger. And, in any case, even when warring among themselves, the gangs exhibit a lively distaste for the hard knocks of hand-to-hand fighting. Their chosen method of battling is to lie down on the ground and shoot. This is more suited to their physique, which is rarely great. The man, as a rule, is stunted and slight of build.

The Kid's rapid work on the present occasion created a good deal of confusion. There was no doubt that much had been hoped for from speedy attack. Also, the generalship of the expedition had been in the hands of the fallen warrior. His removal from the sphere of active influence had left the party without a head. And, to add to their discomfiture, they could not account for the Kid. Psmith they knew, and Billy Windsor they knew, but who was this stranger with the square shoulders and the upper-cut that landed like a cannon-ball? Something approaching a panic prevailed among the gang.

It was not lessened by the behaviour of the intended victims. Billy Windsor, armed with the big stick which he had bought after the visit of Mr Parker, was the first to join issue. He had been a few paces behind the others during the black-jack incident; but, dark as it was, he had seen enough to show him that the occasion was, as Psmith would have said, one for the Shrewd Blow rather

than the Prolonged Parley. With a whoop of the purest
Wyoming brand, he sprang forward into the confused
mass of the enemy. A moment later Psmith and the Kid
followed, and there raged over the body of the fallen leader
a battle of Homeric type.

It was not a long affair. The rules and conditions
governing the encounter offended the delicate
sensibilities of the gang. Like artists who feel themselves
trammelled by distasteful conventions, they were damped
and could not do themselves justice. Their forte was long-
range fighting with pistols. With that they felt *en
rapport*. But this vulgar brawling in the darkness with
muscular opponents who hit hard and often with sticks
and hands was distasteful to them. They could not
develop any enthusiasm for it. They carried pistols, but
it was too dark and the combatants were too entangled
to allow them to use these. Besides, this was not the
dear, homely old Bowery, where a gentleman may fire a
pistol without exciting vulgar comment. It was up-town,
where curious crowds might collect at the first shot.

There was but one thing to be done. Reluctant as they
might be to abandon their fallen leader, they must tear
themselves away. Already they were suffering grievously
from the stick, the black-jack, and the lightning blows
of the Kid. For a moment they hung, wavering; then
stampeded in half a dozen different directions, melting
into the night whence they had come.

Billy, full of zeal, pursued one fugitive some fifty yards
down the street, but his quarry, exhibiting a rare turn of
speed, easily outstripped him.

He came back, panting, to find Psmith and the Kid
examining the fallen leader of the departed ones with
the aid of a match, which went out just as Billy arrived.

'It is our friend of the earlier part of the evening,
Comrade Windsor,' said Psmith. 'The merchant with
whom we hobnobbed on our way to the Highfield. In a
moment of imprudence I mentioned *Cosy Moments*. I

fancy that this was his first intimation that we were in
the offing. His visit to the Highfield was paid, I think,
purely from sport-loving motives. He was not on our trail.
He came merely to see if Comrade Brady was proficient
with his hands. Subsequent events must have justified
our fighting-editor in his eyes. It seems to be a moot
point whether he will ever recover consciousness.'

'Mighty good thing if he doesn't,' said Billy
uncharitably.

'From one point of view, Comrade Windsor, yes. Such
an event would undoubtedly be an excellent thing for
the public good. But from our point of view, it would be
as well if he were to sit up and take notice. We could
ascertain from him who he is and which particular
collection of horny-handeds he represents. Light another
match, Comrade Brady.'

The Kid did so. The head of it fell off and dropped upon
the up-turned face. The hooligan stirred, shook himself,
sat up, and began to mutter something in a foggy
voice.

'He's still woozy,' said the Kid.

'Still – what exactly, Comrade Brady?'

'In the air,' explained the Kid. 'Bats in the belfry. Dizzy.
See what I mean? It's often like that when a feller puts
one in with a bit of weight behind it just where that one
landed. Gum! I remember when I fought Martin Kelly;
I was only starting to learn the game then. Martin and
me was mixing it good and hard all over the ring, when
suddenly he puts over a stiff one right on the point. What
do you think I done? Fall down and take the count? Not
on your life. I just turns round and walks straight out of
the ring to my dressing-room. Willie Harvey, who was
seconding me, comes tearing in after me, and finds me
getting into my clothes. "What's doing, Kid?" he asks.
"I'm going fishin', Willie," I says. "It's a lovely day."
"You've lost the fight," he says. "Fight?" says I. "What
fight?" See what I mean? I hadn't a notion of what had

287

happened. It was a half an hour and more before I could remember a thing.'

During this reminiscence, the man on the ground had contrived to clear his mind of the mistiness induced by the Kid's upper-cut. The first sign he showed of returning intelligence was a sudden dash for safety up the road. But he had not gone five yards when he sat down limply.

The Kid was inspired to further reminiscence. 'Guess he's feeling pretty poor,' he said. 'It's no good him trying to run for a while after he's put his chin in the way of a real live one. I remember when Joe Peterson put me out, way back when I was new to the game – it was the same year I fought Martin Kelly. He had an awful punch, had old Joe, and he put me down and out in the eighth round. After the fight they found me on the fire-escape outside my dressing-room. "Come in, Kid," says they. "It's all right, chaps," I says, "I'm dying." Like that. "It's all right, chaps, I'm dying." Same with this guy. See what I mean?'

They formed a group about the fallen black-jack expert.

'Pardon us,' said Psmith courteously, 'for breaking in upon your reverie; but, if you could spare us a moment of your valuable time, there are one or two things which we should like to know.'

'Sure thing,' agreed the Kid.

'In the first place,' continued Psmith, 'would it be betraying professional secrets if you told us which particular bevy of energetic sandbaggers it is to which you are attached?'

'Gent,' explained the Kid, 'wants to know what's your gang.'

The man on the ground muttered something that to Psmith and Billy was unintelligible.

'It would be a charity,' said the former, 'if some philanthropist would give this blighter elocution lessons. Can you interpret, Comrade Brady?'

'Says it's the Three Points,' said the Kid.

'The Three Points? Let me see, is that Dude Dawson, Comrade Windsor, or the other gentleman?'

'It's Spider Reilly. Dude Dawson runs the Table Hill crowd.'

'Perhaps this *is* Spider Reilly?'

'Nope,' said the Kid. 'I know the Spider. This ain't him. This is some other mutt.'

'Which other mutt in particular?' asked Psmith. 'Try and find out, Comrade Brady. You seem to be able to understand what he says. To me, personally, his remarks sound like the output of a gramophone with a hot potato in its mouth.'

'Says he's Jack Repetto,' announced the interpreter.

There was another interruption at this moment. The bashful Mr Repetto, plainly a man who was not happy in the society of strangers, made another attempt to withdraw. Reaching out a pair of lean hands, he pulled the Kid's legs from under him with a swift jerk, and, wriggling to his feet, started off again down the road. Once more, however, desire outran performance. He got as far as the nearest street-lamp, but no farther. The giddiness seemed to overcome him again, for he grasped the lamp-post, and, sliding slowly to the ground, sat there motionless.

The Kid, whose fall had jolted and bruised him, was inclined to be wrathful and vindictive. He was the first of the three to reach the elusive Mr Repetto, and if that worthy had happened to be standing instead of sitting it might have gone hard with him. But the Kid was not the man to attack a fallen foe. He contented himself with brushing the dust off his person and addressing a richly abusive flow of remarks to Mr Repetto.

Under the rays of the lamp it was possible to discern more closely the features of the black-jack exponent. There was a subtle but noticeable resemblance to those of Mr Bat Jarvis. Apparently the latter's oiled forelock, worn low over the forehead, was more a concession to the general fashion prevailing in gang circles than an expression of personal taste. Mr Repetto had it, too. In his case it was almost white, for the fallen warrior was an albino. His eyes, which were closed, had white lashes and were set as near together as Nature had been able to manage without actually running them into one another. His under-lip protruded and drooped. Looking at him, one felt instinctively that no judging committee of a beauty contest would hesitate a moment before him.

It soon became apparent that the light of the lamp, though bestowing the doubtful privilege of a clearer view of Mr Repetto's face, held certain disadvantages. Scarcely had the staff of *Cosy Moments* reached the faint yellow pool of light, in the centre of which Mr Repetto reclined, than, with a suddenness which caused them to leap into the air, there sounded from the darkness down the road the *crack-crack-crack* of a revolver. Instantly from the opposite direction came other shots. Three bullets flicked grooves in the roadway almost at Billy's feet. The Kid gave a sudden howl. Psmith's hat, suddenly imbued with life, sprang into the air and vanished, whirling into the night.

The thought did not come to them consciously at the moment, there being little time to think, but it was evident as soon as, diving out of the circle of light into the sheltering darkness, they crouched down and waited for the next move, that a somewhat skilful ambush had been effected. The other members of the gang, who had fled with such remarkable speed, had by no means been eliminated altogether from the game. While the questioning of Mr Repetto had been in progress, they had crept back, unperceived except by Mr Repetto himself. It being too dark for successful shooting, it had become Mr Repetto's task to lure his captors into the light, which he had accomplished with considerable skill.

For some minutes the battle halted. There was dead silence. The circle of light was empty now. Mr Repetto

had vanished. A tentative shot from nowhere ripped
through the air close to where Psmith lay flattened on
the pavement. And then the pavement began to vibrate
and give out a curious resonant sound. To Psmith it
conveyed nothing, but to the opposing army it meant
much. They knew it for what it was. Somewhere – it
might be near or far – a policeman had heard the shots,
and was signalling for help to other policemen along the
line by beating on the flagstones with his night-stick,
the New York constable's substitute for the London
police-whistle. The noise grew, filling the still air. From
somewhere down the road sounded the ring of running
feet.

'De cops!' cried a voice. 'Beat it!'

Next moment the night was full of clatter. The gang
was 'beating it'.

Psmith rose to his feet and dusted his clothes
ruefully. For the first time he realized the horrors of war.
His hat had gone for ever. His trousers could never be the
same again after their close acquaintance with the
pavement.

The rescue party was coming up at the gallop.

The New York policeman may lack the quiet dignity
of his London rival, but he is a hustler.

'What's doing?'

'Nothing now,' said the disgusted voice of Billy
Windsor from the shadows. 'They've beaten it.'

The circle of lamplight became as if by mutual consent
a general rendezvous. Three grey-clad policemen, tough,
clean-shaven men with keen eyes and square jaws, stood
there, revolver in one hand, night-stick in the other.
Psmith, hatless and dusty, joined them. Billy Windsor
and the Kid, the latter bleeding freely from his left ear, the
lobe of which had been chipped by a bullet, were the last
to arrive.

'What's bin the rough house?' inquired one of the
policemen, mildly interested.

'Do you know a sportsman of the name of Repetto?' inquired Psmith.

'Jack Repetto? Sure.'

'He belongs to the Three Points,' said another intelligent officer, as one naming some fashionable club.

'When next you see him,' said Psmith, 'I should be obliged if you would use your authority to make him buy me a new hat. I could do with another pair of trousers, too; but I will not press the trousers. A new hat, is, however, essential. Mine has a six-inch hole in it.'

'Shot at you, did they?' said one of the policemen, as who should say, 'Dash the lads, they're always up to some of their larks.'

'Shot at us!' burst out the ruffled Kid. 'What do you think's bin happening? Think an aeroplane ran into my ear and took half of it off? Think the noise was somebody opening bottles of pop? Think those guys that sneaked off down the road was just training for a Marathon?'

'Comrade Brady,' said Psmith, 'touches the spot. He – '

'Say, are you Kid Brady?' inquired one of the officers. For the first time the constabulary had begun to display any real animation.

'Reckoned I'd seen you somewhere!' said another. 'You licked Cyclone Al. all right, Kid, I hear.'

'And who but a bone-head thought he wouldn't?' demanded the third warmly. 'He could whip a dozen Cyclone Al.'s in the same evening with his eyes shut.'

'He's the next champeen,' admitted the first speaker.

'If he puts it over Jimmy Garvin,' argued the second.

'Jimmy Garvin!' cried the third. 'He can whip twenty Jimmy Garvins with his feet tied. I tell you – '

'I am loath,' observed Psmith, 'to interrupt this very impressive brain-barbecue, but, trivial as it may seem to you, to me there is a certain interest in this other little matter of my ruined hat. I know that it may strike you

as hypersensitive of us to protest against being riddled
with bullets, but – '

'Well, what's bin doin'?' inquired the Force. It was a
nuisance, this perpetual harping on trifles when the deep
question of the light-weight Championship of the World
was under discussion, but the sooner it was attended to,
the sooner it would be over.

Billy Windsor undertook to explain.

'The Three Points laid for us,' he said. 'Jack Repetto
was bossing the crowd. I don't know who the rest were.
The Kid put one over on to Jack Repetto's chin, and we
were asking him a few questions when the rest came
back, and started into shooting. Then we got to cover
quick, and you came up and they beat it.'

'That,' said Psmith, nodding, 'is a very fair *précis* of
the evening's events. We should like you, if you will be
so good, to corral this Comrade Repetto, and see that he
buys me a new hat.'

'We'll round Jack up,' said one of the policemen
indulgently.

'Do it nicely,' urged Psmith. 'Don't go hurting his
feelings.'

The second policeman gave it as his opinion that Jack
was getting too gay. The third policeman conceded this.
Jack, he said had shown signs for some time past of asking
for it in the neck. It was an error on Jack's part, he gave
his hearers to understand, to assume that the lid was
completely off the great city of New York.

'Too blamed fresh he's gettin',' the trio agreed. They
could not have been more disapproving if they had been
prefects at Haileybury and Mr Repetto a first-termer who
had been detected in the act of wearing his cap on the
back of his head.

They seemed to think it was too bad of Jack.

'The wrath of the Law,' said Psmith, 'is very terrible.
We will leave the matter, then, in your hands. In the
meantime, we should be glad if you would direct us to

the nearest Subway station. Just at the moment, the
cheerful lights of the Great White Way are what I seem
chiefly to need.'

17 — Guerilla Warfare

Thus ended the opening engagement of the campaign, seemingly in a victory for the *Cosy Moments* army. Billy Windsor, however, shook his head.

'We've got mighty little out of it,' he said.

'The victory,' said Psmith, 'was not bloodless. Comrade Brady's ear, my hat – these are not slight casualties. On the other hand, surely we are one up? Surely we have gained ground? The elimination of Comrade Repetto from the scheme of things in itself is something. I know few men I would not rather meet in a lonely road than Comrade Repetto. He is one of Nature's sand-baggers. Probably the thing crept upon him slowly. He started, possibly, in a merely tentative way by slugging one of the family circle. His nurse, let us say, or his young brother. But, once started, he is unable to resist the craving. The thing grips him like dram-drinking. He sandbags now not because he really wants to, but because he cannot help himself. To me there is something singularly consoling in the thought that Comrade Repetto will no longer be among those present.'

'What makes you think that?'

'I should imagine that a benevolent Law will put him away in his little cell for at least a brief spell.'

'Not on your life,' said Billy. 'He'll prove an alibi.'

Psmith's eyeglass dropped out of his eye. He replaced it, and gazed, astonished, at Billy.

'An alibi? When three keen-eyed men actually caught him at it?'

'He can find thirty toughs to swear he was five miles away.'

'And get the court to believe it?' said Psmith.

'Sure,' said Billy disgustedly. 'You don't catch them hurting a gangsman unless they're pushed against the wall. The politicians don't want the gangs in gaol, especially as the Aldermanic elections will be on in a few weeks. Did you ever hear of Monk Eastman?'

'I fancy not, Comrade Windsor. If I did, the name has escaped me. Who was this cleric?'

'He was the first boss of the East Side gang, before Kid Twist took it on.'

'Yes?'

'He was arrested dozens of times, but he always got off. Do you know what he said once, when they pulled him for thugging a fellow out in New Jersey?'

'I fear not, Comrade Windsor. Tell me all.'

'He said, "You're arresting me, huh? Say, you want to look where you're goin'; I cut some ice in this town. I made half the big politicians in New York!" That was what he said.'

'His small-talk,' said Psmith, 'seems to have been bright and well-expressed. What happened then? Was he restored to his friends and his relations?'

'Sure, he was. What do you think? Well, Jack Repetto isn't Monk Eastman, but he's in with Spider Reilly, and the Spider's in with the men behind. Jack'll get off.'

'It looks to me, Comrade Windsor,' said Psmith thoughtfully, 'as if my stay in this great city were going to cost me a small fortune in hats.'

Billy's prophecy proved absolutely correct. The police were as good as their word. In due season they rounded up the impulsive Mr Repetto, and he was haled before a magistrate. And then, what a beautiful exhibition of brotherly love and auld-lang-syne camaraderie was witnessed! One by one, smirking sheepishly, but giving out their evidence with unshaken earnestness, eleven greasy, wandering-eyed youths mounted the witness-stand and affirmed on oath that at the time mentioned dear old Jack had been making merry in their company in a genial and law-abiding fashion, many, many blocks below the scene of the regrettable assault. The magistrate discharged the prisoner, and the prisoner, meeting Billy and Psmith in the street outside, leered triumphantly at them.

Billy stepped up to him. 'You may have wriggled out of this,' he said furiously, 'but if you don't get a move on and quit looking at me like that, I'll knock you over the Singer Building. Hump yourself.'

Mr Repetto humped himself.

So was victory turned into defeat, and Billy's jaw became squarer and his eye more full of the light of battle than ever. And there was need of a square jaw and a battlelit eye, for now began a period of guerilla warfare such as no New York paper had ever had to fight against.

It was Wheeler, the gaunt manager of the business side of the journal, who first brought it to the notice of the editorial staff. Wheeler was a man for whom in business hours nothing existed but his job; and his job was to look after the distribution of the paper. As to the contents of the paper he was absolutely ignorant. He had been with *Cosy Moments* from its start, but he had never read a line of it. He handled it as if it were so much soap. The scholarly writings of Mr Wilberfloss, the mirth-provoking sallies of Mr B. Henderson Asher, the tender outpourings of Luella Granville Waterman – all these were things outside his ken. He was a distributor, and he distributed.

A few days after the restoration of Mr Repetto to East Side Society, Mr Wheeler came into the editorial room with information and desire for information.

He endeavoured to satisfy the latter first.

'What's doing, anyway?' he asked. He then proceeded to his information. 'Someone's got it in against the paper, sure,' he said. 'I don't know what it's all about. I ha'n't never read the thing. Don't see what any one could have against a paper with a name like *Cosy Moments*, anyway.

The way things have been going last few days, seems it might be the organ of a blamed mining-camp what the boys have took a dislike to.'

'What's been happening?' asked Billy with gleaming eyes.

'Why, nothing in the world to fuss about, only our carriers can't go out without being beaten up by gangs of toughs. Pat Harrigan's in the hospital now. Just been looking in on him. Pat's a feller who likes to fight. Rather fight he would than see a ball-game. But this was too much for him. Know what happened? Why, see here, just like this it was. Pat goes out with his cart. Passing through a low-down street on his way up-town he's held up by a bunch of toughs. He shows fight. Half a dozen of them attend to him, while the rest gets clean away with every copy of the paper there was in the cart. When the cop comes along, there's Pat in pieces on the ground and nobody in sight but a Dago chewing gum. Cop asks the Dago what's been doing, and the Dago says he's only just come round the corner and ha'n't seen nothing of anybody. What I want to know is, what's it all about? Who's got it in for us and why?'

Mr Wheeler leaned back in his chair, while Billy, his hair rumpled more than ever and his eyes glowing, explained the situation. Mr Wheeler listened absolutely unmoved, and, when the narrative had come to an end, gave it as his opinion that the editorial staff had sand. That was his sole comment.

'It's up to you,' he said, rising. 'You know your business. Say, though, someone had better get busy right quick and do something to stop these guys rough-housing like this. If we get a few more carriers beat up the way Pat was, there'll be a strike. It's not as if they were all Irishmen. The most of them are Dagoes and such, and they don't want any more fight than they can get by beating their wives and kicking kids off the sidewalk. I'll do my best to get this paper distributed right and it's a shame if it ain't, because it's going big just now – but it's up to you. Good day, gents.'

He went out. Psmith looked at Billy.

'As Comrade Wheeler remarks,' he said, 'it is up to us. What do you propose to do about it? This is a move of the enemy which I have not anticipated. I had fancied that their operations would be confined exclusively to our two selves. If they are going to strew the street with our carriers, we are somewhat in the soup.'

Billy said nothing. He was chewing the stem of an unlighted pipe. Psmith went on.

'It means, of course, that we must buck up to a certain extent. If the campaign is to be a long one, they have us where the hair is crisp. We cannot stand the strain. *Cosy Moments* cannot be muzzled, but it can undoubtedly be choked. What we want to do is to find out the name of the man behind the tenements as soon as ever we can and publish it; and, then, if we perish, fall yelling the name.'

Billy admitted the soundness of this scheme, but wished to know how it was to be done.

'Comrade Windsor,' said Psmith. 'I have been thinking this thing over, and it seems to me that we are on the wrong track, or rather we aren't on any track at all; we are simply marking time. What we want to do is to go out and hustle round till we stir up something. Our line up to the present has been to sit at home and scream vigorously in the hope of some stout fellow hearing and rushing to help. In other words, we've been saying in the paper what an out-size in scugs the merchant must be who owns those tenements, in the hope that somebody else will agree with us and be sufficiently interested to get to work and find out who the blighter is. That's all wrong. What we must do now, Comrade Windsor, is put on our hats, such hats as Comrade Repetto has left us, and sally forth as sleuth-hounds on our own account.'

'Yes, but how?' demanded Billy. 'That's all right in theory, but how's it going to work in practice? The only thing that can corner the man is a commission.'

'Far from it, Comrade Windsor. The job may be worked more simply. I don't know how often the rents are collected in these places, but I should say at a venture once a week. My idea is to hang negligently round till the rent-collector arrives, and when he has loomed upon the horizon, buttonhole him and ask him quite politely, as man to man, whether he is collecting those rents for himself or for somebody else, and if somebody else, who that somebody else is. Simple, I fancy? Yet brainy. Do you take me, Comrade Windsor?'

Billy sat up, excited. 'I believe you've hit it.'

Psmith shot his cuffs modestly.

18 — An Episode by the Way

It was Pugsy Maloney who, on the following morning, brought to the office the gist of what is related in this chapter. Pugsy's version was, however, brief and unadorned, as was the way with his narratives. Such things as first causes and piquant details he avoided, as tending to prolong the telling excessively, thus keeping him from perusal of his cowboy stories. The way Pugsy put it was as follows. He gave the thing out merely as an item of general interest, a bubble on the surface of the life of a great city. He did not know how nearly interested were his employers in any matter touching that gang which is known as the Three Points. Pugsy said: 'Dere's trouble down where I live. Dude Dawson's mad at Spider Reilly, an' now de Table Hills are layin' for de T'ree Points. Sure.' He had then retired to his outer fastness, yielding further details jerkily and with the distrait air of one whose mind is elsewhere.

Skilfully extracted and pieced together, these details formed themselves into the following typical narrative of East Side life in New York.

The really important gangs of New York are four. There are other less important institutions, but these are little more than mere friendly gatherings of old boyhood chums for purposes of mutual companionship. In time they may grow, as did Bat Jarvis's coterie, into formidable organizations, for the soil is undoubtedly propitious to such growth. But at present the amount of ice which good judges declare them to cut is but small. They 'stick up' an occasional wayfarer for his 'cush', and they carry 'canisters' and sometimes fire them off, but these things do not signify the cutting of ice. In matters political there are only four gangs which count, the East Side, the Groome Street, the Three Points, and the Table Hill. Greatest of these by virtue of their numbers are the East Side and the Groome Street, the latter presided over at the time of this story by Mr Bat Jarvis. These two are colossal, and, though they may fight each other, are immune from attack at the hands of lesser gangs. But between the other gangs, and especially between the Table Hill and the Three Points which are much of a size, warfare rages as briskly as among the republics of South America. There has always been bad blood between the Table Hill and the Three Points, and until they wipe each other out after the manner of the Kilkenny cats, it is probable that there always will be. Little events, trifling in themselves, have always occurred to shatter friendly relations just when there has seemed a chance of their being formed. Thus, just as the Table Hillites were beginning to forgive the Three Points for shooting the redoubtable Paul Horgan down at Coney Island, a Three Pointer injudiciously wiped out another of the rival gang near Canal Street. He pleaded self-defence, and in any case it was probably mere thoughtlessness, but nevertheless the Table Hillites were ruffled.

That had been a month or so back. During that month things had been simmering down, and peace was just preparing to brood when there occurred the incident to which Pugsy had alluded, the regrettable falling out of Dude Dawson and Spider Reilly at Mr Maginnis's dancing saloon, Shamrock Hall, the same which Bat Jarvis had been called in to protect in the days before the Groome Street gang began to be.

Shamrock Hall, being under the eyes of the great Bat, was, of course, forbidden ground; and it was with no intention of spoiling the harmony of the evening that Mr Dawson had looked in. He was there in a purely private and peaceful character.

As he sat smoking, sipping, and observing the revels, there settled at the next table Mr Robert ('Nigger') Coston, an eminent member of the Three Points.

There being temporary peace between the two gangs, the great men exchanged a not unfriendly nod and, after a short pause, a word or two. Mr Coston, alluding to an Italian who had just pirouetted past, remarked that there sure was some class to the way that wop hit it up. Mr Dawson said Yup, there sure was. You would have said that all Nature smiled.

Alas! The next moment the sky was covered with black clouds and the storm broke. For Mr Dawson, continuing in this vein of criticism, rather injudiciously gave it as his opinion that one of the lady dancers had two left feet.

For a moment Mr Coston did not see which lady was alluded to.

'De goil in de pink skoit,' said Mr Dawson, facilitating the other's search by pointing with a much-chewed cigarette. It was at this moment that Nature's smile was shut off as if by a tap. For the lady in the pink skirt had been in receipt of Mr Coston's respectful devotion for the past eight days.

From this point onwards the march of events was rapid.

Mr Coston, rising, asked Mr Dawson who he thought he, Mr Dawson, was.

Mr Dawson, extinguishing his cigarette and placing it behind his ear, replied that he was the fellow who could bite his, Mr Coston's, head off.

Mr Coston said: 'Huh?'

Mr Dawson said: 'Sure.'

Mr Coston called Mr Dawson a pie-faced rubber-necked four-flusher.

Mr Dawson called Mr Coston a coon.

And that was where the trouble really started.

It was secretly a great grief to Mr Coston that his skin

was of so swarthy a hue. To be permitted to address Mr
Coston face to face by his nickname was a sign of the
closest friendship, to which only Spider Reilly, Jack
Repetto, and one or two more of the gang could aspire.
Others spoke of him as Nigger, or, more briefly, Nig –
strictly behind his back. For Mr Coston had a wide
reputation as a fighter, and his particular mode of
battling was to descend on his antagonist and bite him.
Into this action he flung himself with the passionate
abandonment of the artist. When he bit he bit. He did not
nibble.

If a friend had called Mr Coston 'Nig' he would have
been running grave risks. A stranger, and a leader of a
rival gang, who addressed him as 'coon' was more than
asking for trouble. He was pleading for it.

Great men seldom waste time. Mr Coston, leaning
towards Mr Dawson, promptly bit him on the cheek. Mr
Dawson bounded from his seat. Such was the excitement
of the moment that, instead of drawing his 'canister',
he forgot that he had one on his person, and, seizing a
mug which had held beer, bounced it vigorously on Mr
Coston's skull, which, being of solid wood, merely gave
out a resonant note and remained unbroken.

So far the honours were comparatively even, with
perhaps a slight balance in favour of Mr Coston. But now
occurred an incident which turned the scale, and made
war between the gangs inevitable. In the far corner of
the room, surrounded by a crowd of admiring friends, sat
Spider Reilly, monarch of the Three Points. He had
noticed that there was a slight disturbance at the other
side of the hall, but had given it little attention till, the
dancing ceasing suddenly and the floor emptying itself of
its crowd, he had a plain view of Mr Dawson and Mr
Coston squaring up at each other for the second round.
We must assume that Mr Reilly was not thinking what
he did, for his action was contrary to all rules of gang-
etiquette. In the street it would have been perfectly

legitimate, even praiseworthy, but in a dance-hall belonging to a neutral power it was unpardonable.

What he did was to produce his 'canister' and pick off the unsuspecting Mr Dawson just as that exquisite was preparing to get in some more good work with the beer-mug. The leader of the Table Hillites fell with a crash, shot through the leg; and Spider Reilly, together with Mr Coston and others of the Three Points, sped through the doorway for safety, fearing the wrath of Bat Jarvis, who, it was known, would countenance no such episodes at the dance-hall which he had undertaken to protect.

Mr Dawson, meanwhile, was attended to and helped home. Willing informants gave him the name of his aggressor, and before morning the Table Hill camp was in ferment. Shooting broke out in three places, though there were no casualties. When the day dawned there existed between the two gangs a state of war more bitter than any in their record; for this time it was no question of obscure nonentities. Chieftain had assaulted chieftain; royal blood had been spilt.

'Comrade Windsor,' said Psmith, when Master Maloney had spoken his last word, 'we must take careful note of this little matter. I rather fancy that sooner or later we may be able to turn it to our profit. I am sorry for Dude Dawson, anyhow. Though I have never met him, I have a sort of instinctive respect for him. A man such as he would feel a bullet through his trouser-leg more than one of common clay who cared little how his clothes looked.'

19 — In Pleasant Street

Careful inquiries, conducted incognito by Master
Maloney among the denizens of Pleasant Street, brought
the information that rents in the tenements were
collected not weekly but monthly, a fact which must
undoubtedly cause a troublesome hitch in the campaign.
Rent-day, announced Pugsy, fell on the last day of the
month.

'I rubbered around,' he said, 'and did de sleut' act,
and I finds t'ings out. Dere's a feller comes round 'bout
supper time dat day, an' den it's up to de fam'lies what
lives in de tenements to dig down into deir jeans fer de
stuff, or out dey goes dat same night.'

'Evidently a hustler, our nameless friend,' said Psmith.

'I got dat from a kid what knows anuder kid what lives
dere,' explained Master Maloney. 'Say,' he proceeded
confidentially, 'dat kid's in bad, sure he is. Dat second
kid, de one what lives dere. He's a wop kid, an – '

'A what, Comrade Maloney?'

'A wop. A Dago. Why, don't you get next? Why, an
Italian. Sure, dat's right. Well, dis kid, he is sure to be
bad, 'cos his father come over from Italy to work on de
Subway.'

'I don't see why that puts him in bad,' said Billy
Windsor wonderingly.

'Nor I,' agreed Psmith. 'Your narratives, Comrade
Maloney, always seem to me to suffer from a certain lack
of construction. You start at the end, and then you go
back to any portion of the story which happens to appeal
to you at the moment, eventually winding up at the
beginning. Why should the fact that this stripling's

306

father has come over from Italy to work on the Subway be a misfortune?'

'Why, sure, because he got fired an' went an' swatted de foreman one on de coco, an' de magistrate gives him t'oity days.'

'And then, Comrade Maloney? This thing is beginning to get clearer. You are like Sherlock Holmes. After you've explained a thing from start to finish – or, as you prefer to do, from finish to start – it becomes quite simple.'

'Why, den dis kid's in bad for fair, 'cos der ain't nobody to pungle de bones – '

'Pungle de what, Comrade Maloney?'

'De bones. De stuff. Dat's right. De dollars. He's all alone, dis kid, so when de rent-guy blows in, who's to slip him over de simoleons? It'll be outside for his, quick.'

Billy warmed up at this tale of distress in his usual way. 'Somebody ought to do something. It's a vile shame the kid being turned out like that.'

'We will see to it, Comrade Windsor. *Cosy Moments* shall step in. We will combine business with pleasure, paying the stripling's rent and corralling the rent-collector at the same time. What is today? How long before the end of the month? Another week! A murrain on it, Comrade Windsor. Two murrains. This delay may undo us.'

But the days went by without any further movement on the part of the enemy. A strange quiet seemed to be brooding over the other camp. As a matter of fact, the sudden outbreak of active hostilities with the Table Hill contingent had had the effect of taking the minds of Spider Reilly and his warriors off *Cosy Moments* and its affairs, much as the unexpected appearance of a mad bull would make a man forget that he had come out butterfly-hunting. Psmith and Billy could wait; they were not likely to take the offensive; but the Table Hillites demanded instant attention.

War had broken out, as was usual between the gangs,

in a somewhat tentative fashion at first sight. There had been sniping and skirmishes by the wayside, but as yet no pitched battle. The two armies were sparring for an opening.

The end of the week arrived, and Psmith and Billy, conducted by Master Maloney, made their way to Pleasant Street. To get there it was necessary to pass through a section of the enemy's country; but the perilous passage was safely negotiated. The expedition reached its unsavoury goal intact.

The wop kid, whose name, it appeared, was Giuseppe Orloni, inhabited a small room at the very top of the building next to the one Psmith and Mike had visited on their first appearance in Pleasant Street. He was out when the party, led by Pugsy up dark stairs, arrived; and, on returning, seemed both surprised and alarmed to see visitors. Pugsy undertook to do the honours. Pugsy as interpreted was energetic but not wholly successful. He appeared to have a fixed idea that the Italian language was one easily mastered by the simple method of saying 'da' instead of 'the', and tacking on a final 'a' to any word that seemed to him to need one.

'Say, kid,' he began, 'has da rent-a-man come yet-a?'

The black eyes of the wop kid clouded. He gesticulated, and said something in his native language.

'He hasn't got next,' reported Master Maloney. 'He can't git on to me curves. Dese wop kids is all boneheads. Say, kid, look-a here.' He walked out of the room and closed the door; then, rapping on it smartly from the outside, re-entered and, assuming a look of extreme ferocity, stretched out his hand and thundered: 'Unbelt-a: Slip-a me da stuff!'

The wop kid's puzzlement became pathetic.

'This,' said Psmith, deeply interested, 'is getting about as tense as anything I ever struck. Don't give in, Comrade Maloney. Who knows but that you may yet win through?

I fancy the trouble is that your too perfect Italian accent is making the youth home-sick. Once more to the breach, Comrade Maloney.'

Master Maloney made a gesture of disgust. 'I'm t'roo. Dese Dagoes makes me tired. Dey don't know enough to go upstairs to take de Elevated. Beat it, you mutt,' he observed with moody displeasure to the wop kid, accompanying the words with a gesture which conveyed its own meaning. The wop kid, plainly glad to get away, slipped out of the door like a shadow.

Pugsy shrugged his shoulders.

'Gents,' he said resignedly, 'it's up to youse.'

'I fancy,' said Psmith, 'that this is one of those moments when it is necessary for me to unlimber my Sherlock Holmes system. As thus. If the rent collector *had* been here, it is certain, I think, that Comrade Spaghetti, or whatever you said his name was, wouldn't have been. That is to say, if the rent collector had called and found no money waiting for him, surely Comrade Spaghetti would have been out in the cold night instead of under his own roof-tree. Do you follow me, Comrade Maloney?'

'That's right,' said Billy Windsor. 'Of course.'

'Elementary, my dear Watson, elementary,' murmured Psmith.

'So all we have to do is to sit here and wait.'

'All?' said Psmith sadly. 'Surely it is enough. For of all the scaly localities I have struck this seems to me the scaliest. The architect of this Stately Home of America seems to have had a positive hatred of windows. His idea of ventilation was to leave a hole in the wall about the size of a lima bean and let the thing go at that. If our friend does not arrive shortly, I shall pull down the roof. Why, gadzooks! Not to mention stap my vitals! Isn't that a trap-door up there? Make a long-arm, Comrade Windsor.'

Billy got on a chair and pulled the bolt. The trap-door

opened downwards. It fell, disclosing a square of deep blue sky.

'Gum!' he said. 'Fancy living in this atmosphere when you don't have to. Fancy these fellows keeping that shut all the time.'

'I expect it is an acquired taste,' said Psmith, 'like Limburger cheese. They don't begin to appreciate air till it is thick enough to scoop chunks out of with a spoon. Then they get up on their hind legs and inflate their chests and say, "This is fine! This beats ozone hollow!" Leave it open, Comrade Windsor. And now, as to the problem of dispensing with Comrade Maloney's services?'

'Sure,' said Billy. 'Beat it, Pugsy, my lad.'

Pugsy looked up, indignant.

'Beat it?' he queried.

'While your shoe leather's good,' said Billy. 'This is no place for a minister's son. There may be a rough house in here any minute, and you would be in the way.'

'I want to stop and pipe de fun,' objected Master Maloney.

'Never mind. Cut off. We'll tell you all about it tomorrow.'

Master Maloney prepared reluctantly to depart. As he did so there was a sound of a well-shod foot on the stairs, and a man in a snuff-coloured suit, wearing a brown Homburg hat and carrying a small notebook in one hand, walked briskly into the room. It was not necessary for Psmith to get his Sherlock Holmes system to work. His whole appearance proclaimed the newcomer to be the long-expected collector of rents.

20 — Cornered

He stood in the doorway looking with some surprise at the group inside. He was a smallish, pale-faced man with protruding eyes and teeth which gave him a certain resemblance to a rabbit.

'Hello,' he said.

'Welcome to New York,' said Psmith.

Master Maloney, who had taken advantage of the interruption to edge farther into the room, now appeared to consider the question of his departure permanently shelved. He sidled to a corner and sat down on an empty soap-box with the air of a dramatic critic at the opening night of a new play. The scene looked good to him. It promised interesting developments. Master Maloney was an earnest student of the drama, as exhibited in the theatres of the East Side, and few had ever applauded the hero of 'Escaped from Sing-Sing', or hissed the villain of 'Nellie, the Beautiful Cloak-Model' with more fervour than he. He liked his drama to have plenty of action, and to his practised eye this one promised well. Psmith he looked upon as a quite amiable lunatic, from whom little was to be expected; but there was a set expression on Billy Windsor's face which suggested great things.

His pleasure was abruptly quenched. Billy Windsor, placing a firm hand on his collar, led him to the door and pushed him out, closing the door behind him.

The rent collector watched these things with a puzzled eye. He now turned to Psmith.

'Say, seen anything of the wops that live here?' he inquired.

'I am addressing – ?' said Psmith courteously.

'My name's Gooch.'

Psmith bowed.

'Touching these wops, Comrade Gooch,' he said, 'I fear there is little chance of your seeing them tonight, unless you wait some considerable time. With one of them – the son and heir of the family, I should say – we have just been having a highly interesting and informative chat. Comrade Maloney, who has just left us, acted as interpreter. The father, I am told, is in the dungeon below the castle moat for a brief spell for punching his foreman in the eye. The result? The rent is not forthcoming.'

'Then it's outside for theirs,' said Mr Gooch definitely.

'It's a big shame,' broke in Billy, 'turning the kid out. Where's he to go?'

'That's up to him. Nothing to do with me. I'm only acting under orders from up top.'

'Whose orders, Comrade Gooch?' inquired Psmith.

'The gent who owns this joint.'

'Who is he?' said Billy.

Suspicion crept into the protruding eyes of the rent collector. He waxed wroth.

'Say!' he demanded. 'Who are you two guys, anyway, and what do you think you're doing here? That's what I'd like to know. What do you want with the name of the owner of this place? What business is it of yours?'

'The fact is, Comrade Gooch, we are newspaper men.'

'I guessed you were,' said Mr Gooch with triumph. 'You can't bluff me. Well, it's no good, boys. I've nothing for you. You'd better chase off and try something else.'

He became more friendly.

'Say, though,' he said, 'I just guessed you were from some paper. I wish I could give you a story, but I can't. I guess it's this *Cosy Moments* business that's been and put your editor on to this joint, ain't it? Say, though, that's a queer thing, that paper. Why, only a few weeks ago it used to be a sort of take-home-and-read-to-the-kids affair. A friend of mine used to buy it regular. And then suddenly it comes out with a regular whoop, and started knocking these tenements and boosting Kid Brady, and all that. I can't understand it. All I know is that it's begun to get this place talked about. Why, you see for yourselves how it is. Here is your editor sending you down to get a story about it. But, say, those *Cosy Moments* guys are taking big risks. I tell you straight they are, and that goes. I happen to know a thing or two about what's going on on the other side, and I tell you there's going to be something doing if they don't cut it out quick. Mr – ' he stopped and chuckled, 'Mr – Jones isn't the man to sit still and smile. He's going to get busy. Say, what paper do you boys come from?'

'*Cosy Moments*, Comrade Gooch,' Psmith replied. 'Immediately behind you, between you and the door, is Comrade Windsor, our editor. I am Psmith. I sub-edit.'

For a moment the inwardness of the information did not seem to come home to Mr Gooch. Then it hit him. He spun round. Billy Windsor was standing with his back against the door and a more than nasty look on his face.

'What's all this?' demanded Mr Gooch.

'I will explain all,' said Psmith soothingly. 'In the first place, however, this matter of Comrade Spaghetti's rent. Sooner than see that friend of my boyhood slung out to do the wandering-child-in-the-show act, I will brass up for him.'

'Confound his rent. Let me out.'

'Business before pleasure. How much is it? Twelve dollars? For the privilege of suffocating in this compact little Black Hole? By my halidom, Comrade Gooch, that gentleman whose name you are so shortly to tell us has a very fair idea of how to charge! But who am I that I should criticize? Here are the simoleons, as our young friend, Comrade Maloney, would call them. Push me over a receipt.'

'Let me out.'

'Anon, gossip, anon. – Shakespeare. First, the receipt.'

Mr Gooch scribbled a few words in his notebook and tore out the page. Psmith thanked him

'I will see that it reaches Comrade Spaghetti,' he said. 'And now to a more important matter. Don't put away that notebook. Turn to a clean page, moisten your pencil, and write as follows. Are you ready? By the way, what is your Christian name? . . . Gooch, Gooch, this is no way to speak! Well, if you are sensitive on the point, we will waive the Christian name. It is my duty to tell you, however, that I suspect it to be Percy. Let us push on. Are you ready, once more? Pencil moistened? Very well, then. "I" – comma – "being of sound mind and body" – comma – "and a bright little chap altogether" – comma – Why you're not writing.'

'Let me out,' bellowed Mr Gooch. 'I'll summon you for assault and battery. Playing a fool game like this! Get away from that door.'

'There has been no assault and battery – yet, Comrade Gooch, but who shall predict how long so happy a state of things will last? Do not be deceived by our gay and smiling faces, Comrade Gooch. We mean business. Let me put the whole position of affairs before you; and I am sure a man of your perception will see that there is only one thing to be done.'

He dusted the only chair in the room with infinite care and sat down. Billy Windsor, who had not spoken a word or moved an inch since the beginning of the interview, continued to stand and be silent. Mr Gooch shuffled restlessly in the middle of the room.

'As you justly observed a moment ago,' said Psmith, 'the staff of *Cosy Moments* is taking big risks. We do not rely on your unsupported word for that. We have had practical demonstration of the fact from one J. Repetto, who tried some few nights ago to put us out of business. Well, it struck us both that we had better get hold of the name of the blighter who runs these tenements as quickly as possible, before Comrade Repetto's next night out.

That is what we should like you to give us, Comrade
Gooch. And we should like it in writing. And, on second
thoughts, in ink. I have one of those patent non-leakable
fountain pens in my pocket. The Old Journalist's Best
Friend. Most of the ink has come out and is permeating
the lining of my coat, but I think there is still sufficient
for our needs. Remind me later, Comrade Gooch, to
continue on the subject of fountain pens. I have much
to say on the theme. Meanwhile, however, business,
business. That is the cry.'

He produced a pen and an old letter, the last page of
which was blank, and began to write.

'How does this strike you?' he said. ' "I" – (I have left
a blank for the Christian name: you can write it in
yourself later) – "I, blank Gooch, being a collector of rents
in Pleasant Street, New York, do hereby swear" – hush,
Comrade Gooch, there is no need to do it yet – "that the
name of the owner of the Pleasant Street tenements,
who is responsible for the perfectly foul conditions there,
is – " And that is where you come in, Comrade Gooch.
That is where we need your specialized knowledge. Who
is he?'

Billy Windsor reached out and grabbed the rent
collector by the collar. Having done this, he proceeded
to shake him.

Billy was muscular, and his heart was so much in the
business that Mr Gooch behaved as if he had been caught
in a high wind. It is probable that in another moment the
desired information might have been shaken out of him,
but before this could happen there was a banging at the
door, followed by the entrance of Master Maloney. For
the first time since Psmith had known him, Pugsy was
openly excited.

'Say,' he began, 'youse had better beat it quick, you
had. Dey's coming!'

'And now go back to the beginning, Comrade
Maloney,' said Psmith patiently, 'which in the

exuberance of the moment you have skipped. Who are
coming?'

'Why, dem. De guys.'

Psmith shook his head.

'Your habit of omitting essentials, Comrade Maloney,
is going to undo you one of these days. When you get to
that ranch of yours, you will probably start out to gallop
after the cattle without remembering to mount your
mustang. There are four million guys in New York. Which
section is it that is coming?'

'Gum! I don't know how many dere is ob dem. I seen
Spider Reilly an' Jack Repetto an' – '

'Say no more,' said Psmith. 'If Comrade Repetto is
there, that is enough for me. I am going to get on the
roof and pull it up after me.'

Billy released Mr Gooch, who fell, puffing, on to the
low bed, which stood in one corner of the room.

'They must have spotted us as we were coming here,'
he said 'and followed us. Where did you see them,
Pugsy?'

'On de street just outside. Dere was a bunch of dem
talkin' togedder, and I hears dem say you was in here.
One of dem seen you come in, and dere ain't no ways out
but de front, so dey ain't hurryin'! Dey just reckon to pike
along upstairs, lookin into each room till dey finds you.
An dere's a bunch of dem goin' to wait on de street in case
youse beat it past down de stairs while de udder guys is
rubberin' for youse. Say, gents, it's pretty fierce, dis
proposition. What are youse goin' to do?'

Mr Gooch, from the bed, laughed unpleasantly.

'I guess you ain't the only assault-and-batter artists in
the business,' he said. 'Looks to me as if someone else
was going to get shaken up some.'

Billy looked at Psmith.

'Well?' he said, 'What shall we do? Go down and try
and rush through?'

Psmith shook his head.

'Not so, Comrade Windsor, but about as much otherwise as you can jolly well imagine.'

'Well, what then?'

'We will stay here. Or rather we will hop nimbly up on to the roof through that skylight. Once there, we may engage these varlets on fairly equal terms. They can only get through one at a time. And while they are doing it I will give my celebrated imitation of Horatius. We had better be moving. Our luggage, fortunately, is small. Merely Comrade Gooch. If you will get through the skylight, I will pass him up to you.'

Mr Gooch, with much verbal embroidery, stated that he would not go. Psmith acted promptly. Gripping the struggling rent collector round the waist, and ignoring his frantic kicks as mere errors in taste, he lifted him to the trap-door, whence the head, shoulders and arms of Billy Windsor protruded into the room. Billy collected the collector, and then Psmith turned to Pugsy.

'Comrade Maloney.'

'Huh?'

'Have I your ear?'

'Huh?'

'Are you listening till you feel that your ears are the size of footballs? Then drink this in. For weeks you have been praying for a chance to show your devotion to the great cause; or if you haven't, you ought to have been. That chance has come. You alone can save us. In a sense, of course, we do not need to be saved. They will find it hard to get at us, I fancy, on the roof. But it ill befits the dignity of the editorial staff of a great New York weekly to roost like pigeons for any length of time; and consequently it is up to you.'

'Shall I go for de cops, Mr Smith?'

'No, Comrade Maloney, I thank you. I have seen the cops in action, and they did not impress me. We do not want allies who will merely shake their heads at Comrade Repetto and the others, however sternly. We want

someone who will swoop down upon these merry
roisterers, and, as it were, soak to them good. Do you
know where Dude Dawson lives?'

The light of intelligence began to shine in Master
Maloney's face. His eye glistened with respectful
approval. This was strategy of the right sort.

'Dude Dawson? Nope. But I can ask around.'

'Do so, Comrade Maloney. And when found, tell him
that his old college chum, Spider Reilly, is here. He will
not be able to come himself, I fear, but he can send
representatives.'

'Sure.'

'That's all, then. Go downstairs with a gay and jaunty
air, as if you had no connection with the old firm at all.
Whistle a few lively bars. Make careless gestures. Thus
shall you win through. And now it would be no bad idea,
I fancy, for me to join the rest of the brains of the paper
up aloft. Off you go, Comrade Maloney. And, in passing,
don't take a week about it. Leg it with all the speed you
possess.'

Pugsy vanished, and Psmith closed the door behind
him. Inspection revealed the fact that it possessed no
lock. As a barrier it was useless. He left it ajar, and,
jumping up, gripped the edge of the opening in the roof
and pulled himself through.

Billy Windsor was seated comfortably on Mr Gooch's
chest a few feet away. By his side was his big stick.
Psmith possessed himself of this, and looked about him.
The examination was satisfactory. The trap-door
appeared to be the only means of access to the roof, and
between their roof and that of the next house there was
a broad gulf.

'Practically impregnable,' he murmured. 'Only one
thing can dish us, Comrade Windsor; and that is if they
have the sense get on to the roof next door and start
shooting. Even in that case, however, we have cover in the
shape of the chimneys. I think we may fairly say that all

is well. How are you getting along? Has the patient responded at all?'

'Not yet,' said Billy. 'But he's going to.'

'He will be in your charge. I must devote myself exclusively to guarding the bridge. It is a pity that the trap has not got a bolt this side. If it had, the thing would be a perfect picnic. As it is, we must leave it open. But we mustn't expect everything.'

Billy was about to speak, but Psmith suddenly held up his hand warningly. From the room below came a sound of feet.

For a moment the silence was tense. Then from Mr Gooch's lips there escaped a screech.

'This way! They're up – '

The words were cut short as Billy banged his hand over the speaker's mouth. But the thing was done.

'On top de roof,' cried a voice. 'Dey've beaten it for de roof.'

The chair rasped over the floor. Feet shuffled. And then, like a jack-in-the-box, there popped through the opening a head and shoulders.

21 — The Battle of Pleasant Street

The new arrival was a young man with a shock of red hair, an ingrowing Roman nose, and a mouth from which force or the passage of time had removed three front teeth. He held on to the edges of the trap with his hands, and stared in a glassy manner into Psmith's face, which was within a foot of his own.

There was a momentary pause, broken by an oath from Mr Gooch, who was still undergoing treatment in the background.

'Aha!' said Psmith genially. 'Historic picture. "Doctor Cook discovers the North Pole."'

The red-headed young man blinked. The strong light of the open air was trying to his eyes.

'Youse had better come down,' he observed coldly. 'We've got youse.'

'And,' continued Psmith, unmoved, 'is instantly handed a gum-drop by his faithful Esquimau.'

As he spoke, he brought the stick down on the knuckles which disfigured the edges of the trap. The intruder uttered a howl and dropped out of sight. In the room below there were whisperings and mutterings, growing gradually louder till something resembling coherent conversation came to Psmith's ears, as he knelt by the trap making meditative billiard-shots with the stick at a small pebble.

'Aw g'wan! Don't be a quitter!'

'Who's a quitter?'

'Youse a quitter. Get on top de roof. He can't hoit youse.'

'De guy's gotten a big stick.'

320

Psmith nodded appreciatively.

'I and Roosevelt,' he murmured.

A somewhat baffled silence on the part of the attacking force was followed by further conversation.

'Gum! some guy's got to go up.'

Murmur of assent from the audience.

A voice, in inspired tones: 'Let Sam do it!'

This suggestion made a hit. There was no doubt about that. It was a success from the start. Quite a little chorus of voices expressed sincere approval of the very happy solution, to what had seemed an insoluble problem. Psmith, listening from above, failed to detect in the choir of glad voices one that might belong to Sam himself. Probably gratification had rendered the chosen one dumb.

'Yes, let Sam do it!' cried the unseen chorus. The first speaker, unnecessarily, perhaps – for the motion had been carried almost unanimously – but possibly with the idea of convincing the one member of the party in whose bosom doubts might conceivably be harboured, went on to adduce reasons.

'Sam bein' a coon,' he argued, 'ain't goin' to git hoit by no stick. Youse can't hoit a coon by soakin' him on de coco, can you, Sam?'

Psmith waited with some interest for the reply, but it did not come. Possibly Sam did not wish to generalize on insufficient experience.

'*Solvitur ambulando*,' said Psmith softly, turning the stick round in his fingers. 'Comrade Windsor!'

'Is it possible to hurt a coloured gentleman by hitting him on the head with a stick?'

'If you hit him hard enough.'

'I knew there was some way out of the difficulty,' said Psmith with satisfaction. 'How are you getting on up at your end of the table, Comrade Windsor?'

'Fine.'

'Any result yet?'

'Not at present.'

'Don't give up.'

'Not me.'

'The right spirit, Comrade Win – '

A report like a cannon in the room below interrupted him. It was merely a revolver shot, but in the confined space it was deafening. The bullet sang up into the sky.

'Never hit me!' said Psmith with dignified triumph.

The noise was succeeded by a shuffling of feet. Psmith grasped his stick more firmly. This was evidently the real attack. The revolver shot had been a mere demonstration of artillery to cover the infantry's advance.

Sure enough, the next moment a woolly head popped through the opening, and a pair of rolling eyes gleamed up at the old Etonian.

'Why, Sam!' said Psmith cordially, 'this is well met! I remember *you*. Yes, indeed, I do. Wasn't you the feller with the open umbereller that I met one rainy morning on the Av-en-ue? What, are you coming up? Sam, I hate to do it, but – '

A yell rang out.

'What was that?' asked Billy Windsor over his shoulder.

'Your statement, Comrade Windsor, has been tested and proved correct.'

By this time the affair had begun to draw a 'gate.' The noise of the revolver had proved a fine advertisement. The roof of the house next door began to fill up. Only a few occupants could get a clear view of the proceedings, for a large chimney-stack intervened. There was considerable speculation as to what was passing between Billy Windsor and Mr Gooch. Psmith's share in the entertainment was more obvious. The early comers had seen his interview with Sam, and were relating it with gusto to their friends. Their attitude towards Psmith was that of a group of men watching a terrier at a rat-hole. They looked to him to provide entertainment for them, but they realized that the first move must be with the attackers. They were fairminded men, and they did not expect Psmith to make any aggressive move.

Their indignation, when the proceedings began to grow slow, was directed entirely at the dilatory Three Pointers. With an aggrieved air, akin to that of a crowd at a cricket match when batsmen are playing for a draw, they began to 'barrack'. They hooted the Three Pointers. They begged them to go home and tuck themselves up in bed. The men on the roof were mostly Irishmen, and it offended them to see what should have been a spirited fight so grossly bungled.

'G'wan away home, ye quitters!' roared one.

'Call yersilves the Three Points, do ye? An' would ye know what *I* call ye? The Young Ladies' Seminary!' bellowed another with withering scorn.

A third member of the audience alluded to them as 'stiffs'.

'I fear, Comrade Windsor,' said Psmith, 'that our blithe friends below are beginning to grow a little unpopular with the many-headed. They must be up and doing if they wish to retain the esteem of Pleasant Street. Aha!'

Another and a longer explosion from below, and more bullets wasted themselves on air. Psmith sighed.

'They make me tired,' he said. 'This is no time for a *feu de joie*. Action! That is the cry. Action! Get busy, you blighters!'

The Irish neighbours expressed the same sentiment in different and more forcible words. There was no doubt about it – as warriors, the Three Pointers had failed to give satisfaction.

A voice from the room called up to Psmith.

'Say!'

'You have our ear,' said Psmith.

'What's that?'

'I said you had our ear.'

'Are youse stiffs comin' down off out of dat roof?'

'Would you mind repeating that remark?'

'Are youse guys goin' to quit off out of dat roof?'

'Your grammar is perfectly beastly,' said Psmith severely.

'Hey!'

'Well?'

'Are youse guys – ?'

'No, my lad,' said Psmith, 'since you ask, we are not. And why? Because the air up here is refreshing, the view pleasant, and we are expecting at any moment an important communication from Comrade Gooch.'

'We're goin' to wait here till youse come down.'

'If you wish it,' said Psmith courteously, 'by all means do. Who am I that I should dictate your movements? The most I aspire to is to check them when they take an upward direction.'

There was silence below. The time began to pass slowly. The Irishmen on the other roof, now definitely abandoning hope of further entertainment, proceeded with hoots of scorn to climb down one by one into the recesses of their own house.

Suddenly from the street far below there came a fusillade of shots and a babel of shouts and counter-shouts. The roof of the house next door, which had been emptying itself slowly and reluctantly, filled again with a magical swiftness, and the low wall facing into the street became black with the backs of those craning over.

'What's that?' inquired Billy.

'I rather fancy,' said Psmith, 'that our allies of the Table Hill contingent must have arrived. I sent Comrade Maloney to explain matters to Dude Dawson, and it seems as if that golden-hearted sportsman has responded. There appear to be great doings in the street.'

In the room below confusion had arisen. A scout, clattering upstairs, had brought the news of the Table Hillites' advent, and there was doubt as to the proper course to pursue. Certain voices urged going down to help the main body. Others pointed out that that would mean abandoning the siege of the roof. The scout who had brought the news was eloquent in favour of the first course.

'Gum!' he cried, 'don't I keep tellin' youse dat de Table Hills is here? Sure, dere's a whole bunch of dem, and unless youse come on down dey'll bite de hull head off of us lot. Leave those stiffs on de roof. Let Sam wait here with his canister, and den dey can't get down, 'cos Sam'll pump dem full of lead while dey're beatin' it t'roo de trap-door. Sure.'

Psmith nodded reflectively.

'There is certainly something in what the bright boy says,' he murmured. 'It seems to me the grand rescue scene in the third act has sprung a leak. This will want thinking over.'

In the street the disturbance had now become terrific. Both sides were hard at it, and the Irishmen on the roof, rewarded at last for their long vigil, were yelling encouragement promiscuously and whooping with the unfettered ecstasy of men who are getting the treat of their lives without having paid a penny for it.

The behaviour of the New York policeman in affairs of this kind is based on principles of the soundest practical wisdom. The unthinking man would rush in and attempt to crush the combat in its earliest and fiercest stages. The New York policeman, knowing the importance of his own safety, and the insignificance of the gangsman's, permits the opposing forces to hammer each other into a certain distaste for battle, and then, when both sides have begun to have enough of it, rushes in himself and clubs everything in sight. It is an admirable process in its results, but it is sure rather than swift.

Proceedings in the affair below had not yet reached the police interference stage. The noise, what with the shots and yells from the street and the ear-piercing approval of the roof-audience, was just working up to a climax.

Psmith rose. He was tired of kneeling by the trap, and

there was no likelihood of Sam making another attempt to climb through. He walked towards Billy.

As he did so, Billy got up and turned to him. His eyes were gleaming with excitement. His whole attitude was triumphant. In his hand he waved a strip of paper.

'I've got it,' he cried.

'Excellent, Comrade Windsor,' said Psmith. 'Surely we must win through now. All we have to do is to get off this roof, and fate cannot touch us. Are two mammoth minds such as ours unequal to such a feat? It can hardly be. Let us ponder.'

'Why not go down through the trap? They've all gone to the street.'

Psmith shook his head.

'All,' he replied, 'save Sam. Sam was the subject of my late successful experiment, when I proved that coloured gentlemen's heads could be hurt with a stick. He is now waiting below, armed with a pistol, ready – even anxious – to pick us off as we climb through the trap. How would it be to drop Comrade Gooch through first, and so draw his fire? Comrade Gooch, I am sure, would be delighted to do a little thing like that for old friends of our standing or – but what's that!'

'What's the matter?'

Is that a ladder that I see before me, its handle to my hand? It is! Comrade Windsor, we win through. *Cosy Moments'* editorial staff may be tree'd, but it cannot be put out of business. Comrade Windsor, take the other end of that ladder and follow me.'

The ladder was lying against the farther wall. It was long, more than enough for the purpose for which it was needed. Psmith and Billy rested it on the coping, and pushed it till the other end reached across the gulf to the roof of the house next door, Mr Gooch eyeing them in silence the while.

Psmith turned to him.

'Comrade Gooch,' he said, 'do nothing to apprise our

friend Sam of these proceedings. I speak in your best interests. Sam is in no mood to make nice distinctions between friend and foe. If you bring him up here, he will probably mistake you for a member of the staff of *Cosy Moments*, and loose off in your direction without waiting for explanations. I think you had better come with us. I will go first, Comrade Windsor, so that if the ladder breaks, the paper will lose merely a sub-editor, not an editor.'

He went down on all-fours, and in this attitude wormed his way across to the opposite roof, whose occupants, engrossed in the fight in the street, in which the police had now joined, had their backs turned and did not observe him. Mr Gooch, pallid and obviously ill-attuned to such feats, followed him; and finally Billy Windsor reached the other side.

'Neat,' said Psmith complacently. 'Uncommonly neat. Comrade Gooch reminded me of the untamed chamois of the Alps, leaping from crag to crag.'

In the street there was now comparative silence. The police, with their clubs, had knocked the last remnant of fight out of the combatants. Shooting had definitely ceased.

'I think,' said Psmith, 'that we might now descend. If you have no other engagements, Comrade Windsor, I will take you to the Knickerbocker, and buy you a square meal. I would ask for the pleasure of your company also, Comrade Gooch, were it not that matters of private moment, relating to the policy of the paper, must be discussed at the table. Some other day, perhaps. We are infinitely obliged to you for your sympathetic cooperation in this little matter. And now good-bye. Comrade Windsor, let us debouch.'

22 — Concerning Mr Waring

Psmith pushed back his chair slightly, stretched out his legs, and lit a cigarette. The resources of the Knickerbocker Hotel had proved equal to supplying the fatigued staff of *Cosy Moments* with an excellent dinner, and Psmith had stoutly declined to talk business until the coffee arrived. This had been hard on Billy, who was bursting with his news. Beyond a hint that it was sensational he had not been permitted to go.

'More bright young careers than I care to think of,' said Psmith, 'have been ruined by the fatal practice of talking shop at dinner. But now that we are through, Comrade Windsor, by all means let us have it. What's the name which Comrade Gooch so eagerly divulged?'

Billy leaned forward excitedly.

'Stewart Waring,' he whispered.

'Stewart who?' asked Psmith.

Billy stared.

'Great Scott, man!' he said, 'haven't you heard of Stewart Waring?'

'The name seems vaguely familiar, like isinglass or Post-toasties. I seem to know it, but it conveys nothing to me.'

'Don't you ever read the papers?'

'I toy with my *American* of a morning, but my interest is confined mainly to the sporting page which reminds me that Comrade Brady has been matched against one Eddie Wood a month from today. Gratifying as it is to find one of the staff getting on in life, I fear this will cause us a certain amount of inconvenience. Comrade Brady will have to leave the office temporarily in order to go into training, and what shall we do then for a fighting-editor? However, possibly we may not need one now. *Cosy Moments* should be able shortly to give its message to the world and ease up for a while. Which brings us back to the point. Who is Stewart Waring?'

'Stewart Waring is running for City Alderman. He's one of the biggest men in New York!'

'Do you mean in girth? If so, he seems to have selected the right career for himself.'

'He's one of the bosses. He used to be Commissioner of Buildings for the city.'

'Commissioner of Buildings? What exactly did that let him in for?'

'It let him in for a lot of graft.'

'How was that?'

'Oh, he took it off the contractors. Shut his eyes and held out his hands when they ran up rotten buildings that a strong breeze would have knocked down, and places like that Pleasant Street hole without any ventilation.'

'Why did he throw up the job?' inquired Psmith. 'It seems to me that it was among the World's Softest. Certain drawbacks to it, perhaps, to the man with the Hair-Trigger Conscience; but I gather that Comrade Waring did not line up in that class. What was his trouble?'

'His trouble,' said Billy, 'was that he stood in with a contractor who was putting up a music-hall, and the contractor put it up with material about as strong as a heap of meringues, and it collapsed on the third night and killed half the audience.'

'And then?'

'The papers raised a howl, and they got after the contractor, and the contractor gave Waring away. It killed him for the time being.'

'I should have thought it would have had that excellent result permanently,' said Psmith thoughtfully. 'Do you mean to say he got back again after that?'

'He had to quit being Commissioner, of course, and leave the town for a time; but affairs move so fast here that a thing like that blows over. He made a bit of a pile out of the job, and could afford to lie low for a year or two.'

'How long ago was that?'

'Five years. People don't remember a thing here that happened five years back unless they're reminded of it.'

Psmith lit another cigarette.

'We will remind them,' he said.

Billy nodded.

'Of course,' he said, 'one or two of the papers against him in this Aldermanic Election business tried to bring the thing up, but they didn't cut any ice. The other papers said it was a shame, hounding a man who was sorry for the past and who was trying to make good now; so they dropped it. Everybody thought that Waring was on the level now. He's been shooting off a lot of hot air lately about philanthropy and so on. Not that he has actually done a thing – not so much as given a supper to a dozen news-boys; but he's talked, and talk gets over if you keep it up long enough.'

Psmith nodded adhesion to this dictum.

'So that naturally he wants to keep it dark about these tenements. It'll smash him at the election when it gets known.'

'Why is he so set on becoming an Alderman?' inquired Psmith.

'There's a lot of graft to being an Alderman,' explained Billy.

'I see. No wonder the poor gentleman was so energetic in his methods. What is our move now, Comrade Windsor?'

Billy stared.

'Why, publish the name, of course.'

'But before then? How are we going to ensure the safety of our evidence? We stand or fall entirely by that slip of paper, because we've got the beggar's name in the writing of his own collector, and that's proof positive.'

'That's all right,' said Billy, patting his breast-pocket. 'Nobody's going to get it from me.'

Psmith dipped his hand into his trouser-pocket.

'Comrade Windsor,' he said, producing a piece of paper, 'how do we go?'

He leaned back in his chair, surveying Billy blandly through his eye-glass. Billy's eyes were goggling. He looked from Psmith to the paper and from the paper to Psmith.

'What – what the – ?' he stammered. 'Why, it's *it*!'

Psmith nodded.

'How on earth did you get it?'

Psmith knocked the ash off his cigarette.

'Comrade Windsor,' he said, 'I do not wish to cavil or carp or rub it in in any way. I will merely remark that you pretty nearly landed us in the soup, and pass on to more congenial topics. Didn't you know we were followed to this place?'

'Followed!'

'By a merchant in what Comrade Maloney would call a tall-shaped hat. I spotted him at an early date, somewhere down by Twenty-ninth Street. When we dived into Sixth Avenue for a space at Thirty-third Street, did he dive, too? He did. And when we turned into Forty-second Street, there he was. I tell you, Comrade Windsor, leeches were aloof, and burrs non-adhesive compared with that tall-shaped-hatted blighter.'

'Yes?'

'Do you remember, as you came to the entrance of this place, somebody knocking against you?'

'Yes, there was a pretty big crush in the entrance.'

'There was; but not so big as all that. There was plenty of room for this merchant to pass if he had wished. Instead of which he butted into you. I happened to be waiting for just that, so I managed to attach myself to

his wrist with some vim and give it a fairly hefty wrench.
The paper was inside his hand.'

Billy was leaning forward with a pale face.

'Jove!' he muttered.

'That about sums it up,' said Psmith

Billy snatched the paper from the table and extended
it towards him.

'Here,' he said feverishly, 'you take it. Gum, I never
thought I was such a mutt! I'm not fit to take charge of
a toothpick. Fancy me not being on the watch for
something of that sort. I guess I was so tickled with
myself at the thought of having got the thing, that it never
struck me they might try for it. But I'm through. No
more for me. You're the man in charge now.'

Psmith shook his head.

'These stately compliments,' he said, 'do my old heart
good, but I fancy I know a better plan. It happened that
I chanced to have my eye on the blighter in the tall-shaped
hat, and so was enabled to land him among the ribstons;
but who knows but that in the crowd on Broadway there
may not lurk others, unidentified blighters in equally
tall-shaped hats, one of whom may work the same sleight-
of-hand speciality on me? It was not that you were not
capable of taking care of that paper: it was simply that
you didn't happen to spot the man. Now observe me
closely, for what follows is an exhibition of Brain.'

He paid the bill, and they went out into the entrance-
hall of the hotel. Psmith, sitting down at a table, placed
the paper in an envelope and addressed it to himself at
the address of *Cosy Moments*. After which, he
stamped the envelope and dropped it into the letter-box
at the back of the hall.

'And now, Comrade Windsor,' he said, 'let us stroll
gently homewards down the Great White Way. What
matter though it be fairly stiff with low-browed bravoes
in tall-shaped hats? They cannot harm us. From me, if
they search me thoroughly, they may scoop a matter of

eleven dollars, a watch, two stamps, and a packet
of chewing-gum. Whether they would do any better with
you I do not know. At any rate, they wouldn't get that
paper; and that's the main thing.'

'You're a genius,' said Billy Windsor.

'You think so?' said Psmith diffidently. 'Well, well,
perhaps you are right, perhaps you are right. Did you
notice the hired ruffian in the flannel suit who just
passed? He wore a slightly baffled look, I fancy. And
hark! Wasn't that a muttered "Failed!" I heard? Or was
it the breeze moaning in the tree-tops? Tonight is a cold,
disappointing night for Hired Ruffians, Comrade
Windsor.'

23 — Reductions in the Staff

The first member of the staff of *Cosy Moments* to arrive
at the office on the following morning was Master
Maloney. This sounds like the beginning of a 'Plod and
Punctuality', or 'How Great Fortunes have been Made'
story; but, as a matter of fact, Master Maloney was no
early bird. Larks who rose in his neighbourhood, rose alone.
He did not get up with them. He was supposed to be at
the office at nine o'clock. It was a point of honour with
him, a sort of daily declaration of independence, never to
put in an appearance before nine-thirty. On this
particular morning he was punctual to the minute, or
half an hour late, whichever way you choose to look at it.

He had only whistled a few bars of 'My Little Irish
Rose', and had barely got into the first page of his story
of life on the prairie when Kid Brady appeared. The Kid,
as was his habit when not in training, was smoking a
big black cigar. Master Maloney eyed him admiringly.
The Kid, unknown to that gentleman himself, was
Pugsy's ideal. He came from the Plains, and had, indeed,
once actually been a cowboy; he was a coming
champion; and he could smoke black cigars. It was,
therefore, without his usual well-what-is-it-now? air
that Pugsy laid down his book, and prepared to converse.

'Say, Mr Smith or Mr Windsor about, Pugsy?' asked
the Kid.

'Naw, Mr Brady, they ain't came yet,' replied Master
Maloney respectfully.

'Late, ain't they?'

'Sure. Mr Windsor generally blows in before I do.'

'Wonder what's keepin' them.'

334

'P'raps, dey've bin put out of business,' suggested Pugsy nonchalantly.

'How's that?'

Pugsy related the events of the previous day, relaxing something of his austere calm as he did so. When he came to the part where the Table Hill allies swooped down on the unsuspecting Three Pointers, he was almost animated.

'Say,' said the Kid approvingly, 'that Smith guy's got more grey matter under his hatch than you'd think to look at him. I – '

'Comrade Brady,' said a voice in the doorway, 'you do me proud.'

'Why, say,' said the Kid, turning, 'I guess the laugh's on me. I didn't see you, Mr Smith. Pugsy's bin tellin' me how you sent him for the Table Hills yesterday. That was cute. It was mighty smart. But say, those guys are goin' some, ain't they now! Seems as if they was dead set on puttin' you out of business.'

'Their manner yesterday, Comrade Brady, certainly suggested the presence of some sketchy outline of such an ideal in their minds. One Sam, in particular, an ebony-hued sportsman, threw himself into the task with great vim. I rather fancy he is waiting for us with his revolver at this moment. But why worry? Here we are, safe and sound, and Comrade Windsor may be expected to arrive at any moment. I see, Comrade Brady, that you have been matched against one Eddie Wood.'

'It's about that I wanted to see you, Mr Smith. Say, now that things have been and brushed up so, what with these gang guys layin' for you the way they're doin', I guess you'll be needin' me around here. Isn't that right? Say the word and I'll call off this Eddie Wood fight.'

'Comrade Brady,' said Psmith with some enthusiasm, 'I call that a sporting offer. I'm very much obliged. But we mustn't stand in your way. If you eliminate this

Comrade Wood, they will have to give you a chance against Jimmy Garvin, won't they?'

'I guess that's right, sir,' said the Kid. 'Eddie stayed nineteen rounds against Jimmy, and if I can put him away, it gets me into line with Jimmy, and he can't side-step me.'

'Then go in and win, Comrade Brady. We shall miss you. It will be as if a ray of sunshine had been removed from the office. But you mustn't throw a chance away. We shall be all right, I think.'

'I'll train at White Plains,' said the Kid. 'That ain't far from here, so I'll be pretty near in case I'm wanted. Hullo, who's here?'

He pointed to the door. A small boy was standing there, holding a note.

'Mr Smith?'

'Sir to you,' said Psmith courteously.

'P. Smith?'

'The same. This is your lucky day.'

'Cop at Jefferson Market give me dis to take to youse.'

'A cop in Jefferson Market?' repeated Psmith. 'I did not know I had friends among the constabulary there. Why, it's from Comrade Windsor.' He opened the envelope and read the letter. 'Thanks,' he said, giving the boy a quarter-dollar.

It was apparent the Kid was politely endeavouring to veil his curiosity. Master Maloney had no such scruples.

'What's in de letter, boss?' he inquired.

'The letter, Comrade Maloney, is from our Mr Windsor, and relates in terse language the following facts, that our editor last night hit a policeman in the eye, and that he was sentenced this morning to thirty days on Blackwell's Island.'

'He's de guy!' admitted Master Maloney approvingly.

'What's that?' said the Kid. 'Mr Windsor bin punchin' cops! What's he bin doin' that for?'

'He gives no clue. I must go and find out. Could you

336

help Comrade Maloney mind the shop for a few
moments while I push round to Jefferson Market and
make inquiries?'

'Sure. But say, fancy Mr Windsor cuttin' loose that
way!' said the Kid admiringly.

The Jefferson Market Police Court is a little way down
town, near Washington Square. It did not take Psmith long
to reach it, and by the judicious expenditure of a few
dollars he was enabled to obtain an interview with Billy
in a back room.

The chief editor of *Cosy Moments* was seated on a
bench looking upon the world through a pair of much
blackened eyes. His general appearance was dishevelled.
He had the air of a man who has been caught in the
machinery.

'Hullo, Smith,' he said. 'You got my note all right
then?'

Psmith looked at him, concerned.

'Comrade Windsor,' he said, 'what on earth has been
happening to you?'

'Oh, that's all right,' said Billy. 'That's nothing.'

'Nothing! You look as if you had been run over by a
motor-car.'

'The cops did that,' said Billy, without any apparent
resentment. 'They always turn nasty if you put up a
fight. I was a fool to do it, I suppose, but I got so mad.
They knew perfectly well that I had nothing to do with
any pool-room downstairs.'

Psmith's eye-glass dropped from his eye.

'Pool-room, Comrade Windsor?'

'Yes. The house where I live was raided late last night.
It seems that some gamblers have been running a pool-
room on the ground floor. Why the cops should have
thought I had anything to do with it, when I was sleeping
peacefully upstairs, is more than I can understand.
Anyway, at about three in the morning there was the
dickens of a banging at my door. I got up to see what was

doing, and found a couple of policemen there. They told me to come along with them to the station. I asked what on earth for. I might have known it was no use arguing with a New York cop. They said they had been tipped off that there was a pool-room being run in the house, and that they were cleaning up the house, and if I wanted to say anything I'd better say it to the magistrate. I said, all right, I'd put on some clothes and come with them. They said they couldn't wait about while I put on clothes. I said I wasn't going to travel about New York in pyjamas, and started to get into my shirt. One of them gave me a shove in the ribs with his night-stick, and told me to come along quick. And that made me so mad I hit out.'

A chuckle escaped Billy. 'He wasn't expecting it, and I got him fair. He went down over the bookcase. The other cop took a swipe at me with his club, but by that time I was so mad I'd have taken on Jim Jeffries, if he had shown up and got in my way. I just sailed in, and was beginning to make the man think that he had stumbled on Stanley Ketchel or Kid Brady or a dynamite explosion by mistake, when the other fellow loosed himself from the bookcase, and they started in on me together, and there was a general rough house, in the middle of which somebody seemed to let off about fifty thousand dollars' worth of fireworks all in a bunch; and I didn't remember anything more till I found myself in a cell, pretty nearly knocked to pieces. That's my little life-history. I guess I was a fool to cut loose that way, but I was so mad I didn't stop to think.'

Psmith sighed.

'You have told me your painful story,' he said. 'Now hear mine. After parting with you last night, I went meditatively back to my Fourth Avenue address, and, with a courtly good night to the large policeman who, as I have mentioned in previous conversations, is stationed almost at my very door, I passed on into my room, and had soon sunk into a dreamless slumber. At about three o'clock in the morning I was aroused by a somewhat hefty banging on the door.'

'What!'

'A banging at the door,' repeated Psmith.

'There, standing on the mat, were three policemen. From their remarks I gathered that certain bright spirits had been running a gambling establishment in the lower regions of the building – where, I think I told you, there is a saloon – and the Law was now about to clean up the place. Very cordially the honest fellows invited me to go with them. A conveyance, it seemed, waited in the street without. I pointed out, even as you appear to have done, that sea-green pyjamas with old rose frogs were not the costume in which a Shropshire Psmith should be seen abroad in one of the world's greatest cities; but they assured me – more by their manner than their words – that my misgivings were out place, so I yielded. These men, I told myself, have lived longer in New York than I. They know what is done and what is not done. I will bow to their views. So I went with them, and after a very pleasant and cosy little ride in the patrol waggon, arrived at the police station. This morning I chatted a while with the courteous magistrate, convinced him by means of arguments and by silent evidence of my open, honest face and unwavering eye that I was not a professional gambler, and came away without a stain on my character.'

Billy Windsor listened to this narrative with growing interest.

'Gum! it's them!' he cried.

'As Comrade Maloney would say,' said Psmith, 'meaning what, Comrade Windsor?'

'Why, the fellows who are after that paper. They tipped the police off about the pool-rooms, knowing that we should be hauled off without having time to take anything with us. I'll bet anything you like they have been in and searched our rooms by now.'

339

'As regards yours, Comrade Windsor, I cannot say. But
it is an undoubted fact that mine, which I revisited
before going to the office, in order to correct what seemed
to me even on reflection certain drawbacks to my
costume, looks as if two cyclones and a threshing
machine had passed through it.'

'They've searched it?'

'With a fine-toothed comb. Not one of my objects of
vertu but has been displaced.'

Billy Windsor slapped his knee.

'It was lucky you thought of sending that paper by
post,' he said. 'We should have been done if you hadn't.
But, say,' he went on miserably, 'this is awful. Things are
just warming up for the final burst, and I'm out of it all.'

'For thirty days,' sighed Psmith. 'What *Cosy Moments*
really needs is a *sitz-redacteur*.'

'A what?'

'A *sitz-redacteur*, Comrade Windsor, is a gentleman
employed by German newspapers with a taste for *lèse
majesté* to go to prison whenever required in place of the
real editor. The real editor hints in his bright and snappy
editorial, for instance, that the Kaiser's moustache
reminds him of a bad dream. The police force swoops
down *en masse* on the office of the journal, and are met
by the *sitz-redacteur*, who goes with them peaceably,
allowing the editor to remain and sketch out plans for his
next week's article on the Crown Prince. We need a *sitz-
redacteur* on *Cosy Moments* almost as much as a fighting
editor; and we have neither.'

'The Kid has had to leave then?'

'He wants to go into training at once. He very
sportingly offered to cancel his match, but of course that
would never do. Unless you consider Comrade Maloney
equal to the job, I must look around me for some one
else. I shall be too fully occupied with purely literary
matters to be able to deal with chance callers. But I have
a scheme.'

'What's that?'

'It seems to me that we are allowing much excellent material to lie unused in the shape of Comrade Jarvis.'

'Bat Jarvis.'

'The same. The cat-specialist to whom you endeared yourself somewhat earlier in the proceedings by befriending one of his wandering animals. Little deeds of kindness, little acts of love, as you have doubtless heard, help, etc. Should we not give Comrade Jarvis an opportunity of proving the correctness of this statement? I think so. Shortly after you – if you will forgive me for touching on a painful subject – have been haled to your dungeon, I will push round to Comrade Jarvis's address, and sound him on the subject. Unfortunately, his affection is confined, I fancy, to you. Whether he will consent to put himself out on my behalf remains to be seen. However, there is no harm in trying. If nothing else comes of the visit, I shall at least have had the opportunity of chatting with one of our most prominent citizens.'

A policeman appeared at the door.

'Say, pal,' he remarked to Psmith, 'you'll have to be fading away soon, I guess. Give you three minutes more. Say it quick.'

He retired. Billy leaned forward to Psmith.

'I guess they won't give me much chance,' he whispered, 'but if you see me around in the next day or two, don't be surprised.'

'I fail to follow you, Comrade Windsor.'

'Men have escaped from Blackwell's Island before now. Not many, it's true; but it has been done.'

Psmith shook his head.

'I shouldn't,' he said. 'They're bound to catch you, and then you will be immersed in the soup beyond hope of recovery. I shouldn't wonder if they put you in your little cell for a year or so.'

341

'I don't care,' said Billy stoutly. 'I'd give a year later on to be round and about now.'

'I shouldn't,' urged Psmith. 'All will be well with the paper. You have left a good man at the helm.'

'I guess I shan't get a chance; but I'll try it if I do.'

The door opened and the policeman reappeared.

'Time's up, I reckon.'

'Well, good-bye, Comrade Windsor,' said Psmith regretfully. 'Abstain from undue worrying. It's a walk-over from now on, and there's no earthly need for you to be around the office. Once, I admit, this could not have been said. But now things have simplified themselves. Have no fear. This act is going to be a scream from start to finish.'

24 — A Gathering of Cat-Specialists

Master Maloney raised his eyes for a moment from his book as Psmith re-entered the office.

'Dere's a guy in dere waitin' ter see youse,' he said briefly, jerking his head in the direction of the inner room.

'A guy waiting to see me, Comrade Maloney? With or without a sand-bag?'

'Says his name's Jackson,' said Master Maloney, turning a page.

Psmith moved quickly to the door of the inner room.

'Why, Comrade Jackson,' he said, with the air of a father welcoming home the prodigal son, 'this is the maddest, merriest day of all the glad New Year. Where did you come from?'

Mike, looking very brown and in excellent condition, put down the paper he was reading.

'Hullo Smith,' he said. 'I got back this morning. We're playing a game over in Brooklyn tomorrow.'

'No engagements of any importance today?'

'Not a thing. Why?'

'Because I propose to take you to visit Comrade Jarvis, whom you will doubtless remember.'

'Jarvis?' said Mike, puzzled. 'I don't remember any Jarvis.'

'Let your mind wander back a little through the jungle of the past. Do you recollect paying a visit to Comrade Windsor's room – '

'By the way, where *is* Windsor?'

'In prison. Well, on that evening – '

'In prison?'

'For thirty days. For slugging a policeman. More of

343

this, however, anon. Let us return to that evening. Don't you remember a certain gentleman with just about enough forehead to keep his front hair from getting all tangled up with his eyebrows – '

'Oh, the cat chap? *I* know.'

'As you very justly observe, Comrade Jackson, the cat chap. For going straight to the mark and seizing on the salient point of a situation I know of no one who can last two minutes against you. Comrade Jarvis may have other sides to his character – possibly many – but it is as a cat chap that I wish to approach him today.'

'What's the idea? What are you going to see him for?'

'We,' corrected Psmith. 'I will explain all at a little luncheon at which I trust that you will be my guest. Already, such is the stress of this journalistic life, I hear my tissues crying out imperatively to be restored. An oyster and a glass of milk somewhere round the corner, Comrade Jackson? I think so, I think so.'

'I was reading *Cosy Moments* in there,' said Mike, as they lunched. 'You certainly seem to have bucked it up rather. Kid Brady's reminiscences are hot stuff.'

'Somewhat sizzling, Comrade Jackson,' admitted Psmith. 'They have, however, unfortunately cost us a fighting-editor.'

'How's that?'

'Such is the boost we have given Comrade Brady, that he is now never without a match. He has had to leave us today to go to White Plains to train for an encounter with a certain Mr Wood, a four-ounce-glove juggler of established fame.'

'I expect you need a fighting-editor, don't you?'

'He is indispensable, Comrade Jackson, quite indispensable.'

'No rotting. Has anybody cut up rough about the stuff you've printed?'

'Cut up rough? Gadzooks! I need merely say that one critical reader put a bullet through my hat – '

'Rot! Not really?'

'While others kept me tree'd on top of a roof for the space of nearly an hour. Assuredly they have cut up rough, Comrade Jackson.'

'Great Scott! Tell us.'

Psmith briefly recounted the adventures of the past few weeks.

'But, man,' said Mike, when he had finished, 'why on earth don't you call in the police?'

'We have mentioned the matter to certain of the force. They appeared tolerably interested, but showed no tendency to leap excitedly to our assistance. The New York policeman, Comrade Jackson, like all great men, is somewhat peculiar. If you go to a New York policeman and exhibit a black eye, he will examine it and express some admiration for the abilities of the citizen responsible for the same. If you press the matter, he becomes bored, and says, "Ain't youse satisfied with what youse got? G'wan!" His advice in such cases is good, and should be followed. No; since coming to this city I have developed a habit of taking care of myself, or employing private help. That is why I should like you, if you will, to come with me to call upon Comrade Jarvis. He is a person of considerable influence among that section of the populace which is endeavouring to smash in our occiputs. Indeed, I know of nobody who cuts a greater quantity of ice. If I can only enlist Comrade Jarvis's assistance, all will be well. If you are through with your refreshment, shall we be moving in his direction? By the way, it will probably be necessary in the course of our interview to allude to you as one of our most eminent living cat-fanciers. You do not object? Remember that you have in your English home seventy-four fine cats, mostly Angoras. Are you on to that? Then let us be going. Comrade Maloney has given me the address. It is a

345

goodish step down on the East Side. I should like to
take a taxi, but it might seem ostentatious. Let us
walk.'

They found Mr Jarvis in his Groome Street fancier's shop,
engaged in the intellectual occupation of greasing a cat's
paws with butter. He looked up as they entered, and began
to breathe a melody with a certain coyness.

'Comrade Jarvis,' said Psmith, 'we meet again. You
remember me?'

'Nope,' said Mr Jarvis, pausing for a moment in the
middle of a bar, and then taking up the air where he had
left off. Psmith was not discouraged.

'Ah,' he said tolerantly, 'the fierce rush of New York
life. How it wipes from the retina today the image
impressed on it but yesterday. Are you with me, Comrade
Jarvis?'

The cat-expert concentrated himself on the cat's paws
without replying.

'A fine animal,' said Psmith, adjusting his eyeglass.
'To which particular family of the Felis Domestica does
that belong? In colour it resembles a Neapolitan ice more
than anything.'

Mr Jarvis's manner became unfriendly.

Say, what do youse want? That's straight ain't it? If
youse want to buy a boid or a snake, why don't youse say
so?'

'I stand corrected,' said Psmith. 'I should have
remembered that time is money. I called in here partly
on the strength of being a colleague and side-partner of
Comrade Windsor – '

'Mr Windsor! De gent what caught me cat?'

'The same – and partly in order that I might make two
very eminent cat-fanciers acquainted. This,' he said,
with a wave of his hand in the direction of the silently
protesting Mike, 'is Comrade Jackson, possibly the best
known of our English cat-fanciers. Comrade Jackson's

stud of Angoras is celebrated wherever the King's English is spoken, and in Hoxton.'

Mr Jarvis rose, and, having inspected Mike with silent admiration for a while, extended a well-buttered hand towards him. Psmith looked on benevolently.

'What Comrade Jackson does not know about cats,' he said, 'is not knowledge. His information on Angoras alone would fill a volume.'

'Say,' – Mr Jarvis was evidently touching on a point which had weighed deeply upon him – 'why's catnip called catnip?'

Mike looked at Psmith helplessly. It sounded like a riddle, but it was obvious that Mr Jarvis's motive in putting the question was not frivolous. He really wished to know.

'The word, as Comrade Jackson was just about to observe,' said Psmith, 'is a corruption of cat-mint. Why it should be so corrupted I do not know. But what of that? The subject is too deep to be gone fully into at the moment. I should recommend you to read Comrade Jackson's little brochure on the matter. Passing lightly on from that – '

'Did youse ever have a cat dat ate beetles?' inquired Mr Jarvis.

'There was a time when many of Comrade Jackson's felidae supported life almost entirely on beetles.'

'Did they git thin?'

Mike felt that it was time, if he was to preserve his reputation, to assert himself.

'No,' he replied firmly.

Mr Jarvis looked astonished.

'English beetles,' said Psmith, 'don't make cats thin. Passing lightly – '

'I had a cat oncest,' said Mr Jarvis, ignoring the remark and sticking to his point, 'dat ate beetles and got thin and used to tie itself inter knots.'

'A versatile animal,' agreed Psmith.

347

'Say,' Mr Jarvis went on, now plainly on a subject near to his heart, 'dem beetles is fierce. Sure. Can't keep de cats off of eatin' dem, I can't. First t'ing you know dey've swallowed dem, and den dey gits thin and ties theirselves into knots.'

'You should put them into strait-waistcoats,' said Psmith. 'Passing, however, lightly – '

'Say, ever have a cross-eyed cat?'

'Comrade Jackson's cats,' said Psmith, 'have happily been almost free from strabismus.'

'Dey's lucky, cross-eyed cats is. You has a cross-eyed cat, and not'in' don't never go wrong. But, say, was dere ever a cat wit one blue eye and one yaller one in your bunch? Gum, it's fierce when it's like dat. It's a real skiddoo, is a cat wit one blue eye and one yaller one. Puts you in bad, surest t'ing you know. Oncest a guy give me a cat like dat, and first t'ing you know I'm in bad all round. It wasn't till I give him away to de cop on de corner and gets me one dat's cross-eyed dat I lifts de skiddoo off of me.'

'And what happened to the cop?' inquired Psmith, interested.

'Oh, he got in bad, sure enough,' said Mr Jarvis without emotion. 'One of de boys what he'd pinched and had sent to de island once lays for him and puts one over him wit a blackjack. Sure. Dat's what comes of havin' a cat wit one blue eye and one yaller one.'

Mr Jarvis relapsed into silence. He seemed to be meditating on the inscrutable workings of Fate. Psmith took advantage of the pause to leave the cat topic and touch on matter of more vital import.

'Tense and exhilarating as is this discussion of the optical peculiarities of cats,' he said, 'there is another matter on which, if you will permit me, I should like to touch. I would hesitate to bore you with my own private troubles, but this is a matter which concerns Comrade

348

Windsor as well as myself, and I know that your regard
for Comrade Windsor is almost an obsession.'

'How's that?'

'I should say,' said Psmith, 'that Comrade Windsor is
a man to whom you give the glad hand.'

'Sure. He's to the good, Mr Windsor is. He caught me
cat.'

'He did. By the way, was that the one that used to tie
itself into knots?'

'Nope. Dat was anudder.'

'Ah! However, to resume. The fact is, Comrade Jarvis,
we are much persecuted by scoundrels. How sad it is in
this world! We look to every side. We look north, east,
south, and west, and what do we see? Mainly scoundrels.
I fancy you have heard a little about our troubles before
this. In fact, I gather that the same scoundrels actually
approached you with a view to engaging your services to
do us in, but that you very handsomely refused the
contract.'

'Sure,' said Mr Jarvis, dimly comprehending. 'A guy
comes to me and says he wants you and Mr Windsor put
through it, but I gives him de t'run down. "Nuttin' done,"
I says. "Mr Windsor caught me cat." '

'So I was informed,' said Psmith. 'Well, failing you,
they went to a gentleman of the name of Reilly – '

'Spider Reilly?'

'You have hit it, Comrade Jarvis. Spider Reilly, the
lessee and manager of the Three Points gang.'

'Dose T'ree Points, dey're to de bad. Dey're fresh.'

'It is too true, Comrade Jarvis.'

'Say,' went on Mr Jarvis, waxing wrathful at the
recollection, 'what do youse t'ink dem fresh stiffs done
de udder night. Started some rough woik in me own
dance-joint.'

'Shamrock Hall?' said Psmith.

'Dat's right. Shamrock Hall. Got gay, dey did, with

some of de Table Hillers. Say, I got it in for dem gazebos, sure I have. Surest t'ing you know.'

Psmith beamed approval.

'That,' he said, 'is the right spirit. Nothing could be more admirable. We are bound together by our common desire to check the ever-growing spirit of freshness among the members of the Three Points. Add to that the fact that we are united by a sympathetic knowledge of the manners and customs of cats, and especially that Comrade Jackson, England's greatest fancier, is our mutual friend, and what more do we want? Nothing.'

'Mr Jackson's to de good,' assented Mr Jarvis, eyeing Mike in friendly fashion.

'We are all to de good,' said Psmith. 'Now the thing I wished to ask you is this. The office of the paper on which I work was until this morning securely guarded by Comrade Brady, whose name will be familiar to you.'

'De Kid?'

'On the bull's-eye, as usual, Comrade Jarvis. Kid Brady, the coming light-weight champion of the world. Well, he has unfortunately been compelled to leave us, and the way into the office is consequently clear to any sand-bag specialist who cares to wander in. Matters connected with the paper have become so poignant during the last few days that an inrush of these same specialists is almost a certainty, unless – and this is where you come in.'

'Me?'

'Will you take Comrade Brady's place for a few days?'

'How's that?'

'Will you come in and sit in the office for the next day or so and help hold the fort? I may mention that there is money attached to the job. We will pay for your services. How do we go, Comrade Jarvis?'

Mr Jarvis reflected but a brief moment.

'Why, sure,' he said. 'Me fer dat. When do I start?'

'Excellent, Comrade Jarvis. Nothing could be better. I am obliged. I rather fancy that the gay band of Three

Pointers who will undoubtedly visit the offices of *Cosy Moments* in the next few days, probably tomorrow, are due to run up against the surprise of their lives. Could you be there at ten tomorrow morning?'

'Sure t'ing. I'll bring me canister.'

'I should,' said Psmith. 'In certain circumstances one canister is worth a flood of rhetoric. Till tomorrow, then, Comrade Jarvis. I am very much obliged to you.'

'Not at all a bad hour's work,' said Psmith complacently, as they turned out of Groome Street. 'A vote of thanks to you, Comrade Jackson, for your invaluable assistance.'

'It strikes me I didn't do much,' said Mike with a grin.

'Apparently, no. In reality, yes. Your manner was exactly right. Reserved, yet not haughty. Just what an eminent cat-fancier's manner should be. I could see that you made a pronounced hit with Comrade Jarvis. By the way, if you are going to show up at the office tomorrow, perhaps it would be as well if you were to look up a few facts bearing on the feline world. There is no knowing what thirst for information a night's rest may not give Comrade Jarvis. I do not presume to dictate, but if you were to make yourself a thorough master of the subject of catnip, for instance, it might quite possibly come in useful.'

25 — Trapped

Mr Jarvis was as good as his word. On the following morning, at ten o'clock to the minute, he made his appearance at the office of *Cosy Moments*, his fore-lock more than usually well-oiled in honour of the occasion, and his right coat-pocket bulging in a manner that betrayed to the initiated eye the presence of the faithful 'canister'. With him, in addition to his revolver, he brought a long, thin young man who wore under his brown tweed coat a blue-and-red striped jersey. Whether he brought him as an ally in case of need or merely as a kindred soul with whom he might commune during his vigil, was not ascertained.

Pugsy, startled out of his wonted calm by the arrival of this distinguished company, observed the pair, as they passed through into the inner office, with protruding eyes, and sat speechless for a full five minutes. Psmith received the newcomers in the editorial sanctum with courteous warmth. Mr Jarvis introduced his colleague.

'Thought I'd bring him along. Long Otto's his monaker.'

'You did very rightly, Comrade Jarvis,' Psmith assured him. 'Your unerring instinct did not play you false when it told you that Comrade Otto would be as welcome as the flowers in May. With Comrade Otto I fancy we shall make a combination which will require a certain amount of tackling.'

Mr Jarvis confirmed this view. Long Otto, he affirmed, was no rube, but a scrapper from Biffville-on-the-Slosh. The hardiest hooligan would shrink from introducing

352

rough-house proceedings into a room graced by the combined presence of Long Otto and himself.

'Then,' said Psmith, 'I can go about my professional duties with a light heart. I may possibly sing a bar or two. You will find cigars in that box. If you and Comrade Otto will select one apiece and group yourselves tastefully about the room in chairs, I will start in to hit up a slightly spicy editorial on the coming election.'

Mr Jarvis regarded the paraphernalia of literature on the table with interest. So did Long Otto, who, however, being a man of silent habit, made no comment. Throughout the *séance* and the events which followed it he confined himself to an occasional grunt. He seemed to lack other modes of expression. A charming chap, however.

'Is dis where youse writes up pieces fer de paper?' inquired Mr Jarvis, eyeing the table.

'It is,' said Psmith. 'In Comrade Windsor's pre-dungeon days he was wont to sit where I am sitting now, while I bivouacked over there at the smaller table. On busy mornings you could hear our brains buzzing in Madison Square Garden. But wait! A thought strikes me.' He called for Pugsy.

'Comrade Maloney,' he said, 'if the Editorial Staff of this paper were to give you a day off, could you employ it to profit?'

'Surest t'ing you know,' replied Pugsy with some fervour. 'I'd take me goil to de Bronx Zoo.'

'Your girl?' said Psmith inquiringly. 'I had heard no inkling of this, Comrade Maloney. I had always imagined you one of those strong, rugged, blood-and-iron men who were above the softer emotions. Who is she?'

'Aw, she's a kid,' said Pugsy. 'Her pa runs a delicatessen shop down our street. She ain't a bad mutt,' added the ardent swain. 'I'm her steady.'

'See that I have a card for the wedding, Comrade

353

Maloney,' said Psmith, 'and in the meantime take her to
the Bronx, as you suggest.'

'Won't youse be wantin' me today.'

'Not today. You need a holiday. Unflagging toil is
sapping your physique. Go up and watch the animals,
and remember me very kindly to the Peruvian Llama,
whom friends have sometimes told me I resemble in
appearance. And if two dollars would in any way add to
the gaiety of the jaunt – '

'Sure t'ing. T'anks, boss.'

'It occurred to me,' said Psmith, when he had gone,
'that the probable first move of any enterprising Three
Pointer who invaded this office would be to knock
Comrade Maloney on the head to prevent his
announcing him. Comrade Maloney's services are too
valuable to allow him to be exposed to unnecessary
perils. Any visitors who call must find their way in for
themselves. And now to work. Work, the what's-its-
name of the thingummy and the thing-um-a-bob of the
what-d'you-call it.'

For about a quarter of an hour the only sound that
broke the silence of the room was the scratching of
Psmith's pen and the musical expectoration of Messrs
Otto and Jarvis. Finally Psmith leaned back in his chair
with a satisfied expression, and spoke.

'While, as of course you know, Comrade Jarvis,' he
said, 'there is no agony like the agony of literary
composition, such toil has its compensations. The
editorial I have just completed contains its measure of
balm. Comrade Otto will bear me out in my statement
that there is a subtle joy in the manufacture of the well-
formed phrase. Am I not right, Comrade Otto?'

The long one gazed appealingly at Mr Jarvis, who spoke
for him.

'He's a bit shy on handin' out woids, is Otto,' he said.
Psmith nodded.

'I understand. I am a man of few words myself. All

great men are like that. Von Moltke, Comrade Otto, and myself. But what are words? Action is the thing. That is the cry. Action. If that is Comrade Otto's forte, so much the better, for I fancy that action rather than words is what we may be needing in the space of about a quarter of a minute. At least, if the footsteps I hear without are, as I suspect, those of our friends of the Three Points.'

Jarvis and Long Otto turned towards the door. Psmith was right. Someone was moving stealthily in the outer office. Judging from the sound, more than one person.

'It is just as well,' said Psmith softly, 'that Comrade Maloney is not at his customary post. Now, in about a quarter of a minute, as I said – Aha!'

The handle of the door began to revolve slowly and quietly. The next moment three figures tumbled into the room. It was evident that they had not expected to find the door unlocked, and the absence of resistance when they applied their weight had had surprising effects. Two of the three did not pause in their career till they cannoned against the table. The third, who was holding the handle, was more fortunate.

Psmith rose with a kindly smile to welcome his guests.

'Why, surely!' he said in a pleased voice. 'I thought I knew the face. Comrade Repetto, this is a treat. Have you come bringing me a new hat?'

The white-haired leader's face, as he spoke, was within a few inches of his own. Psmith's observant eye noted that the bruise still lingered on the chin where Kid Brady's upper-cut had landed at their previous meeting.

'I cannot offer you all seats,' he went on, 'unless you care to dispose yourselves upon the tables. I wonder if you know my friend, Mr Bat Jarvis? And my friend, Mr L. Otto? Let us all get acquainted on this merry occasion.'

The three invaders had been aware of the presence of the great Bat and his colleague for some moments, and the meeting seemed to be causing them embarrassment.

This may have been due to the fact that both Mr Jarvis and Mr Otto had produced and were toying meditatively with distinctly ugly-looking pistols.

Mr Jarvis spoke.

'Well,' he said, 'what's doin'?'

Mr Repetto, to whom the remark was directly addressed, appeared to have some difficulty in finding a reply. He shuffled his feet, and looked at the floor. His two companions seemed equally at a loss.

'Goin' to start any rough stuff?' inquired Mr Jarvis casually.

'The cigars are on the table,' said Psmith hospitably. 'Draw up your chairs, and let's all be jolly. I will open the proceedings with a song.'

In a rich baritone, with his eyeglass fixed the while on Mr Repetto, he proceeded to relieve himself of the first verse of 'I only know I love thee'.

'Chorus, please,' he added, as he finished. 'Come along, Comrade Repetto. Why this shrinking coyness? Fling out your chest, and cut loose.'

But Mr Repetto's eye was fastened on Mr Jarvis's revolver. The sight apparently had the effect of quenching his desire for song.

' "Lov' muh, ahnd ther world is – ah – mine!" ' concluded Psmith.

He looked round the assembled company.

'Comrade Otto,' he observed, 'will now recite that pathetic little poem "Baby's Sock is now a Blue-bag". Pray, gentlemen, silence for Comrade Otto.'

He looked inquiringly at the long youth, who remained mute. Psmith clicked his tongue regretfully.

'Comrade Jarvis,' he said, 'I fear that as a smoking-concert this is not going to be a success. I understand, however. Comrade Repetto and his colleagues have come here on business, and nothing will make them forget it. Typical New York men of affairs, they close their minds to all influences that might lure them from their business.

Let us get on, then. What did you wish to see me about,
Comrade Repetto?'

Mr Repetto's reply was unintelligible.

Mr Jarvis made a suggestion.

'Youse had better beat it,' he said.

Long Otto grunted sympathy with this advice.

'And youse had better go back to Spider Reilly,'
continued Mr Jarvis, 'and tell him that there's nothin'
doin' in the way of rough house wit dis gent here.' He
indicated Psmith, who bowed. 'And you can tell de
Spider,' went on Bat with growing ferocity, 'dat next time
he gits gay and starts in to shoot guys in me dance-joint
I'll bite de head off'n him. See? Does dat go? If he t'inks
his little two-by-four gang can put it across de Groome
Street, he can try. Dat's right. An' don't fergit dis gent
here and me is pals, and any one dat starts anyt'ing wit
dis gent is going to have to git busy wit me. Does dat go?'

Psmith coughed, and shot his cuffs.

'I do not know,' he said, in the manner of a chairman
addressing a meeting, 'that I have anything to add to the
very well-expressed remarks of my friend, Comrade
Jarvis. He has in my opinion, covered the ground very
thoroughly and satisfactorily. It now only remains for me
to pass a vote of thanks to Comrade Jarvis and to declare
this meeting at an end.'

'Beat it,' said Mr Jarvis, pointing to the door.

The delegation then withdrew.

'I am very much obliged,' said Psmith, 'for your courtly
assistance, Comrade Jarvis. But for you I do not care to
think with what a splash I might not have been immersed
in the gumbo. Thank you, Comrade Jarvis. And you,
Comrade Otto.'

'Aw chee!' said Mr Jarvis, handsomely dismissing the
matter. Mr Otto kicked the leg of the table, and grunted.

For half an hour after the departure of the Three Pointers
Psmith chatted amiably to his two assistants on matters

of general interest. The exchange of ideas was somewhat one-sided, though Mr Jarvis had one or two striking items of information to impart, notably some hints on the treatment of fits in kittens.

At the end of this period the conversation was once more interrupted by the sound of movements in the outer office.

'If dat's dose stiffs come back – ' began Mr Jarvis, reaching for his revolver.

'Stay your hand, Comrade Jarvis,' said Psmith, as a sharp knock sounded on the door. 'I do not think it can be our late friends. Comrade Repetto's knowledge of the usages of polite society is too limited, I fancy, to prompt him to knock on doors. Come in.'

The door opened. It was not Mr Repetto or his colleagues, but another old friend. No other, in fact, than Mr Francis Parker, he who had come as an embassy from the man up top in the very beginning of affairs, and had departed, wrathful, mouthing declarations of war. As on his previous visit, he wore the dude suit, the shiny shoes, and the tall-shaped hat.

'Welcome, Comrade Parker,' said Psmith. 'It is too long since we met. Comrade Jarvis I think you know. If I am right, that is to say, in supposing that it was you who approached him at an earlier stage in the proceedings with a view to engaging his sympathetic aid in the great work of putting Comrade Windsor and myself out of business. The gentleman on your left is Comrade Otto.'

Mr Parker was looking at Bat in bewilderment. It was plain that he had not expected to find Psmith entertaining such company.

'Did you come purely for friendly chit-chat, Comrade Parker,' inquired Psmith, 'or was there, woven into the social motives of your call, a desire to talk business of any kind?'

'My business is private. I didn't expect a crowd.'

'Especially of ancient friends such as Comrade Jarvis.

358

Well, well, you are breaking up a most interesting little symposium. Comrade Jarvis, I think I shall be forced to postpone our very entertaining discussion of fits in kittens till a more opportune moment. Meanwhile, as Comrade Parker wishes to talk over some private business – '

Bat Jarvis rose.

'I'll beat it,' he said.

'Reluctantly, I hope, Comrade Jarvis. As reluctantly as I hint that I would be alone. If I might drop in some time at your private residence?'

'Sure,' said Mr Jarvis warmly.

'Excellent. Well, for the present, good-bye. And many thanks for your invaluable cooperation.'

'Aw chee!' said Mr Jarvis.

'And now, Comrade Parker,' said Psmith, when the door had closed, 'let her rip. What can I do for you?'

'You seem to be all to the merry with Bat Jarvis,' observed Mr Parker.

'The phrase exactly expresses it, Comrade Parker. I am as a tortoiseshell kitten to him. But, touching your business?'

Mr Parker was silent for a moment.

'See here,' he said at last, 'aren't you going to be good? Say, what's the use of keeping on at this fool game? Why not quit it before you get hurt?'

Psmith smoothed his waistcoat reflectively.

'I may be wrong, Comrade Parker,' he said, 'but it seems to me that the chances of my getting hurt are not so great as you appear to imagine. The person who is in danger of getting hurt seems to me to be the gentleman whose name is on that paper which is now in my possession.'

'Where is it?' demanded Mr Parker quickly.

Psmith eyed him benevolently.

'If you will pardon the expression, Comrade Parker,' he said, ' " Aha!" Meaning that I propose to keep that information to myself.'

Mr Parker shrugged his shoulders.

'You know your own business, I guess.'

Psmith nodded.

'You are absolutely correct, Comrade Parker. I do. Now that *Cosy Moments* has our excellent friend Comrade Jarvis on its side, are you not to a certain extent among the Blenheim Oranges? I think so. I think so.'

As he spoke there was a rap at the door. A small boy entered. In his hand was a scrap of paper.

'Guy asks me give dis to gazebo named Smiff,' he said.

'There are many gazebos of that name, my lad. One of whom I am which, as Artemus Ward was wont to observe. Possibly the missive is for me.'

He took the paper. It was dated from an address on the East Side.

'Dear Smith,' it ran. 'Come here as quick as you can, and bring some money. Explain when I see you.'

It was signed 'W. W.'

So Billy Windsor had fulfilled his promise. He had escaped.

A feeling of regret for the futility of the thing was Psmith's first emotion. Billy could be of no possible help in the campaign at its present point. All the work that remained to be done could easily be carried through without his assistance. And by breaking out from the Island he had committed an offence which was bound to carry with it serious penalties. For the first time since his connection with *Cosy Moments* began Psmith was really disturbed

He turned to Mr Parker.

'Comrade Parker,' he said, 'I regret to state that this office is now closing for the day. But for this, I should be delighted to sit chatting with you. As it is – '

'Very well,' said Mr Parker. 'Then you mean to go on with this business?'

'Though it snows, Comrade Parker.'

They went out into the street, Psmith thoughtful and

hardly realizing the other's presence. By the side of the pavement a few yards down the road a taximeter-cab was standing. Psmith hailed it.

Mr Parker was still beside him. It occurred to Psmith that it would not do to let him hear the address Billy Windsor had given in his note.

'Turn and go on down the street,' he said to the driver.

He had taken his seat and was closing the door, when it was snatched from his grasp and Mr Parker darted on to the seat opposite. The next moment the cab had started up the street instead of down, and the hard muzzle of a revolver was pressing against Psmith's waistcoat.

'Now what?' said Mr Parker smoothly, leaning back with the pistol resting easily on his knee.

26 — A Friend in Need

The point is well taken,' said Psmith thoughtfully.

'You think so?' said Mr Parker.

'I am convinced of it.'

'Good. But don't move. Put that hand back where it was.'

'You think of everything, Comrade Parker.'

He dropped his hand on to the seat, and remained silent for a few moments. The taxi-cab was buzzing along up Fifth Avenue now. Looking towards the window, Psmith saw that they were nearing the park. The great white mass of the Plaza Hotel showed up on the left.

'Did you ever stop at the Plaza, Comrade Parker?'

'No,' said Mr Parker shortly.

'Don't bite at me, Comrade Parker. Why be brusque on so joyous an occasion? Better men than us have stopped at the Plaza. Ah, the Park! How fresh the leaves, Comrade Parker, how green the herbage! Fling your eye at yonder grassy knoll.'

He raised his hand to point. Instantly the revolver was against his waistcoat, making an unwelcome crease in that immaculate garment.

'I told you to keep that hand where it was.'

'You did, Comrade Parker, you did. The fault,' said Psmith handsomely, 'was mine. Entirely mine. Carried away by my love of nature, I forgot. It shall not occur again.'

'It had better not,' said Mr Parker unpleasantly. 'If it does, I'll blow a hole through you.'

Psmith raised his eyebrows.

'That, Comrade Parker,' he said, 'is where you make

your error. You would no more shoot me in the heart of
the metropolis than, I trust, you would wear a made-up
tie with evening dress. Your skin, however unhealthy to
the eye of the casual observer, is doubtless precious
to yourself, and you are not the man I take you for if you
would risk it purely for the momentary pleasure of
plugging me with a revolver. The cry goes round criminal
circles in New York, "Comrade Parker is not such a fool
as he looks." Think for a moment what would happen.
The shot would ring out, and instantly bicycle-policemen
would be pursuing this taxi-cab with the purposeful
speed of greyhounds trying to win the Waterloo Cup. You
would be headed off and stopped. Ha! What is this?
Psmith, the People's Pet, weltering in his gore? Death to
the assassin! I fear nothing could save you from the fury
of the mob, Comrade Parker. I seem to see them
meditatively plucking you limb from limb. "She loves
me!" Off comes an arm. "She loves me not." A leg joins
the little heap of limbs on the ground. That is how it
would be. And what would you have left out of it? Merely,
as I say, the momentary pleasure of potting me. And it
isn't as if such a feat could give you the thrill of successful
marksmanship. Anybody could hit a man with a pistol at
an inch and a quarter. I fear you have not thought this
matter out with sufficient care, Comrade Parker. You said
to yourself, "Happy thought, I will kidnap Psmith!" and
all your friends said, "Parker is the man with the big
brain!" But now, while it is true that I can't get out, you
are moaning, "What on earth shall I do with him, now that
I have got him?"'

'You think so, do you?'

'I am convinced of it. Your face is contorted with the
anguish of mental stress. Let this be a lesson to you,
Comrade Parker, never to embark on any enterprise of
which you do not see the end.'

'I guess I see the end of this all right.'

'You have the advantage of me then, Comrade Parker.

It seems to me that we have nothing before us but to go on riding about New York till you feel that my society begins to pall.'

'You figure you're clever, I guess.'

'There are few brighter brains in this city, Comrade Parker. But why this sudden tribute?'

'You reckon you've thought it all out, eh?'

'There may be a flaw in my reasoning, but I confess I do not at the moment see where it lies. Have you detected one?'

'I guess so.'

'Ah! And what is it?'

'You seem to think New York's the only place on the map.'

'Meaning what, Comrade Parker?'

'It might be a fool trick to shoot you in the city as you say, but, you see, we aren't due to stay in the city. This cab is moving on.'

'Like John Brown's soul,' said Psmith, nodding. 'I see. Then you propose to make quite a little tour in this cab?'

'You've got it.'

'And when we are out in the open country, where there are no witnesses, things may begin to move?'

'That's it.'

'Then,' said Psmith heartily, 'till that moment arrives what we must do is to entertain each other with conversation. You can take no step of any sort for a full half-hour, possibly more, so let us give ourselves up to the merriment of the passing instant. Are you good at riddles, Comrade Parker? How much wood would a wood-chuck chuck, assuming for purposes of argument that it was in the power of a wood-chuck to chuck wood?'

Mr Parker did not attempt to solve this problem. He was sitting in the same attitude of watchfulness, the revolver resting on his knee. He seemed mistrustful of Psmith's right hand, which was hanging limply at his side. It was from this quarter that he seemed to expect attack. The cab was bowling easily up the broad street, past rows on rows of high houses, all looking exactly the same. Occasionally, to the right, through a break in the line of buildings, a glimpse of the river could be seen.

Psmith resumed the conversation.

'You are not interested in wood-chucks, Comrade Parker? Well, well, many people are not. A passion for the flora and fauna of our forests is innate rather than acquired. Let us talk of something else. Tell me about your home-life, Comrade Parker. Are you married? Are there any little Parkers running about the house? When you return from this very pleasant excursion will baby voices crow gleefully, "Fahzer's come home"?'

Mr Parker said nothing.

'I see,' said Psmith with ready sympathy. 'I understand. Say no more. You are unmarried. She wouldn't have you. Alas, Comrade Parker! However, thus it is! We look around us, and what do we see? A solid phalanx of the girls we have loved and lost. Tell me about her, Comrade Parker. Was it your face or your manners at which she drew the line?'

Mr Parker leaned forward with a scowl. Psmith did not move, but his right hand, as it hung, closed. Another moment and Mr Parker's chin would be in just the right position for a swift upper-cut . . .

This fact appeared suddenly to dawn on Mr Parker himself. He drew back quickly, and half raised the revolver. Psmith's hand resumed its normal attitude.

'Leaving more painful topics,' said Psmith, 'let us turn to another point. That note which the grubby stripling brought to me at the office purported to come from Comrade Windsor, and stated that he had escaped from Blackwell's Island, and was awaiting my arrival at some address in the Bowery. Would you mind telling me, purely to satisfy my curiosity, if that note was genuine? I have never made a close study of Comrade

Windsor's handwriting, and in an unguarded moment I may have assumed too much.'

Mr Parker permitted himself a smile.

'I guess you aren't so clever after all,' he said. 'The note was a fake all right.'

'And you had this cab waiting for me on the chance?'

Mr Parker nodded.

'Sherlock Holmes was right,' said Psmith regretfully. 'You may remember that he advised Doctor Watson never to take the first cab, or the second. He should have gone further, and urged him not to take cabs at all. Walking is far healthier.'

'You'll find it so,' said Mr Parker.

Psmith eyed him curiously.

'What *are* you going to do with me, Comrade Parker?' he asked.

Mr Parker did not reply. Psmith's eye turned again to the window. They had covered much ground since last he had looked at the view. They were off Manhattan Island now, and the houses were beginning to thin out. Soon, travelling at their present rate, they must come into the open country. Psmith relapsed into silence. It was necessary for him to think. He had been talking in the hope of getting the other off his guard; but Mr Parker was evidently too keenly on the lookout. The hand that held the revolver never wavered. The muzzle, pointing in an upward direction, was aimed at Psmith's waist. There was no doubt that a move on his part would be fatal. If the pistol went off, it must hit him. If it had been pointed at his head in the orthodox way he might have risked a sudden blow to knock it aside, but in the present circumstances that would be useless. There was nothing to do but wait.

The cab moved swiftly on. Now they had reached the open country. An occasional wooden shack was passed but that was all. At any moment the climax of the drama might be reached. Psmith's muscles stiffened for a spring. There was little chance of its being effective, but at least it would be better to put up some kind of a fight. And he had a faint hope that the suddenness of his movement might upset the other's aim. He was bound to be hit somewhere. That was certain. But quickness might save him to some extent.

He braced his leg against the back of the cab. In another moment he would have sprung; but just then the smooth speed of the cab changed to a series of jarring bumps, each more emphatic than the last. It slowed down, then came to a halt. One of the tyres had burst.

There was a thud, as the chauffeur jumped down. They heard him fumbling in the tool-box. Presently the body of the machine was raised slightly as he got to work with the jack.

It was about a minute later that somebody in the road outside spoke.

'Had a breakdown?' inquired the voice.

Psmith recognized it. It was the voice of Kid Brady.

27 — Psmith Concludes His Ride

The Kid, as he had stated to Psmith at their last interview that he intended to do, had begun his training for his match with Eddie Wood, at White Plains, a village distant but a few miles from New York. It was his practice to open a course of training with a little gentle road-work; and it was while jogging along the highway a couple of miles from his training-camp, in company with the two thick-necked gentlemen who acted as his sparring-partners, that he had come upon the broken-down taxi-cab.

If this had happened after his training had begun in real earnest, he would have averted his eyes from the spectacle, however alluring, and continued on his way without a pause. But now, as he had not yet settled down to genuine hard work, he felt justified in turning aside and looking into the matter. The fact that the chauffeur, who seemed to be a taciturn man, lacking the conversational graces, manifestly objected to an audience, deterred him not at all. One cannot have everything in this world, and the Kid and his attendant thick-necks were content to watch the process of mending the tyre, without demanding the additional joy of sparkling small-talk from the man in charge of the operations.

'Guy's had a breakdown, sure,' said the first of the thick-necks.

'Surest thing you know,' agreed his colleague.

'Seems to me the tyre's punctured,' said the Kid.

All three concentrated their gaze on the machine.

'Kid's right,' said thick-neck number one. 'Guy's been an' bust a tyre.'

'Surest thing you know,' said thick-neck number two.

They observed the perspiring chauffeur in silence for a while.

'Wonder how he did that, now?' speculated the Kid.

'Guy ran over a nail, I guess,' said thick-neck number one.

'Surest thing you know,' said the other, who, while perhaps somewhat lacking in the matter of original thought, was a most useful fellow to have by one. A sort of Boswell.

'Did you run over a nail?' the Kid inquired of the chauffeur.

The chauffeur ignored the question.

'This is his busy day,' said the first thick-neck with satire. 'Guy's too full of work to talk to us.'

'Deaf, shouldn't wonder,' surmised the Kid. 'Say, wonder what he's doin' with a taxi so far out of the city.'

'Some guy tells him to drive him out here, I guess. Say, it'll cost him something, too. He'll have to strip off a few from his roll to pay for this.'

Psmith, in the interior of the cab, glanced at Mr Parker.

'You heard, Comrade Parker? He is right, I fancy. The bill – '

Mr Parker dug viciously at him with the revolver.

'Keep quiet,' he whispered, 'or you'll get hurt.'

Psmith suspended his remarks.

Outside, the conversation had begun again.

'Pretty rich guy inside,' said the Kid, following up his companion's train of thought. 'I'm goin' to rubber in at the window.'

Psmith, meeting Mr Parker's eye, smiled pleasantly. There was no answering smile on the other's face.

There came the sound of the Kid's feet grating on the road as he turned; and as he heard it Mr Parker, that eminent tactician, for the first time lost his head. With a

vague idea of screening Psmith from the eyes of the man
in the road he half rose. For an instant the muzzle of the
pistol ceased to point at Psmith's waistcoat. It was
the very chance Psmith had been waiting for. His left
hand shot out, grasped the other's wrist, and gave it a sharp
wrench. The revolver went off with a deafening report,
the bullet passing through the back of the cab; then fell
to the floor, as the fingers lost their hold. The next
moment Psmith's right fist, darting upwards, took Mr
Parker neatly under the angle of the jaw.

The effect was instantaneous. Psmith had risen from
his seat as he delivered the blow, and it consequently
got the full benefit of his weight, which was not small.
Mr Parker literally crumpled up. His head jerked back,
then fell limply on his chest. He would have slipped to
the floor had not Psmith pushed him on to the seat.

The interested face of the Kid appeared at the window.
Behind him could be seen portions of the faces of the
two thick-necks.

'Ah, Comrade Brady!' said Psmith genially. 'I heard
your voice, and was hoping you might look in for a chat.'

'What's doin', Mr Smith?' queried the excited Kid.

'Much, Comrade Brady, much. I will tell you all anon.
Meanwhile, however, kindly knock that chauffeur down
and sit on his head. He's a bad person.'

'De guy's beat it,' volunteered the first thick-neck.

'Surest thing you know,' said the other.

'What's been doin', Mr Smith?' asked the Kid.

'I'll tell you about it as we go, Comrade Brady,' said
Psmith, stepping into the road. 'Riding in a taxi is
pleasant provided it is not overdone. For the moment I
have had sufficient. A bit of walking will do me good.'

'What are you going to do with this guy, Mr Smith?'
asked the Kid, pointing to Parker, who had begun to stir
slightly.

Psmith inspected the stricken one gravely.

'I have no use for him, Comrade Brady,' he said. 'Our

ride together gave me as much of his society as I desire
for today. Unless you or either of your friends are
collecting Parkers, I propose that we leave him where he
is. We may as well take the gun, however. In my opinion,
Comrade Parker is not the proper man to have such a
weapon. He is too prone to go firing it off in any direction
at a moment's notice, causing inconvenience to all.' He
groped on the floor of the cab for the revolver. 'Now,
Comrade Brady,' he said, straightening himself up, 'I am
at your disposal. Shall we be pushing off?'

It was late in the evening when Psmith returned to the
metropolis, after a pleasant afternoon at the Brady
training-camp. The Kid, having heard the details of the
ride, offered once more to abandon his match with Eddie
Wood, but Psmith would not hear of it. He was fairly
satisfied that the opposition had fired their last shot,
and that their next move would be to endeavour to come
to terms. They could not hope to catch him off his guard
a second time, and, as far as hired assault and battery
were concerned, he was as safe in New York, now that Bat
Jarvis had declared himself on his side, as he would have
been in the middle of the desert. What Bat said was law on
the East Side. No hooligan, however eager to make money,
would dare to act against a protégé of the Groome Street
leader.

The only flaw in Psmith's contentment was the
absence of Billy Windsor. On this night of all nights
the editorial staff of *Cosy Moments* should have been
together to celebrate the successful outcome of their
campaign. Psmith dined alone, his enjoyment of the
rather special dinner which he felt justified in ordering
in honour of the occasion somewhat diminished by the
thought of Billy's hard case. He had seen Mr William
Collier in *The Man from Mexico*, and that had given him
an understanding of what a term of imprisonment on
Blackwell's Island meant. Billy, during these lean days,
must be supporting life on bread, bean soup, and water.

Psmith, toying with the *hors d'oeuvre*, was somewhat saddened by the thought.

All was quiet at the office on the following day. Bat Jarvis, again accompanied by the faithful Otto, took up his position in the inner room, prepared to repel all invaders; but none arrived. No sounds broke the peace of the office except the whistling of Master Maloney.

Things were almost dull when the telephone bell rang. Psmith took down the receiver.

'Hullo?' he said.

'I'm Parker,' said a moody voice.

Psmith uttered a cry of welcome.

'Why. Comrade Parker, this is splendid! How goes it? Did you get back all right yesterday? I was sorry to have to tear myself away, but I had other engagements. But why use the telephone? Why not come here in person? You know how welcome you are. Hire a taxi-cab and come right round.'

Mr Parker made no reply to the invitation.

'Mr Waring would like to see you.'

'Who, Comrade Parker?'

'Mr Stewart Waring.'

'The celebrated tenement house-owner?'

Silence from the other end of the wire.

'Well,' said Psmith, 'what step does he propose to take towards it?'

'He tells me to say that he will be in his office at twelve o'clock tomorrow morning. His office is in the Morton Building, Nassau Street.'

Psmith clicked his tongue regretfully.

'Then I do not see how we can meet,' he said. 'I shall be here.'

'He wishes to see you at his office.'

'I'm sorry, Comrade Parker. It is impossible. I am very busy just now, as you may know, preparing the next number, the one in which we publish the name of the owner of the Pleasant Street tenements. Otherwise, I should be delighted. Perhaps later, when the rush of work has diminished somewhat.'

'Am I to tell Mr Waring that you refuse?'

'If you are seeing him any time and feel at a loss for something to say, perhaps you might mention it. Is there anything else I can do for you, Comrade Parker?'

'See here – '

'Nothing? Then good-bye. Look in when you're this way.'

He hung up the receiver.

As he did so, he was aware of Master Maloney standing beside the table.

'Yes, Comrade Maloney?'

'Telegram,' said Pugsy. 'For Mr Windsor.'

Psmith ripped open the envelope.

The message ran:

'Returning today. Will be at office tomorrow morning,' and it was signed 'Wilberfloss'.

'See who's here!' said Psmith softly.

28 — Standing Room Only

In the light of subsequent events it was perhaps the least bit unfortunate that Mr Jarvis should have seen fit to bring with him to the office of *Cosy Moments* on the following morning two of his celebrated squad of cats, and that Long Otto, who, as usual, accompanied him, should have been fired by his example to the extent of introducing a large and rather boisterous yellow dog. They were not to be blamed, of course. They could not know that before the morning was over space in the office would be at a premium. Still, it was unfortunate.

Mr Jarvis was slightly apologetic.

'T'ought I'd bring de kits along,' he said. 'Dey started in scrappin' yesterday when I was here, so today I says I'll keep my eye on dem.'

Psmith inspected the menagerie without resentment.

'Assuredly, Comrade Jarvis,' he said. 'They add a pleasantly cosy and domestic touch to the scene. The only possible criticism I can find to make has to do with their probable brawling with the dog.'

'Oh, dey won't scrap wit de dawg. Dey knows him.'

'But is he aware of that? He looks to me a somewhat impulsive animal. Well, well, the matter's in your hands. If you will undertake to look after the refereeing of any pogrom that may arise, I say no more.'

Mr Jarvis's statement as to the friendly relations between the animals proved to be correct. The dog made no attempt to annihilate the cats. After an inquisitive journey round the room he lay down and went to sleep, and an era of peace set in. The cats had settled themselves comfortably, one on each of Mr Jarvis's knees, and Long

Otto, surveying the ceiling with his customary glassy stare, smoked a long cigar in silence. Bat breathed a tune, and scratched one of the cats under the ear. It was a soothing scene.

But it did not last. Ten minutes had barely elapsed when the yellow dog, sitting up with a start, uttered a whine. In the outer office could be heard a stir and movement. The next moment the door burst open and a little man dashed in. He had a peeled nose and showed other evidences of having been living in the open air. Behind him was a crowd of uncertain numbers. Psmith recognized the leaders of this crowd. They were the Reverend Edwin T. Philpotts and Mr B. Henderson Asher.

'Why, Comrade Asher,' he said, 'this is indeed a Moment of Mirth. I have been wondering for weeks where you could have got to. And Comrade Philpotts! Am I wrong in saying that this is the maddest, merriest day of all the glad New Year?'

The rest of the crowd had entered the room.

'Comrade Waterman, too!' cried Psmith. 'Why we have all met before. Except – '

He glanced inquiringly at the little man with the peeled nose.

'My name is Wilberfloss,' said the other with austerity. 'Will you be so good as to tell me where Mr Windsor is?'

A murmur of approval from his followers.

'In one moment,' said Psmith. 'First, however, let me introduce two important members of our staff. On your right, Mr Bat Jarvis. On your left, Mr Long Otto. Both of Groome Street.'

The two Bowery boys rose awkwardly. The cats fell in an avalanche to the floor. Long Otto, in his haste, trod on the dog, which began barking, a process which it kept up almost without a pause during the rest of the interview.

'Mr Wilberfloss,' said Psmith in an aside to Bat, 'is widely known as a cat fancier in Brooklyn circles.'

375

'Honest?' said Mr Jarvis. He tapped Mr Wilberfloss in friendly fashion on the chest. 'Say,' he asked, 'did youse ever have a cat with one blue and one yellow eye?'

Mr Wilberfloss side-stepped and turned once more to Psmith, who was offering B. Henderson Asher a cigarette.

'Who are you?' he demanded.

'Who am *I*?' repeated Psmith in an astonished tone.

'Who are you?'

'I am Psmith,' said the old Etonian reverently. 'There is a preliminary P before the name. This, however, is silent. Like the tomb. Compare such words as ptarmigan, psalm, and phthisis.'

'These gentlemen tell me you're acting sub-editor. Who appointed you?'

Psmith reflected.

'It is rather a nice point,' he said. 'It might be claimed that I appointed myself. Perhaps we may say, however, that Comrade Windsor appointed me.'

'Ah! And where is Mr Windsor?'

'In prison,' said Psmith sorrowfully.

'In prison!'

Psmith nodded.

'It is too true. Such is the generous impulsiveness of Comrade Windsor's nature that he hit a policeman, was promptly gathered in, and is now serving a sentence of thirty days on Blackwell's Island.'

Mr Wilberfloss looked at Mr Philpotts. Mr Asher looked at Mr Wilberfloss. Mr Waterman started, and stumbled over a cat.

'I never heard of such a thing,' said Mr Wilberfloss.

A faint, sad smile played across Psmith's face.

'Do you remember, Comrade Waterman – I fancy it was to you that I made the remark – my commenting at our previous interview on the rashness of confusing the unusual with the improbable? Here we see Comrade

Wilberfloss, big-brained though he is, falling into the error.'

'I shall dismiss Mr Windsor immediately,' said the big-brained one.

'From Blackwell's Island?' said Psmith. 'I am sure you will earn his gratitude if you do. They live on bean soup there. Bean soup and bread, and not much of either.'

He broke off, to turn his attention to Mr Jarvis and Mr Waterman, between whom bad blood seemed to have arisen. Mr Jarvis, holding a cat in his arms, was glowering at Mr Waterman, who had backed away and seemed nervous.

'What is the trouble, Comrade Jarvis?'

'Dat guy dere wit two left feet,' said Bat querulously, 'goes and treads on de kit. I – '

'I assure you it was a pure accident. The animal – '

Mr Wilberfloss, eyeing Bat and the silent Otto with disgust, intervened.

'Who are these persons, Mr Smith?' he inquired.

'Poisson yourself,' rejoined Bat, justly incensed. 'Who's de little guy wit de peeled breezer, Mr Smith?'

Psmith waved his hands.

'Gentlemen, gentlemen,' he said, 'let us not descend to mere personalities. I thought I had introduced you. This, Comrade Jarvis, is Mr Wilberfloss, the editor of this journal. These, Comrade Wilberfloss – Zam-buk would put your nose right in a day – are, respectively, Bat Jarvis and Long Otto, our acting fighting-editors, vice Kid Brady, absent on unavoidable business.'

'Kid Brady!' shrilled Mr Wilberfloss. 'I insist that you give me a full explanation of this matter. I go away by my doctor's orders for ten weeks, leaving Mr Windsor to conduct the paper on certain well-defined lines. I return yesterday, and, getting into communication with Mr Philpotts, what do I find? Why, that in my absence the paper has been ruined.'

'Ruined?' said Psmith. 'On the contrary. Examine the

returns, and you will see that the circulation has gone
up every week. *Cosy Moments* was never so prosperous
and flourishing. Comrade Otto, do you think you could
use your personal influence with that dog to induce it to
suspend its barking for a while? It is musical, but renders
conversation difficult.'

Long Otto raised a massive boot and aimed it at the
animal, which, dodging with a yelp, cannoned against
the second cat and had its nose scratched. Piercing shrieks
cleft the air.

'I demand an explanation,' roared Mr Wilberfloss
above the din.

'I think, Comrade Otto,' said Psmith, 'it would make
things a little easier if you removed that dog.'

He opened the door. The dog shot out. They could hear
it being ejected from the outer office by Master Maloney.
When there was silence, Psmith turned courteously to
the editor.

'You were saying, Comrade Wilberfloss – ?'

'Who is this person Brady? With Mr Philpotts I have
been going carefully over the numbers which have been
issued since my departure – '

'An intellectual treat,' murmured Psmith.

' – and in each there is a picture of this young man in
a costume which I will not particularize – '

'There is hardly enough of it to particularize.'

' – together with a page of disgusting autobiographical
matter.'

Psmith held up his hand.

'I protest,' he said. 'We court criticism, but this is mere
abuse. I appeal to these gentlemen to say whether this,
for instance, is not bright and interesting.'

He picked up the current number of *Cosy Moments*,
and turned to the Kid's page.

'This,' he said. 'Describing a certain ten-round
unpleasantness with one Mexican Joe. " Joe comes up
for the second round and he gives me a nasty look, but I

378

thinks of my mother and swats him one in the lower ribs. He hollers foul, but nix on that. Referee says, 'Fight on.' Joe gives me another nasty look. 'All right, Kid,' he says; 'now I'll knock you up into the gallery.' And with that he cuts loose with a right swing, but I falls into the clinch, and then – !'''

'Bah!' exclaimed Mr Wilberfloss.

'Go on, boss,' urged Mr Jarvis approvingly. 'It's to de good, dat stuff.'

'There!' said Psmith triumphantly. 'You heard? Comrade Jarvis, one of the most firmly established critics east of Fifth Avenue, stamps Kid Brady's reminiscences with the hall mark of his approval.'

'I falls fer de Kid every time,' assented Mr Jarvis.

'Assuredly, Comrade Jarvis. You know a good thing when you see one. Why,' he went on warmly, 'there is stuff in these reminiscences which would stir the blood of a jelly-fish. Let me quote you another passage to show that they are not only enthralling, but helpful as well. Let me see, where is it? Ah, I have it. "A bully good way of putting a guy out of business is this. You don't want to use it in the ring, because by Queensberry Rules it's a foul; but you will find it mighty useful if any thickneck comes up to you in the street and tries to start anything. It's this way. While he's setting himself for a punch, just place the tips of the fingers of your left hand on the right side of his chest. Then bring down the heel of your left hand. There isn't a guy living that could stand up against that. The fingers give you a leverage to beat the band. The guy doubles up, and you upper-cut him with your right, and out he goes." Now, I bet you never knew *that* before, Comrade Philpotts. Try it on your parishioners.'

'*Cosy Moments*,' said Mr Wilberfloss irately, 'is no medium for exploiting low prize-fighters.'

'Low prize-fighters! Comrade Wilberfloss, you have been misinformed. The Kid is as decent a little chap as you'd meet anywhere. You do not seem to appreciate the philanthropic motives of the paper in adopting Comrade Brady's cause. Think of it, Comrade Wilberfloss. There was that unfortunate stripling with only two pleasures in life, to love his mother and to knock the heads off other youths whose weight coincided with his own; and misfortune, until we took him up, had barred him almost completely from the second pastime. Our editorial heart was melted. We adopted Comrade Brady. And look at him now! Matched against Eddie Wood! And Comrade Waterman will support me in my statement that a victory over Eddie Wood means that he gets a legitimate claim to meet Jimmy Garvin for the championship.'

'It is abominable,' burst forth Mr Wilberfloss. 'It is disgraceful. I never heard of such a thing. The paper is ruined.'

'You keep reverting to that statement, Comrade Wilberfloss. Can nothing reassure you? The returns are excellent. Prosperity beams on us like a sun. The proprietor is more than satisfied.'

'The proprietor?' gasped Mr Wilberfloss. 'Does *he* know how you have treated the paper?'

'He is cognizant of our every move.'

'And he approves?'

'He more than approves.'

Mr Wilberfloss snorted.

'I don't believe it,' he said.

The assembled ex-contributors backed up this statement with a united murmur. B. Henderson Asher snorted satirically.

'They don't believe it,' sighed Psmith. 'Nevertheless, it is true.'

'It is not true,' thundered Mr Wilberfloss, hopping to avoid a perambulating cat. 'Nothing will convince me of it. Mr Benjamin White is not a maniac.'

'I trust not,' said Psmith. 'I sincerely trust not. I have every reason to believe in his complete sanity. What makes you fancy that there is even a possibility of his being – er – ?'

'Nobody but a lunatic would approve of seeing his paper ruined.'

'Again!' said Psmith. 'I fear that the notion that this journal is ruined has become an obsession with you, Comrade Wilberfloss. Once again I assure you that it is more than prosperous.'

'If,' said Mr Wilberfloss, 'you imagine that I intend to take your word in this matter, you are mistaken. I shall cable Mr White today, and inquire whether these alterations in the paper meet with his approval.'

'I shouldn't, Comrade Wilberfloss. Cables are expensive, and in these hard times a penny saved is a penny earned. Why worry Comrade White? He is so far away, so out of touch with our New York literary life. I think it is practically a certainty that he has not the slightest inkling of any changes in the paper.'

Mr Wilberfloss uttered a cry of triumph.

'I knew it,' he said, 'I knew it. I knew you would give up when it came to the point, and you were driven into a corner. Now, perhaps, you will admit that Mr White has given no sanction for the alterations in the paper?'

A puzzled look crept into Psmith's face.

'I think, Comrade Wilberfloss,' he said, 'we are talking at cross-purposes. You keep harping on Comrade White and his views and tastes. One would almost imagine that you fancied that Comrade White was the proprietor of this paper.'

Mr Wilberfloss stared. B. Henderson Asher stared. Every one stared, except Mr Jarvis, who, since the readings from the Kid's reminiscences had ceased, had lost interest in the discussion, and was now entertaining the cats with a ball of paper tied to a string.

'Fancied that Mr White . . .?' repeated Mr Wilberfloss. 'I don't follow you. Who is, if he isn't?'

Psmith removed his monocle, polished it thoughtfully, and put it back in its place.

'I am,' he said.

29 — The Knock-out for Mr Waring

'You!' cried Mr Wilberfloss.

'The same,' said Psmith.

'You!' exclaimed Messrs Waterman, Asher, and the Reverend Edwin Philpotts.

'On the spot!' said Psmith.

Mr Wilberfloss groped for a chair, and sat down.

'Am I going mad?' he demanded feebly.

'Not so, Comrade Wilberfloss,' said Psmith encouragingly. 'All is well. The cry goes round New York, "Comrade Wilberfloss is to the good. He does not gibber."'

'Do I understand you to say that you own this paper?'

'I do.'

'Since when?'

'Roughly speaking, about a month.'

Among his audience (still excepting Mr Jarvis, who was tickling one of the cats and whistling a plaintive melody) there was a tendency toward awkward silence. To start bally-ragging a seeming nonentity and then to discover he is the proprietor of the paper to which you wish to contribute is like kicking an apparently empty hat and finding your rich uncle inside it. Mr Wilberfloss in particular was disturbed. Editorships of the kind which he aspired to are not easy to get. If he were to be removed from *Cosy Moments* he would find it hard to place himself anywhere else. Editors, like manuscripts, are rejected from want of space.

'Very early in my connection with this journal,' said Psmith. 'I saw that I was on to a good thing. I had long been convinced that about the nearest approach to the perfect job in this world, where good jobs are so hard to acquire, was to own a paper. All you had to do, once you had secured your paper, was to sit back and watch the other fellows work, and from time to time forward big cheques to the bank. Nothing could be more nicely attuned to the tastes of a Shropshire Psmith. The glimpses I was enabled to get of the workings of this little journal gave me the impression that Comrade White was not attached with any paternal fervour to *Cosy Moments*. He regarded it, I deduced, not so much as a life-work as in the light of an investment. I assumed that Comrade White had his price, and wrote to my father, who was visiting Carlsbad at the moment, to ascertain what that price might be. He cabled it to me. It was reasonable. Now it so happens that an uncle of mine some years ago left me a considerable number of simoleons, and though I shall not be legally entitled actually to close in on the opulence for a matter of nine months or so, I anticipated that my father would have no objection to staking me to the necessary amount on the security of my little bit of money. My father has spent some time of late hurling me at various professions, and we had agreed some time ago that the Law was to be my long suit. Paper-owning, however, may be combined with being Lord Chancellor, and I knew he would have no objection to my being a Napoleon of the Press on this side. So we closed with Comrade White, and – '

There was a knock at the door, and Master Maloney entered with a card.

'Guy's waiting outside,' he said.

'Mr Stewart Waring,' read Psmith. 'Comrade Maloney, do you know what Mahomet did when the mountain would not come to him?'

'Search me,' said the office-boy indifferently.

'He went to the mountain. It was a wise thing to do. As a general rule in life you can't beat it. Remember that, Comrade Maloney.'

'Sure,' said Pugsy. 'Shall I send the guy in?'

'Surest thing you know, Comrade Maloney.'

He turned to the assembled company.

'Gentlemen,' he said, 'you know how I hate to have to send you away, but would you mind withdrawing in good order? A somewhat delicate and private interview is in the offing. Comrade Jarvis, we will meet anon. Your services to the paper have been greatly appreciated. If I might drop in some afternoon and inspect the remainder of your zoo – ?'

'Any time you're down Groome Street way. Glad.'

'I will make a point of it. Comrade Wilberfloss, would you mind remaining? As editor of this journal you should be present. If the rest of you would look in about this time tomorrow – Show Mr Waring in, Comrade Maloney.'

He took a seat.

'We are now, Comrade Wilberfloss,' he said, 'at a crisis in the affairs of this journal, but I fancy we shall win through.'

The door opened, and Pugsy announced Mr Waring.

The owner of the Pleasant Street tenements was of what is usually called commanding presence. He was tall and broad, and more than a little stout. His face was clean-shaven and curiously expressionless. Bushy eyebrows topped a pair of cold grey eyes. He walked into the room with the air of one who is not wont to apologize for existing. There are some men who seem to fill any room in which they may be. Mr Waring was one of these.

He set his hat down on the table without speaking. After which he looked at Mr Wilberfloss, who shrank a little beneath his gaze.

Psmith had risen to greet him.

'Won't you sit down?' he said.

'I prefer to stand.'

'Just as you wish. This is Liberty Hall.'

Mr Waring again glanced at Mr Wilberfloss.

'What I have to say is private,' he said.

'All is well,' said Psmith reassuringly. 'It is no stranger that you see before you, no mere irresponsible lounger who has butted in by chance. That is Comrade J. Fillken Wilberfloss, the editor of this journal.'

'The editor? I understood – '

'I know what you would say. You have Comrade Windsor in your mind. He was merely acting as editor while the chief was away hunting sand-eels in the jungles of Texas. In his absence Comrade Windsor and I did our best to keep the old journal booming along, but it lacked the masterhand. But now all is well: Comrade Wilberfloss is once more doing stunts at the old stand. You may speak as freely before him as you would before – well, let us say Comrade Parker.'

'Who are you, then, if this gentleman is the editor?'

'I am the proprietor.'

'I understood that a Mr White was the proprietor.'

'Not so,' said Psmith. 'There was a time when that was the case, but not now. Things move so swiftly in New York journalistic matters that a man may well be excused for not keeping abreast of the times, especially one who, like yourself, is interested in politics and house-ownership rather than in literature. Are you sure you won't sit down?'

Mr Waring brought his hand down with a bang on the table, causing Mr Wilberfloss to leap a clear two inches from his chair.

'What are you doing it for?' he demanded explosively. 'I tell you, you had better quit it. It isn't healthy.'

Psmith shook his head.

'You are merely stating in other – and, if I may say so, inferior – words what Comrade Parker said to us. I did not object to giving up valuable time to listen to Comrade Parker. He is a fascinating conversationalist, and it was a privilege to hob-nob with him. But if you are merely intending to cover the ground covered by him, I fear I

must remind you that this is one of our busy days. Have
you no new light to fling upon the subject?'

Mr Waring wiped his forehead. He was playing a
lost game, and he was not the sort of man who plays lost
games well. The Waring type is dangerous when
it is winning, but it is apt to crumple up against strong
defence.

His next words proved his demoralization.

'I'll sue you for libel,' said he.

Psmith looked at him admiringly.

'Say no more,' he said, 'for you will never beat that.
For pure richness and whimsical humour it stands alone.
During the past seven weeks you have been endeavouring
in your cheery fashion to blot the editorial staff of this
paper off the face of the earth in a variety of ingenious
and entertaining ways; and now you propose to sue us
for libel! I wish Comrade Windsor could have heard you
say that. It would have hit him right.'

Mr Waring accepted the invitation he had refused
before. He sat down.

'What are you going to do?' he said.

It was the white flag. The fight had gone out of him.

Psmith leaned back in his chair.

'I'll tell you,' he said. 'I've thought the whole thing
out. The right plan would be to put the complete kybosh
(if I may use the expression) on your chances of becoming
an alderman. On the other hand, I have been studying
the papers of late, and it seems to me that it doesn't much
matter who gets elected. Of course the opposition papers
may have allowed their zeal to run away with them, but
even assuming that to be the case, the other candidates
appear to be a pretty fair contingent of blighters. If I were
a native of New York, perhaps I might take a more fervid
interest in the matter, but as I am merely passing through
your beautiful little city, it doesn't seem to me to make
any very substantial difference who gets in. To be
absolutely candid, my view of the thing is this. If the

People are chumps enough to elect you, then they deserve you. I hope I don't hurt your feelings in any way. I am merely stating my own individual opinion.'

Mr Waring made no remark.

'The only thing that really interests me,' resumed Psmith, 'is the matter of these tenements. I shall shortly be leaving this country to resume the strangle-hold on Learning which I relinquished at the beginning of the Long Vacation. If I were to depart without bringing off improvements down Pleasant Street way, I shouldn't be able to enjoy my meals. The startled cry would go round Cambridge: "Something is the matter with Psmith. He is off his feed. He should try Blenkinsop's Balm for the Bilious." But no balm would do me any good. I should simply droop and fade slowly away like a neglected lily. And you wouldn't like *that*, Comrade Wilberfloss, would you?'

Mr Wilberfloss, thus suddenly pulled into the conversation, again leaped in his seat.

'What I propose to do,' continued Psmith, without waiting for an answer, 'is to touch you for the good round sum of five thousand and three dollars.'

Mr Waring half rose.

'Five thousand dollars!'

'Five thousand and three dollars,' said Psmith. 'It may possibly have escaped your memory, but a certain minion of yours, one J. Repetto, utterly ruined a practically new hat of mine. If you think that I can afford to come to New York and scatter hats about as if they were mere dross, you are making the culminating error of a misspent life. Three dollars are what I need for a new one. The balance of your cheque, the five thousand, I propose to apply to making those tenements fit for a tolerably fastidious pig to live in.'

'Five thousand!' cried Mr Waring. 'It's monstrous.'

'It isn't,' said Psmith. 'It's more or less of a minimum.

388

I have made inquiries. So out with the good old cheque-book, and let's all be jolly.'

'I have no cheque-book with me.'

'I have,' said Psmith, producing one from a drawer. 'Cross out the name of my bank, substitute yours, and fate cannot touch us.'

Mr Waring hesitated for a moment, then capitulated. Psmith watched, as he wrote, with an indulgent and fatherly eye.

'Finished?' he said. 'Comrade Maloney.'

'Youse hollering fer me?' asked that youth, appearing at the door.

'Bet your life I am, Comrade Maloney. Have you ever seen an untamed mustang of the prairie?'

'Nope. But I've read about dem.'

'Well, run like one down to Wall Street with this cheque, and pay it in to my account at the International Bank.'

Pugsy disappeared.

'Cheques,' said Psmith, 'have been known to be stopped. Who knows but what on reflection, you might not have changed your mind?'

'What guarantee have I,' asked Mr Waring, 'that these attacks on me in your paper will stop?'

'If you like,' said Psmith, 'I will write you a note to that effect. But it will not be necessary. I propose, with Comrade Wilberfloss's assistance, to restore *Cosy Moments* to its old style. Some days ago the editor of Comrade Windsor's late daily paper called up on the telephone and asked to speak to him. I explained the painful circumstances, and, later, went round and hob-nobbed with the great man. A very pleasant fellow He asks to re-engage Comrade Windsor's services at a pretty sizeable salary, so, as far as our prison expert is concerned, all may be said to be well. He has got where he wanted. *Cosy Moments* may therefore ease up a bit. If, at about the beginning of next month, you should hear a deafening squeal of joy ring through this city, it will be the infants of New York and their parents receiving the news that *Cosy Moments* stands where it did. May I count on your services, Comrade Wilberfloss? Excellent. I see I may. Then perhaps you would not mind passing the word round among Comrades Asher, Waterman, and the rest of the squad, and telling them to burnish their brains and be ready to wade in at a moment's notice. I fear you will have a pretty tough job roping in the old subscribers again, but it can be done. I look to you, Comrade Wilberfloss. Are you on?'

Mr Wilberfloss, wriggling in his chair, intimated that he was.

30 — Conclusion

It was a drizzly November evening. The streets of
Cambridge were a compound of mud, mist, and
melancholy. But in Psmith's rooms the fire burned
brightly, the kettle droned, and all, as the proprietor had
just observed, was joy, jollity, and song. Psmith, in
pyjamas and a college blazer, was lying on the sofa. Mike,
who had been playing football, was reclining in a
comatose state in an arm-chair by the fire.

'How pleasant it would be,' said Psmith dreamily, 'if
all our friends on the other side of the Atlantic could
share this very peaceful moment with us! Or perhaps not
quite all. Let us say, Comrade Windsor in the chair over
there, Comrades Brady and Maloney on the table, and our
old pal Wilberfloss sharing the floor with B. Henderson
Asher, Bat Jarvis, and the cats. By the way, I think it would
be a graceful act if you were to write to Comrade Jarvis
from time to time telling him how your Angoras are
getting on. He regards you as the World's Most
Prominent Citizen. A line from you every now and then
would sweeten the lad's existence.'

Mike stirred sleepily in his chair.

'What?' he said drowsily.

'Never mind, Comrade Jackson. Let us pass lightly
on. I am filled with a strange content tonight. I may be
wrong, but it seems to me that all is singularly to de
good, as Comrade Maloney would put it. Advices from
Comrade Windsor inform me that that prince of blighters,
Waring, was rejected by an intelligent electorate. Those
keen, clear-sighted citizens refused to vote for him to an
extent that you could notice without a microscope. Still,

391

he has one consolation. He owns what, when the improvements are completed, will be the finest and most commodious tenement houses in New York. Millionaires will stop at them instead of going to the Plaza. Are you asleep, Comrade Jackson?'

'Um – m,' said Mike.

'That is excellent. You could not be better employed. Keep listening. Comrade Windsor also stated – as indeed did the sporting papers – that Comrade Brady put it all over friend Eddie Wood, administering the sleep-producer in the eighth round. My authorities are silent as to whether or not the lethal blow was a half-scissor hook, but I presume such to have been the case. The Kid is now definitely matched against Comrade Garvin for the championship, and the experts seem to think that he should win. He is a stout fellow, is Comrade Brady, and I hope he wins through. He will probably come to England later on. When he does, we must show him round. I don't think you ever met him, did you, Comrade Jackson?'

'Ur-r,' said Mike.

'Say no more,' said Psmith. 'I take you.'

He reached out for a cigarette.

'These,' he said, comfortably, 'are the moments in life to which we look back with that wistful pleasure. What of my boyhood at Eton? Do I remember with the keenest joy the brain-tourneys in the old form-room, and the bally rot which used to take place on the Fourth of June? No. Burned deeply into my memory is a certain hot bath I took after one of the foulest cross-country runs that ever occurred outside Dante's Inferno. So with the present moment. This peaceful scene, Comrade Jackson, will remain with me when I have forgotten that such a person as Comrade Repetto ever existed. These are the real Cosy Moments. And while on that subject you will be glad to hear that the little sheet is going strong. The man Wilberfloss is a marvel in his way. He appears to have gathered in the majority of the old subscribers again.

Hopping mad but a brief while ago, they now eat out of his hand. You've really no notion what a feeling of quiet pride it gives you owning a paper. I try not to show it, but I seem to myself to be looking down on the world from some lofty peak. Yesterday night, when I was looking down from the peak without a cap and gown, a proctor slid up. Today I had to dig down into my jeans for a matter of two plunks. But what of it? Life must inevitably be dotted with these minor tragedies. I do not repine. The whisper goes round, "Psmith bites the bullet, and wears a brave smile." Comrade Jackson – '

A snore came from the chair.

Psmith sighed. But he did not repine. He bit the bullet. His eyes closed.

Five minutes later a slight snore came from the sofa, too. The man behind *Cosy Moments* slept.

Leave it to Psmith

TO MY DAUGHTER LEONORA
QUEEN OF HER SPECIES

Contents

1 — Dark Plottings at Blandings Castle

1

At the open window of the great library of Blandings Castle, drooping like a wet sock, as was his habit when he had nothing to prop his spine against, the Earl of Emsworth, that amiable and boneheaded peer, stood gazing out over his domain.

It was a lovely morning and the air was fragrant with gentle summer scents. Yet in his lordship's pale blue eyes there was a look of melancholy. His brow was furrowed, his mouth peevish. And this was all the more strange in that he was normally as happy as only a fluffy-minded man with excellent health and a large income can be. A writer, describing Blandings Castle in a magazine article, had once said: 'Tiny mosses have grown in the cavities of the stones, until, viewed near at hand, the place seems shaggy with vegetation.' It would not have been a bad description of the proprietor. Fifty-odd years of serene and unruffled placidity had given Lord Emsworth a curiously moss-covered look. Very few things had the power to disturb him. Even his younger son, the Hon. Freddie Threepwood, could only do it occasionally.

Yet now he was sad. And – not to make a mystery of it any longer – the reason of his sorrow was the fact that he had mislaid his glasses and without them was as blind, to use his own neat simile, as a bat. He was keenly aware of the sunshine that poured down on his gardens, and was yearning to pop out and potter among the flowers he loved. But no man, pop he never so wisely, can hope to potter with any good result if the world is a mere blur.

The door behind him opened, and Beach the butler entered, a dignified procession of one.

'Who's that?' inquired Lord Emsworth, spinning on his axis.

'It is I, your lordship – Beach.'

'Have you found them?'

'Not yet, your lordship,' sighed the butler.

'You can't have looked.'

'I have searched assiduously, your lordship, but without avail. Thomas and Charles also announce non-success. Stokes has not yet made his report.'

'Ah!'

'I am re-despatching Thomas and Charles to your lordship's bedroom,' said the Master of the Hunt. 'I trust that their efforts will be rewarded.'

Beach withdrew, and Lord Emsworth turned to the window again. The scene that spread itself beneath him – though he was unfortunately not able to see it – was a singularly beautiful one, for the castle, which is one of the oldest inhabited houses in England, stands upon a knoll of rising ground at the southern end of the celebrated Vale of Blandings in the county of Shropshire. Away in the blue distance wooded hills ran down to where the Severn gleamed like an unsheathed sword; while up from the river rolling park-land, mounting and dipping, surged in a green wave almost to the castle walls, breaking on the terraces in a many-coloured flurry of flowers as it reached the spot where the province of Angus McAllister, his lordship's head gardener, began. The day being June the thirtieth, which is the very high-tide time of summer flowers, the immediate neighbourhood of the castle was ablaze with roses, pinks, pansies, carnations, hollyhocks, columbines, larkspurs, London pride, Canterbury bells, and a multitude of other choice blooms of which only Angus could have told you the names. A conscientious man was Angus; and in spite of being a good deal hampered by Lord Emsworth's amateur assistance, he showed excellent results in his department. In his beds there was much at which to point with pride, little to view with concern.

Scarcely had Beach removed himself when Lord Emsworth was called upon to turn again. The door had opened for the second time, and a young man in a beautifully-cut suit of grey flannel was standing in the doorway. He had a long and vacant face topped by shining hair brushed back and heavily brilliantined after the prevailing mode, and he was standing on one leg. For Freddie Threepwood was seldom completely at his ease in his parent's presence.

'Hullo, guv'nor.'

'Well, Frederick?'

It would be paltering with the truth to say that Lord Emsworth's greeting was a warm one. It lacked the note of true affection. A few weeks before he had had to pay a matter of five hundred pounds to settle certain racing debts for his offspring; and, while this had not actually dealt an irretrievable blow at his bank account, it had undeniably tended to diminish Freddie's charm in his eyes.

'Hear you've lost your glasses, guv'nor.'

'That is so.'

'Nuisance, what?'

'Undeniably.'

'Ought to have a spare pair.'

'I have broken my spare pair.'

'Tough luck! And lost the other?'

'And, as you say, lost the other.'

'Have you looked for the bally things?'

'I have.'

'Must be somewhere, I mean.'

'Quite possibly.'

'Where,' asked Freddie, warming to his work, 'did you see them last?'

'Go away!' said Lord Emsworth, on whom his child's conversation had begun to exercise an oppressive effect.

'Eh?'

'Go away!'

'Go away?'

'Yes, go away!'

'Right ho!'

The door closed. His lordship returned to the window once more.

He had been standing there some few minutes when one of those miracles occurred which happen in libraries. Without sound or warning a section of books started to move away from the parent body and, swinging out in a solid chunk into the room, showed a glimpse of a small, study-like apartment. A young man in spectacles came noiselessly through and the books returned to their place.

The contrast between Lord Emsworth and the new-comer, as they stood there, was striking, almost dramatic. Lord Emsworth was so acutely spectacleless; Rupert Baxter, his secretary, so pronouncedly spectacled. It was his spectacles that struck you first as you saw the man. They gleamed efficiently at you. If you had a guilty conscience, they pierced you through and through; and even if your conscience was one hundred per cent pure you could not ignore them. 'Here,' you said to yourself, 'is an efficient young man in spectacles.'

In describing Rupert Baxter as efficient, you did not overestimate him. He was essentially that. Technically but a salaried subordinate, he had become by degrees, owing to the limp amiability of his employer, the real master of the house. He was the Brains of Blandings, the man at the switch, the person in charge, and the pilot, so to speak, who weathered the storm. Lord Emsworth left everything to Baxter, only asking to be allowed to potter in peace; and Baxter, more than equal to the task, shouldered it without wincing.

Having got within range, Baxter coughed; and Lord Emsworth, recognizing the sound, wheeled round with a faint flicker of hope. It might be that even this apparently insoluble problem of the missing pince-nez would yield before the other's efficiency.

'Baxter, my dear fellow, I've lost my glasses. My glasses. I have mislaid them. I cannot think where they can have gone to. You haven't seen them anywhere by any chance?'

'Yes, Lord Emsworth,' replied the secretary, quietly equal to the crisis. 'They are hanging down your back.'

'Down my back? Why, bless my soul!' His lordship tested the statement and found it – like all Baxter's statements – accurate. 'Why, bless my soul, so they are! Do you know, Baxter, I really believe I must be growing absent-minded.' He hauled in the slack, secured the pince-nez, adjusted them beamingly. His irritability had vanished like the dew off one of his roses. 'Thank you, Baxter, thank you. You are invaluable.'

And with a radiant smile Lord Emsworth made buoyantly for the door, *en route* for God's air and the society of McAllister. The movement drew from Baxter another cough – a sharp, peremptory cough this time; and his lordship paused, reluctantly, like a dog whistled back from the chase. A cloud fell over the sunniness of his mood. Admirable as Baxter was in so many respects, he had a tendency to worry him at times; and something told Lord Emsworth that he was going to worry him now.

'The car will be at the door,' said Baxter with quiet firmness, 'at two sharp.'

'Car? What car?'

'The car to take you to the station.'

'Station? What station?'

Rupert Baxter preserved his calm. There were times when he found his employer a little trying, but he never showed it.

'You have perhaps forgotten, Lord Emsworth, that you arranged with Lady Constance to go to London this afternoon.'

'Go to London!' gasped Lord Emsworth, appalled. 'In

403

weather like this? With a thousand things to attend to in the garden? What a perfectly preposterous notion! Why should I go to London? I hate London.'

'You arranged with Lady Constance that you would give Mr McTodd lunch tomorrow at your club.'

'Who the devil is Mr McTodd?'

'The well-known Canadian poet.'

'Never heard of him.'

'Lady Constance has long been a great admirer of his work. She wrote inviting him, should he ever come to England, to pay a visit to Blandings. He is now in London and is to come down tomorrow for two weeks. Lady Constance's suggestion was that, as a compliment to Mr McTodd's eminence in the world of literature, you should meet him in London and bring him back here yourself.'

Lord Emsworth remembered now. He also remembered that this positively infernal scheme had not been his sister Constance's in the first place. It was Baxter who had made the suggestion, and Constance had approved. He made use of the recovered pince-nez to glower through them at his secretary; and not for the first time in recent months was aware of a feeling that this fellow Baxter was becoming a dashed infliction. Baxter was getting above himself, throwing his weight about, making himself a confounded nuisance. He wished he could get rid of the man. But where could he find an adequate successor? That was the trouble. With all his drawbacks, Baxter *was* efficient. Nevertheless, for a moment Lord Emsworth toyed with the pleasant dream of dismissing him. And it is possible, such was his exasperation, that he might on this occasion have done something practical in that direction, had not the library door at this moment opened for the third time, to admit yet another intruder – at the sight of whom his lordship's militant mood faded weakly.

'Oh – hallo, Connie!' he said, guiltily, like a small boy

caught in the jam cupboard. Somehow his sister always
had this effect upon him.

Of all those who had entered the library that morning
the new arrival was the best worth looking at. Lord
Emsworth was tall and lean and scraggy; Rupert Baxter
thick-set and handicapped by that vaguely grubby
appearance which is presented by swarthy young men of
bad complexion; and even Beach, though dignified, and
Freddie, though slim, would never have got far in a beauty
competition. But Lady Constance Keeble really took the
eye. She was a strikingly handsome woman in the middle
forties. She had a fair, broad brow, teeth of a perfect even
whiteness, and the carriage of an empress. Her eyes were
large and grey, and gentle – and incidentally misleading,
for gentle was hardly the adjective which anybody who
knew her would have applied to Lady Constance.
Though genial enough when she got her way, on the rare
occasions when people attempted to thwart her she was
apt to comport herself in a manner reminiscent of
Cleopatra on one of the latter's bad mornings.

'I hope I am not disturbing you,' said Lady Constance
with a bright smile. 'I just came in to tell you to be sure
not to forget, Clarence, that you are going to London this
afternoon to meet Mr McTodd.'

'I was just telling Lord Emsworth,' said Baxter, 'that
the car would be at the door at two.'

'Thank you, Mr Baxter. Of course I might have known
that you would not forget. You are so wonderfully
capable. I don't know what in the world we would do
without you.'

The Efficient Baxter bowed. But, though gratified, he
was not overwhelmed by the tribute. The same thought
had often occurred to him independently.

'If you will excuse me,' he said, 'I have one or two
things to attend to . . .'

'Certainly, Mr Baxter.'

The Efficient One withdrew through the door in the

bookshelf. He realized that his employer was in fractious mood, but knew that he was leaving him in capable hands.

Lord Emsworth turned from the window, out of which he had been gazing with a plaintive detachment.

'Look here, Connie,' he grumbled feebly. 'You know I hate literary fellows. It's bad enough having them in the house, but when it comes to going to London to fetch 'em . . .'

He shuffled morosely. It was a perpetual grievance of his, this practice of his sister's of collecting literary celebrities and dumping them down in the home for indeterminate visits. You never knew when she was going to spring another on you. Already since the beginning of the year she had suffered from a round dozen of the species at brief intervals; and at this very moment his life was being poisoned by the fact that Blandings was sheltering a certain Miss Aileen Peavey, the mere thought of whom was enough to turn the sunshine off as with a tap.

'Can't stand literary fellows,' proceeded his lordship. 'Never could. And, by Jove, literary females are worse. Miss Peavey . . .' Here words temporarily failed the owner of Blandings. 'Miss Peavey . . .' he resumed after an eloquent pause. 'Who *is* Miss Peavey?'

'My dear Clarence,' replied Lady Constance tolerantly, for the fine morning had made her mild and amiable, 'if you do not know that Aileen is one of the leading poetesses of the younger school, you must be very ignorant.'

'I don't mean that. I know she writes poetry. I mean who *is* she? You suddenly produced her here like a rabbit out of a hat,' said his lordship, in a tone of strong resentment. 'Where did you find her?'

'I first made Aileen's acquaintance on an Atlantic liner when Joe and I were coming back from our trip round the world. She was very kind to me when I was feeling the motion of the vessel . . . If you mean what is her family, I think Aileen told me once that she was connected with the Rutlandshire Peaveys.'

'Never heard of them!' snapped Lord Emsworth. 'And if they're anything like Miss Peavey, God help Rutlandshire!'

Tranquil as Lady Constance's mood was this morning, an ominous stoniness came into her grey eyes at these words, and there is little doubt that in another instant she would have discharged at her mutinous brother one of those shattering comebacks for which she had been celebrated in the family from nursery days onward; but at this juncture the Efficient Baxter appeared again through the bookshelf.

'Excuse me,' said Baxter, securing attention with a flash of his spectacles. 'I forgot to mention, Lord Emsworth, that, to suit everybody's convenience, I have arranged that Miss Halliday shall call to see you at your club tomorrow after lunch.'

'Good Lord, Baxter!' The harassed peer started as if he had been bitten in the leg. 'Who's Miss Halliday? Not another literary female?'

'Miss Halliday is the young lady who is coming to Blandings to catalogue the library.'

'Catalogue the library? What does it want cataloguing for?'

'It has not been done since the year 1885.'

'Well, and look how splendidly we've got along without it,' said Lord Emsworth acutely.

'Don't be so ridiculous, Clarence,' said Lady Constance, annoyed. 'The catalogue of a great library like this must be brought up to date.' She moved to the door. 'I do wish you would try to wake up and take an interest in things. If it wasn't for Mr Baxter, I don't know what would happen.'

And with a beaming glance of approval at her ally she left the room. Baxter, coldly austere, returned to the subject under discussion.

'I have written to Miss Halliday suggesting two-thirty as a suitable hour for the interview.'

'But look here . . .'

'You will wish to see her before definitely confirming the engagement.'

'Yes, but look here, I wish you wouldn't go tying me up with all these appointments.'

'I thought that as you were going to London to meet Mr McTodd . . .'

'But I'm not going to London to meet Mr McTodd,' cried Lord Emsworth with weak fury. 'It's out of the question. I can't possibly leave Blandings. The weather may break at any moment. I don't want to miss a day of it.'

'The arrangements are all made.'

'Send the fellow a wire . . . "unavoidably detained".'

'I could not take the responsibility for such a course myself,' said Baxter coldly. 'But possibly if you were to make the suggestion to Lady Constance . . .'

'Oh, dash it!' said Lord Emsworth unhappily, at once realizing the impossibility of the scheme. 'Oh, well, if I've got to go, I've got to go,' he said after a gloomy pause. 'But to leave my garden and stew in London at this time of the year . . .'

There seemed nothing further to say on the subject. He took off his glasses, polished them, put them on again, and shuffled to the door. After all, he reflected, even though the car was coming for him at two, at least he had the morning, and he proposed to make the most of it. But his first careless rapture at the prospect of pottering among his flowers was dimmed, and would not be recaptured. He did not entertain any project so mad as the idea of defying his sister Constance, but he felt extremely bitter about the whole affair. Confound Constance! . . . Dash Baxter! . . . Miss Peavey . . .

The door closed behind Lord Emsworth.

2

Lady Constance meanwhile, proceeding downstairs, had reached the big hall, when the door of the smoking-room opened and a head popped out. A round, grizzled head with a healthy pink face attached to it.

'Connie!' said the head.

Lady Constance halted.

'Yes, Joe!'

'Come in here a minute,' said the head. 'Want to speak to you.'

Lady Constance went into the smoking-room. It was large and cosily book-lined, and its window looked out on to an Italian garden. A wide fire-place occupied nearly the whole of one side of it, and in front of this, his legs spread to an invisible blaze, Mr Joseph Keeble had already taken his stand. His manner was bluff, but an acute observer might have detected embarrassment in it.

'What is it, Joe?' asked Lady Constance, and smiled pleasantly at her husband. When, two years previously, she had married this elderly widower, of whom the world knew nothing beyond the fact that he had amassed a large fortune in South African diamond mines, there had not been wanting cynics to set the match down as one of convenience, a purely business arrangement by which Mr Keeble exchanged his money for Lady Constance's social position. Such was not the case. It had been a genuine marriage of affection on both sides. Mr Keeble worshipped his wife, and she was devoted to him, though never foolishly indulgent. They were a happy and united couple.

Mr Keeble cleared his throat. He seemed to find some difficulty in speaking. And when he spoke it was not on the subject which he had intended to open, but on one which had already been worn out in previous conversations.

'Connie, I've been thinking about that necklace again.'

409

Lady Constance laughed.

'Oh, don't be silly, Joe. You haven't called me into this stuffy room on a lovely morning like this to talk about that for the hundredth time.'

'Well, you know, there's no sense in taking risks.'

'Don't be absurd. What risks can there be?'

'There was a burglary over at Winstone Court, not ten miles from here, only a day or two ago.'

'Don't be so fussy, Joe.'

'That necklace cost nearly twenty thousand pounds,' said Mr Keeble, in the reverent voice in which men of business traditions speak of large sums.

'I know.'

'It ought to be in the bank.'

'Once and for all, Joe,' said Lady Constance, losing her amiability and becoming suddenly imperious and Cleopatrine, 'I will *not* keep that necklace in a bank. What on earth is the use of having a beautiful necklace if it is lying in the strong room of a bank all the time? There is the County Ball coming on, and the Bachelors' Ball after that, and . . . well, I *need* it. I will send the thing to the bank when we pass through London on our way to Scotland, but not till then. And I do wish you would stop worrying me about it.'

There was a silence. Mr Keeble was regretting now that his unfortunate poltroonery had stopped him from tackling in a straightforward and manly fashion the really important matter which was weighing on his mind: for he perceived that his remarks about the necklace, eminently sensible though they were, had marred the genial mood in which his wife had begun this interview. It was going to be more difficult now than ever to approach the main issue. Still, ruffled though she might be, the thing had to be done: for it involved a matter of finance, and in matters of finance Mr Keeble was no longer a free agent. He and Lady Constance had a mutual banking account, and it was she who supervised the spending of

it. This was an arrangement, subsequently regretted by
Mr Keeble, which had been come to in the early days of
the honeymoon, when men are apt to do foolish things.

Mr Keeble coughed. Not the sharp, efficient cough
which we have heard Rupert Baxter uttering in the
library, but a feeble, strangled thing like the bleat of a
diffident sheep.

'Connie,' he said. 'Er – Connie.'

And at the words a sort of cold film seemed to come
over Lady Constance's eyes: for some sixth sense told
her what subject it was that was now about to be
introduced.

'Connie, I – er – had a letter from Phyllis this morning.'

Lady Constance said nothing. Her eyes gleamed for an
instant, then became frozen again. Her intuition had not
deceived her.

Into the married life of this happy couple only one
shadow had intruded itself up to the present. But
unfortunately it was a shadow of considerable
proportions, a kind of super shadow; and its effect had
been chilling. It was Phyllis, Mr Keeble's step-daughter,
who had caused it – by the simple process of jilting the
rich and suitable young man whom Lady Constance had
attached to her (rather in the manner of a conjurer forcing
a card upon his victim) and running off and marrying a
far from rich and quite unsuitable person of whom all
that seemed to be known was that his name was Jackson.
Mr Keeble, whose simple creed was that Phyllis could
do no wrong, had been prepared to accept the situation
philosophically; but his wife's wrath had been deep and
enduring. So much so that the mere mentioning of the
girl's name must be accounted to him for a brave deed,
Lady Constance having specifically stated that she never
wished to hear it again.

Keenly alive to this prejudice of hers, Mr Keeble
stopped after making his announcement, and had to
rattle his keys in his pocket in order to acquire the

necessary courage to continue. He was not looking at his wife, but he knew just how forbidding her expression must be. This task of his was no easy, congenial task for a pleasant summer morning.

'She says in her letter,' proceeded Mr Keeble, his eyes on the carpet and his cheeks a deeper pink, 'that young Jackson has got the chance of buying a big farm . . . in Lincolnshire, I think she said . . . if he can raise three thousand pounds.'

He paused, and stole a glance at his wife. It was as he had feared. She had congealed. Like some spell, the name Jackson had apparently turned her to marble. It was like the Pygmalion and Galatea business working the wrong way round. She was presumably breathing, but there was no sign of it.

'So I was just thinking,' said Mr Keeble, producing another *obbligato* on the keys, 'it just crossed my mind . . . it isn't as if the thing were a speculation . . . the place is apparently coining money . . . present owner only selling because he wants to go abroad . . . it occurred to me . . . and they would pay good interest on the loan . . .'

'What loan?' inquired the statue icily, coming to life.

'Well, what I was thinking . . . just a suggestion, you know . . . what struck me was that if you were willing we might . . . good investment, you know, and nowadays it's deuced hard to find good investments . . . I was thinking that we might lend them the money.'

He stopped. But he had got the thing out and felt happier. He rattled his keys again, and rubbed the back of his head against the mantelpiece. The friction seemed to give him confidence.

'We had better settle this thing once and for all, Joe,' said Lady Constance. 'As you know, when we were married, I was ready to do everything for Phyllis, I was prepared to be a mother to her. I gave her every chance, took her everywhere. And what happened?'

'Yes, I know. But . . .'

'She became engaged to a man with plenty of money . . .'

'Shocking young ass,' interjected Mr Keeble, perking up for a moment at the recollection of the late lamented, whom he had never liked. 'And a rip, what's more. I've heard stories.'

'Nonsense! If you are going to believe all the gossip you hear about people, nobody would be safe. He was a delightful young man and he would have made Phyllis perfectly happy. Instead of marrying him, she chose to go off with this – Jackson.' Lady Constance's voice quivered. Greater scorn could hardly have been packed into two syllables. 'After what has happened, I certainly intend to have nothing more to do with her. I shall not lend them a penny, so please do not let us continue this discussion any longer. I hope I am not an unjust woman, but I must say that I consider, after the way Phyllis behaved . . .'

The sudden opening of the door caused her to break off. Lord Emsworth, mould-stained and wearing a deplorable old jacket, pottered into the room. He peered benevolently at his sister and his brother-in-law, but seemed unaware that he was interrupting a conversation.

'*Gardening As A Fine Art*,' he murmured. 'Connie, have you seen a book called *Gardening As A Fine Art*? I was reading it in here last night. *Gardening As A Fine Art*. That is the title. Now, where can it have got to?' His dreamy eye flitted to and fro. 'I want to show it to McAllister. There is a passage in it that directly refutes his anarchistic views on . . .'

'It is probably on one of the shelves,' said Lady Constance shortly.

'On one of the shelves?' said Lord Emsworth, obviously impressed by this bright suggestion. 'Why, of course, to be sure.'

Mr Keeble was rattling his keys moodily. A mutinous expression was on his pink face. These moments of

rebellion did not come to him very often, for he loved
his wife with a dog-like affection, and had grown
accustomed to being ruled by her, but now resentment
filled him. She was unreasonable, he considered. She
ought to have realized how strongly he felt about poor
little Phyllis. It was too infernally cold-blooded to
abandon the poor child like an old shoe simply because . . .

'Are you going?' he asked, observing his wife moving
to the door.

'Yes. I am going into the garden,' said Lady Constance.
'Why? Was there anything else you wanted to talk to
me about?'

'No,' said Mr Keeble despondently. 'Oh, no.'

Lady Constance left the room, and a deep masculine
silence fell. Mr Keeble rubbed the back of his head
meditatively against the mantelpiece, and Lord
Emsworth scratched among the book-shelves.

'Clarence!' said Mr Keeble suddenly. An idea – one
might almost say an inspiration – had come to him.

'Eh?' responded his lordship absently. He had found
his book and was turning its pages, absorbed.

'Clarence, can you . . . ?'

'Angus McAllister,' observed Lord Emsworth bitterly,
'is an obstinate, stiff-necked son of Belial. The writer of
this book distinctly states in so many words . . .'

'Clarence, can you lend me three thousand pounds on
good security and keep it dark from Connie?'

Lord Emsworth blinked.

'Keep something dark from Connie?' He raised his
eyes from his book in order to peer at this visionary with
a gentle pity. 'My dear fellow, it can't be done.'

'She would never know. I will tell you just why I want
this money . . .'

'Money?' Lord Emsworth's eye had become vacant
again. He was reading once more. 'Money? Money, my
dear fellow? Money? Money? What money? If I have said
once,' declared Lord Emsworth, 'that Angus McAllister

is all wrong on the subject of hollyhocks, I've said it a hundred times.'

'Let me explain. This three thousand pounds . . .'

'My dear fellow, no. No, no. It was like you,' said his lordship with a vague heartiness, 'it was like you – good and generous – to make this offer, but I have ample, thank you, ample. I don't *need* three thousand pounds.'

'You don't understand. I . . .'

'No, no. No, no. But I am very much obliged, all the same. It was kind of you, my dear fellow, to give me the opportunity. Very kind. Very, very, very kind,' proceeded his lordship, trailing to the door and reading as he went. 'Oh, very, very, very . . .'

The door closed behind him.

'Oh, *damn*!' said Mr Keeble.

He sank into a chair in a state of profound dejection. He thought of the letter he would have to write to Phyllis. Poor little Phyllis . . . he would have to tell her that what she asked could not be managed. And why, thought Mr Keeble sourly, as he rose from his seat and went to the writing-table, could it not be managed? Simply because he was a weak-kneed, spineless creature who was afraid of a pair of grey eyes that had a tendency to freeze.

'*My dear Phyllis*,' he wrote.

Here he stopped. How on earth was he to put it! What a letter to have to write! Mr Keeble placed his head between his hands and groaned aloud.

'Hallo, Uncle Joe!'

The letter-writer, turning sharply, was aware – without pleasure – of his nephew Frederick, standing beside his chair. He eyed him resentfully, for he was not only exasperated but startled. He had not heard the door open. It was as if the smooth-haired youth had popped up out of a trap.

'Came in through the window,' explained the Hon. Freddie. 'I say, Uncle Joe.'

'Well, what is it?'

415

'I say, Uncle Joe,' said Freddie, 'can you lend me a thousand quid?'

Mr Keeble uttered a yelp like a pinched Pomeranian.

3

As Mr Keeble, red-eyed and overwrought, rose slowly from his chair and began to swell in ominous silence, his nephew raised his hand appealingly. It began to occur to the Hon. Freddie that he had perhaps not led up to his request with the maximum of smooth tact.

'Half a jiffy!' he entreated. 'I say, don't go off the deep end for just a second. I can explain.'

Mr Keeble's feelings expressed themselves in a loud snort.

'Explain!'

'Well, I can. Whole trouble was, I started at the wrong end. Shouldn't have sprung it on you like that. The fact is, Uncle Joe, I've got a scheme. I give you my word that, if you'll only put off having apoplexy for about three minutes,' said Freddie, scanning his fermenting relative with some anxiety, 'I can shove you on to a good thing. Honestly, I can. And all I say is, if this scheme I'm talking about is worth a thousand quid to you, will you slip it across? I'm game to spill it and leave it to your honesty to cash up if the thing looks good to you.'

'A thousand pounds!'

'Nice round sum,' urged Freddie ingratiatingly.

'Why,' demanded Mr Keeble, now somewhat recovered, 'do you want a thousand pounds?'

'Well, who doesn't, if it comes to that?' said Freddie. 'But I don't mind telling you my special reason for wanting it at just this moment, if you'll swear to keep it under your hat as far as the guv'nor is concerned.'

'If you mean that you wish me not to repeat to your father anything you may tell me in confidence, naturally I should not dream of doing such a thing.'

Freddie looked puzzled. His was no lighting
brain.

'Can't quite work that out,' he confessed. 'Do you
mean you will tell him or you won't?'

'I will not tell him.'

'Good old Uncle Joe!' said Freddie, relieved. 'A topper!
I've always said so. Well, look here, you know all the
trouble there's been about my dropping a bit on the races
lately?'

'I do.'

'Between ourselves, I dropped about five hundred of
the best. And I just want to ask you one simple question.
Why did I drop it?'

'Because you were an infernal young ass.'

'Well, yes,' agreed Freddie, having considered the
point, 'you might put it that way, of course. But why
was I an ass?'

'Good God!' exclaimed the exasperated Mr Keeble.
'Am I a psycho-analyst?'

'I mean to say, if you come right down to it, I lost all
that stuff simply because I was on the wrong side of the
fence. It's a mug's game betting on horses. The only way
to make money is to be a bookie, and that's what I'm
going to do if you'll part with that thousand. Pal of mine,
who was up at Oxford with me, is in a bookie's office, and
they're game to take me in too if I can put up a thousand
quid. Only I must let them know quick, because the
offer's not going to be open for ever. You've no notion
what a deuce of a lot of competition there is for that sort
of job.'

Mr Keeble, who had been endeavouring with some
energy to get a word in during this harangue, now
contrived to speak.

'And do you seriously suppose that I would . . . But
what's the use of wasting time talking? I have no means
of laying my hands on the sum you mention. If I had,'
said Mr Keeble wistfully. 'If I had . . .' And his eye strayed

to the letter on the desk, the letter which had got as far
as 'My dear Phyllis' and stuck there.

Freddie gazed upon him with cordial sympathy.

'Oh, I know how you're situated, Uncle Joe, and I'm
dashed sorry for you. I mean, Aunt Constance and all
that.'

'What!' Irksome as Mr Keeble sometimes found the
peculiar condition of his financial arrangements, he had
always had the consolation of supposing that they were
a secret between his wife and himself. 'What do you
mean?'

'Well, I know that Aunt Constance keeps an eye on
the doubloons and checks the outgoings pretty narrowly.
And I think it's a dashed shame that she won't unbuckle
to help poor old Phyllis. A girl,' said Freddie, 'I always
liked. Bally shame! Why the dickens shouldn't she marry
that fellow Jackson? I mean, love's love,' said Freddie,
who felt strongly on this point.

Mr Keeble was making curious gulping noises.

'Perhaps I ought to explain,' said Freddie, 'that I was
having a quiet after-breakfast smoke outside the window
there and heard the whole thing. I mean, you and Aunt
Constance going to the mat about poor old Phyllis and you
trying to bite the guv'nor's ear and so forth.'

Mr Keeble bubbled for a while.

'You – you listened!' he managed to ejaculate at length.

'And dashed lucky for you,' said Freddie with a
cordiality unimpaired by the frankly unfriendly stare
under which a nicer-minded youth would have withered;
'dashed lucky for you that I did. Because I've got a
scheme.'

Mr Keeble's estimate of his young relative's sagacity
was not a high one, and it is doubtful whether, had the
latter caught him in a less despondent mood, he would
have wasted time in inquiring into the details of this
scheme, the mention of which had been playing in and
out of Freddie's conversation like a will-o'-the-wisp. But

such was his reduced state at the moment that a reluctant gleam of hope crept into his troubled eye.

'A scheme? Do you mean a scheme to help me out of – out of my difficulty?'

'Absolutely! You want the best seats, we have 'em. I mean,' Freddie went on in interpretation of these peculiar words, 'you want three thousand quid, and I can show you how to get it.'

'Then kindly do so,' said Mr Keeble; and, having opened the door, peered cautiously out, and closed it again, he crossed the room and shut the window.

'Makes it a bit fuggy, but perhaps you're right,' said Freddie, eyeing these manoeuvres. 'Well, it's like this, Uncle Joe. You remember what you were saying to Aunt Constance about some bird being apt to sneak up and pinch her necklace!'

'I do.'

'Well, why not?'

'What do you mean?'

'I mean, why don't you?'

Mr Keeble regarded his nephew with unconcealed astonishment. He had been prepared for imbecility, but this exceeded his expectations.

'Steal my wife's necklace!'

'That's it. Frightfully quick you are, getting on to an idea. Pinch Aunt Connie's necklace. For, mark you,' continued Freddie, so far forgetting the respect due from a nephew as to tap his uncle sharply on the chest, 'if a husband pinches anything from a wife, it isn't stealing. That's law. I found that out from a movie I saw in town.'

The Hon. Freddie was a great student of the movies. He could tell a super-film from a super-super-film at a glance, and what he did not know about erring wives and licentious clubmen could have been written in a sub-title.

'Are you insane?' growled Mr Keeble.

419

'It wouldn't be hard for you to get hold of it. And once you'd got it everybody would be happy. I mean, all you'd have to do would be to draw a cheque to pay for another one for Aunt Connie – which would make her perfectly chirpy, as well as putting you one up, if you follow me. Then you would have the other necklace, the pinched one, to play about with. See what I mean? You could sell it privily and by stealth, ship Phyllis her three thousand, push across my thousand, and what was left over would be a nice little private account for you to tuck away somewhere where Aunt Connie wouldn't know anything about it. And a dashed useful thing,' said Freddie, 'to have up your sleeve in case of emergencies.'

'Are you . . .?'

Mr Keeble was on the point of repeating his previous remark when suddenly there came the realization that, despite all preconceived opinions, the young man was anything but insane. The scheme, at which he had been prepared to scoff, was so brilliant, yet simple, that it seemed almost incredible that its sponsor could have worked it out for himself.

'Not my own,' said Freddie modestly, as if in answer to the thought. 'Saw much the same thing in a movie once. Only there the fellow, if I remember, wanted to do down an insurance company, and it wasn't a necklace that he pinched but bonds. Still, the principle's the same. Well, how do we go, Uncle Joe? How about it? Is that worth a thousand quid or not?'

Even though he had seen in person to the closing of the door and the window, Mr Keeble could not refrain from a conspirator-like glance about him. They had been speaking with lowered voices, but now words came from him in an almost inaudible whisper.

'Could it really be done? Is it feasible?'

'Feasible? Why, dash it, what the dickens is there to stop you? You could do it in a second. And the beauty of the whole thing is that, if you were copped, nobody could say a word, because husband pinching from wife isn't stealing. Law.'

The statement that in the circumstances indicated nobody could say a word seemed to Mr Keeble so at variance with the facts that he was compelled to challenge it.

'Your aunt would have a good deal to say,' he observed ruefully.

'Eh? Oh, yes, I see what you mean. Well, you would have to risk that. After all, the chances would be dead against her finding out.'

'But she might.'

'Oh, well, if you put it like that, I suppose she might.'

'Freddie, my boy,' said Mr Keeble weakly, 'I daren't do it!'

The vision of his thousand pounds slipping from his grasp so wrought upon Freddie that he expressed himself in a manner far from fitting in one of his years towards an older man.

'Oh, I say, don't be such a rabbit!'

Mr Keeble shook his head.

'No,' he repeated, 'I daren't.'

It might have seemed that the negotiations had reached a deadlock, but Freddie, with a thousand pounds in sight, was in far too stimulated a condition to permit so tame an ending to such a promising plot. As he stood there, chafing at his uncle's pusillanimity, an idea was vouchsafed to him.

'By Jove! I'll tell you what!' he cried.

'Not so loud!' moaned the apprehensive Mr Keeble. 'Not so loud!'

'I'll tell you what,' repeated Freddie in a hoarse whisper. 'How would it be if *I* did the pinching?'

'What!'

'How would it . . .?'

'Would you?' Hope, which had vanished from Mr

Keeble's face, came flooding back. 'My boy, would you really?'

'For a thousand quid you bet I would.'

Mr Keeble clutched at his young relative's hand and gripped it feverishly.

'Freddie,' he said, 'the moment you place that necklace in my hands, I will give you not a thousand but two thousand pounds.'

'Uncle Joe,' said Freddie with equal intensity, 'it's a bet!'

Mr Keeble mopped at his forehead.

'You think you can manage it?'

'Manage it?' Freddie laughed a light laugh. 'Just watch me!'

Mr Keeble grasped his hand again with the utmost warmth.

'I must go out and get some air,' he said. 'I'm all upset. May I really leave this matter to you, Freddie?'

'Rather!'

'Good! Then tonight I will write to Phyllis and say that I may be able to do what she wishes.'

'Don't say "may,"' cried Freddie buoyantly. 'The word is "will". Bally will! What ho!'

4

Exhilaration is a heady drug; but, like other drugs, it has the disadvantage that its stimulating effects seldom last for very long. For perhaps ten minutes after his uncle had left him, Freddie Threepwood lay back in his chair in a sort of ecstasy. He felt strong, vigorous, alert. Then by degrees, like a chilling wind, doubt began to creep upon him – faintly at first, then more and more insistently, till by the end of a quarter of an hour he was in a state of pronounced self-mistrust. Or, to put it with less elegance, he was suffering from an exceedingly severe attack of cold feet.

The more he contemplated the venture which he had undertaken, the less alluring did it appear to him. His was not a keen imagination, but even he could shape with a gruesome clearness a vision of the frightful bust-up that would ensue should he be detected stealing his Aunt Constance's diamond necklace. Common decency would in such an event seal his lips as regarded his Uncle Joseph's share in the matter. And even if – as might conceivably happen – common decency failed at the crisis, reason told him that his Uncle Joseph would infallibly disclaim any knowledge of or connection with the rash act. And then where would he be? In the soup, undoubtedly. For Freddie could not conceal it from himself that there was nothing in his previous record to make it seem inconceivable to his nearest and dearest that he should steal the jewellery of a female relative for purely personal ends. The verdict in the event of detection would be one of uncompromising condemnation.

And yet he hated the idea of meekly allowing that two thousand pounds to escape from his clutch . . .

A young man's cross-roads.

The agony of spirit into which these meditations cast him had brought him up with a bound from the comfortable depths of his arm-chair and had set him prowling restlessly about the room. His wanderings led him at this point to collide somewhat painfully with the long table on which Beach the butler, a tidy soul, was in the habit of arranging in a neat row the daily papers, weekly papers, and magazines which found their way into the castle. The shock had the effect of rousing him from his stupor, and in an absent way he clutched the nearest daily paper, which happened to be the *Morning Globe*, and returned to his chair in the hope of quieting his nerves with a perusal of the racing intelligence. For, though far removed now from any practical share in the doings of the racing world, he still took a faint melancholy interest in ascertaining what Captain Curb, the Head Lad, Little Brighteyes, and the rest of the newspaper experts fancied for the day's big event. He lit a cigarette and unfolded the journal.

The next moment, instead of passing directly, as was his usual practice, to the last page, which was devoted to sport, he was gazing with a strange dry feeling in his throat at a certain advertisement on page one.

It was a well-displayed advertisement, and one that had caught the eye of many other readers of the paper that morning. It was worded to attract attention, and it had achieved its object. But where others who read it had merely smiled and marvelled idly how anybody could spend good money putting nonsense like this in the paper, to Freddie its import was wholly serious. It read to him like the Real Thing. His motion-picture-trained mind accepted this advertisement at its face-value.

It ran as follows:

LEAVE IT TO PSMITH!
Psmith Will Help You
Psmith Is Ready For Anything

DO YOU WANT

Someone To Manage Your Affairs?
Someone To Manage Your Business?
Someone To Take The Dog For A Run?
Someone To Assassinate Your Aunt?

PSMITH WILL DO IT
CRIME NOT OBJECTED TO

Whatever Job You Have To Offer
(Provided It Has Nothing To Do With Fish)

LEAVE IT TO PSMITH!

Address Applications To 'R. Psmith, Box 365'

LEAVE IT TO PSMITH!

Freddie laid the paper down with a deep intake of breath. He picked it up again, and read the advertisement a second time. Yes, it sounded good.

More, it had something of the quality of a direct answer to prayer. Very vividly now Freddie realized that what he had been wishing for was a partner to share the perils of this enterprise which he had so rashly undertaken. In fact, not so much to share them as to take them off his shoulders altogether. And such a partner he was now in a position to command. Uncle Joe was going to give him two thousand if he brought the thing off. This advertisement fellow would probably be charmed to come in for a few hundred . . .

Two minutes later, Freddie was at the writing-desk, scribbling a letter. From time to time he glanced furtively over his shoulder at the door. But the house was still. No footsteps came to interrupt him at his task.

5

Freddie went out into the garden. He had not wandered far when from somewhere close at hand there was borne to him on the breeze a remark in a high voice about Scottish obstinacy, which could only have proceeded from one source. He quickened his steps.

'Hallo, guv'nor.'

'Well, Frederick?'

Freddie shuffled.

'I say, guv'nor, do you think I might go up to town with you this afternoon?'

'What!'

'Fact is, I ought to see my dentist. Haven't been to him for a deuce of a time.'

'I cannot see the necessity for you to visit a London dentist. There is an excellent man in Shrewsbury, and you know I have the strongest objection to your going to London.'

'Well, you see, this fellow understands my snappers. Always been to him, I mean to say. Anybody who knows anything about these things will tell you greatest mistake go buzzing about to different dentists.'

Already Lord Emsworth's attention was wandering back to the waiting McAllister.

'Oh, very well, very well.'

'Thanks awfully, guv'nor.'

'But on one thing I insist, Frederick. I cannot have you loafing about London the whole day. You must catch the twelve-fifty train back.'

'Right ho. That'll be all right, guv'nor.'

'Now, listen to reason, McAllister,' said his lordship. 'That is all I ask you to do – listen to reason . . .'

2 — Enter Psmith

At about the hour when Lord Emsworth's train, whirling
him and his son Freddie to London, had reached the half-
way point in its journey, a very tall, very thin, very solemn
young man, gleaming in a speckless top hat and a
morning coat of irreproachable fit, mounted the steps of
Number Eighteen, Wallingford Street, West Kensington,
and rang the front door bell. This done, he removed the
hat; and having touched his forehead lightly with a silk
handkerchief, for the afternoon sun was warm, gazed
about him with a grave distaste.

'A scaly neighbourhood!' he murmured.

The young man's judgement was one at which few
people with an eye for beauty would have cavilled. When
the great revolution against London's ugliness really
starts and yelling hordes of artists and architects,
maddened beyond endurance, finally take the law into
their own hands and rage through the city burning and
destroying, Wallingford Street, West Kensington, will
surely not escape the torch. Long since it must have
been marked down for destruction. For, though it
possesses certain merits of a low practical kind, being
inexpensive in the matter of rents and handy for the buses
and the Underground, it is a peculiarly beastly little
street. Situated in the middle of one of those districts
where London breaks out into a sort of eczema of red
brick, it consists of two parallel rows of semi-detached
villas, all exactly alike, each guarded by a ragged
evergreen hedge, each with coloured glass of an extremely
regrettable nature let into the panels of the front door;

and sensitive young impressionists from the artists'
colony up Holland Park way may sometimes be seen
stumbling through it with hands over their eyes,
muttering between clenched teeth 'How long? How
long?'

A small maid-of-all-work appeared in answer to the
bell, and stood transfixed as the visitor, producing a
monocle, placed it in his right eye and inspected her
through it.

'A warm afternoon,' he said cordially.

'Yes, sir.'

'But pleasant,' urged the young man. 'Tell me, is Mrs
Jackson at home?'

'No, sir.'

'Not at home?'

'No, sir.'

The young man sighed.

'Ah well,' he said, 'we must always remember that
these disappointments are sent to us for some good
purpose. No doubt they make us more spiritual. Will
you inform her that I called? The name is Psmith.
P-smith.'

'Peasmith, sir?'

'No, no. P-s-m-i-t-h. I should explain to you that I
started life without the initial letter, and my father
always clung ruggedly to the plain Smith. But it seemed
to me that there were so many Smiths in the world that
a little variety might well be introduced. Smythe I look
on as a cowardly evasion, nor do I approve of the too
prevalent custom of tacking another name on in front by
means of a hyphen. So I decided to adopt the Psmith. The
p, I should add for your guidance, is silent, as in phthisis,
psychic, and ptarmigan. You follow me?'

'Y-yes, sir.'

'You don't think,' he said anxiously, 'that I did wrong
in pursuing this course!'

'N-no, sir.'

428

'Splendid!' said the young man, flicking a speck of dust from his coat-sleeve. 'Splendid! Splendid!'

And with a courteous bow he descended the steps and made his way down the street. The little maid, having followed him with bulging eyes till he was out of sight, closed the door and returned to her kitchen.

Psmith strolled meditatively on. The genial warmth of the afternoon soothed him. He hummed lightly – only stopping when, as he reached the end of the street, a young man of his own age, rounding the corner rapidly, almost ran into him.

'Sorry,' said the young man. 'Hallo, Smith.'

Psmith gazed upon him with benevolent affection.

'Comrade Jackson,' he said, 'this is well met. The one man of all others whom I would have wished to encounter. We will pop off somewhere, Comrade Jackson, should your engagements permit, and restore our tissues with a cup of tea. I had hoped to touch the Jackson family for some slight refreshment, but I was informed that your wife was out.'

Mike Jackson laughed.

'Phyllis isn't out. She . . .'

'Not out? Then,' said Psmith, pained, 'there has been dirty work done this day. For I was turned from the door. It would not be exaggerating to say that I was given the bird. Is this the boasted Jackson hospitality?'

'Phyllis is giving a tea to some of her old school pals,' explained Mike. 'She told the maid to say she wasn't at home to anybody else. I'm not allowed in myself.'

'Enough, Comrade Jackson!' said Psmith agreeably. 'Say no more. If you yourself have been booted out in spite of all the loving, honouring, and obeying your wife promised at the altar, who am I to complain? And possibly, one can console oneself by reflecting, we are well out of it. These gathering of old girls'-school chums are not the sort of function your man of affairs wants to get lugged into. Capital company as we are, Comrade

429

Jackson, we should doubtless have been extremely in
the way. I suppose the conversation would have dealt
exclusively with reminiscences of the dear old school,
of tales of surreptitious cocoa-drinking in the dormitories
and what the deportment mistress said when Angela
was found chewing tobacco in the shrubbery. Yes, I fancy
we have not missed a lot . . . By the way, I don't think
much of the new home. True, I only saw it from the
outside, but . . . no, I don't think much of it.'

'Best we can afford.'

'And who,' said Psmith, 'am I to taunt my boyhood
friend with his honest poverty? Especially as I myself am
standing on the very brink of destitution.'

'You?'

'I in person. That low moaning sound you hear is the
wolf bivouacked outside my door.'

'But I thought your uncle gave you rather a good salary.'

'So he did. But my uncle and I are about to part
company. From now on he, so to speak, will take the
high road and I'll take the low road. I dine with him
tonight, and over the nuts and wine I shall hand him the
bad news that I propose to resign my position in the firm.
I have no doubt that he supposed he was doing me a good
turn by starting me in his fish business, but even what
little experience I have had of it has convinced me that
it is not my proper sphere. The whisper flies round the
clubs "Psmith has not found his niche!"'

'I am not,' said Psmith, 'an unreasonable man. I realize
that humanity must be supplied with fish. I am not
averse from a bit of fish myself. But to be professionally
connected with a firm that handles the material in the
raw is not my idea of a large life-work. Remind me to tell
you some time what it feels like to sling yourself out of
bed at four a.m. and go down to toil in Billingsgate Market.
No, there is money in fish – my uncle has made a pot of
it – but what I feel is that there must be other walks in
life for a bright young man. I chuck it tonight.'

'What are you going to do, then?'

'That, Comrade Jackson, is more or less on the knees of the gods. Tomorrow morning I think I will stroll round to an employment agency and see how the market for bright young men stands. Do you know a good one?'

'Phyllis always goes to Miss Clarkson's in Shaftesbury Avenue. But . . .'

'Miss Clarkson's in Shaftesbury Avenue. I will make a note of it . . . Meanwhile, I wonder if you saw the *Morning Globe* today?'

'No. Why?'

'I had an advertisement in it, in which I expressed myself as willing – indeed, eager – to tackle any undertaking that had nothing to do with fish. I am confidently expecting shoals of replies. I look forward to winnowing the heap and selecting the most desirable.'

'Pretty hard to get a job these days,' said Mike doubtfully.

'Not if you have something superlatively good to offer.'

'What have you got to offer?'

'My services,' said Psmith with faint reproach.

'What as?'

'As anything. I made no restrictions. Would you care to take at look at my manifesto? I have a copy in my pocket.'

Psmith produced from inside his immaculate waistcoat a folded clipping.

'I should welcome your opinion of it, Comrade Jackson. I have frequently said that for sturdy common sense you stand alone. Your judgement should be invaluable.'

The advertisement, which some hours earlier had so electrified the Hon. Freddie Threepwood in the smoking-room at Blandings Castle, seemed to affect Mike whose mind was of the stolid and serious type, somewhat differently. He finished his perusal and stared speechlessly.

'Neat, don't you think?' said Psmith. 'Covers the ground adequately? I think so, I think so.'

'Do you mean to say you're going to put drivel like that in the paper?' asked Mike.

'I *have* put it in the paper. As I told you, it appeared this morning. By this time tomorrow I shall no doubt have finished sorting out the first batch of replies.'

Mike's emotion took him back to the phraseology of school-days.

'You *are* an ass!'

Psmith restored the clipping to his waistcoat pocket.

'You wound me, Comrade Jackson,' he said. 'I had expected a broader outlook from you. In fact, I rather supposed that you would have rushed round instantly to the offices of the journal and shoved in a similar advertisement yourself. But nothing that you can say can damp my buoyant spirit. The cry goes round Kensington (and district) "Psmith is off!" In what direction the cry omits to state: but that information the future will supply. And now, Comrade Jackson, let us trickle into yonder tea-shop and drink success to the venture in a cup of the steaming. I had a particularly hard morning today among the whitebait, and I need refreshment.'

2

After Psmith had withdrawn his spectacular person from it, there was an interval of perhaps twenty minutes before anything else occurred to brighten the drabness of Wallingford Street. The lethargy of afternoon held the thoroughfare in its grip. Occasionally a tradesman's cart would rattle round the corner, and from time to time cats appeared, stalking purposefully among the evergreens. But at ten minutes to five a girl ran up the steps of Number Eighteen and rang the bell.

She was a girl of medium height, very straight and slim; and her fair hair, her cheerful smile, and the boyish suppleness of her body all contributed to a general effect of valiant gaiety, a sort of golden sunniness – accentuated by the fact that, like all girls who looked to Paris for inspiration in their dress that season, she was wearing black.

The small maid appeared again.

'Is Mrs Jackson at home?' said the girl. 'I think she's expecting me. Miss Halliday.'

'Yes, miss.'

A door at the end of the narrow hall had opened.

'Is that you, Eve?'

'Hallo, Phyl, darling.'

Phyllis Jackson fluttered down the passage like a rose-leaf on the wind, and hurled herself into Eve's arms. She was small and fragile, with great brown eyes under a cloud of dark hair. She had a wistful look, and most people who knew her wanted to pet her. Eve had always petted her, from their first days at school together.

'Am I late or early?' asked Eve.

'You're the first, but we won't wait. Jane, will you bring tea into the drawing-room?'

'Yes'm.'

'And, remember, I don't want to see anyone for the rest of the afternoon. If anybody calls, tell them I'm not at home. Except Miss Clarkson and Mrs McTodd, of course.'

'Yes'm.'

'Who is Mrs McTodd?' inquired Eve. 'Is that Cynthia?'

'Yes. Didn't you know she had married Ralston McTodd, the Canadian poet? You knew she went out to Canada?'

'I knew that, yes. But I hadn't heard that she was married. Funny how out of touch one gets with girls who were one's best friends at school. Do you realize it's nearly two years since I saw you?'

'I know. Isn't it awful! I got your address from Elsa

433

Wentworth two or three days ago, and then Clarkie told me that Cynthia was over here on a visit with her husband, so I thought how jolly it would be to have a regular reunion. We three were such friends in the old days . . . You remember Clarkie, of course? Miss Clarkson, who used to be English mistress at Wayland House.'

'Yes, of course. Where did you run into her?'

'Oh, I see a lot of her. She runs a Domestic Employment Agency in Shaftesbury Avenue now, and I have to go there about once a fortnight to get a new maid. She supplied Jane.'

'Is Cynthia's husband coming with her this afternoon?'

'No. I wanted it to be simply us four. Do you know him? But of course you don't. This is his first visit to England.'

'I know his poetry. He's quite a celebrity. Cynthia's lucky.'

They had made their way into the drawing-room, a gruesome little apartment full of all those antimacassars, wax flowers, and china dogs inseparable from the cheaper type of London furnished house. Eve, though the exterior of Number Eighteen should have prepared her for all this, was unable to check a slight shudder as she caught the eye of the least prepossessing of the dogs, goggling at her from the mantelpiece.

'Don't look at them,' recommended Phyllis, following her gaze. 'I try not to. We've only just moved in here, so I haven't had time to make the place nice. Here's tea. All right, Jane, put it down there. Tea, Eve?'

Eve sat down. She was puzzled and curious. She threw her mind back to the days at school and remembered the Phyllis of that epoch as almost indecently opulent. A millionaire stepfather there had been then, she recollected. What had become of him now, that he should allow Phyllis to stay in surroundings like this? Eve

scented a mystery, and in her customary straightforward
way went to the heart of it.

'Tell me all about yourself,' she said, having achieved
as much comfort as the peculiar structure of her chair
would permit. 'And remember that I haven't seen you for
two years, so don't leave anything out.'

'It's so difficult to know where to start.'

'Well, you signed your letter "Phyllis Jackson". Start
with the mysterious Jackson. Where does he come in?
The last I heard about you was an announcement in the
Morning Post that you were engaged to – I've forgotten
the name, but I'm certain it wasn't Jackson.'

'Rollo Mountford.'

'Was it? Well, what has become of Rollo? You seem to
have mislaid him. Did you break off the engagement?'

'Well, it – sort of broke itself off. I mean, you see, I
went and married Mike.'

'Eloped with him, do you mean?'

'Yes.'

'Good heavens!'

'I'm awfully ashamed about that, Eve. I suppose I
treated Rollo awfully badly.'

'Never mind. A man with a name like that was made
for suffering.'

'I never really cared for him. He had horrid swimmy
eyes . . .'

'I understand. So you eloped with your Mike. Tell me
about him. Who is he? What does he do?'

'Well, at present he's master at a school. But he doesn't
like it. He wants to get back to the country again. When
I met him, he was agent on a place in the country
belonging to some people named Smith. Mike had been
at school and Cambridge with the son. They were very
rich then and had a big estate. It was the next place to
the Edgelows. I had gone to stay with Mary Edgelow – I
don't know if you remember her at school? I met Mike
first at a dance, and then I met him out riding, and then

– well, after that we used to meet every day. And we fell in love right from the start and we went and got married. Oh, Eve, I wish you could have seen our darling little house. It was all over ivy and roses, and we had horses and dogs and . . .'

Phyllis's narrative broke off with a gulp. Eve looked at her sympathetically. All her life she herself had been joyously impecunious, but it had never seemed to matter. She was strong and adventurous, and revelled in the perpetual excitement of trying to make both ends meet. But Phyllis was one of those sweet porcelain girls whom the roughnesses of life bruise instead of stimulating. She needed comfort and pleasant surroundings. Eve looked morosely at the china dog, which leered back at her with an insufferable good-fellowship.

'We had hardly got married,' resumed Phyllis, blinking, 'when poor Mr Smith died and the whole place was broken up. He must have been speculating or something, I suppose, because he hardly left any money, and the estate had to be sold. And the people who bought it – they were coal people from Wolverhampton – had a nephew for whom they wanted the agent job, so Mike had to go. So here we are.'

Eve put the question which she had been waiting to ask ever since she had entered the house.

'But what about your stepfather? Surely, when we were at school, you had a rich stepfather in the background. Has he lost his money, too?'

'No.'

'Well, why doesn't he help you, then?'

'He would, I know, if he was left to himself. But it's Aunt Constance.'

'What's Aunt Constance done? And who *is* Aunt Constance?'

'Well, I call her that, but she's really my stepmother – sort of. I suppose she's really my step-stepmother. My stepfather married again two years ago. It was Aunt

436

Constance who was so furious when I married Mike.
She wanted me to marry Rollo. She has never forgiven
me, and she won't let my stepfather do anything to help
us.'

'But the man must be a worm!' said Eve indignantly.
'Why doesn't he insist? You always used to tell me how
fond he was of you.'

'He isn't a worm, Eve. He's a dear. It's just that he has
let her boss him. She's rather a terror, you know. She
can be quite nice, and they're awfully fond of each other,
but she is as hard as nails sometimes.' Phyllis broke off.
. The front door had opened, and there were footsteps in
the hall. 'Here's Clarkie. I hope she has brought Cynthia
with her. She was to pick her up on her way. Don't talk
about what I've been telling you in front of her, Eve,
there's an angel.'

'Why not?'

'She's so motherly about it. It's sweet of her, but . . .'
Eve understood.

'All right. Later on.'

The door opened to admit Miss Clarkson.

The adjective which Phyllis had applied to her late
schoolmistress was obviously well chosen. Miss
Clarkson exuded motherliness. She was large,
wholesome, and soft, and she swooped on Eve like a hen
on its chicken almost before the door had closed.

'Eve! How nice to see you after all this time! My dear,
you're looking perfectly lovely! And *so* prosperous.
What a beautiful hat!'

'I've been envying it ever since you came, Eve,' said
Phyllis. 'Where did you get it?'

'Madeleine Soeurs, in Regent Street.'

Miss Clarkson, having acquired and stirred a cup of
tea, started to improve the occasion. Eve had always
been a favourite of hers at school. She beamed
affectionately upon her.

'Now doesn't this show – what I always used to say to

437

you in the dear old days, Eve – that one must never despair, however black the outlook may seem? I remember you at school, dear, as poor as a church mouse, and with no prospects, none whatever. And yet here you are – rich . . .'

Eve laughed. She got up and kissed Miss Clarkson. She regretted that she was compelled to strike a jarring note, but it had to be done.

'I'm awfully sorry, Clarkie dear,' she said, 'but I'm afraid I've misled you. I'm just as broke as I ever was. In fact, when Phyllis told me you were running an Employment Agency, I made a note to come and see you and ask if you had some attractive billet to dispose of. Governess to a thoroughly angelic child would do. Or isn't there some nice cosy author or something who wants his letters answered and his press-clippings pasted in an album?'

'Oh, my dear!' Miss Clarkson was deeply concerned. 'I did hope . . . That hat . . .!'

'The hat's the whole trouble. Of course I had no business even to think of it, but I saw it in the shop-window and coveted it for days, and finally fell. And then, you see, I had to live up to it – buy shoes and a dress to match. I tell you it was a perfect orgy, and I'm thoroughly ashamed of myself now. Too late, as usual.'

'Oh, dear! You always were such a wild, impetuous child, even at school. I remember how often I used to speak to you about it.'

'Well, when it was all over and I was sane again, I found I had only a few pounds left, not nearly enough to see me through till the relief expedition arrived. So I thought it over and decided to invest my little all.'

'I hope you chose something safe?'

'It ought to have been. The *Sporting Express* called it "Today's Safety Bet." It was Bounding Willie for the two-thirty race at Sandown last Wednesday.'

'Oh, dear!'

'That's what I said when poor old Willie came in
sixth. But it's no good worrying, is it? What it means is
that I simply must find something to do that will carry
me through till I get my next quarter's allowance.
And that won't be till September . . . But don't let's talk
business here. I'll come round to your office, Clarkie,
tomorrow . . . Where's Cynthia? Didn't you bring
her?'

'Yes, I thought you were going to pick Cynthia up on
your way, Clarkie,' said Phyllis.

If Eve's information as to her financial affairs had
caused Miss Clarkson to mourn, the mention of Cynthia
plunged her into the very depths of woe. Her mouth
quivered and a tear stole down her cheek. Eve and Phyllis
exchanged bewildered glances.

'I say,' said Eve after a moment's pause and a silence
broken only by a smothered sob from their late
instructress, 'we aren't being very cheerful, are we,
considering that this is supposed to be a joyous reunion?
Is anything wrong with Cynthia?'

So poignant was Miss Clarkson's anguish that Phyllis,
in a flutter of alarm, rose and left the room swiftly in
search of the only remedy that suggested itself to her –
her smelling-salts.

'Poor dear Cynthia!' moaned Miss Clarkson.

'Why, what's the matter with her?' asked Eve. She was
not callous to Miss Clarkson's grief, but she could not
help the tiniest of smiles. In a flash she had been
transported to her school-days, when the other's habit
of extracting the utmost tragedy out of the slimmest
material had been a source of ever-fresh amusement to
her. Not for an instant did she expect to hear any worse
news of her old friend than that she was in bed with a
cold or had twisted her ankle.

'She's married, you know,' said Miss Clarkson.

'Well, I see no harm in that, Clarkie. If a few more
Safety Bets go wrong, I shall probably have to rush out

and marry someone myself. Some nice, rich, indulgent man who will spoil me.'

'Oh, Eve, my dear,' pleaded Miss Clarkson, bleating with alarm, 'do please be careful whom you marry. I never hear of one of my girls marrying without feeling that the worst may happen and that, all unknowing, she may be stepping over a grim precipice!'

'You don't *tell* them that, do you? Because I should think it would rather cast a damper on the wedding festivities. Has Cynthia gone stepping over grim precipices? I was just saying to Phyllis that I envied her, marrying a celebrity like Ralston McTodd.'

Miss Clarkson gulped.

'The man must be a *fiend*!' she said brokenly. 'I have just left poor dear Cynthia in floods of tears at the Cadogan Hotel – she had a very nice quiet room on the fourth floor, though the carpet does not harmonize with the wall-paper . . . She was broken-hearted, poor child. I did what I could to console her, but it was useless. She always was so highly strung. I must be getting back to her very soon. I only came on here because I did not want to disappoint you two dear girls . . .'

'Why?' said Eve with quiet intensity. She knew from experience that Miss Clarkson, unless firmly checked, would pirouette round and round the point for minutes without ever touching it.

'Why?' echoed Miss Clarkson, blinking as if the word was something solid that had struck her unexpectedly.

'Why was Cynthia in floods of tears?'

'But I'm telling you, my dear. That man has left her!'

'Left her!'

'They had a quarrel, and he walked straight out of the hotel. That was the day before yesterday, and he has not been back since. This afternoon the curtest note came from him to say that he never intended to return. He had secretly and in a most underhand way arranged for his luggage to be removed from the hotel to a District

Messenger office, and from there he has taken it no one knows where. He has completely disappeared.'

Eve stared. She had not been prepared for news of this momentous order.

'But what did they quarrel about?'

'Cynthia, poor child, was too overwrought to tell me!'

Eve clenched her teeth.

'The beast! . . . Poor old Cynthia . . . Shall I come round with you?'

'No, my dear, better let me look after her alone. I will tell her to write and let you know when she can see you. I must be going, Phyllis dear,' she said, as her hostess re-entered, bearing a small bottle.

'But you've only just come!' said Phyllis, surprised.

'Poor old Cynthia's husband has left her,' explained Eve briefly. 'And Clarkie's going back to look after her. She's in a pretty bad way, it seems.'

'Oh, no!'

'Yes, indeed. And I really must be going at once,' said Miss Clarkson.

Eve waited in the drawing-room till the front door banged and Phyllis came back to her. Phyllis was more wistful than ever. She had been looking forward to this tea-party, and it had not been the happy occasion she had anticipated. The two girls sat in silence for a moment.

'What brutes some men are!' said Eve at length.

'Mike,' said Phyllis dreamily, 'is an angel.'

Eve welcomed the unspoken invitation to return to a more agreeable topic. She felt very deeply for the stricken Cynthia, but she hated aimless talk, and nothing could have been more aimless than for her and Phyllis to sit there exchanging lamentations concerning a tragedy of which neither knew more than the bare outlines. Phyllis had her tragedy, too, and it was one where Eve saw the possibility of doing something practical and helpful. She was a girl of action, and was glad to be able to attack a living issue.

'Yes, let's go on talking about you and Mike,' she said. 'At present I can't understand the position at all. When Clarkie came in, you were just telling me about your stepfather and why he wouldn't help you. And I thought you made out a very poor case for him. Tell me some more. I've forgotten his name, by the way.'

'Keeble.'

'Oh! Well, I think you ought to write and tell him how hard-up you are. He may be under the impression that you are still living in luxury and don't need any help. After all, he can't know unless you tell him. And I should ask him straight out to come to the rescue. It isn't as if it was your Mike's fault that you're broke. He married you on the strength of a very good position which looked like a permanency, and lost it through no fault of his own. I should write to him, Phyl. Pitch it strong.'

'I have. I wrote today. Mike's just been offered a wonderful opportunity. A sort of farm place in Lincolnshire. You know. Cows and things. Just what he would like and just what he would do awfully well. And we only need three thousand pounds to get it . . . But I'm afraid nothing will come of it.'

'Because of Aunt Constance, you mean?'

'Yes.'

'You must *make* something come of it.' Eve's chin went up. She looked like a Goddess of Determination. 'If I were you, I'd haunt their doorstep till they had to give you the money to get rid of you. The idea of anybody doing that absurd driving-into-the-snow business in these days! Why *shouldn't* you marry the man you were in love with? If I were you, I'd go and chain myself to their railings and howl like a dog till they rushed out with cheque-books just to get some peace. Do they live in London?'

'They are down in Shropshire at present at a place called Blandings Castle.'

Eve started.

'Blandings Castle? Good gracious!'

'Aunt Constance is Lord Emsworth's sister.'

'But this is the most extraordinary thing. I'm going to Blandings myself in a few days.'

'No!'

'They've engaged me to catalogue the castle library.'

'But, Eve, were you only joking when you asked Clarkie to find you something to do? She took you quite seriously.'

'No, I wasn't joking. There's a drawback to my going to Blandings. I suppose you know the place pretty well?'

'I've often stayed there. It's beautiful.'

'Then you know Lord Emsworth's second son, Freddie Threepwood?'

'Of course.'

'Well, he's the drawback. He wants to marry me, and I certainly don't want to marry him. And what I've been wondering is whether a nice easy job like that, which would tide me over beautifully till September, is attractive enough to make up for the nuisance of having to be always squelching poor Freddie. I ought to have thought of it right at the beginning, of course, when he wrote and told me to apply for the position, but I was so delighted at the idea of regular work that it didn't occur to me. Then I began to wonder. He's such a persevering young man. He proposes early and often.'

'Where did you meet Freddie?'

'At a theatre party. About two months ago. He was living in London then, but he suddenly disappeared and I had a heart-broken letter from him, saying that he had been running up debts and things and his father had snatched him away to live at Blandings, which apparently is Freddie's idea of the Inferno. The world seems full of hard-hearted relatives.'

'Oh, Lord Emsworth isn't really hard-hearted. You will love him. He's so dreamy and absent-minded. He potters about the garden all the time. I don't think you'll like

443

Aunt Constance much. But I suppose you won't see a great deal of her.'

'Whom *shall* I see much of – except Freddie, of course?'

'Mr Baxter, Lord Emsworth's secretary, I expect. I don't like him at all. He's a sort of spectacled caveman.'

'He doesn't sound attractive. But you say the place is nice?'

'It's gorgeous. I should go, if I were you, Eve.'

'Well, I had intended not to. But now you've told me about Mr Keeble and Aunt Constance, I've changed my mind. I'll have to look in at Clarkie's office tomorrow and tell her I'm fixed up and shan't need her help. I'm going to take your sad case in hand, darling. I shall go to Blandings, and I will dog your stepfather's footsteps . . . Well, I must be going. Come and see me to the front door, or I'll be losing my way in the miles of stately corridors . . . I suppose I mayn't smash that china dog before I go? Oh, well, I just thought I'd ask.'

Out in the hall the little maid-of-all-work bobbed up and intercepted them.

'I forgot to tell you, mum, a gentleman called. I told him you was out.'

'Quite right, Jane.'

'Said his name was Smith, 'm.'

Phyllis gave a cry of dismay.

'Oh, no! What a shame! I particularly wanted you to meet him, Eve. I wish I'd known.'

'Smith?' said Eve. 'The name seems familiar. Why were you so anxious for me to meet him?'

'He's Mike's best friend. Mike worships him. He's the son of the Mr Smith I was telling you about – the one Mike was at school and Cambridge with. He's a perfect darling, Eve, and you would love him. He's just your sort. I do wish we had known. And now you're going to Blandings for goodness knows how long, and you won't be able to see him.'

'What a pity,' said Eve, politely uninterested.

444

'I'm so sorry for him.'

'Why?'

'He's in the fish business.'

'Ugh!'

'Well, he hates it, poor dear. But he was left stranded like all the rest of us after the crash, and he was put into the business by an uncle who is a sort of fish magnate.'

'Well, why does he stay there, if he dislikes it so much?' said Eve with indignation. The helpless type of man was her pet aversion. 'I hate a man who's got no enterprise.'

'I don't think you could call him unenterprising. He never struck me like that . . . You simply must meet him when you come back to London.'

'All right,' said Eve indifferently. 'Just as you like. I might put business in his way. I'm very fond of fish.'

3 — Eve Borrows an Umbrella

What strikes the visitor to London most forcibly, as he enters the heart of that city's fashionable shopping district, is the almost entire absence of ostentation in the shop-windows, the studied avoidance of garish display. About the front of the premises of Messrs Thorpe & Briscoe, for instance, who sell coal in Dover Street, there is as a rule nothing whatever to attract fascinated attention. You might give the place a glance as you passed, but you would certainly not pause and stand staring at it as at the Sistine Chapel or the Taj Mahal. Yet at ten-thirty on the morning after Eve Halliday had taken tea with her friend Phyllis Jackson in West Kensington, Psmith, lounging gracefully in the smoking-room window of the Drones Club, which is immediately opposite the Thorpe & Briscoe establishment, had been gazing at it fixedly for a full five minutes. One would have said that the spectacle enthralled him. He seemed unable to take his eyes off it.

There is always a reason for the most apparently inexplicable happenings. It is the practice of Thorpe (or Briscoe) during the months of summer to run out an awning over the shop. A quiet, genteel awning, of course, nothing to offend the eye – but an awning which offers a quite adequate protection against those sudden showers which are such a delightfully piquant feature of the English summer; one of which had just begun to sprinkle the West End of London with a good deal of heartiness and vigour. And under this awning, peering plaintively out at the rain, Eve Halliday, on her way to the Ada Clarkson

Employment Bureau, had taken refuge. It was she who had so enchained Psmith's interest. It was his considered opinion that she improved the Thorpe & Briscoe frontage by about ninety-five per cent.

Pleased and gratified as Psmith was to have something nice to look at out of the smoking-room window, he was also somewhat puzzled. This girl seemed to him to radiate an atmosphere of wealth. Starting at farthest south and proceeding northward, she began in a gleam of patent-leather shoes. Fawn stockings, obviously expensive, led up to a black crêpe frock. And then, just as the eye was beginning to feel that there could be nothing more, it was stunned by a supreme hat of soft, dull satin with a black bird of Paradise feather falling down over the left shoulder. Even to the masculine eye, which is notoriously to seek in these matters, a whale of a hat. And yet this sumptuously upholstered young woman had been marooned by a shower of rain beneath the awning of Messrs Thorpe & Briscoe. Why Psmith asked himself, was this? Even, he argued, if Charles the chauffeur had been given the day off or was driving her father the millionaire to the City to attend to his vast interests, she could surely afford a cab-fare? We, who are familiar with the state of Eve's finances, can understand her inability to take cabs, but Psmith was frankly perplexed.

Being, however, both ready-witted and chivalrous, he perceived that this was no time for idle speculation. His not to reason why; his obvious duty was to take steps to assist Beauty in distress. He left the window of the smoking-room, and, having made his way with a smooth dignity to the club's cloak-room, proceeded to submit a row of umbrellas to a close inspection. He was not easy to satisfy. Two which he went so far as to pull out of the rack he returned with a shake of the head. Quite good umbrellas, but not fit for this special service. At length, however, he found a beauty, and a gentle smile flickered across his solemn face. He put up his monocle and gazed

searchingly at this umbrella. It seemed to answer every
test. He was well pleased with it.

'Whose,' he inquired of the attendant, 'is this?'

'Belongs to the Honourable Mr Walderwick, sir.'

'Ah!' said Psmith tolerantly.

He tucked the umbrella under his arm and went out.

Meanwhile Eve Halliday, lightening up the sombre
austerity of Messrs Thorpe & Briscoe's shop-front,
continued to think hard thoughts of the English climate
and to inspect the sky in the hope of detecting a spot of
blue. She was engaged in this cheerless occupation when
at her side a voice spoke.

'Excuse me!'

A hatless young man was standing beside her, holding
an umbrella. He was a striking-looking young man, very
tall, very thin and very well dressed. In his right eye there
was a monocle, and through this he looked down at her
with a grave friendliness. He said nothing further, but,
taking her fingers, clasped them round the handle of the
umbrella, which he had obligingly opened, and then with
a courteous bow proceeded to dash with long strides
across the road, disappearing through the doorway of a
gloomy building which, from the number of men who
had gone in and out during her vigil, she had set down as
a club of some sort.

A good many surprising things had happened to Eve
since first she had come to live in London, but nothing
quite so surprising as this. For several minutes she stood
where she was without moving, staring round-eyed, at
the building opposite. The episode was, however,
apparently ended. The young man did not reappear. He
did not even show himself at the window. The club had
swallowed him up. And eventually Eve, deciding that
this was not the sort of day on which to refuse umbrellas
even if they dropped inexplicably from heaven, stepped
out from under the awning, laughing helplessly, and

448

started to resume her interrupted journey to Miss
Clarkson's.

The offices of the Ada Clarkson International
Employment Bureau ('Promptitude – Courtesy –
Intelligence') are at the top of Shaftesbury Avenue, a little
way past the Palace Theatre. Eve, closing the umbrella,
which had prevented even a spot of rain falling on her
hat, climbed the short stair leading to the door and
tapped on the window marked 'Inquiries'.

'Can I see Miss Clarkson?'

'What name, please?' responded Inquiries promptly
and with intelligent courtesy.

'Miss Halliday.'

Brief interlude, involving business with speaking-
tube.

'Will you go into the private office, please,' said
Inquiries a moment later, in a voice which now added
respect to the other advertised qualities, for she had had
time to observe and digest the hat.

Eve passed in through the general waiting-room with
its magazine-covered table, and tapped at the door
beyond marked 'Private'.

'Eve, dear!' exclaimed Miss Clarkson the moment she
had entered, 'I don't know how to tell you, but I have
been looking through my books and I have nothing,
simply nothing. There is not a single place that you
could possibly take. What *is* to be done?'

'That's all right, Clarkie.'

'But . . .'

'I didn't come to talk business. I came to ask after
Cynthia. How is she?'

Miss Clarkson sighed.

'Poor child, she is still in a dreadful state, and no
wonder. No news at all from her husband. He has simply
deserted her.'

'Poor darling! Can't I see her?'

449

'Not at present. I have persuaded her to go down to Brighton for a day or two. I think the sea air will pick her up. So much better than mooning about in a London hotel. She is leaving on the eleven o'clock train. I gave her your love, and she was most grateful that you should have remembered your old friendship and be sorry for her in her affliction.'

'Well, I can write to her. Where is she staying?'

'I don't know her Brighton address, but no doubt the Cadogan Hotel would forward letters. I think she would be glad to hear from you, dear.'

Eve looked sadly at the framed testimonials which decorated the wall. She was not often melancholy, but it was such a beast of a day and all her friends seemed to be having such a bad time.

'Oh, Clarkie,' she said, 'what a lot of trouble there is in the world!'

'Yes, yes!' sighed Miss Clarkson, a specialist on this subject.

'All the horses you back finish sixth and all the girls you like best come croppers. Poor little Phyllis! weren't you sorry for her?'

'But her husband, surely, is most devoted?'

'Yes, but she's frightfully hard-up, and you remember how opulent she used to be at school. Of course, it must sound funny hearing me pitying people for having no money. But somehow other people's hard-upness always seems so much worse than mine. Especially poor old Phyl's, because she really isn't fit to stand it. I've been used to being absolutely broke all my life. Poor dear father always seemed to be writing an article against time, with creditors scratching earnestly at the door.' Eve laughed, but her eyes were misty. 'He was a brick, wasn't he? I mean, sending me to a first-class school like Wayland House when he often hadn't enough money to buy tobacco, poor angel. I expect he wasn't always up to time with fees, was he?'

'Well, my dear, of course I was only an assistant mistress at Wayland House and had nothing to do with the financial side, but I did hear sometimes . . .'

'Poor darling father! Do you know, one of my earliest recollections – I couldn't have been more than ten – is of a ring at the front-door bell and father diving like a seal under the sofa and poking his head out and imploring me in a hoarse voice to hold the fort. I went to the door and found an indignant man with a blue paper. I prattled so prettily and innocently that he not only went away quite contentedly but actually patted me on the head and gave me a penny. And when the door had shut father crawled out from under the sofa and gave me twopence, making threepence in all – a good morning's work. I bought father a diamond ring with it at a shop down the street, I remember. At least I thought it was a diamond. They may have swindled me, for I was very young.'

'You have had a hard life, dear.'

'Yes, but hasn't it been a lark! I've loved every minute of it. Besides, you can't call me really one of the submerged tenth. Uncle Thomas left me a hundred and fifty pounds a year, and mercifully I'm not allowed to touch the capital. If only there were no hats or safety bets in the world, I should be smugly opulent . . . But I mustn't keep you any longer, Clarkie dear. I expect the waiting-room is full of dukes who want cooks and cooks who want dukes, all fidgeting and wondering how much longer you're going to keep them. Good-bye, darling.'

And, having kissed Miss Clarkson fondly and straightened her hat, which the other's motherly embrace had disarranged, Eve left the room.

4 — Painful Scene at the Drones Club

Meanwhile at the Drones Club, a rather painful scene had been taking place. Psmith, regaining the shelter of the building, had made his way to the wash-room, where, having studied his features with interest for a moment in the mirror, he smoothed his hair, which the rain had somewhat disordered, and brushed his clothes with extreme care. He then went to the cloak-room for his hat. The attendant regarded him as he entered with the air of one whose mind is not wholly at rest.

'Mr Walderwick was in here a moment ago, sir,' said the attendant.

'Yes?' said Psmith, mildly interested. 'An energetic, bustling soul, Comrade Walderwick. Always somewhere. Now here, now there.'

'Asking about his umbrella, he was,' pursued the attendant with a touch of coldness.

'Indeed? Asking about his umbrella, eh?'

'Made a great fuss about it, sir, he did.'

'And rightly,' said Psmith with approval. 'The good man loves his umbrella.'

'Of course I had to tell him that you had took it, sir.'

'I would not have it otherwise,' assented Psmith heartily. 'I like this spirit of candour. There must be no reservations, no subterfuges between you and Comrade Walderwick. Let all be open and above-board.'

'He seemed very put out, sir. He went off to find you.'

'I am always glad of a chat with Comrade Walderwick,' said Psmith. 'Always.'

He left the cloak-room and made for the hall, where he desired the porter to procure him a cab. This having drawn up in front of the club, he descended the steps and was about to enter it, when there was a hoarse cry in his rear, and through the front door there came bounding a pinkly indignant youth, who called loudly:

'Here! Hi! Smith! Dash it!'

Psmith climbed into the cab and gazed benevolently out at the new-comer.

'Ah, Comrade Walderwick!' he said. 'What have we on our mind?'

'Where's my umbrella?' demanded the pink one. 'The cloak-room waiter says you took my umbrella. I mean, a joke's a joke, but that was a dashed good umbrella.'

'It was, indeed,' Psmith agreed cordially. 'It may be of interest to you to know that I selected it as the only possible one from among a number of competitors. I fear this club is becoming very mixed, Comrade Walderwick. You with your pure mind would hardly believe the rottenness of some of the umbrellas I inspected in the cloak-room.'

'Where is it?'

'The cloak-room? You turn to the left as you go in at the main entrance and . . .'

'My umbrella, dash it! Where's my umbrella?'

'Ah, there,' said Psmith, and there was a touch of manly regret in his voice, 'you have me. I gave it to a young lady in the street. Where she is at the present moment I could not say.'

The pink youth tottered slightly.

'You gave my umbrella to a girl?'

'A very loose way of describing her. You would not speak of her in that light fashion if you had seen her. Comrade Walderwick, she was wonderful! I am a plain, blunt, rugged man, above the softer emotions as a general thing, but I frankly confess that she stirred a chord in me which is not often stirred. She thrilled my battered old heart, Comrade Walderwick. There is no other word. Thrilled it!'

453

'But, dash it! . . .'

Psmith reached out a long arm and laid his hand paternally on the other's shoulder.

'Be brave, Comrade Walderwick!' he said. 'Face this thing like a man! I am sorry to have been the means of depriving you of an excellent umbrella, but as you will readily understand I had no alternative. It was raining. She was over there, crouched despairingly beneath the awning of that shop. She wanted to be elsewhere, but the moisture lay in wait to damage her hat. What could I do? What could any man worthy of the name do but go down to the cloak-room and pinch the best umbrella in sight and take it to her? Yours was easily the best. There was absolutely no comparison. I gave it to her, and she has gone off with it, happy once more. This explanation,' said Psmith, 'will, I am sure, sensibly diminish your natural chagrin. You have lost your umbrella, Comrade Walderwick, but in what a cause! In what a cause, Comrade Walderwick! You are now entitled to rank with Sir Philip Sidney and Sir Walter Raleigh. The latter is perhaps the closer historical parallel. He spread his cloak to keep a queen from wetting her feet. You – by proxy – yielded up your umbrella to save a girl's hat. Posterity will be proud of you, Comrade Walderwick. I shall be vastly surprised if you do not go down in legend and song. Children in ages to come will cluster about their grandfather's knees, saying, "Tell us how the great Walderwick lost his umbrella, grandpapa!" And he will tell them, and they will rise from the recital better, deeper, broader children . . . But now, as I see that the driver has started his meter, I fear I must conclude this little chat – which I, for one, have heartily enjoyed. Drive on,' he said, leaning out of the window. 'I want to go to Ada Clarkson's International Employment Bureau in Shaftesbury Avenue.'

The cab moved off. The Hon. Hugo Walderwick, after

one passionate glance in its wake, realized that he was getting wet and went back into the club.

Arriving at the address named, Psmith paid his cab and having mounted the stairs, delicately knuckled the ground-glass window of Inquiries.

'My dear Miss Clarkson,' he began in an affable voice, the instant the window had shot up, 'if you can spare me a few moments of your valuable time . . .'

'Miss Clarkson's engaged.'

Psmith scrutinized her gravely through his monocle.

'Aren't *you* Miss Clarkson?'

Inquiries said she was not.

'Then,' said Psmith, 'there has been a misunderstanding, for which,' he added cordially, 'I am to blame. Perhaps I could see her anon? You will find me in the waiting-room when required.'

He went into the waiting-room, and, having picked up a magazine from the table, settled down to read a story in *The Girls' Pet* – the January number of the year 1919, for Employment Agencies, like dentists, prefer their literature of a matured vintage. He was absorbed in this when Eve came out of the private office.

5 — Psmith Applies for Employment

Psmith rose courteously as she entered.

'My dear Miss Clarkson,' he said, 'if you can spare me a moment of your valuable time . . .'

'Good gracious!' said Eve. 'How extraordinary!'

'A singular coincidence,' agreed Psmith.

'You never gave me time to thank you for the umbrella,' said Eve reproachfully. 'You must have thought me awfully rude. But you took my breath away.'

'My dear Miss Clarkson, please do not . . .'

'Why do you keep calling me that?'

'Aren't *you* Miss Clarkson, either?'

'Of course I'm not.'

'Then,' said Psmith, 'I must start my quest all over again. These constant checks are trying to an ardent spirit. Perhaps you are a young bride come to engage her first cook?'

'No. I'm not married.'

'Good!'

Eve found his relieved thankfulness a little embarrassing. In the momentary pause which followed his remark, Inquiries entered alertly.

'Miss Clarkson will see you now, sir.'

'Leave us,' said Psmith with a wave of his hand. 'We would be alone.'

Inquiries stared; then, awed by his manner and general appearance of magnificence, withdrew.

'I suppose really,' said Eve, toying with the umbrella, 'I ought to give this back to you.' She glanced at the dripping window. But it *is* raining rather hard, isn't it?'

'Like the dickens,' assented Psmith.

'Then would you mind very much if I kept it till this evening?'

'Please do.'

'Thanks ever so much. I will send it back to you tonight if you will give me the name and address.'

Psmith waved his hand, deprecatingly.

'No, no. If it is of any use to you, I hope that you will look on it as a present.'

'A present!'

'A gift,' explained Psmith.

'But I really can't go about accepting expensive umbrellas from people. Where shall I send it?'

'If you insist, you may send it to the Hon. Hugo Walderwick, Drones Club, Dover Street. But it really isn't necessary.'

'I won't forget. And thank you very much, Mr Walderwick.'

'Why do you call me that?'

'Well, you said . . .'

'Ah, I see. A slight confusion of ideas. No, I am not Mr Walderwick. And between ourselves I should hate to be. His is a very C3 intelligence. Comrade Walderwick is merely the man to whom the umbrella belongs.'

Eve's eyes opened wide.

'Do you mean to say you gave me somebody else's umbrella?'

'I had unfortunately omitted to bring my own out with me this morning.'

'I never heard of such a thing!'

'Merely practical Socialism. Other people are content to talk about the Redistribution of property. I go out and do it.'

'But won't he be awfully angry when he finds out it has gone?'

'He *has* found out. And it was pretty to see his delight. I explained the circumstances, and he was charmed to have been of service to you.'

The door opened again, and this time it was Miss Clarkson in person who entered. She had found Inquiries' statement over the speaking-tube rambling and unsatisfactory, and had come to investigate for herself the reason why the machinery of the office was being held up.

'Oh, I must go,' said Eve, as she saw her. 'I'm interrupting your business.'

'I'm so glad you're still here, dear,' said Miss Clarkson. 'I have just been looking over my files, and I see that there *is* one vacancy. For a nurse,' said Miss Clarkson with a touch of the apologetic in her voice.

'Oh, no, that's all right,' said Eve. 'I don't really need anything. But thanks ever so much for bothering.'

She smiled affectionately upon the proprietress, bestowed another smile upon Psmith as he opened the door for her, and went out. Psmith turned away from the door with a thoughtful look upon his face.

'Is that young lady a nurse?' he asked.

'Do you want a nurse?' inquired Miss Clarkson, at once the woman of business.

'I want that nurse,' said Psmith with conviction.

'She is a delightful girl,' said Miss Clarkson with enthusiasm. 'There is no one in whom I would feel more confidence in recommending to a position. She is a Miss Halliday, the daughter of a very clever but erratic writer, who died some years ago. I can speak with particular knowledge of Miss Halliday, for I was for many years an assistant mistress at Wayland House, where she was at school. She is a charming, warm-hearted, impulsive girl ... But you will hardly want to hear all this.'

'On the contrary,' said Psmith, 'I could listen for hours. You have stumbled upon my favourite subject.'

Miss Clarkson eyed him a little doubtfully, and decided that it would be best to reintroduce the business theme.

'Perhaps, when you say you are looking for a nurse, you mean you need a hospital nurse?'

'My friends have sometimes suggested it.'

'Miss Halliday's greatest experience has, of course, been as a governess.'

'A governess is just as good,' said Psmith agreeably.

Miss Clarkson began to be conscious of a sensation of being out of her depth.

'How old are your children, sir?' she asked.

'I fear,' said Psmith, 'you are peeping into Volume Two. This romance has only just started.'

'I am afraid,' said Miss Clarkson, now completely fogged, 'I do not quite understand. What exactly are you looking for?'

Psmith flicked a speck of fluff from his coat-sleeve.

'A job,' he said.

'A job!' echoed Miss Clarkson, her voice breaking in an amazed squeak.

Psmith raised his eyebrows.

'You seem surprised. Isn't this a job emporium?'

'This *is* an Employment Bureau,' admitted Miss Clarkson.

'I knew it, I knew it,' said Psmith. ' Something seemed to tell me. Possibly it was the legend "Employment Bureau" over the door. And those framed testimonials would convince the most sceptical. Yes, Miss Clarkson, I want a job, and I feel somehow that you are the woman to find it for me. I have inserted an advertisement in the papers, expressing my readiness to undertake any form of employment, but I have since begun to wonder if after all this will lead to wealth and fame. At any rate, it is wise to attack the great world from another angle as well, so I come to you.'

'But you must excuse me if I remark that this application of yours strikes me as most extra-ordinary.'

'Why? I am young, active, and extremely broke.'

'But your – er – your clothes . . .'

Psmith squinted, not without complacency, down a

459

faultlessly fitting waistcoat, and flicked another speck of dust off his sleeve.

'You consider me well dressed?' he said. 'You find me natty? Well, well, perhaps you are right, perhaps you are right But consider, Miss Clarkson. If one expects to find employment in these days of strenuous competition, one must be neatly and decently clad. Employers look askance at a baggy trouser-leg. A zippy waistcoat is more to them than an honest heart. This beautiful crease was obtained with the aid of the mattress upon which I tossed feverishly last night in my attic room.'

'I can't take you seriously.'

'Oh, don't say that, please.'

'You really want me to find you work?'

'I prefer the term "employment".'

Miss Clarkson produced a notebook.

'If you are really not making this application just as a joke . . .'

'I assure you, no. My entire capital consists, in specie, of about ten pounds.'

'Then perhaps you will tell me your name.'

'Ah! Things are beginning to move. The name is Psmith. P-smith. The p is silent.'

'Psmith?'

'Psmith.'

Miss Clarkson brooded over this for a moment in almost pained silence, then recovered her slipping grip of affairs.

'I think,' she said, 'you had better give me a few particulars about yourself.'

'There is nothing I should like better,' responded Psmith warmly. 'I am always ready – I may say eager – to tell people the story of my life, but in this rushing age I get little encouragement. Let us start at the beginning. My infancy. When I was but a babe, my eldest sister was bribed with sixpence an hour by my nurse to keep an eye on me and see that I did not raise Cain. At the end of the first day she struck for a shilling, and got it. We now pass to my boyhood. At an early age I was sent to Eton, everybody predicting a bright career for me. Those were happy days, Miss Clarkson. A merry, laughing lad with curly hair and a sunny smile, it is not too much to say that I was the pet of the place. The old cloisters. . . . But I am boring you. I can see it in your eye.'

'No, no,' protested Miss Clarkson. 'But what I meant was . . . I thought you might have had some experience in some particular line of . . . In fact, what sort of work . . . ?'

'Employment.'

'What sort of employment do you require?'

'Broadly speaking,' said Psmith, 'any reasonably salaried position that has nothing to do with fish.'

'Fish!' quavered Miss Clarkson, slipping again. 'Why fish?'

'Because, Miss Clarkson, the fish trade was until this morning my walk in life, and my soul has sickened of it.'

'You are in the *fish* trade?' squeaked Miss Clarkson, with an amazed glance at the knife-like crease in his trousers.

'These are not my working clothes,' said Psmith, following and interpreting her glance. 'Yes, owing to a financial upheaval in my branch of the family, I was until this morning at the beck and call of an uncle who unfortunately happens to be a Mackerel Monarch or a Sardine Sultan, or whatever these merchant princes are called who rule the fish market. He insisted on my going into the business to learn it from the bottom up, thinking, no doubt, that I would follow in his footsteps and eventually work my way to the position of a Whitebait Wizard. Alas! he was too sanguine. It was not to be,' said Psmith solemnly, fixing an owl-like gaze on Miss Clarkson through his eye-glass.

'No?' said Miss Clarkson.

'No. Last night I was obliged to inform him that the

461

fish business was all right, but it wouldn't do, and that I proposed to sever my connection with the firm for ever. I may say at once that there ensued something in the nature of a family earthquake. Hard words,' sighed Psmith. 'Black looks. Unseemly wrangle. And the upshot of it all was that my uncle washed his hands of me and drove me forth into the great world. Hence my anxiety to find employment. My uncle has definitely withdrawn his countenance from me, Miss Clarkson.'

'Dear, dear!' murmured the proprietress sympathetically.

'Yes. He is a hard man, and he judges his fellows solely by their devotion to fish. I never in my life met a man so wrapped up in a subject. For years he has been practically a monomaniac on the subject of fish. So much so that he actually looks like one. It is as if he had taken one of those auto-suggestion courses and had kept saying to himself, 'Every day, in every way, I grow more and more like a fish.' His closest friends can hardly tell now whether he more nearly resembles a halibut or a cod . . . But I am boring you again with this family gossip?'

He eyed Miss Clarkson with such a sudden and penetrating glance that she started nervously.

'No, no,' she exclaimed.

'You relieve my apprehensions. I am only too well aware that, when fairly launched on the topic of fish, I am more than apt to weary my audience. I cannot understand this enthusiasm for fish. My uncle used to talk about an unusually large catch of pilchards in Cornwall in much the same awed way as a right-minded curate would talk about the spiritual excellence of his bishop. To me, Miss Clarkson, from the very start, the fish business was what I can only describe as a wash-out. It nauseated my finer feelings. It got right in amongst my fibres. I had to rise and partake of a simple breakfast about four in the morning, after which I would make my way to Billingsgate Market and stand for some hours

knee-deep in dead fish of every description. A jolly life
for a cat, no doubt, but a bit too thick for a Shropshire
Psmith. Mine, Miss Clarkson, is a refined and poetic
nature. I like to be surrounded by joy and life, and I know
nothing more joyless and deader than a dead fish.
Multiply that dead fish by a million, and you have an
environment which only a Dante could contemplate
with equanimity. My uncle used to tell me that the way
to ascertain whether a fish was fresh was to peer into its
eyes. Could I spend the springtime of life staring into
the eyes of dead fish? No!' He rose. 'Well, I will not
detain you any longer. Thank you for the unfailing
courtesy and attention with which you have listened to
me. You can understand now why my talents are on the
market and why I am compelled to state specifically
that no employment can be considered which has
anything to do with fish. I am convinced that you will
shortly have something particularly good to offer me.'

'I don't know that I can say that, Mr Psmith.'

'The p is silent, as in pshrimp,' he reminded her. 'Oh,
by the way,' he said, pausing at the door, 'there is one other
thing before I go. While I was waiting for you to be
disengaged, I chanced on an instalment of a serial story
in *The Girl's Pet* for January, 1919. My search for the
remaining issues proved fruitless. The title was "Her
Honour At Stake," by Jane Emmeline Moss. You don't
happen to know how it all came out in the end, do you?
Did Lord Eustace ever learn that, when he found Clarice
in Sir Jasper's rooms at midnight, she had only gone there
to recover some compromising letters for a girl friend?
You don't know? I feared as much. Well, good morning,
Miss Clarkson, good morning. I leave my future in your
hands with a light heart.'

'I will do my best for you, of course.'

'And what,' said Psmith cordially, 'could be better
than Miss Clarkson's best?'

He closed the door gently behind him, and went out.

Struck by a kindly thought, he tapped upon Inquiries'
window, and beamed benevolently as her bobbed head
shot into view.

'They tell me,' he said, 'that Aspidistra is much fancied
for the four o'clock race at Birmingham this afternoon.
I give the information without prejudice, for what it is
worth. Good day!'

6 — Lord Emsworth Meets a Poet

The rain had stopped when Psmith stepped out into the street, and the sun was shining again in that half blustering, half apologetic manner which it affects on its reappearance after a summer shower. The pavements glistened cheerfully, and the air had a welcome freshness. Pausing at the corner, he pondered for a moment as to the best method of passing the hour and twenty minutes which must elapse before he could reasonably think of lunching. The fact that the offices of the *Morning Globe* were within easy strolling distance decided him to go thither and see if the first post had brought anything in the shape of answers to his advertisements. And his energy was rewarded a few minutes later when Box 365 on being opened yielded up quite a little budget of literary matter. No fewer than seven letters in all. A nice bag.

What, however, had appeared at first sight evidence of a pleasing ebullition of enterprise on the part of the newspaper-reading public turned out on closer inspection, when he had retired to a corner where he could concentrate in peace, a hollow delusion. Enterprising in a sense though the communications were – and they certainly showed the writers as men of considerable ginger and business push – to Psmith they came as a disappointment. He had expected better things. These letters were not at all what he had paid good money to receive. They missed the point altogether. The right spirit, it seemed to him, was entirely absent.

The first envelope, attractive though it looked from the outside, being of an expensive brand of stationery

465

and gaily adorned with a somewhat startling crest, merely contained a pleasantly-worded offer from a Mr Alistair MacDougall to advance him any sum from ten to fifty thousand pounds on his note of hand only. The second revealed a similar proposal from another Scot named Colin MacDonald. While in the third Mr Ian Campbell was prepared to go as high as one hundred thousand. All three philanthropists had but one stipulation to make – they would have no dealings with minors. Youth, with all its glorious traditions, did not seem to appeal to them. But they cordially urged Psmith, in the event of his having celebrated his twenty-first birthday, to come round to the office and take the stuff away in a sack.

Keeping his head well in the midst of this shower of riches, Psmith dropped the three letters with a sigh into the wastepaper basket, and opened the next in order. This was a bulky envelope, and its contents consisted of a printed brochure entitled, 'This Night Shall Thy Soul Be Required Of Thee' – while, by a curious and appropriate coincidence, Number Five proved to be a circular from an energetic firm of coffin-makers offering to bury him for eight pounds ten. Number Six, also printed, was a manifesto from one Howard Hill, of Newmarket, recommending him to apply without delay for 'Hill's Three-Horse Special,' without which – ('Who,' demanded Mr Hill in large type, 'gave you Wibbly-Wob for the Jubilee Cup?') – no sportsman could hope to accomplish the undoing of the bookmakers.

Although by doing so he convicted himself of that very lack of enterprise which he had been deploring in the great public, Psmith placed this communication with the others in the wastepaper basket. There now remained only Number Seven, and a slight flicker of hope returned to him when he perceived that this envelope was addressed by hand and not in typescript. He opened it.

Beyond a doubt he had kept the pick of the bunch to the last. Here was something that made up for all those

other disappointments. Written in a scrawly and
apparently agitated hand, the letter ran as follows:

> If R. Psmith will meet the writer in the lobby of the
> Piccadilly Palace Hotel at twelve sharp, Friday, July
> 1, business may result if business meant and terms
> reasonable. R. Psmith will wear a pink chrysan-
> themum in his buttonhole, and will say to the writer,
> 'There will be rain in Northumberland tomorrow,' to
> which the writer will reply, 'Good for the crops.'
> Kindly be punctual.

A pleased smile played about Psmith's solemn face as
he read this communication for the second time. It was
much more the sort of thing for which he had been hoping.
Although his closest friend, Mike Jackson, was a young
man of complete ordinariness, Psmith's tastes when he
sought companionship lay as a rule in the direction of the
bizarre. He preferred his humanity eccentric. And 'the
writer', to judge him by this specimen of his
correspondence, appeared to be eccentric enough for the
most exacting taste. Whether this promising person
turned out to be a ribald jester or an earnest crank, Psmith
felt no doubt whatever as to the advisability of following
the matter up. Whichever he might be, his society ought
to afford entertainment during the interval before lunch.
Psmith glanced at his watch. The hour was a quarter to
twelve. He would be able to secure the necessary
chrysanthemum and reach the Piccadilly Palace Hotel by
twelve sharp, thus achieving the businesslike
punctuality on which the unknown writer seemed to set
such store.

It was not until he had entered the florist's shop on the
way to the tryst that it was borne in upon him that
the adventure was going to have its drawbacks. The first
of these was the chrysanthemum. Preoccupied with the

rest of the communication, Psmith, when he had read the letter, had not given much thought to the decoration which it would be necessary for him to wear; and it was only when, in reply to his demand for a chrysanthemum, the florist came forward, almost hidden, like the army at Dunsinane, behind what looked like a small shrubbery, that he realized what he, a correct and fastidious dresser, was up against.

'Is that a chrysanthemum?'

'Yes, sir. Pink chrysanthemum.'

'One!'

'Yes, sir. One pink chrysanthemum.'

Psmith regarded the repellent object with disfavour through his eyeglass. Then, having placed it in his buttonhole, he proceeded on his way, feeling like some wild thing peering through the undergrowth. The distressing shrub completely spoiled his walk.

Arrived at the hotel and standing in the lobby, he perceived the existence of further complications. The lobby was in its usual state of congestion, it being a recognized meeting-place for those who did not find it convenient to go as far east as that traditional rendezvous of Londoners, the spot under the clock at Charing Cross Station; and 'the writer', while giving instructions as to how Psmith should ornament his exterior, had carelessly omitted to mention how he himself was to be recognized. A rollicking, slap-dash conspirator, was Psmith's opinion.

It seemed best to take up a position as nearly as possible in the centre of the lobby and stand there until 'the writer', lured by the chrysanthemum, should come forward and start something. This he accordingly did, but when at the end of ten minutes nothing had happened beyond a series of collisions with perhaps a dozen hurrying visitors to the hotel, he decided on a more active course. A young man of sporting appearance had been standing beside him for the last five minutes, and ever and anon this young man had glanced with some impatience at his watch. He was plainly waiting for someone, so Psmith tried the formula on him.

'There will be rain,' said Psmith, 'in Northumberland tomorrow.'

The young man looked at him, not without interest, certainly, but without that gleam of intelligence in his eye which Psmith had hoped to see.

'What?' he replied.

'There will be rain in Northumberland tomorrow.'

'Thanks, Zadkiel,' said the young man. 'Deuced gratifying, I'm sure. I suppose you couldn't predict the winner of the Goodwood Cup as well?'

He then withdrew rapidly to intercept a young woman in a large hat who had just come through the swing doors. Psmith was forced to the conclusion that this was not his man. He was sorry on the whole, for he had seemed a pleasant fellow.

As Psmith had taken up a stationary position and the population of the lobby was for the most part in a state of flux, he was finding himself next to someone new all the time; and now he decided to accost the individual whom the re-shuffle had just brought elbow to elbow with him. This was a jovial-looking soul with a flowered waistcoat, a white hat, and a mottled face. Just the man who might have written that letter.

The effect upon this person of Psmith's meteorological remark was instantaneous. A light of the utmost friendliness shone in his beautifully-shaven face as he turned. He seized Psmith's hand and gripped it with a delightful heartiness. He had the air of a man who has found a friend, and what is more, an old friend. He had a sort of journeys-end-in-lovers'-meeting look.

'My dear old chap!' he cried. 'I've been waiting for you to speak for the last five minutes. Knew we'd met before somewhere, but couldn't place you. Face familiar as the dickens, of course. Well, well, well! And how are they all?'

'Who?' said Psmith courteously.

'Why, the boys, my dear chap.'

'Oh, the boys?'

'The dear old boys,' said the other, specifying more exactly. He slapped Psmith on the shoulder. 'What times those were, eh?'

'Which?' said Psmith.

'The times we all used to have together.'

'Oh, *those*?' said Psmith.

Something of discouragement seemed to creep over the other's exuberance, as a cloud creeps over the summer sky. But he persevered.

'Fancy meeting you again like this!'

'It is a small world,' agreed Psmith.

'I'd ask you to come and have a drink,' said the jovial one, with the slight increase of tensity which comes to a man who approaches the core of a business deal, 'but the fact is my ass of a man sent me out this morning without a penny. Forgot to give me my note-case. Damn careless! I'll have to sack the fellow.'

'Annoying, certainly,' said Psmith.

'I wish I could have stood you a drink,' said the other wistfully.

'Of all sad words of tongue or pen, the saddest are these, "It might have been",' sighed Psmith.

'I'll tell you what,' said the jovial one, inspired. 'Lend me a fiver, my dear old boy. That's the best way out of the difficulty. I can send it round to your hotel or wherever you are this evening when I get home.'

A sweet, sad smile played over Psmith's face.

'Leave me, comrade!' he murmured.

'Eh?'

'Pass along, old friend, pass along.'

Resignation displaced joviality in the other's countenance.

'Nothing doing?' he inquired.

'Nothing.'

'Well, there was no harm in trying,' argued the other.

'None whatever.'

'You see,' said the now far less jovial man confidentially, 'you look such a perfect mug with that eyeglass that it tempts a chap.'

'I can quite understand how it must!'

'No offence.'

'Assuredly not.'

The white hat disappeared through the swing doors, and Psmith returned to his quest. He engaged the attention of a middle-aged man in a snuff-coloured suit who had just come within hail.

'There will be rain in Northumberland tomorrow,' he said.

The man peered at him inquiringly.

'Hey?' he said.

Psmith repeated his observation.

'Huh?' said the man.

Psmith was beginning to lose the unruffled calm which made him such an impressive figure to the public eye. He had not taken into consideration the possibility that the object of his search might be deaf. It undoubtedly added to the embarrassment of the pursuit. He was moving away, when a hand fell on his sleeve.

Psmith turned. The hand which still grasped his sleeve belonged to an elegantly dressed young man of somewhat nervous and feverish appearance. During his recent vigil Psmith had noticed this young man standing not far away, and had had half a mind to include him in the platoon of new friends he was making that morning.

'I say,' said this young man in a tense whisper, 'did I hear you say that there would be rain in Northumberland tomorrow?'

'If,' said Smith, 'you were anywhere within the radius

of a dozen yards while I was chatting with the recent deaf adder, I think it is possible that you did.'

'Good for the crops,' said the young man. 'Come over here where we can talk quietly.'

2

'So you're R. Psmith?' said the young man, when they had made their way to a remote corner of the lobby, apart from the throng.

'The same.'

'I say, dash it, you're frightfully late, you know. I told you to be here at twelve sharp. It's nearly twelve past.'

'You wrong me,' said Psmith. 'I arrived here precisely at twelve. Since when, I have been standing like Patience on a monument . . .'

'Like what?'

'Let it go,' said Psmith. 'It is not important.'

'I asked you to wear a pink chrysanthemum. So I could recognize you, you know.'

'I *am* wearing a pink chrysanthemum. I should have imagined that that was a fact that the most casual could hardly have overlooked.'

'That thing?' The other gazed disparagingly at the floral decoration. 'I thought it was some kind of cabbage. I meant one of those little what-d'you-may-call-its that people do wear in their button-holes.'

'Carnation, possibly?'

'Carnation! That's right.'

Psmith removed the chrysanthemum and dropped it behind his chair. He looked at his companion reproachfully.

'If you had studied botany at school, comrade,' he said, 'much misery might have been averted. I cannot begin to tell you the spiritual agony I suffered, trailing through the metropolis behind that shrub.'

Whatever decent sympathy and remorse the other

might have shown at these words was swept away in the shock resultant on a glance at his watch. Not for an instant during this brief return of his to London had Freddie Threepwood been unmindful of his father's stern injunction to him to catch the twelve-fifty train back to Market Blandings. If he missed it, there would be the deuce of a lot of unpleasantness, and unpleasantness in the home was the one thing Freddie wanted to avoid nowadays; for, like a prudent convict in a prison, he hoped by exemplary behaviour to get his sentence of imprisonment at Blandings Castle reduced for good conduct.

'Good Lord! I've only got about five minutes. Got to talk quick . . . About this thing. This business. That advertisement of yours.'

'Ah, yes. My advertisement. It interested you?'

'Was it on the level?'

'Assuredly. We Psmiths do not deceive.'

Freddie looked at him doubtfully.

'You know, you aren't a bit like I expected you'd be.'

'In what respect,' inquired Psmith, 'do I fall short of the ideal?'

'It isn't so much falling short. It's – oh, I don't know . . . Well, yes, if you want to know, I thought you'd be a tougher specimen altogether. I got the impression from your advertisement that you were down and out and ready for anything, and you look as if you were on your way to a garden-party at Buckingham Palace.'

'Ah!' said Psmith, enlightened. 'It is my costume that is causing these doubts in your mind. This is the second time this morning that such a misunderstanding has occurred. Have no misgivings. These trousers may sit well, but, if they do, it is because the pockets are empty.'

'Are you really broke!'

'As broke as the Ten Commandments.'

'I'm hanged if I can believe it.'

473

'Suppose I brush my hat the wrong way for a moment?' said Psmith obligingly. 'Would that help?'

His companion remained silent for a few moments. In spite of the fact that he was in so great a hurry and that every minute that passed brought nearer the moment when he would be compelled to tear himself away and make a dash for Paddington Station, Freddie was finding it difficult to open the subject he had come there to discuss.

'Look here,' he said at length, 'I shall have to trust you, dash it.'

'You could pursue no better course.'

'It's like this. I'm trying to raise a thousand quid . . .'

'I regret that I cannot offer to advance it to you myself. I have, indeed, already been compelled to decline to lend a gentleman who claimed to be an old friend of mine so small a sum as a fiver. But there is a dear obliging soul of the name of Alistair MacDougall who . . .'

'Good Lord! You don't think I'm trying to touch you?'

'That impression did flit through my mind.'

'Oh, dash it, no. No, but – well, as I was saying, I'm frightfully keen to get hold of a thousand quid.'

'So am I,' said Psmith. 'Two minds with but a single thought. How do *you* propose to start about it? For my part, I must freely confess that I haven't a notion. I am stumped. The cry goes round the chancelleries, "Psmith is baffled!"'

'I say, old thing,' said Freddie plaintively, 'you couldn't talk a bit less, could you? I've only got about two minutes.'

'I beg your pardon. Proceed.'

'It's so dashed difficult to know how to begin the thing. I mean, it's all a bit complicated till you get the hang of it . . . Look here, you said in your advertisement that you had no objection to crime.'

Psmith considered the point.

'Within reason – and if undetected – I see no objection to two-pennorth of crime.'

474

'Well, look here . . . look here . . . Well, look here,' said Freddie, 'will you steal my aunt's diamond necklace?'

Psmith placed his monocle in his eye and bent gravely towards his companion.

'Steal your aunt's necklace?' he said indulgently.

'Yes.'

'You do not think she might consider it a liberty from one to whom she has never been introduced?'

What Freddie might have replied to this pertinent question will never be known, for at this moment, looking nervously at his watch for the twentieth time, he observed that the hands had passed the half-hour and were well on their way to twenty-five minutes to one. He bounded up with a cry.

'I must go! I shall miss that damned train!'

'And meanwhile . . .?' said Psmith.

The familiar phrase – the words 'And meanwhile' had occurred at least once in every film Freddie had ever seen – had the effect of wrenching the latter's mind back to the subject in hand for a moment. Freddie was not a clear-thinking young man, but even he could see that he had left the negotiations suspended at a very unsatisfactory point. Nevertheless, he had to catch that twelve-fifty.

'Write and tell me what you think about it,' panted Freddie, skimming through the lobby like a swallow.

'You have unfortunately omitted to leave a name and address,' Psmith pointed out, following him at an easy jog-trot.

In spite of his hurry, a prudence born of much movie-seeing restrained Freddie from supplying the information asked for. Give away your name and address and you never knew what might happen.

'I'll write to you,' he cried, racing for a cab.

'I shall count the minutes,' said Psmith courteously.

'Drive like blazes!' said Freddie to the chauffeur.

'Where?' inquired the man, not unreasonably.

'Eh? Oh, Paddington.'

The cab whirled off, and Psmith, pleasantly conscious of a morning not ill-spent, gazed after it pensively for a moment. Then, with the feeling that the authorities of Colney Hatch or some kindred establishment had been extraordinarily negligent, he permitted his mind to turn with genial anticipation in the direction of lunch. For, though he had celebrated his first day of emancipation from Billingsgate Fish Market by rising late and breakfasting later, he had become aware by now of that not unpleasant emptiness which is the silent luncheon-gong of the soul.

3

The minor problem now presented itself of where to lunch; and with scarcely a moment's consideration he dismissed those large, noisy, and bustling restaurants which lie near Piccadilly Circus. After a morning spent with Eve Halliday and the young man who was going about the place asking people to steal his aunt's necklace, it was imperative that he select some place where he could sit and think quietly. Any food of which he partook must be consumed in calm, even cloistral surroundings, unpolluted by the presence of a first violin who tied himself into knots and an orchestra in whose lexicon there was no such word as *piano*. One of his clubs seemed indicated.

In the days of his prosperity, Psmith's father, an enthusiastic clubman, had enrolled his son's name on the list of several institutions: and now, although the lean years had arrived, he was still a member of six, and would continue to be a member till the beginning of the new year and the consequent call for fresh subscriptions. These clubs ranged from the Drones, frankly frivolous, to the Senior Conservative, solidly worthy. Almost immediately Psmith decided that for such a mood as was upon him at the moment, the latter might have been specially constructed.

Anybody familiar with the interior of the Senior Conservative Club would have applauded his choice. In the whole of London no better haven could have been found by one desirous of staying his interior with excellently-cooked food while passing his soul under a leisurely examination. They fed you well at the Drones, too, no doubt; but there Youth held carnival, and the thoughtful man, examining his soul, was apt at any moment to have his meditations broken in upon by a chunk of bread, dexterously thrown by some bright spirit at an adjoining table. No horror of that description could possibly occur at the Senior Conservative. The Senior Conservative has six thousand one hundred and eleven members. Some of the six thousand one hundred and eleven are more respectable than the others, but they are all respectable – whether they be numbered among the oldest inhabitants like the Earl of Emsworth, who joined as a country member in 1888, or are among the recent creations of the last election of candidates. They are bald, reverend men, who look as if they are on their way to the City to preside at directors' meetings or have dropped in after conferring with the Prime Minister at Downing Street as to the prospects at the coming by-election in the Little Wabsley Division.

With the quiet dignity which atoned for his lack in years in this stronghold of mellow worth, Psmith mounted the steps, passed through the doors which were obligingly flung open for him by two uniformed dignitaries, and made his way to the coffee-room. Here, having selected a table in the middle of the room and ordered a simple and appetizing lunch, he gave himself up to thoughts of Eve Halliday. As he had confessed to his young friend Mr Walderwick, she had made a powerful impression upon him. He was tearing himself from his day-dream in order to wrestle with a mutton chop, when a foreign body shot into his orbit and blundered heavily against the table. Looking up, he perceived a long, thin, elderly gentleman of pleasantly vague aspect, who immediately began to apologize.

'My dear sir, I am extremely sorry. I trust I have caused no damage.'

'None whatever,' replied Psmith courteously.

'The fact is, I have mislaid my glasses. Blind as a bat without them. Can't see where I'm going.'

A gloomy-looking young man with long and disordered hair, who stood at the elderly gentleman's elbow, coughed suggestively. He was shuffling restlessly, and appeared to be anxious to close the episode and move on. A young man, evidently, of highly-strung temperament. He had a sullen air.

The elderly gentleman started vaguely at the sound of the cough.

'Eh?' he said, as if in answer to some spoken remark. 'Oh, yes, quite so, quite so, my dear fellow. Mustn't stop here chatting, eh? Had to apologize, though. Nearly upset this gentleman's table. Can't see where I'm going without my glasses. Blind as a bat. Eh? What? Quite so, quite so.'

He ambled off, doddering cheerfully, while his companion still preserved his look of sulky aloofness. Psmith gazed after them with interest.

'Can you tell me,' he asked of the waiter, who was rallying round with the potatoes, 'who that was?'

The waiter followed his glance.

'Don't know who the young gentleman is, sir. Guest here, I fancy. The old gentleman is the Earl of Emsworth. Lives in the country and doesn't often come to the club. Very absent-minded gentleman, they tell me. Potatoes, sir?'

'Thank you,' said Psmith.

The waited drifted away, and returned.

'I have been looking at the guest-book, sir. The name

of the gentleman lunching with Lord Emsworth is Mr
Ralston McTodd.'

'Thank you very much. I am sorry you had the trouble.'

'No trouble, sir.'

Psmith resumed his meal.

4

The sullen demeanour of the young man who had
accompanied Lord Emsworth through the coffee-room
accurately reflected the emotions which were vexing his
troubled soul. Ralston McTodd, the powerful young
singer of Saskatoon ('Plumbs the depths of human
emotion and strikes a new note' – *Montreal Star*. 'Very
readable' – *Ipsilanti Herald*), had not enjoyed his lunch.
The pleasing sense of importance induced by the fact
that for the first time in his life he was hob-nobbing with
a genuine earl had given way after ten minutes of his
host's society to a mingled despair and irritation which
had grown steadily deeper as the meal proceeded. It is
not too much to say that by the time the fish course
arrived it would have been a relief to Mr McTodd's
feelings if he could have taken up the butter-dish and
banged it down, butter and all, on his lordship's bald
head.

A temperamental young man was Ralston McTodd.
He liked to be the centre of the picture, to do the talking,
to air his views, to be listened to respectfully and with
interest by a submissive audience. At the meal which
had just concluded none of these reasonable demands had
been permitted to him. From the very beginning, Lord
Emsworth had collared the conversation and held it with
a gentle, bleating persistency against all assaults. Five
times had Mr McTodd almost succeeded in launching
one of his best epigrams, only to see it swept away on
the tossing flood of a lecture on hollyhocks. At the sixth
attempt he had managed to get it out, complete and

sparkling, and the old ass opposite him had taken it in his stride like a hurdle and gone galloping off about the mental and moral defects of a creature named Angus McAllister, who appeared to be his head gardener or something of the kind. The luncheon, though he was a hearty feeder and as a rule appreciative of good cooking, had turned to ashes in Mr McTodd's mouth, and it was a soured and chafing Singer of Saskatoon who dropped scowlingly into an arm-chair by the window of the lower smoking-room a few moments later. We introduce Ralston McTodd to the reader, in short, at a moment when he is very near the breaking-point. A little more provocation, and goodness knows what he may not do. For the time being, he is merely leaning back in his chair and scowling. He has a faint hope, however, that a cigar may bring some sort of relief, and he is waiting for one to be ordered for him.

The Earl of Emsworth did not see the scowl. He had not really seen Mr McTodd at all from the moment of his arrival at the club, when somebody, who sounded like the head porter, had informed him that a gentleman was waiting to see him and had led him up to a shapeless blur which had introduced itself as his expected guest. The loss of his glasses had had its usual effect on Lord Emsworth, making the world a misty place in which indefinite objects swam dimly like fish in muddy water. Not that this mattered much, seeing that he was in London, for in London there was never anything worth looking at. Beyond a vague feeling that it would be more comfortable on the whole if he had his glasses – a feeling just strong enough to have made him send off a messenger boy to his hotel to hunt for them – Lord Emsworth had not allowed lack of vision to interfere with his enjoyment of the proceedings.

And, unlike Mr McTodd, he had been enjoying himself very much. A good listener, this young man, he felt. Very soothing, the way he had constituted himself a willing audience, never interrupting or thrusting himself forward, as is so often the deplorable tendency of the modern young man. Lord Emsworth was bound to admit that, much as he had disliked the idea of going to London to pick up this poet or whatever he was, the thing had turned out better than he had expected. He liked Mr McTodd's silent but obvious interest in flowers, his tacit but warm-hearted sympathy in the matter of Angus McAllister. He was glad he was coming to Blandings. It would be agreeable to conduct him personally through the gardens, to introduce him to Angus McAllister and allow him to plumb for himself the black abysses of that outcast's mental processes.

Meanwhile, he had forgotten all about ordering that cigar . . .

'In large gardens where ample space permits,' said Lord Emsworth, dropping cosily into his chair and taking up the conversation at the point where it had been broken off, 'nothing is more desirable than that there should be some places, or one at least, of quiet greenery alone, without any flowers whatever. I see that you agree with me.'

Mr McTodd had not agreed with him. The grunt which Lord Emsworth had taken for an exclamation of rapturous adhesion to his sentiments had been merely a sort of bubble of sound rising from the tortured depths of Mr McTodd's suffering soul – the cry, as the poet beautifully puts it, 'of some strong smoker in his agony.' The desire to smoke had now gripped Mr McTodd's very vitals; but, as some lingering remains of the social sense kept him from asking point-blank for the cigar for which he yearned, he sought in his mind for a way of approaching the subject obliquely.

'In no other way,' proceeded Lord Emsworth, 'can the brilliancy of flowers be so keenly enjoyed as by . . .'

'Talking of flowers,' said Mr McTodd, 'it is a fact, I believe, that tobacco smoke is good for roses.'

' . . . as by pacing for a time,' said Lord Emsworth, 'in some cool, green alley, and then passing on to the flowery places. It is partly, no doubt, the unconscious working out of some optical law, the explanation of which in everyday language is that the eye . . .'

'Some people say that smoking is bad for the eyes. I don't agree with them,' said Mr McTodd warmly.

' . . . being, as it were, saturated with the green colour, is the more attuned to receive the others, especially the reds. It was probably some such consideration that influenced the designers of the many old gardens of England in devoting so much attention to the cult of the yew tree. When you come to Blandings, my dear fellow, I will show you our celebrated yew alley. And, when you see it, you will agree that I was right in taking the stand I did against Angus McAllister's pernicious views.'

'I was lunching in a club yesterday,' said Mr McTodd, with the splendid McTodd doggedness, 'where they had no matches on the tables in the smoking-room. Only spills. It made it very inconvenient . . .'

'Angus McAllister,' said Lord Emsworth, 'is a professional gardener. I need say no more. You know as well as I do, my dear fellow, what professional gardeners are like when it is a question of moss . . .'

'What it meant was that, when you wanted to light your after-luncheon cigar, you had to get up and go to a gas-burner on a bracket at the other end of the room . . .'

'Moss, for some obscure reason, appears to infuriate them. It rouses their basest passions. Nature intended a yew alley to be carpeted with a mossy growth. The mossy path in the yew alley at Blandings is in true relation for colour to the trees and grassy edges; yet will you credit it that that soulless disgrace to Scotland actually wished to grub it all up and have a rolled gravel path staring up from beneath those immemorial trees! I have already told you how I was compelled to give in to him in the matter of the hollyhocks – head gardeners of any ability

at all are rare in these days and one has to make
concessions – but this was too much. I was perfectly
friendly and civil about it. "Certainly, McAllister," I said,
"you may have your gravel path if you wish it. I make
but one proviso, that you construct it over my dead body.
Only when I am weltering in my blood on the threshold
of that yew alley shall you disturb one inch of my beautiful
moss. Try to remember, McAllister," I said, still quite
cordially, "that you are not laying out a recreation ground
in a Glasgow suburb – you are proposing to make an
eyesore of what is possibly the most beautiful nook in
one of the finest and oldest gardens in the United
Kingdom." He made some repulsive Scotch noise at the
back of his throat, and there the matter rests . . . Let me,
my dear fellow,' said Lord Emsworth, writhing down into
the depths of his chair like an aristocratic snake until
his spine rested snugly against the leather, 'let me
describe for you the Yew Alley at Blandings. Entering
from the west . . .'

Mr McTodd gave up the struggle and sank back, filled
with black and deleterious thoughts, into a tobacco-less
hell. The smoking-room was full now, and on all sides
fragrant blue clouds arose from the little groups of serious
thinkers who were discussing what Gladstone had said
in '78. Mr McTodd, as he watched them, had something
of the emotions of the Peri excluded from Paradise. So
reduced was he by this time that he would have accepted
gratefully the meanest straight-cut cigarette in place of
the Corona of his dreams. But even this poor substitute
for smoking was denied him.

Lord Emsworth droned on. Having approached from
the west, he was now well inside the yew alley.

'Many of the yews, no doubt, have taken forms other
than those that were originally designed. Some are like
turned chessmen; some might be taken for adaptations
of human figures, for one can trace here and there a hat-
covered head or a spreading petticoat. Some rise in solid

blocks with rounded roof and stemless mushroom finial.
These have for the most part arched recesses, forming
arbours. One of the tallest . . . Eh? What?'

Lord Emsworth blinked vaguely at the waiter who had
sidled up. A moment before he had been a hundred odd
miles away and it was not easy to adjust his mind
immediately to the fact that he was in the smoking-
room of the Senior Conservative Club.

'Eh? What?'

'A messenger boy has just arrived with these, your
lordship.'

Lord Emsworth peered in a dazed and woolly manner
at the proffered spectacle-case. Intelligence returned to
him.

'Oh, thank you. Thank you very much. My glasses.
Capital! Thank you, thank you, thank you.'

He removed the glasses from their case and placed
them on his nose: and instantly the world sprang into
being before his eyes, sharp and well-defined. It was like
coming out of a fog.

'Dear me!' he said in a self-congratulatory voice.

Then abruptly he sat up, transfixed. The lower
smoking-room at the Senior Conservative Club is on the
street level, and Lord Emsworth's chair faced the large
window. Through this, as he raised his now spectacled
face, he perceived for the first time that among the row
of shops on the opposite side of the road was a jaunty
new florist's. It had not been there at his last visit to the
metropolis, and he stared at it raptly, as a small boy
would stare at a saucer of ice-cream if such a thing had
suddenly descended from heaven immediately in front
of him. And, like a small boy in such a situation, he had
eyes for nothing else. He did not look at his guest. Indeed,
in the ecstasy of his discovery, he had completely
forgotten that he had a guest.

Any flower shop, however small, was a magnet to the
Earl of Emsworth. And this was a particularly spacious

and arresting flower shop. Its window was gay with summer blooms. And Lord Emsworth, slowly rising from his chair, 'pointed' like a dog that sees a pheasant.

'Bless my soul!' he murmured.

If the reader has followed with the closeness which it deserves the extremely entertaining conversation of his lordship recorded in the last few paragraphs, he will have noted a reference to hollyhocks. Lord Emsworth had ventilated the hollyhock question at some little length while seated at the luncheon table. But, as we had not the good fortune to be present at that enjoyable meal, a brief *résumé* of the situation must now be given and the intelligent public allowed to judge between his lordship and the uncompromising McAllister.

Briefly, the position was this. Many head gardeners are apt to favour in the hollyhock forms that one cannot but think have for their aim an ideal that is a false and unworthy one. Angus McAllister, clinging to the head-gardeneresque standard of beauty and correct form, would not sanction the wide outer petal. The flower, so Angus held, must be very tight and very round, like the uniform of a major-general. Lord Emsworth, on the other hand, considered this view narrow, and claimed the liberty to try for the very highest and truest beauty in hollyhocks. The loosely-folded inner petals of the hollyhock, he considered, invited a wonderful play and brilliancy of colour; while the wide outer petal, with its slightly waved surface and gently frilled edge . . . well, anyway, Lord Emsworth liked his hollyhocks floppy and Angus McAllister liked them tight, and bitter warfare had resulted, in which, as we have seen, his lordship had been compelled to give way. He had been brooding on this defeat ever since, and in the florist opposite he saw a possible sympathizer, a potential ally, an intelligent chum with whom he could get together and thoroughly damn Angus McAllister's Glaswegian obstinacy.

You would not have suspected Lord Emsworth, from

a casual glance, of having within him the ability to move rapidly; but it is a fact that he was out of the smoking-room and skimming down the front steps of the club before Mr McTodd's jaw, which had fallen at the spectacle of his host bounding out of his horizon of vision like a jack-rabbit, had time to hitch itself up again. A moment later, Mr McTodd, happening to direct his gaze out of the window, saw him whiz across the road and vanish into the florist's shop.

It was at this juncture that Psmith, having finished his lunch, came downstairs to enjoy a quiet cup of coffee. The room was rather crowded, and the chair which Lord Emsworth had vacated offered a wide invitation. He made his way to it.

'Is this chair occupied?' he inquired politely. So politely that Mr McTodd's reply sounded by contrast even more violent than it might otherwise have done.

'No, it isn't!' snapped Mr McTodd.

Psmith seated himself. He was feeling agreeably disposed to conversation.

'Lord Emsworth has left you then?' he said.

'Is he a friend of yours?' inquired Mr McTodd in a voice that suggested that he was perfectly willing to accept a proxy as a target for his wrath.

'I know him by sight. Nothing more.'

'Blast him!' muttered Mr McTodd with indescribable virulence.

Psmith eyed him inquiringly.

'Correct me if I am wrong,' he said, 'but I seem to detect in your manner a certain half-veiled annoyance. Is anything the matter?'

Mr McTodd barked bitterly.

'Oh, no. Nothing's the matter. Nothing whatever, except that that old beaver' – here he wronged Lord Emsworth, who, whatever his faults, was not a bearded man – 'that old beaver invited me to lunch, talked all the time about his infernal flowers, never let me get a word in edgeways, hadn't the common civility to offer me a cigar, and now has gone off without a word of apology, and buried himself in that shop over the way. I've never been so insulted in my life!' raved Mr McTodd.

'Scarcely the perfect host,' admitted Psmith.

'And if he thinks,' said Mr McTodd, rising, 'that I'm going to go and stay with him at his beastly castle after this, he's mistaken. I'm supposed to go down there with him this evening. And perhaps the old fossil thinks I will! After this!' A horrid laugh rolled up from Mr McTodd's interior. 'Likely! I see myself! After being insulted like this . . . Would *you*?' he demanded.

Psmith gave the matter thought.

'I am inclined to think no.'

'And so am I damned well inclined to think no!' cried Mr McTodd. 'I'm going away now, this very minute. And if that old total loss ever comes back, you can tell him he's seen the last of me.'

And Ralston McTodd, his blood boiling with justifiable indignation and pique to a degree dangerous on such a warm day, stalked off towards the door with a hard, set face. Through the door he stalked to the cloak-room for his hat and cane; then, his lips moving silently, he stalked through the hall, stalked down the steps, and passed from the scene, stalking furiously round the corner in quest of a tobacconist's. At the moment of his disappearance, the Earl of Emsworth had just begun to give the sympathetic florist a limpid character-sketch of Angus McAllister.

Psmith shook his head sadly. These clashings of human temperament were very lamentable. They disturbed the after-luncheon repose of the man of sensibility. He ordered coffee, and endeavoured to forget the painful scene by thinking of Eve Halliday.

487

5

The florist who had settled down to ply his trade opposite
the Senior Conservative Club was a delightful fellow,
thoroughly sound on the hollyhock question and so
informative in the matter of delphiniums, achilleas,
coreopsis, eryngiums, geums, lupins, bergamot, and early
phloxes that Lord Emsworth gave himself up whole-
heartedly to the feast of reason and the flow of soul; and
it was only some fifteen minutes later that he
remembered that he had left a guest languishing in the
lower smoking-room and that this guest might be
thinking him a trifle remiss in the observance of the
sacred duties of hospitality.

'Bless my soul, yes!' said his lordship, coming out
from under the influence with a start.

Even then he could not bring himself to dash abruptly
from the shop. Twice he reached the door and twice
pottered back to sniff at flowers and say something he
had forgotten to mention about the Stronger Growing
Clematis. Finally, however, with one last, longing,
lingering look behind, he tore himself away and trotted
back across the road.

Arrived in the lower smoking-room, he stood in the
doorway for a moment, peering. The place had been a
blur to him when he had left it, but he remembered that
he had been sitting in the middle window and, as there
were only two seats by the window, that tall, dark young
man in one of them must be the guest he had deserted.
That he could be a changeling never occurred to Lord
Emsworth. So pleasantly had the time passed in the shop
across the way that he had the impression that he had
only been gone a couple of minutes or so. He made his way
to where the young man sat. A vague idea came into his
head that the other had grown a bit in his absence, but
it passed.

'My dear fellow,' he said genially, as he slid into the other chair, 'I really must apologize.'

It was plain to Psmith that the other was under a misapprehension, and a really nice-minded young man would no doubt have put the matter right at once. The fact that it never for a single instant occurred to Psmith to do so was due, no doubt, to some innate defect in his character. He was essentially a young man who took life as it came, and the more inconsequently it came the better he liked it. Presently, he reflected, it would become necessary for him to make some excuse and steal quietly out of the other's life; but meanwhile the situation seemed to him to present entertaining possibilities.

'Not at all,' he replied graciously. 'Not at all.'

'I was afraid for a moment,' said Lord Emsworth, 'that you might – quite naturally – be offended.'

'Absurd!'

'Shouldn't have left you like that. Shocking bad manners. But, my dear fellow, I simply had to pop across the street.'

'Most decidedly,' said Psmith. 'Always pop across streets. It is the secret of a happy and successful life.'

Lord Emsworth looked at him a little perplexedly, and wondered if he had caught the last remark correctly. But his mind had never been designed for the purpose of dwelling closely on problems for any length of time, and he let it go.

'Beautiful roses that man has,' he observed. 'Really an extraordinarily fine display.'

'Indeed?' said Psmith.

'Nothing to touch mine, though. I wish, my dear fellow, you could have been down at Blandings at the beginning of the month. My roses were at their best then. It's too bad you weren't there to see them.'

'The fault no doubt was mine,' said Psmith.

'Of course you weren't in England then.'

'Ah! That explains it.'

'Still, I shall have plenty of flowers to show you when you are at Blandings. I expect,' said Lord Emsworth, at last showing a host-like disposition to give his guest a belated innings, 'I expect you'll write one of your poems about my gardens, eh?'

Psmith was conscious of a feeling of distinct gratification. Weeks of toil among the herrings of Billingsgate had left him with a sort of haunting fear that even in private life there clung to him the miasma of the fish market. Yet here was a perfectly unprejudiced observer looking squarely at him and mistaking him for a poet – showing that in spite of all he had gone through there must still be something notably spiritual and unfishy about his outward appearance.

'Very possibly,' he said. 'Very possibly.'

'I suppose you get ideas for your poetry from all sorts of things,' said Lord Emsworth, nobly resisting the temptation to collar the conversation again. He was feeling extremely friendly towards this poet fellow. It was deuced civil of him not to be put out and huffy at being left alone in the smoking-room.

'From practically everything,' said Psmith, 'except fish.'

'Fish?'

'I have never written a poem about fish.'

'No?' said Lord Emsworth, again feeling that a pin had worked loose in the machinery of the conversation.

'I was once offered a princely sum,' went on Psmith, now floating happily along on the tide of his native exuberance, 'to write a ballad for the *Fishmonger's Gazette* entitled, "Herbert the Turbot". But I was firm. I declined.'

'Indeed?' said Lord Emsworth.

'One has one's self-respect,' said Psmith.

'Oh, decidedly,' said Lord Emsworth.

'It was painful, of course. The editor broke down completely when he realized that my refusal was final. However, I sent him on with a letter of introduction to John Drinkwater, who, I believe, turned him out quite a good little effort on the theme.'

At this moment, when Lord Emsworth was feeling a trifle dizzy, and Psmith, on whom conversation always acted as a mental stimulus, was on the point of plunging even deeper into the agreeable depths of light persiflage, a waiter approached.

'A lady to see you, your lordship.'

'Eh? Ah, yes, of course, of course. I was expecting her. It is a Miss – what is the name? Holliday? Halliday. It is a Miss Halliday,' he said in explanation to Psmith, 'who is coming down to Blandings to catalogue the library. My secretary, Baxter, told her to call here and see me. If you will excuse me for a moment, my dear fellow?'

'Certainly.'

As Lord Emsworth disappeared, it occurred to Psmith that the moment had arrived for him to get his hat and steal softly out of the other's life for ever. Only so could confusion and embarrassing explanations be avoided. And it was Psmith's guiding rule in life always to avoid explanations. It might, he felt, cause Lord Emsworth a momentary pang when he returned to the smoking-room and found that he was a poet short, but what is that in these modern days when poets are so plentiful that it is almost impossible to fling a brick in any public place without damaging some stern young singer. Psmith's view of the matter was that, if Lord Emsworth was bent on associating with poets, there was bound to be another one along in a minute. He was on the point, therefore, of rising, when the laziness induced by a good lunch decided him to remain in his comfortable chair for a few minutes longer. He was in one of those moods of rare tranquillity which it is rash to break.

He lit another cigarette, and his thoughts, as they had

done after the departure of Mr McTodd, turned dreamily in the direction of the girl he had met at Miss Clarkson's Employment Bureau. He mused upon her with a gentle melancholy. Sad, he felt, that two obviously kindred spirits like himself and her should meet in the whirl of London life, only to separate again – presumably for ever – simply because the etiquette governing those who are created male and female forbids a man to cement a chance acquaintanceship by ascertaining the lady's name and address, asking her to lunch, and swearing eternal friendship. He sighed as he gazed thoughtfully out of the lower smoking-room window. As he had indicated in his conversation with Mr Walderwick, those blue eyes and that cheerful, friendly face had made a deep impression on him. Who was she? Where did she live? And was he ever to see her again?

He was. Even as he asked himself the question, two figures came down the steps of the club, and paused. One was Lord Emsworth, without his hat. The other – and Psmith's usually orderly heart gave a spasmodic bound at the sight of her – was the very girl who was occupying his thoughts. There she stood, as blue-eyed, as fair-haired, as indescribably jolly and charming as ever.

Psmith rose from his chair with a vehemence almost equal to that recently displayed by Mr McTodd. It was his intention to add himself immediately to the group. He raced across the room in a manner that drew censorious glances from the local greybeards, many of whom had half a mind to write to the committee about it.

But when he reached the open air the pavement at the foot of the club steps was empty. The girl was just vanishing round the corner into the Strand, and of Lord Emsworth there was no sign whatever.

By this time, however, Psmith had acquired a useful working knowledge of his lordship's habits, and he knew where to look. He crossed the street and headed for the florist's shop.

'Ah, my dear fellow,' said his lordship amiably, suspending his conversation with the proprietor on the subject of delphiniums, 'must you be off? Don't forget that our train leaves Paddington at five sharp. You take your ticket for Market Blandings.'

Psmith had come into the shop merely with the intention of asking his lordship if he happened to know Miss Halliday's address, but these words opened out such a vista of attractive possibilities that he had abandoned this tame programme immediately. He remembered now that among Mr McTodd's remarks on things in general had been one to the effect that he had received an invitation to visit Blandings Castle – of which invitation he did not propose to avail himself; and he argued that if he had acted as substitute for Mr McTodd at the club, he might well continue the kindly work by officiating for him at Blandings. Looking at the matter altruistically, he would prevent his kind host much disappointment by taking this course; and, looking at it from a more personal viewpoint, only by going to Blandings could he renew his acquaintance with this girl. Psmith had never been one of those who hang back diffidently when Adventure calls, and he did not hang back now.

'At five sharp,' he said. 'I will be there.'

'Capital, my dear fellow,' said his lordship.

'Does Miss Halliday travel with us?'

'Eh! No, she is coming down in a day or two.'

'I shall look forward to meeting her,' said Psmith.

He turned to the door, and Lord Emsworth with a farewell beam resumed his conversation with the florist.

7 — Baxter Suspects

I

The five o'clock train, having given itself a spasmodic jerk, began to move slowly out of Paddington Station. The platform past which it was gliding was crowded with a number of the fauna always to be seen at railway stations at such moments, but in their ranks there was no sign of Mr Ralston McTodd: and Psmith, as he sat opposite Lord Emsworth in a corner seat of a first-class compartment, felt that genial glow of satisfaction which comes to the man who has successfully taken a chance. Until now, he had been half afraid that McTodd, having changed his mind, might suddenly appear with bag and baggage – an event which must necessarily have caused confusion and discomfort. His mind was now tranquil. Concerning the future he declined to worry. It would, no doubt, contain its little difficulties, but he was prepared to meet them in the right spirit; and his only trouble in the world now was the difficulty he was experiencing in avoiding his lordship's legs, which showed a disposition to pervade the compartment like the tentacles of an octopus. Lord Emsworth rather ran to leg, and his practice of reclining when at ease on the base of his spine was causing him to straddle, like Apollyon in *Pilgrim's Progress*, 'right across the way'. It became manifest that in a journey lasting several hours his society was likely to prove irksome. For the time being, however, he endured it, and listened with polite attention to his host's remark on the subject of the Blandings gardens. Lord Emsworth, in a train moving in the direction of home, was behaving like a horse heading for his stable. He snorted eagerly, and spoke at length and with emotion of roses and herbaceous borders.

'It will be dark, I suppose, by the time we arrive,' he said regretfully, 'but the first thing tomorrow, my dear fellow, I must take you round and show you my gardens.'

'I shall look forward to it keenly,' said Psmith. 'They are, I can readily imagine, distinctly oojah-cum-spiff.'

'I beg your pardon?' said Lord Emsworth, with a start.

'Not at all,' said Psmith graciously.

'Er – what did you say?' asked his lordship after a slight pause.

'I was saying that, from all reports, you must have a very nifty display of garden-produce at your rural seat.'

'Oh, yes. Oh, most,' said his lordship, looking puzzled. He examined Psmith across the compartment with something of the peering curiosity which he would have bestowed upon a new and unclassified shrub. 'Most extraordinary!' he murmured. 'I trust, my dear fellow, you will not think me personal, but, do you know, nobody would imagine that you were a poet. You don't look like a poet, and, dash it, you don't talk like a poet.'

'How should a poet talk?'

'Well . . .' Lord Emsworth considered the point. 'Well, Miss Peavey . . . But of course you don't know Miss Peavey . . . Miss Peavey is a poetess, and she waylaid me the other morning while I was having a most important conference with McAllister on the subject of bulbs and asked me if I didn't think that it was fairies' tear-drops that made the dew. Did you ever hear such dashed nonsense?'

'Evidently an aggravated case. Is Miss Peavey staying at the castle?'

'My dear fellow, you couldn't shift her with blasting-powder. Really this craze of my sister Constance for filling the house with these infernal literary people is getting on my nerves. I can't stand these poets and what not. Never could.'

'We must always remember, however,' said Psmith gravely, 'that poets are also God's creatures.'

'Good heavens!' exclaimed his lordship, aghast. 'I had forgotten that you were one. What will you think of me, my dear fellow! But, of course, as I said a moment ago, you are different. I admit that when Constance told me that she had invited you to the house I was not cheered, but, now that I have had the pleasure of meeting you . . .'

The conversation had worked round to the very point to which Psmith had been wishing to direct it. He was keenly desirous of finding out why Mr McTodd had been invited to Blandings and – a still more vital matter – of ascertaining whether, on his arrival there as Mr McTodd's understudy, he was going to meet people who knew the poet by sight. On this latter point, it seemed to him, hung the question of whether he was about to enjoy a delightful visit to a historic country house in the society of Eve Halliday – or leave the train at the next stop and omit to return to it.

'It was extremely kind of Lady Constance,' he hazarded, 'to invite a perfect stranger to Blandings.'

'Oh, she's always doing that sort of thing,' said his lordship. 'It didn't matter to her that she'd never seen you in her life. She had read your books, you know, and liked them: and when she heard that you were coming to England, she wrote to you.'

'I see,' said Psmith, relieved.

'Of course, it is all right as it has turned out,' said Lord Emsworth handsomely. 'As I say, you're different. And how you came to write that . . . that . . .'

'Bilge?' suggested Psmith.

'The very word I was about to employ, my dear fellow . . . No, no, I don't mean that . . . I – I . . . Capital stuff, no doubt, capital stuff . . . but . . .'

'I understand.'

'Constance tried to make me read the things, but I couldn't. I fell asleep over them.'

'I hope you rested well.'

'I – er – the fact is, I suppose they were beyond me. I couldn't see any sense in the things.'

'If you would care to have another pop at them,' said Psmith agreeably, 'I have a complete set in my bag.'

'No, no, my dear fellow, thank you very much, thank you a thousand times. I – er – find that reading in the train tries my eyes.'

'Ah! You would prefer that I read them aloud?'

'No, no.' A look of hunted alarm came into his lordship's speaking countenance at the suggestion. 'As a matter of fact, I generally take a short nap at the beginning of a railway journey. I find it refreshing and – er – in short, refreshing. You will excuse me?'

'If you think you can get to sleep all right without the aid of my poems, certainly.'

'You won't think me rude?'

'Not at all, not at all. By the way, am I likely to meet any old friends at Blandings?'

'Eh? Oh no. There will be nobody but ourselves. Except my sister and Miss Peavey, of course. You said you had not met Miss Peavey, I think?'

'I have not had that pleasure. I am, of course, looking forward to it with the utmost keenness.'

Lord Emsworth eyed him for a moment, astonished: then concluded the conversation by closing his eyes defensively. Psmith was left to his reflections, which a few minutes later were interrupted by a smart kick on the shin, as Lord Emsworth, a jumpy sleeper, began to throw his long legs about. Psmith moved to the other end of the seat, and, taking his bag down from the rack, extracted a slim volume bound in squashy mauve. After gazing at this in an unfriendly manner for a moment, he opened it at random and began to read. His first move on leaving Lord Emsworth at the florist's had been to spend a portion of his slender capital on the works of Ralston McTodd in order not to be taken at a disadvantage in the event of questions about them at Blandings: but he speedily realized, as he dipped into the poems, that anything in the nature of a prolonged study of them was likely to spoil his little holiday. They were not light summer reading.

'Across the pale parabola of Joy . . .'

A gurgling snort from the other end of the compartment abruptly detached his mind from its struggle with this mystic line. He perceived that his host had slipped even further down on to his spine and was now lying with open mouth in an attitude suggestive of dislocation. And as he looked, there was a whistling sound, and another snore proceeded from the back of his lordship's throat.

Psmith rose and took his book of poems out into the corridor with the purpose of roaming along the train until he should find an empty compartment in which to read in peace.

With the two adjoining compartments he had no luck. One was occupied by an elderly man with a retriever, while the presence of a baby in the other ruled it out of consideration. The third, however, looked more promising. It was not actually empty, but there was only one occupant, and he was asleep. He was lying back in the far corner with a large silk handkerchief draped over his face and his feet propped up on the seat opposite. His society did not seem likely to act as a bar to the study of Mr McTodd's masterpieces. Psmith sat down and resumed his reading.

Across the pale parabola of Joy . . .

Psmith knitted his brow. It was just the sort of line which was likely to have puzzled his patroness, Lady Constance, and he anticipated that she would come to him directly he arrived and ask for an explanation. It would obviously be a poor start for his visit to confess that he had no theory as to its meaning himself. He tried it again.

Across the pale parabola of Joy . . .

A sound like two or three pigs feeding rather noisily in the middle of a thunderstorm interrupted his meditations. Psmith laid his book down and gazed in a pained way across the compartment. There came to him a sense of being unfairly put upon, as towards the end of his troubles it might have come upon Job. This, he felt, was too much. He was being harried.

The man in the corner went on snoring.

There is always a way. Almost immediately Psmith saw what Napoleon would have done in this crisis. On the seat beside the sleeper was lying a compact little suit-case with hard, sharp edges. Rising softly, Psmith edged along the compartment and secured this. Then, having balanced it carefully on the rack above the sleeper's stomach, he returned to his seat to await developments.

These were not long in coming. The train, now flying at its best speed through open country, was shaking itself at intervals in a vigorous way as it raced along. A few seconds later it apparently passed over some points, and shivered briskly down its whole length. The suit-case wobbled insecurely, hesitated, and fell chunkily in the exact middle of its owner's waistcoat. There was a smothered gulp beneath the handkerchief. The sleeper sat up with a jerk. The handkerchief fell off. And there was revealed to Psmith's interested gaze the face of the Hon. Freddie Threepwood.

2

'Goo!' observed Freddie. He removed the bag from his midriff and began to massage the stricken spot. Then suddenly perceiving that he was not alone he looked up and saw Psmith.

'Goo!' said Freddie, and sat staring wildly.

Nobody is more alive than we are to the fact that the dialogue of Frederick Threepwood, recorded above, is not bright. Nevertheless, those were his opening remarks, and the excuse must be that he had passed through a trying time and had just received two shocks, one after the other. From the first of these, the physical impact of the suit-case, he was recovering; but the second had simply paralysed him. When, the mists of sleep having cleared away, he saw sitting but a few feet away from him on the train that was carrying him home the very man with whom he had plotted in the lobby of the Piccadilly Palace Hotel, a cold fear gripped Freddie's very vitals.

Freddie's troubles had begun when he just missed the twelve-fifty train. This disaster had perturbed him greatly, for he could not forget his father's stern injunctions on the subject. But what had really upset him was the fact that he had come within an ace of missing the five o'clock train as well. He had spent the afternoon in a motion-picture palace, and the fascination of the film had caused him to lose all sense of time, so that only the slow fade-out on the embrace and the words 'The End' reminded him to look at his watch. A mad rush had got him to Paddington just as the five o'clock express was leaving the station. Exhausted, he had fallen into a troubled sleep, from which he had been aroused by a violent blow in the waistcoat and the nightmare vision of Psmith in the seat across the compartment. One cannot wonder in these circumstances that Freddie did not immediately soar to the heights of eloquence.

The picture which the Hon. Frederick Threepwood

had selected for his patronage that afternoon was the
well-known super-super-film, 'Fangs Of The Past,'
featuring Bertha Blevitch and Maurice Heddlestone –
which, as everybody knows, is all about blackmail.
Green-walled by primeval hills, bathed in the golden
sunshine of peace and happiness, the village of Honeydean
slumbered in the clear morning air. But off the train
from the city stepped A Stranger – (The Stranger –
Maxwell Bannister). He inquired of a passing rustic –
(The Passing Rustic – Claude Hepworth) – the way to the
great house where Myrtle Dale, the Lady Bountiful of
the village . . . well, anyway, it is all about blackmail, and
it had affected Freddie profoundly. It still coloured his
imagination, and the conclusion to which he came the
moment he saw Psmith was that the latter had shadowed
him and was following him home with the purpose of
extracting hush-money.

While he was still gurgling wordlessly, Psmith opened
the conversation.

'A delightful and unexpected pleasure, comrade.
I thought you had left the Metropolis some hours
since.'

As Freddie sat looking like a cornered dormouse a
voice from the corridor spoke.

'Ah, there you are, my dear fellow!'

Lord Emsworth was beaming in the doorway. His
slumbers, like those of Freddie, had not lasted long. He
had been aroused only a few minutes after Psmith's
departure by the arrival of the retriever from the next
compartment, which, bored by the society of its owner,
had strolled off on a tour of investigation and, finding
next door an old acquaintance in the person of his
lordship, had jumped on the seat and licked his face with
such hearty goodwill that further sleep was out of the
question. Being awake, Lord Emsworth, as always when
he was awake, had begun to potter.

When he saw Freddie his amiability suffered a shock.

'Frederick! I thought I told you to be sure to return on the twelve-fifty train!'

'Missed it, guv'nor,' mumbled Freddie thickly. 'Not my fault.'

'H'mph!' His father seemed about to pursue the subject, but the fact that a stranger and one who was his guest was present apparently decided him to avoid anything in the shape of family wrangles. He peered from Freddie to Psmith and back again. 'Do you two know each other?' he said.

'Not yet,' said Psmith. 'We only met a moment ago.'

'My son Frederick,' said Lord Emsworth, rather in the voice with which he would have called attention to the presence of a slug among his flowers. 'Frederick, this is Mr McTodd, the poet, who is coming to stay at Blandings.'

Freddie started, and his mouth opened. But, meeting Psmith's friendly gaze, he closed the orifice again without speaking. He licked his lips in an overwrought way.

'You'll find me next door, if you want me,' said Lord Emsworth to Psmith. 'Just discovered that George Willard, very old friend of mine, is in there. Never saw him get on the train. His dog came into my compartment and licked my face. One of my neighbours. A remarkable rose-grower. As you are so interested in flowers, I will take you over to his place some time. Why don't you join us now?'

'I would prefer, if you do not mind,' said Psmith, 'to remain here for the moment and foster what I feel sure is about to develop into a great and lasting friendship. I am convinced that your son and I will have much to talk about together.'

'Very well, my dear fellow. We will meet at dinner in the restaurant-car.'

Lord Emsworth pottered off, and Psmith rose and closed the door. He returned to his seat to find Freddie

regarding him with a tortured expression in his rather
prominent eyes. Freddie's brain had had more exercise
in the last few minutes than in years of his normal life,
and he was feeling the strain.

'I say, what?' he observed feebly.

'If there is anything,' said Psmith kindly, 'that I can
do to clear up any little difficulty that is perplexing you,
call on me. What is biting you?'

Freddie swallowed convulsively.

'I say, he said your name was McTodd!'

'Precisely.'

'But you said it was Psmith.'

'It is.'

'Then why did father call you McTodd?'

'He thinks I am. It is a harmless error, and I see no
reason why it should be discouraged.'

'But why does he think you're McTodd?'

'It is a long story, which you may find tedious. But, if
you really wish to hear it . . .'

Nothing could have exceeded the raptness of Freddie's
attention as he listened to the tale of the encounter with
Lord Emsworth at the Senior Conservative Club.

'Do you mean to say,' he demanded at its conclusion,
'that you're coming to Blandings pretending to be this
poet blighter?'

'That is the scheme.'

'But why?'

'I have my reasons, Comrade – what is the name?
Threepwood? I thank you. You will pardon me,
Comrade Threepwood, if I do not go into them. And now,'
said Psmith, 'to resume our very interesting chat which
was unfortunately cut short this morning, why do you
want me to steal your aunt's necklace?'

Freddie jumped. For the moment, so tensely had the
fact of his companion's audacity chained his interest, he
had actually forgotten about the necklace.

'Great Scott!' he exclaimed. 'Why, of course!'

503

'You still have not made it quite clear.'

'It fits splendidly.'

'The necklace?'

'I mean to say, the great difficulty would have been to find a way of getting you into the house, and here you are, coming there as this poet bird. Topping!'

'If,' said Psmith, regarding him patiently through his eye-glass, 'I do not seem to be immediately infected by your joyous enthusiasm, put it down to the fact that I haven't the remotest idea what you're talking about. Could you give me a pointer or two? What, for instance, assuming that I agreed to steal your aunt's necklace, would you expect me to do with it, when and if stolen?'

'Why, hand it over to me.'

'I see. And what would you do with it?'

'Hand it over to my uncle.'

'And whom would he hand it over to?'

'Look here,' said Freddie, 'I might as well start at the beginning.'

'An excellent idea.'

The speed at which the train was now proceeding had begun to render conversation in anything but stentorian tones somewhat difficult. Freddie accordingly bent forward till his mouth almost touched Psmith's ear.

'You see, it's like this. My uncle, old Joe Keeble . . .'

'Keeble?' said Psmith. 'Why,' he murmured meditatively, 'is that name familiar?'

'Don't interrupt, old lad,' pleaded Freddie.

'I stand corrected.'

'Uncle Joe has a step-daughter – Phyllis her name is – and some time ago she popped off and married a cove called Jackson . . .'

Psmith did not interrupt the narrative again, but as it proceeded his look of interest deepened. And at the conclusion he patted his companion encouragingly on the shoulder.

'The proceeds, then, of this jewel-robbery, if it comes off,' he said, 'will go to establish the Jackson home on a firm footing? Am I right in thinking that?'

'Absolutely.'

'There is no danger – you will pardon the suggestion – of you clinging like glue to the swag and using it to maintain yourself in the position to which you are accustomed?'

'Absolutely not. Uncle Joe is giving me – er – giving me a bit for myself. Just a small bit, you understand. This is the scheme. You sneak the necklace and hand it over to me. I push the necklace over to Uncle Joe, who hides it somewhere for the moment. There is the dickens of a fuss, and Uncle Joe comes out strong by telling Aunt Constance that he'll buy her another necklace, just as good. Then he takes the stones out of the necklace, has them reset and gives them to Aunt Constance. Looks like a new necklace, if you see what I mean. Then he draws a cheque for twenty thousand quid, which Aunt Constance naturally thinks is for the new necklace, and he shoves the money somewhere as a little private account. He gives Phyllis her money, and everybody's happy. Aunt Constance has got her necklace, Phyllis has got her money, and all that's happened is that Aunt Constance's and Uncle Joe's combined bank balance has had a bit of a hole knocked in it. See?'

'I see. It is a little difficult to follow all the necklaces. I seemed to count about seventeen of them while you were talking, but I suppose I was wrong. Yes, I see, Comrade Threepwood, and I may say at once that you can rely on my cooperation.'

'You'll do it?'

'I will.'

'Of course,' said Freddie awkwardly, 'I'll see that you get a bit all right. I mean . . .'

Psmith waved his hand deprecatingly.

'My dear Comrade Threepwood, let us not become

sordid on this glad occasion. As far as I am concerned, there will be no charge.'

'What! But look here . . .'

'Any assistance I can give will be offered in a purely amateur spirit. I would have mentioned before, only I was reluctant to interrupt you, that Comrade Jackson is my boyhood chum, and that Phyllis, his wife, injects into my life the few beams of sunshine that illumine its dreary round. I have long desired to do something to ameliorate their lot, and now that the chance has come I am delighted. It is true that I am not a man of affluence – my bank-manager, I am told, winces in a rather painful manner whenever my name is mentioned – but I am not so reduced that I must charge a fee for performing, on behalf of a pal, a simple act of courtesy like pinching a twenty thousand pound necklace.'

'Good Lord! Fancy that!'

'Fancy what, Comrade Threepwood?'

'Fancy your knowing Phyllis and her husband.'

'It is odd, no doubt. But true. Many a whack at the cold beef have I had on Sunday evenings under their roof, and I am much obliged to you for putting in my way this opportunity of repaying their hospitality. Thank you!'

'Oh, that's all right,' said Freddie, somewhat bewildered by this eloquence.

'Even if the little enterprise meets with disaster, the reflection that I did my best for the young couple will be a great consolation to me when I am serving my bit of time in Wormwood Scrubbs. It will cheer me up. The jailers will cluster outside the door to listen to me singing in my cell. My pet rat, as he creeps out to share the crumbs of my breakfast, will wonder why I whistle as I pick the morning's oakum. I shall join in the hymns on Sundays in a way that will electrify the chaplain. That is to say, if anything goes wrong and I am what I believe is technically termed "copped". I say "if",' said Psmith, gazing solemnly at his companion, 'But I do not intend to be copped. I have never gone in largely for crime hitherto, but something tells me I shall be rather good at it. I look forward confidently to making a nice, clean job of the thing. And now, Comrade Threepwood, I must ask you to excuse me while I get the half-nelson on this rather poisonous poetry of good old McTodd's. From the cursory glance I have taken at it, the stuff doesn't seem to mean anything. I think the boy's *non compos. You* don't happen to understand the expression "Across the pale parabola of Joy," do you? . . . I feared as much. Well, pip-pip for the present, Comrade Threepwood. I shall now ask you to retire into your corner and amuse yourself for a while as you best can. I must concentrate, concentrate.'

And Psmith, having put his feet up on the opposite seat and reopened the mauve volume, began to read. Freddie, his mind still in a whirl, looked out of the window at the passing scenery in a mood which was a nice blend of elation and apprehension.

3

Although the hands of the station clock pointed to several minutes past nine, it was still apparently early evening when the train drew up at the platform of Market Blandings and discharged its distinguished passengers. The sun, taken in as usual by the never-failing practical joke of the Daylight Saving Act, had only just set, and a golden afterglow lingered on the fields as the car which had met the train purred over the two miles of country road that separated the little town from the castle. As they passed in between the great stone gate-posts and shot up the winding drive, the soft murmur of the engines seemed to deepen rather than break the soothing stillness. The air was fragrant with indescribable English scents. Somewhere in the distance sheep-bells tinkled; rabbits, waggling white tails, bolted across the path; and once a herd of agitated deer made a brief appearance among the trees. The only thing that disturbed the magic hush was the fluting voice of Lord Emsworth, on whom the spectacle of his beloved property had acted as an immediate stimulant. Unlike his son Freddie, who sat silent in his corner wrestling with his hopes and fears, Lord Emsworth had plunged into a perfect Niagara of speech the moment the car entered the park. In a high tenor voice, and with wide, excited gestures, he pointed out to Psmith oaks with a history and rhododendrons with a past: his conversation as they drew near the castle and came in sight of the flower-beds taking on an almost lyrical note and becoming a sort of anthem of gladness, through which, like some theme in the minor, ran a series of opprobrious observations on the subject of Angus McAllister.

Beach, the butler, solicitously scooping them out of the car at the front door, announced that her ladyship and Miss Peavey were taking their after-dinner coffee in the arbour by the bowling-green; and presently Psmith, conducted by his lordship, found himself shaking hands with a strikingly handsome woman in whom, though her manner was friendliness itself, he could detect a marked suggestion of the formidable. Aesthetically, he admired Lady Constance's appearance, but he could not conceal from himself that in the particular circumstances he would have preferred something rather more fragile and drooping. Lady Constance conveyed the impression that anybody who had the choice between stealing anything from her and stirring up a nest of hornets with a short walking-stick would do well to choose the hornets.

'How do you do, Mr McTodd?' said Lady Constance with great amiability. 'I am so glad you were able to come after all.'

Psmith wondered what she meant by 'after all,' but there were so many things about his present situation calculated to tax the mind that he had no desire to probe slight verbal ambiguities. He shook her hand and replied that it was very kind of her to say so.

'We are quite a small party at present,' continued Lady Constance, 'but we are expecting a number of people quite soon. For the moment Aileen and you are our only guests. Oh, I am sorry, I should have . . . Miss Peavey, Mr McTodd.'

The slim and willowy female who during this brief conversation had been waiting in an attitude of suspended animation, gazing at Psmith with large, wistful eyes, stepped forward. She clasped Psmith's hand in hers, held it, and in a low, soft voice, like thick cream made audible, uttered one reverent word.

'*Maître!*'

'I beg your pardon?' said Psmith. A young man capable of bearing himself with calm and dignity in most circumstances, however trying, he found his poise wobbling under the impact of Miss Aileen Peavey.

Miss Peavey often had this effect on the less soulful type of man, especially in the mornings, when such men are not at their strongest and best. When she came into the breakfast-room of a country house, brave men who had been up a bit late the night before quailed and tried to hide behind newspapers. She was the sort of woman who tells a man who is propping his eyes open with his fingers and endeavouring to correct a headache with strong tea, that she was up at six watching the dew fade off the grass, and didn't he think that those wisps of morning mist were the elves' bridal-veils. She had large, fine, melancholy eyes, and was apt to droop dreamily.

'Master!' said Miss Peavey, obligingly translating.

There did not seem to be any immediate come-back to a remark like this, so Psmith contented himself with beaming genially at her through his monocle: and Miss Peavey came to bat again.

'How wonderful that you were able to come – after all!'

Again this 'after all' motive creeping into the theme . . .

'You know Miss Peavey's work, of course?' said Lady Constance, smiling pleasantly on her two celebrities.

'Who does not?' said Psmith courteously.

'Oh, *do* you?' said Miss Peavey, gratification causing her slender body to perform a sort of ladylike shimmy down its whole length. 'I scarcely hoped that you would know my name. My Canadian sales have not been large.'

'Quite large enough,' said Psmith. 'I mean, of course,' he added with a paternal smile, 'that while your delicate art may not have a universal appeal in a young country, it is intensely appreciated by a small and select body of the intelligentsia.'

And if that was not the stuff to give them, he reflected with not a little complacency, he was dashed.

'Your own wonderful poems,' replied Miss Peavey, 'are, of course, known the whole world over. Oh, Mr McTodd, you can hardly appreciate how I feel, meeting you. It is like the realization of some golden dream of childhood. It is like . . .'

Here the Hon. Freddie Threepwood remarked suddenly that he was going to pop into the house for a whisky and soda. As he had not previously spoken, his observation had something of the effect of a voice from the tomb. The daylight was ebbing fast now, and in the shadows he had contrived to pass out of sight as well as out of mind. Miss Peavey started like an abruptly awakened somnambulist, and Psmith was at last able to release his hand, which he had begun to look on as gone beyond his control for ever. Until this fortunate interruption there had seemed no reason why Miss Peavey should not have continued to hold it till bedtime.

Freddie's departure had the effect of breaking a spell. Lord Emsworth, who had been standing perfectly still with vacant eyes, like a dog listening to a noise a long way off, came to life with a jerk.

'I'm going to have a look at my flowers,' he announced.

'Don't be silly, Clarence,' said his sister. 'It's much too dark to see flowers.'

'I could smell 'em,' retorted his lordship argumentatively.

It seemed as if the party must break up, for already his lordship had begun to potter off, when a newcomer arrived to solidify it again.

'Ah, Baxter, my dear fellow,' said Lord Emsworth. 'Here we are, you see.'

'Mr Baxter,' said Lady Constance, 'I want you to meet Mr McTodd.'

'Mr McTodd!' said the new arrival, on a note of surprise.

'Yes, he found himself able to come after all.'

'Ah!' said the Efficient Baxter.

It occurred to Psmith as a passing thought, to which he gave no more than a momentary attention, that this spectacled and capable-looking man was gazing at him, as they shook hands, with a curious intensity. But possibly, he reflected, this was merely a species of optical illusion due to the other's spectacles. Baxter, staring through his spectacles, often gave people the impression of possessing an eye that could pierce six inches of harveyized steel and stick out on the other side. Having registered in his consciousness the fact that he had been stared at keenly by this stranger, Psmith thought no more of the matter.

In thus lightly dismissing the Baxterian stare, Psmith had acted injudiciously. He should have examined it more closely and made an effort to analyse it, for it was by no means without its message. It was a stare of suspicion. Vague suspicion as yet, but nevertheless suspicion. Rupert Baxter was one of those men whose chief characteristic is a disposition to suspect their fellows. He did not suspect them of this or that definite crime: he simply suspected them. He had not yet definitely accused

Psmith in his mind of any specific tort or malfeasance. He merely had a nebulous feeling that he would bear watching.

Miss Peavey now fluttered again into the centre of things. On the arrival of Baxter she had withdrawn for a moment into the background, but she was not the woman to stay there long. She came forward holding out a small oblong book, which, with a languishing firmness, she pressed into Psmith's hands.

'Could I persuade you, Mr McTodd,' said Miss Peavey pleadingly, 'to write some little thought in my autograph-book and sign it? I have a fountain-pen.'

Light flooded the arbour. The Efficient Baxter, who knew where everything was, had found and pressed the switch. He did this not so much to oblige Miss Peavey as to enable him to obtain a clearer view of the visitor. With each minute that passed the Efficient Baxter was finding himself more and more doubtful in his mind about this visitor.

'There!' said Miss Peavey, welcoming the illumination.

Psmith tapped his chin thoughtfully with the fountain-pen. He felt that he should have foreseen this emergency earlier. If ever there was a woman who was bound to have an autograph-book, that woman was Miss Peavey.

'Just some little thought . . .'

Psmith hesitated no longer. In a firm hand he wrote the words 'Across the pale parabola of Joy . . .' adding an unfaltering 'Ralston McTodd,' and handed the book back.

'How strange,' sighed Miss Peavey.

'May I look?' said Baxter, moving quickly to her side.

'How strange!' repeated Miss Peavey. 'To think that you should have chosen that line! There are several of your more mystic passages that I meant to ask you to explain, but particularly "Across the pale parabola of Joy" . . .'

512

'You find it difficult to understand?'

'A little, I confess.'

'Well, well,' said Psmith indulgently, 'perhaps I did put a bit of top-spin on that one.'

'I beg your pardon?'

'I say, perhaps it is a little obscure. We must have a long chat about it – later on.'

'Why not now?' demanded the Efficient Baxter, flashing his spectacles.

'I am rather tired,' said Psmith with gentle reproach, 'after my journey. Fatigued. We artists . . .'

'Of course,' said Miss Peavey, with an indignant glance at the secretary. 'Mr Baxter does not understand the sensitive poetic temperament.'

'A bit unspiritual, eh?' said Psmith tolerantly. 'A trifle earthy? So I thought, so I thought. One of these strong, hard men of affairs, I shouldn't wonder.'

'Shall we go and find Lord Emsworth, Mr McTodd?' said Miss Peavey, dismissing the fermenting Baxter with a scornful look. 'He wandered off just now. I suppose he is among his flowers. Flowers are very beautiful by night.'

'Indeed, yes,' said Psmith. 'And also by day. When I am surrounded by flowers, a sort of divine peace floods over me, and the rough, harsh world seems far away. I feel soothed, tranquil. I sometimes think, Miss Peavey, that flowers must be the souls of little children who have died in their innocence.'

'What a beautiful thought, Mr McTodd!' exclaimed Miss Peavey rapturously.

'Yes,' agreed Psmith. 'Don't pinch it. It's copyright.'

The darkness swallowed them up. Lady Constance turned to the Efficient Baxter, who was brooding with furrowed brow.

'Charming, is he not?'

'I beg your pardon?'

'I said I thought Mr McTodd was charming.'

513

'Oh, quite.'

'Completely unspoiled.'

'Oh, decidedly.'

'I am so glad that he was able to come after all. That telegram he sent this afternoon cancelling his visit seemed so curt and final.'

'So I thought it.'

'Almost as if he had taken offence at something and decided to have nothing to do with us.'

'Quite.'

Lady Constance shivered delicately. A cool breeze had sprung up. She drew her wrap more closely about her shapely shoulders, and began to walk to the house. Baxter did not accompany her. The moment she had gone he switched off the light and sat down, chin in hand. That massive brain was working hard.

8 — Confidences on the Lake

I

'Miss Halliday,' announced the Efficient Baxter, removing another letter from its envelope and submitting it to a swift, keen scrutiny, 'arrives at about three today. She is catching the the twelve-fifty train.'

He placed the letter on the pile beside his plate; and, having decapitated an egg, peered sharply into its interior as if hoping to surprise guilty secrets. For it was the breakfast hour, and the members of the house party, scattered up and down the long table, were fortifying their tissues against another day. An agreeable scent of bacon floated over the scene like a benediction.

Lord Emsworth looked up from the seed catalogue in which he was immersed. For some time past his enjoyment of the meal had been marred by a vague sense of something missing, and now he knew what it was.

'Coffee!' he said, not violently, but in the voice of a good man oppressed. 'I want coffee. Why have I no coffee? Constance, my dear, I should have coffee. Why have I none?'

'I'm sure I gave you some,' said Lady Constance, brightly presiding over the beverages at the other end of the table.

'Then where is it?' demanded his lordship clinchingly.

Baxter – almost regretfully, it seemed – gave the egg a clean bill of health, and turned in his able way to cope with this domestic problem.

'Your coffee is behind the catalogue you are reading, Lord Emsworth. You propped the catalogue against your cup.'

'Did I? Did I? Why, so I did! Bless my soul!' His lordship, relieved, took an invigorating sip. 'What were you saying just then, my dear fellow?'

'I have had a letter from Miss Halliday,' said Baxter. 'She writes that she is catching the twelve-fifty train at Paddington, which means that she should arrive at Market Blandings at about three.'

'Who,' asked Miss Peavey, in a low, thrilling voice, ceasing for a moment to peck at her plate of kedgeree, 'is Miss Halliday?'

'The exact question I was about to ask myself,' said Lord Emsworth. 'Baxter, my dear fellow, who is Miss Halliday?'

Baxter, with a stifled sigh, was about to refresh his employer's memory, when Psmith anticipated him. Psmith had been consuming toast and marmalade with his customary languid grace and up till now had firmly checked all attempts to engage him in conversation.

'Miss Halliday,' he said, 'is a very old and valued friend of mine. We two have, so to speak, pulled the gowans fine. I had been hoping to hear that she had been sighted on the horizon.'

The effect of these words on two of the company was somewhat remarkable. Baxter, hearing them, gave such a violent start that he spilled half the contents of his cup: and Freddie, who had been flitting like a butterfly among the dishes on the sideboard and had just decided to help himself to scrambled eggs, deposited a liberal spoonful on the carpet, where it was found and salvaged a moment later by Lady Constance's spaniel.

Psmith did not observe these phenomena, for he had returned to his toast and marmalade. He thus missed encountering perhaps the keenest glance that had ever come through Rupert Baxter's spectacles. It was not a protracted glance, but while it lasted it was like the ray from an oxy-acetylene blowpipe.

'A friend of yours?' said Lord Emsworth. 'Indeed? Of

course, Baxter, I remember now. Miss Halliday is the young lady who is coming to catalogue the library.'

'What a delightful task!' cooed Miss Peavey. 'To live among the stored-up thoughts of dead and gone genius!'

'You had better go down and meet her, my dear fellow,' said Lord Emsworth. 'At the station, you know,' he continued, clarifying his meaning. 'She will be glad to see you.'

'I was about to suggest it myself,' said Psmith.

'Though why the library needs cataloguing,' said his lordship, returning to a problem which still vexed his soul when he had leisure to give a thought to it, 'I can't . . . However . . .'

He finished his coffee and rose from the table. A stray shaft of sunlight had fallen provocatively on his bald head, and sunshine always made him restive.

'Are you going to your flowers, Lord Emsworth?' asked Miss Peavey.

'Eh? What? Yes. Oh, yes. Going to have a look at those lobelias.'

'I will accompany you, if I may,' said Psmith.

'Eh? Why, certainly, certainly.'

'I have always held,' said Psmith, 'that there is no finer tonic than a good look at a lobelia immediately after breakfast. Doctors, I believe, recommend it.'

'Oh, I say,' said Freddie hastily, as he reached the door, 'can I have a couple of words with you a bit later on?'

'A thousand if you wish it,' said Psmith. 'You will find me somewhere out there in the great open spaces where men are men.'

He included the entire company in a benevolent smile, and left the room.

'How charming he is!' sighed Miss Peavey. 'Don't you think so, Mr Baxter?'

The Efficient Baxter seemed for a moment to find some difficulty in replying.

'Oh, very,' he said, but not heartily.

'And such a *soul*! It shines on that wonderful brow of his, doesn't it?'

'He has a good forehead,' said Lady Constance. 'But I wish he wouldn't wear his hair so short. Somehow it makes him seem unlike a poet.'

Freddie, alarmed, swallowed a mouthful of scrambled egg.

'Oh, he's a poet all right,' he said hastily.

'Well, really, Freddie,' said Lady Constance, piqued, 'I think we hardly need *you* to tell us that.'

'No, no, of course. But what I mean is, in spite of his wearing his hair short, you know.'

'I ventured to speak to him of that yesterday,' said Miss Peavey, 'and he said he rather expected to be wearing it even shorter very soon.'

'Freddie!' cried Lady Constance with asperity. 'What *are* you doing?'

A brown lake of tea was filling the portion of the tablecloth immediately opposite the Hon. Freddie Threepwood. Like the Efficient Baxter a few minutes before, sudden emotion had caused him to upset his cup.

2

The scrutiny of his lordship's lobelias has palled upon Psmith at a fairly early stage in the proceedings, and he was sitting on the terrace wall enjoying a meditative cigarette when Freddie found him.

'Ah, Comrade Threepwood,' said Psmith, 'welcome to Blandings Castle! You said something about wishing to have speech with me, if I remember rightly?'

The Hon. Freddie shot a nervous glance about him, and seated himself on the wall.

'I say,' he said, 'I wish you wouldn't say things like that.'

'Like what, Comrade Threepwood?'

'What you said to the Peavey woman.'

'I recollect having a refreshing chat with Miss Peavey yesterday afternoon,' said Psmith, 'but I cannot recall saying anything calculated to bring the blush of shame to the cheek of modesty. What observation of mine was it that meets with your censure?'

'Why, that stuff about expecting to wear your hair shorter. If you're going to go about saying that sort of thing – well, dash it, you might just as well give the whole bally show away at once and have done with it.'

Psmith nodded gravely.

'Your generous heat, Comrade Threepwood, is not unjustified. It was undoubtedly an error of judgement. If I have a fault – which I am not prepared to admit – it is a perhaps ungentlemanly desire to pull that curious female's leg. A stronger man than myself might well find it hard to battle against the temptation. However, now that you have called it to my notice, it shall not occur again. In future I will moderate the persiflage. Cheer up, therefore, Comrade Threepwood, and let us see that merry smile of yours, of which I hear such good reports.'

The appeal failed to alleviate Freddie's gloom. He smote morosely at a fly which had settled on his furrowed brow.

'I'm getting as jumpy as a cat,' he said.

'Fight against this unmanly weakness,' urged Psmith. 'As far as I can see, everything is going along nicely.'

'I'm not so sure. I believe that blighter Baxter suspects something.'

'What do you think he suspects?'

'Why, that there's something fishy about you.'

Psmith winced.

'I would be infinitely obliged to you, Comrade Threepwood, if you would not use that particular adjective. It awakens old memories, all very painful. But let us go more deeply into this matter, for you interest me strangely. Why do you think that cheery old Baxter, a delightful personality if ever I met one, suspects me?'

'It's the way he looks at you.'

'I know what you mean, but I attribute no importance to it. As far as I have been able to ascertain during my brief visit, he looks at everybody and everything in precisely the same way. Only last night at dinner I observed him glaring with keen mistrust at about as blameless and innocent a plate of clear soup as was ever dished up. He then proceeded to shovel it down with quite undisguised relish. So possibly you are all wrong about his motive for looking at me like that. It may be admiration.'

'Well, I don't like it.'

'Nor, from an aesthetic point of view, do I. But we must bear these things manfully. We must remind ourselves that it is Baxter's misfortune rather than his fault that he looks like a dyspeptic lizard.'

Freddie was not to be consoled. His gloom deepened.

'And it isn't only Baxter.'

'What else is on your mind?'

'The whole atmosphere of the place is getting rummy, if you know what I mean.' He bent towards Psmith and whispered pallidly, 'I say, I believe that new housemaid is a detective!'

Psmith eyed him patiently.

'Which new housemaid, Comrade Threepwood? Brooding, as I do, pretty tensely all the time on deep and wonderful subjects, I have little leisure to keep tab on the domestic staff. *Is* there a new housemaid?'

'Yes. Susan, her name is.'

'Susan? Susan? That sounds all right. Just the name a real housemaid would have.'

'Did you ever,' demanded Freddie earnestly, 'see a real housemaid sweep under a bureau?'

'Does she?'

'Caught her at it in my room this morning.'

'But isn't it a trifle far-fetched to imagine that she is a detective? Why should she be a detective?'

'Well, I've seen such a dashed lot of films where the house maid or the parlourmaid or what not were detectives. Makes a fellow uneasy.'

'Fortunately,' said Psmith, 'there is no necessity to remain in a state of doubt. I can give you an unfailing method by means of which you may discover if she is what she would have us believe her.'

'What's that?'

'Kiss her.'

'Kiss her!'

'Precisely. Go to her and say, "Susan, you're a very pretty girl . . ." '

'But she isn't.'

'We will assume, for purposes of argument, that she is. Go to her and say, "Susan, you are a very pretty girl. What would you do if I were to kiss you?" If she is a detective, she will reply, "How dare you, sir!" or, possibly, more simply, "Sir!" Whereas if she is the genuine housemaid I believe her to be and only sweeps under bureaux out of pure zeal, she will giggle and remark, "Oh, don't be silly, sir!" You appreciate the distinction?'

'How do you know?'

'My grandmother told me, Comrade Threepwood. My advice to you, if the state of doubt you are in is affecting your enjoyment of life, is to put the matter to the test at the earliest convenient opportunity.'

'I'll think it over,' said Freddie dubiously.

Silence fell upon him for a space, and Psmith was well content to have it so. He had no specific need of Freddie's prattle to help him enjoy the pleasant sunshine and the scent of Angus McAllister's innumerable flowers. Presently, however, his companion was off again. But now there was a different note in his voice. Alarm seemed to have given place to something which appeared to be embarrassment. He coughed several times, and his neatly-shod feet, writhing in self-conscious circles, scraped against the wall.

'I say!'

'You have our ear once more, Comrade Threepwood,' said Psmith politely.

'I say, what I really came out here to talk about was something else. I say, are you really a pal of Miss Halliday's?'

'Assuredly. Why?'

'I say!' A rosy blush mantled the Hon. Freddie's young cheek. 'I say, I wish you would put in a word for me, then.'

'Put in a word for you?'

Freddie gulped.

'I love her, dash it!'

'A noble emotion,' said Psmith courteously. 'When did you feel it coming on?'

'I've been in love with her for months. But she won't look at me.'

'That, of course,' agreed Psmith, 'must be a disadvantage. Yes, I should imagine that that would stick the gaff into the course of true love to no small extent.'

'I mean, won't take me seriously, and all that. Laughs at me, don't you know, when I propose. What would you do?'

'I should stop proposing,' said Psmith, having given the matter thought.

'But I can't.'

'Tut, tut!' said Psmith severely. 'And, in case the expression is new to you, what I mean is "Pooh, pooh!" Just say to yourself, "From now on I will not start proposing until after lunch." That done, it will be an easy step to do no proposing during the afternoon. And by degrees you will find that you can give it up altogether. Once you have conquered the impulse for the after-breakfast proposal, the rest will be easy. The first one of the day is always the hardest to drop.'

'I believe she thinks me a mere butterfly,' said Freddie,

who had not been listening to this most valuable homily.

Psmith slid down from the wall and stretched himself.

'Why,' he said, 'are butterflies so often described as "mere"? I have heard them so called a hundred times, and I cannot understand the reason . . . Well, it would, no doubt, be both interesting and improving to go into the problem, but at this point, Comrade Threepwood, I leave you. I would brood.'

'Yes, but, I say, will you?'

'Will I what?'

'Put in a word for me?'

'If,' said Psmith, 'the subject crops up in the course of the chit-chat, I shall be delighted to spread myself with no little vim on the theme of your fine qualities.'

He melted away into the shrubbery, just in time to avoid Miss Peavey, who broke in on Freddie's meditations a moment later and kept him company till lunch.

3

The twelve-fifty train drew up with a grinding of brakes at the platform of Market Blandings, and Psmith, who had been whiling away the time of waiting by squandering money which he could ill afford on the slot-machine which supplied butterscotch, turned and submitted it to a grave scrutiny. Eve Halliday got out of a third-class compartment.

'Welcome to our village, Miss Halliday,' said Psmith, advancing.

Eve regarded him with frank astonishment.

'What are you doing here?' she asked.

'Lord Emsworth was kind enough to suggest that, as we were such old friends, I should come down in the car and meet you.'

'Are we old friends?'

'Surely. Have you forgotten all those happy days in London?'

'There was only one.'

'True. But think how many meetings we crammed into it.'

'Are you staying at the castle?'

'Yes. And what is more, I am the life and soul of the party. Have you anything in the shape of luggage?'

'I nearly always take luggage when I am going to stay a month or so in the country. It's at the back somewhere.'

'I will look after it. You will find the car outside. If you care to go and sit in it, I will join you in a moment. And, lest the time hangs heavy on your hands, take this. Butterscotch. Delicious, and, so I understand, wholesome. I bought it specially for you.'

A few minutes later, having arranged for the trunk to be taken to the castle, Psmith emerged from the station and found Eve drinking in the beauties of the town of Market Blandings.

'What a delightful old place,' she said as they drove off. 'I almost wish I lived here.'

'During the brief period of my stay at the castle,' said Psmith, 'the same thought has occurred to me. It is the sort of place where one feels that one could gladly settle down into a peaceful retirement and grow a honey-coloured beard.' He looked at her with solemn admiration. 'Women are wonderful,' he said.

'And why, Mr Bones, are women wonderful?' asked Eve.

'I was thinking at the moment of your appearance. You have just stepped off the train after a four-hour journey, and you are as fresh and blooming as – if I may coin a simile – a rose. How do you do it? When I arrived I was deep in alluvial deposits, and have only just managed to scrape them off.'

'When did you arrive?'

'On the evening of the day on which I met you.'

'But it's so extraordinary. That you should be here, I mean. I was wondering if I should ever see you again.' Eve coloured a little, and went on rather hurriedly. 'I mean, it seems so strange that we should always be meeting like this.'

'Fate, probably,' said Psmith. 'I hope it isn't going to spoil your visit?'

'Oh, no.'

'I could have done with a trifle more emphasis on the last word,' said Psmith gently. 'Forgive me for criticizing your methods of voice production, but surely you can see how much better it would have sounded spoken thus: "*Oh, no!*" '

Eve laughed.

'Very well, then,' she said. 'Oh, *no*.'

'Much better,' said Psmith. 'Much better.'

He began to see that it was going to be difficult to introduce a eulogy of the Hon. Freddie Threepwood into this conversation.

'I'm very glad you're here,' said Eve, resuming the talk after a slight pause. 'Because, as a matter of fact, I'm feeling just the least bit nervous.'

'Nervous? Why?'

'This is my first visit to a place of this size.' The car had turned in at the big stone gates, and they were bowling smoothly up the winding drive. Through an avenue of trees to the right the great bulk of the castle had just appeared, grey and imposing against the sky. The afternoon sun glittered on the lake beyond it. 'Is everything very stately?'

'Not at all. We are very homely folk, we of Blandings Castle. We go about, simple and unaffected, dropping gracious words all over the place. Lord Emsworth didn't overawe you, did he?'

'Oh, he's a dear. And, of course, I know Freddie quite well.'

Psmith nodded. If she knew Freddie quite well, there

525

was naturally no need to talk about him. He did not talk about him, therefore.

'Have you known Lord Emsworth long?' asked Eve.

'I met him for the first time the day I met you.'

'Good gracious!' Eve stared. 'And he invited you to the castle?'

Psmith smoothed his waistcoat.

'Strange, I agree. One can only account for it, can one not, by supposing that I radiate some extraordinary attraction. Have you noticed it?'

'No!'

'No?' said Psmith, surprised. 'Ah, well,' he went on tolerantly, 'no doubt it will flash upon you quite unexpectedly sooner or later. Like a thunderbolt or something.'

'I think you're terribly conceited.'

'Not at all,' said Psmith. 'Conceited? No, no. Success has not spoiled me.'

'Have you had any success?'

'None whatever.' The car stopped. 'We get down here,' said Psmith, opening the door.

'Here? Why?'

'Because, if we go up to the house, you will infallibly be pounced on and set to work by one Baxter – a delightful fellow, but a whale for toil. I propose to conduct you on a tour round the grounds, and then we will go for a row on the lake. You will enjoy that.'

'You seem to have mapped out my future for me.'

'I have,' said Psmith with emphasis, and in the monocled eye that met hers Eve detected so beaming a glance of esteem and admiration that she retreated warily into herself and endeavoured to be frigid.

'I'm afraid I haven't time to wander about the grounds,' she said aloofly. 'I must be going and seeing Mr Baxter.'

'Baxter,' said Psmith, 'is not one of the natural beauties of the place. Time enough to see him when you are compelled to . . . We are now in the southern pleasaunce

or the west homepark or something. Note the refined
way the deer are cropping the grass. All the ground on
which we are now standing is of historic interest. Oliver
Cromwell went through here in 1550. The record has
since been lowered.'

'I haven't time . . .'

'Leaving the pleasaunce on our left, we proceed to the
northern messuage. The dandelions were imported from
Egypt by the ninth Earl.'

'Well, anyhow,' said Eve mutinously, 'I won't come
on the lake.'

'You will enjoy the lake,' said Psmith. 'The newts
are of the famous old Blandings strain. They were
introduced, together with the water-beetles, in the reign
of Queen Elizabeth. Lord Emsworth, of course, holds
manorial rights over the mosquito-swatting.'

Eve was a girl of high and haughty spirit, and as such
strongly resented being appropriated and having her
movements directed by one who, in spite of his specious
claims, was almost a stranger. But somehow she found
her companion's placid assumption of authority hard to
resist. Almost meekly she accompanied him through
meadow and shrubbery, over velvet lawns and past
gleaming flower beds, and her indignation evaporated as
her eyes absorbed the beauty of it all. She gave a little
sigh. If Market Blandings had seemed a place in which
one might dwell happily, Blandings Castle was a paradise.

'Before us now,' said Psmith, 'lies the celebrated Yew
Alley, so called from the yews which hem it in. Speaking
in my capacity of guide to the estate, I may say that when
we have turned this next corner you will see a most
remarkable sight.'

And they did. Before them, as they passed in under the
boughs of an aged tree, lay a green vista, faintly dappled
with stray shafts of sunshine. In the middle of this vista
the Hon. Frederick Threepwood was embracing a young
woman in the dress of a housemaid.

4

Psmith was the first of the little group to recover from
the shock of this unexpected encounter, the Hon.
Freddie the last. That unfortunate youth, meeting Eve's
astonished eye as he raised his head, froze where he
stood and remained with his mouth open until she had
disappeared, which she did a few moments later, led
away by Psmith, who, as he went, directed at his young
friend a look in which surprise, pain and reproof were
so nicely blended that it would have been hard to say
which predominated. All that a spectator could have
said with certainty was that Psmith's finer feelings had
suffered a severe blow.

'A painful scene,' he remarked to Eve, as he drew her
away in the direction of the house. 'But we must always
strive to be charitable. He may have been taking a fly out
of her eye, or teaching her jiu-jitsu.'

He looked at her searchingly.

'You seem less revolted,' he said, 'then one might have
expected. This argues a sweet, shall we say angelic
disposition and confirms my already high opinion of you.'

'Thank you.'

'Not at all. Mark you,' said Psmith, 'I don't think that
this sort of thing is a hobby of Comrade Threepwood's.
He probably has many other ways of passing his spare
time. Remember that before you pass judgement upon
him. Also – Young Blood, and all that sort of thing.'

'I haven't any intention of passing judgement upon
him. It doesn't interest me what Mr Threepwood does,
either in his spare time or out of it.'

'His interest in you, on the other hand, is vast. I forgot
to tell you before, but he loves you. He asked me to
mention it if the conversation happened to veer round in
that direction.'

'I know he does,' said Eve ruefully.

'And does the fact stir no chord in you?'

'I think he's a nuisance.'

'That,' said Psmith cordially, 'is the right spirit. I like to see it. Very well, then, we will discard the topic of Freddie, and I will try to find others that may interest, elevate, and amuse you. We are now approaching the main buildings. I am no expert in architecture, so cannot tell you all I could wish about the façade, but you can see there *is* a façade, and in my opinion – for what it is worth – a jolly good one. We approach by a sweeping gravel walk.'

'I am going in to report to Mr Baxter,' said Eve with decision. 'It's too absurd. I mustn't spend my time strolling about the grounds. I must see Mr Baxter at once.'

Psmith inclined his head courteously.

'Nothing easier. That big, open window there is the library. Doubtless Comrade Baxter is somewhere inside, toiling away among the archives.'

'Yes, but I can't announce myself by shouting to him.'

'Assuredly not,' said Psmith. 'No need for that at all. Leave it to me.' He stooped and picked up a large flower-pot which stood under the terrace wall, and before Eve could intervene had tossed it lightly through the open window. A muffled thud, followed by a sharp exclamation from within, caused a faint smile of gratification to illumine his solemn countenance. 'He *is* in. I thought he would be. Ah, Baxter,' he said graciously, as the upper half of a body surmounted by a spectacled face framed itself suddenly in the window, 'a pleasant, sunny afternoon. How is everything?'

The Efficient Baxter struggled for utterance.

'You look like the Blessed Damozel gazing down from the gold bar of Heaven,' said Psmith genially. 'Baxter, I want to introduce you to Miss Halliday. She arrived safely after a somewhat fatiguing journey. You will like Miss Halliday. If I had a library, I could not wish for a more courteous, obliging and capable cataloguist.'

This striking and unsolicited testimonial made no

appeal to the Efficient Baxter. His mind seemed occupied with other matters.

'Did you throw that flower-plot?' he demanded coldly.

'You will no doubt,' said Psmith, 'wish on some later occasion to have a nice long talk with Miss Halliday in order to give her an outline of her duties. I have been showing her the grounds and am about to take her for a row on the lake. But after that she will – and I know I may speak for Miss Halliday in this matter – be entirely at your disposal.'

'Did you throw that flower-pot?'

'I look forward confidently to the pleasantest of associations between you and Miss Halliday. You will find her,' said Psmith warmly, 'a willing assistant, a tireless worker.'

'Did you . . .?'

'But now,' said Psmith, 'I must be tearing myself away. In order to impress Miss Halliday, I put on my best suit when I went to meet her. For a row upon the lake something simpler in pale flannel is indicated. I shall only be a few minutes,' he said to Eve. 'Would you mind meeting me at the boat-house?'

'I am not coming on the lake with you.'

'At the boat-house in – say – six and a quarter minutes,' said Psmith with a gentle smile, and pranced into the house like a long-legged mustang.

Eve remained where she stood, struggling between laughter and embarrassment. The Efficient Baxter was still leaning wrathfully out of the library window, and it began to seem a little difficult to carry on an ordinary conversation. The problem of what she was to say in order to continue the scene in an agreeable manner was solved by the arrival of Lord Emsworth, who pottered out from the bushes with a rake in his hand. He stood eyeing Eve for a moment, then memory seemed to wake. Eve's appearance was easier to remember, possibly, than some of the things which his lordship was wont to forget. He came forward beamingly.

'Ah, there you are, Miss . . . Dear me, I'm really afraid I have forgotten your name. My memory is excellent as a rule, but I cannot remember names . . . Miss Halliday! Of course, of course. Baxter, my dear fellow,' he proceeded, sighting the watcher at the window, 'this is Miss Halliday.'

'Mr McTodd,' said the Efficient One sourly, 'has already introduced me to Miss Halliday.'

'Has he? Deuced civil of him, deuced civil of him. But where *is* he?' inquired his lordship, scanning the surrounding scenery with a vague eye.

'He went into the house. After,' said Baxter in a cold voice, 'throwing a flower-pot at me.'

'Doing what?'

'He threw a flower-pot at me,' said Baxter, and vanished moodily.

Lord Emsworth stared at the open window, then turned to Eve for enlightenment.

'*Why* did Baxter throw a flower-pot at McTodd?' he said. 'And,' he went on, ventilating an even deeper question, 'where the deuce did he get a flower-pot? There are no flower-pots in the library.'

Eve, on her side, was also seeking information.

'Did you say his name was McTodd, Lord Emsworth?'

'No, no. Baxter. That was Baxter, my secretary.'

'No, I mean the one who met me at the station.'

'Baxter did not meet you at the station. The man who met you at the station,' said Lord Emsworth, speaking slowly, for women are so apt to get things muddled, 'was McTodd. He's staying here. Constance asked him, and I'm bound to say when I first heard of it I was not any too well pleased. I don't like poets as a rule. But this fellow's so different from the other poets I've met. Different altogether. And,' said Lord Emsworth with not a little heat, 'I strongly object to Baxter throwing flower-pots at

531

my guests,' he said firmly, for Lord Emsworth, though occasionally a little vague, was keenly alive to the ancient traditions of his family regarding hospitality.

'Is Mr McTodd a poet?' said Eve, her heart beating.

'Eh? Oh yes, yes. There seems to be no doubt about that. A Canadian poet. Apparently they have poets out there. And,' demanded his lordship, ever a fair-minded man, 'why not? A remarkably growing country, I was there in the year '98. Or was it,' he added, thoughtfully passing a muddy hand over his chin and leaving a rich brown stain, ''99? I forget. My memory isn't good for dates . . . If you will excuse me, Miss – Miss Halliday, of course – if you will excuse me, I must be leaving you. I have to see McAllister, my head gardener. An obstinate man. A Scotsman. If you go into the house, my sister Constance will give you a cup of tea. I don't know what the time is, but I suppose there will be tea soon. Never take it myself.'

'Mr McTodd asked me to go for a row on the lake.'

'On the lake, eh? On the *lake*?' said his lordship, as if this was the last place in the neighbourhood where he would have expected to hear of people proposing to row. Then he brightened. 'Of course, yes, on the lake. I think you will like the lake. I take a dip there myself every morning before breakfast. I find it good for the health and appetite. I plunge in and swim perhaps fifty yards, and then return.' Lord Emsworth suspended the gossip from the training camp in order to look at his watch. 'Dear me,' he said, 'I must be going. McAllister has been waiting fully ten minutes. Good-bye, then, for the present, Miss – er – good-bye.'

And Lord Emsworth ambled off, on his face that look of tense concentration which it always wore when interviews with Angus McAllister were in prospect – the look which stern warriors wear when about to meet a foeman worthy of their steel.

5

There was a cold expression in Eve's eyes as she made her way slowly to the boat-house. The information which she had just received had come as a shock, and she was trying to adjust her mind to it. When Miss Clarkson had told her of the unhappy conclusion to her old school friend's marriage to Ralston McTodd, she had immediately, without knowing anything of the facts, arrayed herself loyally on Cynthia's side and condemned the unknown McTodd uncompromisingly and without hesitation. It was many years since she had seen Cynthia, and their friendship might almost have been said to have lapsed; but Eve's affection, when she had once given it, was a durable thing, capable of surviving long separation. She had loved Cynthia at school, and she could feel nothing but animosity towards anyone who had treated her badly. She eyed the glittering water of the lake from under lowered brows, and prepared to be frigid and hostile when the villain of the piece should arrive. It was only when she heard footsteps behind her and turned to perceive Psmith hurrying up, radiant in gleaming flannel, that it occurred to her for the first time that there might have been faults on both sides. She had not known Psmith long, it was true, but already his personality had made a somewhat deep impression on her, and she was loath to believe that he could be the callous scoundrel of her imagination. She decided to suspend judgement until they should be out in mid-water and in a position to discuss the matter without interruption.

'I am a little late,' said Psmith, as he came up. 'I was detained by our young friend Freddie. He came into my room and started talking about himself at the very moment when I was tying my tie and needed every ounce of concentration for that delicate task. The recent painful episode appeared to be weighing on his mind to some extent.' He helped Eve into the boat and started

533

to row. 'I consoled him as best I could by telling him
that it would probably have made you think all the more
highly of him. I ventured the suggestion that girls worship
the strong, rough, dashing type of man. And, after I had
done my best to convince him that he was a strong,
rough, dashing man, I came away. By now, of course, he
may have had a relapse into despair; so, if you happen
to see a body bobbing about in the water as we row along,
it will probably be Freddie's.'

'Never mind about Freddie.'

'I don't if you don't,' said Psmith agreeably. 'Very well,
then, if we see a body, we will ignore it.' He rowed on a
few strokes. 'Correct me if I am wrong,' he said, resting
on his oars and leaning forward, 'but you appear to be
brooding about something. If you will give me a clue, I
will endeavour to assist you to grapple with any little
problem which is troubling you. What is the matter?'

Eve, questioned thus directly, found it difficult to open
the subject. She hesitated a moment, and let the water
ripple through her fingers.

'I have only just found out your name, Mr McTodd,'
she said at length.

Psmith nodded.

'It is always thus,' he said. 'Passing through this life,
we meet a fellow-mortal, chat awhile, and part; and the
last thing we think of doing is to ask him in a manly and
direct way what his label is. There is something oddly
furtive and shamefaced in one's attitude towards people's
names. It is as if we shrank from probing some hideous
secret. We say to ourselves "This pleasant stranger may
be a Snooks or a Buggins. Better not inquire." But in my
case . . .'

'It was a great shock to me.'

'Now there,' said Psmith, 'I cannot follow you. I
wouldn't call McTodd a bad name, as names go. Don't
you think there is a sort of Highland strength about it? It
sounds to me like something out of "The Lady of the

Lake" or "The Lay of the Last Minstrel." "The stag at eve had drunk its fill adoon the glen beyint the hill, and welcomed with a friendly nod old Scotland's pride, young Laird McTodd." You don't think it has a sort of wild romantic ring?'

'I ought to tell you, Mr McTodd,' said Eve, 'that I was at school with Cynthia.'

Psmith was not a young man who often found himself at a loss, but this remark gave him a bewildered feeling such as comes in dreams. It was plain to him that this delightful girl thought she had said something serious, even impressive; but for the moment it did not seem to him to make sense. He sparred warily for time.

'Indeed? With Cynthia? That must have been jolly.'

The harmless observation appeared to have the worst effect upon his companion. The frown came back to her face.

'Oh, don't speak in that flippant, sneering way,' she said. 'It's so cheap.'

Psmith, having nothing to say, remained silent, and the boat drifted on. Eve's face was delicately pink, for she was feeling extraordinarily embarrassed. There was something in the solemn gaze of the man before her which made it difficult for her to go on. But, with the stout-heartedness which was one of her characteristics, she stuck to her task.

'After all,' she said, 'however you may feel about her now, you must have been fond of poor Cynthia at one time, or I don't see why you should have married her.'

Psmith, for want of conversation, had begun rowing again. The start he gave at these remarkable words caused him to skim the surface of the water with the left oar in such a manner to send a liberal pint into Eve's lap. He started forward with apologies.

'Oh, never mind about that,' said Eve impatiently. 'It doesn't matter . . . Mr McTodd,' she said, and there was a note of gentleness in her voice, 'I do wish you would tell me what the trouble was.'

Psmith stared at the floor of the boat in silence. He was wrestling with a feeling of injury. True, he had not during their brief conversation at the Senior Conservative Club specifically inquired of Mr McTodd whether he was a bachelor, but somehow he felt that the man should have dropped some hint as to his married state. True, again, Mr McTodd had not asked him to impersonate him at Blandings Castle. And yet, undeniably, he felt that he had a grievance. Psmith's was an orderly mind. He had proposed to continue the pleasant relations which had begun between Eve and himself, seeing to it that every day they became a little pleasanter, until eventually, in due season, they should reach the point where it would become possible to lay heart and hand at her feet. For there was no doubt in his mind that in a world congested to overflowing with girls Eve Halliday stood entirely alone. And now this infernal Cynthia had risen from nowhere to stand between them. Even a young man as liberally endowed with calm assurance as he was might find it awkward to conduct his wooing with such a handicap as a wife in the background.

Eve misinterpreted his silence.

'I suppose you are thinking that it is no business of mine?'

Psmith came out of his thoughts with a start.

'No, no. Not at all.'

'You see, I'm devoted to Cynthia – and I like you.'

She smiled for the first time. Her embarrassment was passing.

'That is the whole point,' she said. 'I do like you. And I'm quite sure that if you were really the sort of man I thought you when I first heard about all this, I shouldn't. The friend who told me about you and Cynthia made it seem as if the whole fault had been yours. I got the impression that you had been very unkind to Cynthia. I thought you must be a brute. And when Lord Emsworth told me who you were, my first impulse was to hate you. I think if you had come along just then I should have been rather horrid to you. But you were late, and that gave me time to think it over. And then I remembered how nice you had been to me and I felt somehow that – that you must really be quite nice, and it occurred to me that there might be some explanation. And I thought that – perhaps – if you would let me interfere in your private affairs – and if things hadn't gone too far – I might do something to help – try to bring you together, you know.'

She broke off, a little confused, for now that the words were out she was conscious of a return of her former shyness. Even though she was an old friend of Cynthia's, there did seem something insufferably officious in this meddling. And when she saw the look of pain on her companion's face, she regretted that she had spoken. Naturally, she thought, he was offended.

In supposing that Psmith was offended she was mistaken. Internally he was glowing with a renewed admiration for all those beautiful qualities in her which he had detected, before they had ever met, at several yards' range across the street from the window of the Drones Club smoking-room. His look of pain was due to the fact that, having now had time to grapple with the problem, he had decided to dispose of this Cynthia once and for all. He proposed to eliminate her for ever from his life. And the elimination of even such a comparative stranger seemed to him to call for a pained look. So he assumed one.

'That,' he said gravely, 'would, I fear, be impossible. It is like you to suggest it, and I cannot tell you how much I appreciate the kindness which has made you interest yourself in my troubles, but it is too late for any reconciliation. Cynthia and I are divorced.'

For a moment the temptation had come to him to kill

the woman off with some wasting sickness, but this
he resisted as tending towards possible future
complications. He was resolved, however, that there
should be no question of bringing them together again.

He was disturbed to find Eve staring at him in
amazement.

'Divorced? But how can you be divorced? It's only a
few days since you and she were in London together.'

Psmith ceased to wonder that Mr McTodd had had
trouble with his wife. The woman was a perfect pest.

'I used the term in a spiritual rather than a legal sense,'
he replied. 'True, there has been no actual decree, but
we are separated beyond hope of reunion.' He saw the
distress in Eve's eyes and hurried on. 'There are things,'
he said, 'which it is impossible for a man to overlook,
however broad-minded he may be. Love, Miss Halliday,
is a delicate plant. It needs tending, nursing, assiduous
fostering. This cannot be done by throwing the breakfast
bacon at a husband's head.'

'What!' Eve's astonishment was such that the word
came out in a startled squeak.

'*In* the dish,' said Psmith sadly.

Eve's blue eyes opened wide.

'*Cynthia* did that!'

'On more than one occasion. Her temper in the
mornings was terrible. I have known her lift the cat over
two chairs and a settee with a single kick. And all because
there were no mushrooms.'

'But – but I can't believe it!'

'Come over to Canada,' said Psmith, 'and I will show
you the cat.'

'Cynthia did that! – Cynthia – why, she was always
the gentlest little creature.'

'At school, you mean?'

'Yes.'

'That,' said Psmith, 'would, I suppose, be before she
had taken to drink.'

538

'Taken to drink!'

Psmith was feeling happier. A passing thought did come to him that all this was perhaps a trifle rough on the absent Cynthia, but he mastered the unmanly weakness. It was necessary that Cynthia should suffer in the good cause. Already he had begun to detect in Eve's eyes the faint dawnings of an angelic pity, and pity is recognized by all the best authorities as one of the most valuable emotions which your wooer can awaken.

'Drink!' Eve repeated, with a little shudder.

'We lived in one of the dry provinces of Canada, and, as so often happens, that started the trouble. From the moment when she installed a private still her downfall was swift. I have seen her, under the influence of home-brew, rage through the house like a devastating cyclone . . . I hate speaking like this of one who was your friend,' said Psmith, in a low, vibrating voice. 'I would not tell these things to anyone but you. The world, of course, supposes that the entire blame for the collapse of our home was mine. I took care that it should be so. The opinion of the world matters little to me. But with you it is different. I should not like you to think badly of me, Miss Halliday. I do not make friends easily – I am a lonely man – but somehow it has seemed to me since we met that you and I might be friends.'

Eve stretched her hand out impulsively.

'Why, of course!'

Psmith took her hand and held it far longer than was strictly necessary.

'Thank you,' he said. 'Thank you.'

He turned the nose of the boat to the shore, and rowed slowly back.

'I have suffered,' said Psmith gravely, as he helped her ashore. 'But, if you will be my friend, I think that I may forget.'

They walked in silence up the winding path to the castle.

539

6

To Psmith five minutes later, as he sat in his room smoking a cigarette and looking dreamily out at the distant hills, there entered the Hon. Frederick Threepwood, who, having closed the door behind him, tottered to the bed and uttered a deep and discordant groan. Psmith, his mind thus rudely wrenched from pleasant meditations, turned and regarded the gloomy youth with disfavour.

'At any other time, Comrade Threepwood,' he said politely but with firmness, 'certainly. But not now. I am not in the vein.'

'What?' said the Hon. Freddie vacantly.

'I say that at any other time I shall be delighted to listen to your farmyard imitations, but not now. At the moment I am deep in thoughts of my own, and I may say frankly that I regard you as more or less of an excrescence. I want solitude, solitude. I am in a beautiful reverie, and your presence jars upon me somewhat profoundly.'

The Hon. Freddie ruined the symmetry of his hair by passing his fingers feverishly through it.

'Don't *talk* so much! I never met a fellow like you for talking.' Having rumpled his hair to the left, he went through it again and rumpled it to the right. 'I say, do you know what? You've jolly well got to clear out of here quick!' He got up from the bed, and approached the window. Having done which, he bent towards Psmith and whispered in his ear. 'The game's up!'

Psmith withdrew his ear with a touch of hauteur, but he looked at his companion with a little more interest. He had feared, when he saw Freddie stagger in with such melodramatic despair and emit so hollow a groan, that the topic on which he wished to converse was the already exhausted one of his broken heart. It now began to appear that weightier matters were on his mind.

'I fail to understand you, Comrade Threepwood,' he said. 'The last time I had the privilege of conversing with you, you informed me that Susan, or whatever her name is, merely giggled and told you not to be silly when you embraced her. In other words, she is *not* a detective. What has happened since then to get you all worked up?'

'Baxter!'

'What has Baxter been doing?'

'Only giving the whole bally show away to me, that's all,' said Freddie feverishly. He clutched Psmith's arm violently, causing that exquisite to utter a slight moan and smooth out the wrinkles thus created in his sleeve. 'Listen! I've just been talking to the blighter. I was passing the library just now, when he popped out of the door and hauled me in. And, dash it, he hadn't been talking two seconds before I realized that he has seen through the whole dam' thing practically from the moment you got here. Though he doesn't seem to know that I've anything to do with it, thank goodness.'

'I should imagine not, if he makes you his confidant. Why did he do that, by the way? What made him select you as the recipient of his secrets?'

'As far as I can make out, his idea was to form a gang, if you know what I mean. He said a lot of stuff about him and me being the only two able-bodied young men in the place, and we ought to be prepared to tackle you if you started anything.'

'I see. And now tell me how our delightful friend ever happened to begin suspecting that I was not all I seemed to be. I had been flattering myself that I had put the little deception over with complete success.'

'Well, in the first place, dash it, that dam' fellow McTodd – the real one, you know – sent a telegram saying that he wasn't coming. So it seemed rummy to Baxter bang from the start when you blew in all merry and bright.'

'Ah! That was what they all meant by saying they were glad I had come "after all". A phrase which at the moment, I confess, rather mystified me.'

'And then you went and wrote in the Peavey female's autograph-book.'

'In what way was that a false move?'

'Why, that was the biggest bloomer on record, as it has turned out,' said Freddie vehemently. 'Baxter apparently keeps every letter that comes to the place on a file, and he'd skewered McTodd's original letter with the rest. I mean, the one he wrote accepting the invitation to come here. And Baxter compared his handwriting with what you wrote in the Peavey's album, and, of course, they weren't a dam' bit alike. And that put the lid on it.'

Psmith lit another cigarette and drew at it thoughtfully. He realized that he had made a tactical error in underestimating the antagonism of the Efficient One.

'Does he seem to have any idea why I have come to the castle?' he asked.

'Any idea? Why, dash it, the very first thing he said to me was that you must have come to sneak Aunt Connie's necklace.'

'In that case, why has he made no move till today? I should have supposed that he would long since have denounced me before as large an audience as he could assemble. Why this reticence on the part of genial old Baxter?'

A crimson flush of chivalrous indignation spread itself over Freddie's face.

'He told me that, too.'

'There seem to have been no reserves between Comrade Baxter and yourself. And very healthy, too, this spirit of confidence. What was his reason for abstaining from loosing the bomb?'

'He said he was pretty sure you wouldn't try to do anything on your own. He thought you would wait till your accomplice arrived. And, damn him,' cried Freddie heatedly, 'do you know who he's got the infernal gall to think is your accomplice? Miss Halliday! Dash him!'

Psmith smoked in thoughtful silence.

'Well, of course, now that this has happened,' said Freddie, 'I suppose it's no good thinking of going on with the thing. You'd better pop off, what? If I were you, I'd leg it today and have your luggage sent on after you.'

Psmith threw away his cigarette and stretched himself. During the last few moments he had been thinking with some tenseness.

'Comrade Threepwood,' he said reprovingly, 'you suggest a cowardly and weak-minded action. I admit that the outlook would be distinctly rosier if no such person as Baxter were on the premises, but nevertheless the thing must be seen through to a finish. At least we have this advantage over our spectacled friend, that we know he suspects me and he doesn't know we know. I think that with a little resource and ingenuity we may yet win through.' He turned to the window and looked out. 'Sad,' he sighed, 'that these idyllic surroundings should have become oppressed with a cloud of sinister menace. One thinks one sees a faun popping about in the undergrowth, and on looking more closely perceives that it is in reality a detective with a notebook. What one fancied was the piping of Pan turns out to be a police-whistle, summoning assistance. Still, we must bear these things without wincing. They are our cross. What you have told me will render me, if possible, warier and more snake-like than ever, but my purpose remains firm. The cry goes round the castle battlements "Psmith intends to keep the old flag flying!" So charge off and soothe your quivering ganglions with a couple of aspirins, Comrade Threepwood, and leave me to my thoughts. All will doubtless come right in the future.'

9 — Psmith Engages a Valet

From out of the scented shade of the big cedar on the lawn in front of the castle Psmith looked at the flower-beds, jaunty and gleaming in the afternoon sun; then he looked back at Eve, incredulity in every feature.

'I must have misunderstood you. Surely,' he said in a voice vibrant with reproach, 'you do not seriously intend to *work* in weather like this?'

'I must. I've got a conscience. They aren't paying me a handsome salary – a fairly handsome salary – to sit about in deckchairs.'

'But you only came yesterday.'

'Well, I ought to have worked yesterday.'

'It seems to me,' said Psmith, 'the nearest thing to slavery that I have ever struck. I had hoped, seeing that everybody had gone off and left us alone, that we were going to spend a happy and instructive afternoon together under the shade of this noble tree, talking of this and that. Is it not to be?'

'No, it is not. It's lucky you're not the one who's supposed to be cataloguing this library. It would never get finished.'

'And why, as your employer would say, should it? He has expressed the opinion several times in my hearing that the library has jogged along quite comfortably for a great number of years without being catalogued. Why shouldn't it go on like that indefinitely?'

'It's no good trying to tempt me. There's nothing I should like better than to loaf here for hours and hours, but what would Mr Baxter say when he got back and found out?'

'It is becoming increasingly clear to me each day that I stay in this place,' said Psmith moodily, 'that Comrade Baxter is little short of a blister on the community. Tell me, how do you get on with him?'

'I don't like him much.'

'Nor do I. It is on these communities of taste that life-long attachments are built. Sit down and let us exchange confidences on the subject of Baxter.'

Eve laughed.

'I won't. You're simply trying to lure me into staying out here and neglecting my duty. I really must be off now. You have no idea what a lot of work there is to be done.'

'You are entirely spoiling my afternoon.'

'No, I'm not. You've got a book. What is it?'

Psmith picked up the brightly-jacketed volume and glanced at it.

'*The Man With The Missing Toe*. Comrade Threepwood lent it to me. He has a vast store of this type of narrative. I expect he will be wanting you to catalogue his library next.'

'Well, it looks interesting.'

'Ah, but what does it *teach*? How long do you propose to shut yourself up in that evil-smelling library?'

'An hour or so.'

'Then I shall rely on your society at the end of that period. We might go for another saunter on the lake.'

'All right. I'll come and find you when I've finished.'

Psmith watched her disappear into the house, then seated himself once more in the long chair under the cedar. A sense of loneliness oppressed him. He gave one look at *The Man With The Missing Toe*, and, having rejected the entertainment it offered, gave himself up to meditation.

Blandings Castle dozed in the midsummer heat like a

Palace of Sleep. There had been an exodus of its inmates
shortly after lunch, when Lord Emsworth, Lady
Constance, Mr Keeble, Miss Peavey, and the Efficient
Baxter had left for the neighbouring town of Bridgeford
in the big car, with the Hon. Freddie puffing in its wake
in a natty two-seater. Psmith, who had been invited to
accompany them, had declined on the plea that he wished
to write a poem. He felt but a tepid interest in the
afternoon's programme, which was to consist of the
unveiling by his lordship of the recently completed
memorial to the late Hartley Reddish, Esq, J. P., for so
many years Member of Parliament for the Bridgeford
and Shifley Division of Shropshire. Not even the prospect
of hearing Lord Emsworth – clad, not without vain
protest and weak grumbling, in a silk hat, morning coat,
and sponge-bag trousers – deliver a speech, had been
sufficient to lure him from the castle grounds.

But at the moment when he had uttered his refusal,
thereby incurring the ill-concealed envy both of Lord
Emsworth and his son Freddie, the latter also an unwilling
celebrant, he had supposed that his solitude would be
shared by Eve. This deplorable conscientiousness of hers,
this morbid craving for work, had left him at a loose end.
The time and the place were both above criticism, but,
as so often happens in this life of ours, he had been let
down by the girl.

But, though he chafed for a while, it was not long
before the dreamy peace of the afternoon began to
exercise a soothing effect upon him. With the exception
of the bees that worked with their usual misguided energy
among the flowers and an occasional butterfly which
flitted past in the sunshine, all nature seemed to be taking
a siesta. Somewhere out of sight a lawn-mower had begun
to emphasize the stillness with its musical whirl. A
telegraph-boy on a red bicycle passed up the drive to the
front door, and seemed to have some difficulty in
establishing communication with the domestic staff –

from which Psmith deduced that Beach, the butler, like a good opportunist, was taking advantage of the absence of authority to enjoy a nap in some distant lair of his own. Eventually a parlourmaid appeared, accepted the telegram and (apparently) a rebuke from the boy, and the bicycle passed out of sight, leaving silence and peace once more.

The noblest minds are not proof against atmospheric conditions of this kind. Psmith's eyes closed, opened, closed again. And presently his regular breathing, varied by an occasional snore, was added to the rest of the small sounds of the summer afternoon.

The shadow of the cedar was appreciably longer when he awoke with that sudden start which generally terminates sleep in a garden-chair. A glance at his watch told him that it was close on five o'clock, a fact which was confirmed a moment later by the arrival of the parlourmaid who had answered the summons of the telegraph-boy. She appeared to be the sole survivor of the little world that had its centre in the servants' hall. A sort of female Casabianca.

'I have put your tea in the hall, sir.'

'You could have performed no nobler or more charitable task,' Psmith assured her; and, having corrected a certain stiffness of limb by means of massage, went in. It occurred to him that Eve, assiduous worker though she was, might have knocked off in order to keep him company.

The hope proved vain. A single cup stood bleakly on the tray. Either Eve was superior to the feminine passion for tea or she was having hers up in the library. Filled with something of the sadness which he had felt at the sight of the toiling bees, Psmith embarked on his solitary meal, wondering sorrowfully at the perverseness which made girls work when there was no one to watch them.

It was very agreeable here in the coolness of the hall. The great door of the castle was open, and through it he had a view of lawns bathed in a thirst-provoking sunlight. Through the green-baize door to his left, which led to the servants' quarters, an occasional sharp giggle gave evidence of the presence of humanity, but apart from that he might have been alone in the world. Once again he fell into a dreamy meditation, and there is little reason to doubt that he would shortly have disgraced himself by falling asleep for the second time in a single afternoon, when he was restored to alertness by the sudden appearance of a foreign body in the open doorway. Against the background of golden light a black figure had abruptly manifested itself.

The sharp pang of apprehension which ran through Psmith's consciousness like an electric shock, causing him to stiffen like some wild creature surprised in the woods, was due to the momentary belief that the newcomer was the local vicar, of whose conversational powers he had had experience on the second day of his visit. Another glance showed him that he had been too pessimistic. This was not the vicar. It was someone whom he had never seen before – a slim and graceful young man with a dark, intelligent face, who stood blinking in the subdued light of the hall with eyes not yet accustomed to the absence of strong sunshine. Greatly relieved, Psmith rose and approached him.

'Hallo!' said the newcomer. 'I didn't see you. It's quite dark in here after outside.'

'The light is pleasantly dim,' agreed Psmith.

'Is Lord Emsworth anywhere about?'

'I fear not. He has legged it, accompanied by the entire household, to superintend the unveiling of a memorial at Bridgeford to – if my memory serves me rightly – the late Hartley Reddish, Esq, J. P., M. P. Is there anything I can do?'

'Well, I've come to stay, you know.'

'Indeed?'

'Lady Constance invited me to pay a visit as soon as I reached England.'

'Ah! Then you have come from foreign parts?'

'Canada.'

Psmith started slightly. This, he perceived, was going to complicate matters. The last thing he desired was the addition to the Blandings circle of one familiar with Canada. Nothing would militate against his peace of mind more than the society of a man who would want to exchange with him views on that growing country.

'Oh, Canada?' he said.

'I wired,' proceeded the other, 'but I suppose it came after everybody had left. Ah, that must be my telegram on that table over there. I walked up from the station.' He was rambling idly about the hall after the fashion of one breaking new ground. He paused at an occasional table, the one where, when taking after-dinner coffee, Miss Peavey was wont to sit. He picked up a book, and uttered a gratified laugh. 'One of my little things,' he said.

'One of what?' said Psmith.

'This book. *Songs of Squalor*. I wrote it.'

'You wrote it!'

'Yes. My name's McTodd. Ralston McTodd. I expect you have heard them speak of me?'

2

The mind of a man who has undertaken a mission as delicate as Psmith's at Blandings Castle is necessarily alert. Ever since he had stepped into the five o'clock train at Paddington, when his adventure might have been said formally to have started, Psmith had walked warily, like one in a jungle on whom sudden and unexpected things might pounce out at any moment. This calm announcement from the slim young man, therefore, though it undoubtedly startled him, did not deprive him

of his faculties. On the contrary, it quickened them. His
first action was to step nimbly to the table on which the
telegram lay awaiting the return of Lord Emsworth, his
second was to slip the envelope into his pocket. It was
imperative that telegrams signed McTodd should not lie
about loose while he was enjoying the hospitality of the
castle.

This done, he confronted the young man.

'Come, come!' he said with quiet severity.

He was extremely grateful to a kindly Providence
which had arranged that this interview should take place
at a time when nobody but himself was in the house.

'You say that you are Ralston McTodd, the author of
these poems?'

'Yes, I do.'

'Then what,' said Psmith incisively, 'is a "pale
parabola of Joy"?'

'Er – what?' said the newcomer in an enfeebled voice.
There was manifest in his demeanour now a marked
nervousness.

'And here is another,' said Psmith. ' "The – " Wait a
minute, I'll get it soon. Yes. "The sibilant, scented
silence that shimmered where we sat." Could you oblige
me with a diagram of that one?'

'I – I – What are you talking about?'

Psmith stretched out a long arm and patted him almost
affectionately on the shoulder.

'It's lucky you met me before you had to face the
others,' he said. 'I fear that you undertook this little
venture without thoroughly equipping yourself. They
would have detected your imposture in the first minute.'

'What do you mean – imposture? I don't know what
you're talking about.'

Psmith waggled his forefinger at him reproachfully.

'My dear Comrade, I may as well tell you at once that
the genuine McTodd is an old and dear friend of mine. I
had a long and entertaining conversation with him only

a few days ago. So that, I think we may confidently assert, is that. Or am I wrong?'

'Oh, hell!' said the young man. And, flopping bonelessly into a chair, he mopped his forehead in undisguised and abject collapse.

Silence reigned for a while.

'What,' inquired the visitor, raising a damp face that shone pallidly in the dim light, 'are you going to do about it?'

'Nothing, Comrade – by the way, what is your name?'

'Cootes.'

'Nothing, Comrade Cootes. Nothing whatever. You are free to leg it hence whenever you feel disposed. In fact the sooner you do so, the better I shall be pleased.'

'Say! That's darned good of you.'

'Not at all, not at all.'

'You're an ace – '

'Oh, hush!' interrupted Psmith modestly. 'But before you go tell me one or two things. I take it that your object in coming here was to have a pop at Lady Constance's necklace?'

'Yes.'

'I thought as much. And what made you suppose that the real McTodd would not be here when you arrived?'

'Oh, that was all right. I travelled over with that guy McTodd on the boat, and saw a good deal of him when we got to London. He was full of how he'd been invited here, and I got it out of him that no one here knew him by sight. And then one afternoon I met him in the Strand, all worked up. Madder than a hornet. Said he'd been insulted and wouldn't come down to this place if they came and begged him on their bended knees. I couldn't make out what it was all about, but apparently he had met Lord Emsworth and hadn't been treated right. He told me he was going straight off to Paris.'

'And did he?'

'Sure. I saw him off myself at Charing Cross. That's

why it seemed such a cinch coming here instead of him. It's just my darned luck that the first man I run into is a friend of his. How was I to know that he had any friends this side? He told me he'd never been in England before.'

'In this life, Comrade Cootes,' said Psmith, 'we must always distinguish between the Unlikely and the Impossible. It was unlikely, as you say, that you would meet any friend of McTodd's in this out-of-the-way spot; and you rashly ordered your movements on the assumption that it was impossible. With what result? The cry goes round the Underworld, "Poor old Cootes has made a bloomer!" '

'You needn't rub it in.'

'I am doing so for your good. It is my earnest hope that you will lay this lesson to heart and profit by it. Who knows that it may not be the turning-point in your career? Years hence, when you are a white-haired and opulent man of leisure, having retired from the crook business with a comfortable fortune, you may look back on your experience of today and realize that it was the means of starting you on the road to Success. You will lay stress on it when you are interviewed for the *Weekly Burglar* on "How I Began" . . . But, talking of starting on roads, I think that perhaps it would be as well if you now had a dash at the one leading to the railway station. The household may be returning at any moment now.'

'That's right,' agreed the visitor.

'I think so,' said Psmith. 'I think so. You will be happier when you are away from here. Once outside the castle precincts, a great weight will roll off your mind. A little fresh air will put the roses in your cheeks. You know your way out?'

He shepherded the young man to the door and with a cordial push started him on his way. Then with long strides he ran upstairs to the library to find Eve.

About the same moment, on the platform of Market

552

Blandings station, Miss Aileen Peavey was alighting
from the train which had left Bridgeford some half an
hour earlier. A headache, the fruit of standing about in the
hot sun, had caused her to forego the pleasure of hearing
Lord Emsworth deliver his speech: and she had slipped
back on a convenient train with the intention of lying
down and resting. Finding, on reaching Market
Blandings, that her head was much better, and the heat
of the afternoon being now over, she started to walk to
the castle, greatly refreshed by a cool breeze which had
sprung up from the west. She left the town at almost the
exact time when the disconsolate Mr Cootes was passing
out of the big gates at the end of the castle drive.

3

The grey melancholy which accompanied Mr Cootes like
a diligent spectre as he began his walk back to the town
of Market Blandings, and which not even the delightful
evening could dispel, was due primarily, of course, to
that sickening sense of defeat which afflicts a man whose
high hopes have been wrecked at the very instant when
success has seemed in sight. Once or twice in the life of
every man there falls to his lot something which can
only be described as a soft snap, and it had seemed to Mr
Cootes that this venture of his to Blandings Castle came
into that category. He had, like most members of his
profession, had his ups and downs in the past, but at
last, he told himself, the goddess Fortune had handed him
something on a plate with watercress round it. Once
established in the castle, there would have been a hundred
opportunities of achieving the capture of Lady
Constance's necklace; and it had looked as though all he
had to do was to walk in, announce himself, and be
treated as the honoured guest. As he slouched moodily
between the dusty hedges that fringed the road to Market
Blandings, Edward Cootes tasted the bitterness that only

those know whose plans have been upset by the
hundredth chance.

But this was not all. In addition to the sadness of
frustrated hope, he was also experiencing the anguish
of troubled memories. Not only was the Present torturing
him, but the Past had come to life and jumped out and
bitten him. A sorrow's crown of sorrow is remembering
happier things, and this was what Edward Cootes was
doing now. It is at moments like this that a man needs a
woman's tender care, and Mr Cootes had lost the only
woman in whom he could have confided his grief, the
only woman who would have understood and
sympathized.

We have been introduced to Mr Cootes at a point in
his career when he was practising upon dry land; but
that was not his chosen environment. Until a few months
back his business had lain upon deep waters. The salt
scent of the sea was in his blood. To put it more exactly,
he had been by profession a card-sharper on the Atlantic
liners; and it was during this period that he had loved and
lost. For three years and more he had worked in perfect
harmony with the lady who, though she adopted a variety
of names for purposes of travel, was known to her
immediate circle as Smooth Lizzie. He had been the
practitioner, she the decoy, and theirs had been one of
those ideal business partnerships which one so seldom
meets with in a world of cynicism and mistrust.
Comradeship had ripened into something deeper and
more sacred, and it was all settled between them that
when they next touched New York, Mr Cootes, if still at
liberty, should proceed to the City Hall for a marriage-
licence; when they had quarrelled – quarrelled
irrevocably over one of those trifling points over which
lovers do quarrel. Some absurd dispute as to the proper
division of the quite meagre sum obtained from a cattle
millionaire on their last voyage had marred their golden
dreams. One word had led to another. The lady, after

woman's habit, had the last of the series, and even Mr
Cootes was forced to admit that it was a pippin. She had
spoken it on the pier at New York, and then passed out
of his life. And with her had gone all his luck. It was as
if her going had brought a curse upon him. On the very
next trip he had had an unfortunate misunderstanding
with an irritable gentleman from the Middle West, who,
piqued at what he considered – not unreasonably – the
undue proportion of kings and aces in the hands which
Mr Cootes had been dealing himself, expressed his
displeasure by biting off the first joint of the other's right
index finger – thus putting an abrupt end to a brilliant
career. For it was on this finger that Mr Cootes principally
relied for the almost magical effects which he was wont
to produce with a pack of cards after a little quiet shuffling.

With an aching sense of what might have been he
thought now of his lost Lizzie. Regretfully he admitted
to himself that she had always been the brains of the firm.
A certain manual dexterity he had no doubt possessed, but
it was ever Lizzie who had been responsible for the finer
work. If they had still been partners, he really believed that
she could have discovered some way of getting round the
obstacles which had reared themselves now between
himself and the necklace of Lady Constance Keeble. It
was in a humble and contrite spirit that Edward Cootes
proceeded on his way to Market Blandings.

Miss Peavey, meanwhile, who, it will be remembered,
was moving slowly along the road from the Market
Blandings end, was finding her walk both restful and
enjoyable. There were moments, it has to be recorded,
when the society of her hostess and her hostess's relations
was something of a strain to Miss Peavey; and she was glad
to be alone. Her headache had disappeared, and she
revelled in the quiet evening hush. About now, if she had
not had the sense to detach herself from the castle platoon,
she would, she reflected, be listening to Lord Emsworth's

speech on the subject of the late Hartley Reddish, J.P., M.P.: a topic which even the noblest of orators might have failed to render really gripping. And what she knew of her host gave her little confidence in his powers of oratory.

Yes, she was well out of it. The gentle breeze played soothingly upon her face. Her delicately modelled nostrils drank in gratefully the scent from the hedgerows. Somewhere out of sight a thrush was singing. And so moved was Miss Peavy by the peace and sweetness of it all that she, too, began to sing.

Had those who enjoyed the privilege of her acquaintance at Blandings Castle been informed that Miss Peavey was about to sing, they would doubtless have considered themselves on firm ground if called upon to make a conjecture as to the type of song which she would select. Something quaint, dreamy, a little wistful . . . that would have been the universal guess . . . some old-world ballad, possibly . . .

What Miss Peavey actually sang – in a soft, meditative voice like that of a linnet waking to greet a new dawn – was that curious composition known as 'The Beale Street Blues'.

As she reached the last line, she broke off abruptly. She was, she perceived, no longer alone. Down the road towards her, walking pensively like one with a secret sorrow, a man was approaching; and for an instant, as she turned the corner, something in his appearance seemed to catch her by the throat and her breath came sharply.

'Gee!' said Miss Peavey.

She was herself again the next moment. A chance resemblance had misled her. She could not see the man's face, for his head was bent, but how was it possible . . .

And then, when he was quite close, he raised his head, and the county of Shropshire, as far as it was visible to her amazed eyes, executed a sudden and eccentric dance.

Trees bobbed up and down, hedgerows shimmied like a Broadway chorus; and from out of the midst of the whirling country-side a voice spoke.

'Liz!'

'Eddie!' ejaculated Miss Peavey faintly, and sat down in a heap on a grassy bank.

4

'Well, for goodness' sake!' said Miss Peavey.

Shropshire had become static once more. She stared at him, wide-eyed.

'Can you tie it!' said Miss Peavey.

She ran her gaze over him once again from head to foot.

'Well, if this ain't the cat's whiskers!' said Miss Peavey. And with this final pronouncement she rose from her bank, somewhat restored, and addressed herself to the task of picking up old threads.

'Wherever,' she inquired, 'did you spring from, Ed?'

There was nothing but affection in her voice. Her gaze was that of a mother contemplating her long-lost child. The past was past and a new era had begun. In the past she had been compelled to describe this man as a hunk of cheese and to express the opinion that his crookedness was such as to enable him to hide at will behind a spiral staircase; but now, in the joy of this unexpected reunion, all these harsh views were forgotten. This was Eddie Cootes, her old side-kick, come back to her after many days, and only now was it borne in upon her what a gap in her life his going had made. She flung herself into his arms with a glad cry.

Mr Cootes, who had not been expecting this demonstration of esteem, staggered a trifle at the impact, but recovered himself sufficiently to return the embrace with something of his ancient warmth. He was delighted at this cordiality, but also surprised. The memory of the lady's parting words on the occasion of their last meeting was still green, and he had not realized how quickly women forget and forgive, and how a sensitive girl, stirred by some fancied injury, may address a man as a pie-faced plugugly and yet retain in her inmost heart all the old love and affection. He kissed Miss Peavey fondly.

'Liz,' he said with fervour, 'you're prettier than ever.'

'Now you behave,' responded Miss Peavey coyly.

The arrival of a baaing flock of sheep, escorted by a priggish dog and followed by a couple of the local peasantry, caused an intermission in these tender exchanges; and by the time the procession had moved off down the road they were in a more suitable frame of mind to converse quietly and in a practical spirit, to compare notes, and to fill up the blanks.

'Wherever,' inquired Miss Peavey again, 'did you spring from, Ed? You could of knocked me down with a feather when I saw you coming along the road. I couldn't have believed it was you, this far from the ocean. What are you doing inland like this? Taking a vacation, or aren't you working the boats any more?'

'No, Liz,' said Mr Cootes sadly. 'I've had to give that up.'

And he exhibited the hiatus where an important section of his finger had been and told his painful tale. His companion's sympathy was balm to his wounded soul.

'The risks of the profession, of course,' said Mr Cootes moodily, removing the exhibit in order to place his arm about her slender waist. 'Still, it's done me in. I tried once or twice, but I couldn't seem to make the cards behave no more, so I quit. Ah, Liz,' said Mr Cootes with feeling, 'you can take it from me that I've had no luck since you left me. Regular hoodoo there's been on me. If I'd walked under a ladder on a Friday to smash a mirror over the dome of a black cat I couldn't have had it tougher.'

'You poor boy!'

Mr Cootes nodded sombrely.

'Tough,' he agreed, 'but there it is. Only this afternoon my jinx gummed the game for me and threw a spanner into the prettiest little scenario you ever thought of . . . But let's not talk about my troubles. What are you doing now, Liz?'

'Me? Oh, I'm living near here.'

Mr Cootes started.

'Not married?' he exclaimed in alarm.

'No!' cried Miss Peavey with vehemence, and shot a tender glance up at his face. 'And I guess you know why, Ed.'

'You don't mean . . . you hadn't forgotten me?'

'As if I could ever forget you, Eddie! There's only one tin-type on *my* mantelpiece.'

'But it struck me . . . it sort of occurred to me as a passing thought that, when we saw each other last, you were a mite peeved with your Eddie . . .'

It was the first allusion either of them had made to the past unpleasantness, and it caused a faint blush to dye Miss Peavey's soft cheek.

'Oh, shucks!' she said. 'I'd forgotten all about that next day. I was good and mad at the time, I'll allow, but if only you'd called me up next morning, Ed . . .'

There was a silence, as they mused on what might have been.

'What are you doing, living here?' asked Mr Cootes after a pregnant pause. 'Have you retired?'

'No, *Sir*. I'm sitting in at a game with real worthwhile stakes. But, darn it,' said Miss Peavey, regretfully, 'I'm wondering if it isn't too big for me to put through alone. Oh, Eddie, if only there was some way you and me could work it together like in the old days.'

'What is it?'

'Diamonds, Eddie. A necklace. I've only had one look at it so far, but that was enough. Some of the best ice I've saw in years, Ed. Worth every cent of a hundred thousand berries.'

The coincidence drew from Mr Cootes a sharp exclamation.

'A necklace!'

'Listen, Ed, while I slip you the low-down. And, say, if you knew the relief it was to me talking good United States again! Like taking off a pair of tight shoes. I'm doing the high-toned stuff for the moment. Soulful. *You* remember, like I used to pull once or twice in the old days. Just after you and me had that little spat of ours I thought I'd take another trip in the old *Atlantic* – force of habit or something, I guess. Anyway, I sailed, and we weren't two days out from New York when I made the biggest kind of a hit with the dame this necklace belongs to. Seemed to take a shine to me right away . . .'

'I don't blame her!' murmured Mr Cootes devotedly.

'Now don't you interrupt,' said Miss Peavey, administering a gratified slap. 'Where was I? Oh yes. This here now Lady Constance Keeble I'm telling you about . . .'

'What!'

'What's the matter now?'

'Lady Constance Keeble?'

'That's the name. She's Lord Emsworth's sister, who lives at a big place up the road. Blandings Castle it's called. She didn't seem like she was able to let me out of her sight, and I've been with her off and on ever since we landed. I'm visiting at the castle now.'

A deep sigh, like the groan of some great spirit in travail forced itself from between Mr Cootes's lips.

'Well, wouldn't that jar you!' he demanded of circumambient space. 'Of all the lucky ones! getting into the place like that, with the band playing and a red carpet laid down for you to walk on! Gee, if you fell down a well, Liz, you'd come up with the bucket. You're a human horseshoe, that's what you are. Say, listen. Lemme-tell-ya-sumf'n. Do you know what *I've* been doing this afternoon? Only trying to edge into the dam' place myself and getting the air two minutes after I was past the front door.'

'What! *You*, Ed?'

'Sure. You're not the only one that's heard of that collection of ice.'

'Oh, Ed!' Bitter disappointment rang in Miss Peavey's voice. 'If only you could have worked it! Me and you partners again! It hurts to think of it. What was the stuff you pulled to get you in?'

Mr Cootes so far forgot himself in his agony of spirit as to expectorate disgustedly at a passing frog. And even in this trivial enterprise failure dogged him. He missed the frog, which withdrew into the grass with a cold look of disapproval.

'Me?' said Mr Cootes. 'I thought I'd got it smooth. I'd chummed up with a fellow who had been invited down to the place and had thought it over and decided not to go, so I said to myself what's the matter with going there instead of him. A gink called McTodd this was, a poet, and none of the folks had ever set eyes on him, except the old man, who's too short-sighted to see anyone, so . . .'

Miss Peavey interrupted.

'You don't mean to tell me, Ed Cootes, that you thought you could get into the castle by pretending to be Ralston McTodd?'

'Sure I did. Why not? It didn't seem like there was anything to it. A cinch, that's what it looked like. And the first guy I meet in the joint is a mutt who knows this McTodd well. We had a couple of words, and I beat it. I know when I'm not wanted.'

'But, Ed! Ed! What do you mean? Ralston McTodd is at the castle now, this very moment.'

'How's that?'

'Sure. Been there coupla days and more. Long, thin bird with an eyeglass.'

Mr Cootes's mind was in a whirl. He could make nothing of this matter.

'Nothing like it! McTodd's not so darned tall or so thin, if it comes to that. And he didn't wear no eyeglass all the time I was with him. This . . .' He broke off sharply. 'My gosh! I wonder!' he cried. 'Liz! How many men are there in the joint right now?'

'Only four besides Lord Emsworth. There's a big party coming down for the County Ball, but that's all there is at present. There's Lord Emsworth's son, Freddie . . .'

'What does he look like?'

'Sort of a dude with blond hair slicked back. Then there's Mr Keeble. He's short with a red face.'

'And?'

'And Baxter. He's Lord Emsworth's secretary. Wears spectacles.'

'And that's the lot?'

'That's all there is, not counting this here McTodd and the help.'

Mr Cootes brought his hand down with a resounding report on his leg. The mildly pleasant look which had been a feature of his appearance during his interview with Psmith had vanished now, its place taken by one of an extremely sinister malevolence.

'And I let him shoo me out as if I was a stray pup!' he muttered through clenched teeth. 'Of all the bunk games!'

'What are you talking about, Ed?'

'And I thanked him! *Thanked* him!' moaned Edward Cootes, writhing at the memory. 'I thanked him for letting me go!'

'Eddie Cootes, whatever are you . . .?'

'Listen, Liz.' Mr Cootes mastered his emotion with a strong effort. 'I blew into that joint and met this fellow with the eyeglass, and he told me he knew McTodd well and that I wasn't him. And, from what you tell me, this must be the very guy that's passing himself off as McTodd! Don't you see? This baby must have started working on the same lines I did. Got to know McTodd, found he

wasn't coming to the castle, and came down instead of
him, same as me. Only he got there first, damn him!
Wouldn't that give you a pain in the neck!'

Amazement held Miss Peavey dumb for an instant.
Then she spoke.

'The big stiff!' said Miss Peavey.

Mr Cootes, regardless of a lady's presence, went even
further in his censure.

'I had a feeling from the first that there was something
not on the level about that guy!' said Miss Peavey. 'Gee!
He must be after that necklace too.'

'Sure he's after the necklace,' said Mr Cootes
impatiently. 'What did you think he'd come down for?
A change of air?'

'But, Ed! Say! Are you going to let him get away with
it?'

'Am *I* going to let him get away with it!' said Mr
Cootes, annoyed by the foolish question. 'Wake me up in
the night and ask me!'

'But what are you going to do?'

'Do!' said Mr Cootes. 'Do! I'll tell you what I'm going
to . . .' He paused, and the stern resolve that shone in his
face seemed to flicker. 'Say, what the hell *am* I going to
do?' he went on somewhat weakly.

'You won't get anything by putting the folks wise that
he's a fake. That would be the finish of him, but it
wouldn't get *you* anywhere.'

'No,' said Mr Cootes.

'Wait a minute while I think,' said Miss Peavey.

There was a pause. Miss Peavey sat with knit brows.

'How could it be . . .?' ventured Mr Cootes.

'Cheese it!' said Miss Peavey.

Mr Cootes cheesed it. The minutes ticked on.

'I've got it,' said Miss Peavey. 'This guy's ace-high with
Lady Constance. You've got to get him alone right away
and tell him he's got to get you invited to the place as a
friend of his.'

'I knew you'd think of something, Liz,' said Mr Cootes, almost humbly. 'You always were a wonder like that. How am I to get him alone?'

'I can fix that. I'll ask him to come for a stroll with me. He's not what you'd call crazy about me, but he can't very well duck if I keep after him. We'll go down the drive. You'll be in the bushes – I'll show you the place. Then I'll send him to fetch me a wrap or something, and while I walk on he'll come back past where you're hiding, and you jump out at him.'

'Liz,' said Mr Cootes, lost in admiration, 'when it comes to doping out a scheme, you're the snake's eyebrows!'

'But what are you going to do if he just turns you down?'

Mr Cootes uttered a bleak laugh, and from the recesses of his costume produced a neat little revolver.

'*He* won't turn me down!' he said.

5

'Fancy!' said Miss Peavey. 'If I had not had a headache and come back early, we should never have had this little chat!'

She gazed up at Psmith in her gentle, wistful way as they started together down the broad gravel drive. A timid, soulful little thing she looked.

'No,' said Psmith.

It was not a gushing reply, but he was not feeling at his sunniest. The idea that Miss Peavey might return from Bridgeford in advance of the main body had not occurred to him. As he would have said himself, he had confused the Unlikely with the Impossible. And the result had been that she had caught him beyond hope of retreat as he sat in his garden-chair and thought of Eve Halliday, who on their return from the lake had been seized with a fresh spasm of conscience and had gone back to the library to put in another hour's work before dinner. To decline Miss Peavey's invitation to accompany her down the drive in order to see if there were any signs of those who had been doing honour to the late Hartley Reddish, M. P., had been out of the question. But Psmith, though he went, went without pleasure. Every moment he spent in her society tended to confirm him more and more in the opinion that Miss Peavey was the curse of the species.

'And I have been so longing,' continued his companion, 'to have a nice, long talk. All these days I have felt that I haven't been able to get as *near* you as I should wish.'

'Well, of course, with the others always about . . .'

'I meant in a spiritual sense, of course.'

'I see.'

'I wanted so much to discuss your wonderful poetry with you. You haven't so much as *mentioned* your work since you came here. *Have* you?'

'Ah, but, you see, I am trying to keep my mind off it.'

'Really? Why?'

'My medical adviser warned me that I had been concentrating a trifle too much. He offered me the choice, in fact, between a complete rest and the loony-bin.'

'The *what*, Mr McTodd?'

'The lunatic asylum, he meant. These medical men express themselves oddly.'

'But surely, then, you ought not to *dream* of trying to compose if it is as bad as that? And you told Lord Emsworth that you wished to stay at home this afternoon to write a poem.'

Her glance showed nothing but tender solicitude, but inwardly Miss Peavey was telling herself that *that* would hold him for a while.

'True,' said Psmith, 'true. But you know what Art is. An inexorable mistress. The inspiration came, and I felt that I must take the risk. But it has left me weak, weak.'

'You BIG STUFF!' said Miss Peavey. But not aloud.

They walked on a few steps.

'In fact,' said Psmith, with another inspiration, 'I'm not sure I ought not to be going back and resting now.'

Miss Peavey eyed a clump of bushes some dozen yards farther down the drive. They were quivering slightly, as though they sheltered some alien body; and Miss Peavey, whose temper was apt to be impatient, registered a resolve to tell Edward Cootes that, if he couldn't hide behind a bush without dancing about like a cat on hot bricks, he had better give up his profession and take to selling jellied eels. In which, it may be mentioned, she wronged her old friend. He had been as still as a statue until a moment before, when a large and excitable beetle had fallen down the space between his collar and his neck, an experience which might well have tried the subtlest woodsman.

'Oh, please don't go in yet,' said Miss Peavey. 'It is such a lovely evening. Hark to the music of the breeze in the tree-tops. So soothing. Like a far-away harp. I wonder if it is whispering secrets to the birds.'

Psmith forbore to follow her into this region of speculation, and they walked past the bushes in silence.

Some little distance farther on, however, Miss Peavey seemed to relent.

'You *are* looking tired, Mr McTodd,' she said anxiously. 'I am afraid you really have been overtaxing your strength. Perhaps after all you had better go back and lie down.'

'You think so?'

'I am sure of it. I will just stroll on to the gates and see if the car is in sight.'

'I feel that I am deserting you.'

'Oh, please!' said Miss Peavey deprecatingly.

With something of the feelings of a long-sentence convict unexpectedly released immediately on his arrival in jail, Psmith retraced his steps. Glancing over his shoulder, he saw that Miss Peavey had disappeared round a bend in the drive; and he paused to light a cigarette. He had just thrown away the match and was walking on, well content with life, when a voice behind him said 'Hey!' and the well-remembered form of Mr Edward Cootes stepped out of the bushes.

'See this?' said Mr Cootes, exhibiting his revolver.

'I do indeed, Comrade Cootes,' replied Psmith. 'And, if it is not an untimely question, what is the idea?'

'That,' said Mr Cootes, 'is just in case you try any funny business.' And, replacing the weapon in a handy pocket, he proceeded to slap vigorously at the region between his shoulder blades. He also wriggled with not a little animation.

Psmith watched these manoeuvres gravely.

'You did not stop me at the pistol's point merely to watch you go through your Swedish exercises?' he said.

Mr Cootes paused for an instant.

'Got a beetle or something down my back,' he explained curtly.

'Ah? Then, as you will naturally wish to be alone in such a sad moment, I will be bidding you a cordial good evening and strolling on.'

'No, you don't!'

'Don't I?' said Psmith resignedly. 'Perhaps you are right, perhaps you are right.' Mr Cootes replaced the revolver once more. 'I take it, then, Comrade Cootes, that you would have speech with me. Carry on, old friend, and get it off your diaphragm. What seems to be on your mind?'

A lucky blow appeared to have stunned Mr Cootes's beetle and he was able to give his full attention to the matter in hand. He stared at Psmith with considerable distaste.

'I'm on to you, Bill!' he said.

'My name is not Bill,' said Psmith.

'No,' snapped Mr Cootes, his annoyance by this time very manifest. 'And it's not McTodd.'

567

Psmith looked at his companion thoughtfully. This was an unforeseen complication, and for the moment he would readily have admitted that he saw no way of overcoming it. That the other was in no genial frame of mind towards him the expression on his face would have showed, even if his actions had not been sufficient indication of the fact. Mr Cootes, having disposed of his beetle and being now at leisure to concentrate his whole attention on Psmith, was eyeing that immaculate a young man with a dislike which he did not attempt to conceal.

'Shall we be strolling on?' suggested Psmith. 'Walking may assist thought. At the moment I am free to confess that you have opened up a subject which causes me some perplexity. I think, Comrade Cootes, having given the position of affairs a careful examination, that we may say that the next move is with you. What do you propose to do about it?'

'I'd like,' said Mr Cootes with asperity, 'to beat your block off.'

'No doubt. But . . .'

'I'd like to knock you for a goal!'

Psmith discouraged these Utopian dreams with a deprecating wave of the hand.

'I can readily understand it,' he said courteously. 'But, to keep within the sphere of practical politics, what is the actual move which you contemplate? You could expose me, no doubt, to my host, but I cannot see how that would profit you.'

'I know that. But you can remember I've got that up my sleeve in case you try any funny business.'

'You persist in harping on that possibility, Comrade Cootes. The idea seems to be an obsession with you. I can assure you that I contemplate no such thing. What, to return to the point, do you intend to do?'

They had reached the broad expanse opposite the front door, where the drive, from being a river, spread out into a lake of gravel. Psmith stopped.

'You've got to get me into this joint,' said Mr Cootes.

'I feared that that was what you were about to suggest.
In my peculiar position I have naturally no choice but
to endeavour to carry out your wishes. Any attempt not
to do so would, I imagine, infallibly strike so keen a
critic as yourself as "funny business". But how can I get
you into what you breezily describe as "this joint"?'

'You can say I'm a friend of yours and ask them to
invite me.'

Psmith shook his head gently.

'Not one of your brightest suggestions, Comrade
Cootes. Tactfully refraining from stressing the point that
an instant lowering of my prestige would inevitably ensue
should it be supposed that you were a friend of mine, I
will merely mention that, being myself merely a guest in
this stately home of England, I can hardly go about
inviting my chums here for indefinite visits. No, we must
find another way . . . You're sure you want to stay? Quite
so, quite so, I merely asked . . . Now, let us think.'

Through the belt of rhododendrons which jutted out
from one side of the castle a portly form at this point
made itself visible, moving high and disposedly in the
direction of the back premises. It was Beach, the butler,
returning from the pleasant ramble in which he had
indulged himself on the departure of his employer and
the rest of the party. Revived by some gracious hours in
the open air, Beach was returning to duty. And with the
sight of him there came to Psmith a neat solution of
the problem confronting him.

'Oh, Beach,' he called.

'Sir?' responded a fruity voice. There was a brief pause
while the butler navigated into the open. He removed
the straw hat which he had donned for his excursion, and
enfolded Psmith in a pop-eyed but not unkindly gaze. A
thoughtful critic of country-house humanity, he had long
since decided that he approved of Psmith. Since Lady
Constance had first begun to offer the hospitality of the

castle to the literary and artistic world, he had been
profoundly shocked by some of the rare and curious
specimens who had nodded their disordered locks and
flaunted their ill-cut evening clothes at the dinner-table
over which he presided; and Psmith had come as a
pleasant surprise.

'Sorry to trouble you, Beach.'

'Not at all, sir.'

'This,' said Psmith, indicating Mr Cootes, who was
viewing the scene with a wary and suspicious eye, an
eye obviously alert for any signs of funny business, 'is my
man. My valet, you know. He has just arrived from town.
I had to leave him behind to attend the bedside of a sick
aunt. Your aunt was better when you came away,
Cootes?' he inquired graciously.

Mr Cootes correctly interpreted this question as a
feeler with regard to his views on this new development,
and decided to accept the situation. True, he had hoped
to enter the castle in a slightly higher capacity than that
of a gentleman's personal gentleman, but he was an old
campaigner. Once in, as he put it to himself with
admirable common sense, he would be in.

'Yes, sir,' he replied.

'Capital,' said Psmith. 'Capital. Then will you look
after Cootes, Beach.'

'Very good, sir,' said the butler in a voice of cordial
approval. The only point he had found to cavil at in
Psmith had been removed; for it had hitherto pained him
a little that a gentleman with so nice a taste in clothes
as that dignified guest should have embarked on a visit
to such a place as Blandings Castle without a personal
attendant. Now all was explained and, as far as Beach was
concerned, forgiven. He proceeded to escort Mr Cootes
to the rear. They disappeared behind the rhododendrons.

They had hardly gone when a sudden thought came to
Psmith as he sat once more in the coolness of the hall. He
pressed the bell. Strange, he reflected, how one overlooked

these obvious things. That was how generals lost battles.

'Sir?' said Beach, appearing through the green baize
door.

'Sorry to trouble you again, Beach.'

'Not at all, sir.'

'I hope you will make Cootes comfortable. I think you
will like him. His, when you get to know him, is a very
winning personality.'

'He seems a nice young fellow, sir.'

'Oh, by the way, Beach. You might ask him if he
brought my revolver from town with him.'

'Yes, sir,' said Beach, who would have scorned to betray
emotion if it had been a Lewis gun.

'I think I saw it sticking out of his pocket. You might
bring it to me, will you?'

'Very good, sir.'

Beach retired, to return a moment later. On the silver
salver which he carried the lethal weapon was duly
reposing.

'Your revolver, sir,' said Beach.

'Thank you,' said Psmith.

6

For some moments after the butler had withdrawn in his
stately pigeon-toed way through the green baize door,
Psmith lay back in his chair with the feeling that
something attempted, something done, had earned a
night's repose. He was not so sanguine as to suppose that
he had actually checkmated an adversary of Mr Cootes's
strenuousness by the simple act of removing a revolver
from his possession; but there was no denying the fact
that the feel of the thing in his pocket engendered a
certain cosy satisfaction. The little he had seen of Mr
Cootes had been enough to convince him that the other
was a man who was far better off without an automatic
pistol. There was an impulsiveness about his character

which did not go well with the possession of fire-arms.

Psmith's meditations had taken him thus far when they were interrupted by an imperative voice.

'Hey!'

Only one person of Psmith's acquaintance was in the habit of opening his remarks in this manner. It was consequently no surprise to him to find Mr Edward Cootes standing at his elbow.

'Hey!'

'All right, Comrade Cootes,' said Psmith, with a touch of austerity, 'I heard you the first time. And may I remind you that this habit of yours of popping out from unexpected places and saying "Hey!" is one which should be overcome. Valets are supposed to wait till rung for. At least, I think so. I must confess that until this moment I have never had a valet.'

'And you wouldn't have one now if I could help it,' responded Mr Cootes.

Psmith raised his eyebrows.

'Why,' he inquired, surprised, 'this peevishness? Don't you like being a valet?'

'No, I don't.'

'You astonish me. I should have thought you would have gone singing about the house. Have you considered that the tenancy of such a position throws you into the constant society of Comrade Beach, than whom it would be difficult to imagine a more delightful companion?'

'Old stiff!' said Mr Cootes sourly. 'If there's one thing that makes me tired, it's a guy that talks about his darned stomach all the time.'

'I beg your pardon?'

'The Beach gook,' explained Mr Cootes, 'has got something wrong with the lining of his stomach, and if I hadn't made my getaway he'd be talking about it yet.'

'If you fail to find entertainment and uplift in first-hand information about Comrade Beach's stomach, you must indeed be hard to please. I am to take it, then, that you came snorting out here, interrupting my day-dreams, merely in order to seek my sympathy?'

Mr Cootes gazed upon him with a smouldering eye.

'I came to tell you I suppose you think you're darned smart.'

'And very nice of you, too,' said Psmith, touched. 'A pretty compliment, for which I am not ungrateful.'

'You got that gun away from me mighty smoothly, didn't you?'

'Since you mention it, yes.'

'And now I suppose you think you're going to slip in ahead of me and get away with that necklace? Well, say, listen, lemme tell you it'll take someone better than a half-baked string-bean like you to put one over on me.'

'I seem,' said Psmith, pained, 'to detect a certain animus creeping into your tone. Surely we can be trade rivals without this spirit of hostility. My attitude towards you is one of kindly tolerance.'

'Even if you get it, where do you think you're going to hide it? And, believe me, it'll take some hiding. Say, lemme tell you something. I'm your valet, ain't I? Well, then, I can come into your room and be tidying up whenever I darn please, can't I? Sure I can. I'll tell the world I can do just that little thing. And you take it from me, Bill . . .'

'You persist in the delusion that my name is William . . .'

'You take it from me, Bill, that if ever that necklace disappears and it isn't me that's done the disappearing, you'll find me tidying up in a way that'll make you dizzy. I'll go through that room of yours with a fine-tooth comb. So chew on that will you?'

And Edward Cootes, moving sombrely across the hall, made a sinister exit. The mood of cool reflection was still to come, when he would realize that, in his desire to administer what he would have described as a hot one, he had acted a little rashly in putting his enemy on his guard.

573

All he was thinking now was that his brief sketch of the position of affairs would have the effect of diminishing Psmith's complacency a trifle. He had, he flattered himself, slipped over something that could be classed as a jolt.

Nor was he unjustified in this view. The aspect of the matter on which he had touched was one that had not previously presented itself to Psmith: and, musing on it as he resettled himself in his chair, he could see that it afforded food for thought. As regarded the disposal of the necklace, should it ever come into his possession, he had formed no definite plan. He had assumed that he would conceal it somewhere until the first excitement of the chase slackened, and it was only now that he realized the difficulty of finding a suitable hiding-place outside his bedroom. Yes, it was certainly a matter on which, as Mr Cootes had suggested, he would do well to chew. For ten minutes, accordingly, he did so. And – it being practically impossible to keep a good man down – at the end of that period he was rewarded with an idea. He rose from his chair and pressed the bell.

'Ah, Beach,' he said affably, as the green baize door swung open, 'I must apologize once more for troubling you. I keep ringing, don't I?'

'No trouble at all, sir,' responded the butler paternally. 'But if you were ringing to summon your personal attendant, I fear he is not immediately available. He left me somewhat abruptly a few moments ago. I was not aware that you would be requiring his services until the dressing-gong sounded, or I would have detained him.'

'Never mind. It was you I wish to see. Beach,' said Psmith, 'I am concerned about you. I learn from my man that the lining of your stomach is not all it should be.'

'That is true, sir,' replied Beach, an excited gleam coming into his dull eyes. He shivered slightly, as might a war-horse at the sound of the bugle. 'I do have trouble with the lining of my stomach.'

574

'Every stomach has a silver lining.'

'Sir?'

'I said, tell me all about it.'

'Well, really, sir . . .' said Beach wistfully.

'To please me,' urged Psmith.

'Well, sir, it is extremely kind of you to take an interest. It generally starts with a dull shooting pain on the right side of the abdomen from twenty minutes to half an hour after the conclusion of a meal. The symptoms . . .'

There was nothing but courteous sympathy in Psmith's gaze as he listened to what sounded like an eye-witness's account of the San Francisco earthquake, but inwardly he was wishing that his companion could see his way to making it a bit briefer and snappier. However, all things come to an end. Even the weariest river winds somewhere safe to sea. With a moving period, the butler finally concluded his narrative.

'Parks' Pepsinine,' said Psmith promptly.

'Sir?'

'That's what you want. Parks' Pepsinine. It would set you right in no time.'

'I will make a note of the name, sir. The specific has not come to my notice until now. And, if I may say so,' added Beach, with a glassy but adoring look at his benefactor, 'I should like to express my gratitude for your kindness.'

'Not at all, Beach, not at all. Oh, Beach,' he said, as the other started to manoeuvre towards the door, 'I've just remembered. There was something else I wanted to talk to you about.'

'Yes, sir?'

'I thought it might be as well to speak to you about it before approaching Lady Constance. The fact is, Beach, I am feeling cramped.'

'Indeed, sir? I forgot to mention that one of the symptoms from which I suffer is a sharp cramp.'

'Too bad. But let us, if you do not mind, shelve for the

moment the subject of your interior organism and its
ailments. When I say I am feeling cramped, I mean
spiritually. Have you ever written poetry, Beach?'

'No, sir.'

'Ah! Then it may be a little difficult for you to
understand my feelings. My trouble is this. Out in
Canada, Beach, I grew accustomed to doing my work
in the most solitary surroundings. You remember that
passage in my *Songs of Squalor* which begins "Across the
pale parabola of Joy . . ."?'

'I fear, sir . . .'

'You missed it? Tough luck. Try to get hold of it some
time. It's a bird. Well, that passage was written in a
lonely hut on the banks of the Saskatchewan, miles away
from human habitation. I am like that, Beach. I need the
stimulus of the great open spaces. When I am surrounded
by my fellows, inspiration slackens and dies. You know
how it is when there are people about. Just as you are
starting in to write a nifty, someone comes and sits down
on the desk and begins talking about himself. Every time
you get going nicely, in barges some alien influence and
the Muse goes blooey. You see what I mean?'

'Yes, sir,' said Beach, gaping slightly.

'Well, that is why for a man like me existence in
Blandings Castle has its drawbacks. I have got to get a
place where I can be alone, Beach – alone with my dreams
and visions. Some little eyrie perched on the cliffs of
Time . . . In other words, do you know of an empty cottage
somewhere on the estate where I could betake myself
when in the mood and swing a nib without any possibility
of being interrupted?'

'A little cottage, sir?'

'A little cottage. With honeysuckle over the door, and
Old Mister Moon climbing up above the trees. A cottage,
Beach, where I can meditate, where I can turn the key in
the door and bid the world go by. Now that the castle is
going to be full of all these people who are coming for the

County Ball, it is imperative that I wangle such a haven.
Otherwise, a considerable slab of priceless poetry will be
lost to humanity for ever.'

'You desire,' said Beach, feeling his way cautiously, 'a
small cottage where you can write poetry, sir?'

'You follow me like a leopard. Do you know of such
a one?'

'There is an unoccupied gamekeeper's cottage in the
west wood, sir, but it is an extremely humble place.'

'Be it never so humble, it will do for me. Do you think
Lady Constance would be offended if I were to ask for
the loan of it for a few days?'

'I fancy that her ladyship would receive the request
with equanimity, sir. She is used to . . . She is not
unaccustomed . . . Well, I can only say, sir, that there was
a literary gentleman visiting the castle last summer who
expressed a desire to take sun-baths in the garden each
morning before breakfast. In the nood, sir. And, beyond
instructing me to warn the maids, her ladyship placed
no obstacle in the way of the fulfilment of his wishes.
So . . .'

'So a modest request like mine isn't likely to cause a
heart-attack? Admirable! You don't know what it means
to me to feel that I shall soon have a little refuge of my
own, to which I can retreat and be in solitude.'

'I can imagine that it must be extremely gratifying,
sir.'

'Then I will put the motion before the Board directly
Lady Constance returns.'

'Very good, sir.'

'I should like to splash it on the record once more,
Beach, that I am much obliged to you for your sympathy
and advice in this matter. I knew you would not fail me.'

'Not at all, sir. I am only too glad to have been able to
be of assistance.'

'Oh, and, Beach . . .'

'Sir?'

'Just one other thing. Will you be seeing Cootes, my valet, again shortly?'

'Quite shortly, sir, I should imagine.'

'Then would you mind just prodding him smartly in the lower ribs . . .'

'Sir!' cried Beach, startled out of his butlerian calm. He swallowed a little convulsively. For eighteen months and more, ever since Lady Constance Keeble had first begun to cast her fly and hook over the murky water of the artistic world and jerk its denizens on to the pile carpets of Blandings Castle, Beach had had his fill of eccentricity. But until this moment he had hoped that Psmith was going to prove an agreeable change from the stream of literary lunatics which had been coming and going all that weary time. And lo! Psmith's name led all the rest. Even the man who had come for a week in April and had wanted to eat jam with his fish paled in comparison.

'Prod him in the ribs, sir?' he quavered.

'Prod him in the ribs,' said Psmith firmly. 'And at the same time whisper in his ear the word "Aha!"'

Beach licked his dry lips.

'Aha, sir?'

'Aha! And say it came from me.'

'Very good, sir. The matter shall be attended to,' said Beach. And with a muffled sound that was half a sigh, half a death-rattle, he tottered through the green-baize door.

10 — Sensational Occurrence at a Poetry Reading

I

Breakfast was over, and the guests of Blandings had scattered to their morning occupations. Some were writing letters, some were in the billiard-room; some had gone to the stables, some to the links: Lady Constance was interviewing the housekeeper, Lord Emsworth harrying head-gardener McAllister among the flower-beds: and in the Yew Alley, the dappled sunlight falling upon her graceful head, Miss Peavey walked pensively up and down.

She was alone. It is a sad but indisputable fact that in this imperfect world Genius is too often condemned to walk alone – if the earthier members of the community see it coming and have time to duck. Not one of the horde of visitors who had arrived overnight for the County Ball had shown any disposition whatever to court Miss Peavey's society.

One regrets this. Except for that slight bias towards dishonesty which led her to steal everything she could lay her hands on that was not nailed down, Aileen Peavey's was an admirable character; and, oddly enough, it was the noble side of her nature to which these coarse-fibred critics objected. Of Miss Peavey, the purloiner of other people's goods, they knew nothing; the woman they were dodging was Miss Peavey, the poetess. And it may be mentioned that, however much she might unbend in the presence of a congenial friend like Mr Edward Cootes, she was a perfectly genuine poetess. Those six volumes under her name in the British Museum Catalogue were her own genuine and unaided work: and, though she had

been compelled to pay for the production of the first of
the series, the other five had been brought out at her
publisher's own risk, and had even made a little money.

Miss Peavey, however, was not sorry to be alone: for
she had that on her mind which called for solitary thinking.
The matter engaging her attention was the problem of
what on earth had happened to Mr Edward Cootes. Two
days had passed since he had left her to go and force
Psmith at the pistol's point to introduce him into the
castle: and since that moment he had vanished
completely. Miss Peavey could not understand it.

His non-appearance was all the more galling in that
her superb brain had just completed in every detail a
scheme for the seizure of Lady Constance Keeble's
diamond necklace; and to the success of this plot his aid
was an indispensable adjunct. She was in the position of
a general who comes from his tent with a plan of battle
all mapped out, and finds that his army has strolled off
somewhere and left him. Little wonder that, as she paced
the Yew Alley, there was a frown on Miss Peavey's fair
forehead.

The Yew Alley, as Lord Emsworth had indicated in his
extremely interesting lecture to Mr Ralston McTodd at
the Senior Conservative Club, contained among other
noteworthy features certain yews which rose in solid
blocks with rounded roof and stemless mushroom finials,
the majority possessing arched recesses, forming arbors.
As Miss Peavey was passing one of these, a voice suddenly
addressed her.

'Hey!'

Miss Peavey started violently.

'Anyone about?'

A damp face with twigs sticking to it was protruding
from a near-by yew. It rolled its eyes in an ineffectual
effort to see round the corner.

Miss Peavey drew nearer, breathing heavily. The
question as to the whereabouts of her wandering boy

was solved; but the abruptness of his return had caused
her to bite her tongue; and joy, as she confronted him,
was blended with other emotions.

'You dish-faced gazooni!' she exclaimed heatedly, her
voice trembling with a sense of ill-usage, 'where do you
get that stuff, hiding in trees, and barking a girl's head
off?'

'Sorry, Liz. I . . .'

'And where,' proceeded Miss Peavey, ventilating
another grievance, 'have you been all this darned time?
Gosh-dingit, you leave me a coupla days back saying
you're going to stick up this bozo that calls himself
McTodd with a gat and make him get you into the house,
and that's the last I see of you. What's the big idea?'

'It's all right, Liz. He did get me into the house. I'm
his valet. That's why I couldn't get at you before. The
way the help has to keep itself to itself in this joint, we
might as well have been in different countries. If I hadn't
happened to see you snooping off by yourself this
morning . . .'

Miss Peavey's keen mind grasped the position of
affairs.

'All right, all right,' she interrupted, ever impatient of
long speeches from others. 'I understand. Well, this is
good, Ed. It couldn't have worked out better. I've got a
scheme all doped out, and now you're here we can get
busy.'

'A scheme?'

'A pippin,' assented Miss Peavey.

'It'll need to be,' said Mr Cootes, on whom the events
of the last few days had caused pessimism to set its seal.
'I tell you that McTodd gook is smooth. He somehow,'
said Mr Cootes prudently, for he feared harsh criticisms
from his lady-love should he reveal the whole truth, 'he
somehow got wise to the notion that, as I was his valet,
I could go and snoop round in his room, where he'd be
wanting to hide the stuff if he ever got it, and now he's

gone and got them to let him have a kind of shack in the woods.'

'H'm!' said Miss Peavey. 'Well,' she resumed after a thoughtful pause, 'I'm not worrying about him. Let him go and roost in the woods all he wants to. I've got a scheme all ready, and it's gilt-edged. And, unless you ball up your end of it, Ed, it can't fail to drag home the gravy.'

'Am I in it?'

'You bet you're in it. I can't work it without you. That's what's been making me so darned mad when you didn't show up all this time.'

'Spill it, Liz,' said Mr Cootes humbly. As always in the presence of this dynamic woman, he was suffering from an inferiority complex. From the very start of their combined activities she had been the brains of the firm, he merely the instrument to carry into effect the plans she dictated.

Miss Peavey glanced swiftly up and down the Yew Alley. It was still the same peaceful, lonely spot. She turned to Mr Cootes again, and spoke with brisk decision.

'Now, listen, Ed, and get this straight, because maybe I shan't have another chance of talking to you.'

'I'm listening,' said Mr Cootes obsequiously.

'Well, to begin with, now that the house is full, Her Nibs is wearing that necklace every night. And you can take it from me, Ed, that you want to put on your smoked glasses before you look at it. It's a lalapaloosa.'

'As good as that?'

'Ask me! You don't know the half of it.'

'Where does she keep it, Liz? Have you found that out?' asked Mr Cootes, a gleam of optimism playing across his sad face for an instant.

'No, I haven't. And I don't want to. I've not got time to waste monkeying about with safes and maybe having the whole bunch pile on the back of my neck. I believe in getting things easy. Well, tonight this bimbo that calls himself McTodd is going to give a reading of his poems in the big drawing-room. You know where that is?'

'I can find out.'

'And you better had find out,' said Miss Peavey vehemently. 'And before tonight at that. Well, there you are. Do you begin to get wise?'

Mr Cootes, his head protruding unhappily from the yew tree, would have given much to have been able to make the demanded claim to wisdom, for he knew of old the store his alert partner set upon quickness of intellect. He was compelled, however, to disturb the branches by shaking his head.

'You always were pretty dumb,' said Miss Peavey with scorn. 'I'll say that you've got good solid qualities, Ed – from the neck up. Why, I'm going to sit behind Lady Constance while that goof is shooting his fool head off, and I'm going to reach out and grab that necklace off of her. See?'

'But, Liz' – Mr Cootes diffidently summoned up courage to point out what appeared to him to be a flaw in the scheme – 'if you start any strong-arm work in front of everybody like the way you say, won't they . . .?'

'No, they won't. And I'll tell you why they won't. They aren't going to see me do it, because when I do it it's going to be good and dark in the room. And it's going to be dark because you'll be somewheres out at the back of the house, wherever they keep the main electric-light works, turning the switch as hard as you can go. See? That's your end of it, and pretty soft for you at that. All you have to do is to find out where the thing is and what you have to do to it to put out all the lights in the joint. I guess I can trust you not to bungle that?'

'Liz,' said Mr Cootes, and there was reverence in his voice, 'you can do just that little thing. But what . . .?'

'All right, I know what you're going to say. What happens after that, and how do I get away with the stuff? Well, the window'll be open, and I'll just get to it and

fling the necklace out. See? There'll be a big fuss going
on in the room on account of the darkness and all that,
and while everybody's cutting up and what-the-helling,
you'll pick up your dogs and run round as quick as you
can make it and pouch the thing. I guess it won't be hard
for you to locate it. The window's just over the terrace,
all smooth turf, and it isn't real dark nights now, and you
ought to have plenty of time to hunt around before they
can get the lights going again . . . Well, what do you think
of it?'

There was a brief silence.

'Liz,' said Mr Cootes at length.

'Is it or is it not,' demanded Miss Peavey, 'a ball of
fire?'

'Liz,' said Mr Cootes, and his voice was husky with
such awe as some young officer of Napoleon's staff might
have felt on hearing the details of the latest plan of
campaign, 'Liz, I've said it before, and I'll say it again.
When it comes to the smooth stuff, old girl, you're the
oyster's eye-tooth!'

And, reaching out an arm from the recesses of the yew,
he took Miss Peavey's hand in his and gave it a tender
squeeze. A dreamy look came into the poetess's fine eyes,
and she giggled a little. Dumbbell though he was, she
loved this man.

2

'Mr Baxter?'

'Yes, Miss Halliday?'

The Brains of Blandings looked abstractedly up from
his desk. It was only some half-hour since luncheon had
finished, but already he was in the library surrounded by
large books like a sea-beast among rocks. Most of his
time was spent in the library when the castle was full of
guests, for his lofty mind was ill-attuned to the frivolous
babblings of Society butterflies.

'I wonder if you could spare me this afternoon?' said Eve.

Baxter directed the glare of his spectacles upon her inquisitorially.

'The whole afternoon?'

'If you don't mind. You see, I had a letter by the second post from a great friend of mine, saying that she will be in Market Blandings this afternoon and asking me to meet her there. I must see her, Mr Baxter, *please*. You've no notion how important it is.'

Eve's manner was excited, and her eyes as they met Baxter's sparkled in a fashion that might have disturbed a man made of less stern stuff. If it had been the Hon. Freddie Threepwood, for instance, who had been gazing into their blue depths, that impulsive youth would have tied himself into knots and yapped like a dog. Baxter, the superman, felt no urge towards any such display. He reviewed her request calmly and judicially, and decided that it was a reasonable one.

'Very well, Miss Halliday.'

'Thank you ever so much. I'll make up for it by working twice as hard tomorrow.'

Eve flitted to the door, pausing there to bestow a grateful smile upon him before going out; and Baxter returned to his reading. For a moment he was conscious of a feeling of regret that this quite attractive and uniformly respectful girl should be the partner in crime of a man of whom he disapproved even more than he disapproved of most malefactors. Then he crushed down the weak emotion and was himself again.

Eve trotted downstairs, humming happily to herself. She had expected a longer and more strenuous struggle before she obtained her order of release, and told herself that, despite a manner which seldom deviated from the forbidding, Baxter was really quite nice. In short, it seemed to her that nothing could possibly occur to mar the joyfulness of this admirable afternoon; and it was only when a voice hailed her as she was going through the hall a few minutes later that she realized that she was mistaken. The voice, which trembled throatily, was that of the Hon. Freddie; and her first look at him told Eve, an expert diagnostician, that he was going to propose to her again.

'Well, Freddie?' said Eve resignedly.

The Hon. Frederick Threepwood was a young man who was used to hearing people say 'Well, Freddie?' resignedly when he appeared. His father said it; his Aunt Constance said it; all his other aunts and uncles said it. Widely differing personalities in every other respect, they all said 'Well, Freddie?' resignedly directly they caught sight of him. Eve's words, therefore, and the tone in which they were spoken, did not damp him as they might have damped another. His only feeling was one of solemn gladness at the thought that at last he had managed to get her alone for half a minute.

The fact that this was the first time he had been able to get her alone since her arrival at the castle had caused Freddie a good deal of sorrow. Bad luck was what he attributed it to, thereby giving the object of his affections less credit than was her due for a masterly policy of evasion. He sidled up, looking like a well-dressed sheep.

'Going anywhere?' he inquired.

'Yes. I'm going to Market Blandings. Isn't it a lovely afternoon? I suppose you are busy all the time now that the house is full? Good-bye,' said Eve.

'Eh?' said Freddie, blinking.

'Good-bye. I must be hurrying.'

'Where did you say you were going?'

'Market Blandings.'

'I'll come with you.'

'No, I want to be alone. I've got to meet someone there.'

'Come with you as far as the gates,' said Freddie, the human limpet.

The afternoon sun seemed to Eve to be shining a little less brightly as they started down the drive. She was a kind-hearted girl, and it irked her to have to be continually acting as a black frost in Freddie's garden of dreams. There appeared, however, to be but two ways out of the thing: either she must accept him or he must stop proposing. The first of these alternatives she resolutely declined to consider, and, as far as was ascertainable from his actions, Freddie declined just as resolutely to consider the second. The result was that solitary interviews between them were seldom wholly free from embarrassing developments.

They walked for a while in silence. Then:

'You're dashed hard on a fellow,' said Freddie.

'How's your putting coming on?' asked Eve.

'Eh?'

'Your putting. You told me you had so much trouble with it.'

She was not looking at him, for she had developed a habit of not looking at him on these occasions; but she assumed that the odd sound which greeted her remark was a hollow, mirthless laugh.

'My putting!'

'Well, you told me yourself it's the most important part of golf.'

'Golf! Do you think I have time to worry about golf these days?'

'Oh, how splendid, Freddie! Are you really doing some work of some kind? It's quite time, you know. Think how pleased your father will be.'

'I say,' said Freddie, 'I do think you might marry a chap.'

'I suppose I shall some day,' said Eve, 'if I meet the right one.'

'No, no!' said Freddie despairingly. She was not usually so dense as this. He had always looked on her as a dashed clever girl. 'I mean *me*.'

Eve sighed. She had hoped to avert the inevitable.

'Oh, Freddie!' she exclaimed, exasperated. She was still sorry for him, but she could not help being irritated. It was such a splendid afternoon and she had been feeling so happy. And now he had spoiled everything. It always took her at least half an hour to get over the nervous strain of refusing his proposals.

'I love you, dash it!' said Freddie.

'Well, do stop loving me,' said Eve. 'I'm an awful girl, really. I'd make you miserable.'

'Happiest man in the world,' corrected Freddie devoutly.

'I've got a frightful temper.'

'You're an angel.'

Eve's exasperation increased. She always had a curious fear that one of these days, if he went on proposing, she might say 'Yes' by mistake. She wished that there was some way known to science of stopping him once and for all. And in her desperation she thought of a line of argument which she had not yet employed.

'It's so absurd, Freddie,' she said. 'Really, it is. Apart from the fact that I don't want to marry you, how can you marry anyone – anyone, I mean, who hasn't plenty of money?'

'Wouldn't dream of marrying for money.'

'No, of course not, but . . .'

'Cupid,' said Freddie woodenly, 'pines and sickens in a gilded cage.'

Eve had not expected to be surprised by anything her companion might say, it being her experience that he possessed a vocabulary of about forty-three words and a sum-total of ideas that hardly ran into two figures; but this poetic remark took her back.

'What!'

Freddie repeated the observation. When it had been flashed on the screen as a spoken sub-title in the six-reel wonder film, 'Love or Mammon' (Beatrice Comely and Brian Fraser), he had approved and made a note of it.

'Oh!' said Eve, and was silent. As Miss Peavey would have put it, it held her for a while. 'What I meant,' she went on after a moment, 'was that you can't possibly marry a girl without money unless you've some money of your own.'

'I say, dash it!' A strange note of jubilation had come into the wooer's voice. 'I say, is that really all that stands between us? Because . . .'

'No, it isn't!'

'Because, look here, I'm going to have quite a good deal of money at any moment. It's more or less of a secret, you know – in fact a pretty deadish secret – so keep it dark, but Uncle is going to give me a couple of thousand quid. He promised me. Two thousand of the crispiest. Absolutely!'

'Uncle Joe?'

'*You* know. Old Keeble. He's going to give me a couple of thousand quid, and then I'm going to buy a partnership in a bookie's business and simply coin money. Stands to reason, I mean. You can't help making your bally fortune. Look at all the mugs who are losing money all the time at the races. It's the bookies that get the stuff. A pal of mine who was up at Oxford with me is in a bookie's office, and they're going to let me in if I . . .'

The momentous nature of his information had caused Eve to deviate now from her policy of keeping her eyes off Freddie when in emotional vein. And, if she had desired to check his lecture on finance, she could have chosen no better method than to look at him; for, meeting her gaze, Freddie immediately lost the thread of his discourse and stood yammering. A direct hit from Eve's eyes always affected him in this way.

'Mr Keeble is going to give you two thousand pounds!'

A wave of mortification swept over Eve. If there was

one thing on which she prided herself, it was the belief
that she was a loyal friend, a staunch pal; and now for
the first time she found herself facing the unpleasant
truth that she had been neglecting Phyllis Jackson's
interests in the most abominable way ever since she had
come to Blandings. She had definitely promised Phyllis
that she would tackle this step-father of hers and shame
him with burning words into yielding up the three
thousand pounds which Phyllis needed so desperately for
her Lincolnshire farm. And what had she done? Nothing.

Eve was honest to the core, even in her dealings with
herself. A less conscientious girl might have argued that
she had had no opportunity of a private interview with
Mr Keeble. She scorned to soothe herself with this
specious plea. If she had given her mind to it she could
have brought about a dozen private interviews, and she
knew it. No. She had allowed the pleasant persistence of
Psmith to take up her time, and Phyllis and her troubles
had been thrust into the background. She confessed,
despising herself, that she had hardly given Phyllis a
thought.

And all the while this Mr Keeble had been in a position
to scatter largesse, thousands of pounds of it, to
undeserving people like Freddie. Why, a word from her
about Phyllis would have . . .

'Two thousand pounds?' she repeated dizzily. 'Mr
Keeble?'

'Absolutely!' cried Freddie radiantly. The first shock
of looking into her eyes had passed, and he was now
revelling in that occupation.

'What for?'

Freddie's rapt gaze flickered. Love, he perceived, had
nearly caused him to be indiscreet.

'Oh, I don't know,' he mumbled. 'He's just giving it
me, you know, don't you know.'

'Did you simply go to him and ask him for it?'

'Well – er – well, yes. That was about the strength of it.'

'And he didn't object?'

'No. He seemed rather pleased.'

'Pleased!' Eve found breathing difficult. She was feeling rather like a man who suddenly discovers that the hole in his back yard which he has been passing nonchalantly for months is a gold mine. If the operation of extracting money from Mr Keeble was not only easy but also agreeable to the victim . . . She became aware of a sudden imperative need for Freddie's absence. She wanted to think this thing over.

'Well, then,' said Freddie, 'coming back to it, will you?'

'What?' said Eve, distrait.

'Marry me, you know. What I mean to say is, I worship the very ground you walk on, and all that sort of rot . . . I mean, and all that. And now that you realize that I'm going to get this couple of thousand . . . and the bookie's business . . . and what not, I mean to say . . .'

'Freddie,' said Eve tensely, expressing her harrassed nerves in a voice that came hotly through clenched teeth, 'go away!'

'Eh?'

'I don't want to marry you, and I'm sick of having to keep on telling you so. Will you please go away and leave me alone?' She stopped. Her sense of fairness told her that she was working off on her hapless suitor venom which should have been expended on herself. 'I'm sorry, Freddie,' she said, softening; 'I didn't mean to be such a beast as that. I know you're awfully fond of me, but really, really I can't marry you. You don't want to mary a girl who doesn't love you, do you?'

'Yes, I do,' said Freddie stoutly. 'If it's you, I mean. Love is a tiny seed that coldness can wither, but if tended and nurtured in the fostering warmth of an honest heart . . .'

'But, Freddie – '

'Blossoms into a flower,' concluded Freddie rapidly. 'What I mean to say is, love would come after marriage.'

'Nonsense!'

'Well, that's the way it happened in "A Society Mating".'

'Freddie,' said Eve, 'I really don't want to talk any more. Will you be a dear and just go away? I've got a lot of thinking to do.'

'Oh, thinking?' said Freddie, impressed. 'Right ho!'

'Thank you so much.'

'Oh – er – not at all. Well, pip-pip.'

'Good-bye.'

'See you later, what?'

'Of course, of course.'

'Fine! Well, toodle-oo!'

And the Hon. Freddie, not ill-pleased – for it seemed to him that at long last he detected signs of melting in the party of the second part – swivelled round on his long legs and started for home.

3

The little town of Market Blandings was a peaceful sight as it slept in the sun. For the first time since Freddie had left her, Eve became conscious of a certain tranquillity as she entered the old grey High Street, which was the centre of the place's life and thought. Market Blandings had a comforting air of having been exactly the same for centuries. Troubles might vex the generations it housed, but they did not worry that lichened church with its sturdy four-square tower, nor those red-roofed shops, nor the age-old inns whose second stories bulged so comfortably out over the pavements. As Eve walked in slow meditation towards the 'Emsworth Arms', the intensely respectable hostelry which was her objective, archways met her gaze, opening with a picturesque unexpectedness to show heartening glimpses of ancient nooks all cool and green. There was about the High Street of Market Blandings a suggestion of a slumbering cathedral close. Nothing was modern in it except the moving-picture house – and even that called itself an Electric Theatre, and was ivy-covered and surmounted by stone gables.

On second thoughts, that statement is too sweeping. There was one other modern building in the High Street – Jno. Banks, Hairdresser, to wit, and Eve was just coming abreast of Mr Banks's emporium now.

In any ordinary surroundings these premises would have been a tolerably attractive sight, but in Market Blandings they were almost an eyesore; and Eve, finding herself at the door, was jarred out of her reverie as if she had heard a false note in a solemn anthem. She was on the point of hurrying past, when the door opened and a short, solid figure came out. And at the sight of this short, solid figure Eve stopped abruptly.

It was with the object of getting his grizzled locks clipped in preparation for the County Ball that Joseph Keeble had come to Mr Banks's shop as soon as he had finished lunch. As he emerged now into the High Street he was wondering why he had permitted Mr Banks to finish off the job with a heliotrope-scented hair-wash. It seemed to Mr Keeble that the air was heavy with heliotrope, and it came to him suddenly that heliotrope was a scent which he always found particularly objectionable.

Ordinarily Joseph Keeble was accustomed to show an iron front to hairdressers who tried to inflict lotions upon him; and the reason his vigilance had relaxed under the ministrations of Jno. Banks was that the second post, which arrived at the castle at the luncheon hour, had brought him a plaintive letter from his step-daughter Phyllis – the second he had had from her since the one which had caused him to tackle his masterful wife in the smoking-room. Immediately after the conclusion of his business deal with the Hon. Freddie, he had written to Phyllis in a vein of optimism rendered glowing by

Freddie's promises, assuring her that at any moment he would be in a position to send her the three thousand pounds which she required to clinch the purchase of that dream-farm in Lincolnshire. To this she had replied with thanks. And after that there had been a lapse of days and still he had not made good. Phyllis was becoming worried, and said so in six closely-written pages.

Mr Keeble, as he sat in the barber's chair going over this letter in his mind, had groaned in spirit, while Jno. Banks with gleaming eyes did practically what he liked with the heliotrope bottle. Not for the first time since the formation of their partnership, Joseph Keeble was tormented with doubts as to his wisdom in entrusting a commission so delicate as the purloining of his wife's diamond necklace to one of his nephew Freddie's known feebleness of intellect. Here, he told himself unhappily, was a job of work which would have tested the combined abilities of a syndicate consisting of Charles Peace and the James Brothers, and he had put it in the hands of a young man who in all his life had only once shown genuine inspiration and initiative – on the occasion when he had parted his hair in the middle at a time when all the other members of the Bachelors' Club were brushing it straight back. The more Mr Keeble thought of Freddie's chances, the slimmer they appeared. By the time Jno. Banks had released him from the spotted apron he was thoroughly pessimistic, and as he passed out of the door, 'so perfumed that the winds were love-sick with him', the estimate of his colleague's abilities was reduced to a point where he began to doubt whether the stealing of a mere milk-can was not beyond his scope. So deeply immersed was he in these gloomy thoughts that Eve had to call his name twice before he came out of them.

'Miss Halliday?' he said apologetically. 'I beg your pardon. I was thinking.'

Eve, though they had hardly exchanged a word since

her arrival at the castle, had taken a liking to Mr Keeble; and she felt in consequence none of the embarrassment which might have handicapped her in the discussion of an extremely delicate matter with another man. By nature direct and straightforward, she came to the point at once.

'Can you spare me a moment or two, Mr Keeble?' she said. She glanced at the clock on the church tower and saw that she had ample time before her own appointment. 'I want to talk to you about Phyllis.'

Mr Keeble jerked his head back in astonishment, and the world became noisome with heliotrope. It was as if the Voice of Conscience had suddenly addressed him.

'Phyllis!' he gasped, and the letter crackled in his breast-pocket.

'Your step-daughter Phyllis.'

'Do you know her?'

'She was my best friend at school. I had tea with her just before I came to the castle.'

'Extraordinary!' said Mr Keeble.

A customer in quest of a shave thrust himself between them and went into the shop. They moved away a few paces.

'Of course if you say it is none of my business . . .'

'My dear young lady . . .'

'Well, it *is* my business, because she's my friend,' said Eve firmly. 'Mr Keeble, Phyllis told me she had written to you about buying that farm. Why don't you help her?'

The afternoon was warm, but not warm enough to account for the moistness of Mr Keeble's brow. He drew out a large handkerchief and mopped his forehead. A hunted look was in his eyes. The hand which was not occupied with the handkerchief had sought his pocket and was busy rattling keys.

'I want to help her. I would do anything in the world to help her.'

'Then why don't you?'

'I – I am curiously situated.'

'Yes, Phyllis told me something about that. I can see
that it is a difficult position for you. But, Mr Keeble,
surely, surely if you can manage to give Freddie
Threepwood two thousand pounds to start a book-
maker's business . . .'

Her words were cut short by a strangled cry from her
companion. Sheer panic was in his eyes now, and in his
heart an overwhelming regret that he had ever been fool
enough to dabble in crime in the company of a mere
animated talking-machine like his nephew Freddie. This
girl knew! And if she knew, how many others knew?
The young imbecile had probably babbled his hideous
secret into the ears of every human being in the place
who would listen to him.

'He told you!' he stammered. 'He t-told you!'

'Yes. Just now.'

'Goosh!' muttered Mr Keeble brokenly.

Eve stared at him in surprise. She could not understand
this emotion. The handkerchief, after a busy session,
was lowered now, and he was looking at her imploringly.

'You haven't told anyone?' he croaked hoarsely.

'Of course not. I said I had only heard of it just now.'

'You wouldn't tell anyone?'

'Why should I?'

Mr Keeble's breath, which had seemed to him for a
moment gone for ever, began to return timidly. Relief
for a space held him dumb. What nonsense, he reflected,
these newspapers and people talked about the modern girl.
It was this very broadmindedness of hers, to which they
objected so absurdly, that made her a creature of such
charm. She might behave in certain ways in a fashion
that would have shocked her grandmother, but how
comforting it was to find her calm and unmoved in the
contemplation of another's crime. His heart warmed to
Eve.

'You're wonderful!' he said.

'What do you mean?'

'Of course,' argued Mr Keeble, 'it isn't really stealing.'

'What!'

'I shall buy my wife another necklace.'

'You will – what?'

'So everything will be all right. Constance will be perfectly happy, and Phyllis will have her money, and . . .'

Something in Eve's astonished gaze seemed to smite Mr Keeble.

'Don't you *know*?' he broke off.

'Know? Know what?'

Mr Keeble perceived that he had wronged Freddie. The young ass had been a fool even to mention the money to this girl, but he had at least, it seemed, stopped short of disclosing the entire plot. An oyster-like reserve came upon him.

'Nothing, nothing,' he said hastily. 'Forget what I was going to say. Well, I must be going, I must be going.'

Eve clutched wildly at his retreating sleeve. Unintelligible though his words had been, one sentence had come home to her, the one about Phyllis having her money. It was no time for half-measures. She grabbed him.

'Mr Keeble,' she cried urgently. 'I don't know what you mean, but you were just going to say something which sounded . . . Mr Keeble, do trust me. I'm Phyllis's best friend, and if you've thought out any way of helping her I wish you would tell me . . . You must tell me. I might be able to help . . .'

Mr Keeble, as she began her broken speech, had been endeavouring with deprecatory tugs to disengage his coat from her grasp. But now he ceased to struggle. Those doubts of Freddies' efficiency, which had troubled him in Jno. Banks's chair, still lingered. His opinion that Freddie was but a broken reed had not changed. Indeed, it had grown. He looked at Eve. He looked at her searchingly. Into her pleading eyes he directed a stare that sought to

probe her soul, and saw there honesty, sympathy, and –
better still – intelligence. He might have stood and gazed
into Freddie's fishy eyes for weeks without discovering a
tithe of such intelligence. His mind was made up. This
girl was an ally. A girl of dash and vigour. A girl worth a
thousand Freddies – not, however, reflected Mr Keeble,
that that was saying much. He hesitated no longer.

'It's like this,' said Mr Keeble.

4

The information, authoritatively conveyed to him during
breakfast by Lady Constance, that he was scheduled that
night to read select passages from Ralston McTodd's
Songs of Squalor to the entire house-party assembled in
the big drawing-room, had come as a complete surprise
to Psmith, and to his fellow-guests – such of them as
were young and of the soulless sex – as a shock from
which they found it hard to rally. True, they had before
now gathered in a vague sort of way that he was one of
those literary fellows, but so normal and engaging had
they found his whole manner and appearance that it
had never occurred to them that he concealed anything
up his sleeve as lethal as *Songs of Squalor*. Among these
members of the younger set the consensus of opinion
was that it was a bit thick, and that at such a price even
the lavish hospitality of Blandings was scarcely worth
having. Only those who had visited the castle before
during the era of her ladyship's flirtation with Art could
have been described as resigned. These stout hearts
argued that while this latest blister was probably
going to be pretty bad, he could hardly be worse than
the chappie who had lectured on Theosophy last
November, and must almost of necessity be better than
the bird who during the Shiffley race-week had attempted
in a two-hour discourse to convert them to
vegetarianism.

Psmith himself regarded the coming ordeal with equanimity. He was not one of those whom the prospect of speaking in public afflicts with nervous horror. He liked the sound of his own voice, and night, when it came, found him calmly cheerful. He listened contentedly to the murmur of the drawing-room filling up as he strolled on the star-lit terrace, smoking a last cigarette before duty called him elsewhere. And when, some few yards away, seated on the terrace wall gazing out into the velvet darkness, he perceived Eve Halliday, his sense of well-being became acute.

All day he had been conscious of a growing desire for another of those cosy chats with Eve which had done so much to make life agreeable for him during his stay at Blandings. Her prejudice – which he deplored – in favour of doing a certain amount of work to justify her salary, had kept him during the morning away from the little room off the library where she was wont to sit cataloguing books; and when he had gone there after lunch he had found it empty. As he approached her now, he was thinking pleasantly of all those delightful walks, those excellent driftings on the lake, and those cheery conversations which had gone to cement his conviction that of all possible girls she was the only possible one. It seemed to him that in addition to being beautiful she brought out all that was best in him of intellect and soul. That is to say, she let him talk oftener and longer than any girl he had ever known.

It struck him as a little curious that she made no move to greet him. She remained apparently unaware of his approach. And yet the summer night was not of such density as to hide him from view – and, even if she could not see him, she must undoubtedly have heard him; for only a moment before he had tripped with some violence over a large flower-pot, one of a row of sixteen which Angus McAllister, doubtless for some good purpose, had place in the fairway that afternoon.

599

'A pleasant night,' he said, seating himself gracefully beside her on the wall.

She turned her head for a brief instant, and, having turned it, looked away again.

'Yes,' she said.

Her manner was not effusive, but Psmith persevered.

'The stars,' he proceeded, indicating them with a kindly yet not patronizing wave of the hand. 'Bright, twinkling, and – if I may say so – rather neatly arranged. When I was a mere lad, someone whose name I cannot recollect taught me which was Orion. Also Mars, Venus, and Jupiter. This thoroughly useless chunk of knowledge has, I am happy to say, long since passed from my mind. However, I am in a position to state that the wiggly thing up there a little to the right is King Charles' Wain.'

'Yes?'

'Yes, indeed, I assure you.' It struck Psmith that Astronomy was not gripping his audience, so he tried Travel. 'I hear,' he said, 'you went to Market Blandings this afternoon.'

'Yes.'

'An attractive settlement.'

'Yes.'

There was a pause. Psmith removed his monocle and polished it thoughtfully. The summer night seemed to him to have taken on a touch of chill.

'What I like about the English rural districts,' he went on, 'is that when the authorities have finished building a place they stop. Somewhere about the reign of Henry the Eighth, I imagine that the master-mason gave the final house a pat with his trowel and said, "Well, boys, that's Market Blandings." To which his assistants no doubt assented with many a hearty "Grammercy!" and "I'fackins!" these being expletives to which they were much addicted. And they went away and left it, and nobody has touched it since. And I, for one, thoroughly approve. I think it makes the place soothing. Don't you?'

'Yes.'

As far as the darkness would permit, Psmith subjected Eve to an inquiring glance through his monocle. This was a strange new mood in which he had found her. Hitherto, though she had always endeared herself to him by permitting him the major portion of the dialogue, they had usually split conversations on at least a seventy-five – twenty-five basis. And though it gratified Psmith to be allowed to deliver a monologue when talking with most people, he found Eve more companionable when in a slightly chattier vein.

'Are you coming in to hear me read?' he asked.

'No.'

It was a change from 'Yes,' but that was the best that could be said of it. A good deal of discouragement was always required to damp Psmith, but he could not help feeling a slight diminution of buoyancy. However, he kept on trying.

'You show your usual sterling good sense,' he said approvingly. 'A scalier method of passing the scented summer night could hardly be hit upon.' He abandoned the topic of the reading. It did not grip. That was manifest. It lacked appeal. 'I went to Market Blandings this afternoon, too,' he said. 'Comrade Baxter informed me that you had gone thither, so I went after you. Not being able to find you, I turned in for half an hour at the local moving-picture palace. They were showing Episode Eleven of a serial. It concluded with the heroine, kidnapped by Indians, stretched on the sacrificial altar with the high-priest making passes at her with a knife. The hero meanwhile had started to climb a rather nasty precipice on his way to the rescue. The final picture was a close-up of his fingers slipping slowly off a rock. Episode Twelve next week.'

Eve looked out into the night without speaking.

'I'm afraid it won't end happily,' said Psmith with a sigh. 'I think he'll save her.'

Eve turned on him with a menacing abruptness.

'Shall I tell you why I went to Market Blandings this afternoon?' she said.

'Do,' said Psmith cordially. 'It is not for me to criticize, but as a matter of fact I was rather wondering when you were going to begin telling me all about your adventures. I have been monopolizing the conversation.'

'I went to meet Cynthia.'

Psmith's monocle fell out of his eye and swung jerkily on its cord. He was not easily disconcerted, but this unexpected piece of information, coming on top of her peculiar manner, undoubtedly jarred him. He foresaw difficulties, and once again found himself thinking hard thoughts of this confounded female who kept bobbing up when least expected. How simple life would have been, he mused wistfully, had Ralston McTodd only had the good sense to remain a bachelor.

'Oh, Cynthia?' he said.

'Yes, Cynthia,' said Eve. The inconvenient Mrs McTodd possessed a Christian name admirably adapted for being hissed between clenched teeth, and Eve hissed it in this fashion now. It became evident to Psmith that the dear girl was in a condition of hardly suppressed fury and that trouble was coming his way. He braced himself to meet it.

'Directly after we had that talk on the lake, the day I arrived,' continued Eve tersely, 'I wrote to Cynthia, telling her to come here at once and meet me at the "Emsworth Arms" . . .'

'In the High Street,' said Psmith. 'I know it. Good beer.'

'What!'

'I said they sell good beer . . .'

'Never mind about the beer,' cried Eve.

'No, no. I merely mentioned it in passing.'

'At lunch today I got a letter from her saying that she would be there this afternoon. So I hurried off.

I wanted – ' Eve laughed a hollow, mirthless laugh of a
calibre which even the Hon. Freddie Threepwood would
have found beyond his powers, and he was a specialist –
'I wanted to try to bring you two together. I thought that
if I could see her and have a talk with her that you might
become reconciled.'

Psmith, though obsessed with a disquieting feeling
that he was fighting in the last ditch, pulled himself
together sufficiently to pat her hand as it lay beside him
on the wall like some white and fragile flower.

'That was like you,' he murmured. 'That was an act
worthy of your great heart. But I fear that the rift between
Cynthia and myself has reached such dimensions . . .'

Eve drew her hand away. She swung round, and the
battery of her indignant gaze raked him furiously.

'I saw Cynthia,' she said, 'and she told me that her
husband was in Paris.'

'Now, how in the world,' said Psmith, struggling
bravely but with a growing sense that they were coming
over the plate a bit too fast for him, 'how in the world did
she get an idea like that?'

'Do you really want to know?'

'I do, indeed.'

'Then I'll tell you. She got the idea because she had
had a letter from him, begging her to join him there.
She had just finished telling me this, when I caught sight
of you from the inn window, walking along the High
Street. I pointed you out to Cynthia, and she said she had
never seen you before in her life.'

'Women soon forget,' sighed Psmith.

'The only excuse I can find for you,' stormed Eve
in a vibrant undertone necessitated by the fact that
somebody had just emerged from the castle door and
they no longer had the terrace to themselves, 'is that
you're mad. When I think of all you said to me about poor
Cynthia on the lake that afternoon, when I think of all
the sympathy I wasted on you . . .'

'Not wasted,' corrected Psmith firmly. 'It was by no means wasted. It made me love you – if possible – even more.'

Eve had supposed that she had embarked on a tirade which would last until she had worked off her indignation and felt composed again, but this extraordinary remark scattered the thread of her harangue so hopelessly that all she could do was to stare at him in amazed silence.

'Womanly intuition,' proceeded Psmith gravely, 'will have told you long ere this that I love you with a fervour which with my poor vocabulary I cannot hope to express. True, as you are about to say, we have known each other but a short time, as time is measured. But what of that?'

Eve raised her eyebrows. Her voice was cold and hostile.

'After what has happened,' she said, 'I suppose I ought not to be surprised at finding you capable of anything, but – are you really choosing this moment to – to propose to me?'

'To employ a favourite word of your own – yes.'

'And you expect me to take you seriously?'

'Assuredly not. I look upon the present disclosure purely as a sighting shot. You may regard it, if you will, as a kind of formal proclamation. I wish simply to go on record as an aspirant to your hand. I want you, if you will be so good, to make a note of my words and give them a thought from time to time. As Comrade Cootes – a young friend of mine whom you have not yet met – would say, "Chew on them".'

'I . . .'

'It is possible,' continued Psmith, 'that black moments will come to you – for they come to all of us, even the sunniest – when you will find yourself saying, "Nobody loves me!" On such occasions I should like you to add, "No, I am wrong. There *is* somebody who loved me." At first, it may be, that reflection will bring but scant balm.

Gradually, however, as the days go by and we are constantly together and my nature unfolds itself before you like the petals of some timid flower the rays of the sun . . .'

Eve's eyes opened wider. She had supposed herself incapable of further astonishment, but she saw that she had been mistaken.

'You surely aren't dreaming of staying on here *now*?' she gasped.

'Most decidedly. Why not?'

'But – but what is to prevent me telling everybody that you are not Mr McTodd?'

'Your sweet, generous nature,' said Psmith. 'Your big heart. Your angelic forbearance.'

'Oh!'

'Considering that I only came here as McTodd – and if you had seen him you would realize that he is not a person for whom the man of sensibility and refinement would lightly allow himself to be mistaken – I say considering that I only took on the job of understudy so as to get to the castle and be near you, I hardly think that you will be able to bring yourself to get me slung out. You must try to understand what happened. When Lord Emsworth started chatting with me under the impression that I was Comrade McTodd, I encouraged the mistake purely with the kindly intention of putting him at his ease. Even when he informed me that he was expecting me to come down to Blandings with him on the five o'clock train, it never occurred to me to do so. It was only when I saw you talking to him in the street and he revealed the fact that you were about to enjoy his hospitality that I decided that there was no other course open to the man of spirit. Consider! Twice that day you had passed out of my life – may I say taking the sunshine with you? – and I began to fear you might pass out of it for ever. So, loath though I was to commit the solecism of planting myself in this happy home under false pretences, I could see no other way. And here I am!'

'You *must* be mad!'

'Well, as I was saying, the days will go by, you will have ample opportunity of studying my personality, and it is quite possible that in due season the love of an honest heart may impress you as worth having. I may add that I have loved you since the moment when I saw you sheltering from the rain under that awning in Dover Street, and I recall saying as much to Comrade Walderwick when he was chatting with me some short time later on the subject of his umbrella. I do not press you for an answer now . . .'

'I should hope not!'

'I merely say "Think it over." It is nothing to cause you mental distress. Other men love you. Freddie Threepwood loves you. Just add me to the list. That is all I ask. Muse on me from time to time. Reflect that I may be an acquired taste. You probably did not like olives the first time you tasted them. Now you probably do. Give me the same chance you would an olive. Consider, also, how little you actually have against me. What, indeed, does it amount to, when you come to examine it narrowly? All you have against me is the fact that I am not Ralston McTodd. Think how comparatively few people *are* Ralston McTodd. Let your meditations proceed along these lines and . . .'

He broke off, for at this moment the individual who had come out of the front door a short while back loomed beside them, and the glint of starlight on glass revealed him as the Efficient Baxter.

'Everybody is waiting, Mr McTodd,' said the Efficient Baxter. He spoke the name, as always, with a certain sardonic emphasis.

'Of course,' said Psmith affably, 'of course. I was forgetting. I will get to work at once. You are quite sure you do not wish to hear a scuttleful of modern poetry, Miss Halliday?'

'Quite sure.'

'And yet even now, so our genial friend here informs us, a bevy of youth and beauty is crowding the drawing-room, agog for the treat. Well, well! It is these strange clashings of personal taste which constitute what we call Life. I think I will write a poem about it some day. Come, Comrade Baxter, let us be up and doing. I must not disappoint my public.'

For some moments after the two had left her – Baxter silent and chilly, Psmith, all debonair chumminess, kneading the other's arm and pointing out as they went objects of interest by the wayside – Eve remained on the terrace wall, thinking. She was laughing now, but behind her amusement there was another feeling, and one that perplexed her. A good many men had proposed to her in the course of her career, but none of them had ever left her with this odd feeling of exhilaration. Psmith was different from any other man who had come her way, and difference was a quality which Eve esteemed . . .

She had just reached the conclusion that life for whatever girl might eventually decide to risk it in Psmith's company would never be dull, when strange doings in her immediate neighbourhood roused her from her meditations.

The thing happened as she rose from her seat on the wall and started to cross the terrace on her way to the front door. She had stopped for an instant beneath the huge open window of the drawing-room to listen to what was going on inside. Faintly, with something of the quality of a far-off phonograph, the sound of Psmith reading came to her; and even at this distance there was a composed blandness about his voice which brought a smile to her lips.

And then, with a startling abruptness, the lighted window was dark. And she was aware that all the lighted windows on that side of the castle had suddenly become dark. The lamp that shone over the great door ceased to shine. And above the hubbub of voices in the drawing-room she heard Psmith's patient drawl.

'Ladies and gentlemen, I think the lights have gone out.'

The night air was rent by a single piercing scream. Something flashed like a shooting star and fell at her feet; and, stooping, Eve found in her hands Lady Constance Keeble's diamond necklace.

5

To be prepared is everything in this life. Ever since her talk with Mr Joseph Keeble in the High Street of Market Blandings that afternoon Eve's mind had been flitting nimbly from one scheme to another, all designed to end in this very act of seizing the necklace in her hands and each rendered impracticable by some annoying flaw. And now that Fate in its impulsive way had achieved for her what she had begun to feel she could never accomplish for herself, she wasted no time in bewildered inaction. The miracle found her ready for it.

For an instant she debated with herself the chances of a dash through the darkened hall up the stairs to her room. But the lights might go on again, and she might meet someone. Memories of sensational novels read in the past told her that on occasions such as this people were detained and searched. . . .

Suddenly, as she stood there, she found the way. Close beside her, lying on its side, was the flower-pot which Psmith had overturned as he came to join her on the terrace wall. It might have defects as a cache, but at the moment she could perceive none. Most flower-pots are alike, but this was particularly easily-remembered flower-pot; for in its journeying from the potting shed to the terrace it had acquired on its side a splash of white paint. She would be able to distinguish it from its fellows when, late that night, she crept out to retrieve the spoil. And surely nobody would ever think of suspecting . . .

She plunged her fingers into the soft mould, and straightened herself, breathing quickly. It was not an ideal piece of work, but it would serve.

She rubbed her fingers on the turf, put the flower-pot back in the row with the others, and then, like a flying white phantom, darted across the terrace and into the house. And so with beating heart, groping her way, to the bathroom to wash her hands. The twenty-thousand-pound flower-pot looked placidly up at the winking stars.

6

It was perhaps two minutes later that Mr Cootes, sprinting lustily, rounded the corner of the house and burst on to the terrace. Late as usual.

11 — Almost Entirely About Flower-pots

1

The Efficient Baxter prowled feverishly up and down the yielding carpet of the big drawing-room. His eyes gleamed behind their spectacles, his dome-like brow was corrugated. Except for himself, the room was empty. As far as the scene of the disaster was concerned, the tumult and the shouting had died. It was going on vigorously in practically every other part of the house, but in the drawing-room there was stillness, if not peace.

Baxter paused, came to a decision, went to the wall and pressed the bell.

'Thomas,' he said when that footman presented himself a few moments later.

'Sir?'

'Send Susan to me.'

'Susan, sir?'

'Yes, Susan,' snapped the Efficient One, who had always a short way with the domestic staff. 'Susan, Susan, Susan . . . The new parlourmaid.'

'Oh, yes, sir. Very good, sir.'

Thomas withdrew, outwardly all grave respectfulness, inwardly piqued, as was his wont, at the airy manner in which the secretary flung his orders about at the castle. The domestic staff at Blandings lived in a perpetual state of smouldering discontent under Baxter's rule.

'Susan,' said Thomas when he arrived in the lower regions, 'you're to go up to the drawing-room. Nosey Parker wants you.'

The pleasant-faced young woman whom he addressed laid down her knitting.

'Who?' she asked.

'Mister Blooming Baxter. When you've been here a little longer you'll know that he's the feller that owns the place. How he got it I don't know. Found it,' said Thomas satirically, 'in his Christmas stocking, I expect. Anyhow, you're to go up.'

Thomas's fellow-footman, Stokes, a serious-looking man with a bald forehead, shook that forehead solemnly.

'Something's the matter,' he asserted. 'You can't tell me that wasn't a scream we heard when them lights was out. Or,' he added weightily, for he was a man who looked at every side of a question, 'a shriek. It was a shriek or scream. I said so at the time. "There," I said, "listen!" I said. "That's somebody screaming," I said. "Or shrieking." Something's up.'

'Well, Baxter hasn't been murdered, worse luck,' said Thomas. 'He's up there screaming or shrieking for Susan. "Send Susan to me!" ' proceeded Thomas, giving an always popular imitation. ' "Susan, Susan, Susan." So you'd best go, my girl, and see what he wants.'

'Very well.'

'And, Susan,' said Thomas, a tender note creeping into his voice, for already, brief as had been her sojourn at Blandings, he had found the new parlourmaid making a deep impression on him, 'if it's a row of any kind . . .'

'Or description,' interjected Stokes.

'Or description,' continued Thomas, accepting the word, 'if 'e's 'arsh with you for some reason or other, you come right back to me and sob out your troubles on my chest, see? Lay your little 'ead on my shoulder and tell me all about it.'

The new parlourmaid, primly declining to reply to this alluring invitation, started on her journey upstairs; and Thomas, with a not unmanly sigh, resumed his interrupted game of halfpenny nap with colleague Stokes.

The Efficient Baxter had gone to the open window and was gazing out into the night when Susan entered the drawing-room.

'You wished to see me, Mr Baxter?'

The secretary spun round. So softly had she opened the door, and so noiselessly had she moved when inside the room, that it was not until she spoke that he had become aware of her arrival. It was a characteristic of this girl Susan that she was always apt to be among those present some time before the latter became cognizant of the fact.

'Oh, good evening, Miss Simmons. You came in very quietly.'

'Habit,' said the parlourmaid.

'You gave me quite a start.'

'I'm sorry. What was it,' she asked, dismissing in a positively unfeeling manner the subject of her companion's jarred nerves, 'that you wished to see me about?'

'Shut that door.'

'I have. I always shut doors.'

'Please sit down.'

'No, thank you, Mr Baxter. It might look odd if anyone should come in.'

'Of course. You think of everything.'

'I always do.'

Baxter stood for a moment, frowning.

'Miss Simmons,' he said, 'when I thought it expedient to instal a private detective in this house, I insisted on Wragge's sending you. We had worked together before . . .'

'Sixteenth of December, 1918, to January twelve, 1919, when you were secretary to Mr Horace Jevons, the American millionaire,' said Miss Simmons as promptly as if he had touched a spring. It was her hobby to remember dates with precision.

'Exactly. I insisted upon your being sent because I knew from experience that you were reliable. At that time I looked on your presence here merely as a precautionary measure. Now, I am sorry to say . . .'

'Did someone steal Lady Constance's necklace tonight?'

'Yes!'

'When the lights went out just now?'

'Exactly.'

'Well, why couldn't you say so at once? Good gracious, man, you don't have to break the thing gently to me.'

The Efficient Baxter, though he strongly objected to being addressed as 'man', decided to overlook the solecism.

'The lights suddenly went out,' he said. 'There was a certain amount of laughter and confusion. Then a piercing shriek . . .'

'I heard it.'

'And immediately after Lady Constance's voice crying that her jewels had been snatched from her neck.'

'Then what happened?'

'Still greater confusion, which lasted until one of the maids arrived with a candle. Eventually the lights went on again, but of the necklace there was no sign whatever.'

'Well? Were you expecting the thief to wear it as a watch-chain or hang it from his teeth?'

Baxter was finding his companion's manner more trying every minute, but he preserved his calm.

'Naturally the doors were barred and a complete search instituted. And extremely embarrassing it was. With the single exception of the scoundrel who has been palming himself off as McTodd, all those present were well-known members of Society.'

'Well-known members of Society might not object to getting hold of a twenty-thousand-pound necklace. But still with the McTodd fellow there, you oughtn't to have had far to look. What had he to say about it?'

'He was among the first to empty his pockets.'

'Well, then, he must have hidden the thing somewhere.'

'Not in this room. I have searched assiduously.'

'H'm.'

There was a silence.

'It is baffling,' said Baxter, 'baffling.'

'It is nothing of the kind,' replied Miss Simmons tartly. 'This wasn't a one-man job. How could it have been? I should be inclined to call it a three-man job. One to switch off the lights, one to snatch the necklace, and one to – was that window open all the time? I thought so – and one to pick up the necklace when the second fellow threw it out on to the terrace.'

'Terrace!'

The word shot from Baxter's lips with explosive force. Miss Simmons looked at him curiously.

'Thought of something?'

'Miss Simmons,' said the Efficient One impressively, 'everybody was assembled in here waiting for the reading to begin, but the pseudo-McTodd was nowhere to be found. I discovered him eventually on the terrace in close talk with the Halliday girl.'

'His partner,' said Miss Simmons, nodding. 'We thought so all along. And let me add my little bit. There's a fellow down in the servants' hall that calls himself a valet, and I'll bet he didn't know what a valet was till he came here. I thought he was a crook the moment I set eyes on him. I can tell 'em in the dark. Now, do you know whose valet he is? This McTodd fellow's!'

Baxter bounded to and fro like a caged tiger.

'And with my own ears,' he cried excitedly, 'I heard the Halliday girl refuse to come to the drawing-room to listen to the reading. She was out on the terrace throughout the whole affair. Miss Simmons, we must act! We must act!'

'Yes, but not like idiots,' replied the detective frostily.

'What do you mean?'

'Well, you can't charge out, as you looked as if you wanted to just then, and denounce these crooks where they sit. We've got to go carefully.'

'But meanwhile they will smuggle the necklace away!'

'They won't smuggle any necklace away, not while I'm around. Suspicion's no good. We've made out a nice little case against the three of them, but it's no use unless we catch them with the goods. The first thing we have to do is to find out where they've hidden the stuff. And that'll take patience. I'll start by searching that girl's room. Then I'll search the valet fellow's room. And if the stuff isn't there it'll mean they've hidden it out in the open somewhere.'

'But this McTodd fellow. This fellow who poses as McTodd. He may have it all the while.'

'No. I'll search his room, too, but the stuff won't be there. He's the fellow who's going to get it in the end, because he's got that place out in the woods to hide it in. But they wouldn't have had time to slip it to him yet. That necklace is somewhere right here. And if,' said Miss Simmons with grim facetiousness, 'they can hide it from me, they may keep it as a birthday present.'

2

How wonderful, if we pause to examine it, is Nature's inexorable law of compensation. Instead of wasting time in envy of our mental superiors, we would do well to reflect that these gifts of theirs which excite our wistful jealousy are ever attended by corresponding penalties. To take an example that lies to hand, it was the very fact that he possessed a brain like a buzz-saw that rendered the Efficient Baxter a bad sleeper. Just as he would be dropping off, bing! would go that brain of his, melting the mists of sleep like snow in a furnace.

This was so even when life was running calmly for him and without excitement. Tonight, his mind, bearing

the load it did, firmly declined even to consider the
question of slumber. The hour of two, chiming from
the clock over the stables, found him as wide awake as
ever he was at high noon.

Lying in bed in the darkness, he reviewed the situation
as far as he had the data. Shortly before he retired, Miss
Simmons had made her report about the bedrooms.
Though subjected to the severest scrutiny, neither
Psmith's boudoir nor Cootes's attic nor Eve's little nook
on the third floor had yielded up treasure of any
description. And this, Miss Simmons held, confirmed her
original view that the necklace must be lying concealed in
what might almost be called a public spot – on some
window-ledge, maybe, or somewhere in the hall . . .

Baxter lay considering this theory. It did appear to be
the only tenable one; but it offended him by giving the
search a frivolous suggestion of being some sort of round
game like Hunt the Slipper or Find the Thimble. As a
child he had held austerely aloof from these silly
pastimes, and he resented being compelled to play them
now. Still . . .

He sat up thinking. He had heard a noise.

The attitude of the majority of people towards noises in
the night is one of cautious non-interference. But Rupert
Baxter was made of sterner stuff. The sound had seemed
to come from downstairs somewhere – perhaps from
that very hall where, according to Miss Simmons, the
stolen necklace might even now be lying hid. Whatever
it was, it must certainly not be ignored. He reached for
the spectacles which lay ever ready to his hand on the
table beside him: then climbed out of bed, and, having
put on a pair of slippers and opened the door, crept forth
into the darkness. As far as he could ascertain by holding
his breath and straining his ears, all was still from cellar
to roof; but nevertheless he was not satisfied. He
continued to listen. His room was on the second floor,

one of a series that ran along a balcony overlooking the hall; and he stood, leaning over the balcony rail, a silent statue of Vigilance.

The noise which had acted so electrically upon the Efficient Baxter had been a particularly noisy noise; and only the intervening distance and the fact that his door was closed had prevented it sounding to him like an explosion. It had been caused by the crashing downfall of a small table containing a vase, a jar of potpourri, an Indian sandalwood box of curious workmanship, and a cabinet-size photograph of the Earl of Emsworth's eldest son, Lord Bosham; and the table had fallen because Eve, *en route* across the hall in quest of her precious flower-pot, had collided with it while making for the front door. Of all indoor sports – and Eve, as she stood pallidly among the ruins, would have been the first to endorse this dictum – the one which offers the minimum of pleasure to the participant is that of roaming in pitch darkness through the hall of a country-house. Easily navigable in the daytime, these places become at night mere traps for the unwary.

Eve paused breathlessly. So terrific had the noise sounded to her guilty ears that every moment she was expecting doors to open all over the castle, belching forth shouting men with pistols. But as nothing happened, courage returned to her, and she resumed her journey. She found the great door, ran her fingers along its surface, and drew the chain. The shooting back of the bolts occupied but another instant, and then she was out on the terrace running her hardest towards the row of flower-pots.

Up on his balcony, meanwhile, the Efficient Baxter was stopping, looking, and listening. The looking brought no results, for all below was black as pitch; but the listening proved more fruitful. Faintly from down in the well of the hall there floated up to him a peculiar sound like something rustling in the darkness. Had he reached the balcony a moment earlier, he would have heard the rattle of the chain and the click of the bolts; but these noises had occurred just before he came out of his room. Now all that was audible was this rustling.

He could not analyse the sound, but the fact that there was any sound at all in such a place at such an hour increased his suspicions that dark doings were towards which would pay for investigation. With stealthy steps he crept to the head of the stairs and descended.

One uses the verb 'descend' advisedly, for what is required is some word suggesting instantaneous activity. About Baxter's progress from the second floor to the first there was nothing halting or hesitating. He, so to speak, did it now. Planting his foot firmly on a golf-ball which the Hon. Freddie Threepwood, who had been practising putting in the corridor before retiring to bed, had left in his casual fashion just where the steps began, he took the entire staircase in one majestic, volplaning sweep. There were eleven stairs in all separating his landing from the landing below, and the only ones he hit were the third and tenth. He came to rest with a squattering thud on the lower landing, and for a moment or two the fever of the chase left him.

The fact that many writers in their time have commented at some length on the mysterious manner in which Fate is apt to perform its work must not deter us now from a brief survey of this latest manifestation of its ingenious methods. Had not his interview with Eve that afternoon so stimulated the Hon. Freddie as to revive in him a faint yet definite desire to putt, there would have been no golf-ball waiting for Baxter on the stairs. And had he been permitted to negotiate the stairs in a less impetuous manner, Baxter would not at this juncture have switched on the light.

It had not been his original intention to illuminate the

theatre of action, but after that Lucifer-like descent from
the second floor to the first he was taking no more
chances. 'Safety First' was Baxter's slogan. As soon,
therefore, as he had shaken off a dazed sensation of mental
and moral collapse, akin to that which comes to the man
who steps on the teeth of a rake and is smitten on the
forehead by the handle, he rose with infinite caution to
his feet and, feeling his way down by the banisters, groped
for the switch and pressed it. And so it came about that
Eve, heading for home with her precious flower-pot in
her arms, was stopped when at the very door by a sudden
warning flood of light. Another instant, and she would
have been across the threshold of disaster.

For a moment paralysis gripped her. The light had
affected her like someone shouting loudly and
unexpectedly in her ear. Her heart gave one convulsive
bound, and she stood frozen. Then, filled with a blind
desire for flight, she dashed like a hunted rabbit into the
friendly shelter of a clump of bushes.

Baxter stood blinking. Gradually his eyes adjusted
themselves to the light, and immediately they had done
so he was seized by a fresh frenzy of zeal. Now that all
things were made visible to him he could see that that
faint rustling sound had been caused by a curtain flapping
in the breeze, and that the breeze which made the curtain
flap was coming in through the open front window.

Baxter wasted no time in abstract thought. He acted
swiftly and with decision. Straightening his spectacles
on his nose, he girded up his pyjamas and galloped out
into the night.

The smooth terrace slept under the stars. To a more poetic
man than Baxter it would have seemed to wear that
faintly reproachful air which a garden always assumes
when invaded at unseemly hours by people who ought
to be in bed. Baxter, never fanciful, was blind to this. He

was thinking, thinking. That shaking-up on the stairs had churned into activity the very depths of his brain and he was at the fever-point of his reasoning powers. A thought had come like a full-blown rose, flushing his brow. Miss Simmons, arguing plausibly, had suggested that the stolen necklace might be concealed in the hall. Baxter, inspired, fancied not. Whoever it was that had been at work in the hall just now had been making for the garden. It was not the desire to escape which had led him – or her – to open the front door, for the opening had been done before he, Baxter, had come out on to the balcony – otherwise he must have heard the shooting of the bolts. No. The enemy's objective had been the garden. In other words, the terrace. And why? Because somewhere on the terrace was the stolen necklace.

Standing there in the starlight, the Efficient Baxter endeavoured to reconstruct the scene, and did so with remarkable accuracy. He saw the jewels flashing down. He saw them picked up. But there he stopped. Try as he might, he could not see them hidden. And yet that they had been hidden – and that within a few feet of where he was now standing – he felt convinced.

He moved from his position near the door and began to roam restlessly. His slippered feet padded over the soft turf.

Eve peered out from her clump of bushes. It was not easy to see any great distance, but Fate, her friend, was still with her. There had been a moment that night when Baxter, disrobing for bed, had wavered absently between his brown and his lemon-coloured pyjamas, little recking of what hung upon the choice. Fate had directed his hand to the lemon-coloured, and he had put them on; with the result that he shone now in the dim light like the white plume of Navarre. Eve could follow his movements perfectly, and, when he was far enough away from his base to make the enterprise prudent, she slipped out and

raced for home and safety. Baxter at the moment was
leaning on the terrace wall, thinking, thinking, thinking.

It was possibly the cool air, playing about his bare ankles,
that at last chilled the secretary's dashing mood and
brought the disquieting thought that he was doing
something distinctly dangerous in remaining out here
in the open like this. A gang of thieves are ugly customers,
likely to stick at little when a valuable necklace is at
stake, and it came to the Efficient Baxter that in his light
pyjamas he must be offering a tempting mark for any
marauder lurking – say in those bushes. And at the
thought, the summer night, though pleasantly mild,
grew suddenly chilly. With an almost convulsive rapidity
he turned to re-enter the house. Zeal was well enough,
but it was silly to be rash. He covered the last few yards
of his journey at a rare burst of speed.

  It was at this point that he discovered that the lights
in the hall had been switched off and that the front door
was closed and bolted.

3

It is the opinion of most thoughtful students of life that
happiness in this world depends chiefly on the ability to
take things as they come. An instance of one who may
be said to have perfected this attitude is to be found in
the writings of a certain eminent Arabian author who
tells of a traveller who, sinking to sleep one afternoon
upon a patch of turf containing an acorn, discovered when
he woke that the warmth of his body had caused the
acorn to germinate and that he was now some sixty feet
above the ground in the upper branches of a massive
oak. Unable to descend, he faced the situation equably. 'I
cannot,' he observed, 'adapt circumstances to my will:
therefore I shall adapt my will to circumstances. I decide
to remain here.' Which he did.

Rupert Baxter, as he stood before the barred door of Blandings Castle, was very far from imitating this admirable philosopher. To find oneself locked out of a country-house at half-past two in the morning in lemon-coloured pyjamas can never be an unmixedly agreeable experience, and Baxter was a man less fitted by nature to endure it with equanimity than most men. His was a fiery and an arrogant soul, and he seethed in furious rebellion against the intolerable position into which Fate had manoeuvred him. He even went so far as to give the front door a petulant kick. Finding, however, that this hurt his toes and accomplished no useful end, he addressed himself to the task of ascertaining whether there was any way of getting in – short of banging the knocker and rousing the house, a line of action which did not commend itself to him. He made a practice of avoiding as far as possible the ribald type of young man of which the castle was now full, and he had no desire to meet them at this hour in his present costume. He left the front door and proceeded to make a circuit of the castle walls; and his spirits sank even lower. In the Middle Ages, during that stormy period of England's history when walls were built six feet thick and a window was not so much a window as a handy place for pouring molten lead on the heads of visitors, Blandings had been an impregnable fortress. But in all its career it can seldom have looked more of a fortress to anyone than it did now to the Efficient Baxter.

One of the disadvantages of being a man of action, impervious to the softer emotions, is that in moments of trial the beauties of Nature are powerless to soothe the anguished heart. Had Baxter been of a dreamy and poetic temperament he might now have been drawing all sorts of balm from the loveliness of his surroundings. The air was full of the scent of growing things; strange, shy creatures came and went about him as he walked; down in the woods a nightingale had begun to sing; and there was something grandly majestic in the huge bulk of the castle as it towered against the sky. But Baxter had temporarily lost his sense of smell; he feared and disliked the strange, shy creatures; the nightingale left him cold; and the only thought the towering castle inspired in him was that it looked as if a fellow would need half a ton of dynamite to get into it.

Baxter paused. He was back now near the spot from which he had started, having completed two laps without finding any solution of his difficulties. The idea in his mind had been to stand under somebody's window and attract the sleeper's attention with soft, significant whistles. But the first whistle he emitted had sounded to him in the stillness of early morn so like a steam syren that thereafter he had merely uttered timid, mouse-like sounds which the breezes had carried away the moment they crept out. He proposed now to halt for a while and rest his lips before making another attempt. He proceeded to the terrace wall and sat down. The clock over the stables struck three.

To the restless type of thinker like Rupert Baxter, the act of sitting down is nearly always the signal for the brain to begin working with even more than its customary energy. The relaxed body seems to invite thought. And Baxter, having suspended for the moment his physical activities – and glad to do so, for his slippers hurt him – gave himself up to tense speculation as to the hiding-place of Lady Constance Keeble's necklace. From the spot where he now sat he was probably, he reflected, actually in a position to see that hiding-place – if only, when he saw it, he were able to recognize it for what it was. Somewhere out here – in yonder bushes or in some unsuspected hole in yonder tree – the jewels must have been placed. Or . . .

Something seemed to go off inside Baxter like a touched spring. One moment, he was sitting limply, keenly conscious of a blister on the sole of his left foot; the next, regardless of the blister, he was off the wall and racing madly along the terrace in a flurry of flying slippers. Inspiration had come to him.

Day dawns early in the summer months, and already a sort of unhealthy pallor had begun to manifest itself in the sky. It was still far from light, but objects hitherto hidden in the gloom had begun to take on uncertain shape. And among these there had come into the line of Baxter's vision a row of fifteen flower-pots.

There they stood, side by side, round and inviting, each with a geranium in its bed of mould. Fifteen flower-pots. There had originally been sixteen, but Baxter knew nothing of that. All he knew was that he was on the trail.

The quest for buried treasure is one which right through the ages has exercised an irresistible spell over humanity. Confronted with a spot where buried treasure may lurk, men do not stand upon the order of their digging; they go at it with both hands. No solicitude for his employer's geraniums came to hamper Rupert Baxter's researches. To grasp the first flower-pot and tilt out its contents was with him the work of a moment. He scrabbled his fingers through the little pile of mould . . .

Nothing.

A second geranium lay broken on the ground . . .

Nothing.

A third . . .

The Efficient Baxter straightened himself painfully. He was unused to stooping, and his back ached. But physical discomfort was forgotten in the agony of hope frustrated. As he stood there, wiping his forehead with an earth-stained hand, fifteen geranium corpses gazed up at him in the growing light, it seemed with reproach. But Baxter felt no remorse. He included all geraniums, all thieves, and most of the human race in one comprehensive black hatred.

All that Rupert Baxter wanted in this world now was bed. The clock over the stables had just struck four, and he was aware of an overpowering fatigue. Somehow or other, if he had to dig through the walls with his bare hands, he must get into the house. He dragged himself painfully from the scene of carnage and blinked up at the row of silent windows above him. He was past whistling now. He stooped for a pebble, and tossed it up at the nearest window.

Nothing happened. Whoever was sleeping up there continued to sleep. The sky had turned pink, birds were twittering in the ivy, other birds had begun to sing in the bushes. All Nature, in short, was waking – except the unseen sluggard up in that room.

He threw another pebble . . .

It seemed to Rupert Baxter that he had been standing there throwing pebbles through a nightmare eternity. The whole universe had now become concentrated in his efforts to rouse that log-like sleeper; and for a brief instant fatigue left him, driven away by a sort of Berserk fury. And there floated into his mind, as if from some previous existence, a memory of somebody once standing near where he was standing now and throwing a flower-pot in at a window at someone. Who it was that had thrown the thing at whom, he could not at the moment recall; but the outstanding point on which his mind focused itself was the fact that the man had had the right idea. This was no time for pebbles. Pebbles were feeble and inadequate. With one voice the birds, the breezes, the grasshoppers, the whole chorus of Nature waking to another day seemed to shout to him, 'Say it with flower-pots!'

4

The ability to sleep soundly and deeply is the prerogative, as has been pointed out earlier in this straightforward narrative of the simple home-life of the English upper classes, of those who do not think quickly. The Earl of Emsworth, who had not thought quickly since the occasion in the summer of 1874 when he had heard his father's footsteps approaching the stable-loft in which he, a lad of fifteen, sat smoking his first cigar, was an excellent sleeper. He started early and finished late. It was his gentle boast for more than twenty years he had never missed his full eight hours. Generally he managed to get something nearer ten.

But then, as a rule, people did not fling flower-pots through his window at four in the morning.

Even under this unusual handicap, however, he struggled bravely to preserve his record. The first of Baxter's missiles, falling on a settee, produced no change in his regular breathing. The second, which struck the carpet, caused him to stir. It was the third, colliding sharply with his humped back, that definitely woke him. He sat up in bed and stared at the thing.

In the first moment of his waking, relief was, oddly enough, his chief emotion. The blow had roused him from a disquieting dream in which he had been arguing with Angus McAllister about early spring bulbs, and McAllister, worsted verbally, had hit him in the ribs with a spud. Even in his dream Lord Emsworth had been perplexed as to what his next move ought to be; and when he found himself awake and in his bedroom he was at first merely thankful that the necessity for making a decision had at any rate been postponed. Angus McAllister might on some future occasion smite him with a spud, but he had not done it yet.

There followed a period of vague bewilderment. He looked at the flower-pot. It had no message for him.

He had not put it there. He never took flower-pots to bed.
Once, as a child, he had taken a dead pet rabbit, but
never a flower-pot. The whole affair was completely
inscrutable; and his lordship, unable to solve the mystery,
was on the point of taking the statesmanlike course of
going to sleep again, when something large and solid
whizzed through the open window and crashed against
the wall, where it broke, but not into such small
fragments that he could not perceive that in its prime it,
too, had been a flower-pot. And at this moment his eyes
fell on the carpet and then on the settee; and the affair
passed still farther into the realm of the inexplicable.
The Hon. Freddie Threepwood, who had a poor singing-
voice but was a game trier, had been annoying his father
of late by crooning a ballad ending in the words:

> It is not raining at all:
> It's raining vi-o-lets.

It seemed to Lord Emsworth now that matters had gone
a step farther. It was raining flower-pots.

The customary attitude of the Earl of Emsworth
towards all mundane affairs was one of vague detachment;
but this phenomenon was so remarkable that he found
himself stirred to quite a little flutter of excitement and
interest. His brain still refused to cope with the problem
of why anybody should be throwing flower-pots into his
room at this hour – or, indeed, at any hour; but it seemed
a good idea to go and ascertain who this peculiar person
was.

He put on his glasses and hopped out of bed and trotted
to the window. And it was while he was on his way there
that memory stirred in him, as some minutes ago it had
stirred in the Efficient Baxter. He recalled that odd
episode of a few days back, when that delightful girl, Miss
What's-her-name, had informed him that his secretary
had been throwing flower-pots at that poet fellow,

McTodd. He had been annoyed, he remembered, that
Baxter should so far have forgotten himself. Now, he
found himself more frightened than annoyed. Just as
every dog is permitted one bite without having its sanity
questioned, so, if you consider it in a broad-minded way,
may every man be allowed to throw one flower-pot. But
let the thing become a habit, and we look askance. This
strange hobby of his appeared to be growing on Baxter
like a drug, and Lord Emsworth did not like it at all. He
had never before suspected his secretary of an unbalanced
mind, but now he mused, as he tiptoed cautiously to the
window, that the Baxter sort of man, the energetic,
restless type, was just the kind that does go off his head.
Just some such calamity as this, his lordship felt, he might
have foreseen. Day in, day out, Rupert Baxter had been
exercising his brain ever since he had come to the castle
– and now he had gone and sprained it. Lord Emsworth
peeped timidly out from behind the curtain.

His worst fears were realized. It was Baxter sure
enough; and a tousled, wild-eyed Baxter incredibly clad
in lemon-coloured pyjamas.

Lord Emsworth stepped back from the window. He had
seen sufficient. The pyjamas had in some curious way
set the coping-stone on his dismay, and he was now in a
condition approximating to panic. That Baxter should
be so irresistibly impelled by his strange mania as actually
to omit to attire himself decently before going out on
one of these flower-pot-hurling expeditions of his seemed
to make it all so sad and hopeless. The dreamy peer was
no poltroon, but he was past his first youth, and it came
to him very forcibly that the interviewing and pacifying of
secretaries who ran amok was young man's work. He
stole across the room and opened the door. It was his
purpose to put this matter into the hands of an agent.
And so it came about that Psmith was aroused some few
minutes later from slumber by a touch on the arm and

sat up to find his host's pale face peering at him in the weird light of early morning.

'My dear fellow,' quavered Lord Emsworth.

Psmith, like Baxter was a light sleeper; and it was only a moment before he was wide awake and exerting himself to do the courtesies.

'Good morning,' he said pleasantly. 'Will you take a seat?'

'I am extremely sorry to be obliged to wake you, my dear fellow,' said his lordship, 'but the fact of the matter is, my secretary, Baxter, has gone off his head.'

'Much?' inquired Psmith, interested.

'He is out in the garden in his pyjamas, throwing flower-pots through my window.'

'Flower-pots?'

'Flower-pots!'

'Oh, flower-pots!' said Psmith, frowning thoughtfully, as if he had expected it would be something else. 'And what steps are you proposing to take? That is to say,' he went on, 'unless you wish him to continue throwing flower-pots.'

'My dear fellow . . .!'

'Some people like it,' explained Psmith. 'But you do not? Quite so, quite so. I understand perfectly. We all have our likes and dislikes. Well, what would you suggest?'

'I was hoping that you might consent to go down – er – having possibly armed yourself with a good stout stick – and induce him to desist and return to bed.'

'A sound suggestion in which I can see no flaw,' said Psmith approvingly. 'If you will make yourself at home in here – pardon me for issuing invitations to you in your own house – I will see what can be done. I have always found Comrade Baxter a reasonable man, ready to welcome suggestions from outside sources, and I have no doubt that we shall easily be able to reach some arrangement.'

He got out of bed, and, having put on his slippers, and his monocle, paused before the mirror to brush his hair.

'For,' he explained, 'one must be natty when entering the presence of a Baxter.'

He went to the closet and took from among a number of hats a neat Homburg. Then, having selected from a bowl of flowers on the mantelpiece a simple white rose, he pinned it in the coat of his pyjama suit and announced himself ready.

5

The sudden freshet of vicious energy which had spurred the Efficient Baxter on to his recent exhibition of marksmanship had not lasted. Lethargy was creeping back on him even as he stooped to pick up the flower-pot which had found its billet on Lord Emsworth's spine. And, as he stood there after hurling that final missile, he had realized that that was his last shot. If that produced no results, he was finished.

And, as far as he could gather, it had produced no results whatever. No head had popped inquiringly out of the window. No sounds of anybody stirring had reached his ears. The place was as still as if he had been throwing marsh-mallows. A weary sigh escaped from Baxter's lips. And a moment later he was reclining on the ground with his head propped against the terrace, a beaten man.

His eyes closed. Sleep, which he had been denying to himself for so long, would be denied no more. When Psmith arrived, daintily swinging the Hon. Freddie Threepwood's niblick like a clouded cane, he had just begun to snore.

Psmith was a kindly soul. He did not like Rupert Baxter, but that was no reason why he should allow him to continue lying on turf wet with the morning dew, thus courting lumbago and sciatica. He prodded Baxter in the stomach with the niblick, and the secretary sat up, blinking. And with returning consciousness came a burning sense of grievance.

'Well, you've been long enough,' he growled. Then, as he rubbed his red-rimmed eyes and was able to see more clearly, he perceived who it was that had come to his rescue. The spectacle of Psmith of all people beaming benignly down at him was an added offence. 'Oh, it's you?' he said morosely.

'I in person,' said Psmith genially. 'Awake, beloved! Awake, for morning in the bowl of night has flung the stone that puts the stars to flight; and lo! the hunter of the East has caught the Sultan's turret in a noose of light. The Sultan himself,' he added, 'you will find behind yonder window, speculating idly on your motives for bunging flower-pots at him. Why, if I may venture the question, *did* you?'

Baxter was in no confiding mood. Without replying, he rose to his feet and started to trudge wearily along the terrace to the front door. Psmith fell into step beside him.

'If I were you,' said Psmith, 'and I offer the suggestion in the most cordial spirit of goodwill, I would use every effort to prevent this passion for flinging flower-pots from growing upon me. I know you will say that you can take it or leave it alone; that just one more pot won't hurt you; but can you stop at one? Isn't it just that first insidious flower-pot that does all the mischief? Be a man, Comrade Baxter!' He laid his hand appealingly on the secretary's shoulder. 'The next time the craving comes on you, fight it. Fight it! Are you, the heir of the ages, going to become a slave to a habit? Tush! You know and I know that there is better stuff in you than that. Use your will-power, man, use your will-power.'

Whatever reply Baxter might have intended to make to this powerful harangue – and his attitude as he turned

on his companion suggested that he had much to say –
was checked by a voice from above.

'Baxter! My dear fellow!'

The Earl of Emsworth, having observed the secretary's
awakening from the safe observation-post of Psmith's
bedroom, and having noted that he seemed to be
exhibiting no signs of violence, had decided to make his
presence known. His panic had passed, and he wanted to
go into first causes.

Baxter gazed wanly up at the window.

'I can explain everything, Lord Emsworth.'

'What?' said his lordship, leaning farther out.

'I can explain everything,' bellowed Baxter.

'It turns out after all,' said Psmith pleasantly, 'to be
very simple. He was practising for the Jerking The
Geranium event at the next Olympic Games.'

Lord Emsworth adjusted his glasses.

'Your face is dirty,' he said, peering down at his
dishevelled secretary. 'Baxter, my dear fellow, your face
is dirty.'

'I was digging,' replied Baxter sullenly.

'What?'

'Digging!'

'The terrier complex,' explained Psmith. 'What,' he
asked kindly, turning to his companion, 'were you
digging for? Forgive me if the question seems an
impertinent one, but we are naturally curious.'

Baxter hesitated.

'What were you digging for?' asked Lord Emsworth.

'You see,' said Psmith. '*He* wants to know.'

Not for the first time since they had become
associated, a mad feeling of irritation at his employer's
woolly persistence flared up in Rupert Baxter's bosom.
The old ass was always pottering about asking questions.
Fury and want of sleep combined to dull the secretary's
normal prudence. Dimly he realized that he was
imparting Psmith, the scoundrel who he was convinced

was the ringleader of last night's outrage, valuable information; but anything was better than to have to stand here shouting up at Lord Emsworth. He wanted to get it over and go to bed.

'I thought Lady Constance's necklace was in one of the flower-pots,' he shrilled.

'What?'

The secretary's powers of endurance gave out. This maddening inquisition, coming on top of the restless night he had had, was too much for him. With a low moan he made one agonized leap for the front door and passed through it to where beyond these voices there was peace.

Psmith, deprived thus abruptly of his stimulating society, remained for some moments standing near the front door, drinking in with grave approval the fresh scents of the summer morning. It was many years since he had been up and about as early as this, and he had forgotten how delightful the first beginnings of a July day can be. Unlike Baxter, on whose self-centred soul these things had been lost, he revelled in the soft breezes, the singing birds, the growing pinkness of the eastern sky. He awoke at length from his reverie to find that Lord Emsworth had toddled down and was tapping him on the arm.

'*What* did he say?' inquired his lordship. He was feeling like a man who has been cut off in the midst of an absorbing telephone conversation.

'Say?' said Psmith. 'Oh, Comrade Baxter? Now, let me think. What *did* he say?'

'Something about something being in a flower-pot,' prompted his lordship.

'Ah, yes. He said he thought that Lady Constance's necklace was in one of the flower-pots.'

'What!'

Lord Emsworth, it should be mentioned, was not completely in touch with recent happenings in his home. His habit of going early to bed had caused him to miss

the sensational events in the drawing-room: and, as he
was a sound sleeper, the subsequent screams – or, as
Stokes the footman would have said, shrieks – had not
disturbed him. He stared at Psmith, aghast. For a while
the apparent placidity of Baxter had lulled his first
suspicions, but now they returned with renewed force.

'Baxter thought my sister's necklace was in a flower-
pot?' he gasped.

'So I understood him to say.'

'But why should my sister keep her necklace in a
flower-pot?'

'Ah, there you take me into deep waters.'

'The man's mad,' cried Lord Emsworth, his last doubts
removed. 'Stark, staring mad! I thought so before, and
now I'm convinced of it.'

His lordship was no novice in the symptoms of
insanity. Several of his best friends were residing in those
palatial establishments set in pleasant parks and
surrounded by high walls with broken bottles on them,
to which the wealthy and aristocratic are wont to retire
when the strain of modern life becomes too great. And
one of his uncles by marriage, who believed that he was
a loaf of bread, had made his first public statement on
the matter in the smoking-room of this very castle. What
Lord Emsworth did not know about lunatics was not
worth knowing.

'I must get rid of him,' he said. And at the thought the
fair morning seemed to Lord Emsworth to take on a
sudden new beauty. Many a time had he toyed wistfully
with the idea of dismissing his efficient but tyrannical
secretary, but never before had that sickeningly
competent young man given him any reasonable cause
to act. Hitherto, moreover, he had feared his sister's wrath
should he take the plunge. But now . . . Surely even
Connie, pig-headed as she was, could not blame him for
dispensing with the services of a secretary who thought
she kept her necklaces in flower-pots, and went out into

the garden in the early dawn to hurl them at his bedroom window.

His demeanour took on a sudden buoyancy. He hummed a gay air.

'Get rid of him,' he murmured, rolling the blessed words round his tongue. He patted Psmith genially on the shoulder. 'Well, my dear fellow,' he said, 'I suppose we had better be getting back to bed and seeing if we can't get a little sleep.'

Psmith gave a little start. He had been somewhat deeply immersed in thought.

'Do not,' he said courteously, 'let me keep you from the hay if you wish to retire. To me – you know what we poets are – this lovely morning has brought inspiration. I think I will push off to my little nook in the woods, and write a poem about something.'

He accompanied his host up the silent stairs, and they parted with mutual good will at their respective doors. Psmith, having cleared his brain with a hurried cold bath, began to dress.

As a rule, the donning of his clothes was a solemn ceremony over which he dwelt lovingly; but this morning he abandoned his customary leisurely habit. He climbed into his trousers with animation, and lingered but a moment over the tying of his tie. He was convinced that there was that before him which would pay for haste.

Nothing in this world is sadder than the frequency with which we suspect our fellows without just cause. In the happenings of the night before, Psmith had seen the hand of Edward Cootes. Edward Cootes, he considered, had been indulging in what – in another – he would certainly have described as funny business. Like Miss Simmons, Psmith had quickly arrived at the conclusion that the necklace had been thrown out of the drawing-room window by one of those who made up the audience at his reading: and it was his firm belief that it had been picked up and hidden by Mr Cootes. He had been trying to think ever since where that persevering man could have concealed it, and Baxter had provided the clue. But Psmith saw clearer than Baxter. The secretary, having disembowelled fifteen flower-pots and found nothing, had abandoned his theory. Psmith went further, and suspected the existence of a sixteenth. And he proposed as soon as he was dressed to sally downstairs in search of it.

He put on his shoes, and left the room, buttoning his waistcoat as he went.

6

The hands of the clock over the stables were pointing to half-past five when Eve Halliday, tiptoeing furtively, made another descent of the stairs. Her feelings as she went were very different from those which had caused her to jump at every sound when she had started on this same journey three hours earlier. Then, she had been a prowler in the darkness and, as such, a fitting object of suspicion: now, if she happened to run into anybody, she was merely a girl who, unable to sleep, had risen early to take a stroll in the garden. It was a distinction that made all the difference.

Moreover, it covered the facts. She had not been able to sleep – except for an hour when she had dozed off in a chair by her window; and she certainly proposed to take a stroll in the garden. It was her intention to recover the necklace from the place where she had deposited it, and bury it somewhere where no one could possibly find it. There it could lie until she had a chance of meeting and talking to Mr Keeble, and ascertaining what was the next step he wished taken.

Two reasons had led Eve, after making her panic dash back into the house after lurking in the bushes while Baxter patrolled the terrace, to leave her precious flower-pot on the sill of the window beside the front door. She

had read in stories of sensation that for purposes of
concealment the most open place is the best place: and,
secondly, the nearer the front door she put the flower-
pot, the less distance would she have to carry it when
the time came for its removal. In the present excited
conditions of the household, with every guest an amateur
detective, the spectacle of a girl tripping downstairs with
a flower-pot in her arms would excite remark.

Eve felt exhilarated. She was not used to getting only
one hour's sleep in the course of a night, but excitement
and the reflection that she had played a difficult game
and won it against odds bore her up so strongly that she
was not conscious of fatigue: and so uplifted did she feel
that as she reached the landing above the hall she
abandoned her cautious mode of progress and ran down
the remaining stairs. She had the sensation of being in
the last few yards of a winning race.

The hall was quite light now. Every object in it was plainly
visible. There was the huge dinner-gong: there was the
long leather settee: there was the table which she had
upset in the darkness. And there was the sill of the window
by the front door. But the flower-pot which had been on
it was gone.

12 — More on the Flower-pot Theme

In any community in which a sensational crime has recently been committed, the feelings of the individuals who go to make up that community must of necessity vary somewhat sharply according to the degree in which the personal fortunes of each are affected by the outrage. Vivid in their own way as may be the emotions of one who sees a fellow-citizen sand-bagged in a quiet street, they differ in kind from those experienced by the victim himself. And so, though the theft of Lady Constance Keeble's diamond necklace had stirred Blandings Castle to its depths, it had not affected all those present in quite the same way. It left the house-party divided into two distinct schools of thought – the one finding in the occurrence material for gloom and despondency, the other deriving from it nothing but joyful excitement.

To this latter section belonged those free young spirits who had chafed at the prospect of being herded into the drawing-room on the eventful night to listen to Psmith's reading of *Songs of Squalor*. It made them tremble now to think of what they would have missed, had Lady Constance's vigilance relaxed sufficiently to enable them to execute the quiet sneak for the billiard-room of which even at the eleventh hour they had thought so wistfully. As far as the Reggies, Berties, Claudes, and Archies at that moment enjoying Lord Emsworth's hospitality were concerned the thing was top-hole, priceless, and indisputably what the doctor ordered. They spent a great deal of their time going from one country-house to another, and as a rule found the routine

a little monotonous. A happening like that of the previous
night gave a splendid zip to rural life. And when they
reflected that, right on top of this binge, there was coming
the County Ball, it seemed to them that God was in His
heaven and all right with the world. They stuck cigarettes
in long holders, and collected in groups, chattering like
starlings.

The gloomy brigade, those with hearts bowed down,
listened to their effervescent babbling with wan distaste.
These last were a small body numerically, but very select.
Lady Constance might have been described as their head
and patroness. Morning found her still in a state bordering
on collapse. After breakfast, however, which she took
in her room, and which was sweetened by an interview
with Mr Joseph Keeble, her husband, she brightened
considerably. Mr Keeble, thought Lady Constance,
behaved magnificently. She had always loved him
dearly, but never so much as when, abstaining from the
slightest reproach of her obstinacy in refusing to allow
the jewels to be placed in the bank, he spaciously informed
her that he would buy her another necklace, just as good
and costing every penny as much as the old one. It was at
this point that Lady Constance almost seceded from the
ranks of gloom. She kissed Mr Keeble gratefully, and
attacked with something approaching animation the
boiled egg at which she had been pecking when he came
in.

But a few minutes later the average of despair was
restored by the enrolment of Mr Keeble in the ranks of
the despondent. He had gladsomely assumed overnight
that one of his agents, either Eve or Freddie, had been
responsible for the disappearance of the necklace. The
fact that Freddie, interviewed by stealth in his room,
gapingly disclaimed any share in the matter had not
damped him. He had never expected results from
Freddie. But when, after leaving Lady Constance, he
encountered Eve and was given a short outline of history,

639

beginning with her acquisition of the necklace, and
ending – like a modern novel – on the sombre note of
her finding the flower-pot gone, he too sat him down and
mourned as deeply as anyone.

Passing with a brief mention over Freddie, whose
morose bearing was the subject of considerable comment
among the younger set; over Lord Emsworth, who woke
at twelve o'clock disgusted to find that he had missed
several hours among his beloved flower-beds; and over
the Efficient Baxter, who was roused from sleep at
twelve-fifteen by Thomas the footman knocking on his
door in order to hand him a note from his employer
enclosing a cheque, and dispensing with his services; we
come to Miss Peavey.

At twenty minutes past eleven on this morning when
so much was happening to so many people, Miss Peavey
stood in the Yew Alley gazing belligerently at the stemless
mushroom finial of a tree about half-way between the
entrance and the point where the alley merged into
the west wood. She appeared to be soliloquizing. For,
though words were proceeding from her with
considerable rapidity, there seemed to be no-one in sight
to whom they were being addressed. Only an
exceptionally keen observer would have noted a slight
significant quivering among the tree's tightly-woven
branches.

'You poor bone-headed fish,' the poetess was saying
with that strained tenseness which results from the
churning up of a generous and emotional nature, 'isn't
there anything in this world you can do without
tumbling over your feet and making a mess of it? All I
ask of you is to stroll under a window and pick up a few
jewels, and now you come and tell me . . .'

'But, Liz!' said the tree plaintively.

'I do all the difficult part of the job. All that there was
left for you to handle was something a child of three
could have done on its ear. And now . . .'

'But, Liz! I'm telling you I couldn't find the stuff. I was down there all right, but I couldn't find it.'

'You couldn't find it!' Miss Peavey pawed restlessly at the soft turf with a shapely shoe. 'You're the sort of dumb Isaac that couldn't find a bass-drum in a telephone booth. You didn't *look*!'

'I did look. Honest, I did.'

'Well, the stuff was there. I threw it down the moment the lights went out.'

'Somebody must have got there first, and swiped it.'

'Who could have got there first? Everybody was up in the room where I was.'

'Are you sure.'

'Am I sure? Am I . . .' The poetess's voice trailed off. She was staring down the Yew Alley at a couple who had just entered. She hissed a warning in a sharp undertone. 'Hsst! Cheese it, Ed. There's someone coming.'

The two intruders who had caused Miss Peavey to suspend her remarks to her erring lieutenant were of opposite sexes – a tall girl with fair hair, and a taller young man irreproachably clad in white flannels who beamed down at his companion through a single eye-glass. Miss Peavey gazed at them searchingly as they approached. A sudden thought had come to her at the sight of them. Mistrusting Psmith as she had done ever since Mr Cootes had unmasked him for the imposter that he was, the fact that they were so often together had led her to extend her suspicion to Eve. It might, of course, be nothing but a casual friendship, begun here at the castle; but Miss Peavey had always felt that Eve would bear watching. And now, seeing them together again this morning, it had suddenly come to her that she did not recall having observed Eve among the gathering in the drawing-room last night. True, there had been many people present, but Eve's appearance was striking, and she was sure that she would have noticed her, if she had been there. And, if she had not been there, why should she not have been on the terrace? Somebody had been on the terrace last night, that was certain. For all her censorious attitude in their recent conversation, Miss Peavey had not really in her heart believed that even a dumb-bell like Eddie Cootes would not have found the necklace if it had been lying under the window on his arrival.

'Oh, good morning, Mr McTodd,' she cooed. 'I'm feeling *so* upset about this terrible affair. Aren't *you*, Miss Halliday?'

'Yes,' said Eve, and she had never said a more truthful word.

Psmith, for his part, was in more debonair and cheerful mood even than was his wont. He had examined the position of affairs and found life good. He was particularly pleased with the fact that he had persuaded Eve to stroll with him this morning and inspect his cottage in the woods. Buoyant as was his temperament, he had been half afraid that last night's interview on the terrace might have had disastrous effects on their intimacy. He was now feeling full of kindliness and goodwill towards all mankind – even Miss Peavey; and he bestowed on the poetess a dazzling smile.

'We must always,' he said, 'endeavour to look on the bright side. It was a pity, no doubt, that my reading last night had to be stopped at a cost of about twenty thousand pounds to the Keeble coffers, but let us not forget that but for that timely interruption I should have gone on for about another hour. I am like that. My friends have frequently told me that when once I start talking it requires something in the nature of a cataclysm to stop me. But, of course, there are drawbacks to everything, and last night's rannygazoo perhaps shook your nervous system to some extent?'

'I was dreadfully frightened,' said Miss Peavey. She turned to Eve with a delicate shiver. 'Weren't *you*, Miss Halliday?'

'I wasn't there,' said Eve absently.

'Miss Halliday,' explained Psmith, 'has had in the last few days some little experience of myself as orator, and with her usual good sense decided not to go out of her way to get more of me than was absolutely necessary. I was perhaps a trifle wounded at the moment, but on thinking it over came to the conclusion that she was perfectly justified in her attitude. I endeavour always in my conversation to instruct, elevate, and entertain, but there is no gainsaying the fact that a purist might consider enough of my chit-chat to be sufficient. Such, at any rate, was Miss Halliday's view, and I honour her for it. But here I am, rambling on again just when I can see that you wish to be alone. We will leave you, therefore, to muse. No doubt we have been interrupting a train of thought which would have resulted but for my arrival in a rondel or a ballade or some other poetic morceau. Come, Miss Halliday. A weird and repellent female,' he said to Eve as they drew out of hearing, 'created for some purpose which I cannot fathom. Everything in this world, I like to think, is placed there for some useful end: but why the authorities unleashed Miss Peavey on us is beyond me. It is not too much to say that she gives me a pain in the gizzard.'

Miss Peavey, unaware of these harsh views, had watched them out of sight, and now she turned excitedly to the tree which sheltered her ally.

'Ed!'

'Hello?' replied the muffled voice of Mr Cootes.

'Did you hear?'

'No.'

'Oh, my heavens!' cried his overwrought partner. 'He's gone deaf now! That girl – you didn't hear what she was saying? She said that she wasn't in the drawing-room when those lights went out. Ed, she was down below on the terrace, that's where she was, picking up the stuff. And if it isn't hidden somewheres in that McTodd's

shack down there in the woods I'll eat my Sunday
rubbers.'

Eve, with Psmith prattling amiably at her side, pursued
her way through the wood. She was wondering why she
had come. She ought, she felt, to have been very cold and
distant to this young man after what had occurred
between them last night. But somehow it was difficult to
be cold and distant with Psmith. He cheered her stricken
soul. By the time they reached the little clearing and came
in sight of the squat, shed-like building with its funny
windows and stained door, her spirits, always mercurial,
had risen to a point where she found herself almost able
to forget her troubles.

'What a horrible-looking place!' she exclaimed.
'Whatever did you want it for?'

'Purely as a nook,' said Psmith, taking out his key.
'You know how the man of sensibility and refinement
needs a nook. In this rushing age it is imperative that the
thinker shall have a place, however humble, where he can
be alone.'

'But you aren't a thinker.'

'You wrong me. For the last few days I have been doing
some extremely brisk thinking. And the strain has taken
its toll. The fierce whirl of life at Blandings is wearing me
away. There are dark circles under my eyes and I see
floating spots.' He opened the door. 'Well, here we are.
Will you pop in for a moment?'

Eve went in. The single sitting-room of the cottage
certainly bore out the promise of the exterior. It
contained a table with a red cloth, a chair, three stuffed
birds in a glass case on the wall, and a small horsehair
sofa. A depressing musty scent pervaded the place, as if a
cheese had recently died there in painful circumstances.
Eve gave a little shiver of distaste.

'I understand your silent criticism,' said Psmith. 'You
are saying to yourself that plain living and high thinking
is evidently the ideal of the gamekeepers on the Blandings

estate. They are strong, rugged men who care little for
the refinements of interior decoration. But shall we blame
them? If I had to spend most of the day and night
chivvying poachers and keeping an eye on the local
rabbits, I imagine that in my off-hours practically
anything with a roof would satisfy me. It was in the hope
that you might be able to offer some hints and
suggestions for small improvements here and there that
I invited you to inspect my little place. There is no doubt
that it wants doing up a bit, by a woman's gentle hand.
Will you take a look round and give out a few ideas? The
wall-paper is, I fear, a fixture, but in every other direction
consider yourself untrammelled.'

Eve looked about her.

'Well,' she began dubiously, 'I don't think . . .'

She stopped abruptly, tingling all over. A second glance
had shown her something which her first careless
inspection had overlooked. Half hidden by a ragged
curtain, there stood on the window-sill a large flower-
pot containing a geranium. And across the surface of the
flower-pot was a broad splash of white paint.

'You were saying . . . ?' said Psmith courteously.

Eve did not reply. She hardly heard him. Her mind was
in a confused whirl. A monstrous suspicion was forming
itself in her brain.

'You are admiring the shrub?' said Psmith. 'I found it
lying about up at the castle this morning and pinched
it. I thought it would add a touch of colour to the place.'

Eve, looking at him keenly as his gaze shifted to the
flower-pot, told herself that her suspicion had been
absurd. Surely this blandness could not be a cloak for
guilt.

'Where did you find it?'

'By one of the windows in the hall, more or less wasting
its sweetness. I am bound to say I am a little disappointed
in the thing. I had a sort of idea it would turn the old
homestead into a floral bower, but it doesn't seem to.'

'It's a beautiful geranium.'

'There,' said Psmith, 'I cannot agree with you. It seems to me to have the glanders or something.'

'It only wants watering.'

'And unfortunately this cosy little place appears to possess no water supply. I take it that the late proprietor when in residence used to trudge to the back door of the castle and fetch what he needed in a bucket. If this moribund plant fancies that I am going to spend my time racing to and fro with refreshments, it is vastly mistaken. Tomorrow it goes into the dustbin.'

Eve shut her eyes. She was awed by a sense of having arrived at a supreme moment. She had the sensations of a gambler who risks all on a single throw.

'What a shame!' she said, and her voice, though she tried to control it, shook. 'You had better give it to me. I'll take care of it. It's just what I want for my room.'

'Pray take it,' said Psmith. 'It isn't mine, but pray take it. And very encouraging it is, let me add, that you should be accepting gifts from me in this hearty fashion; for it is well known that there is no surer sign of the dawning of the divine emotion – love,' he explained, 'than this willingness to receive presents from the hands of the adorer. I make progress, I make progress.'

'You don't do anything of the kind,' said Eve. Her eyes were sparkling and her heart sang within her. In the revulsion of feeling which had come to her on finding her suspicions unfounded she was aware of a warm friendliness towards this absurd young man.

'Pardon me,' said Psmith firmly. 'I'm quoting an established authority – Auntie Bell of *Home Gossip*.'

'I must be going,' said Eve. She took the flower-pot and hugged it to her. 'I've got work to do.'

'Work, work, always work!' sighed Psmith. 'The curse of the age. Well, I will escort you back to your cell.'

'No, you won't,' said Eve. 'I mean, thank you for your polite offer, but I want to be alone.'

646

'Alone?' Psmith looked at her, astonished. 'When you have the chance of being with *me*? This is a strange attitude.'

'Good-bye,' said Eve. 'Thank you for being so hospitable and lavish. I'll try to find some cushions and muslin and stuff to brighten up this place.'

'Your presence does that adequately,' said Psmith, accompanying her to the door. 'By the way, returning to the subject we were discussing last night, I forgot to mention, when asking you to marry me, that I can do card-tricks.'

'Really?'

'And also a passable imitation of a cat calling to her young. Has this no weight with you? Think! These things come in very handy in the long winter evenings.'

'But I shan't be there when you are imitating cats in the long winter evenings.'

'I think you are wrong. As I visualize my little home, I can see you there very clearly, sitting before the fire. Your maid has put you into something loose. The light of the flickering flames reflects itself in your lovely eyes. You are pleasantly tired after an afternoon's shopping, but not so tired as to be unable to select a card – *any* card – from the pack which I offer . . .'

'Good-bye,' said Eve.

'If it must be so – good-bye. For the present. I shall see you anon?'

'I expect so.'

'Good! I will count the minutes.'

Eve walked rapidly away. As she snuggled the flower-pot under her arm she was feeling like a child about to open its Christmas stocking. Before she had gone far, a shout stopped her and she perceived Psmith galloping gracefully in her wake.

'Can you spare me a moment?' said Psmith.

'Certainly.'

'I should have added that I can also recite "Gunga Din." Will you think that over?'

'I will.'

'Thank you,' said Psmith. 'Thank you. I have a feeling that it may just turn the scale.'

He raised his hat ambassadorially and galloped away again.

Eve found herself unable to wait any longer. Psmith was out of sight now, and the wood was very still and empty. Birds twittered in the branches, and the sun made little pools of gold upon the ground. She cast a swift glance about her and crouched down in the shelter of a tree.

The birds stopped singing. The sun no longer shone. The wood had become cold and sinister. For Eve, with a heart of lead, was staring blankly at a little pile of mould at her feet; mould which she had sifted again and again in a frenzied, fruitless effort to find a necklace which was not there.

The empty flower-pot seemed to leer up at her in mockery.

13 — Psmith Receives Guests

Blandings Castle was astir from roof to hall. Lights blazed, voices shouted, bells rang. All over the huge building there prevailed a vast activity like that of a barracks on the eve of the regiment's departure for abroad. Dinner was over, and the Expeditionary Force was making its final preparations before starting off in many motor-cars for the County Ball at Shiffey. In the bedrooms on every floor, Reggies, doubtful at the last moment about their white ties, were feverishly arranging new ones; Berties brushed their already glistening hair; and Claudes shouted to Archies along the passages insulting inquiries as to whether they had been sneaking their handkerchiefs. Valets skimmed like swallows up and down corridors, maids fluttered in and out of rooms in aid of Beauty in distress. The noise penetrated into every nook and corner of the house. It vexed the Efficient Baxter, going through his papers in the library preparatory to leaving Blandings on the morrow for ever. It disturbed Lord Emsworth, who, stoutly declining to go within ten miles of the County Ball, had retired to his room with a book on Herbaceous Borders. It troubled the peace of Beach the butler, refreshing himself after his activities around the dinner table with a glass of sound port in the housekeeper's room. The only person in the place who paid no attention to it was Eve Halliday.

Eve was too furious to pay attention to anything but her deleterious thoughts. As she walked on the terrace, to which she had fled in quest of solitude, her teeth were set and her blue eyes glowed belligerently. As Miss Peavey would have put it in one of her colloquial moods, she was mad clear through. For Eve was a girl of spirit, and there is nothing your girl of spirit so keenly resents as being made a fool of, whether it be by Fate or by a fellow human creature. Eve was in the uncomfortable position of having had this indignity put upon her by both. But, while as far as Fate was concerned she merely smouldered rebelliously, her animosity towards Psmith was vivid in the extreme.

A hot wave of humiliation made her writhe as she remembered the infantile guilelessness with which she had accepted the preposterous story he had told her in explanation of his presence at Blandings in another man's name. He had been playing with her all the time – fooling her – and, most unforgivable crime of all, he had dared to pretend that he was fond of her and – Eve's face burned again – to make her – almost fond of him. How he must have laughed . . .

Well, she was not beaten yet. Her chin went up and she began to walk quicker. He was clever, but she would be cleverer. The game was not over . . .

'Hallo!'

A white waistcoat was gleaming at her side. Polished shoes shuffled on the turf. Light hair, brushed and brilliantined to the last possible pitch of perfection, shone in the light of the stars. The Hon. Freddie Threepwood was in her midst.

'Well, Freddie?' said Eve resignedly.

'I say,' said Freddie in a voice in which self-pity fought with commiseration for her. 'Beastly shame you aren't coming to the hop.'

'I don't mind.'

'But I do, dash it! The thing won't be anything without you. A bally wash-out. And I've been trying out some new steps with the Victrola.'

'Well, there will be plenty of other girls there for you to step on.'

'I don't *want* other girls, dash them. I want you.'

'That's very nice of you,' said Eve. The first truculence of her manner had softened. She reminded herself, as she had so often been obliged to remind herself before, that Freddie meant well. 'But it can't be helped. I'm only an employee here, not a guest. I'm not invited.'

'I know,' said Freddie. 'And that's what makes it so dashed sickening. It's like that picture I saw once, "A Modern Cinderella". Only there the girl nipped off to the dance – disguised, you know – and had a most topping time. I wish life was a bit more like the movies.'

'Well, it was enough like the movies last night when . . . Oh!'

Eve stopped. Her heart gave a sudden jump. Somehow the presence of Freddie was so inextricably associated in her mind with limp proposals of marriage that she had completely forgotten that there was another and a more dashing side to his nature, that side which Mr Keeble had revealed to her at their meeting in Market Blandings on the previous afternoon. She looked at him with new eyes.

'Anything up?' said Freddie.

Eve took him excitedly by the sleeve and drew him farther away from the house. Not that there was any need to do so, for the bustle within continued unabated.

'Freddie,' she whispered, 'listen! I met Mr Keeble yesterday after I had left you, and he told me all about how you and he had planned to steal Lady Constance's necklace.'

'Good Lord!' cried Freddie, and leaped like a stranded fish.

'And I've got an idea,' said Eve.

She had, and it was one which had only in this instant come to her. Until now, though she had tilted her chin bravely and assured herself that the game was not over and that she was not yet beaten, a small discouraging voice had whispered to her all the while that this was mere bravado. What, the voice had asked, are you going to do? And she had not been able to answer it. But now, with Freddie as an ally, she could act.

'Told you all about it?' Freddie was muttering pallidly. He had never had a very high opinion of his Uncle Joseph's mentality, but he had supposed him capable of keeping a thing like that to himself. He was, indeed, thinking of Mr Keeble almost the identical thoughts which Mr Keeble in the first moments of his interview with Eve in Market Blandings had thought of him. And these reflections brought much the same qualms which they had brought to the elder conspirator. Once these things got talked about, mused Freddie agitatedly, you never knew where they would stop. Before his mental eye there swam a painful picture of his Aunt Constance, informed of the plot, tackling him and demanding the return of her necklace. 'Told you all about it?' he bleated, and, like Mr Keeble, mopped his brow.

'It's all right,' said Eve impatiently. 'It's quite all right. He asked me to steal the necklace, too.'

'You?' said Freddie, gaping.

'Yes.'

'My Gosh!' cried Freddie, electrified 'Then was it you who got the thing last night?'

'Yes it was. But . . .'

For a moment Freddie had to wrestle with something that was almost a sordid envy. Then better feelings prevailed. He quivered with manly generosity. He gave Eve's hand a tender pat. It was too dark for her to see it, but he was registering renunciation.

'Little girl,' he murmured, 'there's no one I'd rather got that thousand quid than you. If I couldn't have it myself, I mean to say. Little girl . . .'

'Oh, be quiet!' cried Eve. 'I wasn't doing it for any thousand pounds. I didn't want Mr Keeble to give me money . . .'

'You didn't want him to give you money!' repeated Freddie wonderingly.

'I just wanted to help Phyllis. She's my friend.'

'Pals, pardner, pals! Pals till hell freezes!' cried Freddie, deeply moved.

'What *are* you talking about?'

'Sorry. That was a sub-title from a thing called "Prairie Nell", you know. Just happened to cross my mind. It was in the second reel where the two fellows are . . .'

'Yes, yes; never mind.'

'Thought I'd mention it.'

'Tell me . . .'

'It seemed to fit in.'

'Do *stop*, Freddie!'

'Right-ho!'

'Tell me,' resumed Eve, 'is Mr McTodd going to the ball?'

'Eh? Why, yes, I suppose so.'

'Then, listen. You know that little cottage your father has let him have!'

'Little cottage?'

'Yes. In the wood past the Yew Alley.'

'Little cottage? I never heard of any little cottage.'

'Well, he's got one,' said Eve. 'And as soon as everybody has gone to the ball you and I are going to burgle it.'

'What!'

'Burgle it!'

'Burgle it?'

'Yes, *burgle* it!'

Freddie gulped.

'Look here, old thing,' he said plaintively. 'This is a bit beyond me. It doesn't seem to me to make sense.'

Eve forced herself to be patient. After all, she reflected, perhaps she had been approaching the matter a little rapidly. The desire to beat Freddie violently over the head passed, and she began to speak slowly, and, as far as she could manage it, in words of one syllable.

'I can make it quite clear if you will listen and not say a word till I've done. This man who calls himself McTodd is not Mr McTodd at all. He is a thief who got into the place by saying that he was McTodd. He stole the jewels from me last night and hid them in his cottage.'

'But, I say!'

'Don't interrupt. I know he has them there, so when he has gone to the ball and the coast is clear you and I will go and search till we find them.'

'But, I say!'

Eve crushed down her impatience once more.

'Well!'

'Do you really think this cove has got the necklace?'

'I know he has.'

'Well, then, it's jolly well the best thing that could possibly have happened, because I got him here to pinch it for Uncle Joseph.'

'What!'

'Absolutely. You see, I began to have a doubt or two as to whether I was quite equal to the contract, so I roped in this bird by way of a gang.'

'You got him here? You mean you sent for him and arranged that he should pass himself off as Mr McTodd?'

'Well, no, not exactly that. He was coming here as McTodd anyway, as far as I can gather. But I'd talked it over with him, you know, before that and asked him to pinch the necklace.'

'Then you know him quite well? He is a friend of yours?'

'I wouldn't say that exactly. But he said he was a great pal of Phyllis and her husband.'

'Did he tell you that?'

'Absolutely!'

'When?'

'In the train.'

'I mean, was it before or after you had told him why you wanted the necklace stolen?'

'Eh? Let me think. After.'

'You're sure?'

'Yes.'

'Tell me exactly what happened,' said Eve. 'I can't understand it at all at present.'

Freddie marshalled his thoughts.

'Well, let's see. Well, to start with, I told Uncle Joe I would pinch the necklace and slip it to him, and he said if I did he'd give me a thousand quid. As a matter of fact, he made it two thousand, and very decent of him, I thought it. Is that straight?'

'Yes.'

'Then I sort of got cold feet. Began to wonder, don't you know, if I hadn't bitten off rather more than I could chew.'

'Yes.'

'And then I saw this advertisement in the paper.'

'Advertisement? What advertisement?'

'There was an advertisement in the paper saying if anybody wanted anything done simply apply to this chap. So I wrote him a letter and went up and had a talk with him in the lobby of the Piccadilly Palace. Only, unfortunately, I'd promised the guv'nor I'd catch the twelve-fifty home, so I had to dash off in the middle. Must have thought me rather an ass, it's sometimes occurred to me since. I mean, practically all I said was, "Will you pinch my aunt's necklace?" and then buzzed off to catch the train. Never thought I'd see the man again, but when I got into the five o'clock train – I missed the twelve-fifty – there he was, as large as life, and the guv'nor suddenly trickled in from another compartment and introduced him to me as McTodd the poet. Then the guv'nor legged it, and this chap told me he wasn't really McTodd, only pretending to be McTodd.'

'Didn't that strike you as strange?'

'Yes, rather rummy.'

'Did you ask him why he was doing such an extraordinary thing?'

'Oh, yes. But he wouldn't tell me. And then he asked

655

me why I wanted him to pinch Aunt Connie's necklace,
and it suddenly occurred to me that everything was
working rather smoothly – I mean, him being on his way
to the castle like that. Right on the spot, don't you know.
So I told him all about Phyllis, and it was then that he said
that he had been a pal of hers and her husband's for years.
So we fixed it up that he was to get the necklace and hand
it over. I must say I was rather drawn to the chappie. He
said he didn't want any money for swiping the thing.'

Eve laughed bitterly.

'Why should he, when he was going to get twenty
thousand pounds' worth of diamonds and keep them? Oh,
Freddie, I should have thought that even you would have
seen through him. You go to this perfect stranger and
tell him that there is a valuable necklace waiting here to
be stolen, you find him on his way to steal it, and you
trust him implicitly just because he tells you he knows
Phyllis – whom he had never heard of in his life till you
mentioned her. Freddie, really!'

The Hon. Freddie scratched his beautifully shaven
chin.

'Well, when you put it like that,' he said, 'I must own
it does sound a bit off. But he seemed such a dashed
matey sort of bird. Cheery and all that. I liked the feller.'

'What nonsense!'

'Well, but you liked him, too. I mean to say, you were
about with him a goodish lot.'

'I hate him!' said Eve angrily. 'I wish I had never seen
him. And if I let him get away with that necklace and
cheat poor little Phyllis out of her money, I'll – I'll . . .'

She raised a grimly determined chin to the stars.
Freddie watched her admiringly.

'I say, you know, you are a wonderful girl,' he said.

'He *shan't* get away with it, if I have to pull the place
down.'

'When you chuck your head up like that you remind
me a bit of What's-her-name, the Famous Players star –

you know, girl who was in "Wed to A Satyr". Only,' added Freddie hurriedly, 'she isn't half so pretty. I say, I was rather looking forward to that County Ball, but now this has happened I don't mind missing it a bit. I mean, it seems to draw us closer together somehow, if you follow me. I say, honestly, all kidding aside, you think that love might some day awaken in . . .'

'We shall want a lamp, of course,' said Eve.

'Eh?'

'A lamp – to see with when we are in the cottage. Can you get one?'

Freddie reluctantly perceived that the moment for sentiment had not arrived.

'A lamp? Oh, yes, of course. Rather.'

'Better get two,' said Eve. 'And meet me here about half an hour after everybody has gone to the ball.'

2

The tiny sitting-room of Psmith's haven of rest in the woods had never reached a high standard of decorativeness even in its best days; but as Eve paused from her labours and looked at it in the light of her lamp about an hour after her conversation with Freddie on the terrace, it presented a picture of desolation which would have startled the plain-living gamekeeper to whom it had once been a home. Even Freddie, though normally an unobservant youth, seemed awed by the ruin he had helped to create.

'Golly!' he observed. 'I say, we've rather mucked the place up a bit!'

It was no over-statement. Eve had come to the cottage to search, and she had searched thoroughly. The torn carpet lay in an untidy heap against the wall. The table was overturned. Boards had been wrenched from the floor, bricks from the chimney-place. The horsehair sofa was in ribbons, and the one small cushion in the room lay limply in a corner, its stuffing distributed north, south, east and west. There was soot everywhere – on the walls, on the floor, on the fireplace, and on Freddie. A brace of dead bats, the further result of the latter's groping in a chimney which had not been swept for seven months, reposed in the fender. The sitting-room had never been luxurious; it was now not even cosy.

Eve did not reply. She was struggling with what she was fair-minded enough to see was an entirely unjust fever of irritation, with her courteous and obliging assistant as its object. It was wrong, she knew, to feel like this. That she should be furious at her failure to find the jewels was excusable, but she had no possible right to be furious with Freddie. It was not his fault that soot had poured from the chimney in lieu of diamonds. If he had asked for a necklace and been given a dead bat, he was surely more to be pitied than censured. Yet Eve, eyeing his grimy face, would have given very much to have been able to scream loudly and throw something at him. The fact was, the Hon. Freddie belonged to that unfortunate type of humanity which automatically gets blamed for everything in moments of stress.

'Well, the bally thing isn't here,' said Freddie. He spoke thickly, as a man will whose mouth is covered with soot.

'I know it isn't,' said Eve. 'But this isn't the only room in the house.'

'Think he might have hidden the stuff upstairs?'

'Or downstairs.'

Freddie shook his head, dislodging a portion of a third bat.

'Must be upstairs, if it's anywhere. Mean to say, there isn't any downstairs.'

'There's the cellar,' said Eve. 'Take your lamp and go and have a look.'

For the first time in the proceedings a spirit of disaffection seemed to manifest itself in the bosom of her assistant. Up till this moment Freddie had taken his orders placidly and executed them with promptness and civility. Even when the first shower of soot had driven him choking from the fire-place, his manly spirit had not been crushed; he had merely uttered a startled 'Oh, I say!' and returned gallantly to the attack. But now he obviously hesitated.

'Go on,' said Eve impatiently.

'Yes, but, I say, you know . . .'

'What's the matter?'

'I don't think the chap would be likely to hide a necklace in the cellar. I vote we give it a miss and try upstairs.'

'Don't be silly, Freddie. He may have hidden it anywhere.'

'Well, to be absolutely honest, I'd much rather not go into any bally cellar, if it's all the same to you.'

'Why ever not?'

'Beetles. Always had a horror of beetles. Ever since I was a kid.'

Eve bit her lip. She was feeling, as Miss Peavey had so often felt when associated in some delicate undertaking with Edward Cootes, that exasperating sense of man's inadequacy which comes to high-spirited girls at moments such as these. To achieve the end for which she had started out that night she would have waded waist-high through a sea of beetles. But, divining with that sixth sense which tells women when the male has been pushed just so far and can be pushed no farther, that Freddie, wax though he might be in her hands in any other circumstances, was on this one point adamant, she made no further effort to bend him to her will.

'All right,' she said. 'I'll go down into the cellar. You go and look upstairs.'

'No. I say, sure you don't mind?'

Eve took up her lamp and left the craven.

For a girl of iron resolution and unswerving purpose, Eve's

inspection of the cellar was decidedly cursory. A distinct feeling of relief came over her as she stood at the top of the steps and saw by the light of the lamp how small and bare it was. For, impervious as she might be to the intimidation of beetles, her armour still contained a chink. She was terribly afraid of rats. And even when the rays of the lamp disclosed no scuttling horrors, she still lingered for a moment before descending. You never knew with rats. They pretend not to be there just to lure you on, and then came out and whizzed about your ankles. However, the memory of her scorn for Freddie's pusillanimity forced her on, and she went down.

The word 'cellar' is an elastic one. It can be applied equally to the acres of bottle-fringed vaults which lie beneath a great pile like Blandings Castle and to a hole in the ground like the one in which she now found herself. This cellar was easily searched. She stamped on its stone flags with an ear strained to detect any note of hollowness, but none came. She moved the lamp so that it shone into every corner, but there was not even a crack in which a diamond necklace could have been concealed. Satisfied that the place contained nothing but a little coal-dust and a smell of damp decay, Eve passed thankfully out.

The law of elimination was doing its remorseless work. It had ruled out the cellar, the kitchen, and the living-room – that is to say, the whole of the lower of the two floors which made up the cottage. There now remained only the rooms upstairs. There were probably not more than two, and Freddie must already have searched one of these. The quest seemed to be nearing its end. As Eve made for the narrow staircase that led to the second floor, the lamp shook in her hand and cast weird shadows. Now that success was in sight, the strain was beginning to affect her nerves.

It was to nerves that in the first instant of hearing it she attributed what sounded like a soft cough in the sitting-room, a few feet from where she stood. Then a chill feeling of dismay gripped her. It could only, she thought, be Freddie, returned from his search; and if Freddie had returned from his search already, what could it mean except that those upstairs rooms, on which she had counted so confidently, had proved as empty as the others? Freddie was not one of your restrained, unemotional men. If he had found the necklace he would have been downstairs in two bounds, shouting. His silence was ominous. She opened the door and went quickly in.

'Freddie,' she began, and broke off with a gasp.

It was not Freddie who had coughed. It was Psmith. He was seated on the remains of the horsehair sofa, toying with an automatic pistol and gravely surveying through his monocle the ruins of a home.

3

'Good evening,' said Psmith.

It was not for a philosopher like himself to display astonishment. He was, however, undeniably feeling it. When, a few minutes before, he had encountered Freddie in this same room, he had received a distinct shock; but a rough theory which would account for Freddie's presence in his home-from-home he had been able to work out. He groped in vain for one which would explain Eve.

Mere surprise, however, was never enough to prevent Psmith talking. He began at once.

'It was nice of you,' he said, rising courteously, 'to look in. Won't you sit down? On the sofa, perhaps? Or would you prefer a brick?'

Eve was not yet equal to speech. She had been so firmly convinced that he was ten miles away at Shiffey that his presence here in the sitting-room of the cottage had something of the breath-taking quality of a miracle. The explanation, if she could have known it, was simple. Two excellent reasons had kept Psmith from gracing the County Ball with his dignified support. In the first place, as Shiffey was only four miles from the village where he had spent most of his life, he had regarded it as probable, if not certain, that he would have encountered there old friends to whom it would have been both tedious and embarrassing to explain why he had changed his name to McTodd. And secondly, though he had not actually anticipated a nocturnal raid on his little nook, he had thought it well to be on the premises that evening in case Mr Edward Cootes should have been getting ideas into his head. As soon, therefore, as the castle had emptied itself and the wheels of the last car had passed away down the drive, he had pocketed Mr Cootes's revolver and proceeded to the cottage.

Eve recovered her self-possession. She was not a girl given to collapse in moments of crisis. The first shock of amazement had passed; a humiliating feeling of extreme foolishness, which came directly after, had also passed; she was now grimly ready for battle.

'Where is Mr Threepwood?' she asked.

'Upstairs. I have put him in storage for a while. Do not worry about Comrade Threepwood. He has lots to think about. He is under the impression that if he stirs out he will be instantly shot.'

'Oh? Well, I want to put this lamp down. Will you please pick up that table?'

'By all means. But – I am a novice in these matters – ought I not first to say "Hands up!" or something?'

'Will you please pick up that table?'

'A friend of mine – one Cootes – you must meet him some time – generally remarks "Hey!" in a sharp, arresting voice on these occasions. Personally I consider the expression too abrupt. Still, he has had great experience . . .'

'Will you please pick up that table?'

'Most certainly. I take it, then, that you would prefer to dispense with the usual formalities. In that case, I will park this revolver on the mantelpiece while we chat. I have taken a curious dislike to the thing. It makes me feel like Dangerous Dan McGrew.'

Eve put down the lamp, and there was silence for a moment. Psmith looked about him thoughtfully. He picked up one of the dead bats and covered it with his handkerchief.

'Somebody's mother,' he murmured reverently.

Eve sat down on the sofa.

'Mr . . .' She stopped. 'I can't call you Mr McTodd. Will you please tell me your name?'

'Ronald,' said Psmith. 'Ronald Eustace.'

'I suppose you have a surname?' snapped Eve. 'Or an alias?'

Psmith eyed her with a pained expression.

'I may be hyper-sensitive,' he said, 'but that last remark sounded to me like a dirty dig. You seem to imply that I am some sort of criminal.'

Eve laughed shortly.

'I'm sorry if I hurt your feelings. There's not much sense in pretending now, is there? What is your name?'

'Psmith. The p is silent.'

'Well, Mr Smith, I imagine you understand why I am here?'

'I took it for granted that you had come to fulfil your kindly promise of doing the place up a bit. Will you be wounded if I say frankly that I preferred it the way it was before? All this may be the last word in ultra-modern interior decoration, but I suppose I am old-fashioned. The whisper flies round Shropshire and adjoining counties, "Psmith is hide-bound. He is not attuned to up-to-date methods." Honestly, don't you think you have rather unduly stressed the bizarre note? This soot . . . these dead bats . . .'

'I have come to get that necklace.'

663

'Ah! The necklace!'

'I'm going to get it, too.'

Psmith shook his head gently.

'There,' he said, 'if you will pardon me, I take issue with you. There is nobody to whom I would rather give that necklace than you, but there are special circumstances connected with it which render such an action impossible. I fancy, Miss Halliday, that you have been misled by your young friend upstairs. No; let me speak,' he said, raising a hand. 'You know what a treat it is to me. The way I envisage the matter is thus. I still cannot understand as completely as I could wish how you come to be mixed up in the affair, but it is plain that in some way or other Comrade Threepwood has enlisted your services, and I regret to be obliged to inform you that the motives animating him in this quest are not pure. To put it crisply, he is engaged in what Comrade Cootes, to whom I alluded just now, would call "funny business".'

'I . . .'

'Pardon me,' said Psmith. 'If you will be patient for a few minutes more, I shall have finished and shall then be delighted to lend an attentive ear to any remarks you may wish to make. As it occurs to me – indeed, you hinted as much yourself just now – that my own position in this little matter has an appearance which to the uninitiated might seem tolerably rummy, I had better explain how I come to be guarding a diamond necklace which does not belong to me. I rely on your womanly discretion to let the thing go no further.'

'Will you please . . .?'

'In one moment. The facts are as follows. Our mutual friend Mr Keeble, Miss Halliday, has a step-daughter who is married to one Comrade Jackson who, if he had no other claim to fame, would go ringing down through history for this reason, that he and I were at school together and that he is my best friend. We two have sported on the green – ooh, a lot of times. Well, owing to one thing and another, the Jackson family is rather badly up against it at the present . . .'

Eve jumped up angrily.

'I don't believe a word of it,' she cried. 'What is the use of trying to fool me like this? You had never heard of Phyllis before Freddie spoke about her in the train . . .'

'Believe me . . .'

'I won't. Freddie got you down here to help him steal that necklace and give it to Mr Keeble so that he could help Phyllis, and now you've got it and are trying to keep it for yourself.'

Psmith started slightly. His monocle fell from its place.

'Is *everybody* in this little plot! Are you also one of Comrade Keeble's corps of assistants?'

'Mr Keeble asked me to try to get the necklace for him.'

Psmith replaced his monocle thoughtfully.

'This,' he said, 'opens up a new line of thought. Can it be that I have been wronging Comrade Threepwood all this time? I must confess that, when I found him here just now standing like a Marius among the ruins of Carthage (the allusion is a classical one, and the fruit of an expensive education), I jumped – I may say, sprang – to the conclusion that he was endeavouring to double-cross both myself and the boss by getting hold of the necklace with a view to retaining it for his own benefit. It never occurred to me that he might be crediting me with the same sinful guile.'

Eve ran to him and clutched his arm.

'Mr Smith, is this really true? Are you really a friend of Phyllis?'

'She looks on me as a grandfather. Are *you* a friend of hers?'

'We were at school together.'

'This,' said Psmith cordially, 'is one of the most

gratifying moments of my life. It makes us all seem like one great big family.'

'But I never heard Phyllis speak about you.'

'Strange!' said Psmith. 'Strange. Surely she was not ashamed of her humble friend?'

'Her what?'

'I must explain,' said Psmith, 'that until recently I was earning a difficult livelihood by slinging fish about in Billingsgate Market. It is possible that some snobbish strain in Comrade Jackson's bride, which I confess I had not suspected, kept her from admitting that she was accustomed to hob-nob with one in the fish business.'

'Good gracious!' cried Eve.

'I beg your pardon?'

'Smith . . . Fish business . . . Why, it was you who called at Phyllis's house while I was there. Just before I came down here. I remember Phyllis saying how sorry she was that we had not met. She said you were just my sort of . . . I mean, she said she wanted me to meet you.'

'This,' said Psmith, 'is becoming more and more gratifying every moment. It seems to me that you and I were made for each other. I am your best friend's best friend and we both have a taste for stealing other people's jewellery. I cannot see how you can very well resist the conclusion that we are twin-souls.'

'Don't be silly.'

'We shall get into that series of "Husbands and Wives Who Work Together".'

'Where is the necklace?'

Psmith sighed.

'The business note. Always the business note. Can't we keep all that till later?'

'No. We can't.'

'Ah, well!'

Psmith crossed the room, and took down from the wall the case of stuffed birds.

'The one place,' said Eve, with mortification, 'where we didn't think of looking!'

Psmith opened the case and removed the centre bird, a depressed-looking fowl with glass eyes which stared with a haunting pathos. He felt in its interior and pulled out something that glittered and sparkled in the lamp-light.

'Oh!'

Eve ran her fingers almost lovingly through the jewels as they lay before her on the little table.

'Aren't they beautiful!'

'Distinctly. I think I may say that of all the jewels I have ever stolen . . .'

'HEY!'

Eve let the necklace fall with a cry. Psmith spun round. In the doorway stood Mr Edward Cootes, pointing a pistol.

4

'Hands up!' said Mr Cootes with the uncouth curtness of one who had not had the advantages of a refined home and a nice upbringing. He advanced warily, preceded by the revolver. It was a dainty, miniature weapon, such as might have been the property of some gentle lady. Mr Cootes had, in fact, borrowed it from Miss Peavey, who at this juncture entered the room in a black and silver dinner-dress surmounted by a Rose du Barri wrap, her spiritual face glowing softly in the subdued light.

'Attaboy, Ed,' observed Miss Peavey crisply.

She swooped on the table and gathered up the necklace. Mr Cootes, though probably gratified by the tribute, made no acknowledgement of it, but continued to direct an austere gaze at Eve and Psmith.

'No funny business,' he advised.

'I would be the last person,' said Psmith agreeably, 'to

advocate anything of the sort. This,' he said to Eve, 'is Comrade Cootes, of whom you have heard so much.'

Eve was staring, bewildered, at the poetess, who, satisfied with the manner in which the preliminaries had been conducted, had begun looking about her with idle curiosity.

'Miss Peavey!' cried Eve. Of all the events of this eventful night the appearance of Lady Constance's emotional friend in the rôle of criminal was the most disconcerting. 'Miss *Peavey*!'

'Hallo?' responded that lady agreeably.

'I . . . I . . .'

'What, I think, Miss Halliday is trying to say,' cut in Psmith, 'is that she is finding it a little difficult to adjust her mind to the present development. I, too, must confess myself somewhat at a loss. I knew, of course, that Comrade Cootes had – shall I say an acquisitive streak in him, but you I had always supposed to be one hundred per cent soul – and snowy white at that.'

'Yeah?' said Miss Peavey, but faintly interested.

'I imagined that you were a poetess.'

'So I am a poetess,' retorted Miss Peavey hotly. 'Just you start in joshing my poems and see how quick I'll bean you with a brick. Well, Ed, no sense in sticking around here. Let's go.'

'We'll have to tie these birds up,' said Mr Cootes. 'Otherwise we'll have them squealing before I can make a getaway.'

'Ed,' said Miss Peavey with the scorn which her colleague so often excited in her, 'try to remember sometimes that that thing balanced on your collar is a head, not a hubbard squash. And be careful what you're doing with that gat! Waving it about like it was a bouquet or something. How are they going to squeal? They can't say a thing without telling everyone they snitched the stuff first.'

'That's right,' admitted Mr Cootes.

668

'Well, then, don't come butting in.'

The silence into which this rebuke plunged Mr Cootes gave Psmith the opportunity to resume speech. An opportunity of which he was glad, for, while he had nothing of definitely vital import to say, he was optimist enough to feel that his only hope of recovering the necklace was to keep the conversation going on the chance of something turning up. Affable though his manner was, he had never lost sight of the fact that one leap would take him across the space of floor separating him from Mr Cootes. At present, that small but effective revolver precluded anything in the nature of leaps, however short, but if in the near future anything occurred to divert his adversary's vigilance even momentarily . . . He pursued a policy of watchful waiting, and in the meantime started to talk again.

'If, before you go,' he said, 'you can spare us a moment of your valuable time, I should be glad of a few words. And, first, may I say that I cordially agree with your condemnation of Comrade Cootes's recent suggestion. The man is an ass.'

'Say!' cried Mr Cootes, coming to life again, 'that'll be about all from you. If there wasn't ladies present, I'd bust you one.'

'Ed,' said Miss Peavey with quiet authority, 'shut your trap!'

Mr Cootes subsided once more. Psmith gazed at him through his monocle, interested.

'Pardon me,' he said, 'but – if it is not a rude question – are you two married?'

'Eh?'

'You seemed to me to talk to him like a wife. Am I addressing Mrs Cootes?'

'You will be if you stick around a while.'

'A thousand congratulations to Comrade Cootes. Not quite so many to you, possibly, but fully that number of good wishes.' He moved towards the poetess with

669

extended hand. 'I am thinking of getting married myself shortly.'

'Keep those hands up,' said Mr Cootes.

'Surely,' said Psmith reproachfully, 'these conventions need not be observed among friends? You will find the only revolver I have ever possessed over there on the mantelpiece. Go and look at it.'

'Yes, and have you jumping on my back the moment I took my eyes off you!'

'There is a suspicious vein in your nature, Comrade Cootes,' sighed Psmith, 'which I do not like to see. Fight against it.' He turned to Miss Peavey once more. 'To resume a pleasanter topic, you will let me know where to send the plated fish-slice, won't you?'

'Huh?' said the lady.

'I was hoping,' proceeded Psmith, 'if you do not think it a liberty on the part of one who has known you but a short time, to be allowed to send you a small wedding-present in due season. And one of these days, perhaps, when I too am married, you and Comrade Cootes will come and visit us in our little home. You will receive a hearty, unaffected welcome. You must not be offended if, just before you say good-bye, we count the spoons.'

One would scarcely have supposed Miss Peavey a sensitive woman, yet at this remark an ominous frown clouded her white forehead. Her careless amiability seemed to wane. She raked Psmith with a glittering eye.

'You're talking a dam' lot,' she observed coldly.

'An old failing of mine,' said Psmith apologetically, 'and one concerning which there have been numerous complaints. I see now that I have been boring you, and I hope that you will allow me to express . . .'

He broke off abruptly, not because he had reached the end of his remarks, but because at this moment there came from above their heads a sudden sharp cracking sound, and almost simultaneously a shower of plaster fell from the ceiling, followed by the startling appearance of a long, shapely leg, which remained waggling in space. And from somewhere out of sight there filtered down a sharp and agonized oath.

Time and neglect had done their work with the flooring of the room in which Psmith had bestowed the Hon. Freddie Threepwood, and, creeping cautiously about in the dark, he had had the misfortune to go through.

But, as so often happens in this life, the misfortune of one is the good fortune of another. Badly as the accident had shaken Freddie, from the point of view of Psmith it was almost ideal. The sudden appearance of a human leg through the ceiling at a moment of nervous tension is enough to unman the stoutest-hearted, and Edward Cootes made no attempt to conceal his perturbation. Leaping a clear six inches from the floor, he jerked up his head and quite unintentionally pulled the trigger of his revolver. A bullet ripped through the plaster.

The leg disappeared. Not for an instant since he had been shut in that upper room had Freddie Threepwood ceased to be mindful of Psmith's parting statement that he would be shot if he tried to escape, and Mr Cootes's bullet seemed to him a dramatic fulfilment of that promise. Wrenching his leg with painful energy out of the abyss, he proceeded to execute a backward spring which took him to the far wall – at which point, as it was impossible to get any farther away from the centre of events, he was compelled to halt his retreat. Having rolled himself up into as small a ball as he could manage, he sat where he was, trying not to breathe. His momentary intention of explaining through the hole that the entire thing had been a regrettable accident, he prudently abandoned. Unintelligent though he had often proved himself in other crises of his life, he had the sagacity now to realize that the neighbourhood of the hole was unhealthy and should be avoided. So, preserving a complete and unbroken silence, he crouched there in the darkness, only asking to be left alone.

And it seemed, as the moments slipped by, that this modest wish was to be gratified. Noises and the sound of voices came up to him from the room below, but no more bullets. It would be paltering with the truth to say that this put him completely at his ease, but still it was something. Freddie's pulse began to return to the normal.

Mr Cootes's, on the other hand, was beating with a dangerous quickness. Swift and objectionable things had been happening to Edward Cootes in that lower room. His first impression was that the rift in the plaster above him had been instantly followed by the collapse of the entire ceiling, but this was a mistaken idea. All that had occurred was that Psmith, finding Mr Cootes's eye and pistol functioning in another direction, had sprung forward, snatched up a chair, hit the unfortunate man over the head with it, relieved him of his pistol, leaped to the mantelpiece, removed the revolver which lay there, and now, holding both weapons in an attitude of menace, was regarding him censoriously through a gleaming eye-glass.

'No funny business, Comrade Cootes,' said Psmith.

Mr Cootes picked himself up painfully. His head was singing. He looked at the revolvers, blinked, opened his mouth and shut it again. He was oppressed with a sense of defeat. Nature had not built him for a man of violence. Peaceful manipulation of a pack of cards in the smoke-room of an Atlantic liner was a thing he understood and enjoyed: rough-and-tumble encounters were alien to him and distasteful. As far as Mr Cootes was concerned the war was over.

But Miss Peavey was a woman of spirit. Her hat was still in the ring. She clutched the necklace in a grasp of steel, and her fine eyes glared defiance.

'You think yourself smart, don't you?' she said.

Psmith eyed her commiseratingly. Her valorous

attitude appealed to him. Nevertheless, business was business.

'I am afraid,' he said regretfully, 'that I must trouble you to hand over that necklace.'

'Try and get it,' said Miss Peavey.

Psmith looked hurt.

'I am a child in these matters,' he said, 'but I had always gathered that on these occasions the wishes of the man behind the gun were automatically respected.'

'I'll call your bluff,' said Miss Peavey firmly. 'I'm going to walk straight out of here with this collection of ice right now, and I'll bet you won't have the nerve to start any shooting. Shoot a woman? Not you!'

Psmith nodded gravely.

'Your knowledge of psychology is absolutely correct. Your trust in my sense of chivalry rests on solid ground. But,' he proceeded, cheering up, 'I fancy that I see a way out of the difficulty. An idea has been vouchsafed to me. I shall shoot – not you, but Comrade Cootes. This will dispose of all unpleasantness. If you attempt to edge out through that door I shall immediately proceed to plug Comrade Cootes in the leg. At least, I shall try. I am a poor shot and may hit him in some more vital spot, but at least he will have the consolation of knowing that I did my best and meant well.'

'Hey!' cried Mr Cootes. And never, in a life liberally embellished with this favourite ejaculation of his, had he uttered it more feelingly. He shot a feverish glance at Miss Peavey; and, reading in her face indecision rather than that instant acquiescence which he had hoped to see, cast off his customary attitude of respectful humility and asserted himself. He was no cave-man, but this was one occasion when he meant to have his own way. With an agonized bound he reached Miss Peavey's side, wrenched the necklace from her grasp and flung it into the enemy's camp. Eve stooped and picked it up.

'I thank you,' said Psmith with a brief bow in her direction.

Miss Peavey breathed heavily. Her strong hands clenched and unclenched. Between her parted lips her teeth showed in a thin white line. Suddenly she swallowed quickly, as if draining a glass of unpalatable medicine.

'Well,' she said in a low, even voice, 'that seems to be about all. Guess we'll be going. Come along, Ed, pick up the Henries.'

'Coming, Liz,' replied Mr Cootes humbly.

They passed together into the night.

5

Silence followed their departure. Eve, weak with the reaction from the complex emotions which she had undergone since her arrival at the cottage, sat on the battered sofa, her chin resting in her hands. She looked at Psmith, who, humming a light air, was delicately piling with the toe of his shoe a funeral mound over the second of the dead bats.

'So that's that!' she said.

Psmith looked up with a bright and friendly smile.

'You have a very happy gift of phrase,' he said. 'That, as you sensibly say, is that.'

Eve was silent for a while. Psmith completed the obsequies and stepped back with the air of a man who has done what he can for a fallen friend.

'Fancy Miss Peavey being a thief!' said Eve. She was somehow feeling a disinclination to allow the conversation to die down, and yet she had an idea that, unless it was permitted to die down, it might become embarrassingly intimate. Subconsciously, she was endeavouring to analyse her views on this long, calm person who had so recently added himself to the list of those who claimed to look upon her with affection.

674

'I confess it came as something of a shock to me also,' said Psmith. 'In fact, the revelation that there was this other, deeper side to her nature materially altered the opinion I had formed of her. I found myself warming to Miss Peavey. Something that was akin to respect began to stir within me. Indeed, I almost wish that we had not been compelled to deprive her of the jewels.'

' "We"?' said Eve. 'I'm afraid I didn't do much.'

'Your attitude was exactly right,' Psmith assured her. 'You afforded just the moral support which a man needs in such a crisis.'

Silence fell once more. Eve returned to her thoughts. And then, with a suddenness which surprised her, she found that she had made up her mind.

'So you're going to be married?' she said.

Psmith polished his monocle thoughtfully.

'I think so,' he said. 'I think so. What do *you* think?'

Eve regarded him steadfastly. Then she gave a little laugh.

'Yes,' she said, 'I think so, too.' She paused. 'Shall I tell you something?'

'You could tell me nothing more wonderful than that.'

'When I met Cynthia in Market Blandings, she told me what the trouble was which made her husband leave her. What do you suppose it was?'

'From my brief acquaintance with Comrade McTodd, I would hazard the guess that he tried to stab her with the bread-knife. He struck me as a murderous-looking specimen.'

'They had some people to dinner, and there was chicken, and Cynthia gave all the giblets to the guests; and her husband bounded out of his seat with a wild cry, and, shouting "You *know* I love those things better than anything in the world!" rushed from the house, never to return!'

'Precisely how I would have wished him to rush, had I been Mrs McTodd.'

'Cynthia told me that he had rushed from the house, never to return, six times since they were married.'

'May I mention – in passing – ' said Psmith, 'that I do not like chicken giblets?'

'Cynthia advised me,' proceeded Eve, 'if ever I married, to marry someone eccentric. She said it was such fun . . . Well, I don't suppose I am ever likely to meet anyone more eccentric than you, am I?'

'I think you would be unwise to wait on the chance.'

'The only thing is . . .' said Eve reflectively. ' "Mrs Smith" . . . It doesn't *sound* much, does it?'

Psmith beamed encouragingly.

'We must look into the future,' he said. 'We must remember that I am only at the beginning of what I am convinced is to be a singularly illustrious career. "Lady Psmith" is better . . . "Baroness Psmith" better still . . . And – who knows? – "The Duchess of Psmith" . . .'

'Well, anyhow,' said Eve, 'you were wonderful just now, simply wonderful. The way you made one spring . . .'

'Your words,' said Psmith, 'are music to my ears, but we must not forget that the foundations of the success of the manoeuvre were laid by Comrade Threepwood. Had it not been for the timely incursion of his leg . . .'

'Good gracious!' cried Eve. 'Freddie! I had forgotten all about him!'

'The right spirit,' said Psmith. 'Quite the right spirit.'

'We must go and let him out.'

'Just as you say. And then he can come with us on the stroll I was about to propose that we should take through the woods. It is a lovely night, and what could be jollier than to have Comrade Threepwood prattling at our side? I will go and let him out at once.'

'No, don't bother,' said Eve.

14 — Psmith Accepts Employment

The golden stillness of a perfect summer morning brooded over Blandings Castle and its adjacent pleasure-grounds. From a sky of unbroken blue the sun poured down its heartening rays on all those roses, pinks, pansies, carnations, hollyhocks, columbines, larkspurs, London pride, and Canterbury bells which made the gardens so rarely beautiful. Flannelled youths and maidens in white serge sported in the shade; gay cries arose from the tennis-courts behind the shrubbery; and birds, bees, and butterflies went about their business with a new energy and zip. In short, the casual observer, assuming that he was addicted to trite phrases, would have said that happiness reigned supreme.

But happiness, even on the finest mornings, is seldom universal. The strolling youths and maidens were happy; the tennis-players were happy; the birds, bees, and butterflies were happy. Eve, walking in pleasant meditation on the terrace, was happy. Freddie Threepwood was happy as he lounged in the smoking-room and gloated over the information, received from Psmith in the small hours, that his thousand pounds was safe. Mr Keeble, writing to Phyllis to inform her that she might clinch the purchase of the Lincolnshire farm, was happy. Even Head-gardener Angus McAllister was as happy as a Scotsman can ever be. But Lord Emsworth, drooping out of the library window, felt only a nervous irritation more in keeping with the blizzards of winter than with the only fine July that England had known in the last ten years.

We have seen his lordship in a similar attitude and a

like frame of mind on a previous occasion; but then his
melancholy had been due to the loss of his glasses. This
morning these were perched firmly on his nose and he
saw all things clearly. What was causing his gloom now
was the fact that some ten minutes earlier his sister
Constance had trapped him the library, full of jarring
rebuke on the subject of the dismissal of Rupert Baxter,
the world's most efficient secretary. It was to avoid her
compelling eye that Lord Emsworth had turned to the
window. And what he saw from that window thrust him
even deeper into the abyss of gloom. The sun, the birds,
the bees, the butterflies, and the flowers called to him to
come out and have the time of his life, but he just lacked
the nerve to make a dash for it.

'I think you must be mad,' said Lady Constance
bitterly, resuming her remarks and starting at the point
where she had begun before.

'Baxter's mad,' retorted his lordship, also re-treading
old ground.

'You are too absurd!'

'He threw flower-pots at me.'

'Do please stop talking about those flower-pots. Mr
Baxter has explained the whole thing to me, and surely
even you can see that his behaviour was perfectly
excusable.'

'I don't like the fellow,' cried Lord Emsworth, once
more retreating to his last line of trenches – the one line
from which all Lady Constance's eloquence had been
unable to dislodge him.

There was a silence, as there had been a short while
before when the discussion had reached this same point.

'You will be helpless without him,' said Lady
Constance.

'Nothing of the kind,' said his lordship.

'You know you will. Where will you ever get another
secretary capable of looking after everything like Mr
Baxter? You know you are a perfect child, and unless you

have someone whom you can trust to manage your affairs I cannot see what will happen.'

Lord Emsworth made no reply. He merely gazed wanly from the window.

'Chaos,' moaned Lady Constance.

His lordship remained mute, but now there was a gleam of something approaching pleasure in his pale eyes; for at this moment a car rounded the corner of the house from the direction of the stables and stood purring at the door. There was a trunk on the car and a suit-case. And almost simultaneously the Efficient Baxter entered the library, clothed and spatted for travel.

'I have come to say good-bye, Lady Constance,' said Baxter coldly and precisely, flashing at his late employer through his spectacles a look of stern reproach. 'The car which is taking me to the station is at the door.'

'Oh, Mr Baxter,' Lady Constance, strong woman though she was, fluttered with distress. 'Oh, Mr Baxter.'

'Good-bye.' He gripped her hand in brief farewell and directed his spectacles for another tense instant upon the sagging figure at the window. 'Good-bye, Lord Emsworth.'

'Eh? What? Oh! Ah, yes. Good-bye, my dear fel – I mean, good-bye. I – er – hope you will have a pleasant journey.'

'Thank you,' said Baxter.

'But, Mr Baxter,' said Lady Constance.

'Lord Emsworth,' said the ex-secretary, icily, 'I am no longer in your employment . . .'

'But, Mr Baxter,' moaned Lady Constance, 'surely . . . even now . . . misunderstanding . . . talk it all over quietly . . .'

Lord Emsworth started violently.

'Here!' he protested, in much the same manner as that in which the recent Mr Cootes had been wont to say 'Hey!'

'I fear it is too late,' said Baxter, to his infinite relief, 'to talk things over. My arrangements are already made and cannot be altered. Ever since I came here to work for Lord Emsworth, my former employer – an American millionaire named Jevons – has been making me flattering offers to return to him. Until now a mistaken sense of loyalty has kept me from accepting these offers, but this morning I telegraphed to Mr Jevons to say that I was at liberty and could join him at once. It is too late now to cancel this promise.'

'Quite, quite, oh, certainly, quite, mustn't dream of it, my dear fellow. No, no, no, indeed no,' said Lord Emsworth with an effervescent cordiality which struck both his hearers as in the most dubious taste.

Baxter merely stiffened haughtily, but Lady Constance was so poignantly affected by the words and the joyous tone in which they were uttered that she could endure her brother's loathly society no longer. Shaking Baxter's hand once more and gazing stonily for a moment at the worm by the window, she left the room.

For some seconds after she had gone, there was silence – a silence which Lord Emsworth found embarrassing. He turned to the window again and took in with one wistful glance the roses, the pinks, the pansies, the carnations, the hollyhocks, the columbines, the larkspurs, the London pride, and the Canterbury bells. And then suddenly there came to him the realization that with Lady Constance gone there no longer existed any reason why he should stay cooped up in this stuffy library on the finest morning that had ever been sent to gladden the heart of man. He shivered ecstatically from the top of his bald head to the soles of his roomy shoes, and, bounding gleefully from the window, started to amble across the room.

'Lord Emsworth!'

His lordship halted. His was a one-track mind, capable of accommodating only one thought at a time – if that, and he had almost forgotten that Baxter was still there. He eyed his late secretary peevishly.

'Yes, yes? Is there anything . . .?'

'I should like to speak to you for a moment.'

'I have a most important conference with McAllister . . .'

'I will not detain you long. Lord Emsworth, I am no longer in your employment, but I think it my duty to say before I go . . .'

'No, no, my dear fellow, I quite understand. Quite, quite, quite. Constance has been going over all that. I know what you are trying to say. That matter of the flower-pots. Please do not apologize. It is quite all right. I was startled at the time, I own, but no doubt you had excellent motives. Let us forget the whole affair.'

Baxter ground an impatient heel into the carpet.

'I had no intention of referring to the matter to which you allude,' he said. 'I merely wished . . .'

'Yes, yes, of course.' A vagrant breeze floated in at the window, languid with summer scents, and Lord Emsworth, sniffing, shuffled restlessly. 'Of course, of course, of course. Some other time, eh? Yes, yes, that will be capital. Capital, capital, cap – '

The Efficient Baxter uttered a sound that was partly a cry, partly a snort. Its quality was so arresting that Lord Emsworth paused, his fingers on the door-handle, and peered back at him, startled.

'Very well,' said Baxter shortly. 'Pray do not let me keep you. If you are not interested in the fact that Blandings Castle is sheltering a criminal . . .'

It was not easy to divert Lord Emsworth when in quest of Angus McAllister, but this remark succeeded in doing so. He let go of the door-handle and came back a step or two into the room.

'Sheltering a criminal?'

'Yes.' Baxter glanced at his watch. 'I must go now or I shall miss my train,' he said curtly. 'I was merely going to tell you that this fellow who calls himself Ralston McTodd is not Ralston McTodd at all.'

'Not Ralston McTodd?' repeated his lordship blankly. 'But – ' He suddenly perceived a flaw in the argument. 'But he *said* he was,' he pointed out cleverly. 'Yes, I remember distinctly. He said he was McTodd.'

'He is an impostor. And I imagine that if you investigate you will find that it is he and his accomplices who stole Lady Constance's necklace.'

'But, my dear fellow . . .'

Baxter walked briskly to the door.

'You need not take my word for it,' he said. 'What I say can easily be proved. Get this so-called McTodd to write his name on a piece of paper and then compare it with the signature to the letter which the real McTodd wrote when accepting Lady Constance's invitation to the castle. You will find it filed away in the drawer of that desk there.'

Lord Emsworth adjusted his glasses and stared at the desk as if he expected it to do a conjuring trick.

'I will leave you to take what steps you please,' said Baxter. 'Now that I am no longer in your employment, the thing does not concern me one way or another. But I thought you might be glad to hear the facts.'

'Oh, I *am*!' responded his lordship, still peering vaguely. 'Oh, I *am*! Oh, yes, yes, yes. Oh, yes, yes . . .'

'Good-bye.'

'But, Baxter . . .'

Lord Emsworth trotted out on to the landing, but Baxter had got off to a good start and was almost out of sight round the bend of the stairs.

'But, my dear fellow . . .' bleated his lordship plaintively over the banisters.

From below, out on the drive, came the sound of an automobile getting into gear and moving off, than which no sound is more final. The great door of the castle closed with a soft but significant bang – as doors close when

handled by an untipped butler. Lord Emsworth returned
to the library to wrestle with his problem unaided.

He was greatly disturbed. Apart from the fact that he
disliked criminals and impostors as a class, it was a
shock to him to learn that the particular criminal and
impostor then in residence at Blandings was the man for
whom, brief as had been the duration of their
acquaintance, he had conceived a warm affection. He
was fond of Psmith. Psmith soothed him. If he had had
to choose any member of his immediate circle for the
rôle of criminal and impostor, he would have chosen
Psmith last.

He went to the window again and looked out. There
was the sunshine, there were the birds, there were the
hollyhocks, carnations, and Canterbury bells, all present
and correct; but now they failed to cheer him. He was
wondering dismally what on earth he was going to do.
What *did* one do with criminals and impostors? Had
'em arrested, he supposed. But he shrank from the thought
of arresting Psmith. It seemed so deuced unfriendly.

He was still meditating gloomily when a voice spoke
behind him.

'Good morning. I am looking for Miss Halliday. You
have not seen her by any chance? Ah, there she is down
there on the terrace.'

Lord Emsworth was aware of Psmith beside him at the
window, waving cordially to Eve, who waved back.

'I thought possibly,' continued Psmith, 'that Miss
Halliday would be in her little room yonder' – he
indicated the dummy book-shelves through which he had
entered. 'But I am glad to see that the morning is so fine
that she has given toil the miss-in-baulk. It is the right
spirit,' said Psmith. 'I like to see it.'

Lord Emsworth peered at him nervously through his
glasses. His embarrassment and his distaste for the task
that lay before him increased as he scanned his
companion in vain for those signs of villainy which all

well-regulated criminals and impostors ought to exhibit to the eye of discernment.

'I am surprised to find you indoors,' said Psmith, 'on so glorious a morning. I should have supposed that you would have been down there among the shrubs, taking a good sniff at a hollyhock or something.'

Lord Emsworth braced himself for the ordeal.

'Er, my dear fellow . . . that is to say . . .' He paused. Psmith was regarding him almost lovingly through his monocle, and it was becoming increasingly difficult to warm up to the work of denouncing him.

'You were observing . . .?' said Psmith.

Lord Emsworth uttered curious buzzing noises.

'I have just parted from Baxter,' he said at length, deciding to approach the subject in more roundabout fashion.

'Indeed?' said Psmith courteously.

'Yes. Baxter has gone.'

'For ever?'

'Er – yes.'

'Splendid!' said Psmith. 'Splendid, splendid.'

Lord Emsworth removed his glasses, twiddled them on their cord, and replaced them on his nose.

'He made . . . He – er – the fact is, he made . . . Before he went Baxter made a most remarkable statement . . . a charge . . . Well, in short, he made a very strange statement about you.'

Psmith nodded gravely.

'I had been expecting something of the kind,' he said. 'He said, no doubt, that I was not really Ralston McTodd?'

His lordship's mouth opened feebly.

'Er – yes,' he said.

'I've been meaning to tell you about that,' said Psmith amiably. 'It is quite true. I am not Ralston McTodd.'

'You – you admit it!'

'I am proud of it.'

Lord Emsworth drew himself up. He endeavoured to assume the attitude of stern censure which came so naturally to him in interviews with his son Frederick. But he met Psmith's eye and sagged again. Beneath the solemn friendliness of Psmith's gaze hauteur was impossible.

'Then what the deuce are you doing here under his name?' he asked, placing his finger in statesmanlike fashion on the very nub of the problem. 'I mean to say,' he went on, making his meaning clearer, 'if you aren't McTodd, why did you come here saying you were McTodd?'

Psmith nodded slowly.

'The point is well taken,' he said. 'I was expecting you to ask that question. Primarily – I want no thanks, but primarily I did it to save you embarrassment.'

'Save me embarrassment?'

'Precisely. When I came into the smoking-room of our mutual club that afternoon when you had been entertaining Comrade McTodd at lunch, I found him on the point of passing out of your life for ever. It seems that he had taken umbrage to some slight extent because you had buzzed off to chat with the florist across the way instead of remaining with him. And, after we had exchanged a pleasant word or two, he legged it, leaving you short one modern poet. On your return I stepped into the breach to save you from the inconvenience of having to return here without a McTodd of any description. No one, of course, could have been more alive than myself to the fact that I was merely a poor substitute, a sort of synthetic McTodd, but still I considered that I was better than nothing so I came along.'

His lordship digested this explanation in silence. Then he seized on a magnificent point.

'Are you a member of the Senior Conservative Club?'

'Most certainly.'

'Why, then, dash it,' cried his lordship, paying to that

august stronghold of respectability as striking a tribute as it had ever received, 'if you're a member of the Senior Conservative, you can't be a criminal. Baxter's an ass!'

'Exactly.'

'Baxter would have it that you had stolen my sister's necklace.'

'I can assure you that I have not got Lady Constance's necklace.'

'Of course not, of course not, my dear fellow. I'm only telling you what that idiot Baxter said. Thank goodness I've got rid of the fellow.' A cloud passed over his now sunny face. 'Though, confound it, Connie was right about one thing.' He relapsed into a somewhat moody silence.

'Yes?' said Psmith.

'Eh?' said his lordship.

'You were saying that Lady Constance had been right about one thing.'

'Oh, yes. She was saying that I should have a hard time finding another secretary as capable as Baxter.'

Psmith permitted himself to bestow an encouraging pat on his host's shoulder.

'You have touched on a matter,' he said, 'which I had intended to broach to you at some convenient moment when you were at leisure. If you would care to accept my services, they are at your disposal.'

'Eh?'

'The fact is,' said Psmith, 'I am shortly about to be married, and it is more or less imperative that I connect with some job which will ensure a moderate competence. Why should I not become your secretary?'

'You want to be my secretary?'

'You have unravelled my meaning exactly.'

'But I've never had a married secretary.'

'I think that you would find a steady married man an improvement on these wild, flower-pot-throwing bachelors. If it would help to influence your decision, I

686

may say that my bride-to-be is Miss Halliday, probably the finest library-cataloguist in the United Kingdom.'

'Eh? Miss Halliday? That girl down there?'

'No other,' said Psmith, waving fondly at Eve as she passed underneath the window. 'In fact, the same.'

'But I like her,' said Lord Emsworth, as if stating an insuperable objection.

'Excellent.'

'She's a nice girl.'

'I quite agree with you.'

'Do you think you could really look after things here like Baxter?'

'I am convinced of it.'

'Then, my dear fellow – well, really I must say . . . I must say . . . well, I mean, why shouldn't you?'

'Precisely,' said Psmith. 'You have put in a nutshell the very thing I have been trying to express.'

'But have you had any experience as a secretary?'

'I must admit that I have not. You see, until recently I was more or less one of the idle rich. I toiled not, neither did I – except once, after a bump-supper at Cambridge – spin. My name, perhaps I ought to reveal to you, is Psmith – the p is silent – and until very recently I lived in affluence not far from the village of Much Middlefold in this county. My name is probably unfamiliar to you, but you may have heard of the house which was for many years the Psmith headquarters – Corfby Hall.'

Lord Emsworth jerked his glasses off his nose.

'Corfby Hall! Are you the son of the Smith who used to own Corfby Hall? Why, bless my soul, I knew your father well.'

'Really?'

'Yes. That is to say, I never met him.'

'No?'

'But I won the first prize for roses at the Shrewsbury Flower Show the year he won the prize for tulips.'

'It seems to draw us very close together,' said Psmith.

'Why, my dear boy,' cried Lord Emsworth jubilantly, 'if you are really looking for a position of some kind and would care to be my secretary, nothing could suit me better. Nothing, nothing, nothing. Why, bless my soul . . .'

'I am extremely obliged,' said Psmith. 'And I shall endeavour to give satisfaction. And surely, if a mere Baxter could hold down the job, it should be well within the scope of a Shropshire Psmith. I think so, I think so . . . And now, if you will excuse me, I think I will go down and tell the glad news to the little woman, if I may so describe her.'

Psmith made his way down the broad staircase at an even better pace than that recently achieved by the departing Baxter, for he rightly considered each moment of this excellent day wasted that was not spent in the company of Eve. He crooned blithely to himself as he passed through the hall, only pausing when, as he passed the door of the smoking-room, the Hon. Freddie Threepwood suddenly emerged.

'Oh, I say!' said Freddie. 'Just the fellow I wanted to see. I was going off to look for you.'

Freddie's tone was cordiality itself. As far as Freddie was concerned, all that had passed between them in the cottage in the west wood last night was forgiven and forgotten.

'Say on, Comrade Threepwood,' replied Psmith; 'and, if I may offer the suggestion, make it snappy, for I would be elsewhere. I have man's work before me.'

'Come over here.' Freddie drew him into a far corner of the hall and lowered his voice to a whisper. 'I say, it's all right, you know.'

'Excellent!' said Psmith. 'Splendid! This is great news. What is all right?'

'I've just seen Uncle Joe. He's going to cough up the money he promised me.'

'I congratulate you.'

'So now I shall be able to get into that bookie's business and make a pile. And, I say, you remember my telling you about Miss Halliday?'

'What was that?'

'Why, that I loved, her, I mean, and all that.'

'Ah, yes.'

'Well, look here, between ourselves,' said Freddie earnestly, 'the whole trouble all along has been that she thought I hadn't any money to get married on. She didn't actually say so in so many words, but you know how it is with women – you can read between the lines, if you know what I mean. So now everything's going to be all right. I shall simply go to her and say, "Well, what about it?" and – well, and so on, don't you know?'

Psmith considered the point gravely.

'I see your reasoning, Comrade Threepwood,' he said. 'I can detect but one flaw in it.'

'Flaw? What flaw?'

'The fact that Miss Halliday is going to marry *me*.'

The Hon. Freddie's jaw dropped. His prominent eyes became more prawn-like.

'What!'

Psmith patted his shoulder commiseratingly.

'Be a man, Comrade Threepwood, and bite the bullet. These things will happen to the best of us. Some day you will be thankful that this has occurred. Purged in the holocaust of a mighty love you will wander out into the sunset, a finer, broader man . . . And now I must reluctantly tear myself away. I have an important appointment.' He patted his shoulder once more. 'If you would care to be a page at the wedding, Comrade

Threepwood, I can honestly say that there is no one whom I would rather have in that capacity.'

And with a stately gesture of farewell, Psmith passed out on to the terrace to join Eve.

The P G Wodehouse Society (UK)

The P G Wodehouse Society (UK) was formed in 1997 and exists to promote the enjoyment of the works of the greatest humorist of the twentieth century.

The Society publishes a quarterly magazine, *Wooster Sauce*, which features articles, reviews, archive material and current news. It also publishes an occasional newsletter in the *By The Way* series which relates a single matter of Wodehousean interest. Members are rewarded in their second and subsequent years by receiving a specially produced text of a Wodehouse magazine story which has never been collected into one of his books.

A variety of Society events are arranged for members including regular meetings at a London club, a golf day, a cricket match, a Society dinner, and walks round Bertie Wooster's London. Meetings are also arranged in other parts of the country.

Membership enquiries

Membership of the Society is available to applicants from all parts of the world. The cost of a year's membership in 1999 was £15. Enquiries and requests for an application form should be addressed in writing to the Membership Secretary, Helen Murphy, at 16 Herbert Street, Plaistow, London E13 8BE, or write to the Editor of *Wooster Sauce*, Tony Ring, at 34 Longfield Road, Great Missenden, Bucks HP16 0EG.

You can visit their website at:
http://www.eclipse.co.uk/wodehouse